CONTENT

NEW DAWN

1

MARGO

Sunset in Cabo San Lucas was magnificent, and Margo had made sure to watch it every day since her arrival at the resort. The bright azure sky transitioned into an array of rich colors, with deep oranges, fiery reds, pinks, and purples reflecting over the pool's surface in a spectacular mirror-like effect. But as the sun dipped lower, so did the temperature, and the day's heat was replaced by the cool evening air.

Shivering, Margo draped a large pool towel over her bikini-clad body and cast a sidelong look at Lynda, who was collecting her things.

"Leaving already?"

"It's getting cold." Lynda wrapped a towel around herself and tucked the corner to secure it. "Are you coming inside?"

"I'm going to stay a little longer." Margo took off her glasses and put them on the side table. "I'm almost done with this book, and I have to know how the story ends."

Well, it was a romance, so happily ever after was guaranteed, but how the couple overcame the obstacles to get there was what made it interesting. So yeah, real life didn't come with guaranteed happy endings, but if Margo wanted real life, she could watch the news.

Not that all those who reported the news could be trusted to deliver objective truths either, and the view of the world that most of them broadcast was projected through the prism of their own agenda, but it definitely didn't promise happy endings. On the contrary, according to most of the media, the world was full of hate and strife and was about to end soon for one reason or another.

Perhaps they were right, but in either case, Margo preferred to spend her free time reading stories that ended in 'happily ever after.'

Lynda pursed her lips, which was a sure sign that she was going to deliver a lecture on all the ways Margo was disappointing her. "All you did during my bachelorette party was read, read, and read some more." She waved her hand for emphasis. "I've been sitting out here long after my friends left, hoping to have a nice chat with my future sister-in-law, but I should have known that you'd have your nose glued to your phone, reading."

Lynda scoffed at eBooks. She rarely read anything other than fashion magazines—the paper versions.

"I thought you were napping." Margo was well aware that Lynda hadn't been dozing off. She'd been watching the buffed-up lifeguard from behind the safety of her dark eyeglasses.

There was nothing wrong with that, but after what she witnessed during the bachelorette party, Margo wasn't sure that Lynda was faithful to Rob. Not that she was going to say anything to her brother. He would only accuse her of hating Lynda and trying to come between them.

The truth was that she wasn't fond of Lynda, but she didn't hate her either. The woman did have some redeeming qualities. Besides, Margo wasn't the one marrying her, and if Rob was happy with her, she was happy for both of them.

"I wasn't napping," Lynda huffed. "I was resting to conserve my energy for partying later tonight. Unlike you, I'm here to have fun and enjoy my bachelorette party." She pouted.

That pouty expression was what made Rob jump to fulfill Lynda's every demand, and it was also what Margo hated the most about her.

She assumed what she hoped was a pleasant expression. "I've had lots of fun with you and your friends. We drank, we sang karaoke, and we went dancing. It's been an awesome vacation." She smiled. "I'm so glad that you invited me."

That was a lie.

Margo would have been much happier if she hadn't been invited. Lynda hadn't paid for anything, and attending her week-long bachelorette party had eradicated Margo's meager savings. Also, calling the experience fun was an exaggeration. While Lynda and her friends had gotten drunk and flirted with the waiters and the lifeguards, Margo had mainly lounged by the pool, drinking virgin cocktails and catching up on her reading.

"Well, you are Rob's sister, so of course I had to invite you." Lynda sighed while collecting her bag from the back of the lounger. "It's our last night here, so I suggest that you take a break from your reading and join us on an outing." She slipped the strap of her oversized Louis Vuitton over her shoulder. "We are going to the Mandala, which is the most famous club in Cabo." Her eyes sparkled with excitement. "It's a must-see destination, and you can't skip it. You have to come."

"You girls enjoy." Margo cast her a fake apologetic smile. "As you know, I have a problem with loud music. My ears keep ringing for days, but I can join you for drinks later if you are still up for it when you return."

Lynda shook her head. "At this rate, you are going to stay single forever. You don't like any of the men that Rob and I introduce you to, you don't like nightclubs, and you work in an office with a bunch of other women. How are you going to meet any guys?"

"Online dating services." Margo put her glasses back on. "That's what everyone does these days." Except for her, but she wasn't going to admit that to Lynda.

"Oh well." Lynda tossed her artfully frosted tresses over her shoulder and put her feet into her Gucci three-inch-heeled slides. "Call me if you change your mind." She sauntered away.

Closing her eyes, Margo let out a relieved breath.

Everyone kept trying to set her up with someone as if being single was a terminal disease.

Margo went out on occasional dates, and sometimes she pretended she was out while staying home and turning her phone off just so people would leave her be. She even lied to her besties about her so-called dating life, complaining about the imaginary men she was supposedly seeing, who were all turning out to be disappointing.

The truth was that she hated dating. Her mother suspected that she was asexual or preferred members of her own gender, but Margo had proved her mother wrong by showing her the collection of her book boyfriends.

Margo just preferred fantasy over reality, and the heroes of her novels were all magnificent supernaturals. Suspending disbelief that they were as fabulous as the authors described them was easier when she didn't have to compare them to her underwhelming experiences in the real world.

Perhaps maturing too quickly and looking like a woman when she was still a child had something to do with it. At age thirteen, she had found that older men openly lusted after her and had made crude remarks which at the time had frightened and repulsed her, and she had never really gotten over that.

It wasn't rational, and she knew logically that there were plenty of nice men out there who weren't perverts, but it was a struggle not to think about what was going through men's minds when they looked at her and what they were planning to do to her.

Her mother had pressured her to get therapy, but Margo didn't like sharing her inner demons with strangers. She'd read self-help books and enough romance novels to fill up a library, and if that hadn't helped, she reasoned that nothing would.

She wasn't like other young women her age, who were obsessed with finding suitable partners, but she had learned to hide it. Going to bars with Mia and Frankie, Margo had flirted with guys like a pro, but she had never given any of them her phone number or taken any home. The only ones she'd actually gone out with had been friends or acquaintances of friends who had been vetted beforehand.

"Hey, pretty lady."

Margo tensed and opened her eyes, but the guy wasn't talking to her. He was talking to a leggy brunette with a huge hat on her head that hid her entire face from view.

The sun was almost all the way down, so the hat was no longer necessary, but it was an elegant accessory, and the woman looked like someone who paid attention to her accessories even more so than Lynda, and that was saying something.

Her sister-in-law was obsessed with designer labels.

Margo let out a breath and turned her phone on, going back to the eBook she'd been reading before the interruption. Still, she couldn't help but overhear the conversation going on two loungers down from her.

The woman was trying to make the guy leave her alone, but he was obnoxiously persistent.

"I can't join you at the bar," the woman said. "Please, leave. I asked you twice already."

"Just tell me your name, and I'll leave," the guy said.

Yeah, right. If she told him her name, he would ask another question, and when she answered that, another, and so on.

Some men didn't know when to quit.

"You are making me uncomfortable," the woman said. "My boyfriend is the jealous type, and if he sees you talking to me, he will get mad. Please go."

She was probably making up the story about the boyfriend, just like Margo had done countless times before, but the guy was either drunk or obtuse and refused to get the hint.

"Your boyfriend doesn't scare me." He thumped his hairy chest. "If you want a real man, dump the asshole and come with me. I'll show you a real good time, and I won't leave a precious jewel like you alone by the pool."

Margo turned on her side and gave the dude a bright smile. "You should do as she says. Marcello is a beast, and he's crazy. He will beat you up just for looking at Kitty."

"Oh?" The guy turned his attention to her. "What about you, missy? Do you also have a jealous boyfriend?"

"I'm happily married." She discreetly turned her ring around and lifted her hand to show him her fake wedding ring. "Patrick and I are expecting our second child." She rubbed a hand over her flat belly. "I hope it's a boy this time. What do you think about the name Solomon? I want my son to be smart, and King Solomon was supposedly the smartest man ever born."

Mindless chatter about children was a sure way to chase off even the most persistent flirts, but the guy was either smarter than he looked or good at detecting lies because he lifted a brow. "And where is this husband of yours?"

"Home with our daughter. I'm here with my sister-in-law, celebrating her last days as a single woman."

A convincing lie always had an element of truth in it.

The dude shook his head and pushed to his feet. "Slim pickings today." He walked away without saying goodbye.

"Thank you for the save," the woman under the large hat said. "Can I show my gratitude by buying you a drink?"

"Sure." Margo put her phone away and took off her reading glasses. "I'm Margo."

The woman chuckled. "I'm not Kitty. I'm Jasmine, or Jaz for short." She removed her enormous floppy hat, revealing a face that took Margo's breath away.

Jasmine was stunning.

"Is that your real name?" she blurted out. "Because you look too much like the princess from the Aladdin movie for the name to be a coincidence."

Black glossy hair tumbled in thick waves down Jasmine's shoulders, and her warm, olive-toned skin was so perfectly smooth that it seemed to be made of glass. Her almond-shaped eyes were deep brown with amber flakes floating around the pupils, their shade so striking that Margo suspected they were colored contact lenses. The high cheekbones, the straight nose that was slightly hooked at the end, and the full lips that were covered in berry-colored lipstick made Jasmine perfect for the role of an Arabian princess.

Her new friend laughed. "Believe it or not, but that's my real name. After the midwife placed me in my mother's arms, she took one look at my face and named me Jasmine."

Margo lifted a brow. "You looked like this as a newborn?"

"I can show you a picture." Reaching into a large tote bag, Jasmine pulled out her phone and frowned. "I'm so sorry, but you'll have to excuse me. I need to make a phone call first. I'll show you the picture after I'm done."

"The jealous boyfriend?"

Jasmine didn't smile. "Yeah. His name is not Marcello, but you must have some psychic powers because the rest of your description fits." She rose to her feet. "Can you watch my stuff while I take care of this?"

"Sure."

As Margo watched Jasmine walk away, the discomfort in her gut was a sure sign that there was a story there, and it wasn't a good one.

2

NEGAL

After scrubbing all the dirt and gore from his body, Negal stepped out of the shower and checked his nails to make sure they were clean. It was a bitch to get all the dirt and blood from under them, and he'd had to use a brush. He'd worked on them until they bled, but that wasn't a big deal for a god.

The skin healed immediately.

The clothes he had worn on the mission, though, were beyond salvageable, and he'd put them in a trash bag, but he wasn't sure what to do with the bag. The ship didn't have regular cabin service, and if he wanted clean towels and other supplies, he had to get them himself, which he might do after going down to the clinic and checking whether Dagor needed anything.

Dressed in a fresh pair of jeans and a black T-shirt, his hair washed and combed back, Negal finally felt like he was presentable enough to show up at the clinic.

Dagor, on the other hand, hadn't bothered to get properly cleaned up in his rush to see Frankie. He had jumped out of the lifeboat and had swum the last few feet to the ship. By the time the rest of them had gotten on board, he had used a hose to shower while fully clothed and had run to see the woman he loved.

It was very romantic and very unlike the crusty Dagor, but then love changed people, and in Dagor's case, it was for the better.

Hopefully, Frankie was okay. During their journey back to the ship, Dagor had called her every fifteen minutes, and she'd answered every time, so apparently, she wasn't slipping in and out of consciousness like Gabi had.

As Negal opened the door to the front room, the nurse smiled at him. "Can I help you?" Her smile was flirty, and he was about to put on the charm, but then the inner door opened, and Dagor stepped out.

Negal turned to him. "How is Frankie doing?"

"She's doing great." Dagor grinned. "Do you want to come in and see for yourself?"

Negal's eyes widened. Aru hadn't allowed them to see Gabi during her transition, so this was a very unexpected invitation.

"Are you sure she will be okay with me coming in?"

"Yeah. Toven and Mia were here not too long ago, and Frankie was very happy to see both."

"Okay then." Negal waved a hand. "After you."

When they passed through the front office, the nurse gave him an appreciative once-over, and he returned the favor with a smile and a wink.

He had to admit that being the most coveted male around was undeniably enjoyable.

Back on Anumati, Negal was a nobody. Just another guy from a family of modest means who hadn't had overly lofty aspirations. Serving in the interstellar fleet, he was content to slowly advance in the ranks, and the height of his ambition was to one day become a team commander. All positions above that required higher education that was nearly inaccessible for someone of his lowly status.

"Negal," Frankie beamed at him from the patient bed. "It's so nice of you to come visit me."

She looked so good that he had to wonder why the clan doctor was keeping her in the clinic.

"Hi, Frankie. I'm so glad to find you awake. How are you feeling?"

She shrugged. "Except for some fever and occasional nausea, I feel great. I was expecting to suffer much worse during my transition." She waved a hand at the lone chair in the room. "Please, take a seat. I want to hear what you've been up to."

Negal froze.

Did she know about his contribution to Karen's transition into immortality?

It was supposed to be a secret. Karen and Gilbert had asked him to supply his venom to aid in her transition, which was an uncommon thing for a bonded couple to even consider, let alone request. The venom bite was a very intimate act with strong sexual connotations, and Gilbert, who was a newly transitioned immortal, was even more possessive of his mate than he had been before that. But desperate times called for desperate measures, and Negal's godly abilities had been greatly beneficial to the successful completion of the procedure. Still, it wasn't something the couple wished to become fodder for clan gossip.

How had Frankie found out about it?

"What's the matter?" She tilted her head. "You look like you forgot something."

He shook his head. "I didn't. I just don't want to take Dagor's seat."

"It's fine." His friend clapped him on the back. "Sit down and chat with Frankie while I get us coffee. Gertrude doesn't mind as long as I bring her a cup as well."

So that was the nurse's name. Perhaps on his way out, Negal could flirt with her and make arrangements for tonight. The cruise was half over, and after that, there would be no more lovely immortal females vying for his attention.

His team was heading to Tibet to search for the missing Kra-ell pods, and it might be a long time before he found a suitable female to spend a few hours of pleasure with.

Negal wasn't looking forward to it, but he had a duty to perform.

He sat down on the chair and steepled his fingers over his knees for the simple reason that he didn't know what to do with them.

Frankie regarded him with a knowing smile. "You still haven't told me what you've been up to lately, and I don't mean the mission you've just come back from." She grimaced. "As glad as I am that those bad guys were dealt with, I don't want to hear the gruesome details. I'm much more interested in your love life."

He frowned. "What did you hear?"

She chuckled. "That you're very popular with the clan ladies."

Negal let out a breath. Maybe she didn't know about Karen after all and was just fishing.

"Indeed. I'm the only available bachelor on this cruise, so of course I'm popular. I could have warts all over my face and still get more attention than I could ever hope for."

"But you don't have warts. You are a god, and you are absolutely perfect." Frankie pulled out her phone. "Do you mind if I take a picture of you?"

"Why do you want to?"

"I want to show it to my friend Margo." She turned on her side and leaned closer to him. "I'm not supposed to take pictures of anyone on the ship, but we are inside a clinic that has no windows and looks like any other medical facility out there. No one will be able to recognize it, so I hope that whoever is monitoring outgoing calls, texts, and emails will let this one slide."

He really didn't want Frankie to show his picture to her friend and get her hopes up for nothing because he wasn't interested.

Wincing, Negal shifted on the uncomfortable chair. "Are you trying to play matchmaker?"

She rolled her eyes. "Obviously. Mia, Margo, and I are best friends, and two of us are mated to gods. It's only fair that Margo mates a god as well, and you are the only one left."

Negal groaned. "I don't want a mate. I'm perfectly happy being a bachelor and enjoying the attention of the single clan ladies." He leaned closer to Frankie, so they were almost touching noses. "Who are immortal and have the stamina to match. With all due respect to your friend, I don't want to waste the last days of the cruise on a human."

Frankie recoiled as if he had insulted her mother. "You are such a bigot, Negal. I was human until this morning, and yet Dagor chose me. Margo is beautiful, smart, and has the heart of a tiger." She leaned away from him and started scrolling on her phone. "Here. Take a look." She shoved the phone in his face.

Not wanting to antagonize her further, Negal took the phone and looked at the photo of a pretty blond human. She might be beautiful by human standards, but she was quite ordinary when compared to goddesses or even immortal females. That being said, there was a fierceness in her eyes that spoke to him. "I see what you mean by her having the heart of a tiger." He handed Frankie the phone back. "She looks formidable."

Frankie frowned. "That's it? That's all you have to say about her?"

"What did you expect me to say? That I fell in love with her at first sight?"

"Well, yeah." Frankie pouted. "I heard one of the immortals talking about falling in love with the picture of his mate before ever meeting her." She sighed. "Well, that was disappointing. Perhaps I should show Margo's picture to Max." She looked at him with a slight smirk, lifting one corner of her lips. "Perhaps he will react like I hoped you would."

"Max is an excellent choice for your friend." Negal pushed to his feet and dipped his head. "I wish you an easy and successful transition." He turned to leave.

"Wait. What about that picture?"

Taking a deep breath, he turned back to her. "What for? I'm not interested in dating your friend. You should take a picture of Max and send it to her."

"Ugh, Negal. You are such a party pooper."

"I'm sorry." He dipped his head again and walked out.

Outside her room, he found Dagor delivering a cup of coffee to the nurse.

"Leaving so soon?" his friend asked.

"Yeah. Frankie wanted to take a picture of me and send it to her friend. Can you please talk to her and ask her not to try to set me up with anyone?"

Dagor grimaced. "Why won't you give it a try? You might find Margo attractive."

Behind Dagor, the nurse cleared her throat. "Do you really want to have this conversation in front of me?"

Damn. Negal had plans for that nurse. Turning his best smile on her, he lifted his hands in mock surrender. "I'm sorry. I didn't come here expecting matchmaking." He lowered his hands. "I much prefer to court ladies of my own choosing."

3

PETER

Peter sat on the Lido deck and watched the sunset with an Old Fashioned in his hand, swirling the dark liquid around the large ice cube in the middle. It was getting cooler, which was a welcome respite from the day's heat.

He was a little miffed about not having been chosen to join the Guardian force that had dealt with the Doomer and cartel infestation. It would have been a nice break from thinking about Kagra and what had gone wrong in their relationship.

Things had been great between them during the joint Guardian and Kra-ell mission to China, the sex was phenomenal, and for a while Peter had thought that they had something special, but she had made it clear in so many words that he had been merely a passing curiosity. Kagra had wanted to experience what it was like to be with an immortal, and Peter had been conveniently available and willing.

Had she found him lacking compared to the males of her own race? Was that the reason she'd dumped him?

The Kra-ell males were faster, stronger, and could properly challenge her in the cruel Kra-ell mating rituals.

It was ironic that despite his proclivity for dominant bedroom games, he couldn't give her what she needed. Compared to the males of her species, he was too gentle, but he'd naively hoped that she would find his style of lovemaking revelatory.

Oh, well. When it wasn't meant to be, it wasn't meant to be, right?

It was her loss. He was wittier, funnier, and much better mate material than her fellow Kra-ell.

Still, despite the self-pep talk, the sting of rejection lingered.

Whatever. He was tired of mulling over the mysteries of love and the unpredictable nature of relationships.

Evidently, he was more clueless than he'd believed.

"Can I please have a mojito?" An unfamiliar female voice caught his attention.

It was heavily accented and a little nasal, which meant that it belonged to a human, and he had never seen one of the human servers on the Lido deck. It wasn't that they weren't allowed, but they preferred not to mingle with the immortals any more than they had to while serving in the kitchen and the dining hall and keeping the ship tidy.

Given their experience with the Kra-ell, that was perfectly understandable.

These humans were used to having been exploited by the powerful aliens, being treated as serfs at best and slaves at worst. The females had been given very little choice regarding accepting invitations from the male Kra-ell. Once they had produced a hybrid offspring or gotten beyond a certain age, they had been released from that obligation, but it must have been a miserable existence. Logically, they might acknowledge that their rescuers were different than their former masters and that no one would take advantage of them, but he could understand why they were wary of yet another kind of alien overlord.

Turning to look at the female, Peter recognized her as one of the servers from the dining room. Her blue hair and the piercing in her left eyebrow were her calling cards. He didn't like either, but he liked the rest. She was pretty, even beautiful, for a human, with smiling eyes and a mouth made for kissing. Her tiny T-shirt left her midriff exposed, and her waist was so small that he could encircle it with his hands. Low-hung jeans hugged her rounded hips and delectable bottom.

For a brief moment he considered flirting with her, a playful smile forming on his lips, but then he remembered where she had come from and changed his mind. During her time in the Kra-ell compound, she must have been subjected to the whims and desires of the powerful Kra-ell, and she might feel trapped.

The last thing he wanted was for the woman to assume that she had to suffer his advances the same way she had been forced to submit in the Kra-ell compound. He didn't want her to feel obligated to please him or to be caught in a situation where she felt powerless.

He had never asked Kagra about her own experience under Igor's rule. She had also been a victim and had suffered worse than the human females, so when she hadn't volunteered information about that time, he'd respected her choice to put the past behind her. It was better not to draw out pain that was best forgotten.

With a sigh, Peter shifted his eyes away from the woman and continued gazing at the horizon while sipping on his Old Fashioned.

"Is this seat taken?" the blue-haired server asked, standing with her mojito next to his table.

There was an abundance of empty chairs scattered across the outdoor bar, so it was clear that her interest was in him and not the other vacant chair next to his table.

"Not at all, please, have a seat." He waved a hand at the chair. "I'm Peter."

She flashed him a friendly smile. "I'm Marina." She put her drink down on the table and offered him her hand.

Leaning over, he took her slender fingers in the tips of his and resisted the urge to lift her hand to his lips. Instead, he gave it a gentle shake and let go.

"It's such a beautiful day, don't you think?" Marina gracefully settled into the chair across from him.

"It is. That's why I'm sitting up here and enjoying the view." He deliberately shifted his gaze to the ocean so she wouldn't think it was a come-on line.

"That's what I thought as well." She affected a sigh. "And I also thought that it was a shame to drink alone on such a lovely day."

Was she flirting with him?

She sounded a little nervous, so maybe she was, and if so, she was doing it in surprisingly good English. Most of the humans from the former Kra-ell compound spoke Russian and Finnish, and very few spoke English at all, let alone so well.

"You're absolutely right." He smiled to put her at ease. "Your English is excellent, by the way."

"Thank you." She grinned. "I've been studying for several hours every day." She crossed her legs. "My shifts at Safe Haven left plenty of free time, so that's what I dedicated most of it to. When the offer to work on the ship came, I saw it as a great opportunity to practice my new skills." She leaned a little closer, her perfume tickling his nostrils. "The community members in Safe Haven are a little standoffish. We basically keep to ourselves, and they keep to themselves. Still, I'm very grateful to them for inviting us to join them. It's a very nice place to live." She chuckled. "The problem is that we don't get to meet new people, so it gets a little boring."

Peter was pretty sure that she was flirting with him, but he wasn't going to assume anything. If Marina was interested, she would have to do more than hint.

He leaned in a bit just to indicate that he wasn't averse to the idea. "Your people keep to themselves here as well. You are the first human I've seen on this deck."

She shrugged. "It's mostly a language barrier thing. They are all taking classes, but the older ones don't learn as quickly."

"That's a relief." He leaned back. "I was concerned that your people were afraid of us."

"Some are," she admitted. "But I think it's stupid. Your people liberated us. You gave us choices, and you are kind and polite to us. You are nothing like the Kra-ell. It's like night and day."

He was relieved.

"I'm glad that you feel that way. Are you enjoying the cruise so far?"

Marina's expression shifted slightly, and she let out a small sigh. "Honestly, it's mostly work, and as you know, we've been on this ship before, so it's not a novelty either, but the pay is good so I can't complain." She shrugged, her blue hair shimmering in the waning sunlight. "The weather is also much nicer this time around. Sailing through the Arctic wasn't much fun."

"Can I ask you something?"

She smiled. "Of course."

"Why the blue hair?"

4

MARINA

Marina leaned back in her chair, her gaze fixed on Peter. "It's my banner of freedom, my autonomy, my right to do with my body as I please and to paint my life any color I choose."

She'd been observing Peter since the voyage began, not only because he was handsome in a way that stirred something inside of her, but also because he looked lonely and sad. Even when sitting among friends and sharing laughs with them, his eyes had remained clouded and his expression defeated.

He was ripe for the taking, the perfect candidate to help her escape the drudgery of Safe Haven and her mind-numbingly boring job as a maid.

She had spent a lot of time observing the immortals in order to choose the right one, and approaching Peter had been a daring and calculated move.

Hopefully, focusing her attention on him wouldn't be a mistake like choosing to settle at Safe Haven had been. This time, she wasn't letting her emotions make the decisions for her.

She'd voted with the others to move there instead of to the immortals' village out of fear. Like the others, she hadn't wanted to exchange one type of tyranny for another, and just like them, she'd been convinced that humans could never be more than slaves to these powerful immortals.

The Kra-ell had been cruel masters, but she had learned what to expect from them, how to stay out of trouble, and how to minimize her exposure to the meanest amongst them. At the time of the vote, she hadn't known much about the immortals. All she had known about her rescuers was that they had defeated the formidable Kra-ell, which meant that they were even more powerful and scary than her former masters.

Over time, though, she had begun to change her mind about them. Every one of the Guardians posted at Safe Haven had been polite and kind. She'd thought they had been instructed to act that way, but she experienced the same on the ship. Everyone she'd interacted with had treated her like a person, with smiles and kind words. No one had looked down their noses at her, been impatient with her, or snapped at her.

The fortress of fear that had started eroding at Safe Haven had crumbled entirely during the cruise.

"I get it," Peter said. "I can't imagine how difficult it must have been." He took another sip of his drink before putting the empty glass down. "Were you born in the compound, or were you abducted?"

"I was born there." She lifted her hand to tuck a stray strand of hair behind her ear. "And before you ask, both of my parents are human. I'm not part Kra-ell, for which I'm thankful."

He winced. "Not all of them are bad. Igor was terrible, but even the males in his close circle weren't all horrible people. They were his victims, compelled to obey him just like everyone else."

Oops. She must have stepped on a toe. Or whatever the phrase was when someone said something they shouldn't have.

Evidently, Peter was a Kra-ell sympathizer.

"I know that. We watched the televised trial. Lusha did a great job defending them. She made us proud even though she has Kra-ell blood in her."

Lusha's quarter Kra-ell part was dormant, but it had been enough for her to get privileges that pure humans hadn't gotten in the compound. She'd been allowed to attend university and had become an attorney. Marina and others like her had been home-schooled, and their job prospects were limited.

"Lusha did an amazing job," Peter agreed. "Do you know that Jade is now mated to one of us?"

"I heard that. But so what? You are powerful immortals, and you defeated the Kra-ell who enslaved her and killed the males of her tribe. Mating one of you was a step up for her."

"She and Phinas fell in love."

Peter looked like he really believed that, but she doubted a female who had never spared her own daughter a kind look was capable of love.

Perhaps these immortals were a little naive when it came to the Kra-ell, thinking that they were like them.

"I heard that you entrusted the Kra-ell with safeguarding your village in your absence. Do you really trust them to do that?"

Peter nodded. "Jade saved Kian's life, and she's proved herself loyal many times over. Kagra, too."

His voice had hitched a little when he said Kagra's name. Were the two involved? Was being separated from her the reason he looked so lonely and sad?

If so, Marina had bet on the wrong guy.

Affecting a smile, she looked at him from under lowered lashes. "Is there something going on between you and Kagra?"

"Not anymore." He lifted his empty glass to signal to the robotic bartender. "Do you want another drink?"

So that was why he had looked so sad. He was getting over a breakup, which made him even more ripe for the taking. Now, she definitely wanted one more drink so she could keep talking to him.

"Yes, please." Marina emptied the rest of the mojito down her throat. "More of the same. The mint is very refreshing."

After Bob brought them their drinks, Marina leaned back with hers in hand. "So, what happened between you and Kagra?"

"Nothing worth mentioning." His eyes flashed as he sipped on his drink. "It was just a fling, and we both moved on."

Marina had a feeling that there was more to it, but if that was a touchy subject for him, she was perfectly fine with leaving it alone. "Very well. I won't ask about her. Tell me a little about yourself."

Peter regarded her with his intense dark eyes as if trying to read her mind. "What do you want to know?"

"You are a Guardian, right? I've seen you sharing a table with several males whom I recognized from the liberation of the compound and later the sea voyage."

"Yes, I am."

"Do you enjoy what you do?"

"Most days, I do. I've tried a few things throughout my life, but nothing has brought me as much satisfaction as being on the force and saving innocents from bad people, so I came back."

He was perfect. The guy was a protector, and that was precisely the type of male she needed. Someone who would want to take care of her.

"Can you tell me a little about what you do as a Guardian, or is it a secret?"

"It is a secret, but you are going to get your memories wiped after the cruise is over, so it doesn't matter."

That wasn't good. Her plan was to make the immortal fall in love with her, or at least care deeply for her, and invite her to live with him in the village.

"Why would they want to erase our memories? There is no need for that. We are under compulsion to keep the existence of Kra-ell and immortals a secret."

He shrugged. "I'm not the boss, and it's not my decision, so perhaps I'm wrong about that. It's just what they usually do to humans they employ after the job is done."

She let out a breath. "I hope you are wrong because I don't want to forget you."

It was almost jarring to see the change that her words evoked in him. Suddenly, there was desire in his eyes that hadn't been there a moment ago.

Leaning over the table, Peter reached for her hand. "Are you flirting with me, Marina?"

She gave him a coquettish smile. "What if I am?"

5

MARGO

While waiting for her new friend to return, Margo watched the clouds over the horizon. They were outlined in brilliant gold, looking majestic against the backdrop of the darkening sky. It was as if the world was putting on a show to celebrate the final moments of the day.

It would have been a tranquil and relaxing time if not for the unease churning in her stomach and the raucous sounds coming from the pool bar.

Margo had no doubt that the guy who had pestered Jasmine before was part of that bachelor party's rowdy and obnoxious crowd. The snippets of their conversations reaching her were a mix of brash jokes and boisterous toasts that were intermingled with bursts of loud laughter.

Ironically, the laughter was what sounded the most threatening to her. It was tinged with aggression, and she imagined that in that drunken and exuberant state, the men could be easily incited to do harm. She tried to rationalize that they were just having fun and that they might be decent men when they weren't drunk and away from the women in their lives, but right now, the members of that group were sad representatives of the male gender and further validation of why she was still single.

It was better to be alone than settle for a buffoon who spouted chauvinistic crap when in the company of other buffoons who laughed at his crude comments.

"Another round!" one of the men shouted, his voice booming over the others. "To Chuck's last night of freedom! It's drudgery and misery from now on!"

Margo's options to escape the unpleasant sounds were to put in her earbuds and blast music to tune the men out, or to leave.

The pool deck was mostly deserted, and if not for the waiters still circling the area, she might have felt uncomfortable there with all those drunks only fifty or so feet away. If she hadn't had to wait for Jasmine, Margo would have gone to her room.

Not that she would have had any peace and quiet there. Sharing it with Beatrice meant listening to the woman constantly talking loudly on the phone with her kids, with her husband, and mostly with her girlfriends back home.

How could one woman have so many friends?

Margo had only two, but they were the best.

Right now, Frankie and Mia were enjoying an all-expenses-paid vacation and mingling with Perfect Match employees, and she could have been there with them if not for Lynda's bachelorette party that she had been forced to attend.

The Perfect Match Virtual Studios company was supposed to be her next grand adventure. Becoming a beta tester for their revolutionary software was a dream that had kept her awake at night, imagining the possibilities. The beta testing would only be the first stage, an entry-level job that would hopefully give her a chance to present her ideas to whomever was running their marketing department.

Yeah, as if that had worked so well in her current job. She'd accepted an assistant position in an advertising agency in hopes of getting promoted to something more lucrative, but after nearly three years, she was still doing the same job she'd been hired to do initially.

She looked in the direction Jasmine had disappeared to, but there was no sign of her. Her things were still there, including her bag, so she had to return for them, and until she did, Margo was stuck watching them.

Tightening the towel around her, she thought about the ship's delays and the inconsistencies in Frankie and Mia's stories explaining them.

She was sure that the delay was more than just a logistical hiccup, and her conspiracy theory brain was working overtime but coming up empty. Mostly, it hovered around clandestine meetings the enigmatic owners of Perfect Match might have been conducting with other reclusive billionaires. Perhaps the ship had been intercepted by a luxury yacht, and they were negotiating while in international waters because it provided some kind of an advantage.

"Sorry about that." Jasmine plopped down on the lounger next to Margo, startling her out of her reveries. "Alberto checks on me constantly." She let out a breath and smiled apologetically. "What's with men and irrational jealousy?"

Was she being apologetic for making the claim or for the irrational men?

"Women get jealous, too," Margo said. "They are just not as dangerous when their jealousy turns psychotic."

The wince on Jasmine's beautiful face was all the proof Margo needed to confirm her suspicion that the boyfriend was bad news.

"Yeah, tell me about it." Jasmine leaned closer. "I shouldn't have agreed to come here with him. He was so charming and attentive back in Los Angeles that I never suspected he could be—" Jasmine stopped and waved a dismissive hand. "Never mind. I don't want to be a downer. Let's get that drink. What's your poison?"

Margo wanted to find out what Jasmine had stopped herself from saying. She had a feeling that the missing word was abusive, but given that the woman was in a tiny bikini, signs of physical abuse would have been hard to hide.

Maybe she'd meant to say jealous? Possessive?

Those weren't good traits, and they could quickly turn abusive, but it didn't look like Jasmine was in any immediate danger.

"Passionfruit mule," she said. "Have you had one of those? They are delicious."

"Not yet." Jasmine lifted her empty glass to signal for the waiter to come. "I'm going to rectify that oversight now."

After Jasmine placed their orders, she carelessly plopped the huge hat back on her head even though the sun had set, and it was dark. Seeing Margo regarding her with a quizzical look, she took it off. "Sorry. It's a habit. It usually keeps guys from hitting on me."

Margo snorted. "I very much doubt that. The hat might hide your face but not your body, and you have a very good one."

"Thank you." Jasmine gave her a small smile. "So, where are you from?"

"Same place as you. Los Angeles. More precisely, I'm from Pasadena."

"Awesome. We should get together when we get home. When are you leaving?"

"In two days. But I'm not going home right away. I'm going on a cruise that will end at Long Beach."

The amber flakes in Jasmine's eyes seemed to swirl. "I'm curious. Do they check passports on cruise ships?"

"They do. I was told to bring mine, but I needed it to get here anyway. My friend, who boarded the ship in Long Beach, had to show hers before being allowed on board. Why do you ask?"

"Never mind." Jasmine smiled at the waiter who had returned with their drinks. "I was just curious. I've never been on a cruise before."

6

KIAN

"I've changed my mind." Kian gestured for Kalugal to follow him. "Cigars first, and the Doomer's interrogation later."

The leader of the Doomers' Acapulco team was in the ship's brig, the same one that Igor had occupied not so long ago, and although Kian had intended to question him first and relax with a cigar later, he'd decided to reverse the order.

He and Kalugal needed to coordinate their line of questioning. Kalugal would have to ask the questions because he was the compeller, and Kian needed to tell him what to ask.

He was well aware that this was just an excuse to postpone an unpleasant task, but even though it wasn't his usual MO, he was cutting himself some slack for a change.

The cruise should have been about spending time with family and celebrating ten weddings. Instead, he was being forced to deal with the worst filth ever to mar the face of the Earth—vermin who rejoiced in causing pain and suffering—and consequently, he was consumed by rage instead of enjoying a well-earned vacation.

Kalugal grinned. "I'm delighted, cousin. Your cabin, I assume?"

Kian nodded. "Syssi is with Callie and her friends, and my mother has Allegra, so we can have the place to ourselves." He opened the door and motioned for Kalugal to enter. "Brundar might not want a bachelor party, but Callie wants to celebrate like all the other brides."

"I know. Jacki was invited to her bachelorette party, which delighted her to no end." He cast Kian an accusing look. "She wasn't invited to your sisters' parties or Wonder's, and she was starting to feel like a pariah."

He was sure that Kalugal was exaggerating. Jacki was well loved and respected, and she knew that.

Then again, they had invited Carol, who was Jacki's de facto sister-in-law, so perhaps that was why she felt slighted.

"Your wife was a bridesmaid at my sisters' weddings." Kian poured two glasses of whiskey and handed one to his cousin before heading to the balcony.

Kalugal followed him out. "True, but she would have loved to be invited to their bachelorette parties too."

"You should have told me." Kian opened the cigar box and offered it to Kalugal. "I would have dropped a hint to Amanda." He sat on the lounger and cut the tip off his cigar.

He lit his cigar and waited until Kalugal had cut the tip off his before offering him the lighter.

"I'm sure it was just an oversight." Kalugal leaned back on the lounger. "It's not a big deal. Jacki will get over it."

"I'm sorry," Kian said. "I'm glad that Callie invited her. I didn't know that they were close."

"They are not." Kalugal closed his eyes briefly. "I wish all of our troubles were as trivial as this. I'm not looking forward to interrogating that scum. Now that it's over and I have already showered, I don't feel like getting dirty again." He lifted his hands. "Even if I only need to dirty these. Can't it wait until tomorrow?"

"I wish." Kian took a sip of his whiskey. "I wish we could kill him and be done with it, but we have to find out what he knows and, more importantly, what he reported back to the Brotherhood."

Kalugal nodded. "Perhaps you should get Toven to compel Bud."

Kian found it amusing that the Doomers' leader had chosen such a mundane name for himself. Surely, that wasn't what his poor mother had named him.

Not for the first time, Kian wondered about the Dormants who were used to breed Navuh's mercenary army. Did they support his efforts, or did they feel victimized?

The women didn't know that they could be turned immortal, and they were probably just as brainwashed as the sons they birthed. They were told to feel proud for being the means by which the Brotherhood grew, and most of them probably believed that.

"Toven is not the right person for the job." Kian took a sip of his whiskey. "Why would you suggest that?"

Kalugal lifted his hand. "I know what you're thinking, but this is not about me trying to wiggle out of something that I'm not looking forward to doing. Toven is just a stronger compeller."

Kian cast him an amused look. "You are strong enough for Bud, and you are familiar with how the Brotherhood operates. Toven would need much more coaching before he could question the Doomer."

"You are right." Kalugal released a breath. "My knowledge is rusty, though. Perhaps we should have Lokan listen in."

"That's a good idea. If Bud throws names around, Lokan will know who he is talking about."

"I'll text him and ask him to come over." Kalugal pulled out his phone.

Kian grimaced. "I promised your brother a pleasant vacation with the family. I hate that he risked coming here, and then I failed to deliver on my promise."

"I'm sure Lokan will be happy to help." Kalugal put the phone on the side table. "The one I'm worried about is Luis."

"The tour guide?"

Kalugal nodded. "I thralled the two guys we left alive to spread a rumor about him being related to the Colombian cartel boss, but now I think it was a mistake. What if someone decides to use him as a bargaining chip again? The guy and his family have been through enough because of us."

"It wasn't directly because of us." Kian took another puff of his cigar. "But you have a point. What do you want to do with him?"

"We've already left Acapulco, so I'm not sure what we can do at this point."

"We can do plenty." Kian pulled out his phone. "I can arrange plane tickets to Los Angeles for him and his family, and once they are there, we can get them new identities."

Kalugal nodded. "Thank you. That will ease my mind. Luis and his family need trauma counseling after what they have been through. Do you think Vanessa could take them on?"

Kian snorted. "Poor Vanessa has enough on her plate. But I'll ask her. Maybe the volunteers in the sanctuary can help."

"That would be nice. Could Luis work in the sanctuary in some capacity? He will need a new job."

"I doubt it," Kian said. "But I'm sure I can find him something to do."

Kalugal lifted his glass, took a sip, and put it back on the side table. "I've noticed that the ship is going faster again. What's up with that? Now that we are not in a rush, I thought we would be going at a slower pace."

"That was the plan, but I decided to speed up our arrival in Cabo so we could have at least one more stop on the way home. As it is, this trip is a far cry from the vacation everyone expected. I want to salvage what I can."

Kalugal emptied his glass and put it back on the side table. "Higher speed requires exponentially more fuel, which makes it much more expensive, and the increased motion makes sailing uncomfortable. I don't think your guests care about visiting another port city as much as they care about enjoying themselves on the ship."

"I don't feel any difference in the comfort level." Kian took a long puff of his cigar. "And I'd prefer to put as much distance as I can between us and Acapulco as fast as possible."

Kalugal nodded. "That's a good point."

7

MARGO

Margo had a feeling that Jasmine's question about needing to show a passport to get on a cruise ship had to do with her boyfriend. She was an American, and she couldn't have boarded the plane at LAX without a passport. She had either lost it or it had been taken away from her, and Margo was betting on option number two.

The problem was approaching the subject in a way that wouldn't offend or scare Jaz away.

She was very pleasant to be around, and Margo wanted to befriend her. They had been chatting for more than an hour, and she found Jasmine knowledgeable about many subjects but not opinionated, and although she was stunningly beautiful, she didn't act like those women who thought that everyone needed to worship them because of their looks.

What was even more attractive about Jasmine was her ability to enjoy quiet camaraderie without having to fill every moment with sound. She was content to just lounge by the pool next to Margo and say absolutely nothing. It was so refreshing after spending nearly a week with Lynda and her friends, who felt like every moment needed to be filled with words, and every second of silence made them feel awkward.

"The bachelor party left the pool bar," Jasmine said after a while. "Do you want to get another drink before the night crowd arrives?"

They were the only two still lounging by the pool. The other hotel guests had left a long time ago, but some were enjoying drinks at the pool bar, which was just gearing up for nighttime activities.

The band was setting up their instruments on the podium while staff members were collecting the loungers and replacing them with tables and chairs.

"That's not a bad idea." Margo removed the towel that had been keeping her warm and pulled her cover-up from her satchel. It wouldn't shield her from the evening chill, but it was more suitable for the bar. "But this time, I'm buying."

"Don't be silly." Jaz waved a dismissive hand. "I'm putting it on Alberto's tab." She smiled with an evil glint in her eyes. "He said to charge anything I want to the room." She pushed to her feet and pulled a beautiful cover-up dress from her bag. "I bought this today in the hotel boutique."

"It's gorgeous." Margo slid her feet into her flip-flops. "It looks expensive."

"Oh, it was." Jasmine lifted her high-heeled slides and put them in her satchel. "But Alberto won't mind. He loves spending money on me." She winced. "He thinks that it makes everything else okay."

That was an opening Margo could pounce on. "What do you mean by everything else? Is he abusive?"

Jaz shook her head, but it was a very unconvincing gesture. "He's very controlling, so I guess that could be called abusive. But so far, he hasn't done anything physical." She padded toward the bar.

Margo fell into step with her. "I don't like how you said 'so far,' as if you are expecting that to happen soon."

"I didn't mean it that way." Jasmine's smile looked so fake that it would have been comical if not for the seriousness of the subject. "It's not going to happen because I won't let it."

"Good for you." Margo patted Jaz's shoulder. "The moment you suspect that things are about to get ugly, walk away. No guy is worth it, not even one who lavishes presents on you."

"I know." Jaz sat on one of the barstools facing the bar and put her satchel on the floor next to her feet. "But it's not that easy."

"Why not?" Margo sat on the one to her right. "Is it a financial thing? If it is, you can move back with your parents for a while until you get back on your feet."

"It's not financial." Jasmine plastered a bright smile on her face for the barman. "Hi, can we have a couple of Cadillac Margaritas?"

"What's that?" Margo asked after the guy turned to fill their order.

"It's a supercharged margarita with a shot of Grand Marnier in it."

"Oh, my." Margo fanned herself. "I don't think I can handle such a potent drink."

"It's really tasty. But if you want something else, I'll order it for you." Jaz chuckled. "I've just pulled an Alberto, deciding for you what you wanted to drink. I'm sorry."

"It's okay. If I feel like it's going to my head, I'll just stop drinking. Speaking of Alberto, we are not done talking about him and why you are still hanging around despite the warning signs."

"Here you go, ladies." The barman put two large margaritas in front of them.

"Thank you." Jaz lifted hers and took several sips before turning back to Margo. "We haven't been dating for long, and we are not living together." She rolled her eyes. "Thank goodness for that." She leaned closer and whispered, "I'm mad at myself for agreeing to go on vacation to Mexico with him, but on the other hand, I might not have discovered what was hiding under the charm and affluence if I hadn't come here with him." She took another sip from her margarita. "I'll be fine. All I need to do is pretend that I'm having a great time until we get back to Los Angeles, and then I can dump his ass."

Margo wasn't convinced that was true, especially in light of Jasmine's passport question. Given that Jaz was reluctant to speak about her boyfriend within anyone's earshot, Margo leaned closer and whispered in her ear, "You asked me about boarding a cruise ship without a passport. Is Alberto holding yours?"

Jaz's eyes widened for a moment, and then she nodded. "He says that it's unsafe because of pickpockets and that hotel safes are not really secure because every employee knows how to open them. He also took all my credit cards and left me with just forty bucks in my wallet, telling me I could have whatever I wanted and to just charge it to the room. I don't doubt that he will return my things, but his excuse about my so-called safety is bogus. That's just how he ensures that I can't leave the hotel. If he's so concerned, why isn't he here?"

"Good question. Where is he?"

"God knows." Jasmine sighed and cast a furtive look at the barman. "Perhaps we can continue our talk in your room?"

Margo's hackles rose.

What if this was an elaborate setup to rob her? Usually, guys fell for pretty girls with sad stories who needed rescuing, but it seemed that women could also be manipulated that way.

On the other hand, what if Jasmine's story was genuine and she needed help for real?

Margo cast a glance at the woman's large satchel. She could be hiding a machine gun in that thing, and as soon as they were alone in Margo's room, she could rob her at gunpoint.

"I share my room with a friend. Maybe we can go to yours?"

Beatrice was on her way to the Mandala club, but Jasmine didn't have to know that.

Or did she?

Margo hadn't noticed Jasmine until that obnoxious guy had started pestering her, but she could have been there when Lynda had told Margo about her plans for tonight.

Jasmine grimaced. "We could, but I have a feeling that we won't have privacy there either." She pursed her lips. "But maybe we can sit on the balcony." She leaned closer to Margo again. "I suspect that Alberto bugged our suite. I've searched for cameras or hidden bugs as best I could, but I didn't want to be too obvious about it. The balcony might be safe, though. Even if he planted anything there as well, we can sit near the waterfall, where it's really noisy."

The hotel had a huge waterfall running down its front, starting from just below the penthouse and spilling into the artificial lake below, so Jasmine might be right about the balcony being safe. Still, it surprised Margo that the woman suspected her boyfriend of bugging the place.

Someone who had been naive enough to fall for charm and lavish gifts couldn't be an overly suspicious type.

Margo was precisely that type, though, and it tickled her that Jasmine and she might have that in common.

"Why do you suspect that he bugged your hotel suite?"

"Because he never calls to check on me when I'm there. Only when I'm away. He doesn't even try to hide that he knows I'm not in the room. He asks me where I am and what I'm doing."

"That's suspicious."

Jasmine waved a hand. "Right?"

"Totally."

8

BRUNDAR

It had been a good day for Brundar, and he felt a rare sense of contentment.

He'd killed some vermin and made the world a tiny bit better for a little bit of time and for a small enclave of people. It was not even a blip on the tapestry of existence, but it gave him some small measure of satisfaction.

Everyone assumed that finding one's fated mate was a cure-all and that happily ever after was guaranteed, but it wasn't. Brundar loved Callie with all the good that had managed to survive the devastation of his trauma, but most of him still needed to stay deadened most of the time, or he would become overwhelmed by rage.

He still had hordes of demons to deal with.

Most people tried to run away from their tormented pasts, but Brundar had discovered a long time ago that there was nowhere to run. The demons were with him wherever he went. They were there when he woke up, and they were still there when he got to bed at night, keeping him awake until his eyes burned with fatigue and he could no longer hold his eyelids up.

Thankfully, when he finally drifted into sleep, he enjoyed a few hours of peace. Since Callie had entered his life, he no longer suffered from nightmares, so the few hours of shuteye he managed were a reprieve.

Love might not cure all, but for him, it cured some.

Stepping out of the shower, he dried off with practiced, efficient moves, combed out the knots from his ass-long hair, and padded to the closet.

There was still plenty of time until the wedding, so there was no point in getting into his tux, but he pulled out the garment bag and unzipped it, nonetheless.

Perhaps he needed reassurance that it was actually happening.

Callie was his miracle, and his gratitude to the universe for sending her to him was the only good thing he had to say to it, or the Fates, or whatever other sadistic power was in charge.

Sometimes, he mused that perhaps this world was nothing more than a computer game played by an alien sociopathic child.

There was too much suffering and misery in the world for him to believe that the powers that be up there were any more interested in the well-being of people than the politicians down on earth.

When the doorbell rang, he rehung the garment bag, pulled on a pair of workout pants, and padded to the living room to open the door without bothering to take a look at the screen to see who it was.

Only his big brother would come to bother him on the evening of his wedding.

"Come in." He threw the door open.

Anandur arched a brow. "That's a surprise. I expected you to slam the door in my face like you usually do."

"I don't do that anymore."

Anandur chuckled. "That's because Callie is around, and you know it will upset her."

"Usually, you also show up with Wonder, and I don't want to be rude to her." He walked over to the bar and poured himself a shot of whiskey. "What do you want?"

Anandur rubbed the back of his neck. "I came to convince you to attend a little get-together. We will not call it a bachelor party, and I promise not to goof around or even tell jokes. All we will do is smoke good cigars, drink premium whiskey, and share battle stories. You will like that, right?"

For a moment, Brundar was tempted, but he knew he wouldn't be able to handle so much social interaction in one day.

"Sorry, but I can't." He took in a deep breath. "I need this time alone before the wedding."

Anandur shook his head. "What are you going to do here by yourself until then?"

"Watch television."

"Right. You never do that."

That was true. The movies and sitcoms were either too saccharine and made a mockery of real life, or too violent, which was more reflective of how things really were, but he hated the glorifying of killing. There was nothing glorious about it, although he had to concede that heroism was real, and some people went above and beyond the call of duty to save their friends or protect the innocent. He liked to watch those kinds of movies, but there weren't many of them.

"Perhaps I'll take a nap." Brundar walked over to the door and opened it. "When and where am I meeting my groomsmen?"

"We will come here to get you. Be ready by eight-thirty. We need to be in formation precisely at nine."

"I'll be ready."

9

CALLIE

Carol released Callie's hair from the loose, wet bun on the top of her head and spread it over her shoulders. "I love your hair. It's such a pleasure to play around with it."

"How would you know? You've never played with it before."

They had been friends while working together in the café, but they hadn't hung out outside of it. Callie had been busy finishing her degree and serving drinks in Brundar's club at night. That hadn't left time for anything else.

Then Carol had left with Lokan, and they barely talked because it was too dangerous for Carol, or maybe just because she was too busy building a fashion empire in China.

Callie was also busier now than she had been before, even though she'd finished her studies and wasn't working in the café or in Brundar's club. Her restaurant was a full-time job even though it was only open for dinner.

"I imagined doing it so many times." Carol reached for the curler. "I always wanted a little sister."

Sitting on the bed behind them, Wonder sighed. "I miss Tula. For me, it wasn't that long ago since the last time I saw her, but she lived for thousands of years while I was in stasis, and she probably barely remembers me."

"She remembers you," Carol said. "She's never forgotten you or Annani or Esag or Khiann."

Callie tried to see Wonder's expression in the mirror, but Carol was blocking her. The rest of her guests were in the cabin's living room, and given the laughter coming through the open door, they were having fun.

Amanda had brought Onidu with her, and he was mixing drinks for everyone and getting them in a good mood for the wedding.

The successful end of the mission had something to do with the mood as well. Everyone had been worried about the tour guide and his family and what those monsters might be doing to them. Now, the guy and his family were safely home.

Brundar had returned from the mission in a good mood, too, which Callie was thankful for. The wedding was stressing him so having an outlet for the stress had been good.

She didn't want to think about what he had done to release that stress. Sometimes, it was better not to let imagination run free.

"You haven't shown me your wedding dress yet," Carol said. "Is it another one of Amanda's designers?"

"No." Callie smiled. "I went to a wedding shop and bought a ready-made dress. I'm not a designer clothing kind of girl."

Carol paused with the curler. "Are you telling me that Amanda agreed to wear a bridesmaid dress that wasn't custom-made for her?"

"I didn't leave her much choice." Callie chuckled. "Not only that, the tulle inserts are made from nylon. I hope she doesn't have an allergic reaction to the material."

"You'd better not tell her about that." Carol wound another lock of hair around the curler. "She might refuse to wear it, or worse, refuse to be your bridesmaid."

Callie doubted that was true, and Carol was probably exaggerating to poke fun at Amanda.

"That's why I brought the dresses with me and didn't let any of you try them on. I just hope everything fits."

Callie had collected everyone's measurements and delivered them to the bridal shop, so they should be okay, but it made her anxious to think that her bridesmaids might not approve of her choices.

"I'm sure they will fit perfectly," Carol said without much conviction in her voice.

"Now that I think of it, I shouldn't have done that," Callie murmured. "I should have let all of you choose your own dresses, go to the fittings, and have everything done perfectly instead of trying to save time and money. I keep forgetting that I don't have to do that anymore. Brundar makes a very good living as a Guardian, the club is finally making a profit, and my restaurant is doing extremely well. I could have hired Amanda's designer to do all the dresses, including mine."

"Are you unhappy with your choice?" Wonder asked.

"I love the dress." Callie smiled at the mirror. "Wearing it, I feel like Cinderella going to the ball. All I'm missing is a pumpkin-made chariot and mice-made horses. Oh, and glass slippers."

"If you're happy with the dress, that's all that matters." Carol released the curl and wound another section around the device. "I'm glad you didn't hire the designer. I couldn't have made the fitting appointment, and I bet the others would have hated running all around town to try on bridesmaids' dresses for ten weddings."

"That's what I was thinking, but now I'm having second thoughts. What if everyone hates what I've chosen for them?"

Carol shrugged. "I'm sure I'm going to love mine, and even if I don't, it's not a big deal. It's just a dress, and most bridesmaids' dresses are horrible. It's your night, and you are the only one who matters."

"Brundar matters too, and I'm worried about him as well. Anandur is so disappointed that he didn't even agree to a small get-together with the guys. It is difficult for Brundar to be around people. If he spent time with the guys, he would have been emotionally exhausted by the time he needed to show up at the altar. It was one or the other."

Wonder pushed to her feet and loomed over Carol as she looked at Callie through the mirror. "He spends long days with Kian in meetings. How does he handle that?"

"By pretending to be a statue." Callie looked up at her friend. "Everyone thinks that he does that to look intimidating. The truth is that he needs to retreat into himself for self-preservation."

"Ha." Wonder pursed her lips. "It's so obvious now that you say it. I remember him pulling the statue routine when Tim had me describe that woman Anandur had been with. What was her name? Was it Rosie?"

"How should I know?" Carol waved the curler in the mirror. "Does it matter what her name was for the sake of your story?"

"Not really," Wonder admitted. "Anyway, he looked so damn scary. I wish I had known it was an act."

"Well," Callie scrunched her nose. "It's not entirely an act. Brundar can be scary sometimes. He's not the soft and fuzzy type."

"Not even when the two of you are alone?" Carol asked.

"Not even then. If I get a smile out of him, I feel like it's a great accomplishment."

"And yet, you are marrying him." Wonder put a hand on her shoulder. "It must be love."

"It is." Callie smiled. "Brundar is a work in progress, and the road to recovery is still long, but I wouldn't trade him for anyone else. I love him so much."

10

MARGO

"Wow." Margo turned in a circle, taking in the luxurious suite. "I've never been in a presidential suite before. This is amazing."

The opulence was intimidating.

The entrance led to a sprawling living area with floor-to-ceiling windows. Two plush purple sofas faced each other with a massive black marble coffee table between them. The artwork on the walls looked original, probably done by local artists.

"Do you want a tour?" Jasmine asked.

"Of course. Can I take pictures? I want to send them to my besties on the cruise ship."

A brief shadow passed over Jasmine's eyes, but it was gone almost as soon as it appeared. "Of course." She smiled. "Take as many as you want."

As they moved through the suite, Margo was struck by the sheer size of it. There were two master bedrooms, each with a king-sized bed, and the linens and pillows were of much better quality than what she had in her room.

Running her fingers over the fabric of the duvet cover, she marveled at its softness. "I wish all the rooms in this hotel came with this kind of luxury bedding."

Jasmine arched a brow. "They don't? I was sure that hotels used the same linens for all their rooms."

"I thought so too, but I was obviously wrong."

Each of the bathrooms was like a private spa, equipped with rain showers and Jacuzzi tubs that gleamed under the soft lighting. Designer toiletries were lined up neatly on the vanities, and the towels looked so fluffy that she had to run her fingers over one of those, too.

She cast an apologetic look at Jaz "I hope you don't mind that I'm touching your stuff."

"Not at all. Everything in here is clean. The housekeeping comes twice a day to replace all the towels and the toiletries."

"Impressive," Margo murmured under her breath. "I bet this suite costs thousands of dollars a night."

"I have no clue." Jasmine leaned against the vanity and crossed her arms over her chest. "Alberto doesn't share details like that with me. He tells me not to worry my pretty little head over stuff like that."

"Ugh." Margo grimaced. "I like him less and less with each new thing you tell me about him. Does he have any redeeming qualities?"

"He's a generous tipper, and he's friendly and polite toward the staff." Jasmine closed her eyes and sighed. "He's also awesome in bed. In fact, he's one of the best I've ever had, but that's probably because I like dominant assholes. It's a terrible character flaw."

"Which is the character flaw?" Margo put down one of the little soaps that was shaped like a mermaid. "Alberto being a dominant asshole or your attraction to the type?"

"The second one." Jasmine pushed away from the counter. "I should find myself a nice accountant or engineer who will worship the ground I walk on and answer every question with 'yes, honey,' 'of course, honey,' 'as you wish, honey'."

Margo laughed. "You've just described my dream man. We should go hunting together. Maybe we can snag a couple of Google engineers. Computer geeks are my favorite type."

"You're on, sister." Jaz high-fived her.

When they returned to the living room, Margo looked around for the bugs Jasmine had hinted at, but the truth was that she wouldn't know one if it stared her in the face and maybe not even if it landed on her nose. What she knew about spyware came from books and not the illustrated type.

Given that she called herself a conspiracy theorist, that was a gap in her education that she needed to rectify. How could she talk about conspiracies if she didn't know the first thing about espionage?

Nevertheless, Margo could tell that cutting-edge technology was seamlessly integrated into every corner of the suite, with a smart system controlling everything from the lighting to the curtains covering the huge floor-to-ceiling windows. The bar in the corner of the living room was stocked with an array of premium bottles, and there was even a kitchen tucked behind a discreet door where the staff could prepare private meals for the guests of the suite.

"It's too large for just the two of us." Jasmine opened the sliding doors to the terrace. "We have the entire floor to ourselves, and this balcony wraps around the suite. We have the ocean on one side and the city on the other."

"So, this is how the rich live." Margo felt as if she had stepped through the looking glass into another world.

"I'm not rich." Jasmine dragged one of the patio chairs all the way to the railing, where the nearby waterfall was indeed loud enough to drown out their conversation.

Margo hefted the other chair and brought it next to the one Jasmine was sitting on. "I wonder where he could have planted bugs out here."

"You've just said it. The planters," Jaz said without hesitation. "I checked under the chairs and tables, so I know those are clean, but I didn't want to get my hands dirty by sifting through the soil."

It seemed like Jasmine had given this a lot of thought, which once again raised Margo's hackles.

"Were you expecting to invite someone up here?"

"No." Jaz crossed her legs. "I was just curious to what lengths Alberto's possessiveness and jealousy would go. I was afraid to search the interior because I didn't want him to realize that I was suspicious, but out here, it was easier. I pretended to be concerned with real bugs, the type that crawled. If he was watching, I gave him a very convincing show of fearfully checking under the chair and jumping with a scream when I saw a suspicious speck."

Imagining what Jaz had described made Margo laugh. "I hope you added a few juicy curses to make it seem even more convincing."

"I did." Jasmine tossed a lock of hair behind her shoulder. "I acted in school and college productions, so I'm a semi-professional actress."

"Is that what you do for a living?"

Margo hadn't seen Jasmine in any movies, but she couldn't claim that she had seen them all.

"When I get lucky, I play in commercials," Jaz said. "The rest of the time, I work in customer service. I'm the one people call when they don't understand their electrical bill."

"That sounds even more boring than what I do."

"Which is?"

Margo sighed. "I work at an advertising agency, but that sounds much more glamorous than it is. I'm an assistant, which is another term for a paid servant. Whatever my boss says, I do. Thankfully, she is not a total bitch, but she's a workaholic and thinks that everyone around her needs to put in just as much effort even though we are paid a fraction of what she gets."

"Life is not fair." Jasmine pushed to her feet. "Can I get you a drink?"

"Water or Coke would be great. I'm still a little tipsy from that Cadillac Margarita."

"Yeah, me too." Jasmine walked into the living room, leaving Margo alone on the terrace to admire the view.

"It's good to be a queen," she murmured. "Except, neither of us is royal."

11

NEGAL

Negal walked through the sliding doors onto the Lido deck with Gertrude's phone number in his contacts, a promise of a dance at the wedding, and a much better mood.

He wanted to check up on Karen and see whether she was showing any early symptoms of the transition, but he didn't want to call Gilbert because it felt too intrusive. Perhaps the couple or one of their many relatives were enjoying a drink by the pool so he could casually inquire about her.

On second thought, he should limit the inquiry to the people who knew for sure what went down last night, and that was a much smaller group. One of them was Max, and he spotted the Guardian sitting at the bar and talking with one of his friends. Negal walked over and sat down on Max's other side.

"Good evening, gentlemen," he greeted them. "Mind if I join you?"

"Not at all." Max turned to him, which meant that he had his back to the other Guardian. "How did it go last night?" he asked.

The question was general enough not to hint at what Max wanted to know.

"Very well. The mission was accomplished."

"Excellent." Max grinned. "Any plans for tonight?"

"Of course. But with a different lady." Negal tacked on that last sentence to insinuate that they had been talking about his nightly exploits with the single clan ladies. "How about you?" He lifted his hand to get Bob's attention.

Max snorted. "The only single ladies I'm not related to on this cruise are underage or recovering from trauma, so it's another lonely night for me."

"Not for long." Negal turned to Bob, who was waiting expectantly for his order. "I will have a whiskey sour, please."

"Coming up, master."

Max frowned. "What do you mean by not for long?"

"Don't you know? Frankie's friend is coming on board in Cabo, and Frankie plans to introduce you to her. She has her matchmaker hat on."

A grin spread over the Guardian's face. "I was sure she would try to get you for her friend. You know, three best friends all mated to gods and all that."

"I'm not interested." Negal lifted the drink Bob had put in front of him and took a sip. "I like my freedom, and I'm not looking for a mate."

"I hope she's pretty," Max said.

"She is. Frankie showed me a picture." Those fierce blue eyes were what Negal remembered best about her.

They were the eyes of a warrior.

"And…" Max waved his hand. "What does she look like?"

"Blond, blue eyes, the same age as Frankie and Mia, looks fierce."

Max's brow furrowed. "Do you mean angry? Because I don't dig angry women."

"No, not angry, just fierce. Not afraid, not mellow, and not accommodating. It's hard to explain. If you visit Frankie, I'm sure she will show you her friend's picture. Be ready for her to take your photo too and send it to her. She wanted to take mine, but I said that I wasn't interested."

"Oh, so she offered the match to you first. I knew it."

Negal didn't know what to say to that. It was true, and Max seemed offended to be the second choice.

The Guardian sitting on Max's other side snorted. "I'll leave you two to gossip. See you later."

"We are not gossiping," Max said. "We are talking."

"Whatever." The guy waved and walked away.

"Asshole," Max muttered under his breath.

"Are you talking about my brother?" Anandur commandeered the vacated seat.

"No, I was talking about James."

"Aha." Anandur turned to Bob. "Your finest whiskey, please."

"Right away, master."

Anandur glanced at Negal's drink. "What's that?"

"Whiskey sour."

Anandur looked down his nose at the glass. "That's a waste of good whiskey."

"That's how I like it." Negal took another sip. "Did you have an argument with your brother and that's why you are calling him names?"

"I didn't. Max did." Anandur leaned over the bar. "Brundar refused to have a bachelor party, and I'm bummed about it. Not only is it a tradition, but he's my brother, and he's only getting married once. I tried to convince him to at least smoke a cigar with a few of our closest friends, but he's so antisocial that he didn't want to do even that. I have no idea how he runs a club."

"Maybe he likes the people in his club more than he likes us?" Max suggested.

"Not likely." Anandur lifted the whiskey glass to his lips. "He doesn't like anyone other than his bride."

"I'm sure he likes you," Negal said.

"Sometimes, I'm not sure he does. He tolerates me, but he doesn't like me." Anandur took a sip from his drink. "Wonder is with Callie and the other ladies, and I'm all by my lonesome."

"Why aren't you with Kian?" Max asked. "Wasn't he planning on interrogating the prisoner?"

"Kian decided to do that later." Anandur pulled out his phone. "He said he would call me when he was ready to go down there, and I hope he didn't go without me. The Clan Mother would be displeased."

The mention of the princess got Negal's attention. Anandur was close to Kian and, therefore should have more insight into the heir than most.

"Why is she so careful with her son and not her daughters?" Negal asked. "From what I've heard, she doesn't require the daughters to take bodyguards everywhere they go."

Anandur chuckled. "The answer to that is simpler than most people assume, but it's a well-guarded secret, so you can't tell anyone."

Max made a sign over his lips that meant he would keep them shut, and Negal mimicked it.

Anandur leaned closer to Max. "The daughters would have never agreed to that, and the Clan Mother knows which battles are worth waging. She got them to agree to take their Odus with them, but Amanda refused to do even that. She almost never takes Onidu with her to the university."

Max looked doubtful. "That doesn't sound right. Kian is more stubborn than all of his sisters combined, and yet he agreed to the bodyguard rule."

"They made a bargain," Anandur said in a conspiratorial tone. "The Clan Mother agreed to follow a safety protocol that Kian insisted on, provided that he followed hers. The truth is that hers is as minimal as her daughters', but even that was a hard-won concession. The Clan Mother believes that she's invincible, and she might be right, but Kian still worries about her."

"That makes more sense." Max lifted his empty glass to signal to Bob that he wanted it refilled. "Although I'm sure it's not the entire story."

"It never is," Anandur said with a wink.

12

KIAN

"He's ready for you, boss," Anandur said as he walked out of the brig, leaving the door open.

"Thank you." Kian followed the Guardian inside, with Kalugal a step behind him.

The fear in the Doomer's eyes as he and Kalugal entered the antechamber sang to Kian's soul. It was satisfying to see the maggot, who had anointed himself a deliverer of death and suffering, cower before a superior force.

The cell had two sections, with a small area at the front separated from the actual cell in the back with reinforced bars. It had been strong enough to hold Igor, so it was definitely strong enough to hold the Doomer calling himself Bud.

His ankles and wrists were cuffed, even though there was no need for that. He had a feeling that Anandur had insisted on the cuffs as another way to intimidate the guy, but again, Kalugal didn't need the help. His compulsion was enough to make the Doomer sing whatever tune they wanted him to sing.

Roger, the Guardian whom Onegus had chosen to fill in for Brundar, stood with his hand on his sidearm, ready to intervene if needed. The guy was an experienced veteran of the force, and Kian had no doubt that he could step into Brundar's shoes for the next few days.

It hadn't been easy to convince Brundar to take time off after his wedding. Allowing the Guardian to join the mission earlier in the day had been a strategic decision on Kian's part. He'd used the concession as a bargaining chip to pressure Brundar to take a leave of absence.

"What do you want with me?" the Doomer asked in his heavily accented English.

"I want you dead, but first, I want some information." Kian turned to Kalugal. "The stage is yours. Go ahead."

Lokan had seen the guy through the camera feed and hadn't recognized him, which meant that he was a junior commander of no importance in the Brotherhood. Still, he wasn't a complete moron because he could speak English quite well, and that wasn't common in the Brotherhood, even though immortals learned languages easily.

Well, not all immortals, as evidenced by Syssi's difficulty with learning Spanish.

"With pleasure." Kalugal leaned his elbow on his knee and rested his chin on his fist. "What did you report to the Brotherhood about us?"

The Doomer looked at Kalugal with defiance in his eyes. "I don't know who you are, so how could I have reported anything about you?"

The guy knew that Kalugal was a compeller, and he was trying to be smart and work around the compulsion, but it wasn't Kian or Kalugal's first rodeo, and the tactic was not going to work on them.

"Nicely done, evasive answer," Kalugal said. "I'll make sure to be more precise with my questions. After you discovered the bodies and figured out that they were killed by immortals. What did you report to your superiors in the Brotherhood?"

The veins in the guy's neck bulged as he tried to fight the compulsion. "We didn't report anything until we conducted an investigation and found Luis."

Kalugal sighed and cast Kian a sidelong glance. "This is going to take longer than I expected." He shifted his gaze back to the Doomer. "What did you learn from Luis?"

"We pumped him for everything he knew, and then we reported what we suspected."

That was bad news. Kalugal had wiped Luis's memories of them and the incident. He shouldn't have remembered anything useful to the Doomers, but apparently, he had remembered something that had made the Doomers suspicious.

In any case, Kian was glad for Kalugal's insistence on getting Luis away from Acapulco. If Bud reported the tour guide to his superiors in the Brotherhood, whoever was sent to investigate what happened to the unit of missing

Doomers would no doubt search for Luis because he was the only connection they would have.

"That still does not tell me what you learned from Luis," Kalugal said. "What did he tell you that you did not know before?"

The Doomer shook his head like a dog trying to dislodge a tick, but Kalugal's compulsion was a force only a few were immune to, and fortunately, Bud wasn't part of that exclusive club.

"He didn't remember much beyond picking up a bunch of tourists at the harbor and taking them to Tehuacalco," Bud said. "He said that he was injured when some bandits started shooting at them, but he and the tourists managed to escape. We figured that he'd been thralled and his memories had been tampered with."

Kian released a relieved breath. Luis didn't remember anything useful about them.

"What else did he tell you?" The element of compulsion in Kalugal's voice was so strong that it reverberated through the cell.

The Doomer looked like he was about to vomit, but instead of emptying the contents of his stomach, he vomited words. "Luis overheard someone talking about picking up a woman from the Grand Allure all-inclusive resort in Cabo San Lucas."

That was not good.

"Did he tell you the woman's name?" Kalugal asked.

"He didn't remember it."

"What else did Luis tell you?"

"Nothing. That was all Luis remembered." The Doomer looked Kalugal straight in the eyes, but Kian knew he was lying, which should be impossible under the power of Kalugal's compulsion.

Bud must have found a loophole.

Kian leaned sideways toward Kalugal. "He could have sifted through Luis's memories without having him talk. Ask him about that."

"Good point." Kalugal turned to the Doomer. "What else did you pick up straight from Luis's mind when you looked at his memories?"

"Names," the Doomer spat.

"Tell me all the names you or any of the others picked up from Luis's head."

The power of Kalugal's compulsion was so strong that Kian felt like reciting names, but thankfully, the question had been very specific and referred only to the names the Doomer or his friends had learned from Luis.

"Kevin, Gunter, Jacki, Edna, Rufus, Doug, and Frankie."

Kian was grateful for Kalugal's foresight in calling himself Kevin Gunter.

His real name would have been a dead giveaway and endangered all of them more than the incident with the Doomers.

Navuh had never truly believed that his son had died in WW2, and he had been searching for Kalugal for decades. He would have sent half of the Brotherhood to look for him.

His cousin turned to him. "Those were all the passengers in Luis's vehicle. I must have forgotten to erase that from his memory."

"Did Rufsur call himself Rufus?" Kian asked.

Kalugal nodded. "We wanted all the names to sound American, and I had a little fun with playing my favorite alter ego, Professor Gunter. There isn't much they can learn from these names. They are all common."

"They know the name of the hotel in Cabo," Kian pointed out.

"Right." Kalugal turned to the prisoner. "What did your superiors tell you to do with the information?"

"Nothing."

"That doesn't sound right," Kalugal said. "Tell me precisely what your superiors told you to do?"

"They told me to lure the immortals into a trap, catch them, and interrogate them to find out where the rest of them were hiding. After I got that information out of them, I was supposed to hold them captive until my superiors verified the information and wait for further instructions."

"To kill us," Kian said.

The Doomer nodded. "They might have wanted to bring you to the island."

"What about the kidnapped women?" Kalugal asked.

"They were a secondary consideration. We could always get more from other villages. You were the big fish we were told to catch."

Kian's blood boiled in his veins when he imagined another slaughter of innocent villagers and the violation of women and children, but he forced himself not to react. The Doomer would die soon, but before that, they needed to get every morsel of information out of him.

"What are your superiors' plans regarding Cabo?" Kalugal asked.

"I don't know. They didn't tell me."

"Do you know or suspect that they will send a team to the hotel in Cabo?" Kalugal asked.

"When we don't report back, I suspect that they will. They will also send a team to Acapulco to investigate what happened to us."

13

MARGO

Jasmine returned with two cans of Coke and handed one to Margo. "How come you are not partying with your friends tonight?"

Margo frowned. "Have you been watching me?"

"It was hard not to notice your group, and you stuck out like a sore thumb."

"What do you mean?" Margo popped the can open and took a grateful sip.

Jasmine sat down and popped hers. "While the others were chatting, getting drunk, and flirting with the waiters, you were reading. The only reason I know you were with them is because I overheard you talking with that lady with the Gucci slides."

"That was Lynda, my future sister-in-law. It's her bachelorette party."

"Makes sense." Jaz took a sip of her Coke.

"How come I didn't notice you?" Margo asked. "You're hard to overlook."

Jaz chuckled. "It's the hat. I turn invisible when I'm wearing it. Besides, I only got here two days ago, and yesterday, I didn't spend much time at the pool. Alberto took me to the city for lunch and then shopping. After that, he left me alone in our suite and didn't return until late at night. He said something about visiting a friend and playing poker, but it sounded like a brush-off. When I told him so, he got angry, accusing me of being irrational and ungrateful after the good times he showed me, and then he left. He didn't return until morning."

"What did he say?"

Jasmine shrugged. "He gave me a half-assed apology, excusing his behavior with stress at work. The thing is, he never told me what he did for a living except for saying that he was a trader."

Alarm bells went off in Margo's head. "Where is he now?"

"More business meetings, or so he says. I'm not jealous because it doesn't make sense for him to drag me out here and spend so much money on me only to screw around. I'm just suspicious about what he's involved in."

That was precisely what Margo was thinking, too. "What do you suspect?"

"Drugs," Jasmine whispered. "He says he's a trader, but he doesn't tell me what he trades in, and he throws money around like he has an endless supply of it. What else am I supposed to think?"

There were worse things to trade in than drugs, but Margo kept that thought to herself. The woman was distraught enough. Then again, a stunning beauty like Jasmine could be sold for top dollar, so maybe it would be better to warn her.

"Trafficking," Margo said quietly. "I'm worried about you. If that's what he is involved in, and he isn't too attached to you, he might try to sell you. You are like a rare jewel that some perverts would pay a lot of money to possess. Not only that, it's a known tactic of human traffickers to seduce their unsuspecting victims and get them to voluntarily travel to a foreign country, where it is easier to have them disappear. That's why it's called trafficking instead of a more appropriate name that sounds much more brutal."

Jasmine waved a dismissive hand. "I'm flattered by your compliments, but you are exaggerating. I'm not such a great catch." She smoothed a hand over her hip. "No matter how much I exercise and diet, I can't get rid of these thunder thighs."

Margo rolled her eyes. "Your body shape is perfect for your type of beauty, and you are exquisite. You don't need to get rid of anything."

"Thank you." Jasmine smiled. "That's very sweet of you to say, but I know what I see in the mirror."

"It's called body dysmorphia," Margo said. "Only you can see the imaginary imperfection."

"Not true. Alberto sees that, too. He said that I should have plastic surgery to remove these pockets of fat."

What an asshole. "Did he offer to pay for it too?"

"No." Jasmine leaned back in her chair. "That's over the limit of what he's willing to spend on me, and I don't expect him to. We haven't been dating that long, and we didn't make any commitments to each other, although he said that he loved me."

Lies.

The wheels in Margo's head started to spin again. "So, I assume that he never bought you expensive jewelry either."

Jasmine shook her head. "As I said, we've only been dating for a few weeks, so I don't think that's significant."

"He's a rich dude who likes to impress people with his money. If he wanted to keep you long term, he would have bought you an extravagant gift to make you feel obligated."

"He paid for this vacation." Jaz waved a hand over the view. "Which is quite extravagant. This suite probably costs thousands of dollars a night."

Margo shook her head. "And yet he left you here alone."

"True." Jasmine worried her lower lip. "And he took away my passport and my credit cards so I couldn't escape." She winced. "I was so stupid for agreeing to come here with him. I've known him for less than three weeks."

"That's still a lot of time to invest in a woman he intends to sell, but regrettably, the rest of his behavior points in that direction."

"You are right." Jasmine let her head fall back and closed her eyes. "What if those meetings are about me? He might be negotiating my sale as we speak. I can't leave, and if I go to the local authorities with this story, they will laugh in my face."

"Maybe you should go to the American Embassy? I don't think they will dismiss your story, and maybe they can help you get away."

Jasmine shook her head. "I can't believe that's what he's really up to. He's a controlling jerk, but he wouldn't have treated me to a stay in the presidential suite only to sell me. Also, my family knows where I am. I can ask my parents to buy me a plane ticket, but I don't have my passport or even my driver's license. I have no way to prove who I am."

It was a conundrum, and Margo wasn't sure how she could help.

"Perhaps I can get you on that cruise ship if I explain your predicament. It's a private cruise for the employees of Perfect Match, so maybe my friend can speak to the boss and convince him to let you hitch a ride with us. The problem is that even if he agrees, the ship will not get here until Thursday, and if we are right about Alberto's nefarious intentions, it might be too late."

Jasmine's head snapped up. "Did you say Perfect Match?"

"Yeah?

She gaped at Margo. "The same Perfect Match Virtual Adventure Studios that are running commercials on all the channels?"

"Yeah. I hope to get a job as a beta tester for their adventures. But this isn't the time to get excited over virtual reality. We need to figure out how to keep you safe first."

"What if I come to stay in your room? You could hide me."

"Not a good plan. First of all, my roommate won't be leaving until tomorrow, and secondly, a lot of people saw you and me talking and drinking together. My room would be the first place your boyfriend would search." Margo scratched her head. "I can get you a cheap Airbnb somewhere in town. Or even better, I can ask my friend to book it, so it won't be under my name. You can hide there until the ship arrives. But first, I need to call her to see if getting you on board is in the cards."

"Thank you." Jasmine leaned over and took Margo's hands. "I promise to repay you and your friend every penny once I get back home."

Margo needed to call Mia without Jasmine listening in, but was it wise to leave her in the suite and go make the phone call from her room?

On the one hand, it would be better if Margo wasn't there when the boyfriend returned, but on the other hand, she was afraid to leave Jaz alone. Then again, what could she do to help her if the guy decided to abduct both of them and sell them?

She wasn't some ninja fighter, and besides, if Alberto was a thug, he was probably armed.

"I'll call my friend from my room. In the meantime, I suggest that you go back to the bar where you will be surrounded by people. I'll find you when I'm done."

Jasmine nodded. "I need to shower and change first. But as soon as I'm done, I'll head to the pool bar."

Margo pushed to her feet. "Don't take too long."

"I won't."

14

KAREN

Karen sat in front of a mirror and regarded her freshly cleaned face. She looked her age, not younger and not older, which was an improvement over the tired and washed-out look she'd been sporting lately.

It was the venom's effect.

Lifting her hand, she feathered her fingers over the spot where Negal had bitten her. She didn't remember the bite because he had thralled her to ignore him when he had done it, and there was no sign left of it, but she could feel its phantom echo on her skin, a prickling that was most likely psychosomatic.

Since she had no memory of the bite, all she had to rely on was what she'd heard from others, and her imagination.

In the mirror, she saw Gilbert walking out of the shower with a towel wrapped around his hips, looking absolutely perfect. The few pounds he'd been carrying around his middle had disappeared, and he had gained muscles even though he rarely visited the gym.

He smiled at her through the mirror. "Anything?"

She knew what he was asking about and shook her head. "I feel exactly the same as I did before the bite."

Well, that wasn't true. She felt invigorated, which she'd been told was one of the residual effects of the venom.

When Gilbert's venom glands and fangs became functional, she would be able to enjoy these wonderful effects daily.

If she survived.

Heck, if she survived the transition, she would become immortal, and she wouldn't need the energy boost that a venom bite provided. The other benefits were more than enough to look forward to, though.

She vividly remembered the string of orgasms and euphoria that had followed and the psychedelic trip that had lasted for hours.

In her case, it wasn't a question of whether she would enter transition. She was a confirmed Dormant. The question was whether she would survive it.

Letting the towel drop, Gilbert gave her a great view of his ass as he walked toward the closet. "I know better than to offer a little hanky-panky when you are getting ready, but in case you are randy..." He looked at her over his shoulder with a hopeful expression on his face and shook his ass. "Cheryl has the kids in her bedroom, and you know how good the soundproofing is here."

"I do, but I also know our kids. Idina could burst in here at any moment. Besides, I do need to get ready."

He sighed dramatically. "We can lock the door..."

Karen closed her eyes. "I'm sorry, sweetheart. I really need to get ready."

"Yeah, yeah." He pulled on a pair of boxer briefs, walked over to the bed, and turned the television on. "You don't mind if I watch something while you do your makeup, right?" He lay down on the bed without waiting for her response.

"I don't. Enjoy your channel surfing."

Gilbert had always been a virile male with a healthy appetite for sex, but since his transition, he'd become insatiable, and his stamina was through the roof. She tried to keep up, but he was exhausting her, and as much as she hated disappointing him, she couldn't handle one more session.

She would never admit it to him, but she was starting to dread getting in bed.

It was temporary, she reminded herself. Soon, she would be immortal, too, and their energy levels would match.

With a sigh, Karen began her routine, first dabbing a light moisturizer onto her skin and patting it down until it dissolved into a silky smoothness. Next came the foundation, which she'd had formulated to match her exact skin tone.

She used to love the process, the transformation she could achieve with contouring and shading, but her skin no longer looked smooth, and the foundation was accentuating every little wrinkle and crease.

Perhaps it was better to go without?

Nah. No one would see the imperfection in the dim light of the transformed dining room, but the shading and contouring would transform her face.

Reaching for the eyeshadow palette, she opted for earthy tones that complemented her eyes, and blended the colors with gentle, circular motions, creating a soft, smoky effect that was neither too bold nor too understated. After cleaning up the corners, she drew a thin line of black eyeliner along her upper lash line, giving her eyes a defined look.

"You look beautiful," Gilbert said from the bed.

"Thank you." She slanted him a smile. "I'm not done yet."

"You look beautiful without any of the war paint."

She chuckled. "War paint? Is that what it looks like?"

"I'm just teasing. You look great. Which dress are you wearing tonight?"

"The silver one. Why are you asking?"

He shrugged, his shoulders looking so much more defined and muscular now, even though he hadn't increased his exercise routine after his transition. It was just happening, the same way his hair was regrowing, and his midsection had lost its padding of fat.

He turned on his side. "I was just imagining dancing with you, and I needed a dress to go with the fantasy."

"You're weird." She dabbed a hint of blush over her cheeks, bringing a warm, rosy hue to her face.

Gilbert propped his head on his hand. "It's not weird to imagine the good things in life even if they are readily available. It enhances the experience. You should try it. Close your eyes and imagine yourself with me on the dance floor, looking into my eyes and telling me that you love me and that I'm the hunkiest male there."

She narrowed her eyes at him. "Do you imagine yourself telling me that I'm the sexiest, most beautiful woman on the dance floor?"

"I do. That's why I needed to know what dress you are planning to wear."

Shaking her head, Karen picked up a lipstick that was a shade darker than her natural lip color, but then changed her mind and went for something bolder, a deep burgundy red.

As she pressed her lips together to blend the color, Karen admired the overall effect. "Not bad if I say so myself."

"Magnificent," Gilbert said.

She turned to him. "Do you ever imagine how I will look after the transition?"

"I don't have to imagine. I know what you will look like."

"And that's what?"

"The way you looked when I first met you. Although, to tell you the truth, in my eyes you haven't changed. When I look at you, I always see the woman I fell in love with."

15

MARGO

As Margo made her way to her room on the second floor of the hotel, her stomach churned with unease.

She didn't like leaving Jasmine alone and vulnerable in that fancy suite, but she had to concede that there wasn't much she could do for her other than make the call she had promised.

Hopefully, tonight's wedding hadn't started yet, or Mia wouldn't be able to help her with anything. To bother the boss in the middle of the festivities would result in a guaranteed refusal.

Margo wondered whether the weddings were of employees who had met their Perfect Match through the algorithm. If so, it could be a wonderful marketing opportunity. The question was whether anyone would let her pitch her idea.

She was supposed to start as a lowly beta tester, and chances were that no one would want to hear what other things she could bring to the table.

So far, she'd gotten the impression that the boss Mia had been referring to was even more intimidating than Mia's fiancé, which was hard to imagine, but since Tom didn't have the authority to approve Jasmine coming on board, the reclusive partners were the ones in charge. Mia hadn't mentioned which one of them was the boss, but since she referred to 'him,' it was a man, and given the tone of her voice when she talked about him, she had a lot of respect for the guy.

Closing the door behind her, Margo locked it as if that was going to keep her safe, dropped her bag on the floor, and sat down on the single armchair in the room.

The contrast to Jasmine's luxurious suite was stark. The room, which Margo had thought was so nice, suddenly looked cramped and basic. The two queen beds and one armchair took up most of the floor space, and the small table by the armchair couldn't even hold her bag.

The bathroom was basic as well, with a bathtub and shower combo, a shower curtain, a toilet, and a single sink.

Oh well, even that simple room, which she had split the cost of with a roommate, had made a big hole in her savings account. That and the plane ticket. The other things were incidentals that weren't too costly.

Pulling out her phone, Margo placed the call and waited for Mia to answer.

When the call went to voicemail, her heart sank. Mia was probably at the wedding already, and it was too noisy to hear the phone ringing.

Maybe she should call Frankie?

Frankie couldn't help her, though. She wasn't close to the boss, and besides, she was probably at the wedding too.

When her phone rang a few minutes later, Margo let out a relieved breath. "Hi, Mia. I thought you were at the wedding reception already."

"No, not yet. These weddings start really late. I didn't answer because I was in the shower when you called, and Tom was helping me. Did you talk with Frankie today by any chance?"

Margo tensed. "No, why? Is she okay?"

"She's fine. She came down with some sort of a bug, and they put her in the infirmary. But that's not why I asked. I didn't know whether she told you that we were going to get to Cabo tomorrow afternoon instead of the following morning. The boss decided to crank up the speed so we can make an excursion to one more port of call before heading home."

"Great." She would have been thrilled to hear that only this morning, but now she was worried about Jasmine. She needed more time to put her rescue plan in motion.

"You don't sound happy," Mia said. "What's up?"

"I met someone who might be in danger, and I need a favor." She proceeded to explain the situation and her suspicions about Jasmine's boyfriend.

When she was done, there was a long moment of silence. "Are you sure that you are not jumping to conclusions? No offense, but you tend to see a conspiracy around every corner."

"That jerk took her passport, her driver's license, and her credit cards. He left her with forty bucks in her wallet. Don't tell me you don't find that suspicious."

"So, the guy is a controlling asshole. It doesn't mean that he's a trafficker."

"What if he is? Do you want Jasmine's abduction and sale into sex slavery on your conscience?"

"Of course not." Mia sighed. "But I would hate to make a big brouhaha about nothing."

"It's not nothing, and even if it is, I'd rather be wrong than sorry. That's how people get killed, Mia. Those who should recognize the warning signs and do something don't want to believe that bad things are about to happen."

After every big terrorist attack, the news was full of warning signs that should have been heeded but had been ignored. Evidently, those in charge of security often suffered from the same idiotic optimism and false sense of safety as the clueless victims in horror movies.

"Yeah, you're right," Mia sighed. "Better safe than sorry, right? I'll tell Tom what you told me and have him ask the boss if he will allow your friend on board."

"Thank you. You are the best. I need one more favor, though."

"What is it now?"

"I want to rent an Airbnb in town so Jasmine will have a place to hide from her boyfriend, but if I book it, I'll have to use my credit card, and he might be able to trace the place. People saw Jasmine and me hanging out together, so he wouldn't have much trouble figuring out who was helping her. If you book the rental, though, he won't be able to find her."

"That's actually a smart idea. I'll book a place, and I suggest that you join her. If he's the bad apple you think he is, you don't want him coming after you when he searches for his girlfriend."

"Good point. I might even save a few dollars by canceling my extra night in the hotel. I'll pay you back, of course."

"*Pfft.* That's the last thing you need to worry about. I'll try to find a place that's walking distance from the hotel. You don't want to take a taxi because that could also lead him to you."

Margo chuckled. "Look at us. We are like a couple of sleuths. I'll leave my luggage in the hotel and go with just a large satchel. I'll tell Jasmine to do the same."

"I'll call you back once I make the reservation."

"Thanks, Mia. I really appreciate it."

"No problem. I'm happy to help. Getting the boss's approval for your friend to come on board might take a little longer, but at least she will be safe in the meantime."

"True that. If the boss says no, I'll try to get her to the embassy. Maybe they can help, although I doubt it. She can't even prove who she is without at least her driver's license."

"Let's keep our fingers crossed that the boss agrees."

When Mia ended the call, Margo slumped in the armchair, her energy level dropping like a rock now that she had done all she could.

But was it all?

She needed to think creatively. Perhaps one of Jasmine's parents could fly in and bring her birth certificate along with some pictures. That was another way to prove who she was. Or maybe she had an expired passport that they could get. That should be helpful as well. After all, it wasn't uncommon for people to get mugged while abroad and have all of their documents and money taken, and yet they somehow found a way to return home.

16

KIAN

"Do we have time for another cigar before the wedding?" Kalugal glanced at his watch. "Or do you need to get ready?"

Kian chuckled. "How long will it take me to put on a tux? Let's go to my suite."

His cousin grinned. "I was hoping you'd say that. Jacki is still with Callie, so I assume Syssi is too. They are getting dressed in Wonder's suite."

"Can I join?" Anandur asked from behind them. "I was told to stay away from the suite until they were done. My tux is in Brundar and Callie's place, and I'm not in the mood to hang out with my brother. Or I should rather say that he's not in the mood to hang out with me."

"Is he nervous about the ceremony?" Kalugal asked.

Anandur shrugged. "Probably. I can't imagine what his vows to Callie will be like. He does not know how to express his emotions, so this must be difficult for him. I just hope he wrote something because I'm sure Callie did. She doesn't suffer from the same limitations he does. She's a loving, caring sweetheart, and she knows how to express herself in words."

Kian nodded. "He'll be fine even if he doesn't have anything profound prepared. All he needs to say is that he will love her forever, which is a given, and it will be enough for her."

Anandur made a face that indicated he disagreed. "It might be true on the day-to-day, but I bet she is hoping for him to say something more profound in front of the entire clan."

"Your vows were great." Kalugal clapped Anandur on the back. "I laughed so hard, and I even teared up a little."

"Thank you." Anandur put a hand over his chest. "It means a lot to me to hear you say that. I worked on them for months."

"Really?" Kian arched a brow.

He was never sure whether Anandur was serious or joking.

"Really, and hearing that Kalugal was touched by what I wrote makes me so proud."

"Your vows were beautiful." Kalugal sighed dramatically.

Kian rolled his eyes as he opened the door to his suite. "I didn't know you were so emotional, cousin." He ushered his guests inside.

Kalugal batted his eyelashes. "I have many layers."

Snorting, Kian walked over to the bar and pulled out a bottle of whiskey. "As lovely as it is to share this touching moment with you two, I need to think about what we are going to do. I don't want to engage another group of Doomers while I have my entire clan on the ship, and especially my mother." He lined up three glasses on the counter and poured whiskey into them. "Any suggestions?"

As Kalugal and Anandur took their glasses, Kian walked over to the balcony doors and opened them.

The humid heat outside was not as bad this late in the evening, but it was still an adjustment after leaving the air-conditioned space behind.

"We can just keep on sailing." Kalugal followed him to the balcony, with Anandur a couple of steps behind him. "Mia and Frankie will be disappointed, and so will their friend, but that shouldn't influence your decision. Safety first, right?"

Kian opened the humidor he had left outside and presented it to Kalugal. "Maybe we can pick Margo up with a lifeboat. She can head to one of the nearby beaches, and we will collect her from there. I doubt the Doomers will be following her since they don't know who she is." He offered the box to Anandur.

Anandur pulled out a Cuban. "It doesn't feel right to run. We took out those directly responsible for the massacre, but that's not enough. We need to take out the entire leadership, and we can't, which frustrates me."

Kian and Kalugal both nodded.

"Perhaps eliminating the team they sent to Cabo will send a message," Kalugal said.

"What kind of a message?" Kian offered him the cutter. "That we are in charge of this area? We are not. They will send an even larger force, and by the time it gets here, we will be long gone. It's futile to engage them." He lit his cigar and took a grateful puff. "We need to stick to what we have always done, which is hiding the best we can. I don't like it, and I wish we could take on the entire Brotherhood and eliminate them, including Navuh, but we can't, not even by bombing the hell out of their island. There are civilians on that damn island, including your mother and Wonder's sister."

"We can get them out first." Anandur lit up his cigar. "The same way we got Carol out. Her rescue was proof that it could be done."

"My mother doesn't want to leave." Kalugal sat down on a lounger and put his feet up. "We would have to knock her out. But since she is the only one who we could coordinate the rescue plan with, that would be a problem. And even if we managed that, I wouldn't want to be on the receiving end of her wrath if we killed my father. She would be enraged and inconsolable."

Kian couldn't argue with that, and he didn't want to. It was a futile discussion at this point, and he had more urgent matters to think about.

"We are getting carried away." He sat on a lounger next to Kalugal. "We need to decide what to do about Cabo. Let's consider the timeline. By now, the superiors know that something is up because they lost communications with Bud's team. They will want to investigate what happened, and they will want revenge. Bud is right about them sending two teams. One to Acapulco and one to Cabo. But even if they are on the plane right now, it will take them at least eighteen hours to get here. Probably more. They need to fly to the Maldives first, and as far as I know, there are no direct flights from there to Acapulco or any of the other nearby airports. They will have to book a flight with a layover. Then, they will need to get weapons from a local supplier, which will probably take a few more hours. In short, I can't see them being ready to engage us sooner than forty-eight hours or so from now. At the speed we are going, we can dock in Cabo, get Margo, and be out of there before they even get there."

Kalugal puffed on his cigar for a few quiet moments before turning to Kian. "Even if you are right about that, which you might not be, they will ask their buddies in the cartel to intervene."

Anandur snorted. "What can a bunch of humans do to us?"

"Plenty," Kalugal said. "We have less than eighty Guardians, and even with my men, our entire force is just a little over a hundred. Humans can easily overwhelm us with the right weapons. My compulsion is a formidable weapon, but it has to be used strategically. They have to be able to hear my voice, so it won't help us at all if they fire a torpedo at the ship from a safe distance. We are lucky that they don't know for sure we are on a ship or which one. One well-aimed anti-ship cruise missile could sink us."

Kian frowned at his cousin. "What did you mean by if I'm right about the timeline?"

"You are assuming that they will send a force from the island, but that's probably not what they will do." Kalugal took a puff from his cigar. "They probably have teams stationed across Mexico and other South American countries that they can deploy on short notice. They could also send a force from California, where they have a large presence. In my opinion, we can assume that they are already waiting for us in Cabo with a large force stationed at the hotel."

17

MARGO

Margo showered and checked her phone. She got dressed and looked at her phone again. She packed a suitcase and her satchel and checked her phone once more, but there was still no response from Mia.

She thought about checking on Jasmine, but then it occurred to her that they hadn't exchanged phone numbers. Besides, even if she had Jasmine's number, it wouldn't be prudent to call her. Alberto might be monitoring her calls.

In fact, when Jasmine fled to the Airbnb, she should leave her phone behind in the suite so Alberto couldn't trace her.

With a sigh, Margo picked up her phone and headed out to the pool bar, where Jaz was supposed to wait for her. She didn't know why it was taking Mia so long to book the Airbnb. Perhaps there was no availability?

If so, one of the nearby hotels would do. They were all clustered in the same area, and Margo was sure they had rooms available. Maybe she should call Mia to tell her that?

Nah. Mia was smart enough to figure that out on her own. Something else must have caused the delay.

As Margo exited the elevator at the ground level, she had a sudden flare of panic. What if the dastardly boyfriend had shown up while she had been gone and dragged Jasmine away from the bar to deliver her to a buyer?

Shaking her head, Margo chided herself for possibly getting carried away again.

Was she making a logical leap with this situation or was she creating a storm in a teacup by weaving yet another conspiracy theory?

Both scenarios seemed plausible.

She was the first one to admit that she had a penchant for defaulting to the worst possible outcome for any given situation. The thing was, being paranoid didn't mean that she was wrong. The world was decidedly a more nefarious and hostile place than most people believed, and safety was an illusion.

Margo was always prepared for the worst to happen. Well, prepared was an exaggeration. She was mentally ready, but she still didn't own a gun or even have a security alarm in her apartment. If she could, she would rent a place in a secure building with a guard in the lobby, so at least she would be somewhat protected, but she couldn't afford the rent in a place like that.

When she got back, the first thing she would do was contact one of those alarm companies, and the second thing was to apply for a gun permit.

The problem was that not all life's calamities could be blamed on murderers, rapists, terrorists, traffickers, and drug dealers. More people died prematurely from diseases, hereditary defects, and natural disasters than from wars and murders.

Perhaps it had been Mia's heart failure that had turned Margo into such a pessimist.

Mia's mother had died from the same heart defect that had almost killed her daughter years later, but everyone had seemed to think that it wouldn't happen to Mia, including Mia herself.

Then it had, and Mia had almost died, and her legs had been amputated.

It had been like a punch to the gut, a rude wake-up call, making it glaringly apparent to Margo that bad things happened to good people for no good reason. Since then, she had never taken anything for granted again. Not her health, not her safety, and not her happily ever after, which was the biggest lie of all.

Most people didn't get to live a happy life, so why would she be so lucky?

Well, miracles happened; Margo was willing to admit that, and that realization too, was because of Mia, or rather thanks to her. Her bestie had met Tom, a multi-billionaire who had taken her to Switzerland and gotten her the best medical help in the world. The details were a big secret because the procedure had not yet been approved, but Mia was regrowing her legs.

Still, stories like Mia's were so rare that it was safe to assume they didn't happen for the vast majority of people, including Margo.

"Ain't I the cheerful sort." Margo chuckled as she walked through the sliding doors out onto the pool area.

The bar was packed, the music was loud, and people were laughing. Life seemed good for this single moment in time.

Seeing Jasmine sitting at the bar with a drink in her hand, Margo let out a relieved breath. Two guys seemed to be vying for her attention, but given her easy smile, she was doing fine.

Heading toward her new friend, Margo took another glance at her phone, but there was still no message from Mia.

She was almost at the bar when her phone finally rang.

Taking a slight detour, she sat on one of the chairs and answered the call.

"I've got the Airbnb," Mia said. "It's fifteen minutes on foot from the hotel. A nice two-bedroom condo in a secure building. I'll text you the codes for the building's front door and the condo. If you want, you can go there right now. I rented it for five days, starting tonight. In case the boss says no, your friend will have a place to stay until she figures something out."

"Thanks. So, I guess you don't have an answer from the boss yet."

"Regretfully, no. Everyone is busy getting ready for the wedding, so I might not have an answer for you until tomorrow."

"Is there a chance you or Tom could talk to the boss during the wedding?"

"We might, but these parties usually end really late. It might be after three in the morning when Tom can catch a word with him."

"That's fine. Call me or text me the moment you have an answer."

"Will do. Are you going to move with your friend tonight?"

"If Jasmine wants to go, I'll escort her there and come back. Lynda and her friends are leaving tomorrow morning, and I'll never hear the end of it if I don't say goodbye to them."

"Yeah, I hear you. Things got better between you two during this week, right?"

"Yeah. I can tolerate her now, but it takes an effort, and I can only do it for a short period of time. The woman's middle name is entitled. I don't know how Rob can stand her, but I gave up on trying to understand their dynamic a long time ago."

"To each their own." Mia sighed. "Good luck to your friend."

"Thank you. For everything."

"If there's anything else you need, let me know. I can rent you a car, send you cash, just say the word."

"Cash would be nice. I'd rather not use my credit cards because charges can be traced, too. I'll pay you back. You know that."

"Don't be silly. Of course, I do."

18

KIAN

"Thank you for coming so quickly." Kian motioned for Lokan to follow him to the balcony. "We need your input."

"I'm glad you called. With Carol gone, I had nothing to do, and I was bored. Besides, I wouldn't mind a cigar and a glass of whiskey, and the company, of course."

Lokan was already dressed in his tuxedo, which was good since they were pressed for time. The wedding was in less than half an hour, which wasn't enough time to devise a strategy, but it was enough to get Lokan's perspective on the situation. He was still an active member of the Brotherhood and had more insight into its workings than Kalugal and Kian had.

Kian opened the lid of the cigar box. "Choose your poison."

"Since we don't have much time, I'll take the Short Story."

"Good choice." Kian handed him the cutter and poured whiskey into a glass from the bottle he had brought outside.

Lokan cut off the tip of his cigar. "I was hoping for another get-together for Brundar's bachelor party and some male bonding, but given that he participated in the mission earlier, I understand why there hasn't been one."

"It has nothing to do with the mission. He just didn't want to have one. He's not very social."

Lokan nodded. "I've noticed." He took the lighter from Kian. "So, what is this about?" He lit his cigar and took a puff.

Kian handed Lokan the glass. "Kalugal and I interrogated Bud earlier, and it turned out that Kalugal hadn't been as meticulous as he should have been erasing the tour guide's memories. The guy remembered a few things that he'd overheard, and Bud was able to coerce him into revealing them."

"It's not easy to thrall so surgically," Kalugal said. "I couldn't erase all of his memories because that would have been suspicious, so I had to sift through them and decide what needed to go and what could stay, and as you all know, looking into someone's head is not like reading a book."

"We know." Kian put a hand on Kalugal's shoulder. "I'm not accusing you of negligence."

"It sure sounded like you did." Kalugal tapped on his cigar, dislodging a big chunk of ash.

Ignoring his cousin's pout, Kian turned to Lokan. "Anyway, Luis overheard someone mentioning Cabo and the name of the hotel where Mia and Frankie's friend is staying. Kalugal says that the Brotherhood have probably moved locally stationed teams, either from here in Mexico or from California, to investigate what happened to their brethren in Acapulco and to wait for us at the hotel. What's your take on this?"

"Kalugal is right. If time was not a factor, they would have sent teams from the island, but the disappearance of an entire team is an urgent matter, especially since they reported their suspicions about who killed their cartel partners. They have several teams in Mexico and other Latin American countries to oversee their drug operations. Those are the teams they will most likely use."

Kalugal smirked. "That's precisely what I said."

Lokan tilted his head. "What is the plan, then? Are we still stopping at Cabo, or are we sailing past it to the next stop? My advice is to keep going. You don't want a confrontation with the Brotherhood."

"No, I don't." Kian took a puff of his cigar. "What I'm worried about is them figuring out which ship we are on and sending the Mexican navy after us. They don't have any compellers other than Navuh on hand, and no one will dare to ask him to get involved in such a marginal matter, but I bet that they have plenty of Mexican politicians, generals, and admirals who they can either bribe or extort to do their dirty work for them."

Lokan shook his head. "They wouldn't go that far. As much as they want revenge, they need to stay under the humans' radar as much as you do. Starting an international incident over twelve members of the Brotherhood is not reason enough to risk exposure, and neither is the prospect of capturing or killing a few clan members. No one in the Brotherhood's leadership would expect that the entire clan is on one ship. Nothing in the clan's behavior over the centuries would lead them to think that. They are used to you doing your best to hide. If I were the one evaluating the situation, I would assume that several clan members, most likely Guardians, were on vacation or on their way to doing some business in Mexico. They ran into the cartel thugs who were holding the women by chance, and being the goody two-shoes that they are, they appointed themselves the champions of the weak and killed the bad humans. When the Brotherhood's team demanded the victims' return and threatened to harm Luis and his family, the Guardians attacked and killed the team and their human cohorts."

Kian let out a breath. "That's the problem right there. They were prepared for us, and they marshaled a large military force. To overcome them, we had to have a superior force. They would no longer think that they are dealing with just a few members of the clan. They don't know about you or Kalugal or Toven, so they might assume that Annani disabled all those soldiers and made them easy to pick off."

A long moment of silence stretched over the balcony as the others considered what he had said.

"Again, not likely." Lokan pushed to his feet and walked over to where Kian had left the bottle of whiskey. "To assume that the Clan Mother was there in person is a leap of logic none of them would make. They might consider cooperation with the local army or police, though. Or maybe even an aerial attack since we are not that far from the clan's base, which they know is in Los Angeles."

"We left no evidence," Kalugal said. "All the bodies were burned, the vehicles and the weapons were delivered to Turner's arms supplier, and the two boys we left alive were thralled to remember that it was a Colombian cartel attack."

"They'll know that the boys were thralled." Lokan returned to his chair. "Since there will be no bodies for them to find and no vehicles, they might assume a coup. The cartel thugs could have overpowered their immortal overlords. It wouldn't be the first time something like that happened."

Kian snorted. "We should be so lucky." He took a puff from his cigar. "So, what's our next move, gentlemen?"

Kalugal pushed to his feet. "We don't stop in Cabo, and we keep sailing back to Long Beach without stopping anywhere. This ship can defend itself in case of an attack, but a hasty retreat is best."

"I disagree," Lokan said. "Ships get tracked, and it's easy to access that information. The mention of Cabo will lead them to believe that the clan members involved in the attack are traveling by ship, and they can follow all the ships that left Acapulco earlier today and are sailing north. We are already going faster than any cruise ship in the area, which will make us stand out, but if we continue all the way to Long Beach as if the hounds of hell are on our heels, they will figure out right away that the *Silver Swan* is their target and wait for us in Long Beach. We should stop in Cabo as planned and have a few groups go ashore and do all the touristy activities that people do there. If possible, they should disguise themselves to look like humans, meaning older and less attractive."

"Good idea." Kian put his glass down and pulled out his phone. "I need to talk to Eva about disguises. I hope she can do something with what's available."

"One more thing," Lokan said. "You should slow down to a normal cruising speed. First of all, it will appear less suspicious if you are going at the same speed as all the other cruise liners, and secondly, it will give us more time to prepare."

19

MARGO

Since Jasmine seemed to be enjoying herself at the bar, Margo continued chatting with Mia for a few minutes longer. After all, it would have been rude to get what she needed from her friend and not talk with her about the things they usually talked about.

"I have to go," Mia said. "I'm sitting here in my underwear while Tom is already dressed in his tux."

Margo laughed. "I'll let you go. Get dressed and have fun at the wedding."

"I intend to. Stay safe, and get Jasmine to the Airbnb." Mia ended the call.

Mia was the best. It helped that she had a very rich fiancé, who made sure that she didn't lack for a thing.

A tiny pang of envy coursed through Margo, but she quickly shoved it away. If anyone deserved a major happily ever after, it was Mia. She had gone through so much. Losing both her legs at such a young age was terrible, and she had been so brave, learning to walk on dual prostheses, which was a very hard thing to do that not many managed well.

Mia might look small and fragile, but she was a fighter.

At the bar, Jasmine said something to the guy sitting next to her, and he turned to look at Margo with a hostile look before getting up and motioning for her to take his seat.

"Someone isn't happy," she muttered under her breath.

Not that she could blame him. If she were a guy, she would also be mad if her flirting with a gorgeous woman was interrupted.

"See you later, Liam." Jasmine waved.

Margo took the seat Liam had vacated. "You probably won't. My friend got you an Airbnb that's walking distance from the hotel. It's under her name, and the door has a code lock, so you don't even need to meet the owner, and no one can trace you there."

The music was loud, so Margo felt okay talking with Jaz about it in the open. Unless someone had bat hearing, their conversation was private.

"I don't know." Jasmine grimaced. "I'm sorry to have put your friend through all that trouble, but I had some time to think, and I realized that we might have overreacted. If Alberto wanted to sell me, he would have shown me to prospective buyers, but he hasn't introduced me to anyone."

That was a good point. But he didn't need to show her in person. There could be hidden cameras in the hotel penthouse.

"What if he put tiny cameras in the bathroom so prospective buyers could see you naked when you are showering or taking a bath?"

Jasmine recoiled. "I didn't think about that angle. Let's check. It's much harder to hide a camera in the bathroom than in the other rooms. If he put one in the shower, we should be able to find it."

Margo slid off the stool and stood up. "Let's do it."

"One moment." Jasmine signaled for the bartender to come closer. "I need to sign for the drinks."

"Check, please," she said.

He nodded. "Give me a moment."

It took him a little longer than that to put a receipt in front of her with a pen on top of it. "Here you go, ma'am. Sorry for the wait. Have a good night."

Jasmine wrote down her room number, added the tip amount, and signed the check. "Let's go."

They rode the elevator in tense silence, and as it opened on the penthouse level, Jaz rushed out with the card key in hand. Once they were inside, they didn't waste any time and walked straight into the master bathroom.

"The shower is the most logical place," Margo said. "Either that or above the bathtub. Do you take baths?"

"Sometimes, I do." Jasmine walked into the shower and started patting the tiled surface. "But mostly, I take showers. How small can those cameras get? I don't know what I'm looking for."

"I read somewhere that they can be as small as a pinhead."

"Great." Jasmine grimaced. "With this pebbled tiling, he could have hidden it anywhere."

"Not really." Margo took off her shoes and climbed on top of the bathtub platform. "It's not like he had access to it while they were building the place, and a retrofit is never seamless." She pointed her phone's flashlight at the ceiling, methodically scanning the entire expanse.

Jaz stopped her tile patting and leaned against the wall. "What if the suite was built to serve as a viewing room? They could have embedded the cameras in the walls."

Margo chuckled. "And I thought that I was the queen of conspiracy theories."

"Jaz? Where are you?"

They both froze.

"It's Alberto," Jasmine whispered.

Margo winced.

"What are we going to do?"

"Follow my lead and act natural." Jasmine smoothed a hand over the flowing skirt of her halter dress and sauntered out of the bathroom.

"Alberto, you're back," she said with such cheer in her voice that Margo had to admire her acting skills.

"Here you are." A good-looking guy swept Jaz into his arms and planted a kiss on her lips. He stopped kissing her only when he noticed Margo behind his girlfriend. "Who are you?"

Jasmine untangled herself from his arms. "This is my new friend, Margo. We met at the pool and hit it off right away. I was just showing her around the suite."

"This place is amazing." Margo put a hand over her heart. "I've never seen a presidential suite before. I didn't even know rooms like this existed in hotels." She snorted. "This place is so big that it needs its own serving staff."

Alberto plastered a charming smile on his handsome face and offered her his hand. "I am very pleased to meet you, Margo." His handshake was firm but not too hard. "I'm so glad that my Jaz found a friend. Regrettably, the business deal I'm working on requires much more of my time than I expected, and I'm forced to neglect my beautiful Jasmine." He made a pouty face and wrapped his arm around Jaz's waist, pulling her toward him. "My precious jewel should not be left by her lonesome."

"I agree." Margo regarded him from under lowered lashes.

Usually, she was good at reading people, but Alberto was either very good at putting on a show, or he was innocent of the nefarious intentions she'd assigned to him.

"You must join us for drinks and a late supper." Alberto walked Jasmine out of the bedroom. "I'll order room service, and we will get to know each other."

"I would love to." Margo granted him a bright smile.

For a brief moment, she considered that Alberto might want to sell her too. Margo wasn't nearly as beautiful as Jasmine, but she was a natural blonde, had a decent figure, and had a pretty face.

She could fetch a good price.

Nah, she was just an average, nothing-special twenty-seven-year-old. Most of those in the market to buy flesh would regard her as too old. They wanted the young and innocent.

How old was Jasmine, though?

The woman appeared ageless. She could be twenty or thirty or any age in between, but she was far from innocent. She was also one of the most beautiful women Margo had ever seen, so maybe it didn't matter that she wasn't as young as the perverts preferred.

20

BRUNDAR

Brundar stood in front of the mirror and debated whether to gather his long hair at his nape like he usually did or leave it to fan out down his back.

The choice to keep it that long had been about making a statement. He could look as feminine as had been claimed by those who had attacked him as a kid and shattered his innocence forever, but no one would ever think that he was easy prey again. He was lethal, and even those who didn't know him could figure that out with just one look.

Still, he didn't need to make a statement onboard a ship that carried mostly his clan. He was an accepted and respected member of the community, and no one would mistake him for someone who needed protecting or rescuing.

He was the protector and rescuer now, and he was damn good at his job.

Pulling the leather tie from his pocket, he brushed his stick-straight hair back with his fingers, gathered it at the nape, and tied the string around the thick, blond column.

In the other pocket of his tux was the folded piece of paper containing his vows to Callie. He pulled it out, unfolded the page, and read through it once more. By now, he could probably recite them in his sleep.

Anandur had pestered him for weeks about writing his vows and memorizing them, warning him that things might get a little emotional during the wedding ceremony and that he might forget some of the words, but Brundar had enjoyed tormenting his brother by pretending that he didn't care about that and wasn't going to bother.

Had Anandur believed him?

He shouldn't have.

His brother was probably the only one other than Callie who knew that Brundar's stoic appearance was a mask, and that inside he was just as susceptible to the turmoil of emotions as the next person, maybe even more so. Except, as soon as he felt anything, he immediately shoved that feeling into the armored safe inside his mind so it wouldn't interfere with his work or training.

The only emotion that Brundar would allow himself to feel was his love for Callie. He didn't shove that into the safe. Even so, it required a conscious effort not to do so, and that was not because his feelings for her didn't run deep because they did. It was just that he'd gotten so used to suppressing his emotions that it happened on autopilot, and reprogramming himself was still a work in progress.

When the doorbell rang, Brundar took one last look at his reflection and walked into the living room to open the door for his brother.

"I don't have much time." Anandur rushed by him, dripping water from his freshly washed hair. "I have two minutes to get into my tux and tame my hair."

Brundar followed him to the bedroom. "Where did you shower?"

"Kian's place. I figured you needed your alone time before the wedding."

"Thank you. That was uncharacteristically considerate of you."

"You're welcome." Anandur pulled his T-shirt over his head and dropped it on the floor. "Don't get used to it. I'm only making an exception for your wedding. The rest of the time, you're fair game." He dropped his pants in the same unceremonious way.

Brundar shook his head at his brother's nudity. "Do you ever wear underwear?"

"Yeah, I do. But I didn't want to borrow Kian's, and I didn't have any fresh ones with me, now did I?" He unzipped the tux bag and pulled the tux out.

With a sigh, Brundar collected the discarded clothing and carried it to the laundry hamper in the bathroom. "I can give you a fresh pair. I have a pack of new ones."

"Thank you. That would be awesome." Anandur shrugged on a white dress shirt and started buttoning it. "I wanted to wear something fun for your wedding, but since you are not fun, I decided it would be a waste of effort."

"And there goes the one day of reprieve you just promised me." Brundar tossed the package at Anandur.

"Thank you. And that doesn't count because it's the truth. You wouldn't have appreciated my humor."

Brundar shrugged. "I thought that the Superman T-shirt was a nice touch."

"Really?" Anandur's brows hitched nearly to his hairline. "Why didn't you say so?" He tore the plastic bag and pulled out one of the boxer briefs.

"Your head is too big already." Brundar leaned against the dresser, waiting for his brother to be done.

"How do I look?" Anandur asked and turned in a circle.

"Just as good as you did at your own wedding." Brundar pushed away from the dresser. "Do you need cologne?"

"Yes, please."

Anandur's hair was still as messy as always, but they didn't have the time or the products for him to tame it, so Brundar didn't mention it.

"Do you have your vows ready?" Anandur asked after spraying himself with the cologne.

Brundar nodded.

"Did you come up with anything good?"

"I hope so, and if not, Callie will forgive me. She knows I'm a man of few words."

Anandur straightened to his full height and looked down at Brundar. "Yeah, everyone knows that. But you've been more talkative than usual just now. Is it because you are nervous?"

"Not about the wedding. It's just a formality. I'm nervous about having everyone looking at me and expecting the same stoic Brundar they are used to seeing every day."

Anandur frowned. "What are they going to see instead?"

Brundar smiled, and the shock on Anandur's face was just precious. "They are going to see the face I've only shown Callie. It's going to come out for one night in honor of my bride and go back into dormancy tomorrow."

21

CALLIE

Callie stood at the entrance to the beautifully adorned hall and smoothed her hand over the voluminous skirt of her gown. She'd chosen a traditional white dress even though it wasn't her first wedding, because the first time didn't count.

She'd married a monster who would have murdered her if Brundar hadn't shown up in her life and given her the courage to escape the trap of her disastrous marriage.

Her destined mate, the love of her life, had almost died while trying to defend her, and if not for Anandur, who had saved them both, they wouldn't be here today.

But she didn't want to think about that now. The past belonged in the past, and today, or rather tonight, it was about her and Brundar and the love they shared.

This was the only wedding that mattered, and this time she was marrying an angel. He certainly looked like an angel to her, and most of their guests, being family, would share her opinion of her mate, but they probably thought of him as their Guardian angel. There were only a few who knew that he was as beautiful on the inside as he was on the outside.

Brundar might look like a killer to some, and when circumstances called for it, he was, but he was also a savior, a protector. He was a guardian.

As tradition dictated, he hadn't seen her dress yet, and she hoped he would love it as much as she did. Callie had seen it in an online catalog and knew that it was the dress she was going to wear on her special day. A trip to the bridal shop had confirmed her choice. The dress fit her so perfectly that no alterations had been needed, not even the length, even though she was of average height and expected the skirt to be too long.

What made the gown truly stand out were the delicate tulle inserts interspersed within the skirt. The sheer fabric pieces played with the light, creating an ethereal, almost magical quality to the gown. As Callie moved, the tulle pieces swayed gently, making her feel like a fairytale princess.

"You look beautiful," Wonder whispered.

Callie smiled at her soon-to-be sister-in-law. "Thank you." She looked over Wonder's tall frame encased in a peach-colored bridesmaid's dress. "The color really suits you."

"I know, right?" Wonder looked at the other bridesmaids, who all wore the same style of dress, just in different colors.

Amanda had joked that they looked like assorted candy or ice cream cones, which was the kind of look Callie had been going for. The dresses were simple satin sheaths with spaghetti straps and of varying lengths, and all of her bridesmaids looked beautiful in them.

Amanda's was blue, Syssi's was orange, Carol's was pink, and Jacki's was yellow. Cassandra's was bright red, Mey's was purple, and Jin's was emerald.

It had been tough to choose her bridesmaids from her many female friends in the clan, but since Brundar's groomsmen were mostly his fellow Guardians, she'd decided to choose their mates in addition to Carol, Syssi, and Amanda.

"That's our cue," Amanda said as the wedding march started playing.

As the double doors to the dining hall were opened by two Guardians, Callie took a deep breath before taking the first step.

With her bridesmaids flanking her, four on each side, she entered the hall and followed the red carpet to the podium, where Brundar waited for her with his seven groomsmen and one groomsmaid by his side.

In addition to the head guardians, his groomsmen included Kian and Dalhu.

Callie smiled, her eyes trained on Brundar, who surprised her by returning her smile and nodding.

She was so stunned by that smile that her step faltered, and she had to steady herself to regain her footing. She'd been graced by his smiles on rare occasions, but never in public. Was this the start of a new Brundar? Or was he only lowering his shields for this one night?

When Brundar averted his gaze to look at the Clan Mother, Callie was finally able to tear her eyes away from him and shift her attention to the goddess who was presiding over their wedding.

Just as in the three preceding nights, Annani wore a gleaming white gown with long sheer sleeves that looked like angel wings when she raised her arms.

It was a different gown every night, but it was a variation on the same theme.

Shifting her eyes back to Brundar, Callie glided toward him on the wings of love. Or at least it felt like that because all she could feel was the smile stretching her face. It probably looked manic, but she couldn't help it because Brundar was once again smiling at her across the room.

As she and her bridesmaids reached the podium, she took her place by Brundar's side while her bridesmaids joined the groomsmen.

Brundar reached for her hand and clasped it gently, pouring strength into her.

The Clan Mother lifted her arms, and the last of the chatter stopped.

"My dear children. We are gathered here tonight to celebrate the union of Callie and Brundar. It is most fitting that this joyous occasion follows a great victory of good over evil, and on this eve, our hearts are filled with joy and hope for a better future."

Smiling, she lowered her arms and trained her glowing eyes on Brundar. "Brundar's journey has been one of courage and determination, of triumph over adversity and the relentless pursuit of excellence and growth. You have been a staunch defender of the clan. With bravery and skill, you have walked a path of honor, courage, and personal growth. In Callie, you have found a safe harbor of calm water, peace, and unconditional love."

The goddess shifted her warm gaze to Callie. "Callie's journey paralleled Brundar's. With courage and determination, you triumphed over hardship while retaining a spirit bright with optimism and hope, a guiding light of compassion, and a testament to the healing power of love. You are proof that the gentlest of touches can move mountains and that kindness can illuminate the darkest of paths. In each other, you have found love and a mirror reflecting back the best of yourselves, and together, you are stronger than the sum of your parts."

She turned her gaze to their gathered family and friends before returning it to the two of them. "May your joined journey be an odyssey of growth, filled with shared joys and enduring companionship. Your love is a sanctuary, a haven of peace and renewal, not just for yourselves but for all who are touched by it. May you walk hand in hand as partners, mates, and scions of hope and inspiration in the Fates' great tapestry of life."

The goddess smiled, and Callie's heart missed a beat. "In the presence of your family and friends, you may now recite your vows of love and commitment to each other."

22

BRUNDAR

Callie was always beautiful to Brundar, but today she looked like a fairytale princess in her white dress and her low-heeled white slippers that he had to examine to make sure they weren't made from glass.

He might be the last male anyone could mistake for a prince, but Callie was dancing only with him, and if anyone was to find her glass slipper, it would be him.

The silly thought brought a smile to his face, but it melted away when the Clan Mother spoke of love's transformative power. Brundar knew what she was referring to, but he hoped that the rest of the assembled clan did not.

In fact, Annani wasn't supposed to know either, and he wondered who had told her.

It couldn't have been Anandur, who had sworn to take the tale with him beyond the veil, but his mother could have said something to the goddess. She also didn't know the details of what had happened to him, but she'd seen him when Anandur had brought him home, and it hadn't been difficult to guess what had been done to him.

Anandur had protected him as he had always done and prohibited their mother from asking questions.

His secret should have never reached the goddess's ears.

"You may now recite your vows of love and commitment for each other."

Annani's words pulled him out of his thoughts, and he turned to Callie, the love of his life and his savior in so many ways.

Her brilliant smile and the sheen in her eyes melted some of the ice that had formed around his heart, and he smiled back. "I'll go first if you don't mind." He took her hands and waited until she nodded.

"Callie, my light in the darkest of nights. From the moment our paths first crossed, I knew deep in my heart that we were destined to be together. You were married to a monster, but at the time, I didn't know the extent of his monstrosity, and I tried to stay away. But the Fates whispered in my ear to keep an eye on you, to guard you in case you needed my help, and that was my excuse for watching you like a stalker."

Callie smiled. "You were not a stalker. You were my guardian angel, and you saved me. I felt you watching me, and your presence was reassuring rather than threatening. The Fates must have whispered in my ears as well."

Brundar gave her hands a light squeeze. "We saved each other. You have been my guiding light. In your eyes, I found a world filled with hope and a future I didn't think was possible for the likes of me. You have shown me that love is more than a soft feeling. It's a force that can move mountains, heal the deepest wounds, and bring light into the darkest corners. In your love, I have found a sanctuary."

"Oh, Brundar." A single tear slid down Callie's cheek. "I love you so much."

"I love you more than words can express. I vow to honor the love you have given me, to cherish it, nurture it, and protect it against all. In the quiet moments and the chaotic ones, in the challenges and the triumphs, I promise to stand by your side as your partner, your best friend, your guardian, and your greatest ally. I promise to be the warmth in your winter, the breeze in your summer, the harvest of your autumn, and the bloom of your spring."

He'd read the last sentence somewhere, and it had stuck in his memory. Hopefully, Callie wouldn't mind that not all the words in his vows were original.

He had to let go of one of her hands to pull the ring out from his pocket. "We don't need symbols to represent our everlasting love, but it's tradition, so here goes. This ring has no beginning and no end, and symbolizes my eternal love, faith, and commitment." He slid the ring on her finger. "With this ring, I bind my life to yours."

He leaned down and kissed her lightly on the lips. "I know that I'm supposed to wait until the Clan Mother pronounces us joined, but I needed this."

"Me too." She wiped the lone tear that had slid down her cheek.

Taking a deep breath, Callie took his hands. "Brundar, my guardian, my strength. In the tapestry of my life, the threads of darkness were once overwhelming until you entered, bringing light, hope, and incredible courage. When shadows loomed large and the path ahead seemed insurmountable, you became my protector, my shield, my guardian angel. I will never forget that you were willing to sacrifice yourself to save me or the terrible injuries you sustained while rescuing me from a monster. You have shown me what true bravery is. In the solace of your strength, I found the courage to dream, to be unapologetically myself, and most importantly, to love as I will."

This was the only mention of their shared proclivities, and it was subtle enough for most of their guests to gloss over, but those who knew them well and were aware of the games they liked to play smiled and clapped.

Callie gave them a slight nod before continuing, "I vow to honor the sacrifices you've made and to cherish the love you've shown me every step of the way. With every beat of my heart, I promise to be your sanctuary and safe harbor as you have been for me."

She turned to Anandur, who stood first among the groomsmen. "Neither of us would be here if not for you. In our darkest moment, in the crucible of despair, you came to our rescue, and for that and all the other times you stood by your brother's side, you have my eternal gratitude."

For a change, Anandur didn't retort with a jest or a joke. Instead, he put his hand over his heart and dipped his head. "For as long as there is breath in my lungs, you will have my protection. As you know, I take my big-brother responsibilities very seriously, and once you became Brundar's mate, you also became my little sister."

"Thank you." She blew him a kiss before returning her gaze to Brundar. "In the human world, when you marry a man, you marry his whole family. I'm overjoyed to be part of yours." She waved a hand over the gathered crowd. "You are all the best people I've ever met, and I love you all."

As applause and cheers erupted, Callie smiled and waited patiently until they subsided. When the room fell quiet again, she turned back to face Brundar. "Today, as I stand with you, I see a future filled with promise. I vow to weather every storm with you, and to glide through every calm. I promise to support you in every struggle, and to celebrate your every triumph."

Callie extended her hand to Wonder, who placed a ring on her palm.

"This ring is a symbol of my eternal gratitude, my unending love, and my commitment to our joined journey." She slid the ring on his finger. "Brundar, my love, my angel, my knight in shining armor. You are my fated mate."

As the crowd erupted in a new wave of cheers and applause, Annani lifted her arms. "In the presence of all gathered here, I pronounce you bonded for eternity. May your love shine as a symbol of hope and transformation and the unyielding power of the heart." She waved a hand. "You may kiss the bride."

23

MARGO

"The food was delicious." Margo leaned back in her chair and rubbed her tummy. "It's good that I don't get to eat like that every day."

"Why not?" Alberto asked.

She smiled. "I don't want to gain weight."

He waved a dismissive hand. "Women think too much about their weight. Men might like to look at skinny models, but they don't want them in their beds." He threw a charming smile at Jasmine. "They don't want a bag of bones under them. They want their woman to be soft."

His words rubbed Margo the wrong way even though she couldn't totally dispute them. She wouldn't be attracted to a guy that was all bones either, but she wouldn't phrase it like that. She would never say that she didn't want a pile of bones in her bed.

Alberto talked about women as if they were sexual objects and not people with minds, feelings, and thoughts.

It wasn't unusual for men, and maybe even for some women, to think about possible partners exclusively in sexual terms, but it was small-minded and offensive.

"Are you calling me fat?" Jasmine asked teasingly.

"I'm calling you perfect." He took her hand and kissed the back of it. "One of a kind." He kissed it again. "A rare and coveted jewel." He kissed it for the third time.

Hadn't he told Jasmine that she should get plastic surgery to slim her thighs? Maybe Jasmine had made that up?

The guy acted as if he worshiped the ground she walked on, even if he was only infatuated with her body and gorgeous face and couldn't care less about her personality or her mind, both of which Margo found lovely. Jasmine was effortlessly friendly, she wasn't conceited, she didn't act entitled, and she was intelligent.

Jasmine smiled. "You are such a charmer."

That he was, and Margo had reconsidered her initial suspicions about him wanting to sell Jaz, but there was still something about him that bothered her.

Perhaps it was just his Latin machismo.

Not that she knew enough about Latin men to pass judgment. Growing up in Los Angeles, she'd been surrounded by Latinos, but she had never dated one. The truth was that she hadn't dated many men in general, so maybe she just didn't know much about them, regardless of their ethnicity.

Crap, she was committing the same offense she'd accused Alberto of. She wasn't thinking of men in terms of people but in terms of their gender, and that was as wrong as any other generalization.

Okay, so what did she know about Alberto as a person?

He spoke English like a native, which led her to believe that he had studied in the US, and his vocabulary was rich enough to indicate that he had at least some higher education or read a lot. Still, she could easily detect the traces of the Spanish accent he was trying to hide. He might have even been born and raised in the US, but his first language had been Spanish.

The guy was too young to have so much money to throw around, but that didn't necessarily mean that he was a drug dealer or a trafficker. Maybe he came from a wealthy family, and the business deal he was negotiating was on behalf of his family business and had nothing to do with drugs or trafficking.

Lifting her wine glass, Margo turned to Alberto. "You mentioned a deal you are working on. What is it about?"

A shadow passed over his eyes, but his lips lifted in a smile. "I'm afraid it's confidential."

Margo's hackles rose again. "How come?"

He sighed. "I'm trying to negotiate a deal between two large companies. If word got out about the possible merger, it would influence their stock prices, which is a big no-no. Anyone who bought or sold their stocks after hearing about it could be accused of insider trading. I'm therefore very careful about saying anything regarding the merger."

"I don't invest in stocks," Margo said. "I have a 401(k) retirement savings through the company I work for and a savings account. That's all."

Alberto let go of Jasmine's hand and reached for the wine bottle. "You might have friends and family who invest." He refilled her glass. "The bottom line is that I can't tell anyone who isn't directly involved in the talks." He refilled Jaz's glass, and lastly his own.

"Is that why they are conducting the negotiations in Cabo?" Jasmine asked.

He nodded. "It's easier to hide from the media. The executives of both companies are staying in different hotels, and I doubt anyone in the media will figure out the connection between the two companies organizing retreats for their executives at the same time and in the same city."

It all sounded perfectly logical, and Margo's earlier suspicions were diminishing by the minute.

"I thought that you were dealing with local businesspeople," Jasmine said.

"What made you think that?" Alberto asked a little sharply.

Jaz shrugged. "You said something about a long drive. All the hotels are clustered in the same area."

He reached for his wine glass. "They are thinking about building a new manufacturing plant in the area, and we are scouting possible building sites."

Again, it sounded legit, but something about it bothered Margo. Did it make sense for the two companies who were negotiating a possible merger to be already looking for a site for their future joint endeavor?

Shouldn't they conclude the first step before going to the next?

If all of that was an elaborate fiction, Alberto was a skilled liar who could spin tales on the spot, which he might very well be.

Still, Margo's usually suspicious mind was getting a little lazy tonight, and she was more and more convinced that she had overreacted. It didn't make sense for the guy to invest so much time and money in a woman whom he intended to sell. There was no reason for him to put her in the presidential suite or to try to charm her new friend into liking him.

On the other hand, Alberto had taken Jasmine's passport, her California driver's license, and her credit cards, and that was a big-ass red flag.

24

KIAN

"That was so beautiful." Syssi dabbed under her eyes with a cloth napkin. "I never suspected that Brundar could be so poetic."

Amanda snorted. "Don't judge the book by its cover, right? People are more than their appearance."

"That reminds me." Kian drummed his fingers on the table. "Eva will need your help tomorrow. We need to disguise a large number of people to look like humans, and Eva can't handle so many on her own."

"Why do you need to do that?" Dalhu asked.

"So, the Doomers don't suspect this ship is ours." He explained Lokan's arguments and why he agreed with them. "But if we hope to pull it off, we will have to do a really good job of appearing like any other cruise ship. A large percentage of passengers will need to disembark and do touristy things while looking like average cruisers, which means much older and less attractive."

"Eva doesn't have her chest of professional makeup and costumes with her," Amanda said. "How does she hope to create the illusion with what's available to her?"

Kian turned to look at Brundar and Callie walking hand in hand toward the dance floor. "Eva said that she could do it with regular makeup, padding, and coaching on how to act. I assume she means walking hunched over, maybe shuffling a little, but it shouldn't be overdone because it will look obvious."

"What about Margo?" Syssi asked. "They don't know who she is, only that we are supposed to pick up a woman from the hotel. We should tell her to take a taxi to the airport and collect her from there."

That was actually a pretty good idea, and it was much simpler than what he had in mind, which was picking up Margo at a mall or a coffee shop. That still didn't solve the problem of getting her on the ship with the Doomers watching. If he were in their shoes, he would have counted the number of passengers leaving the ship and compared it to the number of those who returned. If there was an excess of one, that would prompt them to further investigate the *Silver Swan,* including boarding it.

There was another problem that he hadn't considered before. If any of the Doomers were lurking nearby, they could sense the immortal males. Still, if only females went ashore, that would appear suspicious as well. Hopefully, they would be watching from some distance. The alarm only worked in close proximity.

"I should tell Mia to contact Margo and tell her what the plan is." He pushed to his feet. "The question is how to explain that to a human who doesn't know who we are."

"Let Mia worry about that," Amanda said. "She can invent some story about the cartels."

"Can't it wait?" Syssi took his hand. "I want to join Brundar and Callie on the dance floor."

"There is no rush." He tugged on her hand. "In fact, it can wait for tomorrow morning. We've slowed down, so we will only get to Cabo in the evening, and Mia will have plenty of time to tell Margo what to do."

Syssi rewarded him with a bright smile. "It would be nice to have at least one night to just enjoy ourselves."

"I couldn't agree more." He led his wife to where several other couples were dancing. "Did I tell you already how stunningly beautiful you look tonight?" He put one hand on her waist and took her hand in the other.

"Yes, you did." She followed his waltz steps. "Several times. You look very handsome tonight as well, my love."

"It's the same tux I wore to the other weddings."

"You've looked dashing every night, but you need to wear your other tux for the upcoming weddings."

He looked down at his pants. "Why? Did I get stains on this one?"

She laughed. "No, but it's no longer in immaculate condition. It's time for a fresh one."

"As you wish, my darling." He dipped his head and kissed her cheek, only because she was wearing lipstick, and he didn't want to mess it up.

Not yet, anyway. Once the wedding was over and they were back in their cabin, he planned to mess up a lot more than just her lipstick.

Syssi chuckled. "I love that lopsided smile of yours. Are you thinking the same thing I'm thinking?"

"That depends on what you were thinking."

"You go first."

He pulled her closer against his chest and whispered in her ear, "I was thinking about messing up your lipstick."

Syssi laughed. "That's all? I was expecting something much naughtier."

He lowered his hand and gave her ass a loving squeeze. "I didn't say how I was going to mess it up."

Predictably, her cheeks pinked. "And how is that?" She licked her lips.

"I think you've got the right idea."

25

PETER

As the vows were concluded and Brundar kissed Callie, Peter cheered and clapped with everyone else, but his eyes scanned the hall for Marina. None of the servers were out, though, and he remembered that they wouldn't be allowed into the event hall until Annani departed.

The Clan Mother never stayed long during the celebrations, usually retreating to her quarters after the ceremony was over, so it wouldn't be long before the servers would start delivering trays of food.

His fellow Guardians were particularly revelrous tonight, which was to be expected after a mission. There was nothing like killing scum who truly deserved it to put everyone in a good mood.

Peter was still clapping when the newlyweds took to the dance floor for their first dance as an officially married couple. Brundar and Callie had been mated for a while, and yet seeing them swaying in each other's arms, lost in their private universe, made him a little emotional.

Thankfully, he wasn't the only one. Anandur was wiping tears from his eyes, and for once, he wasn't pretending.

Who would have thought that the stoic Brundar could deliver such beautiful vows to his bride?

Callie and Brundar's vows had been touching, but then Peter had found all the previous couples' vows moving.

Love was truly a beautiful thing, and he hoped to one day find his own fated mate, but the waiting line was long, and there were many ahead of him.

No one knew for sure why the Fates rewarded some with the boon of a fated mate and not others, but the belief was that it had to do with the sacrifices one had made for other people or the terrible suffering that one had endured.

The only hardship Peter had ever suffered was when Emmett had abducted him, and he'd been afraid of being used as a stud bull for Kra-ell Dormants, but even though it had been a scary experience, he really hadn't been harmed, so it probably didn't count as enduring great suffering.

Bottom line, he wasn't expecting his truelove mate to appear anytime soon.

After Annani departed, Peter waited until the servers emerged with their trays and scanned the room. Looking for a glint of blue hair, he spotted Marina weaving between the tables while expertly balancing a tray laden with champagne flutes.

She'd promised him a dance at the wedding, and he intended to collect on that promise sooner than later. He also had plans for her later that night, and he had a feeling that she would be more than amenable to those plans.

Rising to his feet, Peter made his way through the crowd, zeroing in on Marina.

Seeing him heading her way, her eyes widened, and a smile ghosted her lips. She shook her head slightly, hinting that she wasn't ready for him to collect on her promise, but he was impatient, and he needed to hold her in his arms right away.

Hell, he'd been imagining that since the moment she'd promised him that dance, her lips curving in a seductive smile and the scent of her arousal nearly bringing him to his knees.

It had flared for only a moment, but it had been enough to imprint itself on his psyche for eternity.

Kagra's words suddenly sounded in his mind, chilling his fervor. *You are a romantic, Peter, and you fall too easily. You are enamored with the notion of love.*

So what? Love was the spice of life, and even though neither Kagra nor Marina could be his fated one, he wasn't looking for a forever love. For-now love was good enough, for the simple reason that it was the only kind available to him.

When he reached Marina, he plucked the tray from her hands, put it down on the nearest table, and took her hand. "Come dance with me."

"I can't. I'm working." She reached for the tray.

"You can take a break. If anyone has a problem with that, they can take it up with me."

She still hesitated.

"Just one dance. The world won't crumble if the champagne is served a minute later."

"Fine," she said in a resigned tone. "Just one dance, and if Mila comes to scream at me, I'll point her in your direction." She untied her apron and draped it over the back of a vacant chair.

"Attagirl." He took her hand. "This morning, you spoke of freedom and choices. I'd say choosing to take a break to dance embodies that sentiment."

Marina laughed. "That's a great argument. I wonder what Mila would think of it."

"I don't really care." He wrapped his arms around her, pulling her close against his body.

She laughed again, nervously this time. "This is not a slow dance."

"I don't really care," he repeated. "I've dreamt of doing this since you promised me a dance this morning."

Her eyes sparkled as she looked up at him. "Me too," she whispered.

As an electric charge of attraction pulsed between them, he wanted to kiss her so badly, but he was acutely aware of the eyes on them. Some were smiling, others seemed curious, and still others looked disapproving.

Was it because he was dancing with a human while everyone else on the dance floor was immortal?

Well, that was their problem, not his or Marina's.

Ignoring the looks, he let the melody envelop them and drew Marina even closer, their bodies touching and electrifying one another. He could sense her heartbeat quicken, her breath hitch, and that delicate aroma of her arousal flare.

She wanted him as much as he wanted her, and unlike Kagra, she didn't find him lacking in any way.

To Marina, he was a god.

26

MARINA

Originally, Marina had seen Peter as a mere steppingstone, a part of her calculated strategy to escape the mundane life in Safe Haven. He was supposed to be a means to an end, but it seemed like she was falling into her own trap.

Moving across the dance floor, she was acutely aware of every point of contact between their bodies, of the way Peter's arms felt around her, of how solid his chest was, and of the substantial erection pressing against her stomach.

It had been so long since she'd been with a man, and she missed it.

She was nearing her mid-thirties, so the Kra-ell had lost interest in her a long time ago, and out of the limited selection of human partners in the compound she had chosen Nicolai, who was many years younger than her and had Kra-ell blood in him, which hadn't worked in his favor as far as she was concerned, but the fact that he'd been chosen to attend a university had. It was what had attracted her to him the most.

The problem was that the university offered him many more choices than what was available in the compound, and eventually he had lost interest in her as well.

Marina had been heartbroken for a while, and then the liberation had happened, and then she had found herself in Safe Haven with community members who held on to strange beliefs that were closer to the Kra-ell way of life than what the humans in her former compound practiced. They were into free love, which just meant multiple partners and no individual commitment. It wasn't what Marina wanted out of life, so she had stayed away from them.

She couldn't even remember the last time she'd had sex. It had been during one of Nicolai's monthly mandatory visits from college, but she didn't recall which one.

It seemed like a lifetime ago.

Everything had changed so drastically that looking back to life in the compound seemed like ancient history, when in fact only a couple of months had passed since the liberation.

The problem was that hooking up with an immortal might help her get out of Safe Haven, but it wouldn't get her any closer to having a man to call her own.

Marina wanted children, and she wanted to make a home for her family, but the only way to achieve that was in the outside world, and she wouldn't be allowed to do that. She knew too much, and there was no way to make her forget that two alien species were hiding among humans.

Her plan had been to play coy, to weave a slow web around Peter and make him chase her. She had thought to draw this out, to savor the dance of seduction, but as their bodies moved in perfect harmony, with Peter's gaze so intently focused on her face, her strategy began to crumble. The desire she felt was too intense, too urgent to be stifled, sacrificed on the altar of strategic games.

He seemed to see beyond the calculated façade and stir something within her that she had long given up on.

Escaping the intensity of his gaze, she put her cheek on his chest and inhaled his scent. He had applied his cologne sparingly, for which she was grateful, and not just because she didn't like overpowering scents. It allowed her to smell his own unique scent, and it was much better than anything that could be bought in a store.

As the song reached its crescendo, Marina lifted her head and whispered, mindful of all the immortals around them with their super hearing, "I want you, and I know that you want me." She leaned away and forced her voice to remain steady as she looked into his eyes. "The only question remaining is your place or mine?"

In that instant, the world seemed to stand still. The dance floor, the watching crowd, the twinkling lights—all faded into a distant blur. There was only Peter and the way he looked at her, with eyes that promised a world of passion.

"Mine," he finally said. "I have my own bedroom, but I share the cabin with another Guardian. Are you okay with that?"

She nodded. "Can you sneak me in without him knowing?"

He frowned. "Are you embarrassed about being with me?"

"No, but you might be embarrassed about being seen with me." She chuckled nervously. "Slumming with the human."

His hold on her tightened, becoming almost bruising. "Never say that. I don't slum. Any female who invites me to her bed or invites herself to mine honors me."

Peter looked so offended and so sincere that she couldn't bring herself to doubt him. He'd really meant that, and it eased something in her chest, a memory of past humiliations that she had buried deep inside and pretended that they had never existed.

"What about your roommate? Does he think the same way you do?"

Peter must have realized that he was hurting her because his grip on her loosened a fraction. "The only thing that my roommate will feel is jealousy that a beautiful woman is spending the night with me."

Was that true, or was he just saying it to make her feel good?

She felt compelled to challenge his assertion. "What if I want to stay more than one night?"

He smiled. "Then he would be even more jealous, and I would be even happier and more honored."

"Okay, then. But you have to wait for me to be done for tonight, and it's going to be really late. I can't leave before the kitchen is clean."

"I'll wait for you, and when you come, I'll draw you a bath and massage your aching feet."

The groan that escaped her throat sounded more like a lust-filled moan. "If you keep saying such wonderful things to me, I might fall in love with you."

"Is that bad?"

"Of course, it is. You are immortal, and I'm mortal. There is no future for us."

He dipped his head and took her lips in a gentle kiss. "I'm not thinking about forever love. For-now love is good enough for me."

27

MARGO

"Margo." Alberto lifted his wine glass and leaned back with it in his hand. "We've been talking about me and Jasmine the entire evening, but you didn't tell us anything about yourself."

"What do you want to know?"

"Who are you with? I'm sure a beautiful woman like you isn't vacationing alone."

The guy probably told all the women he talked to that they were beautiful, but Margo couldn't help but feel pleased by it. "I'm attending my future sister-in-law's week-long bachelorette party."

He arched a brow. "So why aren't you celebrating with her tonight?"

Margo didn't want to tell him about Lynda and the others being away in the club. She no longer thought he wanted to sell Jasmine to the highest bidder, but there was a lot about the guy that still seemed shady, and she didn't trust him.

"After nearly a week, I needed a little break from Lynda and her girlfriends."

Alberto smiled knowingly. "Did you have a fight with your future sister-in-law?"

His mocking tone annoyed her. In fact, a lot about the guy grated on her, but she couldn't put her finger on what it was. He was unapologetically chauvinistic, so maybe that was it.

"I didn't have a fight with Lynda." There was really no harm in telling him that Lynda was away from the resort at the moment. It wasn't as if she was a factor in his decisions, even if they were shady. "She and her friends went to a club, and I decided to pass. I don't like the club scene, and I've been a good sport about partying with them so far."

"I can understand that." His tone turned compassionate, and his eyes conveyed commiseration. "How much longer is this bachelorette party going to last? You sound like you've had enough of it."

Now she was back to liking him. The guy was very attuned to her, which meant that he was an attentive listener who heard more than just what was said. He got the emotions behind the words, which was pretty rare for men.

Crap, I'm doing that again. I shouldn't generalize.

It was the wine's fault, and the Cadillac margarita before that, and that other drink she'd had before that one. She really needed to cut back on the alcohol, or she would start acting like Lynda and her girlfriends, flirting with waiters and making a fool of herself.

"It's almost over. Tomorrow is the last day."

The smile Alberto gave her looked predatory. "Are you happy to be going home?"

"I'm not happy about going back to work, but I miss sleeping in my own bed."

She didn't want to tell him about the cruise, and she cast a loaded glance at Jasmine, who nodded that she understood her meaning.

Evidently, she wasn't completely drunk and could still think semi-clearly. The ship might still be an option for Jasmine in case their suspicions proved correct after all, and telling Alberto about it would be stupid.

"What about the person sharing your bed?" Alberto asked. "Are you happy to go back to them?"

It was pretty progressive of him not to assume the gender of her bed partner, but then he might have suspected that her interest in Jasmine was sexual in nature.

"I have no partner at the moment." Margo took another sip of the wine.

"That's a shame. A beautiful woman like you shouldn't be alone. Perhaps I could introduce you to some of my friends? Do you have particular preferences I should know about?"

He was definitely fishing for information about her sexual orientation, and for a moment, Margo considered toying with him and answering vaguely, but perhaps it wasn't a good idea to make a possessive, jealous man think that she was interested in his girlfriend.

Smiling sweetly, she lifted the wine glass to her lips, took a dainty sip, and put it back down. "Tall, handsome, well-educated, and open-minded. The rest is negotiable."

"What about rich?" Alberto reached for the second wine bottle on the table and uncorked it.

"I don't care about money."

He refilled her glass and Jasmine's. "Most women want a man who can take care of them and their children. It might not be politically correct to say that, but that's reality. It's instinctual." He refilled his glass as well.

"Well, I want my dream guy to have a good job and make a decent living. I didn't say that I was willing to settle for a pauper. But I don't need a lot of money to be happy. Just enough to pay the bills and have some saved up for emergencies."

Jasmine laughed a little too loudly. She was definitely drunker than Margo. "With how much everything costs these days, you need to be wealthy just to afford rent and pay for groceries, and rich if you want to go out to restaurants and buy nice stuff from time to time."

Margo nodded. "I've been thinking about renting out the second bedroom in my apartment to make ends meet, but I might not need to do that after I start the new job I'm hoping to get." She took another sip of her wine and then put the glass down when she remembered that she needed to cut down.

The wine was so good, though. Tomorrow, she wasn't going to touch alcohol.

"What kind of a job?" Jasmine asked.

Margo frowned. Hadn't she told Jaz about it? She was sure that she had told her about the cruise being a private retreat for the Perfect Match company staff and that she hoped to get a job as a beta tester for their adventures. She even remembered Jasmine gushing over it.

"Didn't I tell you about it?" Her words came up a little slurred.

How much wine did they drink? They'd finished the first bottle and were on their second, and they had been drinking before that.

She was certainly overdoing it, and so was Jasmine.

"I don't remember." Jasmine lifted a hand to her temple. "I'm not feeling so great. I think I need to lie down for a few moments."

"What's the matter, love?" Alberto asked, rising to his feet.

"I'm dizzy," Margo said, even though his question had been directed at Jasmine. "Maybe I should call it a night and go to sleep." She snorted. "I'm sure to wake up with one hell of a hangover tomorrow."

28

KIAN

"I wish immortality made wearing high heels painless, but I guess that's asking for too much." Syssi plopped down on the chair and kicked off her shoes. "You can go talk to Mia now." She lifted her leg, crossed it over her knee, and started massaging her foot.

"I can also stay here and massage your feet." Kian sat down, took her foot, and put it over his thigh. "After all, it's my fault that your feet are hurting."

She frowned. "How is it your fault? I was the one who wanted to keep on dancing."

"If I wasn't as tall, you wouldn't have felt the need to wear high heels."

On the other side of the table, Amanda snorted. "Men. They think that the sun orbits around them. Syssi is not wearing high heels because you are tall. She's wearing them because they make her look good. Why do you think I always wear them even though I'm tall?"

"Because you are vain?"

She rolled her eyes. "Well, duh. I want to look my best at all times."

"You don't need heels for that." Dalhu draped his arm around her shoulders. "But what do I know? I'm just a simple-minded male."

Amanda chuckled. "Oh, stop it. We all have our hobbies, and one of mine is looking fabulous. Anyone have a problem with that?"

"Nope." Kian reached for Syssi's other foot and lifted it onto his lap. "No one dares."

As the whiz of Mia's motorized wheelchair alerted Kian to her approach, he turned to look at her over his shoulder. "Mia. You're just the person I need to talk to."

"Really? I came over to talk to you." She waited for Toven to move one of the chairs away so she could get closer to the table. "I spoke to Margo earlier, and she asked me to ask you for a favor."

Kian arched a brow. "She isn't supposed to know about me."

"She doesn't. We only refer to you as the boss or Tom's mysterious and eccentric partner, who should remain unnamed."

That got a smile out of him. "I like that. So, what's the favor?"

Mia took a deep breath. "Margo met a woman named Jasmine at the hotel, and they started chatting. Margo thinks that Jasmine's boyfriend is about to sell her. He took her passport, her driver's license, and her credit cards, claiming that he needed to keep them safe from thieves and pickpockets. The bottom line is that Jasmine can't escape him without her passport, and she needs to return to Los Angeles. Margo is asking if she can hitch a ride with us."

Kian grimaced. "It sounds fishy to me. Did that woman ask Margo if she can come aboard?"

"I don't think so, but maybe she did. Margo asked me to book an Airbnb for her so she could hide from her boyfriend until the ship arrived. If you don't allow her to come on board, having a place to hide will give her time to contact her family and have them try to help her. She said that people at the hotel had seen the two of them hanging out together, so if she booked the Airbnb under her name, the boyfriend could easily trace it through her. That's why she wanted me to book it under mine."

Syssi put her feet down and leaned over the table to look at Mia. "Did Jasmine ask her boyfriend for her passport, and he refused to give it back?"

"I don't know. I told Margo that she might be overreacting and making a big fuss over nothing, but her answer convinced me to help Jasmine anyway. She said that she might be wrong, and the boyfriend could be just a controlling jerk, but if she was right and did nothing, it would be forever on her conscience that she hadn't helped Jasmine."

"That's a convincing argument," Toven said. "I think we should allow the woman on board. We already have a group of rescued victims. What's one more?"

Kian sighed. "I might have been agreeable to letting Jasmine on the ship, but there are developments you are not aware of, which will make even getting just Margo here difficult."

"What's going on?" Toven asked.

"We interrogated Bud, the Doomers' leader, and it turns out that Kalugal left some memories in Luis's head that they were able to retrieve. One of them was that we were picking up a woman from the Grand Allure Resort in Cabo San Lucas. They don't know Margo's name, but we expect the Doomers to have a large presence at the hotel."

"That's not good," Toven said. "Are we still going to Cabo?"

"Yes, but we are putting on a charade, pretending to be a ship full of humans. That's why I wanted to talk to you. We slowed down so we wouldn't stand out among the other cruise ships that left Acapulco around the same time we did, and we will be arriving at Cabo late in the evening instead of early afternoon. Several groups will go to local clubs and restaurants, pretending to be tourists, and I plan on having the human staff intermingled with them to reinforce the perception. You need to tell Margo about our late arrival and also make up an excuse as to why we need her to take a taxi to the airport. We will collect her from there and find a way to smuggle her aboard, probably in a supply crate."

Mia chewed on her lower lip for a moment, and then she perked up. "I know what we can do. Jasmine can take a taxi to the airport from the Airbnb, and we can collect her from there together with Margo. If we can smuggle one in a supply crate, I don't see why we can't smuggle two."

Except for the law of unintended consequences, which was a major bitch, Kian couldn't find a fault in Mia's plan.

"They can both go to the Airbnb," Amanda said. "And we can pick them up from there. All the Doomers know is that we are picking a woman up from that hotel. They don't know who she is, so no one is going to watch Margo specifically."

The girl had probably told everyone in her group about being picked up by a cruise ship, and if she was the talkative type, she might have told many people about that. The Doomers could find out who she was very easily, which meant that she might be followed to the airport.

"Here is what I want you to tell Margo." Kian leaned back so he could see both Mia and Toven. "Tell her to go to the Airbnb and stay there until you call her. I will have Guardians watching the Airbnb to check that no one is following her and Jasmine to the airport. If they are compromised, we will have to change plans accordingly."

29

PETER

Peter didn't want to take any chances and risk Marina changing her mind. After everyone had left and the dining room was empty of guests, he started collecting plates with the other servers and putting them into the plastic bins.

"What are you doing?" Marina whispered.

"Helping out so you will be done faster."

"Don't," she hissed. "You're embarrassing me."

Now, that was rich coming from her after she'd accused him of being embarrassed about her spending the night with him.

He leaned to whisper back. "Are you afraid your people will find out about us?"

She stopped collecting dishes, took the plate he was holding, dropped it in the bin, and took his hand. "Come with me." She tugged him behind her out of the dining room.

When they were outside, she turned to him. "You are making everyone in there uncomfortable. They don't want their employers to help them clean up. They want the place devoid of immortals so they can joke and laugh and not worry about appearances."

He could understand that. "If you want me to leave, you'll have to give me something."

"What?"

"A kiss. A good one."

A smile spread over her lovely face. "I can do that." She wound her arms around his neck. "Kiss me."

He shook his head. "Nope. I want you to do it and make sure it's a good one, or I'll go back in there and keep on helping."

A giggle escaped Marina's beautiful lips. "That's the worst blackmail I've ever heard, but fine." She lifted on her toes and pressed a soft kiss to his lips.

Cupping her bottom, he lifted her and urged her to wrap her legs around his middle. He then turned around and pressed her against the wall.

"We can do it right here," she whispered against his lips.

That was a scandalous suggestion, but his kink didn't include exhibitionism. "Tempting, but no." He nibbled lightly on her lower lip. "Our first time is going to be the whole nine yards and not a quickie against the wall."

She leaned away to look into his eyes. "Why are you being so nice to me?"

That was an odd question. "Because I care about you."

"Why? We've just met, and you know nothing about me. What if I'm a horrible person?"

"You are not." He gave her bottom a squeeze. "And I know a lot about you. Probably more than any human male you will ever meet will get to know, and that's even if you spend the rest of your life with him."

Marina closed her eyes. "That's true. But it's also true that there is a lot you don't know about me."

He pretended to frown. "Are you really horrible?"

"No. I don't think so."

"Then that's settled." He transferred her weight to one hand to free the other and cupped the back of her neck. "Let me take care of you, Marina." He dipped his head and nuzzled the curve of her throat, then pressed a kiss to her wildly beating pulse. "Don't be afraid of me. My only wish is to give you pleasure."

"I'm not afraid." She lifted her hands and cupped his face. "I'm excited." She kissed him, and as he parted his lips, she swept her tongue into his mouth, and he let her even though his fangs were starting to elongate.

He allowed her to explore his mouth for a few seconds and then took over the kiss. She melted against him, her lips soft and pliable, her tongue dueling gently with his. He then coaxed her to taste him again, enjoying the freedom of letting her explore.

"Marina!" someone called from the door to the dining room. "*Gde ty?*"

The lights in the corridor had been dimmed, and they were standing in an alcove that wasn't visible from the door, so there was no chance that the human looking for Marina could see them.

She looked dazed when she drew back. Her lips swollen from his attention, she groaned quietly. "*Ya budu tam cherez minutu,*" she called out. Resting her forehead on his, she let out a breath. "I have to go."

He kissed her eyelids, planted one last soft kiss on her lips, and then, reluctantly, let her slide down his body. "Take this." He put a keycard in her hand. "I'm in cabin 305. Let yourself in."

She looked at the card and then lifted her eyes to him. "You trust me with this?"

He smiled. "I'm trusting you with my body and soul. The key is meaningless."

She gave him a crooked smile. "What if I'm an assassin, and I'll sneak up on you when you're asleep?"

"I'll risk it." He pulled her against his body and kissed her one last time before letting her go.

"Thank you." Marina lifted on her toes, planted a quick kiss on his cheek, and scurried away.

A stupid smile stretching his face, Peter stood in the shaded nook for a long moment before commanding his feet to move. He excused it by not wanting to compromise Marina, but the kitchen staff probably knew what she was doing and with whom. Maybe that's why that woman had called her back in? To give her a talking-to for fraternizing with the employers?

Would they make her change her mind about coming to his cabin later tonight?

The thought was too upsetting to be just about losing a night of pleasure with an attractive female. He liked being with Marina even though they hadn't spent more than a few minutes together.

What was it about her that made her special?

The answer to that seemed simple. Other than Kagra, she was the only female to share his bed, knowing who he was. He didn't need to pretend to be human, he didn't need to hide his fangs and glowing eyes, and after she passed out from the euphoric rush of his venom, he wouldn't need to thrall her to forget anything. He also didn't need to leave the bed and could wake up next to her and maybe even go for another round.

But it was more than that.

When she'd told him why she'd dyed her hair blue and put a ring in her brow, it had resonated with him. He had been at the mercy of another only once, and it hadn't been for long, but he had never forgotten how it had felt to be helpless.

Maybe he, too, should dye his hair some crazy color. Purple would look good on him. Or maybe bright red?

Regrettably, piercings were out of the question for immortals except for the fake ones that only looked like piercings and were held by a magnet. But those were for kids and posers, and he was neither.

30

MARINA

Excitement thrumming in her chest, Marina removed her apron and added it to the laundry cart with all the linen collected from the dining room.

Mila eyed her with a knowing look as she dropped her own apron into the cart. "Are you going to indulge that immortal tonight?"

It was nobody's business who she spent the night with, but it irked Marina that Mila thought she was doing so under duress the way it had been in the Kra-ell compound.

"I'm going to indulge myself." She waggled her brows suggestively. "Have you seen the size of his shoulders?"

Not to mention that face, that mischievous look in those dark eyes, and the goatee that made him look devilishly handsome and a little dangerous. Peter was sex on a stick, and he also seemed like a nice guy.

Was he too good to be true?

Yeah, probably.

He was an immortal, and she knew nothing about their sexual practices. The rumor was that they were like human males, only better, but she didn't know what the rumor was based on. So far, none of the humans had admitted to having been with one of them. Well, other than Sofia, but she was part Kra-ell, and she had moved with her boyfriend to the village. Still, she might have been the source of those rumors.

As far as Marina knew, Sofia had never shared a Kra-ell's bed, so even if she was the one who had supplied those flattering rumors about the immortals' sexual prowess, she could only compare her lover to a human man and not the Kra-ell.

Losing her virginity to a Kra-ell had trained Marina to enjoy the sharper edge of sexual pleasure, so even if Peter was more like the Kra-ell males than humans, but not too much so, she would probably like being with him more than she'd enjoyed being with Nicolai.

That would be more than welcome. Having an amazing new lover was the best way to get rid of the specter of the old one.

A throaty laughter shook Mila's ample bosom. "I have to admit that these immortals are much nicer to look at than the Kra-ell." She sighed, and the smile slid off her face. "Be careful, Marina. You might think that you are just having fun tonight, but once the line is crossed, there is no going back. There are many single males on this cruise, and they are a lustful bunch. Others might get the idea that we are free for the taking, and things could get ugly. I don't want us to go back to the way it was with the Kra-ell."

"These immortals are nothing like the Kra-ell. They treat us with respect, and they don't expect us to serve them unless they pay us proper wages for our work."

"I'm talking sexually, Marina."

"They don't expect us to share their beds unless it's our choice, and they are also not as rough."

"And you know that how?"

"I kissed Peter, and he was very gentle with me." Too gentle. She hoped he would loosen up tonight.

Mila pursed her lips. "One kiss is not enough to judge."

"I'll tell you tomorrow how it was." Marina patted Mila's fleshy forearm. "If my experience is good, perhaps you can snag yourself an immortal lover as well."

Mila laughed again. "I'm too old for these immortals to look at with desire in their eyes. Those days are behind me. But even if they are wonderful lovers, don't fool yourself, expecting more than a night or two of pleasure with this Peter or any of the others. If you are smart, you will forget about these immortals and choose a nice boy to marry and have children with."

"I've tried that, but as you know, it didn't work." She gave Mila one last smile. "I'll see you tomorrow at lunch."

Thankfully, she wasn't on the breakfast roster, so she could afford a sleepless night.

It was nearly four in the morning, and Peter had been waiting for over two hours for her, but she didn't intend to head straight to his cabin as he'd suggested.

Her hair and her clothing smelled of cooking and cleaning materials, and even though he had promised her a bath, she didn't want to show up smelling and disheveled for their first time together, or what might be their only time if she disappointed Peter.

Marina really liked him and would have spent the night with him even if she didn't have an ulterior motive, but her plan was to have him like her enough to invite her to live with him.

It was an ambitious plan, and it might not work, but she desperately needed a change, and the village was her only option.

Nicolai was done with his studies and had settled into life at Safe Haven, making her life miserable every time he'd shown up in the staff dining hall with the fiancée that he had brought with him from the university. It wasn't that she still loved him, but he'd hurt her, and seeing him with another woman while she was lonely was like throwing salt in an open wound.

Marina opened the door to her small cabin as quietly as she could, careful not to wake up Alina, who had the morning shift, and tiptoed to the tiny bathroom.

There wasn't time to properly condition her hair and style it, and she knew it would be a frizzy mess the next morning, but she didn't want to make Peter wait any longer than necessary. Gathering it into a tight bun, she secured it with a couple of hairpins and examined her pale face in the mirror.

She was still attractive despite the age showing on her face, but she was a little washed out, and makeup was a necessity even though she was going to bed.

Some lip gloss, a blue liquid eyeliner, and a few strokes with a brown eyebrow pencil took at least five years off her face. A pair of low-cut leggings and a flirty blouse with short puff sleeves that left her midriff exposed made her confident enough to face the immortal, who was physically perfect in every way.

31

PETER

It was after four in the morning when Peter heard the front door to the cabin open.

Jay was already asleep when he entered the cabin earlier, and the door to his bedroom was closed, so he hadn't been able to warn him that he was expecting a visitor.

What if the door opening woke Jay up, and he thought that Marina was an intruder?

What if she couldn't see his open door and opted to go to Jay's bedroom?

The drapes were drawn closed, so not even moonlight could filter through, and the light he had left in his bathroom was enough for him to see clearly, but not for Marina.

Risking scaring her, Peter jumped out of bed and leaped into the living room. "Over here," he whispered.

Her hand flew to her chest. "You scared me," she whispered back. "It's so dark in here. I can't see anything."

As she took a step toward him, he closed the rest of the distance between them and lifted her into his arms. "I see perfectly well in the dark."

Marina smelled freshly showered so he could skip the bath he had promised her. There was always the next time and the time after that. With her, he didn't need to limit himself to just one night, and he didn't plan to.

Her fingers splayed over his bare chest for a brief moment, and she sucked in a breath. "I imagined how you looked without clothes, but the reality of you is so much better."

He never wore clothes to bed, and the only reason he had pants on was because he didn't want to jump her as soon as she came in.

"I'm glad you like what you can't see." He cupped her bottom.

"I see with my hands." She wrapped her legs around his torso and lifted her arms to his neck. "I want you," she whispered.

He could hear her heart racing and her breath hitching, and he hoped it was desire and not fear. Her scent indicated the former, but women often confused the two, which wasn't necessarily a bad thing, and a little fear could enhance their pleasure, but this wasn't a normal situation.

Marina knew that he wasn't human, and she'd had a bad experience with powerful aliens. He didn't want her to think that he was like them or that she would have to do anything she wasn't a hundred percent into.

"I want you, too," he murmured into her hair. "I ache for you. But I want you to know that with one word from you, everything stops. No matter how desperate I am for you, I'm never too far gone to stop. You have nothing to fear from me."

"I don't fear you." She leaned away and frowned. "Your eyes are glowing."

"That's what happens when immortals get excited."

A smile bloomed on her face. "I'm glad that I excite you." She brushed her lips across his and threaded her fingers in his hair.

He took it as a silent invitation, and as his tongue parted her lips, capturing her tongue, she moaned softly against his mouth.

Still kissing her, he carried her to his bedroom and held her up with one hand under her soft bottom so he could gently close the door behind them with the other.

If Jay hadn't woken up while they were in the living room, he didn't want him to be woken by the sound of the door slamming.

"I planned on bathing you and pampering you with a foot massage, but since you've showered already, I'll give you a rain check for the next time." He laid her gently on the bed.

Marina lifted on her forearms and looked at him. "You assume that there will be a next time."

He smirked. "I don't assume. I know." He crawled over her and straddled her legs. "You'll want more of what I will give you tonight."

"So confident," she murmured as he tugged her leggings down. "I need you to promise me something, though."

He paused. "What is it?"

"I want to remember everything precisely as it happened. Promise that you won't thrall me to remember delights that didn't happen."

"You offend me, Marina." He put his hand over his chest. "Do you think I would resort to cheap tricks like that?"

"I don't, but I want to hear you promise that."

"I vow to the Fates that I will not alter your memory of this night or any others that follow. But if the boss decides to erase the memories of this cruise from the minds of all the humans on board, there isn't much I can do about it."

She nodded. "That's good enough for me."

32

MARINA

As Peter started to slowly undress Marina, her insecurities flared. Her breasts were too small, her hips were too big, and she had cellulite. But he looked at her with so much hunger in his eyes that the pressure in her chest eased.

"Beautiful," he murmured as he lowered himself on top of her and kissed her.

She wanted to argue and tell him that he shouldn't lie to her, that she knew she was pretty but far from spectacular, but he didn't let go of her mouth, kissing her with so much passion that all she could do was moan and undulate her hips under him.

He still had his pants on, but they were made from thin nylon, and he wasn't wearing underwear, so she could feel the thick, hard bulge of his erection almost as if he was naked, and if she lifted her hips and moved them just right, she could get the friction she needed.

When he finally let her come up for air, she was too dazed to remember that she'd wanted to argue with his appraisal of her, and then he was sliding down her body, and she didn't need a working brain to know what his intentions were.

No one had pleasured her that way in ages, and Marina was surprised that she was allowing a stranger to perform such an intimate act.

"Beautiful," he murmured again as he spread her thighs to make room for his broad shoulders.

Was that the only word he could think of when he was with her? Or was it something he said to all the women he took to his bed?

Jealousy flared in her chest, but as his finger slid into her wet entrance and then another, filling her deliciously, she forgot what made her feel jealous and surrendered to the pleasure.

Moaning, she rocked her hips, chasing his pumping fingers and needing more.

He blew a breath over her moist petals, and then his mouth was on her, his tongue gently brushing against her clitoris. He was shockingly good at this, building up her pleasure gradually instead of trying to rush her. It was as if he was in her head, knowing exactly how to pleasure her. When she neared the peak, he closed his lips around her clit, sucking it in while his fingers kept pumping, but even though she was teetering on the edge, she couldn't tumble over it.

Was she so out of practice that she couldn't orgasm unless it were her own fingers working the magic?

"Peter," she breathed.

He didn't answer, probably because his lips and tongue were busy, but he lifted a hand to her breast and toyed with her nipple, alternating light pinching with gentle tugging.

The extra stimulation was amazing, and yet she couldn't dive over the edge. He was being too gentle, and she didn't know how to tell him what she needed.

"Please," she murmured instead.

"Please, what?" he growled.

"I need to come, and I can't." It was as close as she could come to admitting her need.

He lifted his head and looked at her with understanding in his glowing eyes. "Close your eyes," he ordered. "And don't move an inch."

A new surge of moisture gathered between her thighs as she obeyed his command.

She heard him open a drawer and then some rustling as he rummaged through it.

What was he looking for?

His hand pushed under her head, and a moment later, she felt a piece of cloth wrapping around her head.

A blindfold.

Was he reading her mind? She'd only made him promise not to change her memories of their time together. She hadn't said anything about him staying out of her head.

"Are you reading my thoughts?" she asked.

"I don't need to. You are an open book to me, Marina."

No one had ever told her that, but maybe this immortal saw her better than most.

When he gripped her wrists and pulled her arms over her head, she suspected that Peter hadn't told her the truth about not peeking into her mind.

The blindfold must have triggered memories of the games she'd played with Nicolai, but it must have been subconscious because she hadn't been aware of thinking about him.

The sad truth was that as much as Marina tried to forget about Nicolai, he was never far from her thoughts. He'd hurt her, eroded her confidence, and she'd spent months obsessing about all the things she might have done better to keep him from leaving her.

Pathetic.

Hopefully, Peter wasn't reading those loser thoughts. She would be mortified if he did.

He didn't say a thing, though, and then she felt another piece of fabric wrapping around her wrists. It wasn't tight, and she could get free if she really wanted to, but it was a reminder to keep her hands where he wanted them, just the way she liked it.

"I know you are reading my mind," she said.

"I told you I'm not." He lifted her legs and delivered a stinging slap to her bottom. "Don't ever doubt my word."

Great Mother, he was perfect.

"I won't make that mistake again." She couldn't help the smile that spread over her face as she planned to do it again as soon as another opportunity presented itself.

"You liked that, didn't you?"

"You know I did."

"Then you are going to like this." His mouth descended on her nipple, sucking and lightly pinching.

Too lightly.

Hadn't he figured out already what she liked?

Suddenly she felt something cold and metallic rub against the wet, turgid peak, and knowing what it was, she sucked in a breath.

As the clamp closed over the sensitive flesh, it stung, and she sucked in another breath, waiting for Peter to do the same to her other nipple.

From experience, she knew that both needed to be clamped for the euphoric rush to wash over her.

As Peter sucked and nipped her other nipple, Marina bit down on her lower lip, stifling the whimpering that threatened to derail this incredible experience. If Peter thought that she was in distress, he would stop, and that was the last thing she wanted.

She just needed that other clamp to even out the torment.

When it finally happened, she could no longer hold the whimper in, and she arched her back, silently begging him to continue what he had started.

"Tell me what you need, beautiful," he murmured against her nipple.

"I need to come," she said shamelessly.

At this point, she was beyond shame.

Peter had already discovered all of her dirty little secrets. If he chose to humiliate her with them, it was too late to do anything about it.

His mouth lowered to where she needed it, and as his tongue flicked against her clit, she detonated, screaming out her climax at the top of her lungs.

33

PETER

The lady was a screamer, which Peter normally loved in a woman. There was no higher compliment for a male than his lady enjoying an explosive orgasm, especially since his venom had nothing to do with it.

Still, it was a little problematic when he was sharing a cabin with another guy. He was sure that Jay had heard Marina scream despite the excellent soundproofing, but since he hadn't barged in, he must have figured out that it was passion and not pain or fear that had produced that sound.

What a sheer stroke of luck it was bringing the cuffs and the little clamps on the cruise.

He'd packed his modest sexual toys arsenal on the remote chance that he would find a suitable companion on one of the shore excursions, but until now, the opportunity hadn't presented itself.

It was as if the Fates had sent Marina to him, knowing that he would be just what the female had been looking for. After all, sex toys were not about the one wielding them. They were about the one on the receiving end, and he loved being the fulfiller of sexual fantasies and the deliverer of memorable sexual experiences that he didn't need to erase or change because they had to do with his fangs or venom.

Kagra had been the only female whose mind hadn't been blown by his masterful ministrations, and it had been a blow to his ego. Marina was the most wonderful antidote to that insult, and he was determined to show his gratitude the best way he could.

Lifting his eyes, Peter smiled at the blissed-out expression on her face. The blindfold, the cuffs, the clamps, she loved all of that, but he needed to see her eyes when he entered her, so the blindfold had to go.

When he removed the scarf he had tied around her eyes, Marina blinked up at him, her gaze unfocused as if she didn't recognize him, but it was all good. She was still riding the high of her orgasm.

"Beautiful," he murmured for the third time tonight.

She blinked again, and then a smile lifted the corner of her lips. "Is that all you can say to me?"

"The word beautiful encapsulates many meanings. Kind of like the word fuck, which is what's next on the menu."

She licked her lips. "Yum. My favorite."

"Is it, now?" He got rid of his pants and got between her legs.

"Are you hungry for this?" He slid his shaft over her slicked folds.

With his other hand, he removed the fabric cuffs holding her wrists.

He expected her to reach for the clamps, but as her arms remained over her head, he removed one, immediately closing his lips over the swollen nub to ease the sting of the blood rushing back in. When he repeated the process with the other, she sighed with relief.

He gave her a moment to catch her breath before pushing the tip of his shaft inside of her. Refraining from surging all the way in was a struggle.

She was tight, thankfully not like a virgin, but more like a woman who hadn't been sexually active in a while, and he wanted to go slowly and let her adjust to him.

Pulling out a fraction, he pushed back, and she lifted up, impaling more of her sheath on his length.

"Patience, beautiful," he said against her ear. "I don't want to rush it."

"Please do," she groaned. "I want you."

He growled and slid a little more of his length inside of her, then forced himself to remain still.

"Oh, Mother of All Life." Marina spread her legs wider to accommodate more of him.

As he rocked his hips, she lowered her arms and cupped her sensitive breasts for a moment before lifting her thumbs to stroke her swollen nipples.

Damn, that was so sexy.

Everything about Marina was so sensual, and if he didn't guard his heart, he could easily fall for her.

Kagra's words once again reverberated in his head. *You are a romantic. You are in love with the notion of love.*

Angry at the memory, he snarled and pushed into Marina until he was buried in her to the hilt, then realizing what he had done, he stilled, letting her adjust to his invasion.

When she started undulating under him, urging him to start moving, he obliged her, and soon he was pounding into her with all the pent-up need that he had been struggling to hold back.

"I...I...." She threw her head back and screamed even louder than before, her body shaking from the force of her orgasm.

Spreading her even wider, Peter pounded into her hard and fast. When he was about to explode, he gripped the top of her head and tilted it to the side.

In a moment of clarity, he saw her eyes widen in fear, but she didn't fight him or say anything, so he took it as consent and licked the spot before sinking his fangs into the smooth column of her neck.

She screamed, but he wasn't sure whether it was in pain or pleasure or a mixture of both. But then her sheath tightened around his shaft, and as she climaxed again, he exploded inside of her, coming so hard and so long that once he was depleted, he felt like he had transferred his life force to her.

It took Peter long moments to regain enough energy to pull out of Marina and then a few moments longer to go grab some washcloths to clean her and the mess their combined issue had made.

She was out, soaring on the blissful clouds of euphoria, and it would probably take her several hours to come down from the venom high, but when she did, he would be there, holding her in his arms, and she would remember every last bit of the immense pleasure they had shared.

It occurred to Peter that Marina hadn't mentioned protection, and neither had he. Hopefully she was on the pill, but if not, it wasn't a big deal.

He couldn't get her pregnant anyway.

34

MIA

Mia drove outside the dining hall and parked her wheelchair in a secluded corner to call Margo. When there was no answer, she waited for Margo's voicemail to kick in and left a message: "Hi, Margo. It's Mia. I guess you fell asleep after all. Call me as soon as you can. I have good news for you and also some instructions, so it's important that you call me."

She ended the recording and put her phone back in her purse.

It was late, so it wasn't surprising that Margo was asleep, and yet worry niggled at her.

Margo was a light sleeper, and the ringing should have woken her up. Perhaps she'd had too much to drink and was passed out?

It was possible.

Perhaps she should call Lynda and ask her to check in on Margo. Except, she really didn't want to do that, especially if Lynda was asleep. The woman was cantankerous when she was in a good mood, and if Mia woke her up, she would definitely not be in a good mood.

But someone needed to check on Margo, and she was the only one there.

Pulling out her phone again, Mia searched her contacts for Lynda's number and placed the call.

The phone kept ringing for a long time, and Mia was about to hang up and call again when it was finally answered. Given how loud the music playing in the background was, Lynda wasn't asleep, and Mia was surprised that she'd even heard the ringing.

"Mia?" Lynda yelled in her ear. "Did something happen? Why are you calling me in the middle of the night?" She sounded a little slurred, but she was still coherent, so she wasn't overly drunk.

Perhaps Margo was with her, and that would explain why she hadn't answered her phone.

"Is Margo with you?"

"No, she decided to stay in the hotel and read. Did you try to call her?"

"I did, and she's not answering. It's not like her. Did any of your friends stay in the hotel who can check up on her?"

"No. We are all here, but as soon as we get back, I'll go to her room and see what's going on. She's probably sleeping with the earplugs in or forgot to charge her phone." Lynda snorted. "Maybe the couple next door is making noises. Get it? Get it? Loud, sexy noises that made Margo jealous because she hasn't gotten any in ages." She snorted again.

Yeah, Lynda was definitely drunk. She never would have talked like that sober. Did Rob know that his fiancée was getting plastered in Cabo?

Whatever. It wasn't Mia's problem.

"Call me as soon as you check on her, okay? Don't forget."

"I won't. I promised Rob that I would keep an eye on his sister. Not that the prude needs a keeper. What could happen to her while she's reading next to the pool in the hotel? I would say sunburn, but she puts on a shitload of sunscreen and keeps reapplying it, so she will be going home just as pale as she left. No one is going to believe that she was in Cabo."

Mia rolled her eyes. "When are you heading back to the hotel?"

"I don't know. Maybe in an hour. This place is open until morning. Isn't that great? This is the most fun I've had in ages."

"Call me no matter what time it is, and if I don't hear from you in the next couple of hours, I'm going to call you."

"Fine. Good night, Mia." Lynda ended the call.

Mia tried Margo's number again, but the call went straight to voicemail. When the same happened the third and fourth time she called, a surge of panic constricted Mia's throat.

Something was wrong.

Driving back into the dining room, she didn't go to her table but straight to Kian's.

When Toven saw the direction she was going, he rose to his feet and headed toward Kian's table as well.

He intercepted her just as she reached her destination. "What happened?"

"Margo is not answering her phone." Mia shifted her gaze to Kian. "I called her four times and each time, the call went to voicemail, and it worried me. Margo was awaiting this call, and even if she fell asleep, she is not a heavy sleeper, and she would have heard the ringing. I called Lynda, her brother's fiancée, but she's at a club with the rest of her girlfriends and won't be back at the hotel for at least another hour, maybe longer. I don't know what to do."

"That's no reason to panic," Kian said. "Maybe Margo has gone to the Airbnb, and there is bad reception there?"

"It's only a fifteen-minute walk from the hotel. There is no reason for it to have worse reception than the resort."

"Can you see if she checked into the Airbnb?" Syssi asked.

"I can call the owner tomorrow morning, but I have a bad feeling that it's going to be too late." Mia lifted a shaking hand to her chest. "Margo suspected that Jasmine's boyfriend was a trafficker, and he wanted to sell her. What if Margo got taken along with Jasmine?"

Toven put a hand on her shoulder. "Let's wait for Lynda to return and check on Margo before we jump to conclusions. She might find Margo asleep in her room, and all this speculation was for nothing."

"I wish." Mia sighed. "I should call Lynda again and ask her to cut her outing short. I need to tell her what Margo told me about Jasmine and her scumbag boyfriend. Maybe that will get her worried enough to get back to the hotel."

Mia wasn't sure it would because Lynda was as selfish as they came, but she had promised Rob to watch over his sister, so there was that. At the very least, it was worth a try.

35

KIAN

Less than an hour later, Mia's phone rang.

"Oh, God." She lifted her shaking hand to her lips. "Did you check the pool bar? Maybe she's there?"

Kian tried to listen to what was being said on the other side, but the music was playing, and it was too loud to hear. Still, the expressions on Mia's face were enough for him to guess what she was being told.

Mia put the phone on the table with a shaking hand. "Margo is not in her room, and she's not in any of the resort's public places either. Lynda called hotel security, and they are searching for her." She trained a pair of teary eyes on Kian. "What do we do now?"

Amanda leaned over the table. "Is there a chance she found a guy to hook up with for the night?"

Mia shook her head. "Margo does not do hookups. She barely even dates. Besides, she was on a mission to save her new friend. She wouldn't have abandoned her to be with some guy. There is no way in hell she would do that."

"We need to send a search party," Toven said. "Perhaps Turner knows a private operator that works in the area. Whatever the costs, I'll cover them."

Kian considered his options.

If Margo was right, and her new friend's boyfriend was indeed a trafficker, and she had somehow got caught in the snare, they couldn't just abandon her to her fate. Mia would never forgive him, and the same went for Toven and Frankie.

The bottom line was that he had no choice but to get involved, which was a real pain in the rear, given that Doomers were lurking in the hotel, waiting for Guardians to show up.

Perhaps it hadn't been the boyfriend but Doomers that had taken Margo?

It was possible that she had talked about joining a cruise, and they had found out about it after interrogating some of the staff and guests.

Talk about a shit storm. That would also reveal that they were arriving by ship. Would the Doomers make the connection? There must be other guests in the hotel who were joining friends on a trip.

Right. That was just wishful thinking.

Kian's philosophy was to always prepare for the worst rather than hope for the best.

"I guess I'm not going to sleep tonight." He leveled his gaze at Toven. "And neither are you. We need to have another emergency meeting with Turner and Onegus and devise a strategy. Given that we suspect the hotel is crawling with Doomers, it's not as simple as sending a search party."

Toven nodded. "Of course. Whatever you need from me is yours."

"Do you need me to attend?" Dalhu asked. "I'll be happy to offer my assistance in any way I can."

The guy sounded excited about getting some action again. Evidently, disposing of the Doomers in Acapulco had just whetted his appetite for more.

"You are welcome to join." Kian pushed to his feet and offered Syssi a hand up. "So are you, but you can also stay and enjoy the rest of the festivities."

Syssi never joined the strategic meetings unless she had something to add, either an insight or a vision, but he needed to offer her the option to make it clear that he valued her opinions even though she was not a strategist.

"I'll stay," she said. "I guess you will be commandeering the suite again."

Kian nodded. "I'm sorry."

"You can use ours," Toven offered. "I'm part of the meeting, and Mia won't be able to sleep anyway."

"Thank you. I appreciate it." Kian was grateful for the offer so Syssi and Allegra could sleep undisturbed.

He leaned and kissed Syssi's cheek. "Are you going to be okay here by yourself?"

"Of course." She gave him a bright smile. "I'll go dancing with Amanda." She turned to his sister. "Are you game?"

"Am I ever?" Amanda rose to her feet. "Let's get Sari and Alena to join."

As the two left to get his other sisters, Kian's gaze followed them. He loved that they loved Syssi and thought of her like another sister.

After the ceremony, Okidu and Onidu had taken the little ones to his mother's cabin, and his mother was watching Allegra, Evie, and Darius with their help. That meant that the parents could enjoy the party for as long as they wanted to without having to worry about the kids, but regrettably, the party was over for him.

Oh, well. There was nothing new about that.

With a sigh, he headed toward Onegus's table with Toven and Dalhu at his side.

"What's going on?" The chief rose to his feet.

Kian explained as the four of them continued to Kalugal's table and got him and Lokan to join them. Then the six of them continued to Turner's table.

"Trouble?" he asked.

"Yes." Kian put a hand on his shoulder. "We need your help." He turned to Bridget. "Perhaps you want to join us as well. It's possibly a case of trafficking. Mia and Frankie's friend Margo is missing, and we suspect she was taken by a trafficker."

"Is there anything I can contribute?" the doctor asked.

"I'm not sure. It's up to you if you want to join the meeting."

The doctor shook her head. "I'd rather stay. If you need me for anything, call me. My watch will vibrate." She lifted her hand to show her smartwatch. "Nifty trick. Now I don't have to worry that I will not hear the ringing when it's noisy."

Kian had hoped that would be her answer. He hated disturbing Brundar's celebration and taking more guests out than was necessary. "Good. Enjoy the party. If we have any questions, Turner or I will call you."

Turner leaned over and kissed her cheek before getting up. "I just need to stop by my suite to get my laptop and notepad."

"We are using Mia and Toven's suite for the meeting tonight," Kian said. "You can meet us there after you get your stuff."

"Good deal." Turner buttoned his tux. "I will also gladly change clothes. Especially if we are going to pull an all-nighter."

"That's a good idea." Kian turned to the small group he had assembled. "We should all get changed. Let's meet in Toven's suite in ten minutes."

As the others nodded their agreement, Kian saw Anandur bee-lining for him.

"What's going on, boss?" he asked.

"Mia's friend is missing. I called an emergency meeting to discuss our options."

"I'm coming."

Kian put a hand on his bicep. "No, you are not. You are staying right here and celebrating your brother's wedding. We are not heading out to war, and I don't need a bodyguard on the ship. Stay with your wife and enjoy the party till it ends."

Anandur didn't look happy, but he knew that Kian was right. "You are the boss." He let out a breath. "Call me if you need me."

36

NEGAL

Negal twirled Gertrude around the dance floor, mimicking the moves of the immortals around him. The weddings were a wonderful opportunity to learn modern human dances and secure partners for the night, just not this time.

It wasn't Gertrude's fault that a pair of fierce eyes kept floating into his mind's eye, regarding him accusatorially when he held her in his arms or when she plastered herself to him during slow dances.

What the hell was wrong with him?

He had briefly glanced at Frankie's friend's picture, and he hadn't even found her all that attractive. She was pretty in a very human way, but not the kind of female poems would be written about. Those eyes, though, had imprinted themselves on his soul, and not because they were remarkably beautiful or uniquely colored. It was the spirit he had seen in them that haunted him, making him feel guilty for holding another woman in his arms.

Was it a psychosomatic response to Frankie's assertion that he was meant to be with her friend?

Had Frankie's conviction that she and her two friends were all destined to mate gods rubbed off on him?

Probably.

The question was what he was going to do about it. He couldn't disappoint Gertrude after promising her a night of passion, and he wouldn't. Somehow, he would power through those annoying fierce eyes and pleasure the immortal like she deserved.

"Something is going on," Gertrude said. "Kian is collecting members of his war council." She pointed with her chin at Turner's table, where Kian, Onegus, Kalugal, Toven, Dalhu, and Kalugal's brother were standing next to the strategist. Toven's mate, Frankie's wheelchair-bound friend, was with them, which made him suspect that it had something to do with the fierce-eyed blond haunting his psyche.

Oh, damn. He knew perfectly well what her name was, so he should stop referring to Margo as Mia or Frankie's friend and pretending that she was nothing to him.

Gertrude's eyes clouded with worry. "Are we being pursued by Doomers?"

"I don't think so. The ship slowed down. It didn't speed up." He watched as the group headed toward the exit. "But perhaps I should find out what's going on. They wouldn't be leaving Brundar's wedding and their mates behind just to smoke cigars. They could have done it right here out on the terrace."

Gertrude nodded. "Mia wouldn't have gone with them if they were going to smoke. She's regrowing her legs, and Bridget told her not to tax her body's healing ability by unnecessarily abusing it. Alcohol and tobacco are unhealthy, and even an immortal's body has to work at counteracting their influence. Please find out what's going on and let me know. My mind is racing with possibilities, and none of them are good."

"Same here. Good things don't necessitate a middle-of-the-night emergency meeting." Negal leaned to kiss Gertrude's cheek. "I'll be back."

He left the dance floor and rushed after the group, catching up to them just as they were entering the elevator. He squeezed inside before the doors closed.

"Hello, gentlemen." He smiled. "Is there an emergency I should be aware of?"

Kian nodded. "Mia's friend is missing. She could have been taken by the Doomers or by an unrelated player."

Negal felt his fangs elongate. "Did she meet someone at the hotel?"

"She met a woman named Jasmine, and the player was the woman's boyfriend. Margo suspected that the guy wanted to traffick Jasmine, and she was trying to help her escape. She might have been caught up in a game she shouldn't have butted her nose into."

Negal didn't know anything about Margo except for the fierceness he had seen in her eyes, but that was enough for him to believe that she would have gotten involved when she suspected that someone was in trouble.

As the door opened on Kian's deck, he followed the regent out. "Do you mind if I join the meeting?"

Kian frowned. "I don't mind, but why would you want to? You should get back to the party and enjoy yourself."

"I feel responsible for Margo." Negal blurted the first thing that came to his mind. "If she needs rescuing, I should be part of the rescue team."

Kian's frown deepened. "You don't even know her."

"I'm aware of that, but Frankie and Mia believe that their friend is destined to mate a god, and I'm the last one available. If they are right, Margo might be my fated mate."

Thankfully, Mia and Toven had already gone to their suite, so Mia wasn't there to dispute his claim.

It was Frankie's idea, not Mia's, to introduce him to Margo, and Negal was quite certain that Margo wasn't his fated mate, but he needed to rescue her, nonetheless. He had to meet her face to face and stop those eyes from haunting him. There was no way the effect could be as profound in person.

Kian regarded him for a long moment before nodding. "We might need your particular talents for this mission. We are meeting in Toven's suite in a few minutes. I'm going to change out of the tux, and I suggest you do the same. It's going to be a long night, and none of us is going to get any sleep any time soon."

"Thank you. I'll be there." Negal darted back toward the elevators.

Should he go down and tell Gertrude that their plans for tonight were not going to happen? Could he just send her a text?

It was bad form to send a text to cancel their plans for tonight, but he was in a rush, and this was a real emergency.

Gertrude would understand.

As the elevator doors opened, he got inside, pressed the button for his level, and pulled out his phone to text the nurse.

37

KIAN

"Whiskey?" Toven asked.

"Definitely." Kian pulled out a chair at the round dining table in Toven and Mia's cabin.

The cabins were equipped with only five dining chairs, so Dalhu brought the missing ones from his and Amanda's cabin. There wasn't enough room around the dining table for the eight of them, but there wasn't much they could do about that.

Mia had chosen to stay by the couch to give them room, but she wasn't going to last long, even though she was worried about her friend. Her eyes were closing, and from time to time, her head was lolling forward.

"You should go to sleep, love." Toven walked over to her and crouched next to her. "Your body is working hard on re-growing your legs, and you know what happens when you deprive it of rest. The growth slows down."

She shook her head. "I need to stay awake. There isn't much I can contribute to the battle plans, but I know Margo. She is resourceful and brave, and if she can find a way to communicate where she is, she will. That's why it's important for me to stay by the phone. And if I fall asleep, you need to answer it for me right away."

Toven nodded. "I'll bring a pillow and a blanket from the bedroom so you can lie down on the couch. Will that work for you?"

"Yes. Thank you."

Casting a sidelong glance at Negal, Kian noted that the god looked pleased by Mia's praise of Margo.

Could he really be feeling a connection to the girl even though he had never met her?

Doubtful.

He'd seen Negal dancing with Gertrude, and the two seemed very cozy. He had no doubt that the god would be later invited to the nurse's bed.

"So, what's the deal?" Onegus asked.

"Let's wait for Toven to be done." Kian took a sip from the whiskey. "I don't want to have to say everything twice."

Once Mia was comfortable on the couch and Toven had sat down next to the table, Kian told everyone what Mia had told him and then glanced at her. "Am I missing anything?"

"No. You've got it all right. I just got a text from Lynda that the hotel security didn't do much to find Margo. Her suitcase and her satchel are still in her hotel room, and Lynda says that they are both packed like Margo was ready to leave, but her purse and her phone are not there. The hotel security people assume she's either partying in one of the clubs or shacking up with a guy, and they are not concerned. They told Lynda to inform the police after Margo had been missing for more than twenty-four hours. Lynda and her friends have early flights tomorrow, and she doesn't know what to do."

"Tell her to go home," Kian said. "There isn't much she can do. She's just going to be in the way, but don't tell her that. I don't want her to know that we are coming. I suspect that the Doomers might have found out who Margo is. She probably talked about joining a cruise ship, and even if she didn't, Lynda or her friends might have talked about it and been overheard."

Mia frowned. "So, you don't think it's the boyfriend?"

"It might be him, but it could also be the Doomers, and in my opinion, they are the more likely suspects. With all due respect to Margo's theory about the boyfriend, it's a little far-fetched."

"I don't think so," Mia insisted. "He took Jasmine's passport, her driver's license, and her credit cards. Why would he do that if he didn't want to do something nefarious to her?"

"Why did she allow it?" Dalhu asked. "She should have refused and called hotel security."

Mia cast him a sad smile. "It's not that simple for women who think that they are in a loving relationship. Her boyfriend gave her a logical excuse, and at that moment, she didn't think it through. Later, she might have thought he was overbearing and that maybe she shouldn't be with him, but she didn't feel an urgency to act immediately until Margo planted in her head the idea of him wanting to trade her."

"Mia is right." Kian let out a breath. "Ella had a similar experience. She met a guy who seemed like a loving boyfriend. He invested a lot of time in her, and she agreed to go with him to visit his family in New York, thinking she was just going for a weekend. She had no idea that she was walking into a trap. Still, that was a very unique situation. The oligarch who ordered her delivery saw her picture in an advertisement and got obsessed with her because she was the spitting image of the love of his life, who had died when he was still a young man. I doubt Jasmine's story is the same."

Toven leaned back in his chair and crossed his arms over his chest. "You know the saying about great minds thinking alike? It's true whether those great minds are good or evil. Perhaps someone ordered Jasmine's abduction."

"That's possible," Kian agreed. "But then why would they also take Margo?"

"So she wouldn't spill?" Kalugal offered. "Margo was a witness. I assume that she's a good-looking young lady, so the perpetrator might have thought to kill two birds with one stone. He eliminated the only witness to Jasmine's abduction and made more money by selling another woman. Win-win for him."

"I still think it's the Doomers," Kian said. "We know that they are in the hotel and that they know we are picking up a woman from there. It's logical to assume that they asked around and heard that there was a woman who talked about getting picked up by a cruise ship." He grimaced. "That means that they know we are arriving by ship, and figuring out which of the ships that left Acapulco earlier today is ours won't be too difficult."

"I don't think the Doomers took her," Dalhu said. "Margo is useless to them as a hostage because they don't know how to contact us. If they could, they would have already done so and stated their demands. The best thing for them to do is to leave her be, watch who she interacts with, wait until she either leaves or gets collected by someone, and then let her lead them to us. My bet is on the boyfriend, although following that logic, the Doomers should have intervened and freed her, so that's a hole in my theory."

"There is another possibility," Kian said. "The Doomers could have decided to do what their brethren in Acapulco did with Luis. Perhaps they wanted to set a trap for us and lure as many of us as possible into coming to search for Margo, expecting us to show up with a big search and rescue team."

38

NEGAL

"Does it matter who took Margo?" Negal asked. "In either case, none of your people can show up at the hotel. You will be immediately recognized by the Doomers. My teammates and I are best suited for this mission. We can enter the hotel shrouded in invisibility and search for Margo, going room to room."

What Negal was concerned about was what was being done to Margo in the meantime. If any of those maggots touched her inappropriately, he would tear the skin off their bodies one inch at a time.

Kian smiled indulgently. "No, you can't. Shrouding doesn't work on surveillance cameras, and I'm sure the first thing the Doomers did was to either take over the control room or hack into it. They will see you even if you shroud yourselves. That being said, you do have one advantage over us. You don't activate the built-in immortal alarm for some reason. You could go in disguise, and they won't know that you are not human."

That was true to some extent. He remembered meeting Magnus and the other immortals for the first time. He'd sensed that they weren't human, but they hadn't known what to think of him and Aru. Later, he had learned that their so-called built-in alarm hadn't been activated by the presence of gods. It only worked with other immortals.

Still, wearing a disguise seemed like such a primitive method. "Can't you do something about the surveillance? Your hacker can access it remotely and put it on a loop. By the time the Doomers figure out that they are watching the same thing over and over again, we will be done."

"That might be doable." Kian put his whiskey glass down. "But a disguise will be much easier to do and with less possible fuckups. You can shroud for only a limited time, and you will need to open doors to search rooms, which will not go unnoticed. I don't have a problem with the ghost stories that will start, but I'm sure the Doomers will figure out what's going on. On the other hand, if you disguise yourself as hotel personnel, let's say plumbers, no one will give you a second glance."

Toven chuckled. "Three extremely good-looking guys with plungers will not go unnoticed. I'm sure they will garner a lot of attention."

"Eva will have to work her magic on them," Kian said. "She can cover their faces with fake beards and pockmarks and whatnot."

"Guys," Mia said from the couch. "You are missing the most important part. If Jasmine's boyfriend took Margo, by the time we get there and Negal and his friends go to investigate, the scumbag could have gotten her and Jasmine very far away from the hotel, and there will be no clues left as to where he took them. Besides, you will need to question the staff and the guests if they saw anything, and how are you going to do that with the Doomers watching the hotel?"

"Good point." Kian sighed. "We need a diversion to draw them away."

Negal lifted a hand. "First, we need to determine that they don't have Margo. Otherwise, creating a diversion will be pointless."

"True." Kian drummed his fingers on the table. "So, you and Aru go in and search the rooms for Margo, pretending to be plumbers or service guys. I doubt Dagor will agree to leave Frankie's side while she's transitioning, so he's not going to come. Once we are sure that Margo is not in the hotel and that the Doomers don't have her, we create a diversion to draw them away. The question is, what kind of diversion?" He looked at Turner. "If you have any ideas, please feel free to share."

"A group of Guardians can enter the hotel and openly start asking questions. The Doomers will not attack with so many human witnesses. They will wait until the Guardians leave and try to ambush them somewhere less public. Except, we will turn the tables on them and ambush them instead."

"Won't they be expecting that?" Kalugal asked. "They know that we know that they are there, or at least they suspect that we know."

"Rank and file Doomers are not that sophisticated," Lokan said. "They will assume that we are the stupid ones who didn't figure out that they are waiting for us. If we wave the proverbial red flag in front of their eyes, they will attack. My concern is the Doomers watching the harbor. I think we should still go ahead with the plan of pretending to be a regular cruise with humans on board and have several groups leave the ship in disguise. Cabo is a tender port, which means that we go ashore using water taxis that can take only a few passengers at a time. That works in our favor. It would have been much more difficult to pull it off in a regular port where everyone disembarks the gangway right onto the dock."

Onegus nodded. "The Guardians who go to the hotel will need to disembark before we get to Cabo by using the lifeboats like we did in Acapulco, and Turner will have to arrange for vehicles once again. When they arrive with cars to the hotel, the Doomers will assume that they drove from Acapulco, which would have taken just as long by land as it will take us by sea, even with the big loop around the Sea of Cortez. Cars can travel much faster than ships."

"I like this plan." Kian reached for the whiskey bottle and refilled his glass. "The force will split into three groups, each arriving separately. First, Negal and Aru will arrive in disguise and search the hotel. If they determine that Margo is not there, a large group of Guardians will continue to the hotel to create the diversion, while the third group will wait on the town's outskirts." He looked at Turner. "What do you think?"

39

KIAN

Turner tapped his pen on his yellow pad. "I think that we are tired and not considering all the possible angles."

The guy was probably referring to everyone other than himself and was just being polite. Turner hadn't said much during the meeting, and he had probably devised a dozen different strategies by now.

Kian wracked his brain, trying to figure out what he and the others might have missed, but he was coming up empty.

"Do you want to guide us through your thought process?" he asked Turner.

"Of course. I'm not saying that I have the answers, only that we weren't methodical in our approach."

Right. The guy was trying to spare their feelings so they wouldn't look dumb when he revealed those different angles they had failed to consider.

Toven pushed to his feet. "I'll brew us coffee. We definitely need the boost."

Turner flipped to a new page on his yellow pad. "Let's analyze the situation methodically." He lifted his eyes to Kian. "To figure out who took Margo, we can have Roni hack into the hotel's surveillance servers and go over the recordings from where Mia last talked with Margo and until she called her and didn't get an answer. The second thing we need to do is trace Margo's phone. The perpetrators probably dumped it somewhere, but even that can give us a clue as to where she was taken to."

What Turner had said sounded so obvious and logical that Kian couldn't understand how he hadn't thought of it. Was he really that tired? Or maybe it was the whiskey?

He pushed the glass away. "We should get Roni in here."

Turner smiled. "I've already sent him a text message. He's on his way. He's just stopping by his cabin to change and grab his laptop."

Kian hadn't noticed Turner texting either, so he really must be tired. "Okay, what else?"

"We need to watch the footage and see if we can identify Doomers. They are pretty easy to spot, so if they are there, ambling around the resort and asking questions, we will know."

"That's true," Onegus said. "They look military but with the added fluidity of movement that only immortals and professional dancers have, and Doomers definitely don't look like dancers."

Lokan chuckled. "If you want to enrage a Doomer, tell him that he looks like a dancer."

Dalhu winced. "Or a painter, a poet, a musician, or any other artistic form of expression. Most of the cultures in that region of the world are incredibly homophobic, and Doomers are among the worst. They think that being artistic is feminine, and if any member of the Brotherhood is even suspected of homosexuality, they are executed, so no one dares to express their creativity even if they possess any." He sighed and ran his fingers through his hair. "I'm ashamed to admit that I was close-minded and ignorant in that regard as well."

"That's illuminating but irrelevant," Turner said. "Let's get back to analyzing what we are likely to face in Cabo. We dealt the Doomers a big blow in Acapulco. We eliminated an entire team of immortals and a large number of cartel thugs. By now, their superiors in the Brotherhood know that, and they also know we are coming to Cabo. They will have a much larger force waiting for us there." He looked at Lokan. "Am I right?"

Lokan nodded. "If they had several teams in the area, they will have called all of them to Cabo. They probably also recruited the help of the local cartel and all the officials they could bribe and extort, including the police, the military, the harbor control, etc."

"Great." Kian groaned. "I really don't want to engage with all that. I hope that Roni can find out what happened to Margo."

Turner regarded him with a sad smile. "We have to deal with them whether we want to or not. They will figure out which ship we are on sooner or later, even if we deploy the disguised teams. Look at it this way—they have no reason to believe that all the ship's passengers are immortal clan members.

They are more likely to assume that several immortals are vacationing among humans. So, seeing humans disembark at Cabo and do touristy things will not remove suspicion from the *Silver Swan*."

Turner was right. The Doomers would question people at the hotel or just thrall them to check their recent memories, and someone would remember talking to Margo, who had mentioned joining a cruise that got delayed several times. From there, it would be easy to find out which ship fit that profile, and it was game over. The Guardians might be able to eliminate the local forces that had arrived there, but then more would be waiting for them in Long Beach.

This called for a drastic change of plans, but he wasn't sure what he should do. Turn back to Acapulco? The Doomers wouldn't be expecting that. He could get everyone off the ship there and fly them to Los Angeles.

The *Silver Swan* would have to stop emitting signals, so it couldn't be easily tracked.

As the doorbell rang, Toven walked over and opened the door.

"So, what are we dealing with now?" Roni walked over to the crowded table and put his laptop down.

"I'll get you a chair," Toven offered.

Roni looked around with a sour expression on his face. "This looks like a command post in a playground sandbox. We need another table. Whose cabin is the closest?"

40

MARGO

Margo's head pounded, and she felt nauseous. She turned on her back and tried to open her eyes, but her eyelids felt as if they weighed five pounds each and refused to open.

Was she in her room?

Was it her head that was swaying, or was it the bed?

Wait, two men were talking in hushed voices on the other side of the room, but she couldn't understand what they were saying. Were they inside her room, or was she hearing voices from the outside?

She must have left the windows open.

Wait, she didn't have windows that opened in her hotel room, just balcony doors, and she never left them open so bugs wouldn't get in.

Trying to focus, Margo listened to the voices until she could discern the words. They were talking in Spanish, which she could understand to some extent, but she was far from fluent.

One of the voices belonged to Alberto or someone who sounded like him. The other one sounded much older and more authoritative, and the two were arguing.

"What did you want me to do with her, *señor*? I had to bring her. She's beautiful in her own way. She is no Jasmine, but then, not everyone is as discriminating as you are, *señor*. I'm sure many men will find her alluring."

Was she dreaming? If she was, this was a nightmare, and everything she had suspected about Alberto was true.

"The hair color is fake. Anyone can be a blond," the older voice said.

"It's not fake. It's real, which is rare and in high demand."

"How do you know that it's real?"

Margo wanted to know that, too. Had Alberto checked her pubic hair?

"It's obvious. She has no dark roots, and the shade is not one that can be achieved with artificial coloring. Just look at it. It looks like spun gold."

"She's too old," the one Alberto called *señor* said. "But she is passable. I can gift her to Carlos. He likes blonds."

Someone exhaled a relieved breath, and she heard a door open and close, but she was still afraid to open her eyes. Heck, she was afraid to breathe.

Listening intently, Margo heard breathing that didn't belong to her and wondered whether Alberto was still in the room. It wouldn't be *señor* because he had sounded impatient and pissed.

Long moments passed as she listened to every sound and registered every sensation. She was swaying, but she wasn't sure whether it was her bed or her head. Was she on a water mattress? It kept moving.

Finally, after what seemed forever, she cracked her eyelids open just a little and peered at the ceiling. When no one said anything and no one moved, she dared to turn her head slightly and look at the room.

The first thing Margo noticed was that there was another woman sleeping on a bed only a few feet away. She was lying on her side with her back facing Margo, but given the black hair spilling from behind her and the hourglass outline of her body, that was Jasmine.

Above her was an oddly shaped window, and Margo tried to figure out what it reminded her of, but her mind was fuzzy. It was dark outside, so it was still night, and she could see the stars and the moon, but they were also swaying.

It finally dawned on her where she was.

The stars and the moon weren't moving, but she was because she was on a boat, and the swaying she'd felt meant that it was moving.

Great. How the hell was she going to escape from a boat in the open sea? Did yachts have lifeboats that she could steal?

Groaning, she forced herself to sit up, then lowered her feet to the floor. She was still wearing the same clothes she had on yesterday, but someone had removed her shoes.

Thank goodness for small mercies. No one had removed her clothing, so she hadn't been violated while she was asleep.

Not asleep.

She'd been drugged.

That's why her head felt so heavy and why her eyelids were not fully cooperating with her brain's demands.

Trying to stand up was a no-go, and she resorted to dropping down to her knees and walking on all fours toward Jasmine's bed.

There couldn't have been more than six feet separating the beds, but she was so badly uncoordinated that it took her several tries until she made it across.

"Jasmine," she whispered while shaking her friend's shoulder. "Wake up, Jaz. We are in big trouble."

She got a groan in response, but that was it. Jasmine must have been even more out of it than she was, and there was no waking her up.

Margo was on her own.

Sitting on the floor by Jasmine's bed, she tried to reconstruct the events that had landed her in this crappy situation.

The second bottle of wine must have been laced with something. Was it the infamous date-rape drug?

Jaz had drunk more than she had, so maybe that's why she seemed more out of it. Margo remembered Alberto filling up his glass from the bottle and lifting it to his lips, but he must have only pretended to drink.

What the hell was she going to do?

Taking another look around the room, or rather cabin, she saw her purse on top of the dresser and almost cried with relief. Her phone was in there. If they weren't too far away from shore, maybe she could call for help.

Crawling to the dresser, she used the handles to hoist herself up and reached for the purse. She pulled it down, catching it before it could hit the floor, and cradled it to her chest as she caught her breath.

The little movement she'd made had exhausted her, and she was so nauseous that she almost threw up. Maybe it was the drugs that were still affecting her like that, or maybe it was the fear she was trying to shove into a corner of her mind so she could think instead of panic.

After resting for a moment, Margo opened her purse and reached inside. Her heart sank. The phone wasn't there.

Of course, it wasn't. That was the first thing they would have gotten rid of, probably tossing it overboard or even before that into a garbage bin.

With a sigh, she closed her eyes and leaned her head against the dresser. How the hell had Alberto managed to carry two unconscious women out of the hotel?

Someone must have helped him.

Margo imagined being stuffed into a laundry cart like she'd seen in the movies, one cart for her and another for Jasmine. A van had probably waited for them next to the service exit, and Alberto and his accomplice had loaded them inside.

Or perhaps it happened some other way. Maybe she and Jasmine had walked out on their own two feet, the drugs making them pliant and obedient like two automatons. She'd seen that in movies, too.

Tomorrow, Mia and Frankie would arrive on the Perfect Match cruise ship, and when they couldn't find her, they would call the police. But what good would that do?

She'd heard about the local police and how corrupt they were. But perhaps it would work to her advantage. Tom could bribe someone to actually make an effort to find her.

Mia would beg him to do that, and Tom didn't refuse Mia anything, so maybe there was hope she would be rescued before Carlos, the guy that *señor* wanted to gift her to, could put his hands on her.

41

NEGAL

Now that they had two tables pushed together, there was plenty of room for everyone, and Roni got to work while the rest of them drank coffee and tried to stay awake.

As Negal peeked at what the kid was doing, he saw that Roni was watching footage from several cameras at once and at ten times the speed. It was difficult for Negal to follow, and given that his senses were superior to the immortals', it was very impressive that the kid was able to take all of that in.

"I'm going to move Mia to the bedroom," Toven said quietly as he walked over to the couch.

She had fallen asleep and didn't wake up when Toven lifted her into his arms and carried her to the bedroom.

Negal was glad that she managed to fall asleep before Turner gave them his assessment. According to him, the situation was much worse than what the rest of them had considered, and he wasn't wrong.

They were all hoping that Roni would find a clue as to Margo's whereabouts, but that would only solve half of the problem. Even if they could retrieve her without engaging the Doomers, the entire ship was at risk, and Kian was thinking about aborting the rest of the cruise and flying everyone home, but not directly to Los Angeles.

He and Turner were discussing sending people to different airports around the country and having them fly to Los Angeles from there.

The question was what to do with the rescued women who had no passports.

"The remaining couples that were supposed to be married on the cruise will be disappointed," Onegus said. "I wish there was a way we could continue as planned, but even taking out all the Doomers in Cabo won't help. That will only make the Brotherhood more rabid about retaliation."

Kalugal smoothed his hand over his short beard. "There must be some way to turn this around, but my brain is too sluggish this late at night to come up with anything."

"I've got something," Roni said when Toven returned to the living room. "I'll slow it for you." He turned the screen around so most of them could see it. "Here is Margo leaving her room last evening."

The camera was in the corridor, and Negal saw one of the doors open, and a woman walk out. She wore a sleeveless dress that was somewhat shapeless and looked like nothing special at first glance, but then she lifted her head and looked straight at the surveillance camera, and Negal's heart lurched into his throat. There was that fierce look that had been haunting him, and it seemed like she was looking at him and challenging him to come to her aid.

"I ran the footage until two other women rushed in. I assume that was her sister-in-law and one of her friends. That means that Margo never returned to her room. She told Mia that Jasmine and her boyfriend were staying in the presidential suite, so I watched that feed next. Margo and Jasmine entered the suite a little over an hour after Margo had left her room, and a few minutes later, the boyfriend walked in." Roni rewound the feed and slowed it down so they could see the boyfriend walking out of the elevator, pulling out his card key, and entering the suite.

"He's a good-looking guy," Onegus said. "But he's not immortal. He's not military, either. He looks too soft."

Negal memorized the maggot's face. If he harmed Margo, he was going to pay.

Roni sped up the recording. "Room service arrived about forty minutes after the boyfriend, and given how packed the cart is, they ordered dinner. There is also a bucket with two bottles of wine."

The waiter entered the suite, and several minutes later, he left. Roni sped up the recording again. "Now things start to get interesting." He slowed the feed again. "About two hours later, the same waiter arrives with a laundry cart, and behind him, another guy is pushing a second one. It's a two-bedroom suite, so two laundry carts wouldn't have been too out of place if it was daytime, but in the middle of the night, I'd say that's suspicious as hell."

"One for each woman," Dalhu said, sounding slurred, not because he was tired or drunk but because his fangs had elongated. "That's how he got them out."

"Correct." Roni sped up the recording until the suite doors opened again, and the two men exited with the carts.

"Where is the boyfriend?" Toven asked.

"Let's see." Roni sped the feed up, but not as fast as he had done before. "Here he comes." The guy left the suite, rolling two suitcases. "That's why he stayed behind. He needed to pack." Roni smirked. "Now we will follow him from camera to camera and find out the vehicle he used. My bet is that the so-called waiters have already loaded the content of the two carts into his car."

42

KIAN

Roni followed the boyfriend through the different surveillance cameras all the way to the service entrance of the hotel, where a Ford Explorer waited for him.

He loaded the suitcases into the back, but given the camera's angle, it was impossible to tell whether the women were inside. They might have been laid out on the back seats, or they might not have been there.

"Let's hope that he's delivering them in person," Turner said.

"Let me check." Roni started clicking with his mouse, flipping from one recording to the next. "Got them," he said triumphantly.

An earlier recording showed the two guys with the laundry carts next to the same SUV. They had been smart about unloading their cargo without leaving recorded evidence, though. Aware of the location of the surveillance camera, they had gone to the other side of the vehicle, which wasn't in the camera's view, and a few moments later, they walked away with their carts.

"They definitely loaded the women into the car," Onegus said. "The vehicle dipped slightly from the added weight."

"I noticed that," Kian confirmed. "Now the question is how we will find out where he took them?"

"Street cameras," Roni said. "I need a little time to hack into the city's network."

While their super hacker got busy, Kian pushed to his feet and walked over to the kitchenette. "Anyone want more coffee?"

A chorus of voices answered in the affirmative.

Dawn was already on the horizon, and the light filtering through the glass doors bathed the cabin in soft hues. It was such a surrealistically tranquil moment, given the storm of their reality, that it gave Kian pause.

Doomers, traffickers, two missing women, and a ship full of his clan that he would probably need to evacuate.

"All in a day's work," he murmured under his breath as he waited for the fresh pot of coffee to brew.

When it was ready, he brought it to the two combined tables and refilled everyone's mugs. "Did you get anything?" He leaned over Roni's shoulder.

"Not yet. I'm working as fast as I can, but it's a lot to go through."

The kid was whizzing through the footage, switching from one camera to the next with dizzying speed, but it seemed that it would take him some time to find the Explorer.

"Got him." Roni zoomed in on a license plate. "He's entering the harbor and heading to the yacht club." Roni kept clicking around for several minutes before lifting his head from the laptop. "I need to hack into the harbor surveillance server, and that will take a while. They have better security than the hotel and the street cameras."

"Take your time." Turner clapped Roni on the back before getting up. "I need to stretch my legs. I'm going to the balcony to watch the sunrise."

"That's a great idea." Toven followed him out.

It was also a great opportunity to light up a cigarillo. Kian patted his pockets and pulled out the small tin box.

Out on the balcony, Kian leaned over the railing, lit his cigarillo, and looked at the horizon where the golden orb cast a pathway of shimmering light across the water's surface. The water rippled gently, disturbed only by the ship's passage.

As his companions talked in hushed voices, Kian turned his face toward the sun, enjoying the warmth, the gentle breeze, and the smell of salt in the air.

Nearly an hour later, the door behind him opened, and Roni poked his head out. "I've got it, guys. You can come back inside."

Kian flicked his cigarillo into the water and followed Roni. "What did you find out?"

"Do you want the good news first or the bad?"

"Makes no difference to me." Kian sat down and took a sip from his coffee, which had cooled down in the time he was outside enjoying the sunrise.

"So, I know where they were taken, but the guy was smart and avoided the cameras. I don't know how they loaded them onto the yacht, but I saw him boarding it with his luggage, so I assume they were either brought there before or after, but it's not on camera."

Kian groaned. "All we have is circumstantial evidence. We have no solid proof that Margo and Jasmine were taken from the hotel, loaded into the SUV, and then transferred onto the yacht."

"We don't need proof," Onegus said. "It's enough that we suspect they are there. Even if we are wrong about them being on the yacht, we need to get the boyfriend and interrogate him about Margo and Jasmine and what he did with them, so in either case, we are storming that boat."

“I think we can be sure they're on the yacht,” Roni said. “I checked in with Frankie and got Margo's phone number. I was able to track the phone to the harbor, but that was as far as it went. He probably dumped both of the phones there."

Turner nodded. "He probably took their purses with him and either brought them to the yacht or dumped them as well."

"As far as storming the boat is concerned, there is one problem," Roni said. "It sailed a little over three hours ago, and it's heading south at a very leisurely pace. It's not in a rush to go anywhere. The good news is that it has a helipad, so if we can get a chopper, we can land it on the boat."

"I can get us one," Turner said.

Leaning back in his chair, Roni crossed his arms over his chest. "We might not need to avail ourselves of your services because I think I know where we can find the helicopter that goes with that boat. The question is whether it will still be there when we get our forces to the mansion of the cartel boss who owns that yacht and the chopper."

43

NEGAL

Turner was quiet for a moment. "Where is the cartel boss's mansion located?" he asked.

"He has many properties." The hacker didn't lift his head from his laptop. "The one I'm talking about is about thirty miles south of Puerto Vallarta, and it has a private bay with a dock for his enormous yacht, so that's where he's taking her."

"Then we are in luck," Kian said. "We are less than an hour away from there." He pulled out his phone. "I'd better tell the captain about our change of plans. We need to stop the ship."

"Don't." Turner lifted his hand. "You can tell him to slow down, but don't tell him to stop. We need to keep up appearances, remember?"

"Right." Kian put his phone down. "So, what do we do? Do we send Guardians in lifeboats to take over the cartel boss's compound and wait for the yacht to arrive? Or do we keep going and intercept it?"

"Give me a moment to think." Turner tapped his pen on his yellow pad. "We know where the yacht is and at what speed it's going." He turned to Roni. "Can you calculate how long it will take it to reach Puerto Vallarta?"

The hacker didn't seem to need time to calculate, answering right away. "About twelve hours if it continues at its current speed."

"We can't wait that long," Negal said. "Fates only know what those thugs are doing to Margo while we wait."

Kian shook his head. "If we want to intercept the yacht instead of going to

Puerto Vallarta, we can do that in about six hours at the current speed or faster if we increase it."

Turner leaned back in his chair. "And then what? The yacht is probably crawling with cartel thugs, and it might even have Doomers on board. Not that I think it's very likely that the Doomers are involved in the kidnapping given what we saw, but we need to be prepared for the possibility that they are."

Kalugal raised his hand. "Compeller here. With a megaphone in hand, I can take care of anyone on that yacht."

"True," Turner admitted, "but then we will have the cartel chasing after us in addition to the Doomers."

"What do you suggest we do?" Kian asked.

Negal was losing his patience. Turner obviously had come up with a plan and was dragging it out instead of just spitting it out, so everyone would appreciate how smart he was, and in the meantime, Margo was suffering.

"We kill several birds with one stone," Turner said.

When the strategist was done explaining his plan, Kian nodded. "We need Andrew to access information about the cartel boss. I'm sure the US government has collected information about him, and Andrew can access it." He looked at Roni. "What's his name?"

"Julio Modana. His brother Carlos is his second in command," the hacker said. "They manage to put up a legitimate front, but everyone knows what they are really about."

Negal wondered whether Roni had found all of that just now or was that cartel boss so well known that he'd heard about him before. If Modana was such a big name, would Turner's simple plan work against what could be a large force?

As Kian pulled out his phone, Negal thought of ways to poke holes in the strategy, but when he couldn't, he had to grudgingly admit that Turner was indeed as brilliant as everyone said he was.

"Hi, Andrew," Kian said as his call was answered. "I need you to check what information the US government has on the Modana cartel. Specifically, I need information about their compound in Puerto Vallarta, if you can find it."

"I'm on it," the guy on the other side said. "Is that where they are holding Frankie and Mia's friend?"

Kian was forever amazed by how fast rumors traveled within the clan.

"It looks like they are being taken there via Modana's yacht." Kian explained in a few words what Roni had found out and what Turner's plan was. "We are most interested in finding out the number of helicopters on the property."

"Give me half an hour or so," the guy said.

"I can give you that, but no more. Our teams are heading out in an hour."

"I might need longer than that."

Kian looked at Turner. "Can we wait?"

Turner shrugged. "It is what it is, and it will take as long as it has to take. We can make changes to the plan while the teams are deployed, improvising as needed."

"Call me whenever you have something," Kian told Andrew.

"I will." The call ended.

"I'm going," Negal said.

"I'm joining as well," Toven said. "You need a strong compeller for this plan to work."

Kian shook his head. "Kalugal will do. With all due respect, you don't have any military training, and this is a military operation."

Toven glared at him. "You didn't mind me going into Kra-ell territory and risking both Mia and myself."

"That was different. You were not part of the assault team. This operation is a commando attack, and you will be a liability instead of an asset."

Toven looked like he was going to strike Kian dead with his eyes, but fortunately for Kian, he didn't have that ability. "The last time Kalugal was part of an active operation was eighty years ago. He's no better equipped to be part of this mission than I am."

"Let's flip a coin." Kalugal pushed his hand into his pocket. "My pockets are empty. Does anyone have a quarter?"

Toven crossed his arms over his chest. "I'm not going to flip a coin over this. I'm going, and that's the end of this discussion."

Kian let out an exasperated breath. "One of you needs to stay on the ship to defend it in case of an attack. Decide between you who will do what."

Negal pushed to his feet. "I'll talk to Aru and Dagor. Hopefully, both will agree to come."

Onegus got up as well. "I will assemble the team. We will meet in forty-five minutes on the promenade deck. Those who intend to join the mission, get dressed to be ready for deployment." He turned to Toven. "I prefer for you to stay on board and defend the ship. Kalugal is more than capable of taking care of a bunch of humans. There is a remote possibility that Modana is hosting Doomers or that one of the thugs is immune, which is why we are taking precautions and assembling a force. If not for that, Kalugal could achieve our objectives all by himself with a megaphone in hand. But since we are leaving the ship with just one-third of the Guardians, we need the stronger compeller to stay here, and that's you."

After a long moment, Toven nodded. "Very well. You are the chief, and if you want me to stay on board, I will bow to your authority."

"Thank you." The chief dipped his head.

Negal was glad that Onegus hadn't objected to his and his two friends' participation in the mission, but he wasn't surprised that neither the chief nor Kian wanted Toven to be in the line of fire. He was a royal, and even here on Earth, where there were supposedly no different classes of gods, Toven was deemed more valuable than three commoner gods.

Not that the royal seemed happy about it. Toven would have preferred to participate, and Negal appreciated that.

Once outside, he typed a long message to his teammates, explaining what was going on and asking whether they were willing to join.

Hopefully, they would respond to the text despite the early hour. If not, he would go to their cabins and ring the bell until someone answered the door.

44

MARINA

Marina woke up after the most wonderful dream. It hadn't lasted long enough, though, and she wished she could return to floating over the beautiful alien landscapes with colors that didn't have a name in any of the languages she spoke.

She was no stranger to the effects of a venom bite, but compared to the Kra-ell, the immortal's was much more potent and delivered twice the euphoric experience.

She was warm and deeply satisfied, but most of all, she felt safe. Peter had his arms wrapped around her, his leg draped over her thighs, caging her in as if he was afraid she would escape while he slept.

Or at least that was what she imagined, what she hoped for.

The night with Peter had been revelatory. Marina had experienced passion and connection that she hadn't expected, and as she looked at Peter, a wave of sweet affection washed through her. He looked so peaceful, his features relaxed in his slumber, and she wanted to believe that it was because he felt as contented as she did.

Lifting her hand, she feathered her fingers over his cheek, the slope of his nose, his forehead. His skin was perfect. There wasn't even a hint of a wrinkle anywhere, not a blemish or even a freckle. It was good that he kept some facial hair, or he would have looked like a boy.

Marina chuckled softly.

Peter was all man, or rather all male, one who knew a hell of a lot about pleasing women. She didn't want to think about the number of bed partners he'd had over his long life.

How old was he?

For all she knew, he could be thousands of years old. All those immortals looked to be in their twenties and early thirties, and they didn't volunteer their age.

Asking was out of the question, and not just because it might be considered rude. It was an unspoken rule for humans to be seen but not heard and to be as unobtrusive as possible.

She'd broken that rule by going to the Lido deck and ordering a drink at the bar like she was a guest. The truth was that she'd expected the robot barman to refuse to serve her and had been surprised when he'd served her with his fake but oddly endearing smile.

She also hadn't expected to find Peter there, sitting alone at the bar.

Marina had taken it as a sign that she should approach him. It couldn't have been a coincidence that the one time she'd gathered the courage to go to the bar, the immortal she'd been watching from the first day of the cruise was there.

Observing Peter during every meal she served, she'd noticed him glancing her way a few times, but as soon as his eyes met hers, he would shift his gaze away, pretending that he was just looking in her general direction but not directly at her.

Sometimes, she was certain that he was watching her, but other times she thought that she imagined it, and approaching him had been difficult.

She was glad that she had. If he hadn't lied about reading her mind, he was perfect for her. Then again, he wouldn't have restraints and nipple clamps on hand if he wasn't into the same kink she was.

"Why are you awake?" he murmured with his eyes closed.

"Am I supposed to be asleep?"

"Definitely." He lazily lifted his eyelids. "You are supposed to be out for hours after a venom bite, soaring on the wings of euphoria."

She smiled. "I was. You forget that this wasn't my first time getting bitten. My body is familiar with the effects, and I don't black out for as long."

His lazy smile wilted. "The Kra-ell?"

She nodded. "Their venom is not as potent as yours, but it still delivers the fun stuff along with the blackouts."

"Were you forced?" he growled.

"Forced is too strong of a word. I was coerced and bribed, but I was given a choice. I could have said no."

He looked skeptical. "Could you really?"

"Rape was not condoned in the compound, but everyone knew that saying no carried consequences. Besides, we all knew that it was impossible to say no to bloodsuckers who could take hold of our minds and convince us that we desired them."

"Was that what happened to you?"

"I don't know for sure. He might have thralled me to think that he was sexy and that I wanted him. He was a nineteen-year-old hybrid whom I found attractive. I was seventeen at the time, but I was born in the compound, and I didn't think that I was too young. I grew up knowing that one day I would be summoned, and when I was, it felt almost like a rite of passage. I was so glad that my first was a hybrid and not a pureblood. I was terrified of them, and I heard that they were brutal. Yogun did his best to be considerate of my inexperience, but with his Kra-ell strength and natural proclivities, he wasn't all that gentle. Not that it was bad. His own natural lubrication and the bite helped make it a good memory."

That had been the first time Marina had realized that she craved some pain with her pleasure and that she enjoyed being dominated.

Perhaps it had been a survival mechanism because that had been her reality, and even if she didn't enjoy that sort of thing, she would have to endure it anyway. Whatever the reason was, the need hadn't gone away when she was with Nicolai, who was technically a human like her, even though he was one-quarter Kra-ell.

Peter's eyes were fully open now, and they were glowing. His fangs were down as well, but not because he was aroused. He was angry, and she regretted telling him too much.

"I assume that there were others," he slurred through his elongated fangs.

"Of course." She affected a smile. "I'm a thirty-two-year-old woman, and other than the last year, I haven't been celibate." It had been probably a little less than a year, but she still couldn't remember when the last time she'd been with Nicolai was.

Peter frowned. "You were liberated only two months ago."

"The Kra-ell stopped inviting me to share their beds when I was approaching thirty. I've never conceived, for which I was grateful, so they must have realized that I was not good for breeding and left me alone. I had a human boyfriend for a while, but we broke up some time ago, and I haven't been with anyone until now." She let out a breath. "Why are we talking about that? It's in the past, and I want to live in the present." She put her hands on his chest and pressed a soft kiss to his sternum. "You fulfilled your promise last night."

"You mean this morning."

She shifted her eyes to look at the scant light the drapes were allowing to filter through. "Okay, this morning, you made good on your promise. You pleased me so well that I want more."

The grin that spread over his handsome face was like warm sunshine despite the enormous fangs protruding over his lower lip. "Right now?"

"Why not? The venom bite is like taking a shot of energy and vitality. I'm rejuvenated, revitalized, and ready for more."

45

PETER

"Is that right?" Peter brushed his fingers over Marina's taut nipple and then drew a circle around it.

Her eyes became hooded. "It is."

He dipped his head and kissed the underside of her breast, lazily making his way to her needy little nub.

He wasn't in a hurry, and neither was she, and he could take his time exploring her with gentle touches and soft kisses.

"I forgot to ask." He slid a hand down her back and cupped her bottom. "Are you on any kind of contraceptives?"

"I've got the shot, and I'm clean. I haven't been with anyone in a long time."

He chuckled. "I'm immortal. I don't get diseases, and I probably can't get anyone pregnant either, but on the remote chance that the impossible happens, you should be protected." He slid a finger down the seam between her ass cheeks, eliciting a hiss and a wiggle.

"Why can't you get anyone pregnant?" she asked.

"Immortals' fertility is incredibly low."

"I'm sorry." She shifted closer to him, so her nipples were rubbing against his chest.

"Nothing to be sorry about. It's just the way it is. Nature makes sure that we don't overpopulate the planet."

"Makes sense."

Gently, he pushed her on her back and lay on his side, his head propped on his forearm, facing her. "I love your breasts." He gave her nipple a little tug. "They are so responsive."

She hissed. "They are still a little tender from what you did to them. The venom didn't take care of that."

"I'm sorry." He dipped his head and gently laved one stiff peak and then the other. "Better?"

"Yes." She smiled. "Don't stop."

"Yes, ma'am." He resumed his tender care for a few more moments and then cupped one breast. "Do you want me to stay away from them?"

"No. Just treat them gently."

It pleased Peter that Marina was instructing him. It meant that she felt comfortable with him and given what she'd been through and who he was, that was no small accomplishment.

He ran his thumb over her nipple and then kissed it and took it between his lips, gently sucking on it.

Marina moaned. "That's good."

He smoothed a hand down her belly, and as he reached the apex of her thighs, she spread them for him, and as he feathered his fingers over her moist slit, he reached behind her with his other hand and did the same to the seam between her ass cheeks.

"You're so bad," she breathed, her face reddening either with excitement or embarrassment or both.

"On the contrary. I think I'm so good." He pressed his thumb against her rear opening and at the same time rubbed his finger over her clit. "Tell me this feels bad."

She bit down on her lower lip and shook her head.

"I didn't hear that. What did you say?" He applied a little more pressure to the small rosette.

"It's bad." She smiled sheepishly.

He laughed. "Liar." He slapped her bottom. "Liars get spanked, Marina. So, let me ask you again? Does it feel bad?" He returned his thumb to her rear entrance.

"It feels good." She worried her lower lip. "But if I say that it feels bad, would you spank me again?"

"You like that, don't you?"

"I hate it."

He laughed and slapped her bottom again, then leaned and sealed her lips with his own.

Working her front and back at the same time, he had her writhing in no time. "Come for me," he commanded as he plunged three fingers into her wet heat and pushed the thumb of his other hand against her rear opening.

She gasped and writhed, and as he added the heel of his palm, pressing it against that most sensitive bundle of nerves, her body arched, and she came, screaming silently this time.

Watching her come apart from just his fingers was satisfying as fuck, and she was so beautiful to him at that moment that he wanted to pull out his phone and take a picture.

Instead, he kept pumping and massaging until her tremors subsided.

Wrapping his arms around her, he pulled her on top of him, and for a long moment, she just lay there, exhausted by her climax, her cheek resting on his chest and her breath fanning over his throat.

He was as hard as a rock, but he didn't want to rush her. Caressing her back, he murmured words of praise, and if she fell asleep on him, it would have been fine as well. But after several minutes, she lifted her head and gifted him with a lazy, satisfied smile.

"I might never want to leave this bed."

"Then don't."

She wiggled, rubbing herself against his hard length. "I owe you an orgasm."

"You don't owe me a thing." He squeezed her bottom. "But if you want to avail yourself of my pleasure stick, you are more than welcome."

She laughed. "Pleasure stick. I haven't heard that one before." She pushed up until she was straddling his thighs and took his erection in her hand. "I want to take a taste."

He lifted his arms and tucked his hands under his head. "Be my guest."

She bent forward and was about to take him into her mouth when his phone rang.

He frowned. It was never good news when he got a call so early in the morning, and the timing sucked. "I hate to interrupt your tasting session, but I have to take it."

Pouting in disappointment, she leaned over to the nightstand and retrieved the phone for him.

"It's my boss." He lifted her off him and sat up. "What's up, Onegus?"

"Meeting in fifteen minutes at the promenade deck. We have another situation."

"On my way, chief."

"See you there." Onegus ended the call.

"What's going on?" Marina regarded him with worried eyes.

"I don't know, but I'm going to find out." He leaned over and kissed her on the lips. "Stay here and get some sleep. I'll let you know what this is about, provided that I'm allowed."

46

MARGO

Margo woke up from a needle prick in her forearm. "What the hell?"

Alberto smiled down at her. "You'll feel amazing in a moment."

What was he talking about?

Margo was still sitting on the floor, propped against the dresser with her purse in her lap. She must have fallen asleep like that, but she couldn't remember why.

For a moment, she tried to concentrate, but then she was flooded with a rush of euphoria, and warmth spread throughout her body. The relaxation was so complete that she let her arms flop by her sides, and her legs extend in front of her. "Wow," was all she managed to say.

She felt relaxed and happy.

Why had she been scared before?

This was amazing.

"I'll get you some food," Alberto said before leaving the cabin.

"I'm floating," Jasmine said from the bed. "Why am I floating?"

Margo giggled. "Because we are on a boat, silly."

In the back of her mind, she knew that this was all wrong and that the happy floating feeling was artificial. She'd been drugged, and if she had her phone, she would search the internet for the kind of drugs that could produce an immediate reaction like that. How long was it going to last?

What would happen once the drug wore off?

Would she start shaking all over like she had seen in the movies?

And why did Alberto do that to her?

It was difficult to think, and even more difficult to worry about anything when she was feeling so amazing. Margo couldn't remember ever feeling so good. No wonder people were willing to do anything for this feeling.

Except, it felt foreign. She was a glass-half-empty type of person, and all this happiness and euphoria felt like an artificial sweetener. It was a good approximation of the real thing, but not quite.

"I need to pee." Jasmine dropped her legs to the floor. "Where is the bathroom?"

"I don't know, and I need to pee too."

Suddenly the urge became overwhelming, and Margo had no choice but to try to stand up and find the bathroom. Using the dresser for support, she managed to haul herself up and then stumbled toward the other door in the cabin, the one Alberto didn't use.

Thankfully, Jasmine was moving even slower than her, so she got to the bathroom first, and barely managed to lower her panties and sit on the toilet when her bladder started to empty itself in a gush.

The door opened before she was done, and Jasmine lurched in. "I'm going to pee in the shower."

Margo laughed, her shoulders heaving as if that was the best joke she'd heard all year. "I don't know you well enough for that, but go ahead. I can't get up from this toilet even if I tried to."

She kept laughing as she watched Jasmine struggle with her underwear, pee on her feet, and then wash it off with the handheld shower head.

"It's not funny." Jasmine grabbed a towel to dry off and then started laughing too. "I take it back. It is funny."

The bathroom door opened, and Alberto poked his head in. "Food is here."

Margo tried to put on an indignant frown. "Can't you see I'm on the toilet? Get out!"

When he closed the door, she started laughing again. "We are so fucked, Jasmine. He drugged us, and it feels so good, but it's so bad. Do you know what he injected us with?"

Jasmine's puzzled expression was comical. "He injected us? I didn't feel anything. I thought he drugged the wine."

Margo had no energy to explain. It took a lot of concentration to just wipe herself clean, flush the toilet, and pull her panties back up.

Somehow, she made it to the sink and washed her hands. "Are you hungry?" she asked Jasmine.

"No. Are you?"

"I'm thirsty." She used the wall to get to the door and open it. "Come on, Jaz. I smell coffee."

Alberto put a tray on the nightstand between the two beds. There were two glasses of orange juice, two cups of coffee, and two plates of fruit, cheese, and crackers.

He waved a hand over the tray. "Five-star service for five-star ladies."

"Where are we?" Margo sat on the bed and reached for the orange juice.

"You are on a yacht." Alberto helped Jasmine to the other bed and then sat on the single chair in the cabin.

The orange juice helped clear some of the cotton candy stuffing Margo's head. "I figured that one out already. Why are we on a yacht, and where are we going?"

Alberto crossed his legs. "You are the guests of Julio Modana, and we are going south to Señor Modana's compound."

"Who is Julio Modana?" Jasmine asked.

"Your new owner."

Jasmine shook her head. "What are you talking about?"

Alberto let out an exasperated breath. "You are so dumb, Jasmine." He glanced at Margo. "You get it, right?"

"Yeah, I think I do. You drugged us, and neither of us can think straight, but I'm a little less affected than Jasmine, who is not dumb at all."

He snorted. "Oh, yes, she is. Dumb as a brick. Otherwise, she wouldn't be here. But she's beautiful, and that's why Señor Modana wants her. He told me to bring her to him, and you just stuck your nose in where it didn't belong, which is why you are here too." He grimaced. "Carlos agreed to take you because you are pretty enough and a natural blonde."

Bits and pieces of the conversation she'd overheard before were floating around in her addled brain. Margo remembered the name Carlos being mentioned.

"Who is Carlos?"

"Julio and Carlos Modana are brothers. Carlos is the younger one."

Margo smiled. "Oh, goodie. I get the young one."

Alberto shook his head. "There is nothing good about it. Julio Modana might be older, but he treats his women well. I can't say the same about Carlos."

"Why did you do that?" Jasmine whispered.

Was she finally sobering up?

Alberto shrugged. "I do what the boss says. He told me to bring you to him, and I did. It was much easier than I thought it would be because you are so fucking stupid."

"I'm not sure who's the stupid one," Margo said. "If your boss wanted Jasmine for himself, he won't like it that you sampled the merchandise." She waggled her finger at him and then burst out laughing. "You are in so much trouble, *Alberrrrto*." She rolled the Rs. "He's going to kill you."

"Shut up." The jerk pushed to his feet. "Modana is not an idiot. He knew what I needed to do to make her come with me voluntarily. Besides, he doesn't care. When he tires of her, which won't take long once he realizes what a bore she is, he will give her to me anyway."

47

PETER

When Peter made it to the promenade deck, many of his fellow Guardians were already there. The sea breeze was cool this early in the morning, which was welcome. He wasn't a fan of the humid heat.

"So here is the situation," Onegus said once everyone gathered around him. "We were supposed to get to Cabo and collect Mia and Frankie's friend from a resort hotel there. Turns out that Luis, the tour guide who was kidnapped by the Doomers, overheard his passengers talking about it, and Kalugal didn't erase that memory. Long story short, we believe that the Doomers are waiting for us there in force."

Crap, that wasn't good.

Onegus waited until the murmurs subsided before continuing, "As it turns out, we don't need to go to Cabo because Margo was abducted along with another woman by someone working for a cartel boss named Julio Modana." The chief continued to explain how Margo got snared in a web that hadn't been meant for her and how Roni had found out what had happened. "They are currently on his yacht, traveling south toward Puerto Vallarta, where his mansion is located. Naturally the place is well guarded by cartel members, and even though Kalugal will join the mission, we need to provide him with backup and support and get him within hearing distance of the guards. I need fifty volunteers to go on this mission. Everyone who wants to join, please step forward."

Fifty guardians were about two-thirds of the force, which meant that Onegus was leaving the ship with skeleton protection.

Peter raised his hand. "Isn't the force left to defend the ship too small?"

Onegus shook his head. "Not with Toven staying behind with a megaphone in hand. Thirty Guardians are enough to man all the battle stations, and if anyone tries to board the ship, he can turn them against each other or tell them to jump overboard and swim ashore."

As some of the Guardians chuckled and joked about all the possible things Toven could command the infiltrators to do, Peter thought about all the other dangers that Onegus hadn't mentioned, like a torpedo attack, or a military drone, or maybe even a military jet. Toven could do nothing to protect the ship from those, but then all the Guardians together couldn't do much either. They had hidden cannons and torpedoes of their own, but they also had very limited experience of operating these weapon systems.

As much as Peter felt bad for Margo and the other woman, his priority was protecting the ship, and while his friends eagerly stepped forward, he stayed behind.

Once the two groups were finalized, Magnus took the group of defenders to one side while Max took the group going on the mission to another.

Magnus divided guard duty among the twenty-seven Guardians staying behind, and Peter got assigned to the Lido deck, where twelve defenders were to be stationed. The others were assigned to man the ship's defensive equipment.

"Is everyone clear on their assignments?" Magnus asked.

"We need to get armed," Jay said.

"Of course." Magnus waved a hand. "Follow me to the armory."

They had to wait their turn until the assault team was done, and then each of them was given a machine gun and a Kevlar vest.

"After you are done, go get something to eat," Magnus said. "Report here in half an hour."

Peter rushed out of the armory first, but instead of heading to the dining room, he headed back up to his cabin. He hadn't asked permission to tell Marina what was going on, but he assumed it was okay.

"Hold up," Jay ran out after him. "Is the woman still in your room?"

"Yes. Why?"

Jay shrugged. "Just checking. Who is she?"

"One of the humans from Safe Haven."

"I know that. Which one?"

"Marina. The girl with the blue hair."

Jay smiled. "She's a looker. How did you get her into your bed? I tried flirting with some of the others but got the cold shoulder. They just pretended not to understand English, but I think they did."

"It's called charm, my friend." Peter clapped Jay on the back.

"Lucky bastard," Jay said. "She's one hell of a screamer."

Peter briefly closed his eyes. "Please don't mention that again. Not to me and not to anyone else. She would be mortified if she found out that you heard her."

Jay put two fingers over his lips and mimed locking them and throwing out the key. "Do you want me to move to another cabin?"

"You can if you want to, but as long as you keep your mouth shut and treat Marina with respect, I have no problem with you staying. If you are nice to her, she might mention you to her friends."

She probably wouldn't, but that would ensure that Jay was on his best behavior around her.

His cabin mate grinned. "I'll keep that in mind."

48

MARGO

After pacing the small cabin while rubbing the back of his neck, Alberto cast Jasmine another disdainful look and sat back down.

Was he being mean to Jaz because he felt guilty for tricking her? Margo suspected that it was easier on his conscience to shift the blame to Jasmine. In his mind, if Jaz was stupid enough to fall for his lies, then she deserved what he had done to her.

It was convoluted logic, and Margo was surprised that she figured it out despite her drugged state. Perhaps the effect was wearing off, and she could think more clearly?

Thankfully, Jasmine was still riding the high, so Alberto's insults didn't seem to bother her. Staring at the window with a grin on her gorgeous face, she looked oblivious to her fate.

Margo put down the toast she'd been eating and took another sip of coffee. "Who is Julio Modana? What does he do?"

"He's a businessman," Alberto said.

"Right." She snorted. "A businessman. Where is he now? Doing business from his posh cabin? Or sleeping?"

"He's not here."

Alberto cast a sidelong glance at Jasmine, that Margo thought was full of guilt, but she didn't trust her judgment in the state she was in.

"I heard him talking with you earlier, so how can he not be here? We are on a yacht in the middle of the ocean."

He looked at her down his nose. "First of all, we are not in the middle of the ocean. We are not far away from the coastline. And secondly, this yacht has a helipad. Señor Modana flew back home after inspecting the merchandise."

Margo grimaced. "You are an asshole, Alberto, but then I'm not telling you anything you don't know. You care for Jasmine, and yet you handed her over to your boss."

"I don't care for her." He shook his head a little too vehemently. "She's just a woman." He pushed to his feet. "I don't know why I'm wasting my time in here with you."

That wasn't good. Margo needed him to stay and keep talking. The more she could learn from him, the better her chances of escape.

"Don't go." She plastered a smile on her face. "Jasmine is half catatonic from the drugs you injected us with, and I need someone to talk to."

He cast another dark look at his former girlfriend and sat back down. "I'll finish my coffee and then go."

"Good." Margo sipped on her coffee for a few moments before firing another question. "So, when is Señor Julio coming back?"

"I don't know. He doesn't tell me his plans. But he will probably want to take another look at her, so he will return sometime later today."

"Why her?" Margo asked. "Was it Jasmine specifically, or would any stunning brunette do?"

He regarded her with suspicion in his eyes but then shrugged. "It doesn't matter what you know. You are not going anywhere." He took another sip from his coffee, and Margo thought that he wasn't going to answer, but then he said, "Señor Modana wanted Jasmine specifically. He'd seen her in a commercial, and he pointed at the screen and said, I want her. Bring her to me, and I'll make it worth your while."

"Did he make it worth your while?"

"He will." Alberto put his coffee cup on the tray and rose to his feet. "I'll come later to give you another dose. You are sobering up too quickly."

Damn, she should pretend to be more out of it than she was. "I'm not. If I were sober, I would be throwing stuff at you or trying to escape or both."

"You can try, but I promise you will regret it." He gave her a salute before opening the door and closing it behind him.

Margo waited to hear the lock engage, and when that didn't happen, she waited a few more moments before getting up and trying the door.

It wasn't locked.

"I'll be damned. We can just walk out of here." She turned to Jasmine. "Do you want to go exploring?"

Jasmine kept staring out the single window in the cabin.

"Come on, Jasmine." Margo snapped her fingers in front of her eyes. "Are you pretending, or are you really out of it?"

"I'm so dumb, but I don't care. I don't care about anything."

Margo sat on the bed next to her. "It's the drugs talking, sweetie. You are not dumb. Alberto was just saying that because he felt guilty for doing this to you."

She shrugged. "Julio Modana might be an improvement over Alberto. Instead of being a small-time crook's girlfriend, I will be a big-time crook's pet."

Margo chuckled. "That's a very smart observation. You see? You are not dumb."

"Why did he drug us?"

"To make us more compliant. But it's not going to work." Margo gave her hand a reassuring squeeze. "Do you know why?"

Jasmine shifted her big brown eyes to her. "Why?"

"Because I am so contrary that even drugs can't make me agreeable. That being said, from now on, I'm going to pretend to be drugged out of my mind, and you keep doing what you're doing. Perhaps it will buy us more time between injections."

49

KIAN

After most of their war council had left, only Kian, Roni, Toven, and Turner remained.

Kian ran his fingers through his hair. "Why do I have a feeling that we are missing something?" He briefly closed his eyes. "I hate making hasty plans, but it's not like we have a choice."

"Your gut feeling is correct," Turner said. "We are missing something, or rather someone." He looked at Roni. "I didn't want to bring it up in front of everyone, but we need Sylvia to join the mission. Without her disabling the surveillance cameras along the way, Modana's people will see our teams coming from miles away. We don't know what kind of firepower they have on the premises, but we need to assume that they have the latest and most advanced weapons at their disposal. Also, the compound is likely to be surrounded by explosives buried in its perimeter, ready to be detonated from the control room inside the compound. It's crucial that we take them by surprise and get Kalugal within hearing distance, and regrettably, shrouding is just not going to cut it."

Great. Kian didn't want a civilian on a mission that involved explosives and machine guns. "You should have mentioned that before. Perhaps we should abandon this ambitious plan of yours and simply continue on an intercept course with the yacht. We will face fewer opponents and retrieve Margo and her friend with little to no effort."

Turner arched a brow. "Did you forget why I came up with this idea in the first place? Doomers and cartel thugs chasing after us?"

"Right." Kian let out a breath. "We need Sylvia." He looked at Roni. "Are you okay with that?"

"Of course, I'm not, but what can I do? Turner is right, and it's not going to work without her. Besides, I can't speak for Sylvia. It's up to her whether she wants to go."

"We need her," Turner said. "If she says no, we have to abort or come up with another plan."

Roni let out a sigh. "Sylvia will say yes. She's too brave for her own good, and she knows what this is about. If we tell her she's needed, no one will be able to stop her from coming."

"Call her," Kian said. "Explain what's going on and have her come to the promenade deck in half an hour."

Roni winced. "Why don't you call her and explain? Sylvia is a sweetheart except for when someone dares to wake her up, but she won't be yelling at you."

Kian stifled a chuckle. "Fine, I'll call her."

Scrolling through his contact list, he found Sylvia's number and placed the call. The first attempt went to voicemail, but he called again, and this time she picked up.

"What?" Sylvia barked, probably without looking at the caller ID.

Or so Kian hoped. He wasn't big on protocol, and he didn't expect deference from his people, but he expected basic courtesy.

"Good morning, Sylvia. This is Kian. I apologize for the wake-up call, but we need your services, and the teams are heading out shortly."

"To rescue Margo?"

"Yes. I'm glad that you know what this is about. The guys can fill you in on the plan on the way, but the gist of it is that we need your special talent for disabling surveillance equipment. It's a dangerous mission, but I will make sure that you are protected. Still, you are a civilian, and you are not obligated to go. If you'd rather not take the risk, we will come up with another plan."

"Of course, I'll go. When and where?"

He chuckled. "I was hoping that would be your response. Half an hour on the promenade deck. Dress like a hiker. You know the drill."

"Someone better bring me coffee," she grumbled.

"I'll prepare a thermos." Roni rose to his feet. "Tell her that I'm on my way."

"I heard that," Sylvia said. "He'd better make it fast."

"Thank you, Sylvia. I appreciate it."

"Yeah, yeah. I need to get ready." She ended the call.

Roni winced. "I told you that she's grumpy in the mornings."

"That's okay." Kian pushed away from the table and walked over to the kitchenette. "I'm grateful for her help, so I would have forgiven her even if she had cussed me out."

"It was a close call." Roni closed his laptop. "I'm going to leave it here and come back after I say goodbye to Sylvia."

Kian nodded. "I'll join you on the promenade in half an hour. I hope that by then, Andrew will have information for me."

50

NEGAL

"Here we go again." Dagor wiped the spray of ocean water from his face.

The lifeboat was going as fast as a speedboat which made the ride bumpy, but Negal didn't mind. The faster they made it to Modana's estate, the faster they would get to Margo.

Naturally, they couldn't go straight to his private bay and just dock there. They needed to land a couple of miles away and make the rest of the way on foot. The clan's techno disruptor was with them, and hopefully, she could disable the surveillance cameras around the cartel boss's compound.

Negal had never heard of an innate talent like Sylvia's, and he was wondering how it came to be. If it was unknown on Anumati, then the gods hadn't coded their genetics for it. It was either a fluke of nature, or she was the descendant of a god who had been given experimental genes.

He and his teammates were tasked with keeping her safe, and Negal had given Roni his word that he would personally ensure her safety.

He didn't like the idea of putting Roni's mate in danger, and he'd even told Turner that they could get a helicopter elsewhere, but Turner rebuffed him by explaining that taking the cartel boss's helicopter was just one objective of the mission and that the others were no less important. Negal had argued that the two objectives didn't have to be achieved simultaneously, but then Turner's winning argument had been that it would take too long to get another helicopter, reminding Negal that they couldn't waste time.

For all they knew, Margo was being subjected to terrible torment and degradation on the yacht, and Negal couldn't think about that without his vision turning red and his fangs punching over his lower lip.

The fastest route to freeing her was getting Modana's helicopter and flying it to the yacht. Negal would have been content to leave the rest of the plan to Kalugal and the Guardians and rushed to save Margo, but he needed Kalugal to do his thing first for the rest of the plan to work. He also needed the clan's helicopter pilot because neither he nor his teammates knew how to operate one.

"I'm surprised that you were willing to leave Frankie," Aru said to Dagor. "That must have been a difficult decision to leave her alone in the clinic during her transition."

Dagor snorted. "Are you kidding me? Frankie commanded me to go and save her friend. On my part, I know that she has Mia and Toven to keep her company, and she's doing great, so I'm not worried. Bridget said that she's not likely to take a turn for the worse."

"Interesting." Aru smiled. "Gabi wasn't happy about me leaving, and she tried to convince me to stay. I guess Frankie cares a lot about Margo."

Dagor shrugged. "She also knows what I'm capable of and trusts me to bring her friend home."

As the two kept talking, Negal turned to Sylvia, who was sitting next to him. "Are you okay?"

"Yeah, why wouldn't I be?"

"I thought that it might be a little scary for a civilian to join a military mission."

She smiled. "This is not my first, nor will it be my last operation. Kian tried to convince me to join the Guardian force and do this full time, but the truth is that there aren't enough missions like this, and I would be wasting my time and sweating through training. I prefer to be an outside consultant, so to speak. He can call on me whenever my talent is needed, but I'm free to do whatever I want with the rest of my time."

"Makes sense," Negal agreed.

It was difficult to keep talking over the noise of the engine and the rush of the waves, and they soon gave up, riding the rest of the way in silence. When the lifeboat hit the sand, Negal and the other males jumped out and hauled the boat to the shore with Sylvia sitting inside it like a queen.

"Thank you." She took his offered hand and stepped out of the lifeboat onto dry sand. "I appreciate not getting wet."

He smiled. "I promised Roni to take care of you."

"This is becoming familiar," Dagor said as they dragged the boats further up until they reached greenery that could act as camouflage.

Unlike the other time, when they had taken a second lifeboat just for appearances, this time the two lifeboats were full of personnel. Not everyone was going to storm the cartel boss's stronghold, though. Most would remain behind as backup in case Doomers were encountered. Given their experience in Acapulco, it seemed that the Brotherhood had close ties to the drug cartels, so it wasn't such a stretch to think that they could be found in Modana's compound.

"Okay, people." Max lifted his hand to get their attention. "Break up into groups of three to five members. Your weapons need to stay hidden in your backpacks. To anyone sighting you, you need to look like backpackers."

They had gone over all of that before boarding the lifeboats, and the clan's disguise expert had done her best to make them look human. Negal wore a bandana around his head, and his jeans were torn and frayed in places. The backpack he was carrying was made from a large potato sack that he had attached straps to, and the machine gun inside was padded by a blanket, so its shape wasn't evident.

Eva had painted a five-o'clock shadow on him and added a large birthmark on his upper left cheek. It might fool people from afar, but not up close. Dagor and Aru had received similar treatment, and so had the other Guardians. There hadn't been much time, so only the bare minimum was done to make them appear more human and less perfect, but hopefully, it would be good enough to fool those watching the feed from the surveillance cameras.

Aru adjusted his earpiece. "Are the three of us on our own?"

Max shook his head. "Kalugal and Dalhu are with you. You worked well together in Acapulco. You are the spear team."

Aru adjusted the straps of his makeshift backpack. "I thought that the plan was for Kalugal to be behind us with another team."

"There was a change of plans." Max tapped his earpiece. "They are still working on the details."

"I just hope the boss and his helicopter are on the premises," Negal said. "I would hate to go to all this trouble for nothing." Especially since they could have sailed ahead and intercepted the yacht.

Max touched his earpiece. "Roni says that the compound has more than one helicopter. If the boss is not there, we can commandeer the other one."

"What if both are gone?" Negal asked.

Max repeated the question to Roni.

"He says that's not likely. Andrew got back to Kian with the information the government has collected on the Modana brothers. One of them is always on the premises, and it's safe to assume that whoever stays behind has a helicopter on standby at his disposal."

51

MARGO

It had taken Jasmine a long time to finally agree to go exploring, which in a way was a blessing. Margo's mind was clearer now, the fog of the drug slowly lifting.

Jasmine was still struggling though, unsteady on her feet, so Margo took her hand and led her to the door. Stepping outside, they found themselves in the lower deck corridor of the yacht.

It didn't look like much, but as they ascended a simple staircase to the next deck, the decor changed drastically, and the contrast to the cramped space they had been confined in made it clear that they had been put in the crew quarters.

This deck was super luxurious, with sleek lines and minimalist decor dominating the space. High-gloss surfaces and metallic accents reflected the light, and the walls were covered with modern art pieces in bold colors. Some were abstract, others depicted faces or objects, and each was signed by the artist.

"It pays to be a drug lord," Margo murmured. "The art alone must be worth a fortune."

Jasmine shrugged. "I don't like any of it. I like pictures of beautiful landscapes or ordinary people doing fun things, like children on swings or people sitting in cafés."

Margo could understand that. In an ugly world where so many suffered, it was important to surround oneself with depictions of peace and tranquility, of happiness.

Margo sighed.

The drugs must really be wearing off if she was once again seeing the glass half empty, but if she wanted to avoid another needle jab, she needed to retain the appearance of still being heavily drugged.

They passed through a lounge area, where floor-to-ceiling windows offered breathtaking views of the sea. Just like in the previous rooms, the furniture was sleek and modern, with clean lines and a monochromatic palette, interrupted only by occasional vibrant throw pillows.

Further exploration brought them to the dining area. A long glass dining table stood at the center, surrounded by high-backed chairs upholstered in white leather. The floor was dark wood, and the simplicity of the design was elegant.

"Look at this." She pointed to a stunning glass staircase that led to the upper deck. The steps were made of clear Plexiglas and seemed to float in the air.

"I'm afraid to step on them," Jasmine said. "What if they break?"

Margo laughed. "They look like a piece of futuristic art, but they serve a function. I'm sure they will not break."

"You go first." Jasmine waved a hand.

"No problem, but I want you right behind me. I don't want us to get separated."

"Okay." Jasmine eyed the staircase as if it were the maw of a leviathan.

When they got to the deck, the expanse of the yacht was revealed in its full glory. The deck was an open, airy space with pieces of contemporary furniture arranged in comfortable groupings. Some of them were under a roof, shaded from the strong sun beaming down on the deck; others were exposed, the sun casting a sparkle across the glass surfaces of the side tables and deck railings.

Beyond the railing, the ocean stretched to the horizon, its surface rippling and shimmering.

Laughing and stumbling to perpetuate the impression of being drugged, Margo looked around the deck and counted six men. They were armed with machine guns that were casually slung over their shoulders, but there was nothing casual about their demeanor.

They looked dangerous and alert, but they seemed to be paying little attention to her and Jasmine.

Evidently, their captors were more concerned with threats from the outside than with them escaping.

Margo's eyes fixed on the vast ocean stretching out before them. They were sailing south from Cabo San Lucas, and in the distance, the shore was visible as a sliver of land. It could have been an illusion, or perhaps the drugs made her see things that weren't there, but seeing the shore gave her hope.

The sun hung low in the sky, casting a warm, golden light that danced on the water's surface. A gentle breeze carried the salty tang of the sea, and as it brushed against her skin, it offered a fleeting sense of freedom.

"We could grab a life vest and swim for it," Margo said, only half jesting, her eyes gauging the distance to the shore. "We can just float, and the tide will bring us in."

Jasmine looked out at the expanse of water between them and freedom. "Are you sure the tide will bring us to the shore?" she whispered.

Their quiet plotting was abruptly shattered by a laugh. Alberto approached with a sneer, the sun casting sharp shadows across his face. "You think you can swim ashore?" he mocked in a derisive tone. "It's much farther than you think. And even if you made it, the men would pick you up before you could shout 'help'." He turned his scornful gaze to Jasmine. "So dumb," he spat.

Anger surged like a wildfire inside Margo, burning away the last vestiges of the artificial good mood the drugs had induced. She wanted to slap the jerk and wipe the smirk off his face, but her brain wasn't addled enough to think that it was a good idea.

Her fists clenched at her sides, she forced herself to take a deep breath and put a stupid smile on her face. "It was my idea. So, I guess I'm dumb, too."

"You said it." Alberto ambled away.

"Don't mind him," Margo whispered. "He's an asshole."

"I know." Jasmine leaned her forearms on the railing and looked at the waves created by the yacht's passage.

Margo leaned on the railing next to her friend and returned her gaze to the line of land that symbolized the life they were being torn away from. With a sigh, she lifted her face to the gentle caress of the sea breeze. It felt as if nature itself was trying to soothe her anger and make this terrible day somehow better.

Well, on the positive side, she got to see how the crooked rich lived, and if she ever got free, she would have one hell of a story to tell Mia and Frankie.

To be frank, it was partially her fault. If she hadn't tried to help Jasmine, she wouldn't be in this mess, but she wasn't the type who could walk away when there was something she could do.

Now, she was trapped at the mercy of a ruthless cartel boss, and escape was a fantasy. She and Jasmine were prisoners in this floating palace, and every moment brought them closer to their terrible fate.

52

NEGAL

Negal handed his backpack to Aru, bent down, and tapped his shoulder. "Come on, Sylvia. Hop onto my back."

"No." She put her hands on her hips. "I can walk."

She and her hacker were a match made by the Fates. She was just as stubborn and contrary as Roni was.

"We can move faster if you ride on my back, and if you are not preoccupied with where your next step should go, you will pay more attention to your surroundings and locate the damn surveillance cameras."

So far, they hadn't encountered any, and Negal was starting to worry that they were missing them. They were less than a mile away from the cartel boss's compound, going through rough terrain that was so steep that the immortals were having difficulty traversing it without injury.

Perhaps that was the reason for the lack of cameras. The cartel boss didn't think anyone would come at him from this side of the estate.

"Fine," Sylvia relented. "But if Roni gets mad at us for getting too close for comfort, I'll point my finger at you."

Negal suppressed an eye roll. "You are a mated female who is faithful to her mate. You smell like Roni, and that's very unattractive to me. I'll have to keep my nose closed the entire time I'm carrying you."

"Then I won't do it." She shrugged and kept going, stumbling and twisting her ankle. "Ouch. Damn it."

"Please, Sylvia," Kalugal said. "If you don't take Negal's offer willingly, I'll have to compel you to take it. You are slowing us down."

"You should be thankful that I'm here," she muttered under her breath as she put her hand on Negal's shoulder. "Crouch lower. I'm injured now. And don't you dare say that you told me so."

"I'm saying nothing." He put his arm under her butt and hoisted her over his back. "Wrap your legs around my middle and hold on like a monkey."

"Great visuals you are giving me," she murmured.

They kept going for another hundred feet or so when her arms tightened around his neck. "Slow down. I see a camera." She lifted a hand and pointed at something high up in the tree, but he couldn't see anything.

"What are you pointing at?"

"It's right there, but don't worry. I've already taken care of it. Keep going."

He did as she said. "How did you see it up there?"

"I sensed it, so I looked for it."

"I didn't know you could do that," Kalugal said. "What does it feel like?"

She chuckled. "Like what you would expect it to feel if you could. It's like a buzz of electricity. When there is a lot of tech around, it's more difficult to isolate the cameras, but there is nothing here, so it's easy."

"We should stop and put our Kevlar vests on," Dalhu said.

"Yeah, good idea." Negal let Sylvia slide down his back. "Especially you, young lady."

She tilted her head. "Are gods bulletproof?"

"Almost," Dagor said. "Our bodies expel bullets so fast that you could say so. That's why we are not putting them on." He waved at Kalugal and Dalhu. "You two, on the other hand, should wear them. The heart and the head should be protected."

"We don't have helmets," Dalhu pointed out. "The vests will have to do."

After the immortals got their vests on, Sylvia hopped onto Negal's back, and the six of them continued at a much slower pace.

"There are not many of them," Sylvia said. "That's just the second one so far."

"What are you doing to them?" Aru asked. "Are they disabled for good?"

"Usually, I would just fritz them out for a few seconds so it would look like a glitch, but because the rest of the force is moving behind us, I'm changing the cameras' angles and getting them stuck in one position instead of fanning out. Whoever is watching the feed sees the canopy of the next tree over."

"Won't it look suspicious?" Dagor moved a branch out of their way.

"Hopefully, they will think that there was a gust of wind that moved the camera. It happens. Like antennas that fall out of alignment in a strong wind."

"Oh shit." Dagor stopped. "Do you hear that?"

Negal heard it a second later. "Dogs barking." He turned around to look at Kalugal. "Please tell me that you can compel animals."

The immortal winced. "They don't understand language, so I can't compel them, but I can try to thrall them. I suggest the rest of you climb up the trees."

As Sylvia released her grip on Negal's neck, he caught her hands. "What are you doing?"

"You can't climb a tree with me on your back."

"Hold on tight and watch me."

Negal rushed to the nearest tree and climbed it effortlessly until he reached a branch that looked strong enough to hold him and Sylvia. "Don't let go."

"I won't." She clung to him so hard that she was choking him.

"You can ease your hold on my neck a little. I promise not to let you fall."

"Sorry." She lowered her arms to wrap them around his chest.

When three large dogs cleared the bushes, the only one remaining on the ground was Kalugal, but the dogs ignored him, and their barking stopped. They put their noses to the ground and sniffed around, but Kalugal must have taken hold of their minds because they whimpered, tucked their tails under their bellies, and ran off.

In the distance, someone cursed in Spanish, and the dogs whimpered some more, and then it got quiet again.

"You can get down now," Kalugal said.

Aru was the first one on the ground. "What did you tell the dogs?"

Kalugal snorted. "I didn't tell them anything. I put an image of a snarling cougar in their pea-sized brains."

53

KALUGAL

"You are clear to proceed," Kalugal said into his earpiece. "The threat has been neutralized."

"You mean the dogs?" Max said in his ear.

Was that a condescending tone that he detected in the Guardian's voice?

"Yeah, the dogs. I thralled them to think I was a cougar. Could you have done that?"

"Not likely," Max said. "I didn't know you could do it."

"Neither did I." Kalugal tapped the earpiece to indicate that he was done.

It had been a neat trick with the dogs, and Kalugal was damn proud of himself. He had never been a dog person, so he'd never bothered trying to get into the brains of dogs or other pets, but apparently, he could do anything he put his mind to.

He chuckled softly at his own pun.

"That was impressive," Negal said. "When we are done with this mission, I would like you to teach me how to do that."

Kalugal tilted his head. "Have you ever tried to get into the mind of an animal?"

The god shook his head. "We have weapons that can neutralize an animal without killing it. Regrettably, we've left them behind."

Kalugal was very interested in those weapons, but given how the gods safeguarded their technology by making it impossible to reverse engineer, it wouldn't have done him much good to get his hands on one of them. Still, he would have liked to hold the weapon and get to use it at least once to get a feel for it.

"Would it be possible for me to play around with your toys?"

Negal cast a sidelong glance at Aru, who shook his head.

"Kian got to see how our tiny spy drones work," Aru said. "So, I can let you play around with one of those, but not our other tech."

"That's a shame. I'm an entrepreneur, and my main interest is in cutting-edge technology. Sometimes, seeing something extraordinary can spark ideas for new products."

Dagor nodded. "I get it. I have ideas for new products all of the time."

Kalugal's interest was piqued. "Perhaps we can get together once this is all over and play around with ideas."

Dagor smiled. "I would like that."

"We should get moving." Negal adjusted Sylvia on his back. "The longer we take, the longer Margo suffers."

Sylvia cast Kalugal a sidelong glance. "I was wondering about something. Kian keeps referring to me as a civilian, but you are a civilian too, and yet he has you going on one mission after another."

"I'm a civilian now, but I have military training, and I'm the only compeller the clan has who knows how to operate modern weapons." He chuckled. "Toven might be a powerful god, but he was never a fighter, and I doubt he can shoot a rifle."

"I see." Sylvia returned her gaze to the canopies. "That's another camera," she said quietly. "We are very close to the compound now, so I expect more of them. We should proceed at a slower pace."

Kalugal reached into his backpack and pulled out his weapon of choice. He didn't carry a semiautomatic like the others in his team.

His weapon was the megaphone.

Sylvia disabled eight more cameras before they reached the backyard fence.

Kalugal motioned for the others to crouch low and hide behind the fence while he peeked over the block wall and noted the positions of the guards.

There were two stationed next to the French doors, and one more was on the roof, but the guard was looking toward the front, not the back. There were probably many more at the front of the house, but hopefully, the megaphone would carry his voice to those guards as well.

"We are in position," Max said in his earpiece.

Kalugal waited until Max informed him that the Guardians were in position before lifting the megaphone to his mouth. "Lay down your weapons," he commanded in Spanish. "Kick them away from you, go down to your knees, and put your hands on your heads."

The two guards next to the French doors complied, their rifles clattering to the ground first and then their knees hitting the soil, followed by their hands going over their heads. The one on the roof took a little longer, but he too was on his knees within seconds.

Thankfully, he didn't fall off the roof. Not that Kalugal cared whether he lived or died, but in case those at the front had not been affected by his command, he didn't want them to be alerted by the guard's fall.

"We are moving in," Max said in his earpiece.

"Stay here," Negal told Sylvia. "The Guardians will come get you once we have the compound secure."

She nodded. "Good luck, Negal. Bring Margo safely to the ship."

As the gods and the Guardians rushed by him, Kalugal proceeded at an easy pace toward the first guard. "Keep your hands on your head, get up, and lead me to your boss, Julio Modana," he commanded the guy.

The strength of his compulsion had the human drooling and glassy-eyed, but he complied with the command and walked toward a pair of French doors.

As soon as the guard opened the doors, Kalugal lifted the megaphone to his lips and repeated the command for everyone to lay down their weapons and go down on their knees in case someone hadn't heard his first command.

All the Guardians and the gods were wearing the specialty earpieces that William had developed especially to filter out his compulsion, so he didn't have to worry about them dropping their weapons in response to his commands.

"Get up," he told the guard who had dropped to his knees once again. "Take me to your boss."

As the guy started walking, the three gods entered through the glass doors and joined Kalugal. "The front of the house is secure."

Kalugal smiled. "Did my compulsion affect everyone?"

"So it would seem," Negal said.

"Excellent. Let's go talk to Señor Modana."

54

NEGAL

As the guard shuffled ahead, Negal followed Kalugal, with Aru and Dagor flanking him.

The place was lavish, and as they passed a pair of grand ornate doors, they entered a living room that was filled with expensive furniture and artwork that was probably original. The soaring ceilings were adorned with detailed moldings, and a large crystal chandelier was suspended from its center. The plush sofas and armchairs, though inviting, were a reminder of the comfort and security that Modana had built at the cost of so many lives.

It was ironic that such a beautiful space hid such ugliness. The money that paid for all that grandeur was tainted with blood and suffering.

As they passed a bar that was as big as that of any hotel, Negal's gaze was drawn to the array of spirits. He could use a drink, but he wouldn't touch anything in this place.

The journey through the house was a silent one, the only sound being the soft tread of their steps on the polished hardwood floor. The dining space they briefly passed was another display of excess, with its large, ornate table that was set up as if expecting a grand feast at any moment.

Finally, they reached the boss's office.

The transition was almost jarring. From the open, airy rooms to a space that was decidedly more utilitarian but no less luxurious. It was a command center, with a large, imposing desk dominating the center of the room. The walls were lined with bookshelves and portraits of Modana and his family, posing like royals in their finery, and cruel expressions on their faces.

At first, Negal thought that the guard had tricked them and that his boss wasn't there, but then he heard the rapid heart rate and shallow breathing coming from somewhere behind the enormous desk.

Peering over it, he was surprised to find a small-sized human kneeling on the hardwood floor, his balding head peeking from under his splayed fingers.

"There you are," Kalugal said in English as he sauntered to the chair Modana must have occupied when he had issued the command for everyone to lay down their weapons and go down on their knees.

"Julio Modana," Kalugal drawled. "What a lovely home you have." He shifted his eyes to the portraits on the walls. "Is that you over there?" He pointed. "You don't look that good from where I'm sitting. The artist did you a favor." He leaned down to look into the man's terrified eyes. "How does it feel to be helpless, Julio? Not so good, eh?"

The guy shook his head.

Kalugal's gaze shifted to a small statue of the Christian goddess, the Madonna. "She would be so disappointed in you, Julio. You've been a very naughty boy, and I'm here to deliver your punishment."

"Who are you?" Modana mumbled.

Kalugal smoothed a hand over his goatee. "Who do you think I am?"

"El Diablo," the boss muttered with a trembling lower lip. "The devil. But why does the devil speak English?"

Kalugal laughed, his laughter booming through the office. "What else would the devil be speaking?"

Negal stifled a chuckle. Kalugal was enjoying this, and he hated to spoil the guy's fun, but they were in a rush.

"El Diablo, forgive me for interrupting." Negal bowed his head mockingly. "But we don't have time for this sinner."

Kalugal laughed again and then leaned down to look Modana in the eyes. "I am indeed in a bit of a rush today, and I'm feeling merciful. I'll give you another chance at redemption, Julio. You will stop selling drugs and cease all of your illegal activities. From now on, you will be a philanthropist dedicated to the betterment of your people. There are several villages near Acapulco that suffered terribly from Cartel activity lately. Do you know anything about it?"

Modana nodded. "I had nothing to do with it. It was Carlos. He's not right in the head. He's dealing with these foreigners who are telling him to do bad things."

They had almost forgotten about the brother.

"Where is Carlos?" Kalugal asked.

"He's in Cabo, meeting with those foreigners. They are bad news, but he made a deal with them, and now it's too late."

"Too late for what?" Kalugal asked.

"Too late to get out of the deal."

Kalugal looked up at Aru. "I hoped we wouldn't have to do this, but we need to take out Carlos and those bad foreigners."

Negal shifted on his feet. "Later. We need to move out."

"Right." Kalugal returned his focus to Modana. "You will give money to these villagers that your brother wronged. You will build a school and a hospital, and you will give out scholarships to kids that do well in your new school and send them to college." He leaned even closer to the man. "I will be checking up on you, Julio. And if I find out that you were a bad boy, I won't give you another chance. Do you understand?"

"Yes, El Diablo. I do." The guy bobbed his head in gratitude.

"There is one more matter we need to settle, Julio. You're holding two women on your yacht against their wishes. I don't approve."

"I will let them go. I promise."

"Yes, you will, and you will do it right now. Where is your helicopter, Julio?"

"On the helipad."

"Get up slowly and lead us to it. We will retrieve the women." Kalugal tapped his earpiece. "I need the pilot."

55

MARINA

As Marina moved around the kitchen, the clink of cutlery and the soft rustle of packing materials was a relaxing soundtrack to her thoughts.

The lunch shift in the dining room was over, the tables were clean, the floor had been vacuumed, and all the dishes had been loaded into the dishwashers. The cooks were already starting to work on dinner, but she had an hour-long break until she needed to be back, and she wanted to spend it with Peter.

He hadn't come to the dining hall for lunch, so she assumed that he was still on duty. She also realized that she didn't have his phone number and he didn't have hers.

Her simple flip phone was a far cry from those fancy smartphones that were like mini-computers, but she could send and receive messages as long as it was with other people on the ship. Communication with the outside world was not permitted, but that was nothing new to her.

The same rules applied at Safe Haven.

The human former members of the Kra-ell compound knew too much to be allowed to roam free or communicate with whomever they pleased on the outside whenever they pleased. No one could erase a lifetime of memories, and the compulsion they were put under to keep the aliens a secret needed periodic reinforcement to stay effective.

Marina understood, but she still hoped that they would one day be allowed more freedom. After all, the students were allowed to attend universities, and to reinforce their compulsion, they had been required to return to the compound once a month. Now that their new home was Safe Haven, they only had to come back every three months.

If she were allowed the same freedom, perhaps she could've done something more with her life than being a maid.

The thing was, Marina had no idea what she would have done if she were free. She hadn't been exposed to enough experience to know what that thing was.

Perhaps the lack of communication had been one of the reasons that her relationship with Nicolai had fallen apart. They had exchanged letters, but knowing that they were being censored precluded any romantic declarations and made the entire thing awkward.

Besides, she wasn't good at expressing herself in writing, and neither was he, and seeing each other for one or two days a month just hadn't been enough to keep the flame alight.

Nicolai had hung in there for a long while, but eventually he'd replaced her with someone who was readily available to him at the university.

Why was she still thinking about him, though?

She'd managed to block thoughts of him for weeks, but now that she was entering a new relationship, she was examining all the ways in which things had gone wrong in the previous one.

But that was stupid.

Peter wasn't human, there was no future for them, and even if she figured out where things had gone wrong with Nicolai, it wouldn't teach her anything useful about keeping Peter.

In a way, it was liberating.

All she had to do was be herself, and if it worked, great, and if it didn't, then it wouldn't be a failure.

She couldn't fail without knowing the rules of engagement, right?

Except, her pragmatic nature refused to just let go and allow her to enjoy the moments of intimacy with Peter until the end of the cruise. Marina had a hard time accepting that she had no control over the situation and was powerless again to direct her own future.

Now that she thought about it, her plan to have him fall in love with her and invite her to live with him was like wishing for Prince Charming to come bearing the glass slipper or some other fairytale combination that even young girls didn't believe in.

She was supposed to be her own savior, and she was working on it. Significantly improving her English skills had been the first step, and the next was to enroll in an online school that would teach her something she could do online, like website design or maybe even translation work, but that was still far in the future.

With a sigh, she finished packing lunch into two cardboard boxes, put them inside a paper bag, and added two cold bottles of water before remembering that Peter was stationed on the Lido deck and could get all the drinks he wanted from Bob.

As she recalled their first meeting at the outdoor bar and how nervous she'd been, a smile lifted the corners of her lips.

Marina hadn't expected things to progress so quickly, but she didn't regret spending the night with Peter, even for a moment.

The sex had been phenomenal, but the memory she cherished the most from last night was how he had looked at her. It was as if he could see beyond the façade she was putting up for the world. How could a male she'd just met see her so clearly when the guy she'd dated for nearly two years hadn't?

It was also possible that she had imagined it.

Peter had figured out her kink without her having to tell him anything, but that wasn't difficult to do, and he also knew that she'd been held by the Kra-ell, but that was the extent of it.

Hefting the bag, she stepped into the elevator and leaned against the side wall. The thing stopped nearly on every floor as it ascended to the Lido deck, and more people got in until she was pushed to the very back of the cab.

Some of the immortals were casting her curious looks, but no one said anything to her or inquired why the human was riding the passenger elevator and not the service one.

Still, she couldn't help but feel like a trespasser, and as the elevator reached its final destination and all of its occupants spilled out, she took her first deep breath since the first stop.

When she walked out through the glass doors, the humid heat enveloped her, and for a moment it felt pleasant after the cool air-conditioned environment inside, but as she made her way through the deck searching for Peter, sweat gathered on the top of her lip and the back of her neck, and she used her hand to wipe it away.

Thankfully, a light breeze began, brushing against her face and cooling it.

When she spotted Peter, her heart skipped a beat, and as he turned to look at her and smiled, the beat accelerated.

"Hey," she greeted, extending the bag with the lunch she'd packed. "I didn't see you at lunch, and I thought we could eat out here."

He surprised her by pulling her to him and planting a kiss on her lips in front of everyone. "Thank you." His eyes danced with mirth as he took the bag from her. "Let's find a table."

56

PETER

No one had ever packed lunch for Peter before, and Marina's gesture warmed his heart. It was such a thoughtful thing to do.

Not even his own mother had done that for him.

Back when he was a kid they had been still living in the Scottish Highlands, and schooling was done by the mothers, who had taken turns teaching the clan kids. Classes had never lasted for more than a couple of hours a day, so there had been no need to pack lunch for school.

"Are you allowed to sit down?" Marina asked as he put the paper bag on the table.

"Of course."

The truth was that Peter had forgotten to signal Mathew that he was taking a break, so he pushed to his feet and waved at the guy. When he got a nod of approval back, he pulled out a chair for Marina and then sat down himself.

She glanced at Mathew, who was standing next to the railing on the other side of the pool. "I should have thought about bringing lunch for all the guards. Now I feel bad." She frowned. "I can give him mine, but then it wouldn't be fair to the others."

"Relax." Peter put a hand over hers. "They all ate already. They packed lunch during breakfast."

"Did you?" She looked embarrassed.

He shook his head. "I'm one of those dumb guys that never plans his meals ahead. If I'm full, I'm not thinking about getting hungry a few hours down the line."

"Good." Marina released a relieved breath. "I mean, it's not good that you don't plan ahead, but it's good that you haven't eaten yet." She smiled. "I was looking forward to sharing lunch with you."

He gave her hand a gentle squeeze. "You have no idea how much that means to me. No one has ever done that for me."

Her eyes widened. "No one has ever brought you lunch?"

"Nope." He opened the cardboard box and took out a beautifully wrapped sandwich. "Did you wrap it, or was it one of the cooks?"

"I did, why?"

"It looks like a present, including a red string for a ribbon."

Marina shrugged, but he could see that she liked his praise. "It's just parchment paper."

"I know. But how did you fold it like that?" He turned the sandwich this way and that, making a big deal of admiring the folds.

She chuckled. "If you start eating it instead of just looking at the wrapping, I'll teach you how to do it."

"You've got yourself a deal."

He carefully peeled the parchment away to reveal what was inside, and it was just as carefully prepared as the outside. The crust had been removed, and the slices were shaped into a perfect square and cut into two perfectly symmetrical triangles. In between was a thick layer of cold cuts, lettuce, tomato, and pickles.

Did she prepare all her sandwiches to look like that, or was it her way to show him that she cared?

"Take a bite," Marina encouraged.

He lifted one of the triangles to his mouth but didn't bite. "You said you will teach me how to do it. Start, and I'll bite."

"Fine." She rolled her eyes and pulled the paper he'd just removed toward her. Pulling out a napkin from the bag, she placed the remaining triangle on it to clear it. "You set the sheet of parchment paper in front of you and place the sandwich in the center."

She stopped and waited for him to take a bite. When he did and moaned his appreciation, she smiled and continued. "Bring the top and bottom edges to the center of the sandwich, line them up, and fold them by half an inch. Make a sharp crease and continue folding while creasing each time until the fold is flush with the sandwich."

Enjoying the dance of her slender fingers on the paper and the sound of her voice explaining what she was doing, Peter kept chewing and humming his approval.

Marina could have been talking about the snow melting in Karelia, and he would have found it fascinating.

She lifted her eyes to his, and seeing how rapt his attention was, continued her tutorial. "Use your fingers to press the opposing edges into the center. It will form a triangle, and you need to press down and crease its edges before tucking them underneath." She lifted the neat square she'd created. "That's it. The whole complicated process."

He finished chewing the last bite of the second triangle and took out a napkin to wipe his mouth. "That was delicious. Thank you for the sandwich and for the lesson, although I doubt I would do as nice of a job as you."

"I don't doubt it at all." She leaned to retrieve another container from the bag. "I knew that one wouldn't be enough for you. There are two more in there, each one different, and there is also dessert."

He pulled out the second sandwich and motioned at the one in front of her that she hadn't touched yet. "I kept you from eating your lunch."

"That's okay." She waved a hand. "I kept snacking on cold cuts and sliced veggies as I was making these. I'm not really hungry."

"You should eat." He leaned closer to her ear. "A woman can't survive on venom alone. You need to replenish your energy stores so we can enjoy ourselves again tonight."

He was surprised when a blush colored her cheeks.

"When does your shift end?" she asked.

"When the others return. I hope it will be in time for tonight's wedding. I want another dance with you."

She cocked a brow. "Just one dance?"

He took her hand and brought it to his lips for a kiss. "I want to dance the night away with you, but I know that you need to work."

"I can switch shifts," she murmured hesitantly.

"Then I'll be honored if you'd agree to be my date at the wedding tonight."

Marina's eyes widened as if she hadn't expected that. "I was just joking. I have nothing nice to wear to a wedding."

He had lived for long enough to know how to respond to that, but this time, he wouldn't be lying. "Anything you wear will look beautiful because it's you. You could make a burlap sack look chic."

Marina laughed. "You are such a charmer, Peter, but I like it. And I can probably do better than a burlap sack. I'll put something together."

"I have no doubt."

57

MARGO

"This is not so bad." Jasmine lifted her martini glass to her lips. "I don't mind lounging on the deck of a luxurious yacht and being served drinks and food."

Drinking while drugged was probably a bad idea, but they needed to pretend to still be under the influence, and the drugs were wearing off.

They had been served a delicious lunch cooked by the yacht's chef and delivered by one of the guards. Everyone was cordial to them, but Margo had caught the sneers.

The only reason no one was molesting them was that they now belonged to the cartel bosses, and the men were afraid to touch them.

Margo leaned back in the ridiculously comfortable armchair and closed her eyes. "It's so peaceful out here. I wish this voyage would never end, and we would never reach our destination, wherever it is."

"Puerto Vallarta," Alberto said. "That's odd." He looked up. "He wasn't supposed to come back. We were supposed to come to him." He cussed in Spanish under his breath. "He will be mad that you were just drugged." A new litany of curses spilled from his lips.

"Who is coming?" Jasmine asked.

"Señor Modana," one of the guards said. "Maybe he's impatient and wants to play with his new toy now."

Jasmine shuddered.

Margo followed Alberto's gaze and looked up at the sky. In the distance, a shape was steadily growing, but she was too loopy to focus her eyes. It wasn't until it was only a few hundred feet away that she realized it was a helicopter.

"Darth Vader arrives," Margo murmured. "Dah, dah, dum," she hummed an ominous sound.

"Come on," Alberto said. "He will be pleased if you are there to welcome him when he arrives."

He probably meant Jasmine, but Margo rose to her feet out of solidarity and walked toward the helipad with her friend.

Alberto stopped them from climbing the stairs to the level above. "That's close enough."

The landing pad was only a few feet higher than where they stood, so they could watch the arrival of the cartel boss. Not that she or Jasmine were looking forward to it, but Margo had never seen a helicopter up close, and she was curious.

The craft cut through the sky, its rotors churning the air and sending a powerful gust across the deck, causing Margo's hair to whip around her face.

It looked like a high-end model, its glossy black exterior gleaming in the waning sunlight. There was some insignia on the side, but she didn't know what it meant.

The pilot skillfully maneuvered the helicopter towards the helipad, making the descent smooth, and then it hovered for a moment above the helipad before gently touching down. The rotors slowed, their deafening whirr diminishing to a low hum, and then, finally, there was silence.

Margo held her breath as the door to the helicopter opened. She knew that whoever was about to step out would hold the key to her and Jasmine's fate.

The setting sun cast long shadows across the deck, adding a dramatic flare to the unscheduled arrival, and as one of the men rushed to open the door, Margo held her breath, praying it was Julio and not Carlos.

So yeah, it was selfish of her, but Alberto had said that Julio treated his women well, and Carlos didn't, so there was that.

The figure emerging from the helicopter matched what she'd imagined the elder Modana looked like. He was short, pudgy, and balding, but instead of wearing a fierce and intimidating expression, he looked like he was either scared or confused.

Margo frowned. She hadn't seen Modana when he'd been in her and Jasmine's cabin, but she'd heard him, and he'd sounded haughty and condescending. Perhaps he'd gotten some bad news?

Would it be too much to hope for that the bad news was the demise of his cruel brother?

Her musings came to an abrupt halt when the next guy stepped out of the helicopter. He was one of the most gorgeous men she'd ever seen, and he had a megaphone in his hand.

That was odd. What did he intend to do with it?

"That's not Carlos, right?" she whispered.

Looking stunned, Alberto didn't answer.

The hottie lifted the megaphone to his lips. "Lay all of your weapons down, get on your knees, and put your hands over your heads."

The command reverberated through her body, and in the next moment, Margo found herself kneeling on the deck with her hands on her head. Next to her, Jasmine and Alberto were doing the same, and so were all of Modana's men, including Modana himself.

"You can get up." The gorgeous man tapped Modana's shoulder. "Tell your men to relax and obey my commands."

Was that magic?

Or was the megaphone some kind of a new weapon that took people's will away and made them obey orders? If so, it was a very dangerous weapon but also very useful in the right hands.

As the megaphone wielder moved aside, another man jumped out of the helicopter, and if she thought that the previous guy was the most gorgeous man she'd ever seen, she now had to revise her assessment because the tall blond was the stuff of fantasies come to life.

"How can you be so stunningly perfect?" she murmured under her breath.

As if he'd heard her, the man turned to look at her, his intense blue eyes boring straight into her soul.

Margo couldn't breathe.

The world tilted, and she was falling, and then there was nothing.

58

NEGAL

Negal recognized Margo right away. She had obeyed Kalugal's command like everyone else on the yacht and was kneeling on the spot, but there was something wrong with her. Her expression indicated shock, and she was swaying on her knees.

When she started to topple sideways, he used his incredible speed to jump from the helipad down to the deck below and catch her before she could hit the deck.

Lifting her into his arms, he walked over to one of the armchairs and sat down.

She was so much smaller than what he'd imagined, and her scent was off, but she was also much more beautiful than the picture he'd seen on Frankie's phone.

Her paleness worried him, and so did the dark circles under her eyes. Some of it was the fault of old, smeared mascara, but the wrongness of her scent indicated disease.

Kalugal walked over and crouched next to him. "What's the matter with her?"

"I don't know, but her scent is off. Can you smell it?"

Kalugal leaned closer, sniffed, and grimaced. "Drugs." He looked at the human male kneeling a few feet away and snarled, "I bet it's his doing." Kalugal pushed to his feet and walked over to where the other woman was kneeling and sniffed her. "She was drugged, too."

Negal tensed. "Is Margo in danger?"

Kalugal returned and crouched next to them again. "Margo's heart rate is normal, and she is breathing fine. Perhaps the drugs combined with the surprise of our arrival were too much for her after all she's been through. She probably just needs a few moments."

Negal didn't know anything about human physiology, but Kalugal's wife used to be a human before she'd transitioned, so he must be knowledgeable on the subject, and he didn't look concerned.

Kalugal shifted his gaze to the other woman, still kneeling with her hands over her head. "Jasmine, you are free to move as you wish."

The woman got to her feet and trained a pair of large brown eyes on him that were a little unfocused and glazed over. "How did you know my name?"

Kalugal smiled. "A little birdie told me." He turned to look at the human male kneeling a couple of feet away. "Is that your scumbag boyfriend?"

"He's not my boyfriend," Jasmine said. "But he is a scumbag." She giggled. "Why am I not mad at him? I should be fuming. It's the damn drugs." She giggled again. "Who are you?"

Kalugal smiled. "If I were single, I would tell you that I'm your knight in shining armor, but I'm taken, so you can think of me as the nice guy who came to rescue Margo and you. You can call me Kevin."

Negal didn't know why Kalugal was bothering with a fake name. In a few hours, Jasmine would board the ship and hear everyone calling him Kalugal.

"Nice to meet you, Kevin." She gave him a dazzling smile. "Are you with the ship that was supposed to pick up Margo in Cabo?"

"Yes, we are."

"Then I'll happily take your offer and hitch a ride back home with you." She turned her eyes to the chopper. "But I don't know whether I want to get there in that."

"You will not." Kalugal patted her shoulder. "We are staying on the yacht for now."

"Why?"

"Because I have work to do." He pointed his finger at Alberto. "You, get up and follow me."

The scumbag rose to his feet like his body was obeying Kalugal's commands and not his own, which was precisely what was happening.

Compulsion was such a useful tool. No wonder the Eternal King hoarded it for his family. The excuse was that compulsion ability couldn't be genetically engineered, but that was just one more lie in the many lies the king was spreading. Everything could be boiled down to genetics, including intelligence and even sexual proclivities.

Jasmine turned to look at him. "Where is he taking Alberto?"

"Don't worry. He's not going to kill him."

"I'm not worried. I'm just curious."

Negal had a feeling that Jasmine was incapable of worrying about anything in her drugged state. "Kevin is going to have a talk with all the men."

"Oh." She walked over and sat down on one of the other outdoor armchairs. "You and Kevin are such gorgeous men. You could play the roles of knights in movies." She crossed her long, tanned legs.

Was she flirting with him? Usually, when women commented on his looks, it was to hint that they were interested.

"I'm taken too," he said.

"I wasn't trying to flirt with you." She giggled. "That's a lie. I totally was. She's a lucky girl, but she might get jealous when she finds out you were holding another woman in your arms like she was your most precious possession."

What in the seven hells was he supposed to say to that?

He wasn't really taken, was he?

And if he was, it was by the woman in his arms, who didn't even know that he existed.

Negal swallowed. "It's fine." The expression covered a lot of different situations, and he hoped it was good enough for this one as well.

Jasmine shifted her eyes to Margo. "Is she okay? Maybe you should take her to see a doctor?"

"Kevin said that she would be fine. She just needs a few moments."

Jasmine tilted her head. "Is Kevin a doctor?"

"No, he's not." Negal tightened his hold on Margo.

What if Jasmine was right?

"Do you have a doctor on the cruise ship?" she asked.

"Yes, we do."

"Then maybe you should take Margo there in that helicopter," Jasmine suggested. "Or you could take her to a nearby hospital, whichever is closer."

She sounded much more lucid than she appeared, so maybe the drugs were wearing off already.

He had to admit that her suggestion had merit.

The helicopter was a four-person small craft that could possibly squeeze in one more, but they had decided to stay on the yacht until it reached the *Silver Swan.*

Negal had negotiated hard to be the only one other than the pilot and Kalugal to accompany Modana to the yacht. The rest of their team had stayed behind to deal with Modana's men and put them through a crash re-education course that was supposed to put them on the right path to assist their boss's new humanitarian endeavors.

He wondered whether it would work, but he couldn't fault the clan for trying to minimize bloodshed. Modana's men were all seasoned killers, but they hadn't committed the kind of atrocities that their counterparts in Acapulco had, so perhaps they were still capable of salvation.

Margo stirred in his arms, and a moment later, she opened her eyes and stared up at him. "Am I dead?"

59

MARGO

Margo was looking at the face of an angel, which meant that she was dead.

Evidently, she'd been wrong about there being no heaven or hell, and she had somehow ended up in heaven.

She hadn't been a bad person, but she hadn't been a very good one either. Or had she? If being good meant volunteering in homeless shelters or donating money to charity, then she hadn't been particularly good because she had done neither. But if being good meant not doing evil, then she qualified.

But wasn't she supposed to go through a trial before being admitted to heaven? There was supposed to be a review of all the bad and good deeds she'd done throughout her life.

The angel frowned. "Why do you think you are dead?"

He sounded a little hoarse as if he had been shouting, or maybe he was thirsty, but angels did none of that. He also smelled of seawater and clean male sweat, and that, too, was something angels didn't do.

"You're not an angel, are you?"

The smile he gave her was so bright that it was blinding. "You thought that I was an angel?"

She lifted her hand to shield her eyes. "You are bright like an angel, but you don't sound like one, and you smell a little sweaty. Not in a bad way, but not in an angelic way."

He laughed, and now she was convinced again that he was an angel because the sound was so beautiful that it stirred something in her soul.

Margo had always believed that music was a portal to the divine, the one thing that made humans superior to animals, and the guy's laughter sounded like the best melody.

Frowning again, he dipped his head and sniffed at his armpit. "I do smell a little. But I assure you that I'm not bright, and I don't have a glow. I'm not a royal."

That was such an odd thing to say. "Royals don't glow."

"They do where I come from."

"And where is that?"

"Portugal."

He said that with a straight face, but it must have been a joke, something about Portugal being a monarchy? Margo had never heard it before, so she didn't laugh. She also suddenly realized that she was staring into his impossibly gorgeous face because he was holding her in his arms.

"Why are you holding me?"

"You fainted."

Somewhere nearby a woman laughed, and as Margo shifted her eyes toward the sound, she recognized the olive-skinned beauty on her left. "Jasmine."

"Yeah, that's still me, and Mr. Angel over there flew like he had wings all the way from the helipad down here to catch you before you fell. I've never seen anyone move that fast." She leaned closer so her face was hovering a few inches above Margo's. "Maybe he has invisible wings that only other angels can see."

"My name is Negal, and I'm not what you call an angel. You only think that you saw me moving so fast because of the drugs. You've both been drugged."

"How do you know that?" Margo asked. "Is it that obvious?"

"I can smell the drugs on you."

"Oh." Jasmine's lips twisted in distaste. "I didn't know they had a smell."

Margo hadn't known that either, and she was mortified that the stunning stranger was smelling her foul smell. "You can let go now. I'm okay."

"Are you sure?" Instead of loosening, his grip on her tightened. "You look very pale."

She wasn't sure of anything, and being held by him felt heavenly even if he wasn't an angel, which she still wasn't convinced was the case.

Could angels lie?

It didn't seem right, given that lying was bad and angels were supposed to be good, but if they were sent to save people on Earth and needed to conceal their identity, lying would be necessary, right?

Except, there was one more thing that angels weren't supposed to do, and the one holding her was definitely doing. She could feel his erection hardening beneath her, and as she shifted a little in his arms, it got harder still.

"What kind of a name is Negal?" Jasmine asked. "I've never met anyone with that name. Is it Portuguese?"

"It's an old name that runs in my family." He didn't even look at Jasmine when he answered her, which pleased Margo.

In fact, it would have pleased her even more if Jasmine had gone away and left her alone with Negal. She was suddenly very possessive of her naughty angel, and she wanted to find out more about him.

"I'm a little warm." Margo put a hand on her forehead. "And I still feel a little faint. Is there a chance you could take me to the salon below? They probably have water in the bar's refrigerator." She lifted a finger to Negal's lips. "You seem thirsty."

His eyes flared with a glow that was for sure heavenly. "You are correct. I am a little thirsty." He pushed to his feet with her still in his arms, effortlessly as if she weighed nothing, and started walking but then stopped. "Where am I going?"

"I'll show you," Jasmine said.

Margo stifled a wince. Her plot to be alone with Negal hadn't worked. Was she a bad person for wanting him all to herself?

Was it a test, and she was failing it because she wanted Jasmine to go away?

Jaz was her friend, and Margo got herself into this mess to help her. So maybe she was allowed a little selfishness.

Winding her arms around Negal's neck, she looked at his glowing eyes and wondered whether it was the drugs' fault. If it wasn't, then all she'd believed about angels had been wrong, and the romance books she'd read about naughty angels who seduced human women or were seduced by them had been right.

60

NEGAL

The salon turned out to be occupied.

That was where Kalugal had taken Modana and his men, including the boyfriend. Negal still planned to punch the guy in the face for kidnapping Margo, even if he had done them all a favor by distancing her from the Doomers.

Worrying about what was being done to Margo had cost Negal a few centuries of his immortal life, and he thanked the Fates that she was mostly unharmed.

It was a miracle that the cartel bosses who had claimed both her and Jasmine had been busy and that no one had forced themselves on the women.

As the three of them passed through the room, Kalugal smiled at them and waved them on before returning his focus to Modana and his men.

The immortal was using his compulsion to reeducate Modana's men and continue his education of the cartel boss himself. The idea was to turn the ruthless killers into do-gooders and to spread misinformation that would reach the ears of the Brotherhood and get them off the clan's tracks. Both were lofty goals, but if anyone had a chance of achieving them, it was Kalugal.

Negal was glad that Onegus had chosen Kalugal to accompany them on the mission and asked Toven to remain on the ship.

He doubted that Toven would have been able to do what Kalugal was doing. The royal was too much of a straight shooter and an idealist. Kalugal, on the other hand, was a creative storyteller who didn't concern himself too much with the truth.

"Is there anywhere else we can go?" Negal asked Jasmine.

She shrugged. "Margo and I went through several areas on our way to the top deck, but I don't remember much of it." She lifted a hand to her forehead. "It was hard to think straight. Let's just keep walking until we find somewhere comfortable to sit." She cast him a sidelong glance. "Unless you are tired of carrying Margo. She must be getting heavy."

"Not at all." He hoisted his precious cargo higher on his chest so her face was closer to his, and he could feel her breath fanning over his skin. "She's practically weightless."

Margo giggled softly. "Thank you. That was the right answer."

He looked down at her. "I didn't know that I was being tested."

She lifted her face to him with a sweet smile. "Don't you know that you are judged on every word you say?"

"By whom?"

"Women," Jasmine said. "We try to determine a man's worth by testing him in every way we can, but I totally suck at it. I fell for Alberto's fake charm."

"He was a scam artist," Margo said. "You should stop beating yourself up over this."

"No, he was right about that. It was stupid of me." Jasmine kept walking, with Negal following.

"The blind leading the blind," Margo murmured into his chest. "She has no idea where she's going."

"Yes, I do." Jasmine looked at them over her shoulder. "If we can't find a good place, we can go back to our cabin."

"It's cramped and crappy." Margo shifted so she could look around. "Let's find the master bedroom suite. I bet it's amazing."

Jasmine snorted. "Do you have naughty ideas for the three of us?"

"Dream on, girl. Negal is mine." She gasped, and her cheeks reddened. "Did I just say that?"

"You certainly did." Call him a peacock and give him glorious tail feathers to spread because that's how he felt right now.

"I'm sorry." She buried her face in his chest. "It's the drugs talking. Don't pay attention to anything I say."

"I liked what you said."

"You don't know me, and I don't know you. You are not mine any more than you are Jasmine's."

"I'll take him," Jaz said.

"We are both drugged." Margo cast her friend a glare. "Her inhibitions are also compromised. You shouldn't listen to either of us."

"What's over here?" Jasmine pushed a door open. "Oh, look. It's the kitchen."

As Negal followed her inside, the smells assaulted his senses, and his stomach growled, reminding him that he hadn't eaten anything since the wedding last night.

"Someone's hungry." Margo laughed. "Put me down, and let's get something to eat."

There were two barstools in the large kitchen, but Negal had no problem eating while standing. He gently lowered Margo to one of the stools and held on to her until he was certain that she wasn't going to tip over.

As Jasmine walked over to the stove and started lifting lids and sniffing the food, a door opened, and a guy in a white coat brandished a gun at them.

"Put up your hands," he said in heavily accented English.

Wondering how the guy had managed to evade Kalugal's compulsion, Negal reached into his mind and changed his perception of what was happening.

They weren't intruders or hostiles taking over his boss's yacht. They were distinguished invited guests, and what was happening in the salon was an important business meeting. Negal also added that the cook should feed them.

"I'm so sorry." The guy lowered his gun and bowed. "I've made a terrible mistake, *señor y señoras*. Let me serve you dinner."

"I'll take that gun." Negal extended his hand.

"Of course, *señor*." The cook rushed over and put the gun in his hand. "Please, make yourself comfortable in the dining room. The kitchen is not the proper place for the distinguished guests of Señor Modana."

61

MARGO

"How did you do that?" Margo asked as Negal lifted her into his arms again. "And I can walk."

"Not yet." He carried her out to the dining room. "I don't want you falling over and hurting yourself."

"That's very kind of you, but you didn't answer my question. How did you make the cook lower his gun and give it to you?"

"I didn't do anything." Negal lowered her into the chair that Jasmine had pulled out for her. "He must have realized that he knew the two of you, and you were Modana's guests."

"What about you? He didn't know you."

"I was with you." Negal treated her to a brilliant smile that took her breath away.

"So, Negal." Jasmine unfurled a cloth napkin and spread it over her lap. "How did you know where to find us?"

It seemed that Jasmine was doing better with the narcotics. She didn't seem as loopy as she was before. Margo still didn't know what kind of drugs Alberto had used on them, and even if she did know, she didn't have her phone with her to search the internet for advice about shaking off the effects.

Negal hesitated for a long moment, then looked around the dining room and shook his head. "I'd better not say. There might be hidden cameras or voice recorders in here."

"Is it such a great secret?" Jasmine said in a teasing tone that grated on Margo's nerves.

She'd really liked the woman until Negal showed up, and suddenly Jasmine started acting like a floozy and flirting with him.

Well, Jasmine wasn't really acting like a floozy, and Margo wasn't sure that she was even trying to flirt with him, but she suddenly felt very possessive over a guy she had no business feeling possessive over.

He was a gorgeous stranger, chivalrous, kind, and intelligent, but that was no reason to act as if he belonged to her.

The thing was, Negal was like one of the supernatural heroes in her romance novels, and he checked all of her boxes and then some, but it must be a fantasy that she was creating in her head.

He was just a good-looking guy who'd saved her, and she was having a damsel in distress moment, fawning over her savior.

"Perhaps I can tell you some of it." Negal reached for the napkin and mimicked Jasmine's move, unfurling it and draping it over his lap. "Mia called Margo, and when Margo didn't answer, Mia got worried and called the sister-in-law, who was partying at a club at the time. When she returned to the hotel, she checked Margo's room, and when she didn't find her, she called hotel security. Hotel security performed a perfunctory search and informed the sister-in-law that she should contact the police after Margo had been missing for more than twenty-four hours. Mia suspected that your so-called boyfriend had something to do with Margo's disappearance, and she told us what Margo had suspected him of. She also remembered that Margo told her that you were staying at the penthouse. We used the services of a hacker to hack into the hotel's surveillance server and check the footage from the camera across the penthouse door. We saw a waiter deliver dinner, and a couple of hours later, the same waiter returned with a laundry cart and another staff member with an additional cart."

"I knew it," Margo exclaimed. "I knew they would use a laundry cart. It's just like in the movies."

Negal nodded. "The two left the penthouse with the laundry carts, and a short time after that, the boyfriend emerged with two pieces of luggage. The hacker followed him from one camera to the next until he saw him get into a large SUV. He didn't see you being loaded into the vehicle because they were careful to do it out of sight of the camera at the loading dock, but we assumed that you were there. The hacker followed the vehicle through the street cameras until it stopped at the yacht club. From there, it was easy to find out who the yacht belonged to, where he lived, and therefore where the yacht was heading to."

Jasmine shook her head. "It's like a James Bond movie. How did a bunch of computer nerds know to do all that?"

Margo chuckled. "Don't you know that geeks and nerds rule the modern world? And these particular computer nerds make the most amazing virtual adventures, which means that they have great imaginations. No wonder they solved the mystery. We are so incredibly lucky." She shivered. "I expected the worst. Alberto said that Carlos was cruel to his women, and I was to be his pet. If not for the drugs keeping me feeling like I could conquer the world, I would have probably thrown myself overboard and drowned. Death would have been better than that fate."

62

NEGAL

At Margo's words, fury washed over Negal, and as his fangs started elongating, he slapped a hand over his mouth. "Excuse me," he mumbled as he shot to his feet.

"What happened?" Margo lifted a pair of worried eyes to him.

Knowing that his eyes were probably glowing, he averted his gaze. "I need to find the bathroom." He rushed out of the dining room.

Finding the bathroom was easy, and after ducking inside, Negal locked the door and leaned against it.

Damn. This hadn't happened to him in a long while. He'd been trained to control his reactions, and he didn't allow his fangs to act on their own accord among humans. Perhaps it had been the time he had spent among immortals where he hadn't needed to hide his godly features that had weakened that mental muscle.

Walking up to the sink, he didn't bother looking into the mirror as he turned on the faucet and gathered water in his palms to splash over his face. After taking a few long breaths, he managed to retract his fangs, and when he finally looked at the mirror, his eyes didn't glow.

He took the opportunity to empty his bladder, washed his hands, and after several additional long breaths, opened the door and returned to the dining room.

While he'd been gone, the chef had served dinner, but neither Jasmine nor Margo were eating. They were waiting for him, he realized.

"I'm sorry. Something must have disagreed with my stomach." He lifted the napkin that had fallen on the floor when he'd made his hasty exit.

Margo smiled. "Now I know for sure that you are really a man and not an angel. Angels don't get upset stomachs."

Neither did he, but he couldn't tell her that. "Thank you for waiting for me." He draped the napkin over his lap. When neither of the women picked up their forks, he frowned. "Is there a special blessing over the meal that needs to be said?"

"Not unless you want to." Margo looked at Jasmine. "Do you want to say anything?"

Jasmine shrugged. "Thanks to the chef?" She waved a hand at the bottle of wine. "We should make a toast to our savior." She smiled at Negal. "We were waiting for you to uncork the wine. The chef just put it on the table without opening it. Usually, whoever serves the wine does the honors."

Margo chuckled. "Not on a yacht owned by a cartel boss. He probably doesn't drink anything that he didn't open himself."

"Good point." Jasmine let out a breath. "I didn't suspect Alberto of anything, so I didn't watch him open the wine bottle, and that was how he got us. He put something into the wine. Probably a roofie."

"What's a roofie?" Negal reached for the bottle, found the opener, and uncorked the wine.

"It's a drug that makes the victim sleepy," Margo said. "It's usually tasteless, and unscrupulous men spike unsuspecting women's drinks to take advantage of them."

Negal commanded his fangs to stay dormant and poured the wine into their three glasses. "I will kill him for you."

Margo's eyes widened. "Are you serious?"

He wasn't sure how he was supposed to answer that. "I want to kill him, but if it will displease you, I won't."

"He's just a maggot." Margo lifted her wine glass. "He's not worth tainting your soul for." She put the glass down without drinking.

Negal took a sip of the wine to refrain from saying that getting rid of vermin would by no means taint him in any way. Margo and Jasmine might have been through a terrifying ordeal, but thankfully, they hadn't seen true evil. If they had, Margo might have had a different view on things.

"Let's make a toast." Jasmine lifted her glass. "To our saviors, who arrived in the nick of time."

That reminded Negal that he hadn't arrived alone, and that the clan pilot and Kalugal were probably hungry as well. "I should tell Kal—I mean Kevin to join us."

Margo put her fork down. "He seemed busy." She frowned. "I wonder how he made all those tough guards obey his command. Come to think of it, why did Jasmine and I drop to our knees as well? We knew that he wasn't talking to us, and yet it was like my body was under his control, obeying his commands and not my own."

"Hypnosis," Negal said the first thing that came to his mind. "Kevin is a powerful hypnotist."

He would have to thrall both women and muddle their memories of what they had witnessed.

Margo grimaced. "That's a very dangerous trick. I'll stay away from that one." She picked up her fork. "Let's eat."

Negal cut a piece off the fragrant roast. "Kevin is a good guy. He only uses his hypnotic power for good."

"Well, thank you." Kalugal walked into the room with the pilot by his side. "I could smell this roast all the way from the salon, and I was salivating. The last meal I had was at the wedding last night."

63

MARGO

The drug must have further worn off, and Margo was starting to feel more like her old skeptical self again.

The third guy who had come with Kevin was nearly as good-looking as his two friends, and that just didn't make sense. What kind of an outfit employed only gorgeous guys?

Frankie had said that her guy looked like a god, and Margo had thought that she was exaggerating, but if he looked anything like these three, then Frankie was right.

"What did you do with Modana and his men?" Negal asked Kevin.

"I left them to contemplate their past and their future." Kevin lifted the small bell that Margo hadn't noticed before and shook it a couple of times.

The chef emerged from the kitchen and frowned at the new guest.

"Please be a good chap and bring out two more plates for me and my friend."

He'd said please, but Margo noted the hypnotic undertones in his voice. Except this time, she hadn't felt compelled to do his bidding as she had the first time. Perhaps it was because he'd addressed the chef as chap, which was obviously not directed at her.

The chef wrung his hands. "Of course, *señor*. Will Señor Modana be joining you?"

"No. He and his men will be dining later."

As the chef dipped his head and scurried into the kitchen, Kevin shifted his gaze to Jasmine and then to Margo. "You two seem to be a little more alert. Are the drugs wearing off?"

"I think so," Margo said. "I know that Alberto was trying to get us addicted, but I hope one dose is not enough to do that. I don't know anyone who's had to go through withdrawal, but if it's as bad as they portray it in movies, then it's nasty."

Jasmine nodded. "I hate to admit it, but I miss the euphoria. Now all I feel is sad." She pouted prettily, and Margo gritted her teeth.

What was happening to her?

She'd never been the jealous type, and she liked Jasmine, but now she was getting angry every time the woman flaunted her superior beauty and allure.

Thankfully, Negal seemed indifferent to her charms, and Kevin seemed amused. The only one who was affected was the third guy, whom no one had bothered to introduce.

Jasmine must have noticed the same thing because she turned her dazzling smile on the guy. "Your friends were remiss and didn't introduce you."

"Edgar, or Ed. I'm the helicopter pilot."

"Nice to meet you, Ed."

"It's a pleasure to make your acquaintance." Ed inclined his head.

Jasmine affected a gasp and put her hand over her chest. "Such beautiful manners you have, Ed."

He laughed. "I would make a Little Red Riding Hood joke, but given the circumstances, I shouldn't."

"Yeah." Jasmine's smile wilted. "I've already met the big bad wolf."

As the two continued talking, Margo was glad that Jasmine was focusing her attention on the pilot instead of flirting with Negal.

The door to the kitchen opened, and the chef came out carrying a tray with two more plates and place settings. While he served the two new dinner guests, Margo thought about what Kevin had said a few moments ago in regard to Modana and his men.

What had he meant by them contemplating their past and future? Had he hypnotized them?

She'd heard that hypnosis was a powerful tool that could be used in therapeutic ways. Was that what Kevin had meant?

Margo waited for the chef to be done and return to the kitchen before turning to Kevin. "Did you use hypnosis on the cartel boss and his men?"

Kevin shot Negal a glance, and Negal nodded, confirming that he had told them about it. "Margo wondered how you were able to make the guards obey your command so readily. I told her that you are a powerful hypnotist."

"Yes." Kevin draped a napkin over his pants. "I am. Hypnosis can be used to address various psychological and medical issues. It can help manage pain, reduce anxiety, treat phobias, and address other behavioral or emotional concerns." He smiled. "In this case, it addressed criminality, which is a deviant behavior. After a couple of sessions, Modana and his men will become the good men their mothers had hoped they would be."

Negal chuckled. "Who said that their mothers wanted that? Perhaps they wanted their sons to be the meanest, baddest criminals around?"

Margo thought about that for a long moment. "In some societies, that might be true. Not everyone has the same values that we hold sacred. Some mothers encourage their sons to become murderers."

Jasmine looked incredulous. "What mother would wish for such a thing and why?"

The woman was really naive or just uninformed. "Religion for one, social pressure for another. Some religions glorify death, and as it happens, those same religions discriminate against women and deprive them of basic rights that you and I take for granted. One of the few ways women can get respect in these societies is to encourage their children to become murderers for the cause."

Across the table, Kevin groaned. "Let's change the subject before I lose my appetite." He smiled at Jasmine. "Tell us a little about yourself. What do you do for a living?"

Ugh, why had she had to open her big mouth and spout depressing stuff?

Margo cast a quick look at Negal, but he smiled at her with affection, so perhaps he didn't mind that she was the glass-half-empty kind of girl.

"I'm an actress," Jasmine said. "I've been cast in a few commercials, and I even got a nice chunk of money for it, but since the roles are unreliable, I continue working in customer service to pay the bills, and what I get from the occasional commercial, I put in my savings account."

"That's smart." Kevin shifted his gaze to Margo. "And you?"

"I work at an advertising agency and hate every moment of it. I can't wait for Mia's boyfriend to get me the job he promised Frankie and me at Perfect Match Virtual Studios. For starters, I'll work at beta testing the new adventures you guys come up with, and then I hope to get promoted to the advertising department. They are doing amazingly well with their commercials, but I have a few ideas on how to improve on that."

Jasmine's eyes widened. "Can you get me a job there as well? I mean in the commercials. I'm not sure I would be good as a beta tester, but I can be a spokeswoman or a participant who describes her experience."

Kevin lifted his hands. "I'm not affiliated with the Perfect Match Studios. You will have to talk to Mia's fiancé."

Margo frowned. "I thought everyone on board was a Perfect Match employee."

"Not everyone." Kevin cut off a piece of the roast. "Some of us are just friends and family."

Very capable friends and family who had managed to take down a cartel boss and rescue two kidnapped women.

Margo regarded the three men.

They looked like models or actors, and if not for what Kevin had just said, she would have assumed that they worked on the production side of Perfect Match. They could have been former Navy SEALs or some other commando unit turned actors.

But according to Kevin, they didn't work for Perfect Match.

Mia had told her and Frankie that the owners of Perfect Match were very reclusive and lived in a secluded compound. She'd also said that they had security on board, which was what these men most likely were.

But why would Kevin say that they were friends and family instead of admitting that they were security?

And what was the deal with how gorgeous they were? Had they been chosen for their good looks or their combat skills?

Something was fishy about these men and about the cruise.

64

KIAN

"Good evening, Mother." Kian leaned to kiss his mother's cheek.

She shifted on the couch, motioning for him to sit beside her. "Thank you for coming over to give me an update in person."

He'd considered calling her, but there was no justification for that, given that her cabin was just down the hallway from his.

"I'll have to make it short because there is still much to do."

"Of course."

"As you have probably guessed, we are not heading to Cabo. We are making a detour and stopping at Puerto Vallarta instead. Hopefully, that will confuse the Doomers, and they won't figure out which ship we are on."

She tilted her head. "You will have to explain your logic, my son, because I do not understand how changing ports will achieve that."

"From what they got out of the tour guide, they learned that he collected his passengers at the port, so they might suspect that we are traveling by ship. They also learned from him that we were supposed to collect a woman from the hotel in Cabo. Margo didn't keep it a secret that she was joining a cruise, and she probably told a number of people about it. The Doomers no doubt interrogated some of the staff and guests and learned who she was. When Margo went missing, we were afraid that they had taken her and were holding her hostage like they did with Luis, but that wasn't what happened. In a way, we were lucky that she befriended a woman in the hotel and got caught up in a plot to kidnap and deliver the other woman to a certain cartel boss, who happened to reside in Puerto Vallarta. I don't want to go into all the details, but thanks to Roni's hacking, we were able to find out what happened to her, and since we were close to Puerto Vallarta, we were able to storm the boss's mansion, get him on his helicopter, fly to the yacht where the women were being held and rescue them." He smiled. "Kalugal compelled the boss to change his ways and become a philanthropist, and he's re-educating the boss's men as we speak. The killers will become do-gooders."

Annani's smile was hesitant. "I love it, provided that this boss and his men were not involved in the atrocities. People like that do not deserve a second chance."

"I agree. None of them are nice people, and they have killed plenty, but there are degrees of evil, and they didn't cross that line." He raked his fingers through his hair. "I'm not a vigilante, and it's not my job to get rid of every thug there is. I limit myself to the worst offenders."

She nodded. "I taught you well, my son."

"I wish I could take credit for this plan, but it was Turner's idea. If we killed Modana and his men, the rest of the cartel would have chased after us, and that was in addition to the Doomers. This way, they won't know what hit them. Kalugal used a combination of compulsion and thralling to convince Modana that the Madonna herself had spoken to him and his men and demanded that they change their ways. Nothing will connect Modana's religious awakening to us. Once Kalugal's done, he will erase the entire episode from their memories, and they won't even remember having Margo and her friend on board."

"That is very smart, but what about the Doomers? They might access the same surveillance cameras that Roni did and follow the breadcrumbs to Modana. They will know what caused his so-called religious awakening."

"Even if they had a capable hacker like Roni, which they don't, they wouldn't have thought to check the penthouse surveillance camera feeds, which is where Margo and Jasmine were when they were drugged and kidnapped. They would have only searched those next to Margo's room. But just in case they do get smart, Roni took care of that footage. He replaced those sections of the recordings with the nothing special footage from before and after."

His mother shook her head. "I have a feeling that we are missing something. It cannot be as easy as that."

Kian sighed. "I know. I was contemplating evacuating the ship and flying everyone home, but that would have been so disappointing for the rest of the couples who were planning a cruise wedding. We will stay in Puerto Vallarta for the night and stay on high alert, watching out for the Doomers." He smiled. "Vlad and Wendy will have their wedding tonight after all."

"I am pleased." His mother patted his hand. "Vlad did not know whether he should have his bachelor party, but his friends convinced him to have it even if the wedding was canceled. Wendy is with the girls and her mother, getting pampered just like the other brides."

"Good. I should let them know that it looks like their wedding is happening." Kian pushed to his feet. "The wedding will have to take place late at night, though. We still need to collect Margo and her friend from the yacht, along with Kalugal, Negal, and Edgar. Once we reach Puerto Vallarta, we will pick up the rest of our people." He rubbed the back of his neck. "Edgar flew Modana, Kalugal, and Negal to the yacht in Modana's helicopter. I could have asked him to fly the women over here and go back, but I don't want anything connecting us with the yacht or the helicopter. We will send a lifeboat to collect our people from the yacht, so if the Doomers or anyone else is watching the signals the vessels are broadcasting, they won't see us stopping next to one another."

Annani nodded sagely. "Very well. What time should I tell Amanda to plan Vlad and Wendy's wedding?"

"Ten-thirty should be fine."

65

NEGAL

Negal spent the rest of dinner in silence, pretending to listen to the others gushing over the wonders of Perfect Match. It was old technology on Anumati, and every interstellar ship was equipped with several chambers that were used for training as well as for entertainment.

No special helmets or wiring were required, and it was as simple as choosing a scenario and walking through a door.

He had done hundreds of those if not thousands, and if these people needed ideas for new adventures, he could provide them with plenty. The problem was that they would have no reference for the different worlds and creatures that he had seen firsthand and then experienced virtually.

Casting a sidelong glance at Margo, he wondered if she would have been brave enough to join him on those adventures. She was brave, as evidenced by her jumping in to help a woman she had just met. But on the other hand, she was reserved, almost shy around him, especially as the drugs she'd been injected with against her will were wearing off.

Negal missed those first moments of their interaction when she'd seemed so uninhibited, so free with her admiration and her attraction to him. But now, she was pulling back and retracting into herself, as if she was inexperienced with males or even fearful.

Perhaps her experience on the yacht had been more difficult than what she and Jasmine had admitted to?

What if those scumbags that Kalugal had attempted to turn into decent people had done bad things to the women?

Across the table, Kalugal cleared his throat quite loudly, drawing Negal's attention. "As I was saying just a few moments ago, it's important to stay calm and not let strong emotions hijack your mind." He stared pointedly at Negal.

Finally, he got the hint and closed his eyes, which were probably glowing. "Excuse me." He pushed away from the table. "I need to use the bathroom again."

"What's the matter?" Margo asked. "Are your contact lenses bothering you? Do you need me to help you get to the bathroom without bumping into anything?"

Kalugal chuckled. "I told Negal that he shouldn't wear them today, but he didn't listen."

The guy was such a resourceful liar.

Negal didn't dare open his eyes, so he had to accept Margo's help. Hopefully, she wouldn't insist on coming into the bathroom with him.

"Thank you for the offer, Margo. It's very kind of you."

"It's the least I can do for the man who leaped to catch me when I fainted and then carried me across the boat like a princess."

He heard her push her chair back, and then her hand clasped his, and his throat went dry.

What the hell was that reaction?

He'd held her in his arms for long moments, and she had put her head on his chest. Their breath intermingled. Why was the touch of her hand making him lose his composure?

"Come on, big guy." She tugged on his hand. "I've had my share of torment with contact lenses, and eventually, I gave up on them. I just use glasses for reading. You should do the same. You are so incredibly good-looking that glasses aren't going to take away from your attractiveness."

A smile tugged on the corner of his lips. "You think that I'm good-looking?"

She snorted. "I might be nearsighted, but I'm not blind." She leaned closer to him, her cheek grazing his forearm. "Did you and Kevin have plastic surgery?"

Gabi had asked Aru the same thing, so maybe he should just say that he had? But he didn't want to lie to Margo more than he already had. "No. I'm just fortunate to have been made with very good genes."

In his home world, they were nothing special, average genes that most commoners were given, but on Earth, they were superior.

"There is no shame in admitting that you had work done. Many men do that these days." She stopped next to the bathroom. "It's a competitive world, and everyone is trying to get a leg up." She opened the door. "Do you need me to help you in there?"

He looked at her from under lowered lashes, admiring the way the light from the windows made her hair look golden. "No, thank you. I'll be fine. I'll just take them out."

"Throw them away." She patted his arm. "I'll be outside the door if you need me."

"Thank you." Negal walked into the bathroom and gently closed the door behind him.

When he looked in the mirror, his eyes were still glowing, but not so intensely that the glow couldn't be explained away as a reflection from misty eyes.

He had sunglasses in his pocket but wearing them inside would be weird. Then again, he could say that the contact lenses irritated his eyes, and that's why he needed to shield them.

Splashing his face with cold water for the second time in less than an hour, he took a few deep breaths, dried his face with a towel, and pulled his sunglasses out.

When he exited the bathroom, he found Margo leaning against the wall right next to the door, just as she had promised.

"Sunglasses?" she asked.

"I know it looks strange, but my eyes are so irritated that even a little bit of direct light is painful."

"My poor hero." She took his hand again. "What did you do with the contact lenses?"

"I threw them away as you suggested."

"Good. Do you have more on the ship?"

He didn't know how to answer that. Did people usually have more than one pair?

"I'll have to check," he hedged. "I might have forgotten to pack the spare pair."

She regarded him with a frown and then shook her head. "Let's get back to the table. The chef is probably serving coffee and dessert."

"Hold on." He tugged on her hand to keep her from walking away. "I hate to do this, but I have to know whether anyone did anything inappropriate to you or to Jasmine."

"You mean other than slip us roofies and then inject us with God knows what?"

Nodding, he let go of her hand. "You know what I mean. Please, don't feel embarrassed about telling me. I just need to know."

Margo let out a breath. "The only one who interacted with us was Alberto, and as far as I know, he didn't touch me that way. But I was out of it for hours, so I don't know that for sure, but I don't think so. He might have taken a peek at my assets, and he jabbed me with a needle, but not with anything else if you know what I mean. I believe that I would have known if he, you know, did that."

66

MARGO

Negal looked confused, as if he wasn't sure what she was implying. Was it a language barrier?

His English was perfect, including a general American accent that wasn't regional, but he'd said something about being from Portugal, so maybe English wasn't his native language, and he didn't get some of the phrases and idioms.

It was either that or he was naive, but that couldn't be the case. The guy looked to be in his late twenties or early thirties, was as gorgeous as a god, and moved like one, too. There was no way he was inexperienced.

He was also very clearly attracted to her, so it wasn't like he didn't know what she'd been talking about.

"So, no one touched you sexually," he said. "You are sure of that?"

"Yes." She smiled and took his hand. "Let's go, or the others will think that we are doing something inappropriate."

He didn't need her to lead him back to the table, but it felt good to hold his hand, and she wanted more of the contact.

"What do you mean?"

She shook her head. "Never mind."

It must have been a language thing.

He looked down at where their hands were conjoined and then back up at her, but his eyes were hidden behind the dark sunglasses, so she didn't know what he was thinking.

Maybe it was not something he was comfortable with?

"I'm sorry." She let go of his hand.

"No, don't be." He reached for her hand and clasped it. "I like it. It's just that I don't know the local customs all that well, so I'm not sure if it's common for strangers to hold hands."

"We are not strangers." She started walking to hide her embarrassment. "You saved me, and I'm grateful. That's how I show my gratitude."

That was such a load of baloney, but if he really wasn't familiar with American culture, he might take her word for it.

"It's nice," he said.

"You sound so American. Are you really from Portugal?"

"I've lived there for a while, but I also travel a lot. My friends and I are flea market bargain hunters."

"No way." She stopped and looked up at him. "How does a bargain hunter become a cartel mob buster?"

"I was a soldier back in the day." He resumed walking.

That explained so much.

He could be from a military family that had traveled all over the world, and then he had become a soldier himself. Negal's English was good, and he sounded like a native because it was his first language, but because he had traveled and lived all over, he hadn't learned all of its nuances.

"Were you homeschooled?" she asked when they entered the dining room.

Frowning, Negal pulled out a chair for her. "I don't know what that means."

"Your mother teaching you to read and write," Kevin said. "I was homeschooled. First by my mother and then by tutors."

There was a buzzing sound and Kevin pulled out his phone. "Oh, good. We should get ready. Our pickup is on its way."

"What pickup?" Jasmine asked. "I thought we were leaving in the helicopter."

"A lifeboat was sent for us from the cruise ship, and it's going to be here in twenty minutes." He looked at Margo. "Is there anything you need to pack?"

"All Alberto brought was my purse and my phone wasn't in it. That was the first thing I checked when I came to on the boat. The rest of my stuff is still at the hotel." It suddenly dawned on her that Lynda was probably worried sick about her. "Oh my God, I need to call my sister-in-law and tell her that I'm okay. She probably has the entire family in an uproar. Can I use one of your phones?"

Kevin shook his head. "I'm sorry, Margo. Just for now, we need to keep a low profile. There is more going on than just the cartel, and we can't let anyone know that we have you."

She turned to Negal, who she had a feeling was the weakest link in the chain and easier to sway. "What's going on, Negal? What are you guys not telling us?"

He swallowed, looking like he wanted to be anywhere but there. "It's complicated. Kalugal is the boss, so you should ask him."

"Who is Kalugal?"

Kevin cleared his throat. "That's me, but you have to keep calling me Kevin for now." He turned to look at Jasmine. "Same goes for you. Call me Kevin."

"Yes, sir." Jasmine saluted him.

Now that Margo knew what to listen for, she'd heard the hypnotic tone and realized how it affected her. She and Jasmine were lucky that he was one of the good guys. Kevin didn't need drugs to make them compliant. All he needed to do was to say the words, and they would obey.

Margo shivered. What if all she'd been told by Mia and Frankie had been lies? This guy could have made them say anything he wanted.

She narrowed her eyes at him. "I have to let my family know that I'm okay, and you didn't give me a reason why I shouldn't do that. You have the cartel boss, and all of his men hypnotized to believe that the Virgin Mary revealed herself to him and commanded him to be good. Who else could be interested in me and whether I've been found, other than my family?"

He let out an exasperated breath. "Can you hold off your questions until we are on the ship? Everything will become clear once you talk to Mia and Frankie."

Yeah, right. Unless he had them and everyone else on that ship under his spell.

"Can I call either of them? Because I'm starting to think that maybe I shouldn't trust you."

If he readily agreed, then she would know that she couldn't trust her friends' words.

"They can't tell you anything over the phone. Besides, we don't have time for that." He rose to his feet. "We need to get ready for the lifeboat. Let's collect your purses and get out of here."

67

NEGAL

As the women left to collect their purses, Kalugal regarded Negal with a raised brow and amusement in his eyes. "What's going on with you?"

"What do you mean?"

"I mean the flashing of fangs and glowing eyes. You need to better control your reactions. These women have been drugged and thralling them while they are experiencing withdrawal might be harmful. I would hate to have to do that to them on top of everything else they have been through."

"You're right." Negal rubbed a hand over the back of his neck. "I'm usually very good at this. It's considered bad form on Anumati to reveal strong emotions, and we are trained from a young age to control our fangs and glowing eyes. But every time I imagine what could have been done to Margo and Jasmine, I get so consumed by rage that I lose hold of my responses."

Kalugal tilted his head. "Do you have a sister?"

"No, why?"

Kalugal shrugged. "I often wonder about Kian's overprotectiveness for females, and I think it stems from him having sisters. Don't get me wrong, it's our duty and privilege to protect the females in our lives and our communities, but Kian often crosses the line by stifling their right to choose. The clan has a very capable female Guardian, but Kian refuses to allow her to participate in missions against Doomers because they are known for their lack of honor, to put it in gentle terms."

Negal scoffed. "You don't need to use gentle terms with me, Kalugal. I've been a soldier for much longer than you have been alive, and I know what you refer to. Regrettably and shamefully, some of the Anumati colonies have succumbed to lawlessness, and females were the first to suffer when they lost the equalizing benefit of culture and technology when brute force became law."

Kalugal tilted his head. "I thought that gods revered females."

Negal let out a breath. "There are deviants in every society, and some manage to convert the weak-minded to their philosophy. From there, it doesn't take long for a few thugs to destroy thousands of years of progress and turn the entire place into a hellhole."

"I know what you mean." Kalugal shifted his weight to his other leg. "My own grandfather was such a deviant god. He abhorred the matrilineal tradition of the gods, and he wanted females to be deprived of all rights. In his insanity, he obliterated nearly all of the gods and plunged humanity into darkness. And don't start me on humans, but that's too lengthy a conversation for now. We should have it over whiskey and cigars when we are not pressed for time."

Negal dipped his head. "Gladly. I'm honored by the invitation."

Kalugal smirked. "Given that I don't have my own cigars, we will have to include Kian, but I'm sure he would enjoy a philosophical and historical discussion. In fact, we should include him regardless of the cigars, or he will think that I'm trying to pump you for information." He leaned toward Negal. "Which I totally am. I'm very curious about those colonies, the law-abiding and the lawless, but I don't mind Kian hearing about it, too." He frowned. "I hope it will be okay with your boss."

"I don't see why not. Aru would most likely love to join."

"Excellent." Kalugal clapped him on the back. "If my former brethren leave us alone, and we are not under attack tomorrow, I will organize a get-together in my cabin."

"Thank you. I would also love to hear about how you escaped the Brotherhood and what motivated you to do so."

"Oh, yes." Kalugal's eyes clouded over. "That's not nearly as interesting as your tale." He turned toward the staircase. "I should check on Modana and his men before we leave."

Talking with Kalugal had an oddly calming effect on Negal. Or maybe it was the fact that Margo wasn't near. He was different around her, and he didn't like that mindless version of himself.

It could be the protector in him that had surged to the surface because of the potential crimes that might have been perpetrated against Margo and Jasmine. It was hardwired into every male god to treat females with the utmost respect and never assume their favors, but even gods sometimes deviated from their genetic programming because not everything could be determined genetically. Free will existed, and fortuitous accidents happened, for better and for worse.

The other thing that could be responsible for this psychosis was the thought that Frankie had planted in his mind about Margo being his fated mate. Logically he knew it wasn't true, but a small part of his heart, a remnant from his youth, hoped that she was right and that he could have his happily ever after like Aru and Dagor.

It was just the placebo effect.

Margo was pretty but not exceptional, and the fierceness he'd seen in her photo was not as evident in person. He'd caught glimpses of it, but it was by no means as potent as he'd imagined.

Still, he couldn't ignore the fact that he wasn't attracted to Jasmine, who was as beautiful as any of the immortal females and could even rival some of the commoner goddesses, especially since her type of beauty was unusual on Anumati. Normally, he would have zeroed in on a stunning beauty like her, and the fact that he hadn't was significant.

Taking one last look at the opulent dining room, with its glass-top table, white leather chairs, and a chandelier that looked like a glass sculpture, Negal turned on his heel and headed toward the staircase. He was glad to leave the symbol of wealth purchased with blood money, but he wasn't sure he was glad to return to the cruise ship. To preserve his sanity, he might be better off renewing his trek through Tibet on his own.

68

MARGO

When Margo and Jasmine entered the cabin, Jaz walked over to the bed and sat down. "I miss the rush of euphoria. I've never felt so good in my life." She sighed. "It's going to be rough, you know. Have you ever seen anyone withdrawing from heroin? It's brutal."

"How do you know it was heroin?" Margo collected her purse and checked that everything was there.

Jasmine shrugged. "I don't, but what else would he use? I had a friend who got addicted, and she went through hell trying to quit."

"We will get through this together." Margo walked over to her and offered her a hand up. "We should tell Kevin to search Alberto's pockets and his cabin for your passport and credit cards."

Jasmine's eyes widened. "Of course. Why didn't I think of that? If I can get my stuff back, I can book a flight from Puerto Vallarta back home, and I don't need to hitch a ride on your cruise ship."

Margo should have been happy to get rid of the competition, but she wasn't. She'd grown attached to Jasmine, and she didn't want her to go. "Are you in such a rush to get rid of me?"

"Of course not." Jasmine wrapped her arm around Margo's middle. "You are my best friend." She leaned her head on Margo's shoulder, which couldn't be comfortable because she was half a head taller. "You have your besties waiting for you on board the cruise ship, and I know that I'm going to be jealous because you will no longer be mine."

It was probably the drugs talking because they hadn't known each other long enough to become best friends, but Margo was touched, nonetheless.

"Oh, Jaz." She patted Jasmine's head. "I will always be your friend. You can be the fourth member of our group."

Jaz lifted a pair of hopeful puppy eyes at her. "Do you mean it?"

"Of course. Imagine how much fun we are going to have when we are not being drugged by Alberto the scumbag or about to be sexually assaulted by vile cartel bosses."

A shiver rocked Jasmine's body. "It's just now starting to sink in. I didn't have much of a life to leave behind, but it was infinitely better than what was waiting for me with Modana. In a way, I'm grateful for the drugs. This would have been harrowing without them."

Margo had a feeling that Jasmine was starting to crash after the high.

She was feeling some of that, too, but it hadn't hit her as hard yet. It just felt like a low after a high, kind of like the way she felt before and after attending her favorite rock group's concerts.

Maybe that was why she'd been so taken by the pretty-faced guy. She had been still riding the high, and now that she was starting to come down, Negal would no longer look as beautiful and angelic to her.

When they got to the top deck, Negal had his back to them, and as he turned to look at her, Margo was proven wrong. It felt like being hit in the chest. He was even more stunning than she'd remembered.

"Looks aren't everything," she murmured under her breath as she and Jasmine walked toward their rescuers.

"Where is Alberto?" Jasmine asked Kevin.

The hypnotist frowned. "Why do you want to know?"

"He has my passport, my driver's license, and my credit cards. I bet he brought them with him. Can you use your hypnosis on him to give them back?"

"Of course. Give me a moment." Kevin trotted down the stairs.

"Where is he keeping the men?" Margo asked Negal.

"The grand salon. They won't move from there until he okays it."

"How is he going to do that after we are gone?"

Negal shrugged. "I don't know, and I don't care." He pointed at the boat heading their way. "Our transport is here."

"Awesome." Margo lifted her hand to shield her eyes. "Where is the ship?"

"Beyond the horizon."

"That far away?" Jasmine asked.

"For a ship to be beyond the horizon, it needs to be only about three miles away. That's not so far."

"Oh, I didn't know that." Jasmine smiled in that coquettish way of hers. "I feel so stupid."

"Stop saying that," Margo snapped. "You are not stupid. I didn't know that either."

As the boat came alongside the idling yacht, one of the guys inside stood and pointed at the ladder. "Who wants to go first?"

"I'll go," Edgar volunteered.

He made it down the ladder in seconds and made it look so easy that Margo offered to go next.

As she carefully made her way down, the guy in the lifeboat put his hands on her hips to help her jump the last couple of feet, and she thought that she heard Negal growl, but she must have imagined it.

When he made it to the lifeboat, though, he glared at the guy, and she thought that maybe she'd heard it right.

"Got it!" Kevin waved a passport from the railing. "I have your other stuff, too."

"Thank you," Jasmine called back.

He made his way into the boat with the same agility as his two companions, and when everyone was seated, one of the guys who came with the boat pushed it away from the yacht while the other revved the engine.

As the lifeboat sped away, Margo watched the yacht getting smaller and smaller the farther away from it they got, and a knot of tension that had been hiding deep inside of her loosened.

This part of her so-called adventure was over, and a new chapter was beginning. The question was whether it would be a love story or a drama.

ECLIPSE OF THE HEART

1

NEGAL

The phrase 'fish out of water' had never resonated with Negal as strongly as it did while sitting next to Margo. There was plenty of space on the rescue boat bench, but she'd shifted closer to him until their thighs were almost touching, and it was making him uncomfortable.

Perhaps she found his proximity reassuring?

After all, he'd rescued Margo and her friend Jasmine from a terrible fate, even if his role had been auxiliary. Kalugal had done the heavy lifting with his compulsion ability, commanding the cartel thugs to drop their weapons and go to their knees, but Negal had been the one who caught Margo when she fainted, so in her mind, he was her savior.

Regrettably, though, that seemed to be the only reason she sought his nearness. Margo wasn't trying to flirt with him. Of that, he was sure. He would have scented her desire if she had been interested in him in that way.

These were new and uncharted waters for him.

Since arriving on Earth, Negal had never encountered a situation where he was attracted to a female who wasn't attracted to him. His perfect, genetically engineered physique made sure of that. He'd also never had a problem speaking to women before. Flirting came naturally to him, but with Margo, it wasn't that simple.

Why was he so tongue-tied around her?

Perhaps losing control over his fangs and glowing eyes twice in her presence had eroded his confidence, or maybe it was because her initial awed response to his godly looks had diminished along with the influence of the drugs she'd been given against her will.

Or maybe it was the odd in-between situation he found himself in, needing to pretend to be human only until they got to the cruise ship and then waiting to drop the pretense until after Margo's friends broke the news to her about what was really going on.

For the past five years, Negal had been pretending to be human with women he was seducing, and he'd learned how to do that quite well. He could shoot the breeze with the best of them, talking about music, films, or even politics if the woman was so inclined. Other times, he would just let the lady talk, compliment her a few times, and, as soon as she was ready, lead her to the nearest bed or even a darkened corner.

Some females enjoyed a little thrill to enhance their pleasure, which Negal always found ironic, given who he was. For a human, it didn't get any more thrilling than an interlude with a god, and not just because he was an immortal alien with tremendous mind-manipulating powers. The pleasure he delivered couldn't be matched by a human lover.

It wasn't boasting. It was physiology.

Immortals probably provided a similar experience, but that was because they were descendants of the gods and had the fangs and venom that did the heavy lifting where the female's pleasure was concerned.

Margo would soon discover that the cruise ship she was boarding wasn't a Perfect Match company retreat and that the majority of its passengers were immortals. She would also learn that her two best friends were mated to gods and that he was a god as well.

How would she react to the news?

Would she freak out?

Would she run away from him once she discovered who he was, or would she want him because he was a god?

Negal dreaded both scenarios. He didn't want Margo to fear him because he wasn't human or reject him for the same reason, and he also didn't want her to be enamored with the idea that he was a god and pursue him for that reason. He wanted her to like him for who he was as a person and not because of his superior godly genes.

In either case, though, he wouldn't have to pretend to be human for much longer. In fact, he could tell her right now if he wanted, but she might not believe him or she might believe him and be frightened by it. It would be better if she found out about gods and immortals from her friends.

The bottom line was that he would have preferred for the lifeboat to go faster so he would have an excuse to remain silent because talking over the noise was difficult. Instead, the slow speed lent itself to pleasant conversation.

Thank the merciful Fates for Kalugal and his penchant for inspired storytelling because the Guardian piloting the small lifeboat didn't seem in a rush to get back to the ship. The immortal's motive was probably to make the journey more pleasant for the two human women he was transporting, but that meant prolonging Negal's torment.

As it was, Kalugal was keeping Jasmine and Margo entertained by telling them a modified version of how the cartel boss's mansion had been overtaken without a single shot fired or one drop of blood spilled. Naturally, Kalugal had taken the credit for it, which was his due, but he could have given some recognition to the Guardians and gods who had gotten him to where he'd needed to be to wield his compulsion ability.

"How did you become such a powerful hypnotist?" Jasmine asked. "Is there a special school for that?"

"It's a natural ability for me," Kalugal said. "I discovered at a young age that I could influence people, and I practiced the ability until I became very good at it."

That was an excellent answer because Kalugal hadn't lied. He hadn't told the whole truth either, but if either of the women confronted him after discovering that he was an immortal with special paranormal talents, they couldn't accuse him of lying.

"Is that what you've been doing on the Perfect Match ship?" Margo asked. "Entertaining the guests with hypnotic demonstrations?"

Kalugal laughed. "I'm just a guest on this cruise, and I don't perform for a crowd. I use my special skills in other ways."

Margo frowned. "Like what?"

A mischievous smirk lifted one corner of Kalugal's mouth. "Making a killing on the stock market."

Margo gasped. "Are you serious? What do you do? Lurk at cafés near Wall Street and hypnotize people to give you insider trading information?"

Negal expected Kalugal to deny that, but the guy surprised him by nodding.

"That's how I made my seed money. Later, I became an investor, specializing in innovative technologies, and I no longer use my ability that way."

"Ah, now I get it." Margo gave him a smile. "You invested in Perfect Match Virtual Studios. That's why you were invited onto their company cruise."

Kalugal sighed dramatically. "Regrettably, I didn't get the opportunity to invest in this tech. My cousin beat me to it and bought the company from the founders. I'm on this cruise just as a family member of the owners, not an investor."

"I see." Margo shifted on the bench, her thigh momentarily brushing Negal's and sending sparks of arousal through him. "Can you tell me a little about your cousin? The only thing Mia told me about him and his wife was that they were very rich and very reclusive."

"They are," Kalugal confirmed. "My cousin is a good guy, and his wife is a sweetheart. In fact, she was the one who convinced him to purchase a controlling interest in the company. Later, my uncle bought the remaining stock." He smiled. "It's all in the family now, but I wasn't invited to join." He pouted. "I would be lying if I said that I wasn't seriously peeved. The technology behind Perfect Match is revolutionary, and it has tremendous growth potential."

"It can also be dangerous," Negal said. "If humans are not careful with it, they might get addicted to the enhanced experiences in the virtual reality world and stop functioning in the real one."

Jasmine arched a brow. "Humans?"

Cursing inwardly, Negal waved a dismissive hand. "I meant people. There was talk about testing how animals respond to virtual reality and whether it would work on them."

It was such a lame save that he doubted it would fly. Obviously, he didn't have Kalugal's talent for spinning tales without actually lying.

Across from him Kalugal was trying hard not to laugh, but thankfully, Jasmine and Margo's attention was on Negal.

"That's absurd." Jasmine crossed her arms over her chest. "Do they even know what dogs think or dream about?"

"They don't." Kalugal came to his rescue. "That's why that idea was dead on arrival. Perhaps in the future, they will find a way to engage animals in the simulations, but for now, all the animals inside the virtual world are animated by the program's artificial intelligence."

"Do they have dragons?" Jasmine asked.

Kalugal shrugged. "I'm not familiar with all the available scenarios, but I'm sure you could request a dragon adventure if that is what tickles your fancy. There is plenty of room for customization."

2

MARGO

Dragon shifters were among Margo's favorite romance heroes, but there was no way she was going to say that in front of Negal. The guy seemed to think that virtual reality was dangerous, so he might sneer at her choice of fantasy book boyfriends.

Negal was nice, chivalrous, even sweet, but he was also a strange dude who didn't talk much and was difficult to read. Maybe he was just the strong, silent type, which was a polite way to describe boring men.

Margo used to think that she was good at reading people, but after her experience with Alberto, she wasn't so sure anymore. Evidently, she was a sucker for charm and as easy to manipulate as Jasmine had been.

She wished she could blame whatever the thug had put in the wine for addling her brain, but long before he'd slipped her and Jasmine the roofie he'd put in that second bottle, he'd somehow managed to convince her that he genuinely cared for Jasmine, and for some inexplicable reason, Margo had ignored all the warning signs and alarm bells going off in her head.

Come to think of it, plenty of warnings had gone through her mind about Jasmine as well, and she had ignored them because, for an equally inexplicable reason, she liked her and wanted to be friends with her.

It was peculiar how at ease Jasmine seemed with their rescuers. She didn't seem traumatized by what she had gone through, and she no longer looked drugged either. The only indication that she had been through anything was a rumpled dress and slight smudges of makeup under her big brown eyes.

Jaz also didn't seem nervous or intimidated by the rescue team's unnaturally good looks, chatting with them like they were old friends. But then Jasmine was a beautiful lady herself, so there was that. Margo couldn't complain about the gifts nature had bestowed on her, but next to Jasmine, she felt like one of Cinderella's ugly sisters.

"What do you think, Margo?" Jasmine asked.

She hadn't been listening.

"About what?"

"A dragon Perfect Match adventure. It's a good idea, right?"

"Last I checked, they had three of them. In one, you can be a dragon shifter or the dragon shifter's mate. In another, you can be a dragon rider, and in yet another, you can be a dragon slayer or the dragon slayer's mate."

She couldn't wait to try the first, but not the third. Margo liked to think of dragons as magical creatures who were intelligent and could communicate their thoughts to humans. She didn't want to think of them as monsters.

"You seem to know a lot about Perfect Match adventures," Negal said. "Have you participated in any?"

She chuckled. "I can't afford them on what I make, but once I become a beta tester, I hope to try as many as I can. Just not the dragon slayer one."

A smile lifted his perfectly shaped lips. "Not even if the dragons are killing people, eating entire flocks of sheep, and destroying crops? Don't they deserve slaying?"

That sounded like a typical epic fantasy scenario, so maybe the guy was a reader, and there was still hope for him. He wasn't a complete bore.

Margo tilted her head. "You also seem to know a lot about dragons. Are you a fantasy reader?"

Negal winced as if her question made him uncomfortable, and he averted his gaze. "I've seen a few movies."

"Which ones? I've probably seen every dragon movie ever made."

He swallowed. "I don't remember the titles."

"What were they about? If you tell me even a little bit, I can probably recognize which one it is and tell you the title."

"*Raya and the Last Dragon,*" Jasmine said. "It was a cute movie. Also, *How to Train Your Dragon*."

There was still no response from Negal.

Had he lied about watching dragon movies? Why would he?

"*Dragonheart,*" said the guy piloting the ship. "Corny as hell, but I liked the dragon."

"There is nothing to like about them," Negal sneered. "They are mindless beasts and a menace."

He was talking about dragons as if they were real. The guy was so weird.

"Oh, well." Kevin sighed loudly. "Flying lizards seem to be a point of contention, so let's change the subject." He turned to Jasmine. "What kind of virtual adventure would you like to try out?"

"I don't know what's available. I really liked Sisu, the shifter dragon in *Raya*, so if they have anything like that, I would love to be her. I like fairytales in general, so I would also enjoy *Sleeping Beauty* or *Cinderella*."

Margo snorted. "Funny that you should say that. You're the last person to identify with Cinderella unless you've already met the fairy godmother, and she gave you those looks for keeps."

What was really funny was that Margo had just been thinking about feeling like one of the wicked stepsisters.

Jasmine's eyes clouded. "You'd be surprised how much I identify with her. Only in real life, I have two evil stepbrothers instead of two wicked stepsisters."

Now Margo felt like an ass. Being beautiful didn't necessarily mean having a charmed life, and she should know that better than most. Not that she was in Jasmine's league, but she'd experienced the darker side of being considered attractive.

There were many advantages to having pleasing looks, but for women and girls, it also meant being more alluring to predators.

"When you talked about your parents, I assumed that they were together," Margo said as gently as she could. "You didn't mention them being divorced."

Jasmine shrugged, but there was pain in her eyes. "My mother died when I was five, my father married a divorced woman with two sons, and they made my life miserable because they blamed my father for their parents' divorce."

"I'm so sorry." Margo put her hand on Jasmine's. "It must have been tough."

She wanted to find out more, but it was obvious that it pained Jasmine to talk about it. They were going to spend several days together on the cruise, and if Jaz felt like telling her more, she would.

Jasmine pushed a strand of dark hair behind her ear. "My stepmother was nice to me until the wedding, so my father thought that he'd found a great substitute mother for me, but she was only nice when my father was around. She wasn't really mean when he wasn't, and she didn't abuse me, but she was resentful and treated me like a nuisance." Jaz let out a breath. "She was jealous of my father's love for me." She gave Margo a tight smile. "But I'm all grown up now, and things are better between us when we don't have to see each other too often."

"What about your stepbrothers?" Edgar asked.

"They are still assholes, but thankfully, I only have to see them once a year."

It made sense now why Jasmine had said that she didn't have much of a life to leave behind. At the time, Margo had wondered about it because she assumed that a beauty like Jasmine had to lead a glamorous life with a ton of friends, but apparently, that wasn't the case.

Most people wanted to project a confident and happy façade for the world to see, but underneath, many were carrying pain, insecurities, grief, or a combination of all three, and Jasmine was no different.

Casting Negal a sidelong glance, Margo wondered what he was hiding under his perfect exterior and stoic expression.

So far, she'd learned three things about him, or was it four?

He had been a soldier at some point in his life, he needed corrective lenses but contact lenses irritated his eyes, so he had to wear dark sunglasses, and he hated dragons.

He also saved damsels in distress in his spare time.

3

KIAN

Toven rose to his feet and stretched his back. "If you don't need me, I would like to catch a couple of hours of shuteye." He looked at Kian.

None of them had gotten any sleep, wanting to stay awake until the mission was completed and Margo and her friend were safe and sound on board the *Silver Swan.*

The god had been needed mostly as a safety measure in case the ship was attacked and they needed his compulsion ability to defend it, but now that most of the Guardians who had raided Modana's compound were back and Kalugal was only minutes away, there was no reason for him to stay awake.

"Thank you for your help," Kian said.

Toven chuckled. "I didn't do much other than stay awake and keep you guys company."

"Having you on standby in case of an attack was what we needed, and I'm grateful for your presence aboard the ship." Kian stood up and offered Toven his hand. "Frankly, since you and Kalugal joined the clan, things have been much easier for us. I didn't realize how useful compulsion could be until it was readily available to us."

Toven cast him an amused glance as he shook his hand. "You had it all along but didn't want to use it. Annani is just as capable a compeller as I am, and probably more so."

Kian grimaced. "She doesn't like using compulsion, so she doesn't have the years of practice required to wield it with the same precision that you and

Kalugal do. Besides, she didn't use to spend much time in the village. In fact, her visits have been quite rare, and she's never stayed for long, so she wasn't always available when I needed a capable compeller."

Kian blamed himself for that. His good intentions had kept his mother away. He'd been so worried about her safety that he had tried to stifle her freedom, and she wouldn't stand for it. Lately, though, she had been much less inclined to get into mischief, and it was probably because she'd lost Alena as her reluctant partner in crime.

For some time now Annani had seemed down, subdued, giving Kian a new reason to worry, but then Aru had arrived with tales of Anumati and her grandparents, and suddenly, there was a new spark in Annani's eyes.

The threat of his great-grandfather, the Eternal King, was worrisome in the extreme and certainly no reason for an improved mood. However, Annani was excited about communicating with her grandmother, who, according to Aru, was overjoyed to discover that her granddaughter had survived.

Hopefully, the report was true, and the queen of Anumati would become a positive force in Annani's life, but that still remained to be seen.

Toven smiled benevolently. "And yet, despite Annani being here on the ship, with all of her considerable power, you prefer me to defend your clan. I don't want to be the one to point it out, but you are a bit of a chauvinist, Kian."

"I've been called worse, and if that means keeping the Clan Mother safe, then it's fine with me. I won't apologize for it."

Toven put a hand on his shoulder and gave it a gentle squeeze. "You're a good male, Kian, even if you are a chauvinist." The god laughed on his way to the bedroom.

"Do you want us to leave?" Kian called after him.

It hadn't bothered Mia that they had turned her and Toven's cabin into their war room, and she'd gone to sleep knowing that they were all there, but it would be awkward to remain in the living room of their cabin while both Toven and Mia slept in the bedroom.

Toven waved a dismissive hand. "You can stay."

When the door closed behind him, Kian sat back down and looked at Turner. "You should get some sleep as well."

"I'm okay." The strategist lifted his half-empty mug of coffee. "I want to talk to Kalugal and hear from him how Modana and his men are doing. As inspired as the idea of a religious revelation and awakening was, I need to know how well it will hold. Unless Kalugal had some seeds to work with, the compulsion could lose its power pretty quickly."

"Kalugal told me that Modana had a statue of the Madonna on his desk, so he must be a believer, and Kalugal knows what he's doing. He wouldn't have used that tactic if he thought it wouldn't work."

Turner's brows lifted to indicate his skepticism. "Modana is a cartel boss. He didn't become one by being morally gray. He's as black as they come. Suddenly leaving a life of crime and brutality behind to do good will look suspicious to everyone whom Kalugal didn't compel, and I'm mostly worried about the brother." Turner glanced at his yellow pad. "Carlos is rumored to be even more ruthless than Julio, and we might have to arrange an accident for him if we want the rest of the plan to work."

"I don't have a problem with one less evildoer in the world." Kian leaned back in his chair. "Except that Carlos is currently in Cabo, maybe even dealing with the Doomers, and I have no intention of going there. We will stop at Ensenada or some other port, and then we will continue to Long Beach." He turned to look at Roni. "How is the naval hacking going?"

"It's a bitch," Roni grumbled. "I had to ask for help, and I hate doing that."

Kian felt the blood drain from his face. "What do you mean? Who did you ask?"

"Relax." The kid waved a hand in dismissal. "The guy who's helping me needs to stay under the radar even more than we do, but he has experience with naval systems, and since you needed this done expeditiously, that was the only way I could do it." He lifted his head and trained a pair of tired eyes on Kian. "I'm one of the best there is, but it would have taken me days or even weeks to crack that encryption. Scorpion has already done it."

"Scorpion?" Turner chuckled. "Is that his code name?"

It seemed that the strategist wasn't concerned about the involvement of the other hacker, so Kian let out a breath and tried to relax.

They needed the record of the ship's sailing plan altered and all the changes they had made in their itinerary erased. Once it was done, it would appear as if the *Silver Swan* had never intended to arrive at Cabo San Lucas, and after leaving Acapulco, Puerto Vallarta had always been its destination.

"What's wrong with Scorpion?" Roni sounded offended on the other hacker's behalf. "It's a great code name."

"It's a cliché," Turner said. "What's yours? The Black Widow?"

"No." Roni smirked. "Guess again."

"Just tell him," Kian said. "We are too tired to play this game, and you are busy."

"I'm the Blue Badger," Roni said as if he was issuing a challenge.

Turner pursed his lips and nodded his approval. "I like it. At least it's original, and it fits you."

4

NEGAL

When the *Silver Swan* became visible in the distance, gleaming under the afternoon sun, Negal released a relieved breath as if he were coming home.

"Finally. There she is," he said, more to himself than to his companions, but it got their attention. Their conversation halted, replaced by an air of anticipation.

For Margo, it was no doubt about reuniting with her friends.

Mia would probably be waiting for her, maybe accompanied by Toven if he was free. Frankie was most likely still in the clinic, but Negal wouldn't be surprised if she'd managed to convince the doctor to let her go so she could greet her friend.

Looking at Jasmine, it was hard to tell what she was thinking as she watched the ship with wide-eyed anticipation, but the others were probably happy to be back so they could get a proper meal, rest, and prepare for tonight's festivities.

Negal was just glad to finally get away from Margo's disturbing presence and have time to relax and decompress before he had to see her again at the wedding, which reminded him that he'd promised Gertrude to be her companion for the party tonight.

If Margo attended, he would be disturbed and distracted by her just as he was now, and he would be a lousy companion to the nurse.

Worse, Gertrude would also expect him to make good on everything else he had promised her last night and failed to deliver, and he already knew that there was no way he could do that.

It was all because of the woman sitting next to him.

Casting a sidelong glance at Margo, he saw her looking at the ship with a smile on her face.

"Excited about finally getting together with your friends?" he asked.

She turned to him. "Of course. But I've also never been on a cruise ship before. Frankie said that it was a small one, but it looks huge to me."

"It's a matter of scale and perspective. When you see it next to the big cruise ships, it will look like a small car next to a semi-trailer."

"It's the same with airplanes," Kalugal said and then proceeded to tell them about the different models and how they compared to one another.

Turned out that the guy had a private jet capable of transatlantic crossing, and Negal wondered if he would be willing to lend it to their team along with a pilot. It could make their search for the missing Kra-ell pods a little easier, but not by much. They still needed to trek on foot and interview locals about strange artifacts and unexplained disturbances to radio and cellular transmissions, so asking Kalugal for a favor was probably not needed.

They would book a commercial flight to one of the major airports and continue from there. Some of the journey could be made by jeep, but a lot of the area they needed to cover didn't even have roads and had to be traversed on foot.

How the hell did Dagor expect Frankie to do that so soon after her transition?

The reality was that she couldn't join them, and Dagor had to accept it. Thankfully, it wasn't Negal's job to break the news to him. Aru was the leader of their team, and that unpleasant task would fall to him.

Once the boat aligned with the cruise ship's lower deck, the Guardians aboard the larger vessel sprang into action, securing the smaller one with ropes to ensure its stability against the gentle sway of the waves.

As a platform extended from the gangway, serving as the transitional bridge between the boat and the ship, Negal was the first to hop on, and then he turned around and offered a hand up to Margo.

"Thank you." She put her hand in his, and given her startled reaction, she'd felt the electrical current passing between them.

He let go as soon as she was stable on her feet and offered his hand to Jasmine. This time there was no reaction, even though she gifted him with a dazzling smile.

The woman was truly beautiful, sexy, and flirty, and she also seemed like a nice person. Normally, he would have zeroed in on a female like that in a heartbeat, and by now, they would be heading to his cabin for some afternoon delight, but he found himself almost indifferent to her. He appreciated her beauty and her charm, but she didn't stir anything in him, and once again, it was all Margo's fault.

He was obsessed with her and didn't even know why.

The rest of the boat's passengers didn't need his help, so he guided the ladies inside.

As he'd expected, Mia was there with her motorized wheelchair, and next to her, Frankie was seated in a simpler, manual version with Gertrude standing behind her and holding the handles.

Damn. That wasn't good.

Negal had hoped to have more time before he needed to deal with the nurse, and the bright smile and hand wave she offered him were like a knife to his gut. He truly hated to disappoint her, but they wouldn't be spending the night together. He would be her date for the wedding, though. That part of the promise he could still deliver.

The one he hadn't expected. but wasn't surprised to see there, was the clan's sole female Guardian. Her task was probably to escort Jasmine to the lower decks, where she would stay until the ship returned to Long Beach.

There was no way Kian would allow the human to roam the ship unaccompanied.

"Frankie!" Margo rushed to her friend. "What happened? Why are you in a wheelchair?"

"I'm fine." Frankie rose to her feet and embraced her friend. "The doctor wouldn't let me come here unless I agreed to sit in a wheelchair and have the nurse take me." She turned to Gertrude. "This is my friend Margo. Margo, this is Gertrude, the ship's lovely nurse."

"Nice to meet you." Margo offered Gertrude her hand and immediately turned back to Frankie. "You still didn't tell me why you needed medical supervision in the first place."

Looking tired, Frankie sat back in the wheelchair. "It's a long story, and your new friend is waiting for you to introduce her."

"Oh, that's right." Margo turned to Jasmine. "Jaz, these are my friends Mia and Frankie. Besties, this is Jaz."

"So nice to finally meet you." Jasmine offered her hand to Mia. "I've heard a lot about you."

Mia's eyes clouded with worry. "What did you hear?"

"That you are a famous children's book author and illustrator and that you met your fiancé in a Perfect Match adventure. I would love to hear everything you can tell me about it." She laughed. "I should say whatever you are willing to tell me. From what I've heard, a lot of scrumptious naughtiness happens inside those adventures."

"Oh, my." Mia blushed prettily. "That's true. But I'll gladly share everything else. And just to clarify, I'm not even close to famous."

"You will be," Margo said. "Your illustrations are inspired. The characters pop off the pages."

Negal didn't wait for the introductions to continue. "If you'll excuse me, I'll take my leave." He smiled at Margo and Jasmine. "It was a pleasure to make your acquaintance. I'll see you both later."

He was pretty sure that he wasn't going to see Jasmine until they reached Long Beach, but he didn't need to be the one to tell her that.

"Wait," Gertrude called after him. "Are we still on for tonight?"

Looking over his shoulder, he forced a smile. "Of course." Negal turned around and kept on walking.

5

MARGO

A bolt of pain pierced through Margo's heart.

Negal and the nurse were an item?

So what if they are? I have no claim on the guy.

He hadn't even tried to flirt with her.

Negal had caught her when she'd fainted, held her in his arms, and then carried her across the yacht until they had reached the kitchen, but that didn't mean that he was interested in her, just that he was a nice guy who took his savior gig a bit too seriously.

So what if she found that adorable?

Oh, well. It was a damn shame that he was taken. She would have loved to get to know Negal a little better. Maybe there could have been something there.

With a sigh, she turned to her friends, who were both looking at her with amusement in their eyes.

"What are you two smiling about?"

Frankie lifted her eyes as if to look at Gertrude, who was standing behind her, and then batted her lashes twice. "We are so happy that you are finally here. I can't wait to show you our cabin. We have a whole suite to ourselves."

Clearly, Frankie had meant to signal that what she'd really wanted to say couldn't be said in front of the nurse, so it had to do with Negal. But whatever she was thinking, she could stop because Margo had no intention of fighting over him with another woman.

Shaking her head, Margo turned to Jasmine. "I'm sure it's not as fancy as the suite you had at the hotel, but since it comes with two awesome ladies instead of a jerk who lied to you, manipulated you, and delivered you to a cartel boss for a price, I'd say it's a huge improvement."

The tall woman with the broad shoulders who had been standing next to Mia cleared her throat. "I'm afraid that Jasmine will have to do with much less fancy accommodations." She cast Jaz an apologetic look. "I'm here to escort you to a cabin in the lower decks."

"Why?" Margo asked. "Can't Jasmine stay with Frankie and me?"

"I'm afraid not," the woman said. "Not my call, so don't blame me." She looked at Jasmine again. "The boss granted you permission to hitch a ride with us, but he wants you to stay on one of the lower decks for the duration of the trip."

Jasmine's eyes flared with panic. "Am I to be confined to quarters?"

"Not exactly." The woman rubbed a hand over the back of her neck. "We have other passengers staying in the staff quarters. You are free to use the staff dining hall and other amenities. You just can't go to the upper decks. It's a matter of security."

Looking deflated, Jasmine nodded. "I understand." She turned to Margo. "I was hoping we could have a fun time together, but I'm not complaining. Your friends saved me from a terrible fate, and if I have to stay in the staff quarters until we get back to Los Angeles, it's not a big deal."

Margo didn't know what to say or why the boss didn't want Jasmine around while he was okay with her being there. She wasn't an employee yet, and she hadn't signed any paperwork, so she was just as much of a security risk as Jasmine.

Did her friendship with Mia give her a special status?

That was most likely the reason.

After all, Mia's fiancé was part owner of the company.

"It probably has to do with Perfect Match," Margo said. "If they are discussing future plans that are supposed to stay a secret, I can understand why they don't want anyone who is not an employee to be there." She smiled apologetically at Jasmine. "I bet that I'll have to sign a nondisclosure agreement and accept an employment contract before I'm allowed to hang out with the other employees, and if I don't, I'll have to stay in the lower decks with you."

The tall woman nodded. "We are big on nondisclosures here."

"We will come with you to check out your cabin," Frankie told Jasmine. "The clinic is on the lower decks." She turned to look at the nurse. "I would hate to drag you along. Margo can push my chair, and if I faint, Mia can show her the way to the clinic."

The nurse hesitated for a moment. "Call me if you need me. You have my number."

"Will do." Frankie smiled at her.

"I can push the chair," the tall woman offered.

"What's your name?" Margo asked.

"My name is Kri."

Jasmine regarded the woman with open admiration. "Are you a security officer?"

"I'm a Guardian, which is like a security officer on steroids."

"What does the steroids part mean?" Jasmine asked. "Special clearance? Better training?"

Pushing Frankie's chair in the same direction the nurse had gone a moment ago, Kri took her time to answer. "I have Special Forces training, which means that I'm way more lethal than the average security guard."

Given the size of the woman's shoulders and the fluid way in which she moved, Margo had no doubt that Kri was as lethal as she claimed. It was probably overkill to have Special Forces' trained people serving as ship security, but she was grateful for it. "Your bosses take security very seriously. Is there a special reason for that or just general paranoia?"

Kri laughed. "Both."

That didn't say much, but Margo had a feeling that Kri was a woman of few words, and she wouldn't say more no matter how many questions were lobbed at her. Hopefully, once she was alone with Frankie and Mia, they would explain what was going on, and why the owners of Perfect Match employed a large security detail with Special Forces training.

She followed Kri and the two wheelchairs into the elevator. "You still didn't tell me what's wrong with you and why you need to be wheeled around. I hope it's not out of solidarity with Mia."

"I had a procedure done," Frankie said. "But it's not something I'm comfortable talking about right now."

Translation—not in front of Jasmine.

What the hell could it be that Frankie was embarrassed to reveal?

Oh, wait. Frankie was tiny, and she always lamented about wanting to be taller. What if she had gone through something similar to what Mia had undergone, just instead of regrowing new legs, she was elongating hers?

Nah, that made no sense. Frankie had gotten up from the chair to hug her, so she obviously hadn't had her legs operated on. She was just too weak to stand for more than a few seconds.

What else could it be, though?

Maybe a boob job? Not that Frankie needed any help in that department.

Besides, she was wearing a thin T-shirt, and Margo could clearly see the bra underneath. It wasn't one of those post-operation contraptions she'd seen online. So that wasn't it either.

Liposuction, perhaps?

Whatever, there was no point in guessing. Once they were alone, Frankie would tell her.

After all, they were besties, and they told each other everything.

6

NEGAL

As Negal entered the cabin, his hopes for a few moments of solitude were dashed. Aru and Dagor were there, both still wearing Eva's makeup and so-called disguises, with Aru straddling a barstool and Dagor holding a whiskey bottle.

"What are you two doing here?" He walked past them, heading for his bedroom.

"Waiting to hear how it went, of course," Dagor said. "Are Margo and Jasmine okay?"

Negal knew what they were really asking about. "No one touched them."

Aru let out a breath. "That's a relief. I was worried."

They all had been.

"Thank the merciful Fates." Dagor lifted the bottle. "Should we drink to that?"

Negal had a feeling that if he refused, Aru would order him to stay and submit a report.

The mission they had just been on had nothing to do with what their team had been sent to do on Earth, so technically, Aru had no authority over him in that regard, but he was still the team's leader, and Negal still answered to him.

"Why not?" Negal changed trajectory and walked over to where Aru was sitting. "I just had two glasses of wine, but I could use a real drink."

"Wine?" Aru asked.

"Yeah, on the yacht. I had dinner with Margo, Jasmine, Kalugal, and Edgar. Have you two eaten anything yet?"

Dagor grimaced. "We've just gotten back, so we haven't had a proper meal yet, but Gabi went to the kitchen to get us something to tide us over. In the meantime, Aru and I finished all the snacks in the fridge." He opened the appliance to show Negal the empty shelves. "We need to resupply."

"After the wedding." Negal took the glass that Dagor filled for him. "I want to shower and get in bed for a couple of hours. When is the party?"

"Ten-thirty," Aru said. "We have plenty of time, but I would like to shower and rest as well, so give me a condensed report. How did it go on Modana's yacht? Did you beat up the boyfriend?"

"No." Negal emptied the glass down his throat and put it down for Dagor to refill. "There was no time. Margo fainted as soon as we landed, so I leaped to catch her, and then one thing led to another, and we ended up in the dining room, with Modana's chef serving us dinner."

Aru frowned. "Why did she faint? Had they done something to her?"

Negal pulled the refilled glass toward him. "The bastard boyfriend drugged them, no doubt on his boss's orders, and they were in the sun, and then the helicopter landed, and it got to be too much for Margo to handle. She's fine now. Frankie and Mia are with her."

"How is Margo's friend doing?" Dagor asked.

"Better than expected. Kalugal entertained her and Margo on the way here, and his stories seem to have had a relaxing influence on them."

Dagor arched a brow. "His stories or his compulsion?"

"He didn't use compulsion on them." Negal took a sip from the whiskey, savoring it this time instead of gulping it like it was water. "I wish I had the guy's talent for storytelling and engaging people in conversation. He makes it look so easy."

Aru regarded him with a smirk playing on his lips. "I've never known you to have trouble engaging ladies in conversation. In fact, out of the three of us, you are probably the best at it. You always seem so cool, so debonair."

Negal snorted. "Debonair? Me? Not really. I lost my cool around Margo. Every time I thought about what could have been done to her, my eyes started glowing and my fangs elongated."

"You care for her." Dagor stated it like it was a fact.

"It was the situation, not the woman herself. I've never been as vicious as I was when we discovered those poor women near Acapulco. Nothing enrages me more than the willful abuse, torment, and murder of females and children.

Nothing." He threw the rest of the whiskey down his throat and put the glass down for Dagor to refill. "It's different when innocents are unintended casualties of war. I can deal with that."

"I know what you mean." Aru put a hand on his shoulder. "But I have a feeling that you are not being honest with us. It was more than that with Margo."

He wanted to tell Aru that it was none of his business, but that would have been hypocritical of him. Not too long ago, he was giving Aru unsolicited advice about Gabi.

Instead, Negal shook his head. "It's a placebo effect."

Aru's forehead furrowed. "How does fake medicine have anything to do with that?"

"It's just an analogy. Frankie filled my head with nonsense about how she and Mia were mated to gods, so their other best friend must also be destined to mate a god, and since I was the only one available, I must be her fated one. She even showed me a picture, hoping that I would fall in love with Margo right then and there." He looked at Dagor. "No offense, but that's a load of romantic crap. I didn't want to offend your mate by telling her that, so I just said that I wasn't interested, but the thought must have taken root in my head." He lifted the glass of whiskey to his lips but then thought better of it and put it down. "I should get showered, and so should you. By the way, who is getting married tonight?"

"Vlad and Wendy," Dagor said. "A young couple with an interesting story, but I won't bother you with the details when you are in a rush to get cleaned up."

"When did you learn about their story?" Aru asked.

"Frankie heard it from Gertrude, and then she told me. It's even better than Negal and Margo's story."

"There is no Negal and Margo story." He changed his mind about the drink and emptied it in two gulps instead of savoring it. "I'm escorting Gertrude to the wedding tonight."

Why had he said that? To prove that he had no feelings for Margo? It was a lie, and besides, it was none of their business.

Aru pushed to his feet. "You don't seem happy about it."

"I promised to be her date for tonight to compensate for leaving early yesterday." Negal stood up and headed toward his room. "And I never break my promises."

The more accurate statement would be that he hadn't broken a promise yet. The only way he could avoid breaking this one was to have Gertrude lose interest in him so she wouldn't demand it, but to do so, he would have to act like a jerk or a fool, and even that might not be enough to turn her off. Besides, it would be just as dishonest as any other type of lie, and she deserved better from him.

7

MARGO

When Kri opened the door to a small windowless cabin, Margo tried not to wince. The place wasn't so bad, but compared to the luxurious suite Jasmine had stayed in with Alberto, it was pretty utilitarian.

Still, it was bigger than the one they had been put into on Modana's yacht, so there was that.

Letting out a sigh, Jasmine plopped down on one of the twin beds. "So, I'm to be all alone in here for the next five and a half days?"

There was barely enough room between the two beds for the wheelchairs, so Margo sat down next to Jasmine while Kri sat on the other bed.

She felt like she'd overpromised and under-delivered even though she actually hadn't done either. Well, not about the ship, but about her friends. She'd promised Jasmine she would spend time with her along with Mia and Frankie, but since Jasmine wasn't allowed on the upper decks, she couldn't take part in the activities available to guests, and the opportunities for interaction would be scarce. And it wasn't as if Margo could ask Mia and Frankie to spend time with her on the staff deck so Jasmine wouldn't feel abandoned.

"I can stay with you," she offered. "I'm sure Frankie will appreciate having the cabin all to herself and her new guy, right?" She turned to her friend. "That way, you don't have to keep quiet. You can make all the noise you want unless you are concerned about the people in the next cabin over."

"This ship has excellent soundproofing." Frankie waved a hand in dismissal. "Besides, I don't know when the doctor will clear me for strenuous activities, and that's a quote, so don't think that I suddenly became shy about sex. That's how she refers to it."

Mia laughed. "That's so like Bridget."

Margo looked Frankie over, trying again to guess what procedure she'd had. "Are they offering cosmetic surgeries on this cruise?"

Frankie shook her head. "It's not what you're thinking." She shifted her gaze to Kri. "Are you staying because you enjoy our company, or are you waiting to give Jasmine more instructions?"

Talk about a hint the size of an elephant. It was almost as bad as asking Kri to leave, but then Frankie had never been known for having much tact.

The Guardian seemed oblivious to the hint. "I want to give Jasmine a tour of the facilities and explain about her neighbors."

"Right." Frankie's face fell. "About that. Won't it be a problem?"

"Aren't these the staff quarters?" Margo asked.

"Not everyone here is staff." Kri leaned back and looked at Jasmine. "Do you speak Spanish?"

Jaz shook her head. "People often mistake me for a Latina because of my looks, but that's not where my parents are from. My mother was Iranian, and my father is of Russian descent, but I look more like my mother."

"That's such an interesting combination," Mia said. "No wonder you are stunning."

"Thank you." Jaz smiled. "You are all beautiful women, and I'm not saying that to repay the compliment. The men who rescued us were also gorgeous beyond belief. Is that a Perfect Match thing? Do they only hire attractive people?"

One of Kri's blond eyebrows lifted, but she schooled her features so quickly that Margo had almost missed it. "Yeah. I guess so. People in the fantasy business have to look good, right?"

"What about the programmers and the office staff?" Margo blurted. "Not everyone is a model or an actor and has to be pretty, right?"

If Perfect Match hired only good-looking people, they were asking for trouble. Someone was going to sue them for discrimination.

"No, they don't have to be." Kri put her hands on her thighs and pushed to her feet. "Let's get the tour over with so you can get washed up and changed. We have a wedding tonight."

Margo and Jasmine didn't have anything to change into. Hopefully, her friends could loan them some things. The problem was that both Frankie and

Mia were petite, so their clothing was going to be too small for Margo and definitely for Jasmine, who was much taller.

"Speaking of getting changed." Margo followed the security guard up. "Do you know what happened to our luggage?"

"I don't, but I can find out."

"I can lend you things," Frankie said. "I brought so much clothing with me that it's ridiculous." She cast a quick glance at Jasmine. "Nothing of mine will fit you, though. You are too tall."

Margo's things were at the hotel, and she hoped to collect them when the ship stopped at Cabo. She also needed to let Lynda and Rob know that she was okay.

Hopefully, they hadn't told her parents anything.

"I'm five-ten," Jaz said and looked at Kri. "How tall are you?"

"I'm six feet even, but I can find a few T-shirts and some jeans that will fit you." Her gaze shifted to Jasmine's chest. "I'm also a DD bra size. I think that will fit you."

Jasmine's olive-toned cheeks deepened in color. "Thank you. I'll gladly take any shirts and pants you can spare, but I have a thing about wearing someone else's intimate clothing. I'll just wash what I have on tonight and hang it up to dry. Hopefully, it will be good to go tomorrow morning."

Margo frowned. "We should have asked Alberto if he packed your things. I'm pretty sure he did because he needed to make it look as if you had checked out of the hotel."

"Good point," Kri said. "From what I was told, the yacht is heading to Modana's mansion, and we have people stationed nearby. We can have someone search for your things, and if they are there, you can get them before bedtime tonight."

"Is that where we are heading?" Margo asked.

Kri nodded. "We will be docking in Puerto Vallarta in less than an hour."

A sliver of fear rushed down Margo's spine. "Is that safe? What if Kevin's hypnosis doesn't work and Modana attacks the ship?"

For a brief moment, Kri looked confused, but then her eyes flashed with understanding. "Don't worry. It will hold. Besides, Modana and his thugs are no match for our force. The ship is well protected."

If they had left people near Modana's estate, there were fewer of them to protect the ship, but Kri seemed confident that it was safe, and Margo had to take her word for it. "Before we got sidetracked, you started to say something about the other people staying on this deck."

"Oh, yes." Kri turned to Jasmine. "If they don't talk to you, don't try to engage them. None of them speaks anything but Spanish. The staff speaks Russian, so if you know any, you are welcome to use it."

"I don't speak Russian," Jasmine said. "And I don't speak Persian either. Languages are not my forte."

Mia shook her head. "That doesn't cover it, Kri. Some of the Spanish-speaking women are very skittish." She turned to Jasmine. "Try not to startle them by talking loudly, making any sudden movements, or even looking at them for too long. They are easily frightened."

That didn't sound right, and Margo's suspicious mind immediately latched on to that. "Why are they so skittish? Are you smuggling illegals into the United States?"

Kri laughed. "Yes, we are, but not for any nefarious reasons, so you can wipe that accusing expression off your face. These women have been victimized, and we are taking them to where they can get help and a chance of a better life. I can't say any more about it without putting them at risk, so you will have to be satisfied with that."

Margo must have looked skeptical because Mia reached for her hand. "That's the truth, Margo. We are doing a good thing for these women, and the best way you and Jasmine can help them is by pretending that you've never seen them or heard anything about them."

Jasmine nodded. "Got it. See no evil, hear no evil, and speak no evil."

Kri regarded her with a raised brow. "Not really applicable in this situation, but if you substitute evil with traumatized women, it works."

"That's what I meant." Jasmine lifted her hands in the air. "Evil was done to these women, and I'm going to pretend not to see it or hear it, and I won't speak it."

The Guardian shrugged her massive shoulders. "Works for me."

8

NEGAL

While Negal brushed his teeth and shaved, the hot water was running in the shower and filling the enclosure with steam.

Unlike his two teammates, his face was clean of makeup because he'd washed it at Modana's mansion, and he didn't want to dwell on why he had taken that extra ten seconds in the bathroom before rushing to board the helicopter.

The makeup had just felt like he had mud on his face. It wasn't because he'd wanted Margo to see him in all of his godly glory, and when she'd fainted, he hadn't hoped it was because of her response to him.

Not at all.

He was such a miserable liar.

The truth was that he truly believed it was Frankie's fault. If she hadn't planted the thought in his head, he would have never thought of Margo in terms of a likely fated mate or even a woman that he was interested in.

She was an attractive female, intelligent and pleasant to be around, and he liked her spirit, but her response to him hadn't been what he was used to from someone he was interested in.

Margo seemed to like and admire him, and she'd expressed her gratitude several times, but the only time he'd scented a whiff of arousal from her was when he'd held her in his arms. Still, the smell of drugs had been so potent that he couldn't be sure he'd gotten it right.

Especially since he hadn't smelled it again.

She'd been nice to him, escorting him to the bathroom when she'd thought he had trouble with his contact lenses, and a few times he had caught her glaring at Jasmine when she'd thought that the woman was acting flirtatious, but he could have been wrong about that as well.

Human jealousy smelled like rotting citrus fruit to him, and he hadn't smelled anything like that from Margo. It was as if she was intellectually possessive of him, but her feelings for him didn't run deep enough to evoke arousal or jealousy.

Some humans emitted less emotional scents than others, but that wasn't the case with Margo. When she was angry or suspicious, her scent indicated that very clearly.

Maybe she wasn't into males?

She could be interested in Jasmine, and then her annoyance at the woman's flirting would make sense. Except, it hadn't bothered Margo when Jasmine turned her attention to the pilot.

Confusing female.

With a sigh, Negal removed his clothing, put it in the laundry basket, and stepped into the shower.

The steam relaxed his tense muscles, and as he shampooed his hair and soaped his body, getting rid of the last of the lingering smells of Modana and his men, he relaxed further. He hadn't realized how much they had bothered him until he had gotten rid of the clothing and scrubbed his body clean.

It was hot and humid in Puerto Vallarta, so the body odor hadn't been surprising, but to him, it reeked like rotten meat, and he'd come to associate it with evil. Since he didn't have Dalhu's ability to actually smell it, he knew that it was just an association his mind was making.

That was precisely the reason why he suspected that his fascination with Margo was the product of Frankie's suggestion and his mind's tendency to expand on it and attach meaning where it didn't belong.

Margo was just an attractive human, who was possibly a Dormant, who could possibly become immortal, and who could possibly be his fated mate.

Damn it. He was doing it again.

Closing his eyes, Negal tilted his head back and let the spray fall on his face, hoping the scalding water would wash the nonsense away,

Except, it did the exact opposite.

Margo's mirage appeared behind his closed lids, and unlike in real life, she smiled at him suggestively and beckoned him with a hooked finger. "Come to me," she seemed to say. "I want you."

With a groan, Negal planted one hand on the marble wall, leaned into his shoulder, and palmed his straining erection with the other. "You don't want me," he said to the phantom image.

"I do." She licked her lips and then blew him a kiss.

"Then show me."

He didn't have to explain himself to the product of his imagination.

Smiling, she pulled her dress over her head, tossing it aside, and of course, she wasn't wearing anything underneath. And, of course, she was even more magnificent in the nude than clothed.

"So beautiful," he said. "Play with yourself for me."

"Like this?" She cupped her breasts.

"It's a good start."

He was losing his fucking mind, but he didn't care. This fantasy felt too good to stop, even though he knew he would hate himself for it later.

Fueling his obsession was not a smart move.

Margo abandoned one breast to slide her hand over her belly and down between her legs. "Is this better?"

"Yes. Keep going." The hand on his shaft moved faster, squeezed harder.

With the finger of one hand buried between her legs and the fingers of the other pinching her nipple, Margo closed her eyes, threw her head back, and opened her mouth in a silent scream.

As her body shivered with the force of her climax, Negal's orgasm hit him like a thunderbolt, barreling through his body, and as he erupted, he grabbed a sponge and bit into it.

The soapy taste should have killed the fantasy, but it didn't. All he saw behind his closed lids was Margo's head thrown back and his fangs embedded deep in her creamy white neck.

As long as the images kept playing in his head, the climax kept going. His mind refused to let go, and his hand refused to release his shaft until there was nothing more to milk. The problem was that he didn't need long to recuperate, and in less than a minute, he was going at it again.

Negal lost count of how many times he had orgasmed, and when he was finally done, he was glad on two counts. One was that he was in the shower, and the mess he'd made would be easy to clean up. The second one was that his mind was clearer than it had been for the past two days, so maybe now he could get a handle on things and free himself from the obsession called Margo.

9

KIAN

"Good afternoon, my esteemed colleagues," Kalugal said as he entered Toven's cabin, which was still functioning as their makeshift war room.

Kian regarded his cousin. "You look good for someone who hasn't slept since yesterday."

Kalugal's hair was wet, and he was wearing fresh clothing, indicating that he had taken a shower before coming to report. Max, who had arrived a few minutes earlier, was still covered in dirt and makeup and was wearing a pair of khaki pants with frayed edges.

"I wish I could say the same about you." Kalugal scanned their faces as he pulled out a chair across from Kian and sat down. "Where is the kid genius?"

"Roni is done for now," Onegus said. "He was anxious to reunite with his mate and see for himself that she wasn't hurt."

Kalugal arched a brow. "Sylvia traveled with me, Dalhu, and three gods. What could have happened to her?"

"Not much," Kian admitted.

Still, he could empathize with Roni. If it had been Syssi out there, he would have been tearing his hair out from worry.

"I'm glad you agree." Kalugal slanted a look at the coffee carafe. "Is that fresh?"

Since he could no doubt smell that it was, the question was meant as a hint that he wanted some.

"It is." Onegus pushed to his feet. "I'll get you a mug."

"Thank you." Kalugal dipped his head in appreciation. "So, if Roni is done, I assume that the *Silver Swan*'s travel itinerary has been fixed."

Turner nodded. "It was. According to the doctored records, the ship was never intended to stop at Cabo San Lucas. Unless anything new comes up, we are going to stay tonight and the entire day tomorrow in Puerto Vallarta and then continue to Ensenada. One of my contractors will watch the Ensenada port and report any suspicious activity. Another one is checking the Cabo area. If we are lucky, the Doomers will get tired of waiting for us to show up and leave."

Kalugal frowned. "What about Carlos? He's in Cabo, right?"

"Not for long," Turner said. "As soon as he hears about his brother's spiritual rebirth, he will head home faster than a speeding bullet." He chuckled. "Pun intended."

Kian shook his head. "We don't want Carlos to kill Julio. We need the older Modana alive to do all that humanitarian work in Acapulco."

"I was just joking." Turner reached for the carafe and refilled his mug.

Exhaustion had a strange effect on the guy. Instead of getting cranky like the rest of them, he seemed to loosen up. He'd been smiling and cracking jokes for the past couple of hours, and it was a little freaky, given how humorless and focused on the task at hand he usually was.

"Speaking of spiritual awakening, your thralling and compulsion are still working their magic," Onegus told Kalugal. "The guys in the control center reported that Modana and his men are praying and asking the Madonna for forgiveness. Modana even vowed to build a chapel in his mansion and bring in a priest to assist them on their journey from sinners to sainthood."

Kalugal pursed his lips in a mock affront. "Did you expect it not to work?"

The chief shrugged. "When it goes against everything a person holds dear, compulsion and thralling might unravel sooner than later. If it was that simple to turn evildoers into good people, we could have had hundreds of Doomers serving in our army instead of slumbering in stasis in our catacombs."

Kalugal smoothed a hand over his goatee. "Compared to most of those Doomers, Modana is a baby bad guy. He hasn't been doing bad things for as long as they did. Also, he was raised in a religious home, so I didn't have to create something from nothing, and the same was true for most of his men."

"Given the right slant, religion can be used for good." Kian sighed. "As long as it holds life sacred, that is. Regrettably, that's not always the case."

Kalugal nodded. "My grandfather did not hold life sacred, and the religion my father created from his teachings does not value life either. His followers are like cancer cells, growing too rapidly and killing the organism that feeds them. I wonder when they will realize that they are working diligently to rot the branch they are sitting on."

Kian was too tired to engage in a philosophical discussion, and he wasn't sure what Kalugal had meant by the Brotherhood killing the organism that fed it. They wanted to enslave humans, and they didn't care how many would die to fulfill that goal, but their aim wasn't to eliminate them all. Still, perhaps Kalugal knew something that Kian didn't. Tomorrow, they could talk about it over whiskey and cigars. Today, or what was left of it, Kian planned to get a few hours of sleep before the wedding.

"I was thinking." Max looked at Turner. "Perhaps your contractor in Cabo can plant a woman in the hotel that will start talking about a ship she is boarding. We could get her a ticket on one of the big cruise liners currently docking there. The Doomers won't go after her on a ship with thousands of passengers and staff. That way, we will remove the last of the breadcrumbs leading to us."

"That's not a bad idea." Kalugal lifted his coffee mug. "We also need to get Margo's luggage out of the hotel." He finished what was left of the coffee.

"That's already done," Turner said. "My contractor has a cousin who works in the hotel. She removed the luggage and put it in storage without marking it or logging it anywhere. We did that while Roni was hacking into the surveillance so it wouldn't show on the recordings."

"What about Jasmine?" Kalugal asked. "I saw Kri talking to her, so I assume you ordered her stashed in the lower decks."

Kian nodded. "The less she is exposed to us, the better. Kri reported that Jasmine doesn't speak Spanish, so she won't be able to communicate with the rescued women. Barely any of the staff speaks English, so she won't be able to talk to them either, but she is free to use the staff lounge and the other facilities available to them."

"I'm not worried about any of them." Kalugal waved a dismissive hand. "Toven and I made sure that none of them would say anything they were not supposed to. The victims don't remember how they were saved, and the staff is under compulsion not to mention their alien employers." He shifted on the chair, so he was facing Kian. "On an entirely different but related subject, why don't we have a damn helicopter on this ship? Wasn't having one the plan all along?"

Kian winced. "It was, and I blame myself for the oversight. It has somehow fallen between the cracks, so to speak. But we have already rectified the situation. Thanks to Turner, we are getting one in Puerto Vallarta. That's one of the reasons we are staying there longer than we would have otherwise."

"That and taking care of Carlos," Turner added. "Modana is on his way back home, and Carlos will soon follow."

10

MARGO

Margo pushed Frankie's wheelchair into the elevator. "I feel so bad about leaving Jasmine down there."

Mia drove into the cab, turned around, and pressed the button for one of the upper decks. She was maneuvering that chair like a pro, but then she'd always been a quick study, with focus and determination that not many possessed.

Noticing that the numbers on the buttons were positive for the decks above the promenade and negative for those below, it occurred to Margo that it kind of reflected the reality of the ship.

The paying guests got the nice spacious cabins with balconies and a view of the ocean, while the staff had cramped, windowless accommodations.

Jasmine wasn't part of the staff, and Margo would have loved for her to be treated as a guest, but since neither of them was paying for the privilege, they really shouldn't complain or make demands.

Frankie tilted her head up to look at Margo. "Don't worry about Jaz. She will be fine."

"I'm not worried about her, but I'm worried about you. You don't look so good." Frankie had dark circles under her eyes, and her face was gaunt and pale. "Don't tell me that you are taking that weight loss drug everyone is talking about lately. I've seen pictures of celebrities who were taking it, and their faces looked like yours."

"You mean beautiful?" Frankie batted her eyelashes.

"I mean gaunt and hollow but also beautiful."

Frankie looked tired, but oddly, she also looked younger. Maybe it was the lack of makeup. The girl usually wore so much of it that it was easy to forget what she looked like underneath.

"Well, thank you." Frankie fanned herself with her hand. "Soon, everything will be revealed, so stop trying to guess what's wrong with me." She smirked. "The better question is, what's right with me."

Margo rolled her eyes. "If too much sex put you in a wheelchair, I need to have a talk with your new boyfriend."

Frankie laughed. "That's a good one, and you are getting warm."

What the hell?

"Was this supposed to be a joke? What's going on?"

"Patience, my friend. Patience."

As the elevator doors opened, Mia drove herself out, and Margo pushed Frankie's chair. She followed Mia down the corridor, and when she stopped in front of one of the doors, Frankie pulled out a phone and opened it with an application.

"That's cool." Margo pushed the chair in, and Mia followed them in hers.

The cabin's living area was spacious and looked well put together and cozy, but it was a far cry from the opulence of the presidential suite in the hotel. Although, in Margo's opinion, the cabin's warm earth tones and Tuscany style decor were much more inviting than the cold modern look of the hotel penthouse, but that was a matter of personal taste.

"So, what do you think?" Mia asked. "Nice, right?"

"It's perfect, and I'm glad that it's not too fancy. It makes me feel a little less guilty about Jaz staying on the lower decks."

Mia frowned. "This is not fancy? What are you comparing it to?"

"The presidential suite at the resort." Margo helped Frankie get out of the chair and sit on the couch. "That's where Jasmine was staying with her fake boyfriend. I still don't understand why he bothered to spend so much money on such a fancy suite if all along he intended to deliver her to his boss. He could have rented a much cheaper room, and Jaz wouldn't have had a problem with that." She sat next to Frankie on the couch.

"Maybe the presidential suite is permanently rented out to the cartel bosses," Mia said. "I bet that's where his brother is staying right now."

Margo shivered. "Don't remind me. I want to forget about that scumbag. Although, to be fair, I don't think he even knew that his brother intended to gift me to him."

"That doesn't make him any less of a scumbag." Mia crossed her legs, which took Margo's breath away.

It was such a simple thing that most people took for granted, but Mia had never done that when she'd still worn a prosthesis. Now that her legs were almost fully regrown, she was finally able to do it. Soon, Mia would walk on her own two legs, which was proof that miracles could happen.

Margo felt tears prickling the back of her eyes. "What do you know about Carlos?" she asked, still staring at Mia's crossed legs.

"Not much," Mia admitted. "Toven said that he was worse than his brother. I mean Tom. Toven is Tom's other name."

"Like a middle name?" Margo asked.

Mia winced. "His real name is Toven, but it's so unusual that he goes by Tom with everyone other than his close family and friends."

Margo had never heard of a name like that before, but that wasn't unusual in a country with immigrants from all over the world. It also wasn't difficult to pronounce.

Frankie chuckled. "Consider that just one tiny tidbit of information out of everything we are going to tell you. I think you will need a stiff drink to hear the rest."

Margo's heartbeat sped up. "I've just been through a nightmare. I'm not sure I can handle any more."

"Don't worry." Mia drove her chair toward the kitchenette. "Everything we are going to tell you is great news, so don't be scared."

Margo narrowed her eyes at Mia. "So why do I need a drink?"

"Because you need to keep an open mind and suspend your disbelief, and it's not easy for you to do either."

"That's not true. I'm very open-minded. I read about shifters, for crying out loud. Talk about suspending disbelief."

"You've got a point there." Mia opened the under-counter fridge and pulled out a bottle of vodka, a container of orange juice, and another of cranberry juice. "Which one do you like better?"

Margo pushed to her feet and walked over to the bar. "The cranberry, but I'll do the mixing. I've been drugged, so I don't want to overdo it with the alcohol. I'll just put a tiny bit of vodka in it for the taste."

Mia's eyes widened. "You should have said something. What did they give you?"

"I don't know. Jasmine thinks it was heroin. Alberto, that's the scumbag fake boyfriend, injected both of us with it." She sighed. "I hate to admit it, but it felt damn good. Of course, I will never do that willingly, but I can understand people who get addicted to the stuff."

As Mia and Frankie exchanged knowing glances, Margo's hackles rose. "What? Did either of you try it and not tell me?"

"We didn't try heroin," Frankie said.

Margo glared at her. "But you've tried some other illicit drug."

"It's not illicit." Mia waved a hand at the three bottles. "Mix the drinks, Margo, and let's sit down. As promised, everything shall soon be revealed."

11

WENDY

The living room of the cabin Margaret and Bowen shared with Stella and Richard was packed with Wendy's friends.

Not too long ago, Wendy had been a lonely girl who couldn't relate to anyone, and now look at her. She had so many friends that it had been hard to decide who to invite to her bachelorette party. The cabin's living room wasn't big enough to accommodate all the females whom she considered friends.

She would have to apologize to so many people for not inviting them.

"Here you go." Jin handed her a margarita. "Tell me what you think."

Jin had appointed herself as their barmaid and was mixing drinks according to online recipes.

Wendy took a sip, making sure to lick some of the salt. "'It's excellent. You should apply for a job at Atzil's bar."

"No, thank you." Jin returned to her mixing station. "I have a job. Besides, the bar is not open yet."

"How is that going?" Aliya asked. "I mean your business, not the bar."

"Good," Mey answered. "We are not making any money yet, but at least we are not losing any, and we are negotiating a contract with a well-known national chain that is interested in our line."

"Which chain is it?" Wendy asked.

"We can't say." Jin brought a margarita without salt to Carol. "It's confidential."

Wendy chuckled. "Who are we going to tell?"

When Jin lifted a brow, Wendy winced. "I'm not the same person I was then. You can trust me."

Jin waved a dismissive hand. "That's not what I implied. Your sordid past is ancient history, and in your defense, you were young and naive and thought the paranormal program was the only way to have a better future. But now, you work in the village café and interact with a lot of people every day. One slip-up and the whole clan would be talking about it, and eventually, someone would say something to someone on the outside, and Mey and I would lose our chance. If we get this contract, our brand will become a household name."

"Fine, keep your secret." Wendy took another sip from the margarita. "Can you believe that it has only been a year and a half since we joined the clan?"

She and Jin had met in the paranormal program. They hadn't been friends, but they had been friendly toward each other. That was before Wendy had betrayed them the first chance she'd gotten, though, and she hadn't expected Jin to ever forgive her for that, but here they were.

"It is hard to believe." Mey walked over to the table and collected a fistful of nuts. "You'd think that being immortal would speed time up, but it seems to work the other way around. Not that I'm complaining. I've never been happier. I just wish Jin and I could bring our parents to the village, and then everything would be perfect."

"We can't make them immortal," Jin said. "And it seems cruel to dangle that in front of them."

"Right." Mey sighed. "We can't have everything we want. We should thank the Fates for what we have."

While Mey and Jin's adoptive parents did not possess the immortal gene, the sisters had grown up in a loving and supportive home.

Wendy hadn't been so lucky.

Her father had been an abusive monster, and he had driven her mother away when Wendy was a baby. But she had her mother with her now, and her father had been dealt with. She couldn't think of a single thing that would have made her life more perfect than it was right now.

"I have everything I want." Wendy looked at her mother. "Against all odds, I have my mom back, I'm mated to the best male in the world, and I'm about to marry him, and I have many wonderful friends. I can even fit into a size six wedding dress with ease. Life is good." She lifted her margarita glass. "To happily ever afters!"

As her friends raised their glasses, a chorus of female voices echoed her toast.

Across from her, Sharon chewed on her lower lip. "I'm stressed and excited at the same time. It didn't hit me until now that Robert and I are next in line."

Wonder patted her shoulder. "You have another twenty-four hours until you need to start stressing. Think of today as a grand rehearsal for tomorrow."

"None of the couples have had rehearsal dinners," Anastasia said, "but having one wedding after the other with the same people attending fills that gap. Although, to be frank, and I don't mean to offend anyone, I don't like this production line style. I think each couple should have their special day with ample time between one celebration and the next."

"It's not practical," Stella said. "It's difficult to get every member of the clan in one place, and having all these weddings on the cruise was the only way to do it."

"That's not true." Carol kicked off her shoes and tucked her legs under her butt. "We have endless time, and I don't get why everyone was in a rush to have a human-style wedding. We could make it a tradition for the entire clan to gather in one place once or twice a year, like during the solstices, and schedule a wedding for each gathering. It's not like we would get too old while waiting our turn."

"Vlad and I are young," Wendy murmured. "But neither of us wanted to wait. It was so frustrating to have the cruise delayed over and over again. I was starting to think that it was a bad omen and that we shouldn't get married at all."

She hadn't voiced that concern to anyone before, not even Vlad, but it had been gnawing at her, and it had gotten worse after what had happened in Acapulco.

Tessa waved a hand. "Don't say that. Ten couples were in the same boat as you, and none of them were thinking that it was a bad omen."

"Dalhu did," Carol said. "Especially after what happened on the day of his and Amanda's wedding. But Amanda turned his argument on its head. She said that it was a good omen because it implied that their future would be filled with more good deeds or something to that effect."

"What about everything that happened before the ship even sailed?" Wendy asked. "First, it was saving Jade and the Kra-ell, and then the three gods showed up, and the village was locked down because Kian didn't know who they were and what they wanted, and I was really scared both times, not just because our wedding was postponed, but because I was afraid this wonderful life I had in the village was going to change, or worse, end." Her voice wavered as tears prickled the corners of her eyes. "I know how easily everything can be taken away from me, so I never take anything good for granted."

"Oh, sweetie." Her mother squeezed into the small space between her and the armrest and wrapped her arm around her shoulders. "It's the survivors' curse. We are always afraid that good things are not going to last because we are haunted by our pasts. I wish there was an exorcism that could be performed on those toxic memories."

"I disagree," Ella said. "We need to be aware of the evils lurking in dark places and the wolves in sheep's clothing who hide in plain sight. The world is full of predators, and to pretend that they don't exist is foolish. I still have nightmares about what I went through, but I don't want to forget it. How else could I warn others to be vigilant?"

Wendy tried really hard not to look at Tessa, who out of everyone in the cabin had suffered the worst, but she couldn't help it.

"It's okay," Tessa said quietly. "Most of us here are survivors, and each of us has found a way to deal with it in her own way." She smiled. "Carol became a major badass, Wendy became super social, and Margaret found peace with Bowen. Ella and I help others through our work in the sanctuary by showing them that not everything is dark and perverted, that there are good people out there who are willing to help, that life goes on, and that it's possible to find love and happiness, and it's okay to feel those good feelings without being terrified that they will be torn asunder at any moment."

Carol raised her glass. "I'll drink to that."

12

ANNANI

"My dear nephews." Annani embraced Kalugal, kissed his cheek, and then did the same to Lokan. "This is a rare treat to have you both here. Areana will be overjoyed."

"Indeed." Lokan dipped his head to hide his momentary shock at the rare show of familiarity, which the goddess typically reserved for her children and their mates. "Thank you for providing me this opportunity to talk with my mother."

"I thought it would be wonderful if we could all talk to her today. I just wish the communicator had a live video option, but we cannot have all we wish for, can we?" She sat down in the middle of the couch and gestured for her nephews to sit beside her. "William assures me that we will have a clear connection the same way we have from the village and the sanctuary." She put the phone on the coffee table, propped up on the little leg that came with the case. "William will connect us in a few moments. Can I offer you something to drink while we wait? Perhaps some tea?"

"Thank you, Clan Mother," Lokan said. "Maybe later."

She mock glared at him. "I am Aunt Annani to you, or just Annani."

Kalugal smiled at the exchange. "Perhaps after the call, we can have tea together, Aunt Annani."

"Very well." She leaned back and adjusted the folds of her gown.

It would have been wonderful if she could share with her nephews the news about their great-grandmother, or with Areana for that matter, but it was too big of a secret, and she still did not trust them or their mother a hundred percent, each one for a different reason.

Kalugal's loyalty was first and foremost to himself, and he was an ambitious fellow. He might have an issue with Annani being chosen by the queen over his own mother. Areana was the older sister, but since she was Ahn's daughter from a concubine and not the official spouse, she was not a legitimate heir to the throne.

Lokan was straddling the fence between the clan and the Brotherhood, and even though his loyalty was to his mate and her clan, he cared deeply about the fate of the people on his father's island and hoped one day to free them. Right now, his and the clan's goals were aligned, but that might change in the future.

As for Areana, she loved her mate.

She was willing to hide things from Navuh as long as they did not pose a threat to him, but the moment she suspected that he was in danger, there was no doubt in Annani's mind that her sister would betray her to save her mate.

She did not hold it against her.

That was how fated mates were, but it pained Annani that the Fates had matched her sweet and kind sister with a monster like Navuh. Perhaps it had been the only way to save Areana, though, and if that had been the case, Annani was grateful to the Fates for sparing her sister's life.

Besides, the secret was so big that no one outside of Aru, Kian, and their three co-conspirators on Anumati knew about it, and it had to stay that way. Syssi probably knew as well, but the secret was safe with her.

When the phone rang, Annani activated the speaker. "Hello, William. Is Areana on the line?"

"Here she is. Go ahead."

"Hello, sister of mine," Areana said. "How do you fare this Wednesday?"

"I am wonderful, and I have a lovely surprise for you. Both of your sons are here with me."

Areana's gasp was audible. "That is indeed a lovely surprise. Hello, my loves."

"Hello, Mother," Lokan said.

Kalugal repeated the greeting and then spent a few moments updating his mother about Darius and Jacki. Naturally, he did not mention the adventures he had encountered on the cruise.

Hearing about the atrocities would have upset Areana, whether Navuh had ordered them or the local team commander had acted on his own, but even that would not be enough to make her leave her fated mate.

In fact, Annani was sure that nothing could.

When it was Lokan's turn, he entertained Areana with stories about Carol and how happy she was to be with her family.

"She's been a bridesmaid in most of the weddings so far. My mate is very popular."

"I am delighted to hear that," Areana said. "I will be even more delighted when my sister marries the two of you in a proper ceremony, and you start working on a grandchild for me."

Lokan uttered a quiet groan that her sister hopefully did not hear. "When Carol and I get married, I would love to have my mother at my wedding."

Areana sighed. "I wish I could be, but regrettably, it is not my destiny to enjoy my sons and grandchildren in person. The best I can hope for is knowing that the two of you are happy and that my grandchildren are growing up in loving homes and a wonderful community."

"You could be with us if you left him."

Areana sighed again. "I cannot, Lokan. Would you leave Carol for any reason under the sun?"

"I would not, but Carol is not a monster."

"And neither is your father. But I do not wish to talk about this. We have talked about it enough. Tell me about the weddings."

Leaning back, Lokan waved a hand at his brother. "She's all yours."

Kalugal looked at Annani. "Since your sister officiated over all the weddings, I think the honor should be hers."

Annani laughed. "Of course. What would you like me to tell you?"

"Tell me about the couples and what is special about each one."

"That would take much longer than the time allotted to us. Instead, I want to hear about you and Tula. What is new with you?"

"With me, not much, and as for Tula, it is more of the same as well."

"Is she still with the young man we talked about?"

Tula had taken a liking to Kaia's friend Anthony, a fellow bioinformatician who had been lured to the island and imprisoned in Navuh's harem to be used as a breeder. Anthony not only fit the program's revamped characteristics criterion of superior intelligence, but he also bore a physical resemblance to Navuh. This allowed Navuh to claim as his own any sons that Anthony might father. Except, Tula did not want to become pregnant only to have to surrender her child, either to Navuh's mercenary army or to his Dormant breeding program, and she was consuming an herb that was supposed to prevent conception.

"Yes, she is." Areana sighed. "But she is endangering the male by claiming him as her own and not sharing him. If he fails to produce a child, Navuh will be displeased, and he might remove him from the harem."

"Is Tula in love with the boy?"

Areana laughed. "She is not. She loves what is stored in his head, and she is possessive and protective of him."

Tula lived in the lap of luxury in the harem but in total isolation from the world, and she craved freedom and knowledge. Kaia's friend, who was very smart and well-educated, could not help her with the first item, but he could provide her with the second.

"That could develop into love." Annani let out a sigh. "People fall in love for all kinds of reasons."

"I do not think that Tula is capable of love," Areana said solemnly. "Something inside of her died when everyone she loved perished. She is afraid to love again."

Annani could understand that. If not for her children, she might have closed off her heart to love as well. Not that having a child could help poor Tula. If anything, it would only further devastate her when her baby was taken away from her.

"Let me tell you about Wonder's wedding. You can tell Tula about it. I am sure it will gladden her heart."

13

MARGO

Margo finished mixing the drinks, brought them to the coffee table, and went back to the kitchenette to look for snacks. "So, which one of you is finally going to tell me what's going on? You've been throwing out hints the size of boulders at me, but I still have no clue."

She had a feeling it would be Mia and not Frankie who told her, even though so far, Frankie had done most of the talking.

Mia ran a hand over her short hair. "I don't know where to start. There is so much to tell."

"Start with the girl," Frankie said. "Tell her what Lisa said about us."

"Lisa?" Margo remembered her. She was a relative of Tom, or rather Toven. "What does she have to do with any of it, whatever it is?" She found a bag of mixed nuts and another one of popcorn and brought them to the table.

"Lisa has a special talent," Mia said. "She can sense godly genes in people."

"Godly?" Margo burst out laughing. "Me?" She sat down next to Frankie on the couch. "I was drugged, but even when I was high, I didn't have delusions of grandeur or a god complex."

When neither Mia nor Frankie smiled, Margo frowned. "You are serious, aren't you?"

She'd heard about the god particle, although she didn't know what it was exactly, but she'd never heard about a god gene. Was there a connection?

Frankie looked at Mia. "Perhaps you should start with the gods."

Mia glared at her. "Do you want to tell the story?"

"I don't know enough to do it justice." Frankie crossed her arms over her chest. "You've been part of this world for a lot longer than me."

"That's true." Mia reached for her glass of mostly orange juice with a few drops of vodka in it and took a sip. "Bridget will be so mad at me for this." She put the glass down. "Okay. So, let's start with the gods." She looked at Margo. "You know how the mythologies of the Greeks, the Romans, the Egyptians, the Sumerians, and others are all similar?"

At least that was familiar ground.

Still a fantasy, though. Everyone knew that mythologies had been invented by people to explain the unexplainable. "I know that the Greek and the Roman pantheons are nearly identical, just with different names for the gods, but I don't know much about the others. Where are you leading with this?"

"They are similar for a reason. They are all based on real people, and the Sumerian stories are the original." Mia smiled. "After we are done, I'll send you a few digital books about Sumerian mythology, and you will see how much more robust and realistic their myths are than the later ones that were copied from them. Some of the copycats took tidbits of stories and combined them, while others elaborated and changed things to fit their cultures and agendas."

"It's like fan fiction," Frankie said. "Sometimes it can be better than the original, but in most cases, it's not."

"I wouldn't know." Margo took a long swig of her spiked cranberry juice. "I don't read fan fiction. But back to mythology, it doesn't matter if the original authors were better. It's still fiction."

Mia cast her a condescending smile. "It's as much fiction as what we learned in history class. The facts get twisted and embellished, and we all know that history is written by the victors, and myths are no different. The bottom line is that the gods were not invented by humans. In fact, it's the other way around. Humans were invented and created by the gods. They actually made us by combining some of their genetic material with that of our predecessors to create a leap in evolution. The thinking human would have eventually emerged without outside intervention, but it would have taken hundreds of thousands of years longer. The stories in the Bible are a simplified version of what actually happened. The gods came from another planet for reasons that we don't need to get into right now, and they needed workers, so they created humans. Many generations later, contact with the home planet was severed, again for reasons that we don't need to get into right now, and the gods who were stuck on Earth faced extinction because their genetic pool was too limited. They took human lovers, and the children born to them were immortals who possessed a weakened version of their godly parent's power. When those immortals took human lovers, though, the children born to them were human. Some of them had the godly genes in them, but those genes needed to be activated." She paused to take another sip of her juice.

Margo was still trying to process Mia's long monologue, but one item in particular stood out as needing further explanation. "Let's assume for a moment that everything you've said is true. How did they activate the genes?"

"We will talk about that later. I want to give you an overview first."

Mia had always been a good storyteller, and Margo wasn't about to interrupt her flow. Maybe her friend was venturing into adult books and was trying out a story idea on her?

Yeah, that was probably what was going on.

"It's an excellent story, Mia. Please, continue."

Mia frowned at her but then sighed and resumed her narrative. "Long after nearly all the gods were killed by one of their own, all that remained of them were a few immortal descendants and dormant carriers of the genes. Those genes kept on passing from mother to child, but with no one to activate them, they remained undetected. I was such a dormant carrier before Toven activated my godly genes. Now to the heart of the matter. Since Dormants and immortals feel a special affinity toward each other, and the three of us have been inseparable since kindergarten, we suspected that the two of you were Dormants as well. Lisa confirmed that when she came to see you. Frankie is already transitioning into immortality, which is why she's weak and needs a wheelchair while the transformation is taking place, and now it's your turn."

Margo clapped her hands. "Awesome story, Mia. You should definitely write it."

Mia groaned. "It's not a story idea, Margo, and I'm not pulling your leg. Everything is true."

Frankie nodded. "We would never invent something like that and try to convince you that it was real. You know us."

She shook her head. "You two are my best friends, and I trust you more than anyone, but do you have proof to substantiate this crazy story?"

Maybe her friends were on drugs?

They had admitted to being on something that was supposedly not illicit, but it could be a new compound that some chemist had cooked up in a laboratory that hadn't been identified as an illegal substance yet.

Frankie tapped a finger on her lower lip. "Remember what Jasmine said about everybody being so good-looking? That's not because all the people on this ship are Perfect Match employees who were hired for their good looks. It's because most of the passengers of this ship are immortals and gods, and the closer they are to the godly source, the more gorgeous they are."

As Negal's face appeared in Margo's mind, she remembered thinking that he was an angel.

"Is Negal an immortal?" she asked.

"Even better." Frankie grinned. "He is a god."

14

VLAD

"Come on, Vlad." Bowen held the open cigar box in front of him. "You have to smoke one. It's a tradition."

"I'll take one." Gordon snatched a thick cigar out of the box. "Cubans are the best."

The box was a present from Kian, who had gotten one for each of the ten grooms, along with two bottles of very expensive whiskey. It was a nice gesture, and Vlad appreciated both gifts, but he didn't smoke. Apparently, though, his childhood friend had developed a taste for cigars while studying in the UK.

He snorted. "Do you get to smoke a lot of them at Oxford?"

"You'd be surprised." Gordon cut the end of the fat cigar. "I can't afford the real thing, but I get to smoke a fake one from time to time. It helps with philosophical discussions. Others prefer pot, but I promised my mother that I wouldn't touch the stuff." He took the lighter Jackson handed him, lit the cigar, and took a puff. "Oh, yeah. That's what I'm talking about. Superb."

Who would have thought that an airhead like Gordon would be getting a master's degree in philosophy? He'd never been studious and had displayed the depth of a puddle on a summer's day, but evidently there was more to him than met the eye. He was finishing his master's at one of the most prestigious universities in the world and intended to continue to a PhD program.

It was so good to see him.

"Are you going to take one or not?" Richard reached behind Bhathian, pulled out a cigar, and put it in Vlad's mouth. "Try it, and if you don't like it, give it to me. I'll finish it for you."

"Fine."

As the balcony door slid open and Roni stepped out, cheers sounded all around.

"Thank you." Roni took a bow. "If I'd known that everyone would be so glad to see me, I would have come earlier."

"I thought that you were still busy hacking," Vlad said. "Are you done?"

"For now." Roni took a cigar. "I'm sure I'll be needed later."

Nick wrapped his arm around Roni's shoulders. "If you need help, I'm here for you, buddy."

Roni frowned. "Why didn't I think of you sooner? The Guardians are setting up a hidden surveillance network at Modana's mansion. I'm sure they could use your expertise." He pulled out his phone, stuck the unlit cigar in his mouth, and started texting. "I'm reminding Turner about you," he said around the cigar.

Bowen came over with a bottle of whiskey and two glasses. "I'm sure Turner didn't forget. The guy's mind is like a computer." He poured a glass for Vlad and another one for Bhathian.

Roni took the cigar out of his mouth. "That's a misconception. I've worked closely with the guy on several occasions, and he uses a damn yellow pad to organize his thoughts. He's just very methodical about it."

"If you say so." Bowen took two more glasses off the tray Vlad had prepared and poured whiskey for Roni and Jackson before turning back to Vlad. "Excited about tonight?"

"I'm glad that it's finally happening. Wendy and I were afraid that the wedding wouldn't happen because of the mission, and we would lose our spot. We were even discussing the possibility of having a lunchtime wedding tomorrow in case the Guardians were delayed."

It wouldn't have been the wedding Wendy had dreamt about, but it was better than postponing it once again.

When everyone had a lit cigar in one hand and a glass of whiskey in the other, Vrog raised his glass. "To my amazing son and my lovely daughter-in-law. May tonight be all that you hoped it would be and tomorrow even better than that."

"I'll drink to that." Vlad clinked his glass with his father's and then turned to clink it with Richard's. "To my father and to my mother's mate. Thank you for making our family complete."

Richard clapped him on the back. "It's not complete until you and Wendy have a kid, and hopefully, your mother and I will give you a little brother or sister as well."

"I'll drink to that too." Vlad clinked his glass with Richard's again. "And I hope to get another sibling from Vrog and Aliya." He clinked his glass with his father's.

"It's a happy day." Jackson wrapped his arm around Vlad's shoulders. "Who would have thought that you would be standing here today, with your father on one side and your stepdad on the other?"

Vlad chuckled. "Not me, that's for sure. The saying that life is stranger than fiction proves to be true once again." He smiled at his childhood friend. "When are you and Tessa going to tie the knot? And will you invite Mo-red's sons to be your groomsmen?"

Jackson sighed. "I should, but then I'll have to disappoint some of my good friends, so I probably won't. But there is plenty of time to think about that. Tessa and I are not in a rush."

"Do you know what sucks about these cruise weddings?" Gordon asked.

Everyone turned to him with frowns on their faces, but it was Leon who asked, "What?"

"No strippers."

Vlad was glad to hear the chorus of boos. "I wouldn't have strippers at my bachelor party even if Wendy and I were getting married in Vegas. The whole idea is repulsive."

Gordon lifted his hands in mock surrender, a cigar in one and a glass of whiskey in the other. "You are all a bunch of prudes, but whatever."

"We don't need strippers to celebrate," Jackson said. "Good friends, good whiskey, and a good cigar are good enough for me."

"Wise words." Bhathian raised his glass. "Let's drink to that and to many more happy occasions to celebrate with family and friends."

15

MARGO

N*egal is a freaking god.*

What did that even mean?

After dropping that grenade at her feet, Frankie and Mia had kept talking, telling her that they were both mated to gods, and the enormity of that explosion was still reverberating in Margo's mind, screaming that one word over and over again.

Gods! Gods?

Like Thor and Loki? Zeus and Poseidon?

"I need to lie down," she interrupted something Frankie was saying. "I don't feel so good."

"She's in shock," Mia said. "Perhaps I should have suggested coffee instead of having her mix us drinks."

"You think?" Frankie glared at Mia.

"It was your idea to give her alcohol."

"And you always listen to me?"

"Stop." Margo lifted her hand. "I'm fine, and there was barely any alcohol in any of our drinks. I put mere drops in. It's just that I've had enough excitement over the last twenty-four hours to last me a lifetime, and now you are telling me that the two of you are mated to gods and that Negal is a god as well, and it all sounds like something from a fantasy novel. I don't know if it's real or I'm suffering from some sort of weird withdrawal symptoms." She rubbed her temples. "If Jasmine is going through the same thing, she shouldn't be alone. I'd better go down there and stay with her."

Frankie reached for her hand. "You can't tell Jasmine anything. You need to stay here and try to process what we've told you. Then, once Toven wakes up from his nap, he will come over and compel you to keep everything we told you a secret."

"Compel me? What do you mean by that?"

"It's the damn drugs," Mia murmured. "Come on, Margo. Try to focus that sharp mind of yours. That's what Kalugal did to Modana and his men to make them put down their weapons. You were there when he did it."

It took her a moment to connect the dots. "You mean Kevin? He hypnotized them. Is that what you mean by compulsion?"

"Yes." Mia let out a breath as if relieved that Margo's brain was back online. "Except, compulsion is to hypnosis what vodka is to wine. It's much more potent."

"Why did he call himself Kevin?"

Mia tilted her head. "For the same reason that Toven calls himself Tom. Generic names don't stand out. It's not like gods and immortals advertise their presence. They go to great lengths to hide it." She put her chair in reverse, turned it around, and drove to the kitchenette. "I'm making you some coffee."

Margo doubted caffeine would help clear the jumbled mess in her head.

She shifted her gaze to Frankie.

"So, your boyfriend Doug, otherwise known as Dagor, is a god."

Frankie grinned. "Yes, he is. And I'm on my way to becoming immortal."

"What's the difference between gods and immortals? And how did the gods die if they can't be killed?"

Her friend smiled indulgently. "You didn't hear a word of what we were saying, did you?"

"I heard the word god, and it was so loud that I couldn't hear anything after that."

"I get it." Frankie patted her knee. "It's weird to see you freaking out like that when you are usually the voice of reason, the pillar of strength that Mia and I depend on. But that's okay. It's our turn to repay the support you have provided us throughout the years."

Margo rolled her eyes. "Yeah, yeah. Now, can you please be kind enough to explain again the difference between gods and immortals and how the hell you became immortal?"

Frankie lifted her hand.

"One thing at a time." She took in a deep breath. "I'm new to all this, so I might not be the best person to explain it, but here goes. Gods and immortals are stronger and faster than humans. They have better eyesight, hearing, sense of smell, and other talents. But the most important thing is their ability to heal incredibly fast, and since gods heal even faster than immortals, it's really hard to kill them. It must be a massive injury that their bodies can't repair fast enough. Immortals can also manipulate human minds like you've seen Kalugal do, but most of them cannot manipulate the minds of other immortals. Kalugal can, but he's unique in that. Gods can manipulate the minds of both humans and immortals." She looked at Mia. "Am I explaining it right?"

"More or less." Mia left the coffee machine to brew and drove her chair back. "The easiest way to think about the differences is that gods are to immortals like immortals are to humans. Most can't compel, though. It's a rare ability for gods and immortals alike. They can all thrall, though."

It was all so confusing.

"What's the difference?" Margo asked.

"That's a good question. Compulsion forces the person to do as the compeller says, even if they are trying to resist. Thralling is changing what they remember and how they think about things. Those under compulsion will, in most cases, know what's happening to them. Those who are thralled will not. A good example is what Kalugal did to Modana and his men. He compelled them to put down their weapons, but he thralled them to believe that the Madonna appeared before them and demanded that they change their ways and become good people."

That made sense to Margo, and it also made her realize how dangerous Kalugal was.

How dangerous all these aliens were.

"What about Negal? Did he use any compulsion or thralling on Jasmine and me?"

"Negal can't compel," Mia said. "He can only thrall, but I doubt he used it on you or on Jasmine unless it was to erase from your memory anything that could reveal that he and his companions were not human. The good guys follow a strict code of conduct, which restricts the use of thralling to only when it is necessary to protect their identity or to save lives. The bad guys, on the other hand, use it as they please to control humans."

"The bad guys? How do I tell the good from the bad? And is Negal good?"

"Negal is good," Mia said. "And everyone on this ship follows that code of conduct. The bad guys are called Doomers, and you don't need to worry about them."

Margo snorted. "You know me better than that. Of course, I'm worried about the bad guys. I need to know who they are and how to avoid them."

16

MARINA

Lost in thought, Marina walked out of the kitchen and headed back to her cabin.

She was excited about going to the wedding as Peter's date, but after the looks she'd gotten from the staff and guests during her lunch shift, she also dreaded it.

Perhaps if she had a beautiful evening gown, she could pretend that she belonged among all those immortals, but she didn't have even a simple nice dress. All she'd brought with her were clothes that were appropriate for work and a couple of nicer tops for after-hours.

What the hell was she going to wear?

The more important question was, what the hell was she doing getting involved with an immortal?

She might enjoy a few blissful days with Peter, pretending to be a modern-day Cinderella, but unlike the fairytale, there was no fairy godmother to conjure a beautiful dress for her, and no happy ending after the magic expired at the proverbial midnight. When the cruise ended, it was back to cleaning rooms in Safe Haven.

Marina sighed.

Then again, this might be her only opportunity to experience life on the other side. The life of a human was short and mostly miserable, so she should enjoy whatever crumbs of happiness she could find, and Peter was a pretty tasty crumb.

A smile tugged at her lips at the memory of the night they had spent together and how perfect it had been between them.

It had been so good that even though they'd made love again this morning, she'd been so charged up with arousal that she'd played with herself in the shower before leaving her cabin for the lunch shift.

If only Peter were human, she would have thought herself the luckiest woman. But that was a silly thought because she wouldn't have approached him if he were just a regular guy.

Her plan had been to seduce an immortal who would be so infatuated with her that he would invite her to live with him in the immortals' village.

Peter was supposed to be her ticket out of the drudgery of Safe Haven.

The joke was on her, though. Despite her initial manipulative intentions, she found herself genuinely drawn to him, and it wasn't just about the mind-blowing sex, although she had to admit that was a large chunk of it.

Peter was the perfect lover who knew precisely how to bring her to the heights of passion, and he was also kind and attentive, stirring emotions in her she hadn't expected to feel again.

A small thing like his appreciation of the simple lunch she'd packed for him had been so genuine and surprising. Marina would have never expected an immortal to treat it as though it was some grand gesture. Her former Kra-ell masters wouldn't have even thanked her, and Nicolai would have taken it for granted as well.

Hell, she could have cooked a five-course meal for him, and he would have thought nothing of it.

Why was she even thinking about him?

One day with Peter should have been enough to wipe away the memory of her old boyfriend for good.

Marina sighed.

She shouldn't get attached to the immortal. As wonderful as being with him was, it wasn't going to last. Even if he was entertaining the thought of keeping her, she could just imagine what his friends and family would think when he brought 'the help' as his date for the wedding.

As she entered her cabin, she found her roommate lying on her belly, her chin propped on her fist and a book open in front of her.

Larisa looked up at her and smirked. "Where have you been? Cavorting with your new immortal boyfriend?"

Larisa had a sharp tongue, but she didn't mean anything by it. They all had a history of dealing with powerful aliens, and a lot of it hadn't been good.

"Not since this morning. Did you happen to bring anything nice to wear? Peter's invited me to accompany him to the wedding tonight."

Larisa flopped to her side. "He did what?"

"You heard me. But unless I can find something to wear that will make me look like I belong, I won't go."

Larisa snorted. "You could be wearing a designer gown, and you still wouldn't fit in. You are human, and you are a servant."

Marina sat on the bed. "Being a servant is a job, not who I am. And I won't be the only human in there. There are several of them who live with the immortals, and they brought two human women aboard earlier."

Larisa shrugged. "I don't have anything nice." She turned back on her belly. "We came here to work, not to party."

"Do you mind if I take a look at your closet?"

"Go ahead." Larisa waved a hand without looking at her. "But you won't find anything. You might want to check with Mila. Maybe she has something."

Mila liked to wear dresses, but she was also three sizes bigger than Marina, and there was no time to make alterations. Besides, Mila's simple dresses were not suitable for a wedding.

As Marina sifted through Larisa's stuff, she had to agree with her roommate that there was nothing in her closet she could use.

She sat on her bed and sighed. "My only other option is Sofia, but I feel weird about asking her. She's one of them now."

Larisa turned to look at her. "If you can date one of them, you can ask one of them to lend you a dress, but Sofia is so skinny that nothing of hers will fit you."

Pretending to be mad, Marina tossed a pillow at her roommate. "Are you calling me fat?"

"You're not fat." Larisa tossed the pillow back. "But Sofia is a twig. She has the body of a tall twelve-year-old girl."

"It's her Kra-ell genes. She has their body shape."

"And yet, that immortal fell in love with her. What's his name?"

"Marcel."

"Yeah. He's okay. I hope your Peter is also a decent guy."

"He is very nice."

Larisa arched a brow. "Then what are you doing with him? You don't date nice guys." She snorted. "We all know that Nico is a jerk."

"I'm turning over a new leaf." Marina pushed to her feet. "Besides, it's probably only going to last until the end of the cruise. After that, Peter goes back to his village, and I go back to Safe Haven." She let out a breath. "But I'm not going to worry about that. Right now, I need to find a dress."

17

MARGO

"That should do it," Toven said after reciting a long and detailed list of all the things that Margo wasn't allowed to talk about with anyone who was not immortal.

"What about Lisa and the other kids who are still human?" Margo asked. "Mia told me that the girls can't transition until they are adults, but she didn't tell me why it's different for the boys."

As bizarre as Mia's initial overview of the story of gods and immortals had been, it had been well organized, but after that, they had been jumping from one subject to the next, and even though Margo was starting to get a picture of what was going on, she was well aware of the huge gaps in information that still needed to be filled in.

Toven took another sip of his coffee. "Let's leave some details for another time. If you try to learn everything there is about us in one sitting, your head will explode."

Margo's head was just fine. Given the number of startling revelations she'd received in the span of three hours, she was doing quite well, if she said so herself. Not to mention that she was diving into this rabbit hole after having just experienced a terrifying ordeal.

To be frank, though, it hadn't been all that frightening because she'd been drugged, but still, she'd been through a lot, and she was doing great. She was probably coasting on a wave of adrenaline and would crash soon, but for now, she was good.

She shook her head. "I still can't believe that you are a god and that you are seven thousand years old. You don't look a day over thirty-three."

"Thank you." He put his mug down and rose to his feet. "We should start getting ready for the wedding, and Frankie needs to return to the clinic, or Bridget will send Guardians to drag her back there."

Turning to look at Frankie, Margo winced. She looked like she was about to fall asleep. "I'll take you there, and then I'll go check on Jasmine."

Frankie didn't put up a fight. "I hoped to attend the wedding tonight, but I'm exhausted. I'm surprised that Dagor hasn't come looking for me yet. He came to the clinic straight from the field, and then I came up here, and he was supposed to have a short meeting with Aru and Negal and come back to shower and change."

"He probably fell asleep in Aru's cabin," Toven said.

Frankie yawned. "Can you check on him? I hate to think of him sleeping on the couch in his dirty clothes and makeup caked on his face."

"Makeup?" Margo asked.

"It was to camouflage their good looks," Frankie said. "Negal had some on as well."

"He didn't. He was holding me in his arms, and my face was inches away from his. I would have noticed if he had makeup on. He must have washed it off." Margo frowned. "He also said that he had contact lenses that bothered him, and now I know that he lied about it. Why would he do that?"

Hiding a smile, Toven cleared his throat. "You will have to ask him about it when you see him." He turned to Frankie. "I'll check on Dagor and tell him to go shower and get changed. You should get some rest, though, so you can at least attend the next wedding."

Frankie gave him a thumbs-up, but the smirk on her face was for Margo. She was probably waiting for Toven to leave to ask Margo what she'd been doing in Negal's arms.

She was wrong.

Frankie didn't wait to ask. "What were you doing in Negal's arms?"

"I fainted, and he caught me."

Mia groaned. "We were in such a rush to tell you about all of this that we didn't ask you about your experience. Tomorrow, you are going to tell us everything." She glanced at the new phone that Toven had brought for Margo. "Or even better, I'll call you later."

"Not fair," Frankie said. "I want to hear all about it too, but as soon as I'm back in bed, I'll fall asleep. I'm so tired."

"Call me when you wake up." Margo took the device and put it in her purse. "Thank you again for the phone."

She could call anyone on the ship, but she couldn't make outside calls, which meant that she still couldn't call her family and tell them that she was alive.

"You're welcome." Toven moved aside to let Mia through. "Are you coming to the wedding tonight?"

Margo thought back to the exchange between Negal and the nurse. Gertrude had asked him if they were still on for tonight, and Negal had said sure. It would be too upsetting to watch them dance, or worse, smooch on the dance floor and then leave together.

Frankie and Mia were all about making a match between her and Negal, and it was sweet of them, but he wasn't into her.

"I think I'll pass. I'm tired, and besides, I have nothing to wear."

"You can have any dress of mine you want." Frankie waved her hand at the door to her bedroom. "I have many to choose from."

"Even if I wanted to attend the party and provided that I could squeeze into one of your dresses, I wouldn't be able to squeeze into your shoes. You have ridiculously small feet."

"Come to the party," Mia implored. "It's a great opportunity to meet everyone in an informal setting."

Margo let out a breath. "I'll think about it. But first, I need to get Frankie to the clinic and visit Jasmine. I'm worried about her." She offered Frankie a hand up and helped her into the wheelchair.

"Call me," Mia said before heading to the door. "If you decide to come, Toven and I will come to get you so you don't have to enter the event hall alone."

"Thank you." Margo waited for the two of them to leave before crouching in front of Frankie. "Do you need anything to take with you to the clinic?"

"I have everything I need down there except for Dagor. I should just call him and see what's going on."

"Do it now. I can wait."

"No, it's fine. I'll wait for Toven to wake him up. He will call me right away."

It suddenly occurred to Margo that the nurse might be in the clinic, but then, she had nothing against the woman. The immortal. She seemed like a nice person.

"Let's get you down there." She pushed Frankie's chair toward the door and opened it. "Can I ask you a favor?"

"Anything," Frankie said.

"I need to let my family know that I'm okay, but Kevin, I mean Kalugal, said that I can't call them for some reason. Something about the cartel thugs finding out about this ship. Is there a way you can call Lynda for me and ask her to tell Rob and my parents?"

Frankie was quiet for a moment. "Calling them might not be a good idea, but I can call my cousin Angelica and ask her to stop by and deliver the message in person. She can tell them that you can't call, but we will have to come up with an excuse why. Any suggestions?"

"First of all, thank you. You are a genius for thinking about your cousin delivering the message in person. And as for the excuse, you can tell Angelica about Jasmine and what Alberto tried to do to her and that I was involved, but we both got away, and now we are in a witness protection program until the bad guys get arrested and that's why I can't call them. Just don't mention any names."

"Sounds good to me. The elevators are that way." Frankie pointed in the opposite direction.

"Right." Margo turned the chair around. "So, how do I tell the immortals from the humans? Everyone who's gorgeous is an immortal, and everyone who is not is a human?"

Frankie chuckled. "More or less. The human staff know about us. It's just the rescued women who don't, and the advice Kri gave Jasmine goes for you, too. Unless you speak Spanish, there isn't much you can do for them. When you see them in the dining hall or the staff lounge, just smile and be nice."

"I can do that."

Frankie turned to look at Margo over her shoulder. "I know you can. I'm so glad that you are finally here. And Negal is not your only option if you don't like him. I told you about Max. He's the Guardian who led the team that took over Modana's mansion, and he's hot."

"I didn't say that I didn't like Negal. What's not to like? But he's not interested in me."

"Are you sure about that?"

"Pretty sure. He's taking Gertrude to the wedding tonight."

"So?"

"So, he's seeing someone."

"Pfft." Frankie waved a dismissive hand. "He's a player. He probably shags a different female each night."

"Then you are right. I'm not interested in him. You know my opinion about players."

18

FRANKIE

"My wayward patient," Bridget greeted Frankie with a wry smile. "I've been waiting for you."

The doctor wore a white coat that was open, revealing a sundress with an above-the-knee hemline and a large white flower print over a yellow background. It was a very cheerful outfit for such a serious woman.

Frankie smiled sweetly. "Hi, doctor. This is my friend Margo. Margo, this is Doctor Bridget. My jailer."

Shaking her head, Bridget offered Margo her hand. "Welcome aboard, Margo. How far down the rabbit hole have you fallen so far?"

Margo chuckled. "Pretty far. My head is spinning, but that could be a withdrawal symptom. I was injected with a drug to relax me so I wouldn't panic over being abducted and about to be gifted to a cartel boss's brother."

Bridget's expression turned from amused to concerned, two creases making an appearance between her red eyebrows. "Do you know what they injected you with?"

It should have occurred to her to have Kalugal ask Alberto what was in the syringe, but it hadn't, and now it was probably too late. "I have no prior experience with drugs, so I can't tell you which one it was, but my fellow abductee thinks it was heroin."

"How long ago were you injected?" Bridget asked.

"It was very early this morning."

"How did it feel?"

"Too damn good." Margo sighed. "At first, it was an intense rush, and I felt like floating. I was so happy, even euphoric, and that's unlike me." She looked at Frankie. "My friends can attest that's not my natural state."

Frankie nodded. "Margo is a bit crusty, and she sees a conspiracy around every corner."

Margo snorted. "I didn't see this one coming." She waved a hand around. "Although given that I believe our government is hiding contact with aliens, discovering that immortals and gods live among us is not so far-fetched. After all, the gods are aliens, and the immortals are part human and part god. The funny thing is that our government has no clue that either exists. Or does it?"

Bridget's face brightened. "We fly under the radar, so to speak. I'm glad that your mind seems to be working just fine despite the onset of withdrawal, but you might not have been hit with it yet. Do you feel anxious or restless?"

"I do, but I don't think it's the drug's effect. As you noted so aptly before, I fell down one hell of a rabbit hole, and I'm still reeling from the rebound."

"Yes, that's understandable." Bridget regarded her with curious eyes. "Any sweating, runny nose, or excessive yawning?"

"No."

"Good. You are not out of the woods yet, but you'll probably be fine. If you experience nausea, muscle pain, bone pain, or any other flu-like symptoms in the next twenty-four to seventy-two hours, it might be withdrawal. If it gets really uncomfortable, come see me, and I'll give you something to help with the symptoms."

"Thank you."

Frankie chuckled. "You've just described all the symptoms of my transition. I didn't know that they were the same as withdrawal from heroin."

"Are you still feeling them?" Bridget asked.

Frankie scrunched her nose. "I was so excited to see Margo that I wasn't paying attention, but now that I think about it, I haven't been nauseous all day. I still have some muscle pain, though, and I get tired easily."

"How long is this stage of the transition going to last?" Margo asked. "Frankie told me that only the beginning is difficult, and then the changes continue under the hood, so to speak."

Evidently, Margo had retained more information than Frankie had expected her to, and the rebound from her fall down the rabbit hole hadn't messed with her sharp brain.

"I'll know more once I check Frankie's vitals," Bridget said. "It might already be over."

Frankie's heart leaped in her chest. "Am I ready for the test?"

The doctor shook her head. "You are transitioning as fast as a teenager, but unlike the teenagers, you're still full of Dagor's venom, and that might skew the results. We need to wait another day or two until it leaves your system."

Damn. Not wanting to scare Margo, Frankie and Mia hadn't told her about the fangs and venom yet, and knowing her suspicious friend, she would latch on to Bridget's slip-up like a baby monkey to its mama.

Wincing, Frankie turned to look at Margo, who was gaping at her with wide, shocked eyes. "Venom? What is she talking about?"

"We didn't get that deep into the rabbit hole yet. Toven told you that there is a lot more for you to learn."

"It will have to wait." Bridget took command of the wheelchair. "Frankie needs to rest." She pushed the chair to the other room.

"Do you need help getting onto the bed?" Margo asked.

"I'm good." Frankie put her hand on the railing and pulled herself up. She used the step stool to climb into the bed. "As much as I hate to admit it, I really need to lie down." She stretched out and let out a sigh. "I don't want to fall asleep, though. I haven't seen Dagor since he went to the meeting with Aru."

"Do you need help changing into a nightgown?" Margo asked.

Frankie shook her head. "I don't have the energy. I'm wearing comfy things, so I'll just take off the bra and go to sleep like this."

"You're not going to sleep yet." The doctor wrapped a blood pressure cuff around Frankie's arm. "I need to check your heartbeat, your temperature, the length of your limbs, etc., etc. You know the drill."

Frankie winced. "Yeah, I do."

"Do you need me to leave?" Margo asked the doctor.

"It's a little cramped in here, so I would appreciate you waiting in the front room until I'm done. It's not going to take more than ten minutes."

"No problem." Margo blew Frankie an air kiss, left the room, and closed the door behind her.

"How is Margo taking it?" Bridget asked.

"Denial at first, and then acceptance. I was in Margo's shoes only a few days ago, so I know what she's going through. It's wonderful and terrifying at the same time." Frankie closed her eyes. "It feels like it has been weeks since I boarded this ship, months even. Are we in a time warp?"

Bridget snorted softly. "The perception of time changes based on the number of new experiences. That's why when a lot is happening, it feels like time is slowing down, and when everything is just routine, we look back and think where did the time go?"

"Makes sense." Frankie opened her eyes and leveled her gaze on Bridget.

"Were you serious about not wanting to test me because of Dagor's venom still circulating in my blood?"

"I don't jest about things like that." Bridget finished noting the blood pressure results and pulled out a measuring tape from her pocket. "It's fascinating how every Dormant's transition is different. You might be doing it so fast because of Dagor's potent godly venom, or because you are close to the source, or a combination of both."

"Is there a way to know?"

"Not yet, but there will be. Kaia is working on it."

Kaia was William's mate, and according to rumors, she was a prodigy, but Frankie didn't know what she was working on. It probably had to do with genetics, and it wasn't a subject she knew a lot about, but perhaps once she was out of the clinic and back on her feet, she could ask Kaia to explain it to her in layman's terms.

After all, Frankie had eternity to learn any subject she wanted, even if some took an extraordinarily long time to do.

"Ain't no mountain high enough..." she sang quietly.

"What was that?" Bridget asked.

"Oh, nothing. I was just reminded of a song."

19

MARGO

It had been such a relief not to run into the nurse, but Margo felt ridiculous for thinking that way. She had no reason to feel animosity toward the immortal just because she was Negal's date. It wasn't as if she wanted to take her place.

No, thank you.

Margo didn't do hookups or one-night stands, and she stayed away from players. Male bimbos was a better term.

What was the point of sleeping with a different woman every night?

It was devoid of any emotional connection and therefore reduced sex to an animalistic level.

Not her thing.

Not now and not ever. It was either the whole nine yards or nothing.

Besides, Negal wasn't interested in her that way, which was a good thing. Margo would have hated having to deflect his advances after he'd come to her rescue like an avenging angel.

How could a guy be so perfect in some ways and so imperfect in others? Maybe it was nature's way of balancing things. If Negal were perfect in every way, he would be a god...

Ugh. He *was* a damn god. Margo let out a sound that was part sigh and part groan. Perhaps she was already in a Perfect Match virtual adventure? It must have started yesterday when she'd met Jasmine, and it was still going, but who was her partner in the game?

It had to be Negal because she hadn't met anyone else who could fit the bill of a romantic interest.

The clinic door banging open startled her from her musings, and for a moment, she wondered if it was also part of the simulation, but as the dark-haired male with a wild look in his blue eyes walked in, she knew who he was from Frankie's descriptions, and she also knew that it didn't make sense for her besties and their boyfriends to be part of the virtual fantasy.

She'd read enough about it to know that the program didn't work that way.

Doug, or rather Dagor, had smeared makeup on his face and was wearing dirty clothing, but she knew the reason was an unsuccessful attempt at camouflaging his unnatural beauty. Otherwise, she would have thought he was a vagrant.

A gorgeous vagrant despite his ugly makeup and haggard appearance.

"Hi, Dagor. You can't go in right now. Doctor Bridget is examining Frankie."

He stopped with his hand on the handle and turned around, his eyes widening as if he'd just noticed she was there. "Margo?"

"In the flesh." She offered him her hand. "It's nice to finally meet you."

"Welcome to the clan." He shook her hand. "How much were you told?"

It was a great opportunity to get some information out of the guy. Getting men talking was always easier than women. They were much less guarded around the so-called weaker sex.

Ha, the joke was on them.

"A lot and not enough," she said. "What's the deal with the venom in Frankie's system that Doctor Bridget mentioned? What's that all about?"

He swallowed, and his eyes darted to the side as if he were looking for a poster that would tell him how to answer that. "I'm really not the one who should be telling you about it."

"Then who?"

"Frankie, Mia, Negal. Even Bridget would be better than me."

The only name that struck her as odd in that list was Negal's. "Is that something Negal should have told me on the way?"

"No." Dagor rubbed a hand over the back of his neck and then grimaced. "Sorry about my disheveled appearance. I fell asleep on the couch, and when Toven woke me up, I rushed down here to see Frankie. How is she doing?"

"Tired. Bridget said that she could have been ready for the test, whatever that is, if she wasn't pumped full of your venom. She said it would skew the results. Care to explain?"

Dagor had just woken up, and he didn't know how to handle the situation. If she pressed hard enough, he might cave in and give her an explanation.

"I really don't." He winced. "Sorry, but it's a delicate type of answer, and I'm not the one who should be doing it. Perhaps after Bridget is done examining Frankie, you can go in and ask her."

"Maybe I will." Margo leaned against the nurse's desk and crossed her arms over her chest.

She was anxious to see Jasmine, but she had a feeling that the answer to the venom question was crucial. Venom usually went together with fangs, but none of the immortals and gods she'd met so far had them. Could it be that their semen was venomous?

She chuckled. It gave credence to the infamous term: a one-eyed trouser snake.

"What's so funny?" Dagor asked.

Margo lifted a brow. "Oh, I don't know if I should tell you that. It's probably something that you need to hear from Frankie."

He laughed. "Touché."

They waited another minute or so for the door to open and for the doctor to step out. "You can go in," she told Dagor and then turned to Margo. "I need you to stay for a moment."

"Of course."

The doctor waited until Dagor closed the door behind him. "You said that both you and Jasmine were injected with the drug, correct?"

"Yes."

"Then I should check on her as well. She might have more severe withdrawal symptoms than you, and she won't know who to turn to."

Margo nodded. "She seemed fine the last time I saw her, but that was several hours ago, and she might have taken a turn for the worse. I probably should come along, though. I think Jaz will be less intimidated by you if I'm there."

The petite doctor frowned. "I'm not intimidating."

"Perhaps not to the people who know you, but you have a formidable presence, and poor Jasmine has been through a lot. She might be a little skittish." The doctor was also a gorgeous redhead, and it would be really difficult to explain why everyone on the ship was so damn good-looking.

"Fine. Let's go." The doctor turned to leave.

"Can you wait a moment for me to say goodbye to Frankie?"

"I don't have a lot of time." Bridget turned back around and glanced at her smartwatch. "I still need to get ready for the wedding." She lifted her head and looked up at Margo. "Are you going to attend?"

"I don't think so. It's been a very long and exciting day for me. I want to take a long bath, crawl into bed with a gallon of ice cream, and watch sitcom reruns."

"I hear you." The doctor sighed. "That actually sounds like a dream, but I have to attend, and so should you. If you are to become a member of this community, you should start mingling and getting to know people, and there is no better time to do it than when everyone is in a good mood." She leaned closer to Margo. "And that's especially true in regard to our esteemed regent. Kian is cranky on a good day, and you haven't seen intimidating until you've met him. But he loves weddings, and that means he's always in a good mood during celebratory times."

That was excellent advice, and Margo decided to follow it even if it meant seeing Negal with the nurse.

"Thank you for the advice, doctor. I'm going to take it."

"Smart girl." Bridget patted her arm. "Now go and say goodbye to your friend, and don't take too long. We need to check on Jasmine."

20

PETER

Holding a stack of fresh towels and a change of linen in his arms, Peter made his way back to his cabin, and as he thought about the reason for the need to change the bedding, he started whistling a happy tune.

Marina was amazing, and it wasn't just the sex.

The memory of their time together on the Lido deck filled him with a sense of warmth and contentment, and he couldn't help but smile as he replayed their conversation in his mind.

She was so easy to be with, probably because he didn't need to be careful around her. He didn't need to hide his fangs or his glowing eyes or think about every word that left his mouth.

That had been one of the main things that had attracted him to Kagra, but things hadn't worked out between them, and not for lack of trying on his part. She just wasn't interested in anything long-term with him, and once her curiosity was sated, she moved on to the next guy.

Still, Marina was human, and she couldn't be more than a passing curiosity for him either, and what a damn shame that was.

She was a great playmate who enjoyed all the things that he did, and he hadn't had one of those in a long time. Kagra was the opposite of Marina, and it had been exciting to make the switch for a while, but Peter had to admit that he enjoyed himself much more with the human than with the Kra-ell.

As he entered the cabin, he was surprised to find the woman who had occupied his thoughts sitting on the couch in the living room with Jay seated on an armchair across from her.

Smart guy.

Peter wouldn't have liked him being any closer to her.

"Hi." Marina rose to her feet. "I wanted to talk to you, but I still don't have your number, so I couldn't call." She lifted her hand with an old-style tiny flip phone clutched in it. "Your roommate kindly let me in."

Jay cleared his throat. "I'll be in my room if you need me." He smiled at Marina. "It was nice to meet you." He ducked into the bedroom and closed the door.

For some reason, it felt suddenly awkward between them, and Peter didn't like it. Reaching for Marina, he wrapped his arm around her tiny waist and pulled her to him. "I missed you." He kissed her softly. "Did you miss me?"

She smiled at him. "I thought about you a lot. Does that count?"

He pouted. "Not the same, but I'll take it. Can I get you something to drink or eat?"

"No, thank you. I'm good. I just came to tell you that I can't accompany you to the wedding tonight. I have to work." She averted her eyes, a clear indication that she wasn't telling him the truth.

He could also smell the lie on her, and if it weren't intertwined with a smell of disappointment, he would have been angry. Something must have caused her to change her mind, but it wasn't work, and she wasn't happy about it.

Leaning closer to her ear, he whispered, "Liars get spanked. Is that what you want?"

The scent of sad lies was immediately overpowered by the scent of her arousal. "Yes, but that's not why I lied."

At least she was wise enough to admit it.

"Why did you lie? And which part was untrue? The bit about you having to work tonight or the one about not being able to accompany me to the wedding?"

She averted her gaze again. "The one about having to work. I can switch shifts if I want, but I really can't come to the wedding as a guest. I asked all my friends, and none of them brought evening attire to the cruise. I can't show up wearing my work clothes."

He leaned away and looked her over. She still had the same cropped top from this morning and a pair of fitted black jeans, and she looked beautiful.

"You are perfect as you are. I won't wear a tux either, so we will both be dressed casually."

She shook her head. "It's going to offend the bride and groom if you come to their ceremony wearing jeans. Besides, I'm not allowed in the dining room until after the ceremony, so we can't arrive together anyway."

He'd forgotten about that.

Kian didn't want the staff to be exposed to his mother even though they were under compulsion to keep quiet about what they saw on the ship, so they were not allowed in the dining room until the ceremony was over and she left. The human staff were also not allowed on the top deck where Annani, Kian and his sisters' cabins were. The Odus took care of cleaning that deck, and Annani dined in her cabin.

"I have to be there for the ceremony, but as soon as the doors open, I'll come out to get you."

"Please, Peter. I can't. It would have been awkward enough to be your date for the evening even if I had the fanciest gown, but it would be unbearable to come dressed in jeans."

"I'll get you a dress."

"From where?"

He waved a hand. "This ship is full of my cousins, and even my mother might have something that you could borrow."

Her eyes widened, and her hand flew to her chest. "Your mother is here?"

"Of course. Why wouldn't she be? The whole idea behind this cruise was for us to gather in one place to attend the weddings."

"Are you related to some of the people getting married?"

The humans didn't know how large or small the clan was, and they also didn't know that most of them were related, and he wasn't supposed to reveal that.

In the grand scheme of things it was a small revelation, almost insignificant compared to all the things he normally needed to hide from his bed partners, so he wasn't too concerned about the slip-up, but that wasn't what was bothering him.

He realized that Marina meant more to him than just another bed partner.

You are in love with the notion of love, Kagra's words sounded in the back of his mind.

"Yeah. As I said, I have many cousins," he said, making the statement as general as he could. "Don't worry about my mother. She won't bother you. We are not very close."

Marina swallowed. "Now that I know your mother is here, I really don't think I should come as your date. I'm human."

As if her humanity was a newsflash to him.

"That's irrelevant. You're coming, and I don't want to hear another word about it." He took the phone she was still clutching. "I'll call myself from your phone so you will have my number, and I'll have yours."

"Do you even know how to use this ancient device?"

He smiled. "You forget that I'm not as young as I look. I've probably used every communication device ever invented."

21

MARGO

Margo knocked on Jasmine's cabin door, and when there was no answer, she knocked again. "Maybe she's sleeping."

"Try the doorbell," Bridget suggested.

"If she's sleeping, I don't want to wake her up."

"I need to check on her." Bridget pressed the doorbell button.

When there was no answer, the doctor rang the bell again, and when that didn't get a response, she pulled out her phone and used the same application Margo had downloaded into her new phone earlier, but unlike hers, which could open only her and Frankie's cabin, it seemed like the doctor could enter any cabin she wished.

It made sense for her to have the ability. In fact, it would be great if paramedics could do that with people's door locks in life-threatening situations.

Margo pushed the door open and entered the empty cabin. The bed was made, and nothing looked out of place. It was as if Jaz had never been there.

"Jasmine is not here," she stated the obvious.

"Let's check the staff lounge and dining room." The doctor closed the door and started walking down the hall. "It's one deck down. We can use the stairs."

Margo fell into step with her. "I wish Toven had brought another phone like mine to give to Jasmine. He could have programmed it so she could call only me."

"That's a good idea." Bridget turned into the staircase. "The problem is that we might not have a spare one. We knew that you were joining the cruise, so we prepared one for you, but we didn't expect Jasmine."

"Who should I ask about it?"

Bridget gave her a curious sidelong glance. "I'll ask the guy in charge of communications for you."

Margo couldn't decipher that look. "Am I overstepping my boundaries?"

"No, you're not. I'm just surprised at how quickly you are adjusting and immediately taking charge. I like that."

"Thank you. It's just that I feel responsible for Jasmine, and I don't want to burden anyone with her care more than I have to." Margo smiled sheepishly. "I'm the rude guest who brought along another guest."

"You asked permission, and it was granted." The doctor opened a door into a sprawling lounge that was bustling with activity.

Some people were lounging on couches and watching a movie with Russian dubbing, while others were sitting around tables and playing cards, checkers or chess, chatting, drinking, and snacking.

The atmosphere was relaxed and upbeat at the same time, and no one paid her and Bridget any mind. Perhaps they were used to seeing the doctor down here.

Scanning the room, Margo found Jasmine sitting at one of the tables with three other women and holding playing cards in her hand. "There she is." She started walking toward her with Bridget at her side.

Jaz didn't notice their approach until they were only a few steps away and then turned her head and smiled. "Hi. I thought that you were not coming, so I came here and found these lovely ladies playing my favorite game. Do you want to join in? We are playing poker and gambling with potato chips."

There was a large stack of Pringles next to Jasmine and nearly none next to her companions.

"Who are your new friends?" Margo asked.

"This is Mila." Jaz waved at a plump older woman.

"*Dobryy vecher*," said Mila and inclined her head.

"This is Lina," Jaz said.

"Hello." The young woman smiled and did a little wave with the hand that wasn't holding cards.

"And that's Helga."

"*Hyvää iltaa*." The forty-something woman with ruddy cheeks nodded.

"Nice to meet you all. I'm Margo." She patted her chest.

"Hello, Jasmine." The doctor offered Jaz her hand. "I'm Bridget, one of the ship's doctors. I would like to have a word with you and check how you are doing after your ordeal."

The fact that Bridget hadn't introduced herself to the other three confirmed Margo's assumption that everyone in the lounge knew the doctor.

"Of course." Jasmine put her cards face down on the tabletop and rose to her feet.

Bridget motioned for her to step away from the table and leaned toward her. "Margo told me about the drugs you two were injected with. I wanted to make sure that you were doing okay with the withdrawal symptoms," she said, so quietly that no one other than Jasmine and Margo could have heard her.

"I feel a little nauseous, which is why I came to the lounge to look for something salty to snack on." Jasmine didn't even try to keep her voice down. "I found these lovely ladies playing poker and asked to join their game."

Margo lifted a brow. "How? You said that you didn't speak Russian."

She turned and smiled at the youngest of the poker players. "Lina speaks English, Russian, and Finnish, and she translates for us."

"Your friend is killing us," Lina said. "It's like she can read our minds."

Jasmine laughed. "The three of you have such obvious tells that a baby could guess what kind of cards you are holding. You really need to work on your poker faces."

When Lina translated, the other two didn't look happy, and a discussion in Russian ensued.

It was strange that Jaz could read these women, whom she'd just met, so easily, but she'd been blind to Alberto's manipulation. Evidently, it was not only men who got stupid around beautiful women. It worked the other way around, too.

"I can give you something for the nausea," Bridget said to Jasmine.

"No need." Jaz snatched one of her winnings. "These do the job." She popped it into her mouth.

"As you wish." Bridget regarded her with the same scrutiny she'd regarded Margo with before. "If your symptoms worsen, let Lina or one of the others know. They can find me or one of the other doctors."

The smile slid off Jasmine's face. "Thank you. Can't I just come up to the clinic? All I need to do to get there is walk up two flights of stairs, and I didn't see anyone stationed there to stop me."

Aha, so she'd tried to push her boundaries already. Margo didn't blame her. She would have done the same.

Bridget smiled indulgently. "There are surveillance cameras in all the public spaces, and if you had tried to go to the upper decks, someone would have intercepted you. You are welcome at the clinic any time, but there is no one there at night. That's the reason I told you to inform Lina so she could find a way to get in touch with one of the doctors."

Frankie was staying in the clinic overnight, and Margo wondered who was going to watch over her if all the medical staff was at the wedding. Dagor would no doubt be there, but he was not a healthcare provider.

Bridget must have realized what she was thinking because she patted her arm. "Don't worry about your friend. I can see all the readouts from the monitoring equipment on my phone, and if anything goes wrong, the application will sound the alarm, and I'll be there in moments."

"That's good to know."

"What's wrong with Frankie?" Jasmine asked.

"She was bitten by a snake and had a reaction to the venom." Margo somehow managed to say that with a straight face. "Frankie is a little embarrassed about the circumstances of that bite, so she doesn't want to talk about it, and I can't really say more."

Bridget snorted. "That's a good one, Margo."

Jasmine frowned. "What's funny about a snake bite?"

"Nothing." Bridget snorted again. "It's just a little insider joke."

22

NEGAL

A loud ringing pierced through the haze of Negal's restless sleep, and as he tried to figure out whether the sound was in his dream or in the real world, he debated whether he should force himself to wake up.

He knew that he was dreaming, but it still felt realistic as hell. Well, hell was precisely where he'd gone in his dream, and it wasn't a product of his imagination. He'd served on that gods-forsaken colony, and his experience there had been pretty close to how humans described the afterlife of sinners.

It was one of Anumati's less desirable settlements, where volcanic activity was the norm, and creatures similar to the dragons of human lore were wreaking havoc on the meager existence of the colonists. After endless requests for help, he and his team had been sent to secure the large engineering crew that had been tasked with building better defenses against the flying lizards. Their job hadn't been to kill the creatures. In fact, they had been instructed to refrain from doing that unless it was necessary to protect the building crews.

The creatures were the apex predators of the planet, and the powers that be had decided that hunting them into extinction was not a good idea because they kept the predators further down the line in check. Without the dragons, the others would rapidly multiply and cause even more trouble to the settlers.

At least the dragons didn't reproduce as readily as the other indigenous nasties, of which there were plenty. Also, the winged lizards were highly territorial and destroyed each other's eggs if they could find them, ensuring that no new hatchlings grew up to encroach on their turf and further reducing their population.

Dragons went to great lengths to hide and protect their nests, which Negal didn't hold against them, but they were also destroying crops, eating livestock, and sometimes roasting entire villages. Most of the gods recovered thanks to their rapid healing, but not all. It was also one of the places the Eternal King sent those he was displeased with, increasing the chances of them meeting with an untimely demise.

Still, the undesirables were just a small fraction of the planet's population. The majority of the settlers were just unlucky to have been randomly picked from the pool of Anumatians destined for the colonies.

As the ringing stopped, Negal released a relieved breath and turned on his side, but then the noise resumed, and he was forced to open his eyes.

Perhaps it was better to wake up instead of returning to the nasty dream. But why weren't his roommates opening the door?

As the cobwebs of sleep receded, Negal remembered that there was no one in the cabin when he'd gotten in bed. Dagor was probably in the clinic with Frankie, and Aru and Gabi might have returned but were busy in their room.

He grabbed his phone off the nightstand, found the application that controlled the lock, and brought up the camera view.

His eyes widened when he saw Gertrude standing outside the door, decked out in an evening gown and tapping her foot on the floor.

Was he late?

What time was it?

He shifted his gaze to the clock display and sucked in a breath. He had overslept, and Gertrude had been waiting for him for the past twenty minutes.

She'd asked him to share a drink with her before the wedding, and he'd promised to meet her in the bar on the main deck.

Why hadn't she called first?

She probably had, but he hadn't heard it because he'd been dreaming about dragons, and their roars had filled his dream.

Grabbing the towel he'd dropped on the floor after showering, Negal wrapped it around his hips and padded to the living room to open the door.

"Took you long enough." As Gertrude's eyes shifted to his bare chest, her indignant expression turned lustful, and the scent of her arousal overpowered the combined smells of her irritation and perfume.

Normally, the scent of a female's arousal would have elicited a corresponding response from him, but now it left him indifferent, which was a testament to how far he had fallen down the crater his mind had created.

"I'm so sorry," he said. "I overslept."

"Obviously." Her eyes roamed over his body, and then a smile lifted one corner of her red-colored lips. "Aren't you going to invite me in?"

She didn't wait for his answer and put a hand on his chest to push him inside.

He could have resisted, but to what end? He owed her a drink and an apology, or maybe the other way around.

"Let me get you a drink." He padded to the kitchenette that also served as the bar. "You can sit down on the couch and relax with a glass of good whiskey while I get dressed."

Instead of sitting on the sofa, Gertrude followed him and sat down on a stool, or rather leaned her bottom against it. "Don't rush to get dressed. I like the view."

Smiling tightly, Negal stifled the urge to adjust the towel around his hips to make sure it stayed in place. He didn't like the hungry look in Gertrude's eyes, and for a moment, she reminded him of the dragon creatures he had just dreamt about.

That was such a nasty thought that he shook his head to dispel it. Gertrude was kind and beautiful, and the only reason she reminded him of the dragon was her assertiveness, which he normally liked in a female.

If not for Margo, he would have been thrilled to spend the night with Gertrude.

Negal pulled out a bottle of whiskey. "Do you like it straight or in a cocktail?"

"Straight if it's good whiskey, and this one is." She wasn't looking at the bottle.

She was looking at him.

"Coming up." He put the bottle on the counter and pulled out two whiskey glasses. "I should get dressed." He poured the golden liquid into them. "We can still make it to the bar if you are in the mood."

"I don't mind skipping that." Gertrude leaned over the counter, the neckline of her dress dipping low and her ample breasts nearly spilling out. "In fact, we can skip the wedding altogether and celebrate right here." She smiled suggestively. "No one is going to miss us."

He returned a forced smile. "With Dagor staying in the clinic with Frankie, Aru won't like it if I don't show up as well. I must attend the wedding."

Frowning, Gertrude leaned back. "Why do I have a feeling that you are suddenly uncomfortable with me?"

Because it was true, but he didn't know how to say that without hurting her feelings.

"It's not that. I really must attend the wedding." He lifted the glass of whiskey, intending to take a sip, but ended up emptying it down his throat. "I'm going to get dressed."

"Stop." Gertrude lifted a hand. "If you are no longer interested in being with me, just say so instead of putting us both through this awkwardness. It's not fair to me, and it seems painful to you."

She was so perceptive.

Negal closed his eyes. "I promised to show you a good time, and I'm not the kind of guy who breaks his promises."

She laughed, but it sounded bitter. "I'm not an obligation, Negal. I'm a prize." She took the whiskey glass, drank it in one go, and pushed away from the stool. "I'll see you around." She walked toward the door.

"I'm sorry," he said after her. "You're an amazing female, and you deserve better. I didn't mean for it to happen like this."

She turned to look at him over her shoulder. "Don't sweat it, Negal. When it's not meant to be, it's not meant to be. I'll get over it." She opened the door and walked out.

He expected her to slam it, but she closed it gently behind her.

"I'm sorry," he murmured again.

23

MARGO

After Bridget left, Jasmine gave most of her Pringles back to her poker crew, thanked them for inviting her to their game, and took Margo's hand. "Come sit with me and tell me what's going on with this cruise. I tried to pump Lina for information, but she wouldn't tell me anything except that most of the staff was working at the party tonight, so they had to wrap up the game early."

That explained why the couches were being vacated, and the lounge was emptying.

"I think that the wedding is starting so late because of us," Jasmine said. "Who ever heard of a wedding that starts at ten-thirty at night?"

Perhaps she was right, and the wedding was happening so late because of the rescue mission their hosts had to pull off to save them, or maybe all immortal weddings happened late.

Margo gave Jaz a once-over. With her face clean of makeup and her long dark hair gathered in a ponytail, she looked younger and not even slightly less beautiful. She had a pair of fitted jeans on and a black T-shirt with a pink rhinestone heart stitched on the front.

"I see that Kri got you the clothes she promised." Margo sat on the low couch and crossed her legs at the ankles. "I would have never suspected her of owning anything with rhinestones or pink."

Jaz looked down at the T-shirt and laughed. "I was surprised, too. She's really sweet once she drops the tough guard façade."

"I don't think it's a façade. Did you see the size of her shoulders? They are almost as broad as Negal's."

"Oh, Negal," Jasmine said in a dreamy voice. "What a hunk of a man. Have you seen him since we got here?"

Jasmine's wistful tone was like nails on a chalkboard in Margo's ears, but she stifled her reaction to the annoyance and answered in what she hoped sounded like an indifferent voice. "I've only been with Frankie and Mia, and I met Mia's fiancé and Frankie's boyfriend. Then I took Frankie back to the clinic and met the doctor, and we came straight here. I was worried about you." She leaned back on the low couch, sinking into the cushions.

It was ridiculously comfortable, and Margo fought the urge to lie down and close her eyes.

"That's so sweet." Jaz surprised her by leaning over and kissing her cheek. "But you don't need to worry about me. I'm a big girl, and as long as I don't get blindsided by a charming snake, I can take care of myself." She tilted her head. "Did Frankie really get bitten by one?"

"How else would she get a reaction to venom?"

Sometimes, to avoid an answer, it was better to turn it into a question. Margo only hoped that her poker face was better than those of Jasmine's game buddies.

"It could have been a poisonous spider or even a toad," Jaz said.

"Frankie didn't tell me the particulars, so I assumed that it was a snake, and since Bridget didn't refute that assumption, I must have been right." Margo shifted on the couch. "So, what have you been doing all this time? Swindling Russian ladies out of Pringles?"

"I wasn't swindling them. It was a fair game that I just happened to be very good at. And no, that's not what I was doing the entire time. Kri and I chatted a little when she brought me the clothes. Did you know that she's getting married in two days?"

"Now, I do."

"Turns out that this cruise is all about weddings, and there is a different one every night. I asked Kri if she met her fiancé in a Perfect Match adventure, and she said no. Then I asked her if the other people getting married were Perfect Match couples, and she said that it was confidential and wouldn't say anything else. I wonder what all that secrecy is about."

Margo would have loved to share what she'd learned, but she was under compulsion to keep her mouth shut. Besides, Jaz wouldn't have believed her even if she told her.

Heck, she was still having a hard time believing it herself.

"It has to do with Perfect Match and their strict client confidentiality policy. If the couples getting married met on Perfect Match, and I'm not saying that they did, but if they did and didn't want that to be known, then it makes sense that access to their party would be restricted."

That's what Margo had thought before Frankie and Mia had told her the truth about the passengers on the ship. Margo still didn't know who was getting married and why there was a wedding every night. Maybe she should return to Frankie's room at the clinic and see if she was still awake. Maybe she could answer more questions for her.

Jasmine's eyes widened. "Now I get it. The weddings are of clients who met through the program but want to keep it a secret."

Margo gestured turning a key over her lips. "Can't confirm or deny it."

"Did they have you sign a confidentiality agreement?"

Technically, what Toven had done could count as one, so Margo nodded. "It's ironclad. I can't say a word without suffering terrible consequences."

Toven had warned her that trying to break through the compulsion would cause a bad headache, so she shouldn't try.

"Oh." Jasmine's face fell. "That's a shame. I hoped to live vicariously through you and get all the juicy details about what's going on upstairs. Talk about feeling like Cinderella, except I'm not invited to the ball, and there is no prince waiting for me."

Margo laughed. "Maybe I can tell you about the decorations and the food at the wedding. Not everything is strictly confidential."

"Please do." Jasmine leaned back against the fluffy couch cushions. "It's not bad down here. I like the casual setting, and the people are nice. It's good that I know a thing or two about Russians, though, so their sourpuss expressions don't scare me. I know they are not mean and that it's cultural."

Margo frowned. "I didn't notice any sourpusses."

"That's because you are an upstairs lady. They are playing nice with you. They gave me the stink eye aplenty when I walked into the lounge, but I know how to work a crowd. I had them eating out of my hand in no time."

"I bet."

Jasmine tilted her head. "So, what's the deal with you and Negal? He seemed really into you, and you weren't indifferent to him."

The second part was true, but regrettably, the first one was not.

"He was just being chivalrous. He's not interested in me. Besides, Frankie told me that he takes a different woman to his bed every night. That's not the kind of guy I'm interested in."

Jasmine leaned closer to her. "Then reform the rogue. Isn't that what all the historical romance novels are about? The lord with the kinky tastes entertains all the loose ladies of the town and then falls for the blushing virgin, who turns out to have kinky tastes herself, and they live happily ever after."

Laughter bubbled up from Margo's chest. "What kind of books have you been reading?"

"I just told you. Historical romance novels."

"You did. I just can't believe you read that nonsense."

Looking offended, Jaz leaned away. "Oh, yeah? What kind of books do you read? *Pride and Prejudice? War and Peace? Anna Karenina?*"

"Touché. I've read all the books you mentioned and many more classics, but what I read for fun are shifter romances," Margo admitted. "Dragon shifters are my guilty pleasure."

"That's why you knew so much about all the dragon adventures that Perfect Match offers."

Margo nodded. "I know a lot about all the adventures, not just those with dragons. I tried to learn as much as I could before coming here. I really want this job."

Jasmine frowned. "I thought that it was in the bag."

"I only signed a nondisclosure agreement. I've not been offered a contract yet."

"You'll get it." Jaz patted her thigh. "Don't forget to put in a good word for me. I would love to be part of this world."

Margo's gut clenched. "I will."

Unless by some miracle Jasmine was also a dormant carrier of godly genes, she would never be part of this world, but that didn't mean she couldn't work for Perfect Match Studios out in the human world.

First, though, Margo needed to find out if she had what it took to remain here. She still didn't know if she possessed the godly genes or how those genes were activated.

24

KIAN

Kian stood in front of the closet and debated whether he should put his tux on. The wedding was starting in about an hour, but he still had to stop by Turner's cabin, which was their makeshift war room's new location, and get an update from the team who had just returned from Modana's estate.

"Are you debating which tux to put on?" Syssi asked quietly from the bed.

Allegra had already been asleep when he'd returned to the cabin, and Syssi had joined him in bed for a short nap, which had been delightful even though he'd only held her in his arms.

"I'm debating whether to put the tux on now or after the meeting in Turner's cabin."

She frowned. "Why are you having another meeting? Did something happen while we were asleep?"

He turned around, sat on the bed, and took her hand. "There is nothing to worry about. Modana's yacht is in his private dock, he's back at his mansion, and our people who stayed behind to monitor the situation are back on board so they can come to the wedding. We are meeting in Turner's cabin to get an update from Theo, who was in charge of that team."

The *Silver Swan* had docked in Puerto Vallarta a while ago, but it had taken the yacht longer to get there.

So far, Carlos was a no-show, and Kian wondered what Turner's people were reporting from Cabo and from Ensenada, although he doubted that the

Doomers had found out about the ship or where it was heading. If he was lucky, and he prayed to the Fates that he was, the Brotherhood hadn't zeroed in on his ship and was still in the dark as to where the force had come from that had demolished their team and their cartel minions.

"You should put on the tux." Syssi sighed. "I guess I will be meeting you at the event."

He lifted her hand to his lips and kissed her knuckles. "I'll come back here to get you. There is no way I'm letting you enter the dining hall without me."

She gifted him with a bright smile. "In that case, you can put the tux on when you return for me. That way, it will look crisp for the wedding."

"That's what I'll do." He leaned down and kissed her on the lips. "I wish I could stay in bed with you."

"Yeah, I wish you could." She glanced at their daughter, who was sleeping peacefully in her portable crib. "I think I'll leave her with Okidu tonight. My mother offered to watch her, but I don't want her to miss the wedding." She smiled. "I want her to have as much fun as possible on this cruise, so maybe she will change her mind about finally retiring and moving into the village."

Kian doubted anything would make Anita retire. The woman was going to work for as long as she could. For her, being a physician was more than a calling. It defined who she was, and the day she stopped doing what she loved, she would probably wither away and die.

"What about Lisa?" he asked. "Can't she come over and watch Allegra?"

"Lisa is babysitting Evie at Amanda's, and I don't want to wake Allegra up by moving her to Amanda's cabin. Cheryl is babysitting her brothers and sister, and Parker is too inexperienced to watch over a baby."

Kian no longer thought of their daughter as a baby. Heck, he often considered her an adult. Allegra was unlike any other young child he had ever seen, and it wasn't just because she was his daughter. Sometimes, he could see such wisdom in her eyes that it was startling.

He pretended to frown. "Parker is more than capable of watching over Allegra. Okidu is here, so it's not like he's going to be on his own, and he needs to start getting experience if he hopes to get babysitting gigs in the future. Don't discriminate against the boy because of his gender."

"Yes, sir." She saluted. "It shall be done."

He snorted. "That was easy."

"When you are right, you're right." She shrugged. "I don't want to be accused of misandry."

"I get accused of chauvinism almost daily." He pushed to his feet and pulled out a pair of jeans from the closet. "But I don't care." He pulled the jeans on.

"By whom?"

"Today, it was Toven." Kian took a shirt off a hanger and shrugged it on. "He said that my mother was just as capable a compeller as he was, and yet I preferred to choose him to defend our clan time and again."

"He has a point. You turn to him because he's a male."

Kian started on the buttons. "If I had a powerful female compeller available to me who wasn't my mother, and I also had Toven, I don't think that I would have chosen him over her. In fact, I'm pretty sure that I would have chosen the female. My mother is the most important member of our community, and I prioritize her safety, but Toven is also important because he's the oldest being on Earth, and he knows so much more than he has shared with us so far."

"You think?" Syssi pushed up on the pillows. "Why would he hide things from us?"

"He's not hiding things to keep them from us." Kian pushed his feet into a pair of loafers. "He just doesn't like to talk about a past that he's not proud of."

Syssi's eyes softened. "I don't blame him. Not everyone is made from the stuff your mother is made of. Her resilience is awe-inspiring. To live through all that she's lived through, to lose as much as she did, and to still retain a positive attitude is even more extraordinary than all of her other attributes. She's a true queen."

Kian tried to control the shudder that coursed through his body. "As strong as she is, I don't think she will ever be ready to take over for her grandfather. My mother is not ruthless enough, and I don't want her to be. She's perfect the way she is."

"I agree, but it's not up to you or me. It's up to her."

"Wise words as always." He leaned down and kissed the top of Syssi's head. "I need to go, but I promise to be back on time to put on the tux and escort my gorgeous wife to the wedding."

25

NEGAL

Negal drank two more shots of whiskey before shuffling back into his room and pulling on some clothing. A pair of clean jeans, a gray T-shirt, and a pair of flip-flops that he usually only wore to the pool.

He was in a lousy mood, and he was hungry, and he didn't know where he could get a meal without showing his sorry face in the dining hall. He hadn't lied about needing to attend the wedding, but maybe he could just duck in for the ceremony and then duck out. Since all the weddings were televised on the ship's closed-circuit network, figuring out the timing was no problem. He'd just turn the television on and wait for the right moment.

Besides, all the previous ceremonies had started close to midnight, and this one would be no different. He had plenty of time to mope around.

Maybe he could somehow sneak into the kitchen without anyone noticing. Or better yet, he could go to the staff kitchen and see if there were any leftovers he could eat.

It was cowardly of him, but he felt like an ass for hurting Gertrude's feelings, and he couldn't face her. If only he was a better actor, he could've pretended to be more into her and given her a good time tonight. After all, it wasn't like she'd expected them to become a couple. She'd known it was supposed to be a one-time thing.

Then again, she might have hoped for more, so it was good that he'd stopped that runaway train from hurtling toward the disastrous end of the road.

Look at him. He was using analogies from the human world like a pro.

As a knock sounded on Negal's bedroom door, his gut clenched, thinking that it was Gertrude coming back to rage at him. Maybe slap him.

Hell, he would have welcomed it. Maybe he would feel a little less guilty.

Why the hell was he feeling the need to be loyal to a female who had shown only a passing interest in him and did not desire him? He could have been with Gertrude, who was very interested and clearly lusted after him.

Reluctantly, he walked to the door and opened it.

Aru looked him over. "Why aren't you dressed?"

"I'll come later to the ceremony. I'm not in the right mood for a party."

"Why?"

Negal shrugged. "Do I need a reason? I'm just not in the mood."

Standing behind Aru, Gabi leaned to the side to peek at him. "Does this have anything to do with Frankie's friend?"

"Who, Margo? Of course not. Why do you ask?"

She gave Aru a slight shove to move aside. "Come out here so we can talk. I want to know what happened to put you in such a foul mood."

Frowning, Negal did as she instructed. "I'm not in a bad mood. I'm just not in the mood for a party."

Gabi looked at his feet. "You are wearing flip-flops, and I've only seen you wearing them once when you went to the pool. It's the equivalent of an old T-shirt, which is what I wear when I'm depressed." She glanced at Aru's worried face and smiled. "Correction. What I used to wear when I got depressed. I don't anymore. Since you entered my life, it's all sunshine for me."

"That's better." Aru wrapped his arm around her waist and pulled her against his side.

Negal still didn't get the analogy between his choice of footwear and Gabi's T-shirt, but he was in no frame of mind to ask for clarification. Curiosity demanded a certain level of energy that implied an upbeat attitude, and he was anything but.

"Sit." Gabi pointed at the couch.

"Yes, ma'am." He planted his butt on the sofa.

"Tell me who rained on your parade?"

He didn't know that phrase either, but it was easy to guess its meaning. "I did."

"What did you do?"

"I disappointed someone who didn't deserve it, and I feel bad about it."

She arched a brow. "Can you be a little less cryptic? Aru and I still need to stop by the clinic, and I don't want to be late for the wedding. I don't have time to pull it out of you one syllable at a time."

He really didn't want to tell her, but knowing Gabi, she would pester him until she got it out of him, so it was better to just get it over with. Besides, maybe she could offer suggestions on how he could make it up to Gertrude.

Negal let out a breath. "Last night, I promised Gertrude a fun time, but I had to leave on the mission, so I promised to make it up to her tonight. I only meant to show her a good time at the wedding and fulfill the promise that way, but she showed up here with other ideas, and I wasn't as responsive as she'd hoped." He let out another breath, hoping Gabi wouldn't need further clarification.

She smoothed a hand over the skirt of her evening gown. "I see. Is there a reason you suddenly didn't feel like entertaining Gertrude the way she hoped? Did she do something to turn you off?"

He shook his head. "It wasn't her fault." He closed his eyes. "For reasons that I cannot explain, I'm drawn to someone else, but she's not interested in me that way."

"Who is she?" Aru asked.

Gabi cast her mate an incredulous look as if she couldn't understand how he hadn't guessed it, but she didn't say anything, waiting for Negal to admit it.

"It's Margo. Frankie planted in my head the idea that Margo and I were destined to be together because Mia and Frankie were mated to gods, so their best friend had to be mated to one as well, and I was the last unmated male god available. I dismissed it as nonsense, but the idea must have burrowed itself into my head because all of a sudden, I felt guilty about holding Gertrude in my arms while we danced, and that was even before I met Margo." He shook his head. "I was glad to have an excuse to leave last night so I wouldn't have to make good on my promise to Gertrude." He released a long breath. "I sound like a lunatic even to myself. I wish I could talk with the ship's counselor."

Gabi leaned forward. "I'm not a counselor or a therapist, but I know that hiding from what's troubling you is not the answer. Why do you think that Margo is not interested in you?"

He looked her in the eyes. "I'm a god. Do I need to say more? There wasn't even a whiff of desire."

Well, there was, but only briefly and not very strong.

Gabi grimaced. "That's the thing I hate most about being immortal. I could do without smelling everyone's arousal and everyone smelling mine. But putting that aside, Margo might not be a very sexual woman. She might be interested in you, but she could be sexually repressed for some reason, and letting herself feel arousal is not something she can do spontaneously. She might need some gentle coaxing."

That was possible. Negal had met many goddesses that hadn't reacted to him in the way he'd hoped, but that was because on Anumati he was a nobody, and his godly good looks were nothing unusual. He'd grown spoiled on Earth, and even more so on this cruise, where almost every single female showed interest in him.

"So, what do you suggest I do?"

Gabi smiled. "Put on your tux and your dress shoes, come to the wedding, and ask Margo to dance. Don't assume anything, and just woo her gently as if she is a virgin."

Negal laughed. "I've never wooed a virgin before. I wouldn't know what to do."

"Improvise." Gabi waved a dismissive hand.

Aru rose to his feet. "We should go." He lifted a paper bag. "I need to drop a change of clothes off at the clinic for Dagor." He cast an accusing glance at Negal. "He tried to call you, but you didn't answer your phone."

"I was asleep, and I didn't hear the ringing."

That was what had gotten him in trouble with Gertrude. If she hadn't come to the cabin, the entire fiasco could have been avoided. Then again, perhaps it was for the best, and what the Fates had intended so he could be free to court Margo.

26

MARGO

With a guilty heart and a promise to come see Jaz tomorrow morning, Margo left her in the lounge and took the stairs back up to the clinic.

The door to the front room was opened, so she walked in and then knocked on the interior door leading to Frankie's room.

Dagor opened up, still looking as disheveled as he had been before. "Hi, come in."

"You're back." Frankie smiled and waved from the bed. "I thought you wouldn't return until tomorrow."

"And I thought that you would be asleep. Is Dagor keeping you awake?" Margo slanted an accusing glance at the god.

"Actually, I napped a little, and then Dagor got me coffee, and I feel much more energized now."

"I'm glad." Margo looked at the single chair in the room.

"Go ahead." Dagor motioned for her to sit down. "Aru and Gabi are on their way with a change of clothes for me, so I'll take advantage of you being here and hop into the shower."

"Thank you." Sitting down, Margo thought about the state she was in, which wasn't as bad as Dagor's, but she definitely needed a shower and a change of clothing as well.

So much had happened today that she wasn't sure how she was still on her feet.

It was probably the adrenaline that was keeping her going, or maybe it was the effect of the drugs. Margo's knowledge about drugs was nearly nonexistent, but she knew that heroin was an opioid and those were used as painkillers, so it made sense that heroin was a relaxant and not a stimulant.

She should ask Bridget about it when she saw her at the wedding.

Was she going, though?

It would have been a no-brainer with Frankie by her side, but Frankie wasn't coming, and Mia was with Toven, who for some reason intimidated Margo much more than Dagor did.

Perhaps it was because her future job at Perfect Match was dependent on him, or maybe it was the god himself. He seemed so much more regal than Dagor, which shouldn't surprise her since he was as old as human civilization.

How the hell was she supposed to wrap her head around that? She and Mia were the same age, and Margo couldn't fathom what an ancient being like Toven could possibly have in common with a twenty-seven-year-old woman.

Mia and Toven were both artists, so there was that, and evidently, it was enough for them to fall in love.

"What's going through your head?" Frankie asked. "You look stressed."

"Bridget convinced me to attend the wedding, and I was thinking that it would have been so much better if you were there with me."

"Go, Bridget." Frankie lifted a fist. "I'm so happy that she managed to convince you. How did she do it?"

"She said that if I wanted to become part of this community, I should start getting to know people. But what if I don't have those godly genes? What's the point of befriending people who I will be thralled to forget?"

Frankie scrunched her nose. "If you want to find out whether you are a Dormant, you really need to get to know at least one of them intimately."

Margo's heartbeat accelerated as she thought about the one person whom she would have liked to get to know that way, but then it occurred to her that Frankie had said that it was a requirement to find out whether she had those godly genes.

"What has one got to do with the other?"

Frankie was about to answer when there was a knock on the door. "That's probably Gabi and Aru with Dagor's clothes," she said. "Can you get the door?"

"Of course."

When Margo opened the door, she was glad that she knew who Aru was and was prepared for his godly beauty, or she would have fainted like she had when she'd first seen Negal. Thankfully, Dagor's looks had been dulled by the ugly makeup and dirty clothing, so her reaction to him had been more muted.

"You must be Margo." The woman standing next to the god offered Margo her hand. "I'm Gabi. Or Gabriella, but everyone calls me Gabi."

She was beautiful, too, but in a much more human way.

"Nice to meet you." Margo shook Gabi's hand and then turned to the god. "Hello, Aru."

He smiled. "I'm glad that your ordeal had a happy ending."

"Thank you, and I mean for everything. Negal told me that you and Dagor helped take over Modana's compound."

As he smiled again, a dimple appeared on his left cheek. "It was mostly Kalugal's doing. We were just the backup." He looked at the door to the bathroom. "Is Dagor in there?"

She nodded. "He's taking a shower."

"I'd better give him this." Aru lifted a large paper bag.

Margo stepped aside, letting the two enter the tiny patient room.

"I love your dress," she said to Gabi after Aru ducked into the bathroom. "It's gorgeous."

The fabric had a slight sheen to it, and the color was blue with a purple hue. The bodice was tight, and the skirt was voluminous, reminiscent of fifties style but with a modern twist.

"Thank you." Gabi did a little twirl that was limited by the cramped space. "It's a bit much, but I just couldn't resist getting it." She chuckled. "Do you have any idea how difficult it is to shop for ten different evening gowns for ten weddings?"

"I can't imagine. I have trouble buying one."

"That's why I don't buy them," Frankie said. "It's such a waste of money. I just borrowed them from my cousins."

Margo cast her a smile. "Not all of us are lucky to have a big, close-knit family."

"Speaking of evening wear," Gabi said. "Why aren't you dressed yet? Do you need to borrow a dress? You can have one of mine." She looked Margo over. "We are about the same size."

Gabi was a little plumper, but that wasn't something one woman could say to another without offending her.

"Thank you for the offer, but I intend to raid Frankie's closet."

"Awesome." Gabi grinned. "For a moment there, I thought that you were planning to skip the wedding, and that would have been a shame."

Margo winced. "In fact, that was precisely what I planned, but Bridget convinced me to attend. I should probably rush back to the cabin to shower and find a dress I can squeeze into." She looked at her feet. "I'll try to match it to these shoes because they are the only ones I have."

"What size do you wear?" Gabi asked.

"Eight. But Frankie wears size six, so nothing of hers fits me."

"I have a brand new pair of black pumps in size eight and a half that are a little too small on me, which means that they will fit you perfectly. I'll go back up and drop them by your cabin door."

"Thank you."

The bathroom door opened, and Aru stepped out. "Are you ready, my love?" He offered his arm to Gabi.

"I am, but we need to go back to the cabin. I have a pair of shoes that I want to give to Margo. A lady can't survive with just one pair, right?"

Frankie nodded enthusiastically. "Shoes are what I spend most of my clothing budget on."

Aru turned to Margo. "I'm so glad that you are coming to the wedding. Negal will be happy to see you."

Her heart felt as if the god had driven a spike through it. "I doubt he will even notice I'm there."

"Oh, he will definitely notice." Aru grinned with a knowing glint in his dark eyes.

Did he know something she didn't?

27

KIAN

There was a fresh carafe of coffee in front of Turner when Kian entered the cabin, and he looked at it longingly.

Reading his expression, Turner reached for it. "I'll pour you a cup."

The guy looked like crap, with bags under his eyes and his hair sticking out in all directions. Theo sat across from Turner and didn't look much better than the strategist. Onegus, on the other hand, looked just fine even though Kian doubted he had gotten any sleep either.

Kian felt guilty for being the only one who had taken a break to catch a short nap. "I guess none of you has gotten any shuteye." He pulled out a chair and sat down.

"There was no time," Turner said.

"I slept for an hour, so I'm good." Theo waved a hand over his face. "I look like crap because I didn't have time to shower, and this makeup is making me look like one of Modana's thugs." He scrubbed a hand over his face, then looked at the makeup smear on his fingers and grimaced. "I don't know how women put up with this stuff."

"Or high heels," Turner murmured. "It's vanity. If the makeup made you look better instead of worse, you wouldn't mind as much."

Leaning back, Theo grinned. "There is no improving on this." He waved a hand over his face.

As Onegus rolled his eyes and came back with a witty retort, Kian took a grateful sip from the coffee and then put the mug down. "Let's make it quick so you can grab a shower before the wedding. What's going on at Modana's place?"

"He returned to his mansion and immediately organized a group prayer with the men on the estate." Theo chuckled. "I wouldn't have believed it if I didn't see it with my own eyes, I mean the cameras' eyes. We followed Nick's advice and hooked into Modana's surveillance network instead of installing the stuff we had, which wasn't nearly as good as what was already in place." He cast Turner an accusing glance. "Your contractor supplied us with crap. It was old technology with cameras too large to hide or camouflage."

Turner shrugged. "I can't always pull off a miracle, and that was all my guy could get on such short notice."

"I hope the helicopter he's getting for us is better than that," Kian muttered under his breath. "I'm paying top dollar for it."

"It is," Turner said. "Top of the line in its class."

Kian nodded and shifted his eyes to Theo. "What about the rest of the thugs? Were there any voices of dissent?"

"Nope. Kalugal did an excellent job with them, but I don't know what will happen when the brother returns with his men. I wish Kalugal could do the same thing to them."

"If they arrive tomorrow, we can have Kalugal work on them as well. Still, there is no way we will be able to convert every last thug in Modana's cartel. What else do you have for me?"

"That's it." Theo leaned back. "The guys in the control room are monitoring the situation in the mansion. How long are you going to continue with that?"

Kian had been wondering the same thing. "I want to say only until we are back in the village, but I'm curious to see how long Kalugal's compulsion will hold and if Modana will do what we told him in Acapulco. Once we know that's going well, I'll probably stop spying on him. It's not like I have any long-term plans to influence the Mexican cartel situation."

"Got it." Theo finished the last of his coffee and rose to his feet. "If that's all, I would like to go." He put the mug in the sink.

"That's all," Onegus said. "Thank you, Theo."

The Guardian dipped his head and walked out the door.

"Jasmine's suitcase was delivered to her," Onegus said. "Naturally, we searched it and put it through the bug detector before giving it to her. She went over her things and reported that only her phone was missing. We assume that it was disposed of in the ocean. Regrettably, William didn't bring any spares with him, so we can't give her one."

"Did you meet her?" Kian asked.

Onegus shook his head. "I put Kri in charge of our guest, and she delivered the suitcase."

"What's Kri's impression of her?" Turner asked.

Onegus leaned back and crossed his arms over his chest. "Kri says that it's hard to tell. Jasmine doesn't broadcast much as far as emotional scents go, and what she does emit doesn't match what she seems to feel at the moment. It could be the lingering effect of the drugs, though. Bridget met Jasmine, but she didn't report anything unusual. She said that it could take up to seventy-two hours for the chemicals to clear from her system."

"We should keep an eye on her," Kian said. "Monitor her through the surveillance cameras. If she tries to snoop around, let her. I want to see what she will do."

"Probably nothing. She's confused, overwhelmed, and suffering from withdrawal." Onegus uncrossed his arms. "Let's move to the next item on the agenda before we have to leave." He looked at Turner. "What's your guy in Cabo reporting?"

"It would seem that the Doomers are still there. My guy reported that Carlos Modana was seen entering a meeting in the Antario hotel with two men who looked like military types, so we should assume that they were Doomers. My contractor is monitoring the main highways and the airport through the local authorities' surveillance equipment, and he didn't see any large groups of men leaving the area, but then they could have done it in smaller groups of three or four and escaped his notice."

"What about the decoy?" Kian asked.

Turner shook his head. "I decided against it. The Doomers most likely heard about the missing woman after Margo's sister-in-law involved hotel security. In my opinion, that's confusing enough to throw them off, and we should leave it at that."

"Agreed." Kian pushed to his feet. "Anything from Ensenada?"

"Nothing yet," Turner said. "But it's too early to celebrate. If there is still no suspicious activity near the port two days from now, we can proceed with our new itinerary."

"Maybe we shouldn't stop there at all," Onegus suggested.

"I wish we could just go home," Turner said. "But if we want to be sure that they don't suspect the *Silver Swan* and won't wait for it in Long Beach, we need to follow our new itinerary or have Roni's buddy doctor the plan logs again. Any change in our official route will draw attention to us, and that's the last thing we need."

28

MARINA

Marina read the message Peter had sent, and a smile lifted the corners of her lips. *I have five evening dresses waiting for you in my cabin. Come up here, and we will get ready together.*

Hopefully, one of those dresses would fit her and would be long enough to cover her feet. She didn't have any evening shoes either, but she didn't want Peter to bother his cousins again, or worse, his mother.

That piece of information had been hard to swallow, and it was still wreaking havoc on Marina's sensitive stomach. It would be difficult to enjoy the party while thinking about Peter's mother watching her with disapproving eyes.

Even a human mother wouldn't have wanted her son to date an uneducated nobody with no prospects for the future, let alone the mother of an immortal Guardian.

The Guardians were held in high regard by these immortals, and she'd heard that they trained for decades before being accepted as full-fledged members of the force.

Marina still needed to shower, do her hair, and apply makeup before going to Peter's cabin, but first she needed to grab a Coke from the staff lounge to soothe the churning in her stomach.

Whenever she was stressed or anxious, her tummy would respond with unpleasant symptoms, and she'd found out that Coke worked wonders to calm things down.

She managed to type a message to Peter using the tiny keys on her phone, telling him that she needed at least an hour before she could come to his cabin.

He replied right away. *Be here in an hour, or I'm coming to get you.*

She had no doubt that he would, and her bottom tingled pleasantly as she thought about the way he would punish her if she didn't show up on time.

Returning her phone to the back pocket of her jeans, Marina chuckled at her own silliness and walked into the lounge.

With most of the staff busy preparing the feast for tonight, the place was mostly empty, and it was hard to miss the beautiful dark-haired woman she hadn't seen before sitting at one of the tables and playing a card game by herself.

Feeling Marina's gaze on her, the woman lifted her head and cast her a dazzling smile. "Hi, I'm Jasmine."

She must be one of the two women who had been rescued from the cartel boss's yacht. Marina didn't know their names, only that one was a friend of the human who'd gotten injured during the previous rescue mission.

"Hi." Marina walked over to her and offered her hand. "I'm Marina."

"Nice to meet you." The brunette tilted her head. "Can I interest you in a game of cards? Almost everyone has left to prepare the wedding dinner, and those two don't speak a word of English." She gestured at the two men sitting on the couch and watching a movie with subtitles.

"I wish I could, but I'll have to take a rain check."

Jasmine's face fell. "I see. Are you also working tonight?"

Marina shook her head. "Actually, I'm accompanying one of the guests as his date."

She didn't want Jasmine to think that she was providing escort services, but she was very limited in what she could tell her. The compulsion prevented her from saying anything about immortals or Kra-ell to any human, and Jasmine was very obviously not an immortal despite her striking looks.

"That's great." The woman pouted. "I envy you. I'm not allowed on the upper decks, and I'm dying of curiosity about those weddings. The couples must be famous people who don't want anyone to find out that they met via the Perfect Match service."

Marina had no idea what Jasmine was talking about. "I can't tell you anything. All the staff is sworn to secrecy."

Jasmine nodded. "My friend Margo told me that they had her sign an iron-clad nondisclosure agreement. Did you have to sign one as well?"

Marina nodded even though she didn't know what that was. It sounded like keeping secrets, though. "I wish I could stay and chat, but I just came to grab a Coke. I need to get ready."

"Do you need help? I'm great with makeup and hair. I'm an actress, so I know all the professional tricks."

That was an offer Marina couldn't refuse. "I would love that. Are you sure you want to do it, though?"

It was a kind offer, but the woman had just met her.

"Of course." Jasmine pushed to her feet. "I'm bored, and I love giving makeovers. Get your Coke, and let's go to my cabin. My suitcase has just been delivered, and I have all my equipment with me." She looked Marina over. "What color dress are you going to wear?"

"I don't know," Marina admitted. "I didn't bring any evening wear with me because I only expected to work, but my date for tonight borrowed several dresses from his relatives for me to choose from."

Jasmine's eyes brightened, and Marina noticed that she had golden flakes surrounding her pupils that started to swirl. "I have something that will look stunning on you. It will match your blue hair beautifully."

Marina was still mesmerized by Jasmine's eyes. "Do you know that you have swirling golden flakes in your eyes?"

Jasmine winced as if it was an insult. "It's a condition. It's loose pigment."

"Is it dangerous?"

"It could be if the pigment clogs my tear ducts, but I have it under control."

"I'm glad. I mean, I'm not glad that you have a condition. I'm glad that you are taking care of yourself." Marina walked over to the fridge and pulled out two Cokes. "Do you want one?"

"No, thanks. I'll get a bottle of water."

Marina pulled one out and handed it to Jasmine. "It's a shame that something so beautiful is a sign of things not working right. Your eyes are mesmerizing."

Jasmine's smile was tight. "Not everyone thinks of them that way. I've been called a witch on more than one occasion. People are weird and sometimes even dangerous."

Marina's stomach twisted painfully again. "Why? What did they do to you?"

Jasmine shook her head. "Never mind. It was a long time ago." She threaded her arm through Marina's. "I'm excited about giving you a makeover. I will turn you into a ravishing beauty for this wedding. Not that you are not beautiful already, but there is always room for improvement, right?"

Marina laughed. "Are you my fairy godmother?"

That seemed to please Jasmine. "I sure am. But instead of a magic wand, I wield a magic makeup brush." She waved with her hand.

"Do you happen to have glass slippers by any chance? Because I need shoes too."

Jasmine glanced at her feet. "I don't have glass slippers. But how about Gucci?"

"What's that?"

Jasmine frowned. "Where did you come from that you've never heard of Gucci?" She waved a hand. "Never mind, that was a stupid question. You are from Russia, like everyone else down here. It's just that your English is so good that I almost didn't notice the accent."

"Thank you. I worked very hard on that."

"Good for you." Jasmine clapped her on the back. "As the saying goes, when in Rome, you should speak Italian, right?"

"I guess so."

29

NEGAL

Negal adjusted his black bowtie, so its center was precisely aligned with the buttons of his white shirt, tugged on the lapels of his jacket, and looked at his shoes to make sure they were polished.

Why was he paying so much attention to his appearance when he intended not to move from the table and to slink away as soon as it was polite to do so?

He'd been a fool to let Gabi convince him to go.

Frankie had probably already introduced Margo to Max and seeing them together on the dance floor was going to slay him.

Not to mention that seeing Gertrude would make him feel like a worm. How the hell was he going to make it up to her? Find her a Dormant male and bring him to her spread out on a silver platter?

That was probably a task even more difficult than finding the missing Kra-ell pods. If only there was a way to identify humans with the right genes, it would make things so much easier for these people.

Except, the Fates probably liked it that way. According to the lore, prayers were the currency the Fates dealt in, and what better way to get a rainfall of prayers than to have a clan of people desperate for mates?

Whatever.

It was all a bunch of nonsense that a hardened trooper like him had no business indulging in. Seeing his two buddies so happy with their mates must have softened him and made him subconsciously wistful.

As he heard the front door to the cabin open, Negal frowned. Aru and

Gabi should be at the wedding already, Dagor was spending the night at the clinic, and no one else was supposed to have access to their cabin.

It could be the cleaning crew, but he doubted they were providing services at night.

Frowning, he walked out of his room. "Why are you back?" he asked Aru while Gabi ducked into their bedroom. "Did you forget something?"

"Gabi is getting shoes for Margo. She has nothing of her own to change into." Aru looked him over. "You look good, especially given how bad you looked before we left."

"Thank you." Negal rubbed a hand over his clean-shaven jaw. "I hate to ask, but do you know if Frankie introduced Max to Margo?"

"Why would she?"

"When I told her that I wasn't interested in her friend, she said that she would introduce her to Max."

"I don't think she did." Gabi walked into the living room with a shoebox under her arm. "We've just been there, and Margo was with Frankie, and neither of them mentioned Max. In fact, Margo said that she hadn't planned on attending, but Bridget had convinced her that she should. That didn't sound like she was going with anyone." She gave him a bright smile. "She is all yours. Don't blow it this time."

"I didn't blow it the other time," he muttered under his breath. "I was the perfect gentleman and treated Margo with care and respect. I don't know what else I was supposed to do."

Gabi regarded him with a frown. "You've never had to work for it, have you?"

"Work for it?"

"Try hard to woo a woman. You're so handsome that all you need to do is show up."

He snorted. "On Earth, yeah, but on Anumati, I was rejected more times than I care to admit."

"Good." She waved a hand. "I mean, it's not good that you got rejected because it sucks, but at least you have experience with wooing females and overcoming objections."

"Not really." He rubbed a hand over the back of his neck. "That's not how it works on Anumati."

She turned to Aru. "What does he mean? You didn't tell me anything about the courtship rules on your home planet."

Aru sighed. "Of course, they are different. There isn't much guesswork when everything is determined genetically. If there is attraction, both partners know right away if it's reciprocated, and if the socioeconomics are compatible, they get together. It's simple."

Gabi shook her head. "And it's also boring and uninspired. Where is the fun in that?"

Aru took her hand and brought it to his lips for a kiss. "Don't dismiss it so quickly. What I described was just the initial stage. To build a relationship, other factors are required, like mutual interests, goals, etc. Sex is simple. Love never is."

"It is for fated mates," Negal said. "But that's rare." He looked at Aru and Gabi and the way they gravitated toward each other like there was a magnet in each of their chests that reacted just to the one inside their mate. "You two are lucky, and so are Dagor and Frankie."

"There are many fated couples among the immortals," Aru said. "I think that the Fates are working overtime on Earth."

Gabi brushed a hand over her skirt. "If those Fates of yours are only in charge of matching immortals, and they are only assigned to Earth, then they don't have a lot of work because there are so few of us. That could explain why nearly every match is fated."

"That's an interesting hypothesis." Aru led Gabi toward the door. "But we have a wedding to attend, so we will have to ponder it some other time." He looked over his shoulder at Negal. "Are you coming?"

"Yes. Of course." He followed them outside.

When the elevator stopped on Frankie's deck, Aru and Gabi walked out, and several immortals walked in.

Negal decided to stay inside. "I'll see you later in the dining hall."

30

PETER

Peter laid out the five dresses on his bed and tried to guess which one Marina would choose. The red one was from his mother, who had arched a brow at his request and had made a comment about the foolishness of getting involved with a human but had contributed to the effort, nonetheless. The long black one was from Beatrice, who had seemed tickled by the idea of him showing up to the wedding with one of the humans, another black dress that was shorter had come from Shirley, the pink one from Becky, and the purple one from Rachel.

The two black ones were the most likely to be chosen, and he personally preferred the shorter one that would reveal Marina's long, shapely legs, but he wasn't going to express his opinion. She would choose the one she liked best.

When the doorbell rang, he walked out of his bedroom and opened the door.

As he took in Marina's appearance, his breath caught in his throat. "Wow," he murmured, his eyes roaming over her. "You look incredible."

He didn't know where she'd gotten the dress, but it was more spectacular than all of the five he had prepared for her.

The subtle shimmer of the dress caught the soft glow of the cabin lights, making her look like a fairytale princess, and the midnight blue fabric hugged her curves in all the right places.

But the dress was only one part of the transformation. Her hair cascaded down her shoulders in waves of blue, framing her face like a work of art.

Peter had never paid much attention to makeup, but given the magical transformation Marina had undergone, turning her from beautiful to stunning and sophisticated, he took note of the details.

Her eyes were framed by smoky eyeshadow that accentuated their blue hue. Her lashes were coated with layers of mascara, and to complement the smoky eye look, her brows had been shaped in perfect twin arches.

The one thing he regretted was that her freckles had been covered with a thin layer of foundation, but on the other hand, it gave her complexion a radiant luminosity. A touch of highlighter had been applied to her cheekbones, and a bold red color had been artfully applied to her lush lips. It was the perfect finishing touch to her glamorous look.

Was he a despicable lecher for imagining those full, red lips wrapped around his shaft?

"Do you like it?" Marina smiled coquettishly.

"I love it. Where did you get the dress?" Peter stepped aside, motioning for her to enter the cabin with a wave of his hand.

"From Jasmine, the woman who was rescued earlier today from the cartel boss. I met her in the staff lounge, and when she heard that I was attending the wedding as a guest, she offered me a makeover. She also loaned me this dress and shoes to match." Marina laughed. "I wished for a fairy godmother, and I got one." She twirled in place. "I've never looked better in my life."

Her giddiness infected him, and he laughed. "So, if the dress is from your fairy godmother, does it mean that when the clock strikes midnight, the dress will disappear, and you will be naked?"

Striking a pose with her hand on her hip, Marina eyed him from under lowered lashes. "Do you want me to be naked in front of all the guests? Because the ceremony will not be over by midnight, so all of them will still be there."

He winced. "Perhaps a couple of hours later, then, and in the privacy of my cabin."

"That's better." She sauntered closer to him. "I wasn't late, you know. But if you still want to spank me later, I'm game."

"Definitely." He had to adjust himself as he imagined doing that.

Marina's gaze followed his hand, and when she noted the evidence of his excitement, her tongue darted out, and she licked those blood-red lips of hers. "I'm in the mood for a little aperitif before the party." She put a hand on his chest and pushed him toward his bedroom.

"What do you have in mind?"

"Oh, I think you can guess." She kept walking, or rather sauntering, her hips sashaying most enticingly.

"I don't want to mess up your makeup."

"You won't." She pushed the door closed behind her. "This lipstick doesn't come off."

"What about your hair?"

"You will have to be careful." Marina threw her evening bag on his bed and dropped to her knees.

Peter hissed. "Sweet merciful Fates, woman. We don't have time for this."

She smiled up at him. "It's not going to take long."

31

MARINA

Marina didn't know what had gotten into her. They were probably going to be late for the wedding, but the urge to drop to her knees in front of this magnificent male had just been overwhelming.

She would give him a gift of pleasure before the party, so even if things went wrong and people looked at her with derision, he would be too blissed out to pay them any attention.

No, that wasn't why she was doing this.

Maybe it was the way he looked at her as if she was just as beautiful as the immortal females he was surrounded by or more, or maybe it was the desire in his eyes that had ignited a corresponding fire in her. Or perhaps it wasn't about that at all, and it was a power play because after the makeover, she felt more powerful than ever before, a Cinderella turned princess, seductress, a femme fatale.

Or maybe it was just the buzz of the insatiable arousal coursing through her. She'd been numb ever since Nicolai had ended things between them, and Peter had blasted off the lid she'd put on her needs.

He groaned when she reached for his belt buckle, his eyes blazing as he watched her loosen his belt, unbutton his trousers, and free his length.

He was beautiful all over, so perfectly made that her mouth salivated for a taste of him. When she took him into her mouth, he jerked, and as she fisted him and squeezed hard, he hissed.

Glancing up at him, she saw his fangs punch over his lower lip, and her core squeezed at the sight of them and the memory of his bite. She'd never experienced pleasure so intense, had never climaxed so hard or so many consecutive times, and she couldn't wait until he bit her again, but it wasn't going to happen now.

Right now, it was about his pleasure and his pleasure alone. Later, when they returned to his cabin after the wedding, he could reciprocate.

Sliding her hand up and down his length in sync with her lips, she took him as deep down her throat as she could, and the hiss he emitted was her reward.

"Marina," Peter growled as he combed his fingers through her hair, fisting it as he thrust shallowly in and out of her mouth. "Those lips of yours will be my undoing."

His hand still tugging on her hair, he cupped her chin with his other one, and she was utterly at his mercy, but she didn't feel even a smidgen of trepidation. She knew he would never take her too roughly and that he would be careful with her, ensuring that she could breathe through it.

Peter had claimed that he couldn't read her mind, but she was still unsure about that because he did everything so perfectly that it couldn't be just experience or intuition guiding him.

The way his fist locked in her hair, tugging just the right way, not too gently and not too roughly, the way he glided his length in and out of her throat, almost to the end but not hitting the back of it so she wouldn't choke, it was as if he was so attuned to her that he could read her every response and adjust accordingly.

In and out, he was controlling everything, and she was just a vessel for his pleasure, but there was power in that, immense satisfaction, and yes, also erotic delight.

When his fingers locked even tighter against her scalp, and the fingers of his other hand tightened over her jaw, he began to thrust harder, deeper, and as she looked up at his face, the primal desire she saw in his blazing eyes, his elongated fangs, electrified her.

She could come like this without even touching herself, and the idea of spending the entire evening with panties that were soaked with the evidence of her desire mortified and excited her at the same time.

All these immortals with their keen sense of smell would know that she wanted this male, that she craved him, and she wondered whether they would envy him or pity him for having her as his partner—the lowly human servant, all dressed up as if she was a princess.

The thought was like a bucket of ice on the fire of her desire.

"Hey," he murmured, his fingers on her jaw, tilting her head so she was looking into his glowing eyes. "Where did you go just now?"

It was hard to answer when her mouth was full of his erection, so she closed her eyes briefly and opened them again, hoping to convey that it didn't matter, that she was okay.

Peter must not have liked what he saw in her eyes because he pulled out and knelt in front of her.

"What just went through your head that spoiled your fun?"

"It was nothing."

He hooked a finger under her chin and brought his lips to hers, kissing her softly, gently, as if he loved her. But this wasn't a fairytale, and the prince wasn't about to fall for her.

"My turn." He put his hands on her waist, lifted her, and sat her down on the edge of the bed.

"What are you doing?" she whispered as he flipped her dress up and moved the soaked gusset of her panties aside.

"Your smell is driving me insane. I have to taste you."

He didn't wait for her permission before extending his tongue and driving it into her, once, twice, three times, and when he flicked it over her engorged clit, she erupted with a scream.

He kept licking and sucking until she could take it no more, and when she pushed on his head, he lifted a pair of smiling eyes to her and grinned with a mouth full of fangs.

"Mission accomplished." He returned her panties to where they were supposed to be, pulled the skirt of her dress down over her legs, rose to his feet, and offered her a hand up. "Shall we, my lady?"

32

MARGO

"This one has to work." Margo sucked in her tummy and pulled up the side zipper.

The dress was so tight that she couldn't expand her chest fully and take a proper breath, but it was the only one that fit her at all. Frankie was tiny, and apparently so were all of her cousins who had contributed their evening attire.

Margo knew many of them, and just like Frankie, they seemed larger than they were because of the life energy they exuded. They were loud, they made big gestures with their arms when they talked, and they hugged everyone in greeting, even if they didn't know them.

In contrast, her own parents rarely hugged her and Rob, let alone strangers.

Growing up, Margo had spent so much time in Frankie's house that her mother used to complain that she had moved in. It had been so much more fun with Frankie's large, warm family, especially compared to how quiet and cold her own home had been.

She also loved visiting Mia's grandparents, but since they had moved into the secret compound to be near Mia and Toven, she didn't get to see them as often.

Oh, wow. Suddenly, it made perfect sense why they had done that.

The compound wasn't the private retreat of the Perfect Match reclusive owners. It was where the gods and immortals lived, and humans were not allowed unless they were related to the immortals. She should have realized that as soon as Mia had explained that her miraculous healing wasn't the result of some experimental treatment but of her transition into immortality.

Talk about a dive down the rabbit hole, but thankfully, many had made that journey before her, and her besties were there to guide her. The big question was if she was destined to join them or would have to leave.

With a sigh, Margo glanced at the shoebox on the floor and regretted not taking them out before putting on the dress. It was so tight that the zipper would pop if she tried to bend, and there was no way she was opening it and closing it again.

Sitting on the bed, she flipped the lid off with her toes and somehow managed to fish the pumps out of the box and slip them on. They were a little too big, but she didn't mind. They were black, like her dress, high quality, and they made her legs look great. The dress was full length, but it was shorter in the front and longer in the back, which meant that having a fabulous pair of shoes wasn't going to be a waste.

Pushing to her feet, Margo walked over to the mirror and checked her hair.

She hadn't had time to wash and dry it, so she gathered it into a classy chignon and pinned it in place. Frankie's coloring was much darker than hers, so using her foundation was a no-go, but a dab of blush on her cheeks, black mascara on her eyelashes, and red-colored lipstick was more than enough.

Anything more, and she would have looked like a clown.

Rummaging through Frankie's collection of fashion jewelry, she found a pair of fake diamond earrings and clipped them on.

"Not bad," she said to her reflection in the mirror. "Not bad at all."

Her new phone went into a black evening purse that she'd also borrowed from Frankie, and she was ready to go.

No, she wasn't.

She was fighting exhaustion, and the dress was too tight. It was so tempting to stay in the cabin and go to sleep, but that wasn't how she was made. She could power through the fatigue.

Margo squared her shoulders, strode out of the bedroom, and walked out of the cabin.

She would sit at Mia and Toven's table, they would introduce her to some of their friends, and she might even meet the formidable regent that Bridget had warned her about.

It didn't matter if Negal was escorting the nurse. There were plenty of other fish in the sea, as Mia's grandmother liked to point out, and they were all gorgeous and immortal, and hopefully, some of them were also nice and smart. Frankie had mentioned a Guardian called Max, but since she wasn't attending the wedding, she wouldn't be there to introduce him to her tonight.

Maybe she could ask Mia to point him out to her.

"Right." Margo chuckled as she pressed the button for the elevator. The introduction would have to wait.

There was no one else in the corridor, and as the elevator doors opened, there was no one inside either. Everyone was probably already at the event, and Margo hoped they were still in the reception part of the evening because it would be awkward as hell to walk in alone if everyone was seated.

When the elevator announced the dining hall deck, she started to take a deep breath but then remembered that she couldn't and took a couple of small ones instead.

As the doors opened, she was greeted by the sounds of soft music, murmurs of conversation, and laughter. It was so normal, so like any other event she'd been to, and the anxious knot in her belly eased up a little.

Taking a look at the large mirror across from the elevator, she turned this way and that, enjoying how the cascading tiered tulle ruffles moved. It was really a gorgeous gown if a bit over the top for Margo's taste. Not that it revealed anything, but the tight corset-style bodice and the layers of tulle made it look like a black bridal gown. Thankfully, there was no such thing as a black wedding dress, so she wouldn't court the bride's ire.

"Looking good." A guy with smiling eyes stood next to her and checked his bowtie in the mirror. "Margo, I presume?"

She turned to him. "How do you know who I am?"

"Easy. I know everyone on board, and I haven't seen you before." He offered her his hand. "I'm Max."

Talk about serendipity.

Unless there was more than one guy named Max on this cruise, this was the Guardian Frankie wanted her to meet. The one who had led the attack on Modana's complex.

"It's nice to meet you, Max." She put her hand in his. "Thank you for the rescue."

"It was my pleasure." He lifted her hand to his lips and brushed them over the back of it. "May I have the privilege of offering my arm and accompanying you to the ball, my lady?"

"I'd be honored," she replied, slipping her arm through his.

33

NEGAL

Negal regretted coming, and it wasn't just because he didn't want to see Margo with Max. She hadn't arrived yet, so maybe she wasn't going to. Aru had said that the Guardian's name hadn't been mentioned, so there was still a chance that she would arrive alone, and Negal would have to follow Gabi's advice and woo her.

Yeah, right. He knew nothing about winning over a woman who showed no interest in him. To make fire, kindling and sparks were needed, and in their absence, he had no chance, no matter how hard he tried.

When Gilbert and Karen joined their table, Karen smiled politely and said all the right things, asking about the mission and how it went, and when he lifted his brow in question, she understood what he was asking about and shook her head.

She wasn't transitioning yet, and it was worrisome. If he couldn't induce her, the only one who might have a better chance was the royal, but Toven was mated, and he probably couldn't force himself to do that even if he wanted to help.

It was a shitty situation, and after shaking her head, Karen was doing everything to avoid meeting Negal's eyes again, while Gilbert seemed oblivious to how uncomfortable his mate was.

Was she blaming Negal for failing her?

Since she was a confirmed Dormant, it should have worked, and the fact that it hadn't could indicate that there was a health problem she wasn't aware of. Negal had heard that the body needed to be healthy to enter transition, so Karen should speak with the clan's doctor about it instead of blaming him.

Not that he knew for a fact that she did. Maybe she was just uncomfortable around him because of the enforced intimacy they had shared.

Perhaps he should excuse himself and walk over to the bar.

Negal pushed to his feet. "I'm getting myself a drink. Does anyone want me to get them anything?"

Gilbert arched a brow. "We have several bottles of fine whiskey on the table. What else do we need?"

"I'm in a mood for a cocktail." He tugged on the lapels of his tux. "Ladies? Can I interest you in anything?"

"I'm good," Gabi said.

"I'll pass." Karen finally met his eyes. "I'll stick with wine tonight."

"As you wish." He inclined his head and headed toward the bar, breathing easier with every step until his eyes landed on Gertrude.

She gave him a tight smile, waved, and went back to talking with a guy sitting next to her at the table.

What a classy lady.

Negal wished things could have ended better between them, but it was what it was. He needed to get rid of that uncomfortable feeling churning in his gut.

Finding a vacant spot next to the bar, he ordered a whiskey sour from Bob, who had been moved there from the Lido deck.

Leaning against the tall counter, Negal cast a glance at the entrance to the dining hall. In part, he was hoping to see Margo walk in, and in part, hoping that she wouldn't. It was already eleven at night, and she was late.

The ceremony would start soon, and the doors to the dining hall would close. If she didn't arrive before that, she wouldn't be allowed in until after the ceremony was over and the princess departed.

Had anyone prepared Margo for Annani?

Had she been told the truth about him being a god?

Frankie and Mia had probably filled her in, but it was impossible to cram everything there was to know about gods and immortals into one conversation, so maybe they hadn't told her that he and his teammates had not originated on Earth.

"Here is your drink, master." Bob put the drink in front of him.

"Thank you." Negal lifted the glass, took a sip, and smiled at the cyborg bartender. "It's excellent as always."

Bob smiled with his metallic lips, which never failed to amuse him. It was such a quirky and oddly human-looking smile.

"Thank you, master. It's my pleasure to serve you." He dipped his head and then zipped to the other side of the bar to serve another customer.

Turning around, Negal glanced at the entrance again and nearly choked on his drink.

Margo was almost unrecognizable in the black evening gown she was wearing, and she looked stunning, but as he felt his fangs elongating, it wasn't because he was overcome by desire.

She was walking in with Max, her arm threaded through his, and she was laughing at something he was saying. The Guardian looked smug as can be, and Negal felt like punching him in his smiling face.

Calm down, he ordered himself.

It wasn't Max's fault that Negal was an idiot and had given up his chance with Margo. The guy was an excellent trooper and a good male all around.

Nevertheless, Negal couldn't take his eyes off her. She looked regal in the black dress, her long blond hair twisted and pinned on the back of her head. He watched as Max escorted her to Mia and Toven's table, pulled out a chair for her, said something that had her smiling and nodding, and then walked away.

Could it be that they weren't together?

Negal watched the Guardian as he walked across the converted dining room and sat down at a table with several of his Guardian friends and a few females who were probably their mothers.

What was going on?

Margo had arrived on Max's arm as if she was his date for tonight, but if that was the case, they would have sat together.

Hope surged in Negal's chest.

He wasn't good at wooing, but he could dance at least as well as the immortals. As soon as the newlyweds took to the dance floor as a married couple, he would rush to Margo and ask her to dance before Max had a chance to beat him to it, and he wouldn't let go of her until the party was over so the Guardian couldn't steal her from him.

Luckily, Negal's table was much closer to Toven and Mia's than Max's, so unless the guy could fly over the dance floor which bisected the room, he had no chance of making it to Margo first.

Lifting his face to the ceiling, Negal offered a quick thank you to the Fates, and then took his drink and headed back to his table, but at the last moment changed directions and walked toward Margo's.

34

MARGO

As Margo saw Negal making his way toward her, looking devastatingly handsome in his tuxedo, her breath hitched.

Next to her, Mia chuckled. "Someone is zeroing in on you like a heat-seeking missile."

Margo couldn't respond even if she wanted to. Her throat was dry, and she reached for her glass of water and sipped on it to avoid looking at the approaching god.

Why had everything with Negal become so difficult? They'd been doing great until they reached the ship, and he'd confirmed his plans with Gertrude for tonight. Ever since that moment, a sense of loss had taken residence in Margo's heart.

It wasn't rational, and it wasn't fair to Negal or to Gertrude, but there wasn't much Margo could do about the way she felt.

Maybe it was connected to the drug withdrawal?

While she'd been high, she'd felt on top of the world, and when she'd dropped from that peak, she had suddenly felt defeated.

Both emotions were foreign to her.

Margo had never been overly brazen. She was reserved and cautious, but she was also confident and assertive. That didn't mean, though, that she was willing to take a guy from another woman even if she could.

Margo wouldn't like it if someone else went after a man she was dating.

She lived by the motto of not doing unto others that which would upset her if it was done to her.

Why wasn't Negal with the nurse, though? Maybe she hadn't arrived yet?

"Hi." Negal pulled out a chair from the next table over, sat right in front of her, and put his drink on the table. "You look stunning tonight. I almost didn't recognize you when you walked in on Max's arm."

Margo didn't know how to answer that. Should she thank him for the compliment or tell him that it was none of his business whose arm she'd walked in on?

Mia cleared her throat. "Good evening, Negal."

He shifted his incredibly blue eyes to her. "Hello, Mia. You also look lovely." His gaze returned to Margo. "Just in case Max somehow beats me to it, I came over now to ask you to reserve the first dance of the night for me. In fact, I would like you to reserve all subsequent dances for me as well."

Was he drunk?

"I don't think Gertrude will be okay with that."

His expression darkened. "Gertrude doesn't mind one way or another. She and I are not together."

Margo frowned. "I heard you making plans with her for tonight. Did something happen?"

He just looked at her for a long moment, pinning her with his intense gaze. "Yeah. Something happened. You." It sounded like an accusation.

"Oh, boy," Mia murmured and reached for her drink.

"Me?" Margo lifted a brow. "What did I do?"

He shook his head. "Forgive me. I'm being as smooth as a bed of nails."

Margo frowned. "I've never heard that expression before. Is it a literal translation from your language back home? And I don't mean Portugal."

As Negal cast a glance at Mia, she nodded. "Margo knows about you. Frankie and I told her that you are a god." She chuckled. "I got so used to referring to Toven and you three as gods that it only strikes me as odd saying that to someone who hasn't heard about you. I'd call you Anumatians, but Toven was born on Earth, so that doesn't apply to him, and calling you aliens brings up images of little gray people with big, all-black, slanted eyes."

Toven had been awfully quiet throughout the exchange, and as Margo glanced at him, she caught his amused smirk before he schooled his features and looked away.

"On Earth, the term god implies divinity," Negal said. "Which I don't claim to be, but that's what my people call themselves in relation to created species. In our language, god and creator are synonymous. The bottom line is that I'm not human, but neither is Max. Well, he's part god and mostly human, but still, he's more like me than he is like you."

"I know," Margo said. "But why are you so focused on Max?"

"He's my competition."

No one could compete with Negal, but she wasn't about to tell him that and watch the smug expression on his face. Still, it bothered her that he was so focused on competing with Max.

Was it a cultural thing?

Maybe on his home planet males competed for female attention differently?

What if duels to the death were a thing there?

Suddenly, she remembered what he'd said about dragons, and it occurred to her that he might have actually encountered real beasts like that and had maybe even slain one or two as tribute to a lady.

"I think we need to talk." She tried to take a deep breath, but the bodice of her dress was too tight. "I don't want anyone fighting over me or slaying dragons to win my heart."

Negal frowned. "Who said anything about slaying dragons? I've been on Earth for five years, and the only dragons I've encountered were in movies and myths."

On Mia's other side, Toven started laughing and then pushed to his feet. "Come on, Mia. Let's give these two some space so they can clear out the misconceptions they have about each other."

Margo wanted to tell Mia to stay and run interference between her and this new Negal, who was nothing like the chivalrous guy who had caught her when she'd fainted and then cradled her in his arms like she was precious to him. But she wasn't a coward, and Toven was right. She and Negal needed to have a talk, but not here and not now.

"The clearing of misconceptions will have to wait." Margo looked up at Toven. "The ceremony is about to start soon, so I don't think you should wander off."

Hopefully, it wasn't considered rude to suggest to a god what to do.

Toven lifted his wrist and glanced at his watch. "You are right." He sat back down and looked at Negal. "You're welcome to stay here, but I believe that you are supposed to sit with Aru and Gabi."

For a long moment, Negal looked undecided, but then he took his drink, pushed to his feet, and leveled his gaze at her. "Don't forget. The first dance is mine."

Margo crossed her arms over her chest. "Did I promise you a dance? Or better yet, did you ask me if I wanted to dance with you? I know that you are military, and you might be used to issuing orders, but I'm not under your command, and if you want anything from me, the word please should be included in your request. "

He frowned. "Would you please reserve the first dance for me?"

"That's better."

"Is that a 'yes'?"

She was tempted to tell him that it was a maybe, but she wasn't into playing games, and she wanted to feel his arms around her again.

"Yes, I'll save the first dance for you, but I'm not making any promises about the rest of the night."

"Understood." Negal bowed to her. "Thank you."

35

WENDY

Wendy stood a few feet away from the entrance to the dining hall with her mother and Stella flanking her and her bridesmaids standing in formation before her.

She was breaking the clan's tradition of the bride and groom not being accompanied by their parents, but her situation was unique, and she hoped her new family would be understanding.

She'd just found her mother and having her by her side as she walked down the aisle was a wish she hadn't even dared to dream about, and now that it was a reality, she wasn't willing to give it up for anything short of not having a wedding at all.

Fortunately, no one had said anything when she'd explained how she wanted the ceremony to proceed.

Vlad had been accompanied by Vrog and Richard as he'd made his way to the altar, and Wendy hoped this hadn't elicited any disapproving looks from the attendees. Bowen, her mother's mate, served as one of the groomsmen.

When the music started, her eight bridesmaids entered first, four rows of two ladies each, wearing silver-colored calf-length gowns.

Their dresses were very different from hers, which was also sleeveless but fitted through the torso. The bodice was covered in lace overlay and transitioned to a wide, voluminous skirt, where layers of tulle cascaded down to the ground, creating a cloud-like effect.

Subtle embellishments of delicate beads and tiny, shimmering sequins were scattered across the dress, catching the light and adding a hint of sparkle without being too much.

Once the bridesmaids joined the eight groomsmen and the music changed to the traditional bridal song, Margaret and Stella threaded their arms through Wendy's, and the three of them walked in, using the measured strides they had practiced.

At the altar, Vlad stood a head taller than all his groomsmen, with only his father matching his impressive height. His raven black hair was slicked back, and his smile was so broad that it made his handsome face glow.

Or was the glow coming from his eyes? One blue and one green, they were both beautiful, but not as beautiful as the soul behind them.

Vlad was one of a kind, made of goodness and love, of kindness and warmth, and she was the luckiest girl on the planet to be loved by a rare jewel like him.

When he turned a little to the side, revealing the goddess standing on the dais behind him, it occurred to Wendy that the glow might have been emanating from Annani. Still, she was sure that at least some of it was coming from Vlad.

Upon reaching the podium, her mother and Stella let go of her arms and joined Vrog and Richard. Vlad extended his hand to her, and when she took it, both of them faced the goddess and bowed their heads.

Annani lifted her glowing arms, and when the crowd hushed down, she lowered them and smiled.

"Welcome, my children, to yet another happy occasion, the joining of Wendy and Vlad. Two young souls who found each other against overwhelming odds and who stand before you as a symbol of the resilience of love.

"In the tapestry of life, every thread of joy, challenge, and triumph contributes to the masterpiece of our existence. Wendy and Vlad's journey to this moment has been woven with threads both dark and bright, painting a picture of strength and commitment. Their story is a testament to the fact that love, in its purest form, transcends the barriers of past pains and the shadows of doubt.

"It is not often that we see two people so uniquely suited to support and understand one another. Wendy and Vlad's relationship was born from a complex weave of emotions and experiences and has blossomed into a partnership defined by mutual respect, understanding, and an unbreakable bond. Through trials and tribulations, they have learned the power of forgiveness, the strength found in vulnerability, and the courage it takes to trust again."

The goddess turned her gaze to the two of them. "Wendy, you are proof that it is possible to move beyond the scars of the past and embrace a future filled with hope and love. Vlad, with your kindness and your capacity for forgiveness, you embody the beauty of true acceptance and the transformative power of believing in someone, even when they struggle to believe in themselves.

"Today, as you pledge your lives to each other, you remind us of the profound impact of love and the miraculous ways it can heal and unite. Your joining is a beacon of hope for all who believe that out of the ashes of doubt and fear, the phoenix of love can rise brighter, stronger, and more beautiful than ever before.

"Wendy and Vlad, may your love continue to be a source of strength and inspiration to you and all who know and care for you. May you face every challenge with the knowledge that together, there is nothing you cannot overcome. And may your love, so beautifully begun, only deepen and grow stronger in the years to come. May your life together be filled with joy, growth, and endless adventures."

As the crowd cheered, the goddess waited patiently until they were done and then smiled at Wendy and Vlad. "Before I pronounce you partners for life, would you like to recite your vows to each other?"

Vlad nodded. "We would, Clan Mother."

36

VLAD

Vlad had agonized over his vows to Wendy for weeks. He'd even considered painting her a picture that would express his feelings better than anything he could verbalize, or writing a musical piece that would touch her soul, but tradition demanded that he put his feelings into words, and that was also what Wendy expected.

Looking at him with her chocolate brown eyes, so full of love and warmth, she gave his hand a gentle squeeze in encouragement.

He returned the squeeze and took a deep breath.

"Wendy, my love, the other half of my soul. Standing here with you today is a culmination of a journey that has taught us the true meaning of strength, trust, and love. When I met you, I saw a reflection of my own fears and insecurities but also an incredible resilience. Your courage to face a past that tried to dim your bright spirit has inspired me to do the same and embrace our future with open arms.

"I've learned from you that vulnerability isn't a weakness but a gateway to genuine connection. Today, I vow to be your sanctuary and your partner in every adventure that lies ahead. I promise to listen with an open heart, to understand beyond words, to support you in every challenge, and to celebrate with you in every victory.

"I vow to love you for all that you are and all that you're yet to become, embracing every layer of you. I promise to be your confidant, your ally, and your greatest supporter. Together, we will build a future where fear has no stronghold, where love triumphs, and where our shared dreams become our reality. Wendy, you are my heart's echo, a reminder that even in our darkest moments, love can shine bright. I choose you today, and I'll choose you every day for the rest of our lives. Let's kick fear in the ass together and step into our destiny, hand in hand, heart in heart."

Seeing the tears brimming in her eyes, he leaned down and kissed her softly on the lips.

"Now comes the ring part." He removed the simple gold band from his little finger and slid it over her ring finger. "I, Vlad, son of Stella and Vrog, pledge myself to you, Wendy, daughter of Margaret and adopted daughter of Bowen." He lifted the hand with the ring he'd just put on her finger and kissed it.

"That was beautiful," she whispered.

"Thank you," he whispered back.

Patting the corners of her eyes with her fingers, Wendy took a shuddering breath.

"Vlad, my love, my soul, my far better half. In the tapestry of my life, every thread has been woven with caution, every color shaded with the past's scars. Yet, in the palette of your love, I found hues of understanding and acceptance that I never knew existed. Today, I stand before you, not just as the woman you've come to love, but as a testament to the transformative power of your kindness and patience.

"You have shown me that the shadows of my past do not define the light of our future together. With every fear you've soothed and every insecurity you've quelled, you've gifted me a strength I thought was beyond my reach. For that, and for so much more, I am eternally grateful.

"I vow to embrace the vulnerability that comes with love and to trust not just in you but in this incredible community that has accepted me and embraced me despite the sins of my past. I promise to support you, to uplift you, and to remind you of your worth, just as you have done for me. In your eyes, I've seen the reflection of a woman I will always aspire to become, one who dares to love, to hope, and to dream, and who is no longer a slave to fear.

"As we journey through life together, I commit to growing alongside you and contributing to our shared story with every beat of my heart. I vow to listen with empathy, to speak with honesty, and to act with compassion, ensuring that our home is always a haven of peace and understanding.

"You've taught me that love is not just a feeling but that it is also an action, a decision to stand by someone through the ebbs and flows of life. So, I choose you today and every day as my partner, my confidant, and my friend.

In your love, I've found the courage to face tomorrow with a smile, to believe in the goodness within us, and to step into our future with confidence. You are my light, my love, and my life. I vow to always be by your side, as your wife, your partner, and your best friend, through all that life brings our way."

Smiling, Wendy removed the ring she had worn on her thumb and put it on Vlad's ring finger. "I, Wendy, daughter of Margaret and adopted daughter of Bowen, pledge myself to you, Vlad, son of Stella and Vrog."

The Clan Mother extended her hands to the two of them, and as Wendy put her hand in the goddess's tiny one, it felt like getting zapped with a boost of energy.

"By the power the Fates vested in me, I now pronounce you bonded mates. Vlad, you may kiss the bride, and Wendy, you may kiss the groom." Annani laughed, the sound raising goosebumps on Wendy's arms. "There is no tradition that cannot be improved on."

As the crowd erupted in cheers, hoots, and applause, Vlad wrapped his arms around Wendy and lifted her so he was looking up into her smiling face. "Kiss me, my love."

37

MARGO

As Margo watched the glowing goddess on top of the podium, she had to remind herself to stop gaping.

Toven, Aru, Negal, and Dagor called themselves gods, but they were aliens who used the term god to describe themselves as creators. They looked human, only better, and it was easy to forget that they were something else. However, there was no doubt that the petite, glowing, angelic beauty was the real thing. She might not be a deity, but Margo was sure she had unimaginable powers that far surpassed what the other so-called gods could do.

Suddenly, she was reminded of the odd comment that Negal had made when she'd told him that he was as bright as an angel. He'd said that he wasn't bright and didn't have a glow because he wasn't royal. At the time, Margo had thought that he might have meant it metaphorically, and she'd said that royals didn't glow, and to that, he'd replied that they did where he came from. When she'd asked him where that was, he'd said Portugal, which had obviously been a lie.

Had he meant that royals on Anumati were bright like the goddess officiating over the ceremony? And did that mean that this tiny glowing goddess was a queen?

Frankie and Mia hadn't said anything about a visiting royal, so maybe she was a permanent resident on Earth.

There was still so much Margo didn't know, so much that she needed to ask, but even though she was sitting at a table with one of those so-called gods, she had to wait until after the ceremony to question him about the goddess.

For now, all she could do was gape, marvel, and let her imagination run wild.

Talk about a dive down the rabbit hole.

Alice had also encountered queens in Wonderland. The Queen of Hearts, and the red and white queens. Was there a symbolism in the story that Margo could relate to? Something that would help her grapple with the world she found herself in?

She shook her head. Lewis Carroll hadn't known about gods and immortals, and his story was an attempt to explain complex themes like the fluidity of time and the inversion of logic.

Surprisingly, though, there was nothing illogical about this world. In fact, so many of Margo's so-called conspiracy theories suddenly made sense.

She'd always believed that aliens were real and that the governments of the world were well aware of their existence and engaged in misinformation and smear campaigns to discredit witnesses. There was no better way to discredit people than to make fun of them, but it wasn't easy to do when those witnesses were fighter jet pilots, navy commanders, and the heads of other countries' space programs. Then there were the pyramids—marvels of engineering that required precision that shouldn't have been possible with the tools available to the ancients, the transatlantic cultural influences, which had existed long before established history claimed travel and migration over the Atlantic was possible, the ancients' knowledge of the solar system, and countless other things. Heck, there were probably plenty of conspiracy theories she'd never heard about that could be explained by the influence of gods and immortals.

When the ceremony ended with the couple exchanging vows and rings, the audience erupted in deafening cheers and applause, and as the music started playing again, Margo saw the goddess leave through a side door, surrounded by several guards and two butlers.

That was odd. Why would a goddess have human butlers? But there was no other way to describe the two guys who looked like twins.

Margo added them to the list of strange things she needed to ask about later, and continued clapping.

As the newlyweds took to the dance floor, the audience quieted down, and Margo wanted to take the opportunity to whisper her questions about the goddess to Mia, but as she leaned toward her friend, she saw Negal walking over.

The guy had been striking in street clothes, but he was devastating in a tux, and as much as she wanted to appear indifferent, she couldn't take her eyes off him.

Dipping his head, he offered her his hand. "Would you do me the honor of joining me on the dance floor, Margo?"

That was a very polite invitation and a great improvement on his previous attempt. Had he gotten coaching from Gabi on how to do it properly?

Margo put her hand in Negal's. "I would be delighted, but we should wait until the newlyweds' parents join them on the dance floor."

He frowned. "Is that the tradition?"

"At human weddings, it is." She rose to her feet. "But I don't know what the immortals' tradition is." She turned to Toven. "Perhaps you can tell us?"

The god shrugged. "We make it up as we go."

"Oh? I assumed that such ancient beings would have many traditions."

"It's complicated," Mia said quietly. "I see Stella and Richard getting up, and also Margaret and Bowen. Vrog and Aliya probably won't." Mia's eyes widened. "I was wrong. They are heading to the dance floor as well."

Margo followed Mia's gaze. The two couples who joined the newlyweds on the dance floor looked only a few years older than Wendy and Vlad, but that wasn't surprising. All these immortals looked more or less the same age. But the third couple drew her attention.

The guy was Vlad's father, and he was just as tall as his son, and the woman had been one of Wendy's bridesmaids, but Margo had been so focused on the goddess that she hadn't paid the bridesmaids much attention. Looking at the female now, though, she noted her impressive height, her impossibly slim waist, and her eyes, which were way too large for her face. She was definitely not like the other immortals in the room, and Margo remembered Negal's comment about the aliens calling themselves gods in relation to their created species, emphasis on the plural.

Evidently, humans were not the only creation of the gods.

"I think it's safe to join them now." Negal put his hand on the small of her back, sending a shiver down her spine.

"Yes, it is." She tore her gaze away from the tall female and smiled up at him.

He was so gorgeous that it was almost painful to look at him, and Margo couldn't understand why he was pursuing her with such tenacity, especially given all the beautiful women in the room. Compared to them, she was a plain Jane.

Had Frankie put him up to it?

Oh, hell, hopefully Frankie hadn't done anything to break Negal and the nurse apart just so Margo would have a chance with him, but she had a sinking feeling that it had been precisely what her meddling friend had done.

Before the ceremony, Negal had accused Margo of being the reason his plans with Gertrude had fallen apart, and at the time, she hadn't known what he could have possibly meant by that, but now she knew whose fault it was.

"Did Frankie say anything to you?" she asked as he led her to the dance floor.

"About what?" He placed his right hand on her back, just below her shoulder blades, and took her right hand in his, holding it out to the side.

She put her left hand on his shoulder. "About entertaining me tonight."

"Of course not."

"Then why aren't you with Gertrude?"

"I told you. We are not together. She changed her mind about accompanying me."

Margo shook her head. "You said that it was because of me, but since I didn't even talk to Gertrude, I couldn't have been the reason she changed her mind. Did Frankie say something to her?"

Negal winced. "I wouldn't know what the nurse and her patient discuss, but I can assure you that it wasn't Frankie's fault."

"Then whose was it? Because it sure wasn't mine."

38

NEGAL

Negal didn't know how to answer that without revealing the confusion that had taken root in his mind, so he decided to go on the offensive instead.

"What about you and Max? He escorted you into the dining hall, but he didn't join you at your table or invite you to his. Did something happen to change his mind or yours?"

Margo smirked. "I'll answer your question if you answer mine."

As the waltz ended, an upbeat piece started playing, and the couples around them switched into free-style dancing, which Negal wasn't a great fan of. "Would you like to step out onto the terrace for some fresh air?" he asked her.

"Sure, if it will get me the answers I want."

Now that Margo's personality was no longer muted by the drug, the strength of it was coming through, and it had done nothing to diminish his attraction to her. On the contrary, it only added fuel to it.

He loved females who challenged him.

Nodding, he took her hand and weaved between the dancing couples to cross the dance floor to the other side of the event hall and the doors leading to the terrace.

As soon as he stepped outside, he was hit by the humid air, but the temperature was pleasant, not too hot or too cold. Then again, he wasn't as sensitive to changes in temperature as humans were, and he was wearing a jacket while Margo's arms and shoulders were exposed.

Shrugging his jacket off, he offered it to her.

She looked at him with puzzlement in her eyes. "Do you want me to hold it for you?"

"Aren't you cold?"

"Why would I be?"

She had an annoying tendency to answer a question with another question, but since he was guilty of doing the same, he couldn't complain about it.

"My body is better equipped at regulating temperature than yours, and I'm covered with clothing while you are exposed, so I thought that it might be a little chilly for you." His gaze traveled to the sheer side panels of the corset top of her dress. It was beautiful, but it didn't provide protection from the elements.

"Thank you, but I'm fine." She crossed her arms over her chest. "So, about Gertrude. Tell me what happened."

He slung the jacket over his arm. "It's really not something I should say because it is between me and her."

Margo shook her head. "Not good enough, Negal. You said that it was my fault, and I need to know in what way."

He scrubbed a hand over his face. "Frankie showed me your picture."

"And? What does that have to do with anything?"

"I couldn't stop thinking about you."

"That's flattering." She let out a breath. "But it still doesn't explain anything. When we got back to the ship, you told Gertrude that the two of you were on for tonight. Am I really going to have to pull it out of you one word at a time?"

Margo had seemed so sweet and mellow when he'd held her in his arms after she'd fainted, but apparently that had been the drug's effect, softening her, and once she'd sobered up her real nature came forth. The woman was stubborn, and she wouldn't relent until she got what she wanted.

Why the hell did he find that sexy?

The more assertive she got, the harder his erection pulsated inside his slacks.

Turning around, Negal leaned against the railing and crossed his arms over his chest, mimicking her pose. "Do you want the truth?"

"Always."

"Even if it's not what you want to hear?"

"The truth shall set you free."

"Very well. When Frankie showed me your picture, playing matchmaker, I told her that I wasn't interested, and I meant it. I thought that you were very pretty, so it wasn't about me not appreciating your beauty, but I didn't want Frankie to set me up with you just because she got it into her head that you had to mate a god because she and Mia were mated to gods, and since I was the only single god left, that meant me. I happen to enjoy my unattached status and to prove that she was wrong, I made plans with Gertrude last night."

"I see." Margo turned to look out at the harbor, but Negal hadn't missed the hurt in her eyes.

He couldn't smell her emotions, though, probably because her scent was overpowered by the strong smell of the ocean.

"Still, despite what I told Frankie and what I told myself, I couldn't stop thinking about you. Those fierce eyes of yours haunted me, and when Mia found out that you were missing and Kian started assembling a task force to deal with the situation, I knew that I had to take part in the rescue mission. It happened during last night's wedding, and I told Gertrude that I had to leave but that I would make it up to her tonight. That's why she asked me about it as soon as I was back. I had made her a promise, and I couldn't go back on it no matter how intrigued I was by you and how much I wanted to spend tonight with you, so I had to agree."

"I didn't know that you felt that way about me." Margo's entire face softened. "I thought that you were just being chivalrous." She chuckled. "The picture Frankie showed you must have been incredibly flattering, and I'm surprised that you weren't disappointed with what you found, especially given the state I was in."

"To tell you the truth, I hoped you would be much less interesting in person and that I could finally stop obsessing over you, but my obsession has only gotten worse."

She arched a brow. "You could have fooled me. I was sure that you weren't interested." She narrowed her eyes at him. "Maybe you're the competitive type who gets interested in a woman only when another guy enters the picture? Frankie told you that she would introduce me to Max, and then you suddenly wanted me. You did call Max your competitor."

39

MARGO

"Is he?"

Margo really wanted to answer in the affirmative, but she also hated playing games. "Max is a great guy, but I'm not interested in him."

He chuckled. "Funny that you would say that because I thought that you weren't interested in me either. So maybe you are also the competitive type who wants a male only if another female desires him?"

She huffed out a breath. "Don't flatter yourself. I would never chase a guy who belonged to another woman, and I wouldn't have agreed to dance with you if you were still with her."

His smile was pure male satisfaction. "So, does that mean that you are attracted to me?"

Margo swallowed. "You are a god, and you came to save me. How could I be indifferent to you?"

He groaned. "You are doing it again. You are answering my question with a question."

She was. "But it's true. I'm awed by you, by this world, by the glowing goddess who presided over the ceremony. How can you expect me to answer this as if you were just some guy I met?"

"Can you pretend that's what I am? Just a guy? Would you be interested in me then?"

There was a vulnerability in his eyes that she didn't know how to interpret. Did he want her to pretend that he was human? Wasn't he proud of being a god?

Or maybe he just wanted her to like him for who he was as a person and not his genetic makeup. But how could she separate the two?

"You're also gorgeous and chivalrous."

"Thank you, but that doesn't answer my question."

He was using her own tactics on her, and she had to admit that they were annoying.

Margo didn't know what he wanted to hear. Well, that wasn't true. He wanted her to say that she wanted him, and she did, but if he had any chance of seducing her body, he had to seduce her mind first.

That wasn't what most males wanted to hear, and it didn't matter if they were human, gods, or immortals. She could read the need in his expression, in the way his eyes glowed, but her needs were different.

Margo had to form a connection before anything sparked inside of her and she could feel physical desire, but that took time that most men weren't willing to dedicate to the pursuit.

"I am very interested in getting to know you better, Negal. Right now, all I know is that you are gorgeous, kind, and polite, and that's a great start, but I also know that you are unlike any guy I have ever met, and I can't judge you by the same criteria. You talk about fighting dragons like someone talks about hunting crocodiles, not that I know anything about that either. You are an alien who has been on Earth for only five years, and yet you speak as if you were born in the US, and you can easily pass for a human, that is, until your eyes start glowing and you need to pretend that your nonexistent contact lenses are bothering you."

He winced. "I'm sorry about lying to you. I usually have great control over my eyes and fangs, but with you around, nothing about me is business as usual."

Fangs? Had he just said fangs?

Margo's heart started beating faster, and her hands started feeling clammy. "What fangs? You don't have fangs. Your teeth are normal."

After what Bridget had said about venom, Margo had paid attention to what was inside these immortals' mouths, but all she had seen were normal teeth, some having a little pointier than normal canines, but nothing to cause alarm.

Negal frowned. "Didn't your friends tell you anything?"

"They told me a lot, but not about fangs."

Closing his eyes, he let out an exasperated breath. "Male gods and immortals have fangs and venom glands. It's one more thing that makes us different from humans. When we get aggressive or aroused, our fangs elongate, and our venom glands fill up."

Margo lifted a shaky hand to her lips. "So that's what she meant by venom. I thought that your...you know, was venomous in some way."

"I don't understand. Who said what, and what did you think is venomous?"

"The doctor said that Frankie was transitioning as fast as a teenager, but because she was full of Dagor's venom, it might skew the results of the immortality test. She wanted to wait for the venom to clear Frankie's system before administering the test. I wondered about what she'd said, and since none of you had fangs, I assumed that Bridget meant some kind of chemical that gods had in their you-know-what."

Margo's cheeks felt as if they were on fire, but she hoped Negal couldn't see the color in the dimly illuminated terrace.

His eyes widened for a moment, and then he laughed. "You mean in our semen?"

Margo nodded. "What else was I supposed to think?"

He laughed even harder.

"Don't laugh at me. It was a legitimate assumption." She chuckled, but then it turned into laughter, and she couldn't help what came out of her mouth next, "It gave credence to the one-eyed-trouser-snake phrase."

"A what?" Negal started wheezing and wiping at his teary eyes. "I've never heard that one. A one-eyed trouser snake? Does that mean what I think it does?"

She slanted a look at him. "What else could it mean?"

"Dear Fates." He wiped the tears from his eyes. "You're funny."

She grimaced. "No one has ever accused me of that."

"It's not an accusation. It's a compliment. No one has made me laugh so hard in ages. It's just that..." Negal shook his head. "Never mind." He took a long breath to calm himself. "The you-know-what that our one-eyed trouser snake produces..." He started heaving with laughter again. "It's not venomous in the same way as the venom from our fangs is."

She glared at him. "So, I was right! It is venomous."

"It might have some of the same chemicals in lower concentrations, but I'm really not the person to ask about that. The doctor should know much more about the transition process."

Another piece of the puzzle fell into place.

It was like in the vampire stories. The vampires had fangs, and they drank blood, but in order to turn a human into a vampire, they forced the human to drink their blood, which was venomous.

Margo lifted a hand. "Hold on. Are you telling me that the venom is needed for the transition?"

"That's what I've been told," Negal said. "I've also witnessed the transitions of Aru and Dagor's mates, so I know that it works."

"You didn't know about it before?"

Negal shook his head. "We didn't even know that immortals existed. Gods are not supposed to procreate with the created species. It's forbidden, but the gods who were exiled to Earth broke the rules. We found out what they had done when we found the immortals."

That was a side of the story she hadn't heard from her friends. Had they omitted that on purpose? In the same way that they had omitted mentioning the fangs and venom that were needed for the transition?

"I think I need to have a long talk with Mia and Frankie. They left a lot out of the story they told me."

40

NEGAL

"You can do that, or I can tell you what I know."

Negal felt bad for laughing, but it was funny the way she'd tried to avoid saying semen, and her joke about the one-eyed trouser snake was hilarious.

He had never heard that expression before, but he could see how it came to be. Humans had many derogatory names for the male organ, and this one wasn't half bad.

"It doesn't seem like you know much," Margo said. "And I think that Frankie and Mia don't know enough either. I think I should talk to the doctor."

He nodded. "That's a good idea. Maybe we can talk to her together?"

Margo narrowed her eyes at him. "Why do you want to talk to her?"

"If I am to induce your transition, I should know everything there is to know about the process."

He felt guilty about not telling her that he had participated in an induction before and that he probably knew all there was to know about it, but it wasn't his secret to reveal.

"Wait." She lifted her hand. "What do you mean by inducing my transition? Why would you be the one to do it, and how?"

"Isn't that obvious?"

"Now you are the one answering a question with a question. Can you just be straight with me?"

Gabi had told him to woo Margo as if she were a virgin, and given her attitude toward anything that had to do with sex, Gabi had been right.

Could it be that a woman her age was indeed still a virgin? If she was, he had no idea how to talk to her about all of this or how to even approach her.

For some reason, humans were touchy about female virginity, and some even thought that it was a big prize, but to him, it meant inexperience, and it wasn't something he wanted to deal with. He preferred females who knew precisely what they wanted.

"I shouldn't have brought it up yet." Negal rubbed a hand over the back of his neck. "It's not something I'm comfortable discussing with you so early in our relationship. You seem more…how should I say it, traditional than other human females I've been with."

"I'm not a prude, which is what I think you are trying to say."

He arched a brow. "The one-eyed trouser snake term is funny, but it also suggests that you are uncomfortable talking about things pertaining to sex."

"Try me." She looked at him with a challenge in her eyes.

"Are you sure?"

"Positive."

"Okay, here goes. Your friends believe that you are a dormant carrier of godly genes."

She nodded. "I know, but the evidence for that is flimsy. All they had to go on is some vague notion of affinity and the claim of a teenage girl who thinks she can sense Dormants."

"It worked for Frankie, so there is a good chance that it would work for you as well."

"Let's assume that it's true and that I'm a Dormant. How are you supposed to induce my transition?"

There was no easy way to say that, and Margo claimed to value the truth. "Unprotected sex and a venom bite." When her eyes widened, and she opened her mouth to protest, he lifted his hand to stop her. "What I meant by unprotected is without a barrier. My semen needs to enter you to do its thing. You can be on birth control pills or some other chemical way of preventing pregnancy, just not a condom. Since I can't carry or transmit diseases, you don't need to worry about that either. Gods and immortals bite during sex, which is the second part necessary. The venom. And again, you shouldn't worry about that because it's extremely pleasurable. Not only will my venom deliver a string of the best orgasms you've ever had, but it will also send you on a euphoric trip that will make what you experienced with that drug you were injected with pale by comparison."

As Margo gaped at him, he hooked a finger under her chin and closed her mouth. "Don't look at me like that. You asked for the truth, and I gave it to you."

She blinked a couple of times, swallowed, and averted her eyes. "I did. Thank you for being so brutally honest with me."

"You're welcome."

"I need a drink," she murmured.

"Do you want to go inside?"

She shook her head. "Could you please get me one? I need a few moments to process what you've told me."

"Of course. What would you like me to get you?"

"A margarita. A Cadillac Margarita."

"What's that?"

"Just tell the barman. He will know." She waved a hand without looking at him.

"I'll be right back." He hesitated. "Are you going to be okay out here on your own?"

She snorted. "What could possibly happen to me on a ship full of immortals?"

He had the urge to laugh and make a joke about a stealth attack by the trouser snake, but he knew that she wouldn't appreciate the humor right now.

"You look a little shell-shocked."

"No, not really. I should have suspected what you've told me from the bits and pieces I've gathered. It just seemed so outlandish that my mind rejected the picture it was putting together." Margo walked over to one of the loungers and sat down. "I just need a moment to think."

41

MARGO

A wave of exhaustion crashed down on Margo as soon as she sat down. It had been a long day, and she'd plowed through it fueled by adrenaline or maybe the drug that Alberto had injected her with, and now all she wanted was to close her eyes and let herself drift into oblivion.

She didn't want to think about what Negal had told her or the fact that he assumed he would be the one inducing her transition and talking about having sex with her as if he was talking about sharing a cup of coffee. She'd asked him to be honest, and he'd complied with her request, but it had been jarring to realize how casually he thought about all this.

Why was he even volunteering to do it?

Under normal circumstances, she would have assumed that he just wanted an excuse to get her in bed, but she was not a great catch on this ship full of beautiful immortal females who most likely didn't have hang-ups about sex and who had no problem with hookups and one-night stands.

Maybe it was an ego trip for Negal? Perhaps it was considered an honor for a god to induce a Dormant?

It wouldn't surprise her if it was.

If Margo were in Negal's shoes and had that kind of power, she would have considered it a privilege to assist in turning someone immortal, and if she were a male, she would probably have the same casual attitude toward sex.

It wasn't his fault that the prospect disturbed her and not because of the fangs and venom. With the many romance novels she'd read about vampires and shifters who were into biting their mates, the bite part was more intriguing than frightening, and according to Negal, it was supposed to be extremely pleasurable.

What she found disturbing was his clinical approach to the induction. She couldn't get intimate with a guy who only thought about the benefit she would gain from it, which was admirable and commendable but not good enough.

She could only be with a man who wanted her and cared deeply for her and who she wanted and cared deeply for in return.

Then again, Negal had told her that he was obsessed with her and that it had started even before he'd met her just from seeing her eyes in a picture.

Could that be true?

She had no reason to think that Negal had lied.

He'd only admitted that after she had pressured him.

Still, an obsession wasn't a good thing. It didn't mean that he cared for her or even liked her. People got obsessed with people who they could barely stand.

There was no way she could jump into bed with Negal without forming a meaningful emotional connection first, and it wasn't because she was a prude or because she adhered to some outdated societal conventions. She just wasn't capable of that, not even for the prospect of immortality.

The only way it could happen was if the doctor drugged her or knocked her out, but she doubted Negal was into sex with a compromised or unresponsive partner.

What was she going to tell him when he returned?

How was she going to face him?

If she had the energy, Margo would have gotten up and slinked away to her cabin before he returned with her drink.

No, she wouldn't have.

It would have been a cowardly and offensive move, and Negal didn't deserve that. She would somehow marshal the dregs of her energy, finish this talk with him, say goodnight, and then go to her cabin and collapse into bed.

When the terrace door swished open, she braced herself as best she could, but given that her dress didn't allow a deep breath, it wasn't much.

"I've got you a Cadillac Margarita." Negal handed her the drink. "But after seeing what went into it, I'm not sure that you are in any state to drink it." He pulled a lounger closer to hers. "You look like you are about to faint again."

She noticed that he hadn't gotten a drink for himself, or maybe he had and had finished it at the bar.

The drink was supposed to give her liquid courage, but Negal was right. It would knock her out.

"You are right. I'm exhausted. I don't know how I'm even still functioning after the twenty-four hours I've had."

He smiled. "By sheer stubbornness."

Margo chuckled. "For a guy who has just met me, you seem to know me quite well."

"I want to get to know you even better."

She grimaced. "I bet."

He narrowed his eyes at her. "I don't mean carnally, although, of course, I want that as well. I mean, get to know you as a person. Your likes and dislikes, what interests you, what bores you, what foods you like, do you like a thick blanket or a thin one, and whether you prefer your eggs done with butter or with olive oil."

Margo chuckled. "Those are very specific questions. I don't think any guy has ever asked me how I liked my eggs. Do you like cooking?"

He smiled sheepishly. "Eggs are the only thing I know how to cook. I tried pasta once, and it didn't come out well. The noodles fell apart."

"You probably overcooked them. I can teach you. I make a wicked pasta primavera."

"Why is the pasta wicked?"

"It's a colloquial usage of the term, and it means that it's very good."

"I see." He braced his elbows on his knees. "It's good that there are kitchens in the cabins, so maybe you could teach me how to make that evil pasta before the cruise ends."

As Margo laughed, she wondered if he was confusing the words on purpose to lighten the mood after their previous conversation from before.

Probably.

He hadn't mentioned transition or induction since returning with her drink.

"What did I say?" Negal pretended to look puzzled.

"It's wicked pasta. Not evil pasta."

"My bad." He cast her that dazzling smile again, the one that probably had other women dropping their panties for him.

"I should go back to my cabin and get some sleep." She tried to get up, but with how tight her dress was, it was difficult.

When she tried the second time, she found herself in Negal's arms. "I'll carry you to your cabin. You look like you are about to pass out."

Margo wound her arms around his neck for balance, not because it felt good to do that, and she was going to stick to that claim no matter what.

Still, she needed to make sure that he didn't have any unrealistic expectations.

Except, she didn't know how to say that without sounding both presumptuous and ungrateful. If she told him that there was no chance that she was inviting him to her bed tonight, it would sound as if she assumed that was his intention, and it might not be. On the other hand, if it was, and she made it clear that it wasn't going to happen, she would sound like she didn't appreciate all that he had done for her and all that he was still willing to do.

42

NEGAL

"Can you please get my purse?" Margo asked. "It's on the table next to the margarita."

Negal had a feeling that there was something else she'd wanted to say, but she seemed frazzled, and he didn't want to push her any further than he already had.

"Of course." He bent his knees, held her to his chest with one arm, and grabbed the purse off the table. "Here you go." He handed it to her.

"You are incredibly strong," she murmured.

"I am. It's part of my enhancements." He walked down the terrace to where there was an additional set of doors that opened to the lobby.

Margo hadn't said anything when he had picked her up, but he had no doubt that she wouldn't want him to carry her through the dining room in view of all the guests.

"Enhancements? Do you mean as compared to a human or compared to other gods?"

He smiled. "I'm glad that even when you are so tired, you are just as sharp as usual. I've been genetically engineered to be stronger than many of the gods. I was destined to be a soldier."

Her expression soured. "Is that common where you come from? Are people's lives decided on even before they are born?"

"To some extent, yes. But once my tour of duty is over, I can do whatever I want."

That wasn't entirely true, but it was close enough. He could do whatever he wanted within the parameters of his class provided that he got approval, which often took decades or even centuries.

The bureaucrats took their sweet time going over every application and voting on every candidate's suitability for the particular colony they applied for. It was all done in the name of democracy and equality, supposedly ensuring fair treatment, but it was anything but.

"When will your tour be over?" Margo asked.

"You don't want to know." He entered the lobby and headed toward the elevators. "Which deck are you on?"

"Deck three, and I do want to know."

He should have expected her to say that. Margo was inquisitive, and she wasn't afraid of hard answers to her questions. Still, he was hesitant about revealing his age. Eventually she would ask, and he would have to answer, but for now, he preferred not to go there.

"My tour could have already been over, but I signed up for another one." He decided to take the stairs just because it would allow him to hold her in his arms for a little longer.

"Why did you do that?"

"It's only two stories up, and it will save us from bumping into someone in the elevator."

"I didn't mean the stairs. Why did you sign up for another tour of duty?"

"Because being a trooper is all I know, and I'm good at it. Besides, with what I've saved so far during my service, I could only afford to live in the type of colonies that are not particularly appealing to me. When I have more saved up, the selection will improve."

A smile bloomed on her tired face. "Are there many of them with dragon-like creatures?"

"Thankfully, there's only one. But who knows, the gods might decide to introduce the pest to other worlds." He exited the stairwell on deck three and proceeded down the corridor. "What's your cabin number?"

"It's that one." Margo pointed at the next door over. "I need to open it with the phone." She took the device out of her purse and pointed it at the lock. "I want to keep talking to you, but I don't think I can keep my eyes open for much longer." She opened the door.

That sounded like an invitation but with reservations, or maybe he was reading it wrong, and it was her polite way of saying that she was tired and wanted him to leave.

Negal walked in and headed to her bedroom. "That's okay. We can continue talking tomorrow over breakfast."

She looked worried as he lowered her onto the bed. "How did you know that this was my bedroom?"

"It smelled like you."

She frowned. "What do I smell like?"

He sniffed. "Sweet with some spicy undertones."

Margo chuckled. "You are making it up."

"I am. But it's hard to explain. Every person has a unique smell, and you have yours. It's a very pleasant scent." He rubbed a hand over his neck. "Do you mind if I stay in the living room and watch some television?"

She seemed both relieved and surprised.

"Why?"

"I don't feel like leaving you alone. You've been drugged, and I don't know what the withdrawal symptoms are and whether you are in danger. Frankie is not here to keep an eye on you, so it has to be me. Anyway, I won't be able to sleep while worrying about you."

"That's so incredibly sweet, but you should go back to the party. You didn't get to eat anything, and they are probably serving dinner now."

"You didn't eat either."

"I snacked, and I'm too tired to eat anyway."

"If you give me the code to your cabin, I can go down, get the staff to pack two plates for us, and come back."

It was a test to see if she trusted him.

Margo chewed on her lower lip. "If you intend to sleep on the couch, you should change out of this tux while you are at it."

His heart flipped inside his chest as if she'd just declared her love for him. "I'll do that."

"Give me your phone number, and I'll text you the room number. That way, we will also have each other's phone numbers."

It was an unexpected victory, and Negal congratulated himself for following his instincts and doing what his heart demanded, which was not leaving Margo alone for the night even if he wasn't going to share her bed.

After he had given her his phone number and she'd texted him the code to the lock, he hesitated for a moment before leaving. "If you get in bed before I'm back, leave the door to your bedroom open just a crack. So, if you fall asleep, I can hear you breathing."

"I will."

He nodded, turned on his heel, and headed toward the cabin's main door.

"Thank you," Margo called after him. "For everything."

Negal smiled. "You're most welcome."

43

MARINA

"Where is your boyfriend?" Mila asked. "Wasn't he supposed to come for you after the ceremony?"

"He was," Marina murmured. "I don't know what's keeping him."

The human staff was not allowed in the dining hall during the ceremony, so Marina couldn't walk in with Peter like the other guests. She'd had to wait for him to come get her once it was over, and she'd decided to do that in the kitchen and help out in the meantime.

She'd expected him to walk in as soon as the kitchen doors were unlocked, but that had been at least half an hour ago, and there was no sign of him.

Perhaps he'd gotten confused and thought that she would come out to meet him.

Not likely.

She clearly remembered telling him how awkward she would feel coming out of the kitchen all dressed up, and he'd said that she was overthinking it and that it would be fine because he would be with her.

So where was he?

When she finally saw Peter walking in as if he owned the place, she pretended not to notice.

"Where is my girl?" He looked around until he spotted her. "What are you doing?"

"What does it look like?" She was next to the platter station, wearing an apron over the dress Jasmine had lent her and artfully arranging pieces of artichokes around slices of beef. "What took you so long?"

"I'm sorry." He stood behind her, wrapped his arms around her, and nuzzled her neck as if they weren't surrounded by a bunch of cooks and servers, who were all watching them as if it were the best show on television. "I was ambushed by my mother and two of my aunts. I couldn't get away from them until now."

She turned around in his arms. "What did they want?"

"Oh, the usual. When am I going to visit, and whether I'm climbing the ranks in the force, and how is this cousin and that cousin doing."

He sounded sincere, but she knew he wasn't because the story didn't add up. No one new had arrived on the cruise apart from the rescued women, so his mother and his aunts had been on this cruise since the ship had left Long Beach and should have exhausted all of those types of questions a long time ago. The only new item of gossip was his relationship with her, and she had no doubt that was what the conversation had been about.

It bothered Marina that Peter could lie so easily to her, but then she hadn't been entirely honest with him either. She hadn't told him that she'd been watching him since the beginning of the cruise and planning to use him.

"Tell me the truth. Did they ask you about me?"

His dark brows lifted, making him look even more devilish than ever. "How did you do that? Are you a mind reader?"

"Very funny, Peter. That's usually my question. So, was I right?"

He nodded. "The blue-haired vixen might have come up in the conversation."

"Vixen?" She wasn't sure what the word meant. "What is a vixen?"

"A female fox and also a spirited and attractive lady."

"So, it's a good thing?"

"Of course." He leaned and kissed her nose and then untied her apron. "Come, my beautiful vixen. Let's dance."

Casting a sidelong glance at Mila, Marina caught her smirking and murmuring under her breath in Russian something about the immortal having a few drinks too many.

"Have you been drinking?" Marina asked as she tossed the apron into the laundry cart.

"Of course. I wouldn't be a Scotsman if I didn't." He led her out of the kitchen and into the dining room.

The dance floor was packed, with those who were still seated busy talking and drinking and laughing, and no one seemed to pay her any attention, which was good.

Well, for tonight, it was. She wouldn't have dyed her hair blue and pierced her eyebrow if she wanted to go unnoticed.

Pulling her behind him, Peter managed to squeeze between the dancing bodies until he reached the center of the dance floor and wrapped her in his arms.

Everyone around them was waving their arms and moving this way and that, but Peter seemed to think it was a slow dance and wouldn't let go of her.

Marina couldn't shake the feeling of unease gnawing at her insides. The eyes of the other guests seemed to bore into her, and she had the feeling that their whispers and murmurs were about the outsider among them.

"This is embarrassing," she hissed into Peter's ear. "Let go of me."

He seemed oblivious to her discomfort, his arms holding her tightly and his nose buried in the crook of her neck. "Not yet," he murmured, his breath warm against her skin. "I need to hold you for a little longer."

Peter was definitely buzzed but despite that, she found herself melting into his embrace, the tension in her body slowly abating, and as they moved together, she tried to convince herself that she was imagining the whispers and stares and that no one was paying attention to the only couple slow dancing among them.

Lost in the rhythm of the music and the warmth of Peter's touch, she had a few blissful moments, but as the song came to an end and the crowd began to disperse, she could no longer pretend that no one was looking or that some of the murmurs weren't about her.

Marina didn't have an immortal's hearing, but she'd heard the words 'human' and 'blue hair' spoken from several directions.

Finally, Peter released her from his embrace and leaned back to look her over. "What's the matter? Why are you so tense?"

She leaned to whisper in his ear. "Everyone is looking at me."

"Of course they are. You are gorgeous." He wrapped his arm around her waist and tugged her along with him. "I know what you need."

"And what's that?"

"A drink."

44

PETER

Were people looking?

Of course they were. Peter was well aware of the looks despite being a little drunk, and Marina was uncomfortable, thinking that everyone had a problem with her being his human date, which wasn't true. She didn't know that most of those immortals, who she thought were judging her, were hooking up with humans on a regular basis.

The only difference was that it was happening on this cruise, which was almost the same as if he had invited a human to the village. Not that it should have been so shocking. After all, the humans from the Kra-ell compound had been offered a place in the village, and if they hadn't decided that they liked Safe Haven better, they would have been living there now.

So yeah, it was a small oddity, but it was by no means the big deal Marina thought it was.

"Bob." Peter waved over to the bartender. "A drink for the lady."

Bob zoomed over and grinned. "What would the mistress like?"

"A mojito, please." She leaned against Peter's side as if trying to disappear into him.

"Marina." Jay walked over and offered her his hand. "Good to see you. Are you enjoying the party?"

"I'm trying to." She gave him a tight smile. "I feel strange being here all dressed up instead of serving tables."

"You look spectacular," Jay said. "I don't think anyone recognizes you as the server they've been seeing every other meal in the dining room."

"You are such a sweet liar." She wound a lock of her hair around her finger. "But with my blue hair, I'm hard to miss or to confuse with someone else."

He shrugged. "Does it matter? Every single guy here is envying Peter for snagging such a beautiful lady as his date for tonight, and I bet tomorrow, he will be approached by a dozen different guys asking him how he managed to get you to agree to be his partner."

That seemed to be the right thing to say, and Marina's posture lost some of its rigidity. "I hope you are right." She looked around at the people crowding the bar. "It's probably all in my head."

"Here is your mojito, mistress." One of Bob's hands put the drink in front of her while his other three served three other drinks.

Jay leaned against the bar and scanned the room. "Who is that redhead over there? The one balancing a tray on her shoulder."

"That's my roommate, Larisa."

Jay grinned. "Can you put in a good word for me? Perhaps she would like to be my date for tomorrow's wedding."

The smile that bloomed on Marina's face was priceless. "I can do that right now. Do you want to come with me to say hello?"

Jay glanced at Peter. "Is it okay with you?"

"Sure." If it made Marina happy, he would gladly watch her introducing his friends to hers for the rest of the party.

Well, not the entire time, of course.

He wasn't done dancing with her, and he wanted her sitting by his side, eating dinner and chatting with his table companions. And once the party was done, he wanted her in his bed, screaming his name.

Simple wishes of a guy with simple needs.

It was the simple things in life that made him happy. He didn't need status or riches or even the admiration of his friends to feel good about himself, and he hoped the same was true for Marina.

They might not have a future together, but they had the present, and not everything was about tomorrow. If more people lived for today, the world would be a happier place.

Marina's friend almost dropped her tray as Jay introduced himself, and Peter could see her blush across the room. But she nodded and smiled, and judging by Jay's corresponding grin, he had a date for tomorrow.

"Success?" Peter asked when they returned to the bar.

Jay nodded and turned to Marina. "Just don't introduce any more of your friends to mine, or there will be no one left to serve dinner tomorrow."

"Don't worry. Larissa is the only single one other than me. All the rest are older and in relationships."

Jay's smile got even wider. "Thank the merciful Fates for putting me in the right place at the right time. If I came over a moment later, you might have introduced the lovely Larisa to someone else."

"Lucky you." Marina took another sip from her mojito and then put the half-empty glass on the bar before turning to Peter. "Do you want to go back to the dance floor?"

She was in a much better mood now than she had been only moments ago, and he had Jay to thank for that.

"Let's go." He poured the rest of the tequila shot down his throat and put the empty glass on the bar next to Marina's.

As they returned to the dance floor, it was like he was with a different lady. Gone was the hesitant and unsure woman from scant minutes ago, and in her place was a confident vixen who danced like she owned the dance floor.

Peter was captivated by the grace and energy of her movements and the vibrant spirit that seemed to radiate from her. He couldn't take his eyes off her.

How had Jay known what Marina needed to feel comfortable among his friends and family, to feel like she belonged?

His friend must have an empathic talent he hadn't fessed up to.

Dancing with renewed spirit and free of inhibition, Marina was a sight to behold, and Peter wasn't the only one paying attention. From the corner of his eye, he could see his mother watching his date with a smile tugging on her lips, and if that didn't constitute one hell of an achievement, he didn't know what did.

45

ARU

As Aru led Gabi to the dance floor, he observed the mass of writhing bodies, each with their own unique flair. Some were spinning and twisting across the floor, others were incorporating dips into their routines, and some were simply swaying on their feet and waving their arms around, but as long as they were moving to the rhythm of the music, the skill level didn't matter.

It was about having fun, which he was, but he wished his teammates were with him.

Since arriving on Earth, Aru had spent so much time with Dagor and Negal that it was odd that their absence bothered him, especially since he had his mate in his arms, but out of everyone on Earth, the three of them were the only ones who were alike, and like gravitated toward like.

Dagor was with Frankie at the clinic, and Aru had seen Negal with Margo heading to the terrace, but that had been a while ago, and they hadn't returned yet.

Hopefully, things were going well between them.

Negal seemed to be taken with the woman, and it couldn't have made her friends happier, but Aru wondered about how it was going to turn out. Negal wasn't like him or Dagor, and he seemed satisfied with his life as a trooper and a bachelor. He hadn't been looking for a mate, but then neither had Dagor or Aru.

The Fates were busy matchmaking, and since they had done wonderfully for him, he trusted them to do the same for his friend, but it wasn't without complications. Their trip to Tibet was turning into an expedition, and Aru had a feeling that he would have to hire some locals to help them on the way. The ladies wouldn't like to rough it like he and his buddies were used to doing. They would need tents, and inflatable mattresses under the sleeping bags, and some yaks would be needed to carry all that equipment.

"Aru." Gabi snapped her fingers in front of his face. "Where did you go just now?"

He arched a brow. "I'm right here."

"Your body might be here, standing in the middle of the dance floor and swaying from side to side, but your mind was somewhere else."

"I'm sorry." He put his hand on the small of her back. "I was thinking about the logistics of traveling through Tibet with three ladies and how to make it more comfortable for you."

Gabi laughed. "So, you've already decided that Negal and Margo are fated for each other?"

"I didn't decide anything, but the Fates' hands seem to be involved. Do you see them anywhere?"

Gabi looked around the room. "I don't see the Fates or Margo and Negal." She leaned into him and whispered. "Do you think they snuck out and went to her cabin?"

Aru pretended to be offended. "I don't follow the love lives of my teammates. I only make plans accordingly."

Gabi said something to him, but he couldn't hear her because he was distracted by the sensation of the channel in his mind opening.

Can you talk? Aria asked.

Give me a few moments, he answered.

I will wait. It is important.

"Forgive me, love." He leaned down to Gabi's ear. "I need to visit the men's room."

She looked surprised because she was usually the one who needed frequent bathroom breaks. "Did you eat something that disagreed with your stomach?"

Aru hated lying to her. "Evidently." He winced.

Looking worried, she waved him off. "Go. I'll wait for you at our table."

He smiled. "Save some of the appetizers for me."

After leaving Gabi at their table, he rushed out of the dining hall and into the nearest bathroom.

It wasn't as if anyone could hear his mental conversation with his sister, but he looked like he was zoning out when he was talking to her, and people noticed.

Entering one of the stalls, he closed the door, lowered the lid on the toilet, and sat down.

I am alone. What is going on?

The queen is ready to talk with her granddaughter. The day after tomorrow, same time as now.

This wasn't good. That would be during another wedding, and although Annani would be done officiating a little after midnight, the party would continue, and if he and Kian left so early, it would look suspicious.

There was no doubt in Aru's mind that Kian would want to be present. The guy was extremely protective of his mother, and he wouldn't want her to be alone with Aru.

He would have to coordinate a good excuse with Kian, maybe something in connection to the cartel boss and his despicable brother.

Is there any way it can be done at a different time? he asked Aria while looking at his watch. It was nearly one o'clock in the morning.

It is when the queen can come to the temple, and since the project of collecting the prophecies has begun, the rest of the plan needs to fall into place. Going forward, it will be the same time every day unless the queen cannot make it.

I will arrange it.

Thank you, Aru. I need to go now.

Be well, sister of mine.

You too, Aru. She closed the channel.

He needed to talk to Kian as soon as possible. He would have to wait until tomorrow and ask for a private audience with the princess and her son.

46

PETER

As soon as Peter closed his bedroom door behind him, he lifted Marina and sealed his lips over hers as he carried her to his bed. Her hands pulled at his hair as she deepened the kiss, and he let her, savoring the feeling of her tongue inside his mouth, swirling around his fangs as if she had no care about how sharp they were.

She was just as hungry for him as he was for her. He could feel it in the way she frantically rubbed herself against him, the small moans escaping her mouth as she kissed him, and the strong scent of her desire that was scrambling his senses.

His ravenous little vixen.

As Peter's knees hit the bed, he crawled across the mattress with Marina in his arms and her mouth still on his. He flipped them around so that he was beneath her and she was straddling him, her long evening gown bunched around her thighs, and her scant panty-clad center rubbing over the erection imprisoned in his underwear and slacks.

When she finally released his mouth so she could suck some air into her lungs, she lifted her head and looked at him with so much fire in her eyes that they were almost glowing and yet unfocused. Her mouth was slightly open, her jaw slackened, and she was panting.

He wanted to rip the dress off her, shred his own clothing, and get inside of her, and he knew she would welcome him, but the dress wasn't hers, and he didn't want her to be upset after she came down from the high of their lovemaking.

Besides, he was wearing his only tux, and there were still five weddings he had to attend.

Smiling with a mouth full of fangs, Peter tucked his hands under his head. "If you want to return this dress to your friend in one piece, you'd better take it off yourself."

For a moment, she didn't seem to track his meaning, but then her gaze came into focus, and a smile tugged her swollen lips.

"You want me to take it off?" She reached for the side zipper and pulled it down agonizingly slowly. "What if I don't?"

"Then I'll have to rip it off you, and your new friend will be upset."

"We can't have that, now, can we?" She gathered the skirt, bunching it in her hands before pulling it over her head.

He sucked in a breath as he beheld her hard nipples. "No bra?"

She cupped her breasts, her thumbs teasing the reddened peaks. "They were too sensitive after what you did to them last night."

At the memory of them clamped and swollen, his erection kicked up. "Then I have to remember to be gentle with them tonight."

They should have been just fine after his venom bite, which was supposed to take care of all the little aches and pains of the rough lovemaking, but perhaps he had overdone it a little, and even the venom's healing properties hadn't been enough to undo that.

That wasn't very likely, though.

The other option was that she had played with herself after he'd escorted her to the kitchen.

When she'd come to his cabin all sexed up, he had pleasured her with his tongue, and she'd climaxed screaming his name, but perhaps she'd still been hungry and had continued without him.

"Did you play with your sweet berries after I left you in the kitchen earlier?"

Her eyes widened. "I did not. You saw me. I was helping with the prep."

"The lady doth protest too much, methinks. Did you play with yourself before coming to my cabin, then?"

Actually, he was sure that was what had happened. When she'd shown up all sexed up and dropped to her knees in front of him, he had been too pleased to ponder why, but it was clear to him now.

The guilty look in her eyes was all the confirmation he needed.

"Naughty girl. You've just earned yourself a spanking."

She pouted, but the scent of her arousal flared. "You didn't say anything about me not being allowed to touch myself."

Her protest was part of the game and given the intensity of her scent and her labored breathing, she enjoyed playing it just as much as he did.

"It should have been self-explanatory." He moved her hands aside, cupped her breasts, and trailed his thumbs softly over her taut nipples. "From now on, you don't touch yourself unless I allow it." He pinched both at the same time, eliciting a gasp.

Still, there was a challenge in her eyes. "What about when you are not around?"

"Then you are free to do as you please." He leaned up, taking one nipple between his lips and flicking his tongue over it to soothe the sting. "But as long as we are together, which is for the duration of this cruise, your pleasure is mine." He bit down lightly.

Marina groaned and rocked her panty-clad center against his throbbing erection, but he detected the whiff of disappointment intermingled in the smell of her arousal.

Did she expect a happily-ever-after with him?

Peter hoped Marina didn't have any such illusions. As much as he enjoyed being with her, they couldn't have anything more than a few days of pleasure together. Getting involved with a mortal was a prescription for pain, and even though he sometimes enjoyed being on the receiving end of it, he wasn't a masochist. Besides, he'd had enough heartache to last him for a while.

Easier said than done, though.

He had a feeling that he wouldn't be saved from another heartache anyway, and saying goodbye to Marina at the end of the cruise would be tough no matter what. He needed to harden himself and be strong for both of them.

Seemingly over her temporary mood swing, Marina attacked the buttons of his dress shirt, and when she exposed his chest, she leaned down and flicked her tongue over his nipple.

He moaned as she explored him, her tongue, lips, and teeth tormenting one nipple while her fingers pinched the other.

He hissed when she bit hard enough to draw blood, but then she licked the small hurt away.

Lifting her head, she smiled apologetically at him. "Sorry. I didn't mean it to hurt."

"That's okay." He cupped her ass cheeks, which were exposed thanks to the skimpy thong she had on. "I enjoyed that."

"Good." She shifted up and lowered her head to kiss him on the lips.

Peter let her push her tongue inside his mouth, controlling the kiss. And even though he was hard as a rock and fought the need to take over, he tried to appear as if he was in no hurry, and she had all the time in the world to do whatever she pleased with him until she grew tired of it, which he knew would be soon.

Marina might enjoy a few moments of role reversal, but she enjoyed it much more when he was in charge.

47

MARINA

Marina hadn't intended to bite Peter's nipple hard enough to draw blood, and she'd regretted it immediately. She was grateful that it hadn't turned him off and even more grateful that his fast immortal healing had erased the bite marks along with any lingering pain.

Her frustration was at fault.

She'd tried to overcome it by drowning the feeling in the frenzy of sex, but it had seeped through and taken over, forcing the vindictive act.

It had dampened her fervor in an instant.

The surge of assertiveness she'd felt before was gone, and to salvage the situation, she needed to relinquish control to Peter.

Lifting one knee, she un-straddled him and lay on her back next to him.

"Had enough being on top?" he teased as he sat up and shrugged off his tux jacket and then the shirt she'd unbuttoned.

He was such a good sport about it, and his smile eased the knot that had formed in her stomach.

Marina managed a teasing smile. "I didn't want to rumple your tux. What would you wear for tomorrow's wedding? Me?"

"Such a smart mouth." He crushed his lips over hers in a brutal kiss.

Oh, yeah. That was what she needed.

Her body responded with an inferno igniting inside her core, and Peter didn't waste any time, tugging his slacks off with one hand while tearing her thong off with the other. Without bothering with buildup, he was inside of her with one brutal thrust and then going from zero to a hundred in three seconds flat.

It was glorious and just what she needed to take her mind off things. All she could do was hang on as he pounded into her, and then he was coming, and so was she, but the bite she'd expected didn't come.

Breathing hard, Peter kept rocking his hips, and his erection wasn't showing any signs of shrinking.

"Why didn't you bite me?" she whispered.

He lifted his head and smiled with those huge fangs of his filling his mouth. "Disappointed?"

"Yes," she admitted. "It was out of this world last night."

He was still rocking inside of her, and with every passing moment, his erection was growing thicker and longer, swelling inside of her.

"I didn't want it to end yet, and it would have if I bit you and you passed out." He trailed soft kisses over her face. "I like being inside of you. We fit well together."

Yes, they did, but it was cruel of him to tell her that when he had no plans to keep her.

A tear glided down her cheek, but Peter was too busy shifting their bodies to notice. Moving to his knees, he held her pressed against his chest.

She folded her legs around his bottom and wrapped her arms around his torso, rocking against him as he gently thrust up into her.

It was so intimate being held by him like that, so close, their chests pressed against each other.

Too intimate.

As tears gathered at the corners of her eyes, she tightened her hold on him and kissed him, biting his lower lip with her blunt front teeth, but not hard enough to draw blood this time.

He'd admitted to enjoying a little pain with his pleasure, and given his response, the little nibble had delivered just the right dose.

Groaning, Peter clamped his hands over her hips, lifted her until she was perched on the very tip of him, and then slammed her down on his hard length until he was buried in her to the hilt. As he did that over and over, the coil inside her tightened again, readying for him to spring it. And then he was supporting her weight with one hand while playing with her clit with the fingers of the other, and the coil was sprung.

Throwing her head back, Marina climaxed.

Peter kept massaging her clit. "Again," he growled as he continued rubbing that oversensitive spot. "Come for me again."

She shook her head. "It's too much. I can't."

"Yes, you can." He rammed up into her, hitting that spot inside of her once, twice, while his fingers kept on their gentle assault.

This time, the orgasm was a whisper instead of a roar, and Peter didn't climax at all. He didn't bite her either.

Maybe he didn't need to bite every time he had sex?

Dazed, Marina suddenly found herself flipped over, her head down on the mattress, her bottom sticking up in the air, and Peter behind her, gripping her hips with an almost bruising force.

It was the perfect pose for spanking, but she was too spent to enjoy that now. The fit was tight at this angle, bordering on uncomfortable, but it was exhilarating, and as his thrusting became frantic, she knew that he would bite her this time, and she would get to soar again.

Nothing could compare to that feeling.

When Peter exploded inside of her, Marina tilted her head, elongating her neck, and when the hiss came, she braced for the brief pain that followed.

Then, there was bliss, and she shot up to the clouds.

48

MARGO

Margo woke up to the smell of eggs frying in butter.

Frankie must be back, and if she was making breakfast, she must be feeling much better. Last night, she'd been too tired and weak to attend the wedding, so her being on her feet was a major improvement. But hadn't Bridget said that she needed to wait until Dagor's venom was out of her system to conduct the immortality test?

She wouldn't have released Frankie from the clinic without it. Or would she?

Oh, well, there was only one way to find out, and it required Margo to get out of bed.

Yawning, she stretched her arms over her head, wiggled her toes, and then tossed the duvet aside.

After a quick visit to the bathroom, she shrugged Frankie's flimsy robe on, padded to the living room, and stopped in her tracks as soon as she saw who was in the kitchen.

"Negal? What are you doing here?"

He smiled at her. "Good morning. I made three kinds of eggs because you never told me what you liked. I have scrambled, sunny side up, and hard-boiled."

"Good morning," she murmured.

Tightening the nearly sheer robe around her, Margo considered ducking back into the bedroom. Frankie's nightgown was so short on her that her ass was probably showing, and the matching robe was not much better.

"What's your pleasure?" Negal asked. "I mean egg-wise."

He was wearing jeans and a navy-blue T-shirt, his hair was tussled like he hadn't combed it after waking up, and he was so handsome that she could barely breathe.

"Scrambled," Margo managed with an effort. "Did you sleep here?"

"Did you forget? I told you that I didn't feel comfortable leaving you alone in here."

"I didn't forget. I just didn't think that you would still be here in the morning."

"I wouldn't have left before you woke up." He pulled out a chair for her. "Please, sit down."

"I should get dressed first."

"The eggs will get cold. Come on." He patted the chair. "I also brewed coffee and made toast."

A god had cooked her breakfast.

Talk about surreal.

She padded to the chair and sat down. "I must be still dreaming."

He arched a brow. "Has no man ever cooked breakfast for you?"

"Even if someone had, he wouldn't have been a god. I feel like I've stepped into an alternate reality."

"I get it." He pushed her chair in and then put a plate with scrambled eggs and toast in front of her. "As someone who has visited many planets, I'm familiar with the feeling, although I have grown to like it. It makes life more interesting." At her puzzled expression, he continued, "Every colony is like a different world, especially those that have been around for a long time and developed their own cultures and traditions. Some of them deviated a lot from my home planet."

She remembered him mentioning something about it last night, but her memory of everything they had talked about was a little hazy. Well, not the part about him having fangs and venom or the part about him having to bite her during sex to induce her transition. That, she remembered very clearly.

"Coffee?" Negal asked.

"Yes, please. And thank you for making breakfast for me. It was very kind of you."

Where did he even get eggs? She'd looked in the fridge before getting dressed for the wedding, and there had been no eggs in there.

"I was hungry, and when I sensed that you were waking up, I started on breakfast." He poured them both coffee and put the mugs on the table.

"You sensed it? How?"

He smiled sheepishly. "You stopped snoring and made this cute sound like you were stretching and yawning at the same time."

"Oh, my God." She closed her eyes. "Are you serious? I'm so embarrassed."

More like mortified. Margo rarely snored and only when she was overtired, which she had been last night.

"Why? It's natural for mortals to snore. Even gods and immortals sometimes do that, even though that shouldn't be possible. Our bodies should adjust to any condition."

He was probably just saying that to alleviate her discomfort. Perfectly healthy bodies, which the gods and immortals enjoyed, didn't snore.

"If you say so." She reached for the coffee mug and took a sip only to grimace. "Is there cream and sugar?"

"There should be." Negal pushed to his feet, opened one of the cabinets, and returned with both.

"Thank you." Margo got busy stirring two packets of sugar into her coffee and two little containers of half-and-half, buying herself time to think.

"So, did you watch any good movies last night?" she asked.

It was such a lame question, but it was the best she could do first thing in the morning while sitting in a sheer nightgown and robe across from a god who had heard her snoring and had made her breakfast.

"After I came back last night, I watched the live streaming of the wedding while eating dinner, and then I fell asleep. I still have a plateful of food for you in the fridge, so if you don't like my eggs, I can warm it up for you in the microwave."

"Did you get the eggs last night, too?"

He nodded. "I was in the kitchen, waiting for one of the cooks to prepare plates to go for us, and I thought about our conversation. I asked her if I could have some eggs and butter, and she packed both for me."

"That was nice of her." Margo scooped some on her fork and brought it to her mouth.

The eggs were cold, and they needed more salt, but it was the thought that mattered, and Negal was looking at her expectantly.

"They are very good." She washed them down with a sip of coffee.

"You don't have to lie to spare my feelings." He pinned her with his incredibly blue stare. "Truth shall set you free."

Damn. He remembered her saying that to him.

"They are not bad. It's just that they've gotten cold, and I like a little more salt on my eggs."

He smiled. "Now, that was the truth."

She eyed him from under lowered lashes. "Am I that transparent, or can you read my mind?"

49

NEGAL

"I can't read your mind," Negal said. "And you are probably not transparent to other humans, but I'm good at detecting emotions, especially when they are strong. Although, in the case of the eggs, your face said it all."

"So, I am transparent." Margo cradled her coffee mug, looking at him from over its rim.

Repeating that word was making it hard for him to keep his eyes on her face. Her damn nightgown and robe combo were so transparent that he could see the color of her nipples through both layers of flimsy fabric, but he refused to look where she didn't want him to look. Margo seemed very self-conscious about her state of dress, or rather undress, and he'd already embarrassed her enough by mentioning her snoring.

"A little," he admitted. "But at least now I know how you like your eggs."

Negal was trying to keep it light today and avoid the mistake of dumping too much information on her like he had done last night, but the truth was that if she wanted him to induce her transition, they didn't have time to dance around the topic.

Then again, he didn't have to be the one she chose for that. Margo could take her time and choose any of the single immortals on the ship.

Except, he didn't like that idea. Not at all. In fact, thinking about her with any other male was making him so angry that his fangs were starting to elongate.

Great. Now, he was going to scare her.

Pushing to his feet, Negal walked to the refrigerator and pretended to look for something inside just to buy himself time to get his damn fangs under control.

"Would you like some orange juice?" he asked without looking at her.

"No, thank you."

He pulled out the container and poured himself a glass, even though he didn't want juice either.

"I'm very curious about all those planets you visited," Margo said. "Can you tell me about them?"

"Right now?"

She chuckled. "Whenever you are in the mood for storytelling. I'm sure you have plenty of fascinating tales to tell."

"You seem to be particularly interested in dragons. Is there a reason for that?"

Margo blushed. "There is, but it's a little embarrassing to talk about."

"Now, you've really made me curious. What could possibly be embarrassing about flying lizards?"

She took another sip of coffee and put the mug down. "The dragons you encountered were obviously just dumb, destructive creatures. The dragons I'm fascinated with are mythical shapeshifters who can shift between their dragon and human forms."

"Oh, I see. You are referring to magical beings in children's stories."

She laughed. "The stories I'm talking about are more suitable for adults."

"Adult fairytales?"

"Yes. Precisely." She lifted her coffee mug and took another sip.

Myths could be called adult fairytales, and his team had researched those quite thoroughly while searching for clues about what had happened to the exiled gods. There were myths about dragons in many cultures, but none about dragons who could shapeshift into humans. Myths usually had a kernel of truth at their core, and dragon-like creatures could have existed on Earth at some point, but shapeshifting was just not possible. The closest any creature came to this was changing skin and eye colors, puffing up and shrinking down. But no creature could turn into another creature just by willing it.

"I would love to read those myths. Can you tell me where I can find them?"

Margo almost choked on her coffee, and as she coughed, a few drops landed on her hand. "I don't think you will enjoy reading them." She wiped them off.

"Why not?"

"Because they are usually more enjoyable to ladies."

Now he was really confused. "I didn't know that myths were based on gender preferences."

Margo closed her eyes and let out an exasperated breath. "Do you know what romance novels are?"

"Of course. They are stories about romantic love."

"Yes, well, there are many different kinds of romance novels, and some of them feature protagonists who are shapeshifters. There are wolves, bears, panthers, lions, eagles, and even dragons."

"Oh, now I get it. And you like dragons in particular?"

She shrugged. "To each her own, right? Jasmine likes historical romance novels about lords and ladies, and I like dragon shifters."

"That's an interesting choice." He leaned back in his chair and leveled his gaze at her. "Can you tell me why you are drawn to those kinds of stories?"

"Because they make suspension of disbelief easier for me. I can let myself imagine the perfect lover as a mythical creature who does not exist in my reality. I can't imagine regular humans being all that great."

Negal grinned. "I'm not a regular human."

"No, you are not."

50

MARGO

Margo took another sip of coffee just so she could hide behind the mug.

Negal wasn't human; she'd known that, but only now had it really sunk in. He wasn't a shifter, but he was kind of a vampire, with all the good things the lore said about them and without any of the bad.

He was beautiful, had mind control ability, was stronger and faster than a human, with much better eyesight, hearing, and sense of smell, and he also had venom that could turn her immortal. He didn't suck blood, and he didn't burn to a crisp when exposed to the sun. He also couldn't teleport or fly.

Nevertheless, he was the closest she would ever get to being with someone like the male protagonists in her stories. The biggest difference was that she wouldn't get a happily ever after with him, but even a happy for now was better than she could have ever hoped for.

Maybe she could use that to trick her mind into getting intimate with him sooner rather than later.

How long could she hope he would wait?

"What is going through your head?" Negal asked.

"I'm thinking about the things you told me yesterday."

The smile slid off his face. "What about them?"

"How long do I have?" She dared to look up at him.

His eyes started glowing. "Do you mean how long will my offer to induce you stand?"

She nodded.

"Why? Are you hoping for other offers?"

Her eyes widened. "Of course not. That's not it at all. It's just that I…"

Damn, she couldn't say that.

If he were a normal guy, she would have told him that she needed to date him for a couple of months before she would consider having sex with him, and in most cases, that was enough to discourage most guys from seeing her again.

But he wasn't just a guy, and what he offered her was so much more than just a night of passion. He was offering her immortality and telling him that she needed a couple of months was kind of rude.

Suddenly, she remembered a comment he'd made about not knowing that immortals even existed because gods were forbidden from fraternizing with the species they created. The gods of old had been rebels, and they had taken human mates, but so had his teammates. Aru and Dagor were both mated to transitioned humans.

Negal's eyes softened. "What were you trying to say, Margo? You can tell me absolutely anything, and I promise not to judge you or get offended or any of the things that might make you hesitate to speak openly with me."

"Are you a rebel?"

Despite his assertions from a moment ago, Negal seemed taken aback. "That's an odd question. Why do you ask?"

"You said that gods were forbidden to fraternize with created species, and yet your friends are mated to former Dormants, and you are offering your induction services to me."

His facial muscles relaxed, and he unclenched his jaw. "You are right. That makes us rebels. But you are wrong about me offering you just my induction services. I'm offering you my courtship, and I'm sweetening the deal by offering to induce you. I hope that you will accept."

That sounded so much nicer than what he had told her last night. It sounded like an offer of a romance and not a clinical transaction.

Margo let out a breath. "Thank you. I accept."

Negal seemed surprised. "I thought that I would need to work harder at winning you over."

"Oh, you will." She grimaced. "If you are up to it. I have a feeling that our views on what constitutes courtship differ."

"Isn't it about getting to know one another?"

"It is." There was no way around it. She just had to spell it out for him and be done with it. "I can't have sex with you before I get to know you. It's not because I'm a prude or that I want to prove anything. It's just the way I am. I need more time."

He nodded as if that was perfectly normal, and that was a huge relief. Maybe on his home world, people took their time and didn't engage in bed-hopping like her generation of humans did.

"I have only until the end of the cruise. After that, my teammates and I and their mates are heading to Tibet. We have a mission we need to complete."

That was news to her. "Frankie didn't tell me anything about going to Tibet with Dagor."

Was Negal making it up?

If he were a human, she would have suspected that he was saying that to pressure her to hurry up, but she was starting to realize that he operated according to a better code of conduct, and deceiving his partners was not part of it.

"Maybe it has slipped her mind," Negal said. "Or maybe she plans on joining us a little later because of her transition. I hope Aru will agree to wait a few more days before heading out to give her time to recover. But yes, that's the plan." He rubbed a hand over the back of his neck. "But if you need more time and you enjoy hiking, you could join us, and we could get to know each other over a longer period of time. I don't want you to feel pressured."

That actually sounded lovely, but there were two big problems with his idea.

"Given that Frankie needs medical supervision during her transition, I assume that I will need it as well, so I can't transition while trekking through Tibet. Also, I'm supposed to start working for the Perfect Match Virtual Reality Studios as a beta tester. Is there any way that the trip could be postponed by a few months?"

"We have our orders." Negal sighed. "But perhaps we can negotiate something. I need to talk to Aru."

"Orders from whom?"

"Our commander. I can't really say more."

She nodded. "I understand. I truly appreciate your willingness to make an effort to give me more time."

Reaching over the small table, he took her hand. "The best things in life are worth waiting for, and since you are the best, so are you."

Margo could fall in love with Negal just for saying that, and she refused to let her suspicious mind ruin the moment by doubting his sincerity.

"That's one of the nicest things anyone has ever said to me."

51

NEGAL

Finally, Negal had managed to say something right.

There were tears in Margo's eyes, but he knew they weren't the result of sadness. She was emotional in a good way.

He lightly squeezed her hand. "I'm not good with words, but I promise to do my best to say more nice things to you that will make you happy."

Margo chuckled. "Don't sell yourself short. What counts is the sincerity of what you said rather than the words you used to say it. In this instant-gratification world, it is rare to meet someone who is not in a rush and is willing to take his time."

Should he say what he really thought about her statement or try to say what she wanted to hear him say?

It was a dilemma.

On the one hand Margo appreciated the truth, but on the other hand, if he told her that he was the farthest from patient she could imagine, she would get defensive again and retract into her shell.

The truth was that he was dying to kiss her, to put his hands on those beautiful breasts, which were on display through the sheer fabric of her nightgown and robe, and that he had been sporting one hell of an erection ever since she'd stepped out of her bedroom in those flimsy garments.

If he were eloquent, he could have found a roundabout way to say that without being so blunt or causing her alarm, but he wasn't. He could say the truth, or he could lie, and lying was not a good strategy when trying to win a female's heart.

Releasing her hand, he let out a breath. "I'm not patient, and if not for your reluctance, I would have picked you up, carried you to the bedroom, and shown you why you shouldn't wait. But I resolved to think of you as a skittish virgin and to let you set the pace." He narrowed his eyes at her deer-in-the-headlights expression. "You are not a virgin, are you?"

Margo was still gaping at him, and he struggled to resist the urge to lean over, hook a finger under her chin, and close her mouth, or conversely, cover those lush lips with his and kiss her like she should be kissed.

He was willing to bet that all of her inhibitions would fly out the window once she got a taste of what being with a god entailed and how none of her prior experiences could prepare her for that.

Finally, Margo closed her mouth and shook her head. "I'm not a virgin. I gave away my virginity on my eighteenth birthday."

He had a feeling that there was a story there, but since she hadn't said that it had been taken away from her or stolen, it had been consensual.

"Giving it away is not a term I have heard before. Humans usually refer to it as losing their virginity. And your eighteenth birthday is a very particular date. Did you choose it on purpose?"

A small smile bloomed on her face. "You're paying attention. Two more merit points to Negal."

"Thank you, but that's not an answer."

She drank what was left in her coffee mug and put it back on the table. "It was the summer before college, and all my friends were boasting about their experiences. Well, Mia didn't, but Frankie did, and most of the girls in my class did. I'd been dating a boy for all of senior year, but we never took the final step. We were not going to the same college, and I knew that I was running out of time. We promised each other that we would stay true and continue our relationship over the phone and on vacations, but I knew that wasn't likely, so I decided to give him a parting present."

Her expression was so revealing that Negal didn't need any empathic ability to guess how that had gone. "Did he like his present?"

She laughed. "What eighteen-year-old boy wouldn't? Of course he did. But we were both virgins, and neither of us knew what we were doing. Roger's only reference was porn, and mine was romance novels, and I don't know which one of us was more delusional. Anyway, it wasn't fun. The second time was better, and the third was better than the second, but none inspired me to pursue sex. In fact, several years passed until I tried again."

"What happened to Roger?"

"He found a new girl a month into the semester. He's the type of guy who needs a woman and can't be without one, not because of the sex but because he's not good at being alone. They got married five years ago and have three kids together."

There had been no envy in her tone, but there was awe.

"So, your high school sweetheart got his happily ever after. What about you?"

Margo shrugged. "There weren't even any maybes. My mother says that I'm too choosy."

"You are, and that's a good thing." He grinned. "You were waiting for me."

52

MARGO

"Don't talk like that. You barely know me, and you are talking as if we were fated to be together. We haven't even kissed yet. What if I'm a terrible kisser?"

What if she was terrible at lovemaking?

Her lukewarm experiences hadn't been totally the guys' fault. She'd had a total of four lovers so far, including Roger, so that wasn't a big sample, but Margo was a realist. It took two to play, and if she were better at it, perhaps she would have enjoyed it more.

Certainly, it had to do with her attitude. She had a problem with smells; even faint ones were enough to turn her off, she hated to get someone else's sweat on her, and the whole thing seemed animalistic to her, which was kind of ironic since she was so much into shapeshifters.

"I'm sure that you are a wonderful kisser." Negal's eyes started glowing, which she now knew indicated arousal or excitement. "But just so we are clear, I'm going to wait until you kiss me. I'm not going to initiate." He leaned back and crossed his arms over his chest as if he was issuing a challenge.

She had to admit that it was incredibly cute. "You are so sure that you are irresistible."

"I'm not sure of anything. I intend on spending as much time with you as possible, getting to know you, and giving you every opportunity to kiss me." He uncrossed his arms and leaned over the table. "So, what are your plans for today?"

"I haven't really thought about that. I need to check on Frankie and Jasmine, and if Mia is available, spend some time with her. I also need to find out whether the Perfect Match deal is still on or was just an excuse to get Frankie and me to come to the cruise so we can find out whether we are Dormants like Lisa suspected." She paused to take a breath. "What did you plan for today?"

"I had a little more time to think about it when you were asleep, and it occurred to me that you would like to go shopping. Your suitcase stayed in the hotel, and you have nothing to wear that's your own." His eyes traveled to her cleavage, but to his credit, they didn't linger there. "I have a feeling that you would have never chosen this type of sleepwear."

"Why, because it's too revealing? I told you that I'm not a prude. I'm just reserved."

The more accurate term was repressed but reserved sounded better. It indicated a choice rather than a problem.

"It's too small on you, as was the beautiful dress you wore last night. You could barely breathe in it. I'm sure we can find nice stores in Puerto Vallarta where you can find evening wear for the next five weddings. You also need everyday clothing and other personal items."

He was right. She needed to buy new underwear, a couple of T-shirts and leggings, and maybe a pair of flip-flops. As for evening gowns, though, she wasn't sure she had the budget for that.

Lynda's bachelorette party had demolished her savings, so whatever she bought would have to be on a credit card, but she hated having a balance that carried over. She always paid off the card so she wouldn't have to pay the insane interest banks charged on credit card debt.

Then again, she didn't want to have to wear the same dress to all five events, and none of Frankie's other dresses fit her.

But what about the cartel thugs?

Kevin, otherwise known as Kalugal, had thralled and compelled them to change their ways, but she didn't really trust that it would hold, and Puerto Vallarta was not a big place. Someone from the yacht might recognize her. Heck, she could even bump into Alberto.

Actually, that wouldn't be such a bad thing.

Now that she was sober, and the drug was no longer making her giddy for no reason, she wanted to punch the scumbag in the face, and with Negal as backup she could do that with impunity.

A smile tugged at her lips. "I will take you up on your offer, the one about going shopping with me." She tagged on the last part in case he misunderstood her meaning.

"Great." He pushed to his feet. "I hope you can borrow something to wear, though. I'm not taking you to Puerto Vallarta wearing that." He waved a hand over her attire.

Margo laughed. "Wouldn't dream of it. But I can't go right away. I told you that I need to check on my friends first." She chewed on her lower lip. "Would it be okay if I brought Jasmine along? The poor girl is stuck on the lower decks. I'm sure she would love to get out of there and go shopping."

Negal looked as if she had fed him a sour lemon. "Whatever makes you happy is fine with me, but Kian might have a problem with her leaving the ship. You will have to ask him if it's okay to take her."

Kian was the big boss, who Mia had said was intimidating when he was in a good mood and scary when he was irritated.

"I've heard that he's not an easy guy to talk to."

Negal arched a brow. "The courageous Margo who was willing to take on the cartel for her friend is afraid of a guy with a bit of a grumpy attitude?"

"Well, yes. I was supposed to mingle last night, and Mia was supposed to introduce me to him, but someone lured me out onto the terrace and then carried me to my cabin, and I missed my opportunity. Where am I even going to find him?"

"I'm sure Mia can help you with that, and when you meet Kian, you can tell him that someone is at fault for preventing you from introducing yourself last night, and it is not you."

53

KAREN

"Karen, sweetheart, it's time to wake up."

"Just a few minutes longer." Karen lifted her hand and patted Gilbert's cheek without opening her eyes.

They had stayed late at the party, dancing and drinking and enjoying themselves. The little ones had been sleeping in Cheryl's bedroom when they came back to the cabin so, of course, they had also made love, and Karen was still a mere human and deserved proper rest.

"The kids are demanding to see their mommy. I kept them from barging in here and waking you up for as long as I could, but Idina is throwing a tantrum, and the boys are crying."

With a sigh, Karen forced her eyes to open. "Let them in here. They can climb in bed with me and watch some kid shows. I don't have the energy to get up." She let her eyelids drop and turned on her side.

"Are you okay?" Gilbert asked.

"Just tired," she murmured.

"Okay. I'm going to open the door. Brace yourself."

Karen smiled. One of the best things in life was having her kiddos jump on her in the morning. Their slobbery kisses and tight hugs were the best way to wake up.

"Mommy!" Idina was the first one to climb on the bed and crawl to her. "Why are you still sleeping?" She put her little arms around Karen's neck and pressed her lips to her cheek. "You are so warm." She laid her head on the pillow facing Karen, so close that her breath tickled her nose.

"Do you want to get under the blanket with me?"

Before Idina had a chance to answer, Gilbert dropped her little brothers on the bed to join the party, and they crawled as close as they could to her, trying to wedge themselves between their mom and their sister.

"Stay over there," Idina ordered. "Mommy is not feeling well."

"I'm just tired," Karen corrected.

"No, you have the feverish," Idina insisted.

"You mean that I feel feverish, sweetie."

"Yes. You are so warm."

Karen lifted a hand to her own forehead, and it felt warm, but it was probably from lying on the pillow and being under the blanket.

"Let me check." Gilbert sat on the bed on her other side and put his palm on her forehead. "She's right. You do feel a little warm."

Karen's heart skipped a beat, and she turned on her back. "Maybe it's starting?"

The color leached from Gilbert's face. "I'm calling Bridget."

"Don't. It might be nothing."

He shook his head. "I don't want to wait for you to lose consciousness. I need to wake Cheryl up so she can watch the kids, and then we are going to the clinic. Let the expert decide if you are transitioning or not."

Karen let out a breath. "Fine. But first, I need to go to the bathroom and get dressed."

He nodded and pushed to his feet. "Do you need help getting to the bathroom?"

"I'm good." She took his offered hand, though, and used it to pull herself up.

"Where are you going, Mommy?" Idina regarded her with worried eyes.

"For now, just to the bathroom. Tell Daddy which show you want to watch so he can put it on for you."

"*The Backyardigans*."

Karen smiled. It was such an old show, but the ship's server had it, and once Idina discovered it, she fell in love. She was singing along, and her brothers seemed to enjoy watching it too, probably because of how colorful and cute the animal pals were.

In the bathroom, she took care of the necessities and then hopped in the shower even though she'd showered after making love last night, or rather this morning. If she was going to the clinic and being probed by the doctor, she'd better be squeaky clean.

After the shower, she felt so refreshed that she was sure there was no fever, and there was no reason to go to the clinic, but she didn't want to let the hope die so soon after it had sparked.

Bridget would probably determine that she wasn't transitioning, but until she did, Karen could keep the hope alive.

When she stepped out, Cheryl was in the bed, occupying the same spot that Karen had just vacated.

"Is it happening?" she asked.

In case it was, there was no point in denying it, so Karen nodded. "Maybe. Cross your fingers for me."

Her daughter was much too perceptive to have been oblivious to what had happened with Negal. She might not know the how, but she knew that something was going on.

Thankfully, she also had enough tact not to ask how it could have happened when Gilbert didn't have what was needed to induce Karen's transition.

"Good luck, Mom." Cheryl lifted her arms, inviting Karen for a hug.

Smiling, Karen leaned down and embraced her daughter. "Thank you for always being there when I need you."

Cheryl's arms tightened around her. "Thank you for being the best mom. Just come back to us."

"I will." Karen straightened. "Probably sooner than I want to because this is a false alarm."

"It's not," Cheryl said. "I have a feeling that this is it."

The knot in Karen's stomach became tighter. "What else is your feeling telling you?"

Cheryl smiled. "That you're going to be okay. You are a fighter, Mom. You will fight to stay with us."

54

MARGO

Ditching the god hadn't been easy, and just thinking that had Margo chuckle.

Life was good when a god wanted to spend every moment with her, but she needed to talk to Frankie privately, so she'd convinced Negal to take Dagor to the dining room with him for a proper late breakfast.

Frankie groaned. "If Bridget doesn't let me out of here today, I'm mutinying." She turned on her side. "Can a passenger mutiny? Is that even a verb?"

"I don't know, but if you need help breaking out of here, I'm your girl." Margo chuckled. "And I think that you can get three gods to assist you as well. That's one hell of a formidable force."

"Not against Bridget." Frankie groaned. "She could incapacitate them with one of her frosty looks."

"I can believe that." Margo cast Frankie one of her own hard looks. "I had an interesting talk with Negal last night, and it turned out that you and Mia omitted the most important details about how a Dormant gets induced."

Frankie hissed and scrunched her nose. "We didn't want to overwhelm you, and we didn't expect Negal to spill the beans so soon. What did he tell you?"

"That to transition, I will need to have unprotected sex with him, and he will have to bite me, injecting me with his venom."

"Yep, that's the gist of it."

Margo arched a brow. "Is that all? Or are there any more shocking details that I need to know that you have conveniently forgotten to mention?"

"Well, it doesn't have to be Negal. Any immortal male would do, but he is your best chance because he's a god, the original artifact, and his venom is the most potent. The other thing is that the transition is not without risks, but since you are young and healthy, chances are that you will be just fine, especially if Negal is the one inducing you. I have no doubt that I'm doing so great because of Dagor's venom."

Margo wanted to ask Frankie how she'd reacted when she'd found out about all that, but she stopped when the door opened and the doctor walked in.

"I have good news for you, Frankie," Bridget said. "You are free to go." Bridget pulled out her measuring tape. "I just need to take a few measurements first."

Frankie sat up in bed. "You didn't even administer the test yet, and you are letting me go?"

Bridget motioned for Frankie to lie back. "Karen is transitioning, and I need the room for her. I'll come up later to your cabin and do the test there." She stretched the tape from Frankie's hip bone to her heel. "It's just a formality. You're obviously transitioning. You've grown half an inch in two days."

"Wow. No wonder everything hurts."

The doctor lifted her head. "I'll give you medication to take with you."

"Thanks." Frankie lifted her arm for the doctor to measure.

Margo cleared her throat to get Bridget's attention. "I have a question."

"Go ahead," the doctor said without looking at her.

"Frankie said that there are risks involved with the transition, but because I'm young and healthy, I should be fine. She also said that having Negal induce me will improve my chances. Is all of that correct?"

This time, Bridget paused what she was doing and turned around. "Twenty-seven is not that young as far as transitioning goes. We've had younger Dormants than you who had a rough time going through it. Also, every transition is unique, so there are no guarantees. That being said, having a god induce you might be beneficial. Mia was induced by Toven, and given how poor her health was before that, she did remarkably well. Frankie didn't have any serious health problems, but her transition was one of the easiest I've seen, so that's additional evidence of the benefit of a god's venom. Still, I would be remiss if I told you that you shouldn't worry at all, and even if everything goes well, you might go through a much tougher time than Frankie."

Frankie peeked at her from behind the doctor. "Don't let her scare you. The tiny risk is worth it when the prize is immortality. And even better, unlimited time with your hunky god."

Bridget snorted. "That's one way of putting it."

Margo shook her head. "You are both assuming that Negal and I are going to end up together. Given that we met only a day ago, I'd say that it's very premature."

"Not really," Frankie said. "Dagor and I hit it off immediately. We met only five days ago, and it feels as if I've known him for years. We are like an old couple already. Do you know what we did last night?"

Bridget cast her a stern look. "Do I want to hear that?"

"You have a dirty mind, doctor. We watched five episodes of *How I Met Your Mother.* Does it get any cozier than that?"

Bridget didn't look impressed. "That's only because I told you that you are not allowed to engage in strenuous physical activities. If you could, you would."

A smirk lifted one corner of Frankie's lips. "That's true. And since you are letting me go, does it mean that the prohibition is lifted?"

The doctor let out a breath. "Wait until I do the test. If you heal as fast as I think you will, then the answer is yes."

"Yay!" Frankie clapped her hands. "I can't wait to tell Dagor."

Margo envied her friend's openness and lack of sexual inhibitions. If she were more like Frankie, she could start working on her transition tonight.

But the truth was that she didn't want to rush it. As Negal had said, all good things were worth waiting for, and she preferred to let their relationship grow at a rate that felt right to her. If they were destined to be together, they should savor these early days instead of rushing them.

55

NEGAL

Negal piled two plates with cold cuts and fruit, one for him and one to bring to Margo.

His attempt at cooking her breakfast hadn't been as successful as he'd hoped, and she was probably hungry. She hadn't said anything about meeting him in the clinic or in the cabin, but he had her phone number so he could call her and tell her that he had a proper breakfast for her.

When he returned to the table, Dagor had his phone out and was reading a text. "I need to go. Bridget is releasing Frankie." He pushed to his feet.

Negal remained standing with the two plates in his hands. "Wait. Does that mean that her transition is over? I mean, the first stage?"

"No, but Bridget needs the room. Karen started transitioning."

Negal's mouth dried up in an instant. It was finally happening, but now that it was, his worry about it not starting was replaced with worry for Karen. Perhaps he should do what Dagor had done for Frankie and sneak in a blood transfusion or two?

But how could he explain even visiting Karen in the clinic?

Maybe he could use Margo as an excuse.

He could convince her that she should witness the initial stages of transition and accompany her to see Karen. He could give her the transfusion while thralling Margo not to pay attention to what he was doing.

"Are you just going to stand there?" Dagor asked. "You said that you wanted to come with me when I go back to the clinic."

Negal looked at the two plates in his hands. "You didn't pack anything for Frankie. What if she's hungry?"

Dagor frowned. "I don't know if she's allowed to eat food like this. Bridget kept her on an easy-to-digest diet. I should ask her first."

"Right." Negal followed him out of the dining room. "There is so much to learn about human physiology. Now that I'm courting Margo, I realize how little I know."

"How is that going? Is she receptive to the idea?" Dagor took the stairs instead of waiting for the elevator.

"She is." Negal smiled. "Surprisingly so."

"Why surprising?" Dagor kept up a brisk pace, indifferent to Negal's struggles to keep up while balancing the plates.

"Because I rarely say the right thing. But I managed to say a couple of things she liked."

"Like what?"

"It's private."

Dagor looked at him over his shoulder with a smirk on his face. "You really like her, don't you?"

"I wouldn't be courting her if I didn't."

"That's not a given. You might have been on a quest for good deeds, offering your godly induction services. I understand that they are in high demand, and you are the only unmated male god available."

Negal halted his descent. "You knew about that?"

Dagor shrugged. "It's difficult to keep anything a secret on this ship. These immortals are terrible gossips."

Letting out a breath, Negal rounded the landing and kept going down the stairs. "How many know?"

"I don't know."

"How did you find out about it?"

"That's confidential." Dagor exited the stairwell and continued down the corridor to the clinic.

Negal needed to know who spilled the beans, and if it was Max, he was going to punch the guy in the face, and it had nothing to do with him being interested in Margo.

Nothing at all.

"Did Frankie tell you?" he asked.

Dagor opened the door to the clinic. "I'm not telling."

The door to the inner room opened, and Bridget came out. "Good, you are here. Frankie is getting dressed, and once she's done, you can take her to her cabin."

"Thank you, doctor," Dagor said. "Anything I should watch for?"

She cast him a guarded look. "I'll give you some pain medication for Frankie. You can give her one pill every four hours. That should be enough."

"Got it."

Negal looked at the door, waiting for it to open and for Margo to come out. He had no doubt that she was still there. She wouldn't leave her friend alone at a time like that.

When the door opened a few minutes later, he was proven right.

Frankie came out beaming with happiness and jumped into Dagor's arms as if she hadn't seen him for days, and behind her was his Margo, smiling indulgently and carrying a bag that was probably filled with Frankie's things.

She walked around the two, who were now kissing, like there was no one with them in the tiny reception area.

"Hi." Margo looked at the plates in his hands. "Is that for Frankie or for me?"

"It's for you. Dagor said that he needed to ask Bridget what Frankie is allowed to eat."

Hearing her name spoken, Frankie let go of Dagor's mouth and looked at the plates. "I'm allowed to eat whatever I want, and these cold cuts look yummy."

"You can have mine," Margo said. "Negal made me eggs earlier, so I'm full."

She hadn't eaten the eggs he'd made her, and she was probably hungry, but that was so like Margo to give up her meal so her friend could have it.

"There is more of this in the dining room, and no one has to give up anything. I can get more."

"Awesome." Frankie smiled at him. "Margo and I will share until you get us more. Please and thank you."

56

KIAN

As Kian read the message from Aru, he knew what the private meeting the god was requesting was about.

Aru must have received a communication from his sister about the time of the first meeting between the queen of Anumati and her granddaughter.

Kian walked out the door and headed across the corridor to his mother's cabin.

Syssi had taken Allegra to her parents' cabin, and since Andrew, Nathalie and Phoenix were there as well, she wouldn't be back anytime soon. His excuse for not visiting was that he had to meet with Onegus and Turner about the situation on Modana's estate, but that could wait. What Aru had to tell him and his mother took precedence.

Kian rang the bell, and a moment later, the door swung open.

"Good morning, master." Oridu bowed. "The Clan Mother is on the balcony, enjoying the sun. Would you like to join her?"

"I would." Kian strode past the Odu and pulled out his sunglasses from his shirt pocket before opening the sliding door.

The sun was glaring this time of the day, and as he'd expected, his mother was wearing her goggle-style protective shades.

She smiled at him. "Good morning, my son. To what do I owe the pleasure?"

He leaned down and kissed her cheek. "Can't a son visit his mother for no other reason than to bask in her presence?"

She laughed. "Yes, but mine is too busy and never does. So, what news do you bring?"

"Aru messaged me requesting a private meeting. Since I assume it has to do with the queen and when she wants your first meeting to happen, I thought I would invite him to your cabin where we would have the most privacy."

His mother sat up and turned to him. "Of course. Let us go inside. I will ask my Odus to prepare a light mid-morning meal."

"That's a great idea." He pushed to his feet and offered her a hand up.

She accepted his offer gracefully, placing her tiny hand in his. It never ceased to amaze him how a small female like her had carried him in her womb until term and then gave birth to him.

His mother smiled up at him. "What troubling thought did you have right now that you are frowning?"

"How did you manage to give birth to me?"

Annani laughed. "It was not easy, but just so you do not feel guilty, I will let you know that Alena was an even larger baby at birth. She was my largest and first baby. Imagine how difficult that birth was. I thanked the merciful Fates for my fast healing, but giving birth to Alena without pain-reducing medication was something I will never forget, and it has been a while."

He opened the balcony door for her. "More than two thousand years is a long time to remember labor pains."

"Indeed." Annani took off her protective eyewear as soon as she was inside. "Nevertheless, I thank the Fates every day for Alena and for my other four children. Each of you has given me so much joy that it was worth the pain of bringing you into the world and even the pain and grief of losing Lilen. I am glad that I had him with me for the centuries I did." She walked over to the couch and sat in the middle of it as she usually did.

Kian swallowed the lump in his throat that the mention of his only brother always brought about. "As the saying goes, 'tis better to have loved and lost than never to have loved at all, and it's true for all types of love, not just the romantic kind." He sat on the couch next to his mother and pulled out his phone. "I should text Aru to tell him to come here."

Annani nodded. "Add to the text that I want to speak with him so he will have a good excuse in case someone sees him coming here and wonders why."

"I'm sure he can come up with an excuse on his own, but I'll do as you say."

His mother laughed. "If only it was so easy every time I ask you to do something."

Kian paused his typing and lifted his head to look at her. "When do I defy your wishes?"

"You do not defy them. You just argue your point until I agree to a compromise."

"That's how civilized people negotiate. I see nothing wrong with that."

"Neither do I." She patted his arm. "I was just teasing. You are the best son a mother could hope for, and I am very proud of you. I do not say it to you often enough."

Kian was touched, and her praise felt good even though he didn't need it, which was a lesson he should learn. He nearly never praised the people working for him, assuming that they knew he was satisfied with their performance when he didn't complain about it, but that was not the same as praise.

He dipped his head and took his mother's hand. "Thank you, Mother. I appreciate your kind words." He gave her hand the lightest of squeezes before gently putting it back on her thigh.

"I need to send out this text before Aru starts to think that I'm ignoring him."

57

ANNANI

Aru and his teammates had a cabin on the same deck as Annani and her family, so it did not take long until her doorbell rang.

Still, it had been enough time for her Odus to prepare the light meal she had asked them to make.

Her instructions had been to assemble a tray of canapés with some cut fruit and a couple of bowls of nuts, which her two Odus had done in minutes.

As Oridu opened the door and welcomed Aru, Kian pushed to his feet and walked over to him to escort him to the dining table.

The god bowed low. "Good morning, Your Highness."

"Good morning, Aru, and please, call me Annani or Clan Mother." She had asked him to do that before, but he seemed to have difficulty complying with her request.

He smiled sheepishly. "My apologies, Clan Mother. I keep forgetting. But can you blame me? You are the personification of royal grace."

"Well, thank you." She rearranged the folds of her gown. "Perhaps I should dim my glow the next time you request an audience with me so it will be easier for you to remember to call me by my given name."

"Fates forbid. I feel so honored every time I am in your luminous presence."

Laughter bubbled from Annani's chest. "Please, sit down, Aru. I am starting to think that I am not built to be a queen someday. It is not that I do not enjoy attention and admiration, but this is too much flattery even for me."

This was the first time she had said out loud that she was considering taking up the quest of becoming the queen of Anumati, and given the startled look on Kian's face, he had not missed that.

Smiling, Aru unfurled a napkin and draped it over his knees. "I will have to dial it down, then, Clan Mother." He gave her a cheeky grin. "I could never bring myself to call you by your given name, though."

"You will have to get used to it." Annani reached for one of the canapés to signal that it was okay to begin the light meal. "My grandmother is going to call me Annani, and if you and your sister translate it into Your Highness each time, it will be a waste of time. Using my name is so much more efficient."

"How about ma'am?" Aru asked. "That is acceptable even for royalty on Earth following the first formal address."

Kian groaned. "Ma'am is fine. Can we please get to the reason for this meeting?"

Aru nodded. "My sister informed me last night that the queen is ready for her first conversation with her granddaughter."

Annani's heart fluttered with excitement. "That is wonderful news. What time?"

"That's the problem. It was one o'clock in the morning when my sister contacted me, and that was the precise time the queen indicated for the day after tomorrow. I asked if it could be moved to another time, but Aria said that this was when the queen was visiting the temple. We have to somehow make it work." He looked at Kian. "The Clan Mother usually departs right after the ceremony and returns to her cabin, but you and I usually stay until late. It will be difficult to excuse our departure."

Annani had to agree. Even her diva reputation would not suffice to explain summoning her son and Aru to her cabin in the middle of the night.

Kian raked his fingers through his hair. "If not for your buddies, we could have made up a story about a spiritual ritual that was conducted at that time on Anumati, but they would know it's a lie."

Both Kian and Aru turned to her. "Any ideas?" Kian asked.

"Perhaps an emergency in one of your European companies that requires Aru's expertise on something? A new contract or something of that nature."

"Shai knows of every deal that's on the table now or ever, and he would know it's not true." Kian shook his head. "I can't believe that between the three of us, we can't come up with a plausible story."

"I can thrall Shai," Aru offered. "I can put in his head a memory of a pending contract that you are eager to get."

"How long will the session be?" Annani asked.

"I was not told," Aru said. "But I do not think it would be more than an hour."

"The two of you will have to come up with separate excuses, then. I can call Kian to come to my cabin for any reason." She smiled at Kian. "You are my son, and I can seek your company at any time of the day or night because of some concern that I suddenly have, and the truth is that you do not really need to be there." She turned to Aru. "You, however, will have to come up with a different excuse. Could it be something about communicating with your commander on the patrol ship?"

He sighed. "It could work once, but not every night, which is what the queen intends to do from now on."

"I see." Annani reached for the cup of tea Oridu had poured for her. "Then I will have no choice but to play the spoiled diva. I will demand your presence at one o'clock in the morning every day to tell me about the history of Anumati because that is the time I feel the strongest connection to the home of my ancestors." She looked at Kian. "And you, my poor son, will have to accompany Aru during his visits with your demanding and eccentric mother."

"It's not great, but it's the best we have."

"On another subject," Aru said. "I had another bizarre request today. Negal asked me if we could delay the trip to Tibet so he would have more time to pursue Margo and eventually induce her transition."

Kian shrugged. "I have no objections to that, but those were your marching orders from your commander. What are you going to tell him?"

Aru chuckled. "I need another creative story. Any ideas?"

Annani lifted her arms. "Do not look at me. I've supplied my share of ideas for today. Now it is your turn."

58

SHARON

"Oh, Eva." Sharon put her hand over her heart as she looked at what Eva had done to her cabin. "Where did you get all these decorations?"

Her boss and mentor put an arm around her shoulders. "I brought them with me, and Tessa helped me put them up."

White and blue swaths of fabric had been elegantly draped from the ceiling and were interspersed with strings of twinkling light that cast a soft glow throughout the cabin's living room, creating an ambiance of starlight reflected on the water.

Eva and Tessa had also placed silver-framed photos of Sharon and Robert on the coffee table and the bar, capturing happy moments as well as just snapshots of everyday life. Sharon hadn't even known that Eva had taken the photos, which was a sad testament to her detective skills.

Then again, she hadn't been in detective mode while relaxing at home, or in Eva's office, or around the village.

"When did you take all these photos?" she asked her boss.

"It wasn't me. It was Nick."

Sharon shook her head. "The sneaky bastard. I'll have words with him when I see him."

Nick was with Robert, celebrating the last moments of her mate's bachelor life, even though he hadn't been a bachelor since the day they had met. He'd been hers and only hers ever since.

Above the bar, a fabric banner bore the words "Sharon's Final Voyage" in elegant, flowing script, a playful nod to the nautical setting and the new journey Sharon was about to undertake, which, again, would not really be new.

She and Robert had been together for over four years, so they were already like an old married couple, and not much would change after their wedding, but it was a cute touch, nonetheless.

"Whose idea was the banner?"

"Mine." Carol sauntered over with a margarita in hand. "You like?"

"I should have known that was you." Sharon hugged Robert's former girlfriend. "I'm so glad that you came."

Carol leaned away with an arched brow. "To your bachelorette party or the cruise?"

"Both. If not for you, I would have never met Robert." Sharon smiled. "I've never thanked you properly for that."

Carol seemed taken aback. "Thank me for what exactly?"

Too late, Sharon realized that thanking Carol for bringing Robert into her life was like thanking her for getting caught by Robert's sadistic boss and being tortured for days on end.

Forcing a smile, she said, "For kicking Robert out, of course. If you'd kept him, I might never have met the love of my life. So, I owe you one."

Carol let out a soft laugh. "That was my intention when I kicked him out. I knew that I was doing both of us a favor, and I hoped Robert would find a wonderful mate who would love him and appreciate him, and that was precisely what happened. You two are perfect for each other, and I found my perfect match as well."

"I love happy endings," Eva said. "What's your poison, Sharon?"

Sharon glanced at the array of bottles lined up on the bar. "Surprise me. You know what I like."

"That I do." Eva clapped Sharon on her back.

"As do I." Ella took Sharon's hand and led her to the table. "I infiltrated the kitchen and made your favorite delights."

Sharon's eyes widened. "Marzipan and mascarpone cake with summer fruit, chocolate, and marzipan croissants, and chocolate-dipped plums with Armagnac marzipan." She turned to her friend. "Did you really make these?"

Ella was a great cook, but this was on a different level.

"My mom helped. We joined a class in the sanctuary about working with marzipan, and knowing how much you loved it, we brought two pounds of it on the trip. The rest of the ingredients were supplied by the cruise kitchen."

Tears prickled Sharon's eyes. Ella had noticed and remembered that she loved marzipan, and she'd gone to all that effort to make her celebration sweet.

"Taste one," Ella prompted.

"Just one? I'm going to taste all of them."

"Then you'll need a drink to wash them down." Eva handed her a glass with orange-colored liquid and black cherries floating around.

"What's that?"

"It's called whiskey sour, but it's not sour at all. It's sweet and tangy."

"Just how I love it." Sharon took a sip.

Eva raised her own glass. "To Sharon, who is finally ready to tie the knot with Robert in the midst of our clan's season of love."

As everyone raised their glasses, Sharon clinked hers with Eva and Ella, then with Tessa, Nathalie, and Ruth. Carol was the last one.

"To love," Carol said.

As the music started playing in the background, and her friends sat on the couch and armchairs, the doorbell rang.

"That must be Amanda." Eva walked over to open the door. "It wouldn't be a proper bachelorette party without the matchmaker who made it happen, right?"

Sharon grinned. "I wondered where she was."

Amanda walked in, dressed to the nines as usual, in a dark blue tuxedo jumpsuit and four-inch heels, and with Kri behind her, wearing jeans and sneakers.

"Hello, darlings. I'm sorry for being late."

"No, you are not." Sharon hugged her. "You just like to make an entrance." She moved to hug Kri. "Did she make you wait outside?"

"Actually, it was my fault. I was playing poker with Jasmine and didn't notice that it was getting late. Amanda came to get me."

"I was curious about the woman, so I used getting Kri as an excuse, and it was good that I did. Jasmine was killing her."

Eva frowned. "Really? A human was beating you at poker? How is that possible?"

"I couldn't smell her." Kri snatched one of the marzipan delights and straddled a chair. "We were snacking on Doritos, and they have such a strong smell that they overpower the delicate emotional scents."

"What about her tells?" Sharon asked.

Kri grimaced. "She's a damn good actress. She projected false tells, and I fell for it time and again."

"How much did you lose?" Ella asked.

"All of the Doritos. We were playing for chips."

"I need to pay this Jasmine a visit," Eva said. "No one is that good of an actress. Not to fool an immortal Guardian."

"We can go together," Sharon offered. "I'm good at reading people."

"Yes, you are, my dear." Eva raised her glass in salute. "That's what makes you such a good detective."

"Your detective work can wait for tomorrow," Amanda said. "Right now, I want to see the dress." She glared at Eva. "The one that you insisted on commissioning for your girl without using any of my recommended designers."

Wincing, Sharon hid behind her drink.

Amanda and Eva had waged a war over who was going to help her choose her wedding dress, and although Sharon trusted Amanda more with everything that had to do with fashion, Eva was like a mother to her, and she'd felt obligated to let her do that.

"It's a beautiful dress." Eva rose to her feet. "Do you want to show it off?"

Sharon put her drink on the coffee table. "Are you kidding me? That's the highlight of the party." She joined her boss. "That's what everyone here has been waiting for."

Ella rose to her feet. "I want to check out the bridesmaids' dresses. You didn't let us see them before, and I want to try mine on."

"You will look great in yours," Eva said.

Sharon paused at the door to Eva's bedroom, where her dress was waiting. "It's too early for me to get dressed, but you are welcome to come take a look."

The ladies crowded at the doorway, craning their necks to catch a glimpse of the wedding dress that was carefully hung on a dress form.

Sharon had found the design in one of the gossip magazines that had featured a story about a famous singer getting married in Hawaii. The dress was gorgeous, and Sharon had fallen in love. Eva had taken the picture to a seamstress, and the woman had done an admirable job of replicating it.

Made of delicate lace and soft, flowing fabric, the dress was a fusion of traditional and modern, with a fitted bodice adorned with intricate beading leading down to a full skirt.

"You can come inside," Eva said.

Her friends oohed and aahed, but she didn't know whether they were just being supportive or if they really liked the dress.

It didn't really matter. What mattered was that she loved it and looked fabulous in it.

"It's so uniquely you," Eva said. "It came out even better than I expected."

Tessa clapped her hands. "Oh, Sharon! It's like something out of a fairy tale! You're going to look like a princess!"

Carol stepped forward and smoothed her hand over the fabric. "It's beautiful. Robert won't know what hit him when he sees you walking down the aisle."

Amanda pursed her lips. "I have to admit that it's much better than I expected." She clapped Eva on her back. "Good job finding that seamstress."

"I can give you her contact info," Eva teased, knowing perfectly well that Amanda would never use a lowly seamstress for anything other than alterations.

Ruth, who hardly ever said anything, walked over to Sharon and put her hand on her shoulder. "It's not just the dress that makes the bride beautiful. It's the love and happiness she radiates. And you, my dear Sharon, are already glowing even before you put the dress on."

59

FRANKIE

"Is here okay?" Frankie pointed at the couch.

Bridget nodded. "It's fine."

Gabi chuckled. "I did mine sitting on the kitchen counter in Kian's penthouse."

Frankie had heard the story before, but she preferred the couch so Dagor could sit next to her and hold her hand. She wasn't scared of a little cut, not after being shot, but she was excited and a little nervous, and she drew strength from his support.

There was no doubt in anyone's mind that she was turning immortal, so she wasn't worried about that, but she wanted to be one of those who healed fast, which would indicate that her genes were strong and that she was close to her godly source.

After all, she was mated to a god, and she wanted to be worthy of him. Not that the strength or concentration of her godly genes made her any more or less worthy, but still, it would be awesome to heal rapidly.

Mia, Margo, Toven, Negal, and Gabi gathered around. Mia remained in her wheelchair with Toven standing behind her, with Margo and Negal each occupying an armchair. Aru couldn't come because of some prior engagement, but that was okay.

What wasn't okay was that Frankie's family back home had no clue about any of this and couldn't be there, and she hadn't figured out yet what she was going to do about those of her family who were Dormants. Perhaps she could approach them one at a time, but she would need Toven to be there to compel them to keep quiet about it. The problem was that she suspected even Toven's compulsion wouldn't be strong enough to keep her family from talking.

"Ready?" Bridget asked.

"Whenever you are, doc." Frankie extended her hand and put on a brave smile to mask her nervousness.

"Who wants to hold the timer?" Bridget scanned the faces of the small group of witnesses.

Margo lifted her hand. "I will."

"Do you have your phone with you?" Bridget asked.

"I do." She pulled it out from the side pocket of her leggings, a pair that Frankie recognized as hers.

The doctor nodded. "When I say go, activate the stopwatch."

"Yes, ma'am." Margo got busy with the phone.

"Who will do the filming?" the doctor asked.

"I will." Toven lifted the phone he was clutching in his hand. "Ready when you are."

Bridget put the tray with her surgical equipment between her and Frankie on the couch.

"Let's do it." She took Frankie's hand and turned it palm up. "First, disinfecting, even though it's probably not necessary, just in case your healing ability is not fully online yet, it's better to exercise caution. We don't want the wound to get infected." She swiped Frankie's palm with the disinfectant and then lifted her scalpel.

The thing was tiny, but that didn't mean that it wouldn't hurt, and Frankie took a deep breath.

On her other side, Dagor gave her hand a gentle reassuring squeeze.

"Go for it, doc," Frankie said.

Bridget made the incision with swift precision, and before the pain could register, she motioned to Margo. "Go!"

The sensation of pain bloomed at the same moment Margo started the timer, and Frankie couldn't help a tiny hiss. She'd planned on being brave and watching the doctor with an impassive expression as she administered the test, but she hadn't figured on the sting being so bad.

The room fell into a hushed silence, with the only sounds being the distant hum of the ship and the collective breathing of her witnesses. As everyone watched the blood welling over the incision, Frankie held her breath.

Bridget wiped away the blood, allowing everyone to take a look at the results of the test. The tiny wound began to show signs of her new extraordinary healing ability, with the blood flow stopping and the skin slowly knitting itself together.

When the wound was fully healed, Margo stopped the timer. "One minute and twelve seconds."

"Is that good?" Frankie asked.

"It's excellent." Bridget smiled. "Welcome to immortality, Frankie."

"Congratulations." Dagor brought her hand to his lips for a kiss and then lifted the one that had been wounded only moments ago and kissed her palm over the incision. "You were very brave."

"Hold on." Frankie turned to Bridget. "Is a minute and twelve seconds considered fast, slow, or average?"

"It's average," the doctor said. "But on the faster side of the scale."

A grin spread over Frankie's face. "Yay. I'm better than average."

"You are the best." Dagor kissed her cheek.

Margo hugged Frankie tightly. "Congratulations on turning immortal. I still can't believe any of this is happening even though I just saw it with my own two eyes."

Frankie patted Margo's back. "I hope to be witnessing your positive test results soon."

Her friend's cheeks reddened, and she cast a quick look at Negal, who was being a sport about it and pretending he hadn't heard.

He really was a great guy, and Frankie was holding her proverbial fingers crossed for the two of them to prove her right and end up together as fated mates.

60

GILBERT

"I'll leave you two alone to get settled." Bridget pointed at the hospital gown folded on the bed. "Put it on and call me when you are ready."

"Okay." Karen didn't argue.

They'd had to wait in the recovery room for the bed in the clinic to become available, but thankfully, Karen hadn't lost consciousness. Her fever was rising, though, and Gilbert's stomach was churning with worry.

"What if I'm not transitioning, and this is just the flu or a cold?" Karen asked. "The human staff and the rescued women could have brought viruses aboard."

Bridget grimaced like she'd heard the same rebuttal too many times and was tired of it. "Even if I could test for antibodies, it wouldn't tell me whether this is a virus or the transition because the body reacts the same way to both. It takes time until it recognizes that the change is not a malicious invasion. Bottom line, I need you monitored, and if you pass out, I will need to put a catheter and an IV in. So, I need you to put on the gown."

"I get it." Karen sighed. "I'm sorry about ruining your vacation. First, it was Frankie and all those poor women, and now it's me."

Bridget shrugged. "I love welcoming Dormants into immortality, and I love what I do." She smiled. "For a long time, I thought that running the administration of the rescue missions would be more fulfilling than working as a physician, and I transferred a lot of my duties to my son, but I missed it too much. So, I made a deal with Julian. He helps me with the rescue missions, and I get to spend more time in the clinic doing what I love most, which is taking care of patients."

When the doctor stepped out of the room and closed the door, Gilbert turned to Karen. "Do you need help undressing?"

She nodded. "I hate feeling sick and weak. My limbs feel as if they are filled with lead."

Gilbert put his hands on her waist and hoisted her on the bed. "They are as beautiful and sexy as ever." He crouched at her feet and removed her shoes.

Karen chuckled. "You know one of the things I'm looking forward to the most after my transition?"

He arched a brow. "Incredible stamina?"

"Well, that too. But I'm excited about not having to shave my legs ever again. Kaia told me that all her body hair just fell off after her transition, what little she had. With her blond hair, it was barely visible."

"You could have gotten it laser removed." He leaned up and lifted her up a little to tug her leggings off.

"It was too time-consuming. I didn't have time for multiple visits to the place."

As he removed her shirt, her bra, and her underwear, it was a struggle not to cop a feel, but he forced himself to behave and helped her into the hospital gown.

Karen lay down and sighed. "I'm exhausted just from walking here from the recovery room. What was it, less than twenty feet?"

"More or less." He covered her with the blanket. "Do you want me to raise the back of the bed?"

"Yes, please." She waited until the back was at about forty-five degrees. "That's good."

"Great. Should I call the doctor in?"

Karen nodded. "Can you check with Kaia and Cheryl that the little ones are okay?"

Smiling, he leaned over and brushed a strand of hair away from her forehead. "Stop worrying. Your daughters are capable young women, and they can handle the three little brats until you are back on your feet."

"Please? For me?"

He let out a breath. "That's not fair. You know exactly what to say to get me to do anything you want."

Karen smiled. "Of course."

Gilbert walked over to the door and opened it. "She's ready."

"I'll send Hildegard in a moment."

"No rush." He left the door open and walked back to the bed. "Do you want to call them yourself?"

"I don't even have the energy to hold the phone, but if you activate the speakerphone, we can talk to them together."

"As you wish, my love." He sat on the single chair in the room and called Kaia.

It rang for a while until Kaia answered. "Hi, Gilbert. How is Mom doing?"

The ruckus in the background brought a smile to his face, and as he switched the call to speakerphone, Karen winced.

"She's right here with me, and she wants to know how things are going with the little demons."

Kaia laughed. "As can be expected. Thing One and Thing Two stole Idina's dolls, and she's chasing them around. The twins used to be so sweet, but they are turning out to be worse than her."

"You sound cheerful," Karen said. "So, it can't be too bad."

"It's not. I'm used to the chaos and enjoy it, but after this, poor William will never want to have kids."

"Can you put Idina on?" Karen asked.

"Sure. Idina! Mommy wants to talk to you."

"I don't want to talk to her," their daughter shouted at the top of her lungs.

"Why not?" Kaia asked.

"Because she's mean and gave me two stinky brothers instead of sisters. I hate them!"

"No, you don't," Kaia cooed. "You love your brothers."

"I hate them!" Idina shrieked.

Gilbert stifled a snort. "I see that you have your hands full. Call me when things quiet down."

"Then you mean never?" Laughing, Kaia ended the call.

Karen let out a long-suffering sigh. "You know what? I kind of like being here and having a couple of days of peace and quiet to myself."

61

MARGO

The sun-kissed streets of Puerto Vallarta welcomed Margo with the promise of unique finds, but she couldn't shake the uneasy feeling of being watched. It was probably all in her head.

"What are you looking for?" Negal asked as her eyes darted from side to side.

"I know it's silly, but I keep expecting to bump into Alberto or one of the other goons."

They should have been arrested for kidnapping her and Jasmine, but given how corrupt everything was here, that wouldn't have happened, and if it had, Modana would have arranged for his people to be released. She used to think that stuff like that happened only in third-world countries, but things were not much better in the US or the rest of the so-called first-world countries. Money talked much louder than justice, and corruption was the norm rather than the exception.

Kalugal's method was much better.

Turning the evildoers into Samaritans wasn't normally possible, but when it could be done, it was the better solution.

Negal's arm around her tightened. "Don't worry about them. They are all on Modana's estate, making plans for all the good deeds Kalugal compelled them to do. But even if we bump into some of them, and even if they have somehow shaken off the compulsion, you have nothing to fear. You are with me."

From anyone else that would have sounded like boasting, but from Negal, it was a mere statement of fact. He'd told her about his ability to take control of human minds with the same effect as Kalugal's compulsion, just on a more limited scale. Where Kalugal could compel anyone within hearing distance, Negal could seize control of the minds of up to about a dozen humans at a time. Also, he could move much faster than any human, and his body was impervious to bullets. Well, that wasn't quite accurate. He could get injured, but his body would expel the bullets immediately and heal the injury.

That was how Dagor had saved Frankie, shielding her with his body from the many bullets aimed at them.

Frankie hadn't told her the whole story about her and Dagor's run-in with the traffickers in Acapulco, only that they had saved a group of women from their clutches and that she'd been injured during the altercation, but not seriously, thanks to Dagor's intervention. Margo couldn't wait to hear the full story, and she intended to pump Frankie for information tomorrow.

The plan was for the three of them to meet up on the Lido deck.

She smiled up at Negal and then leaned her head on his bicep. "It's nice to have a god by my side." She saw yet another woman gawk at him and glared at her until the woman looked away. "But there are downsides as well."

He chuckled. "Oh, yeah? Like what?"

"Every woman we pass, and even some of the men, are devouring you with their eyes, and I feel like punching them in the face."

Negal's smirk was all about male satisfaction. He was smart enough not to say anything, but he strutted like a peacock.

She had to take control of this new jealous streak she'd developed since meeting Negal. She had no right to feel possessive over a guy she hadn't even kissed yet, although she planned to remedy that as soon as possible.

With every moment she spent with Negal she was getting more and more drawn to him, and the need to touch him, to kiss him, was growing along with her attachment.

If he were just a guy, Margo would have been alarmed at the rate at which her response to him was intensifying and would have sought to put some distance between them, but given the unique situation she found herself in, she welcomed the rapid development.

The sooner she got over her hesitance to get intimate with him, the better.

"Do you see any store you would like to visit?" Negal asked.

"Not yet."

She'd been so busy thinking about how she felt about him that she had barely paid attention to the beautifully designed outdoor mall.

La Isla Shopping Village seemed more like a lavish resort than a collection of stores. High-end boutiques showcased the latest fashions in their storefronts, and as they meandered through the open-air corridors, Margo admired the water features and lush greenery.

Her eyes were drawn to the Apple Store, where the latest technology was displayed like works of art, but she hadn't come here to shop for a new phone or a laptop. She needed evening dresses for the upcoming weddings.

"They have many nice stores here, but not what I'm looking for. Perhaps we should check out Liverpool, like the taxi driver suggested."

"No problem. Let's go there."

Liverpool was a high-end department store, supposedly known for its upscale products and great service, or at least that was what the very helpful taxi driver had claimed.

Once they were inside, it didn't take Margo long to zero in on the right section of the store. Judging by what was on display, though, she might not be able to afford what they were selling.

"This one looks good." Negal pointed at the dress in the display.

"It also looks expensive."

"Don't worry about it. Just find the dresses and shoes you like, and I'll take care of the rest."

"Thank you for the very generous offer, but I can't accept that. I can buy one dress and wear it to all the remaining weddings. Let's keep walking. Perhaps we can find a store with nice evening dresses that don't cost as much as my monthly rent."

He didn't argue with her, but given the tight line of his lips, he had no intention of giving up.

Well, he was going to learn that Margo was not a pushover and that she didn't let anyone take over unless she absolutely had to. If any of the cartel thugs showed up, she would gladly let Negal take care of that, but she was perfectly capable of paying for her own stuff.

62

ROBERT

Robert leaned against the balcony railing, a cigar in one hand and a glass of whiskey in the other and listened to the soft hum of male voices. Bathed in the gentle glow of the setting sun reflecting off the water, the balcony provided the perfect ambiance for celebrating his last moments of bachelorhood with his friends—his new family, or rather, the only family he'd ever had.

He could hardly remember his mother or what life had been like in the Brotherhood's Dormants' enclosure. It had been so long ago. But he remembered vividly his first day in the training camp, and those weren't good memories. He'd been lucky to be a big guy and quite strong at thirteen, so he could defend himself and hold his own against the others, but fighting had never been in his nature, and he'd suffered through every moment of the training and the years that had followed.

Getting picked up by Sharim to be his assistant had been a liberation because it had taken him off the battlefield, but working for a monster had proven to be another form of torture even though Sharim had never hurt him.

Watching the sadist at work had been its own hell, but even though Robert had been miserable, he never would have gathered the courage to escape if not for Carol. Her suffering had been the catalyst that had ejected him from the Brotherhood once and for all, and for that, he would be forever grateful to her.

He might have saved her from Sharim and the daily torture she had endured, but she had saved him from an immortal's lifetime of horror.

Turning around, he looked at the shimmering ocean water and regretted that the ship was docked near the port of Puerto Vallarta and not out at sea.

He'd felt calmer during the voyage—had to struggle less with the demons of his past that refused to leave him alone. Surrounded by the infinite expanse of the sea, he'd felt adrift, and for some reason, it had been a good feeling.

Still, he was grateful to be here, with a small, tight-knit circle of unlikely allies, the rich, earthy scent of their smoldering cigars intermingling with the briny sea air and creating this moment suspended in time.

Bhathian, who was standing beside him, raised his glass. "Robert, my friend, this is to you and the crooked path that led you to this happy day." He clinked his glass to Robert's. "May all of your tomorrows be at least as joyful as today."

"I'll drink to that." Robert downed the shot in one go and extended his hand to Charlie, who was holding the bottle. "A refill, if you will, my friend."

His former roommate filled his glass to the brim. "To Robert, the myth, the legend, the man."

Robert chuckled. "I didn't know I was a myth."

"But you are. Every member of the clan, including those in Scotland and Alaska, knows the story of you saving Carol from the sadist, and it's going to be told for many generations to come. That's what myths are made of, my friend. It's just a shame that the two of you didn't end up together. It would have made for an even better story."

"I don't share your view." Robert puffed on his cigar. "The way I see it, Carol and I saved each other so we could go on and find our fated mates. I found mine in Sharon, and Carol found hers in Lokan." He chuckled. "Maybe the Fates were confused between me and him because we were both members of the Brotherhood, and once they realized their mistake, they convinced Carol to end things between us."

"Technically, Lokan is still a Doomer," Dalhu said. "He's still a member of the Brotherhood."

Robert exchanged looks with Dalhu, an unspoken understanding passing between them. The two of them were not friends, but they had a common past, and that bound them whether they liked it or not.

Out of everyone here, Dalhu was the only one who truly got where Robert had come from, and the shadow of the past still loomed over him despite the home he had found in the clan.

They were both still battling similar demons.

Ed, reclining on a lounger with his feet propped up, nodded thoughtfully, swirling the whiskey in his glass. "Lokan is a brave dude. I admire him for what he's doing. I would be terrified to spy on the Brotherhood for the clan, and if I had a mate, I would never endanger her like that. They are both insane for coming on this cruise." He looked at Robert. "Love's not just about the sunny days. It's about weathering the storms together. But enough about your former girlfriend and your former boss. Sharon is a badass in her own right, and you are one lucky dude to have snagged her. What is it about you that attracts these tough women?"

Robert shrugged. "Beats me. I'm as boring as they come, so maybe that's the attraction. They have enough turmoil in the outside world and prefer calm waters at home."

Nick nodded with a sage expression on his face. "You are onto something. Opposites attract and all that. My Ruth is an introvert, and I'm an extrovert, and we get along splendidly."

Bhathian snorted. "Your theory falls apart with me and Eva. She's a major badass, but so am I. We are more alike than we are different."

"Yeah," Roni snorted. "But thankfully, she's much better looking than you."

Robert had thought that the guy was asleep on the lounger, but apparently, he'd been listening to the conversation.

Jackson, who was usually the one talking the most, hadn't contributed to the banter so far and seemed a little broody. Maybe he was regretting passing on the opportunity to get married on the ship.

Hopefully, there would be another wedding cruise, this time without all the excitement.

Robert glanced at Julian. "Next time, you and Ella?"

The doctor released a plume of smoke. "We are not in a rush. We are happy the way we are."

Robert nodded. "These weddings are more for our community than they are for us. Everyone loves weddings."

"Yeah." Ed lifted his drink. "I love being stuffed into a tuxedo and feeling like a penguin."

Charlie punched him in the shoulder playfully. "Yeah, yeah. I saw you tearing up at Brundar and Callie's wedding."

"I had something in my eye," Ed protested.

As laughter intermingled with banter, the cigars emitted fragrant smoke, and the whiskey flowed.

Puffing on his cigar, Robert regarded his companions with fondness and appreciation. He was blessed, not only with a wonderful mate who got him and accepted him the way he was, warts and all, but with good friends who accepted him as well.

63

MARGO

As Margo and Negal strolled through the mall, they ended up back in front of the exclusive boutique and the stunning evening dress in the window that Margo had been pining for since the moment she'd laid eyes on it but knew that she couldn't afford.

The deep emerald fabric shimmered under the boutique's strategically positioned lighting, and she just knew that it would look perfect on her.

"Shall we?" Negal gestured towards the entrance, a soft smile playing on his lips. "You seem to really like this dress, and you should try it on."

"It's beautiful." She let out a breath.

Perhaps she could splurge this one time on something spectacular. After all, she would attend those weddings with a spectacular male by her side, so a killer dress was a must.

"Excuses, excuses," she murmured under her breath.

Negal glanced at her with a frown. "Excuses?"

"Yeah. I'm trying to talk myself into splurging on a dress that I shouldn't," she said quietly so the enthusiastic sales lady with the barracuda smile wouldn't hear her. "I'm giving myself a bunch of excuses for why it's okay to go into debt for a dress."

"I'm paying for it, and I don't want to hear any arguments about it." He leaned closer and whispered in her ear, "I have a large allowance to spend however I please, and I can't keep what I don't spend. I assure you, the intergalactic fleet that provides this allowance will not be impoverished by the cost of this dress."

"It's still not right," she whispered back.

"Yes, it is."

She turned to look at him. "How will you justify the expense to your commanders? I'm sure you need to provide a list of the things you spend your allowance on."

"No, I don't. It would be impractical to keep track of every expense made over hundreds of years."

Margo swallowed. He was talking about centuries the same way she talked about weeks or months.

Would her perspective of time change once she became immortal? Probably not right away. She was willing to bet that Frankie and Mia were still thinking in human time frames. It would take time to adjust.

"May I help you?" asked the barracuda lady with too many teeth in her mouth in heavily accented English.

"Yes," Negal said. "We would like to try this dress on." He pointed at the display.

"That's an excellent choice." She looked Margo over. "We only have it in two sizes, but I believe that the one in the display will fit your wife perfectly."

He grinned. "I believe so, too."

"It's a beautiful dress." The sales lady reached for the dress and removed it from the mannequin. "Let me show you to a dressing room."

As they followed her, Margo wondered if Negal knew that he couldn't come in with her.

"You need to stay outside."

"Oh, no." The sales lady gave him a bright smile. "We have a special room where the husbands can watch." She removed a bracelet that had a key attached to it and opened the door to a dressing room.

Margo swallowed.

This was going to be awkward as hell. Thankfully, there was a screen she could change behind, but the rest of the setup was meant for rich dudes who bought stuff for their mistresses.

A couch at one end of the room faced the wall of mirrors on the other end, where the flimsy screen had been put up just for appearances. The panels weren't even solid, and Negal would be able to see her naked silhouette when she changed.

"It's perfect." Negal walked over to the couch and sat down. "If you'd be so kind as to bring more dresses for my wife? We have several events to attend, and the airline lost our luggage."

"How terrible." The saleslady affected a sorrowful tone, but her eyes sparkled with dollar signs. "I'll just hang this masterpiece up here and then collect a selection of dresses for your beautiful wife."

When the woman left, closing the door behind her, Margo walked over to the dress and brushed her fingers over the silk, feeling the weight and texture of the fabric.

Slanting a glance at Negal, she chuckled at the pose he'd assumed. He looked the part of a gorgeous mobster with his arm draped over the back of the couch and his legs spread out in a very macho pose.

"Are you enjoying yourself?"

"Tremendously. This room is the best find of this shopping expedition."

She narrowed her eyes at him. "Just don't get any ideas."

He seemed genuinely puzzled by her comment. "About what?"

"Never mind."

It was her own dirty mind that had conjured every fitting-room sex scene she'd ever read, and there had been plenty.

"Go ahead, try it on." Negal's tone was casual, but there was an underlying note of eagerness. He was either eager to see her taking off what she had on or to see her in the evening gown.

Damn, why did she find it arousing?

Was it because, after spending so many hours in his company, she was finally feeling comfortable enough around him to let down her guard and allow herself to feel her attraction to him? The nascent sparks of arousal?

God, it had been so long since she'd felt that tingling in her lady parts at the thought of being with a man. Usually, it only happened after reading a hot scene in a book and not in response to a flesh and blood man, or god as it were.

Except, the one sitting on the couch was a fascinating mixture of a flesh and blood male and every paranormal and science fiction romance novel hero she'd ever read about.

Margo quickly took off the leggings and T-shirt she'd borrowed from Frankie and slipped into the dress. The silk cascaded down her figure like liquid, and as she zipped it up effortlessly, she had to admit that the dress looked and felt like it had been made for her.

Staring at her reflection in the mirror, she felt a sense of rightness settle over her, and as she stepped out to show Negal she was met with his hot gaze, his intense blue eyes glowing with inner light and something deeper, more intimate.

"It looks like it was made for you," Negal said, his voice sounding husky with desire.

It sent Margo's heart aflutter.

64

NEGAL

"I feel like a different person," Margo admitted, turning slightly to view the dress from another angle. "The dress I borrowed from Frankie last night was gorgeous, but this one is fit for a queen." She chuckled. "And I can breathe in it, which is a big plus." She twirled on the spot, letting the silk glide over her legs.

Negal pushed to his feet and walked over, lost for words. Saying that she looked beautiful sounded empty even though it was true. The emerald dress clung to her form, and the rich, deep green contrasted stunningly with her pale skin and blond hair. It was long and straight, with a slight golden hue interspersed with the platinum, and it took on a new dimension against the backdrop of the dress, its strands shimmering like a halo in the soft lighting of the dressing room.

The plunging neckline hinted at the soft contours of her collarbones and led his eyes to the graceful line of her neck, an understated invitation to gaze. Yet, it was the way the dress moved with her that was truly captivating. Each step she took was accentuated by the gentle flow of the fabric.

But what made the dress so sexy was not just the way it draped over Margo's body or the subtle reveal of skin through its expertly placed cutouts. It was the confidence Margo exuded while wearing it.

Not that she hadn't been confident before.

Margo was assertive, intelligent, and beautiful, and she knew how to carry herself. Her only insecurity seemed to be about intimacy, and it made him wonder whether she'd had a bad experience that had made her more cautious and reserved than most of the human females he'd met and engaged with.

He was about to ask her that when the door opened, and the saleslady came in with an armful of dresses and other clothing items.

"You said that the airline lost your luggage, so I took the liberty of assembling some wardrobe essentials." She started hanging all the items on hooks that were placed behind the screen. "I also brought some intimates." She pulled several skimpy, lacy things from the bag she'd slung across her body. "How many nights are you staying in Puerto Vallarta?"

"My wife needs items for five more days," Negal said.

"Perfect." The saleslady spread out the lacy panties over the table on the other side of the elevated stage. "There are seven sets in here. Do you also need a bathing suit?"

"Yes," Negal said.

Margo glared at him, but she didn't say anything. Instead, she turned to the saleslady. "Thank you. I will try on the dresses and the other items and pick out the ones I like."

"I will also bring shoes. What size heel do you find comfortable?"

Margo hesitated for a moment. "No higher than four inches. Three and a half would be best."

"Perfect." The woman grinned, more at Negal than at Margo, probably understanding which one of them was willing to spend the money and which one was putting on the brakes. "You are such a beautiful couple. Are you newlyweds?"

"Yes, we are." Negal wrapped his arm around Margo's shoulders. "Margo is the love of my life."

"Oh, how lovely." The saleslady put a hand over her chest. "Congratulations. May you enjoy many happy years together."

"Thank you," Negal said. "We will."

After the woman left, Margo looked at him from under lowered lashes. "Do you always lie with such ease?"

"I didn't lie." He tried to stifle his smile but failed.

"Oh, yeah? I'm not your wife or the love of your life."

"But you will be. I was merely seeing the future."

When she opened her mouth to protest, he put a finger over her lips. "Would you call a seer a liar just because the events in her vision are not happening right now?" He rubbed his thumb over her lips.

Margo wanted to ask him whether there was really any such thing as a seer, but his thumb gently stroking over her lips was distracting her. Her eyes became hooded, and when the scent of her arousal hit his nostrils, Negal's erection punched out against the zipper of his jeans.

"Margo," he whispered as he dipped his head so their lips were mere inches apart.

His thumb was still brushing gently over her lips, so she couldn't say anything, but the way she tilted her head up and closed her eyes spoke volumes.

Still, he didn't want to take anything for granted. Besides, he'd told her that she would have to ask him to kiss her. "If you don't want me to kiss you," he murmured. "Tell me now."

Those were not the exact words he'd used before, but it was close enough. Verbal consent was as good as her asking.

Margo opened her eyes and looked at him with so much smoldering heat that he could have caught on fire just from looking into their depths, and then she did something he would have never expected from her.

Reaching with her hand, she pushed his finger aside, lifted on her toes, and closed the distance between their lips.

65

MARGO

It had been an impulse to close the distance between their mouths and kiss Negal, and as their lips touched, a rush of heat swept through Margo. She moaned as he slipped his tongue past her lips, her arms going around his neck and holding on tight.

When she wrapped her tongue around his, teasing and licking, he groaned, but he still held back, allowing her to explore. She knew he wouldn't last long, though, and as he deepened the kiss, his tongue taking the lead, she melted into him.

Holding on to Negal, Margo reveled in the powerful muscles of his neck and his shoulders.

Her fingers threading through his hair, she pressed herself to him, seeking some friction for her aching nipples.

He was hard, she could feel the bulge in his jeans through the delicate silk of her dress, which reminded her where she was and that they shouldn't be doing this while the saleswoman was due to return any moment with a bunch of shoes.

With a groan, Margo let go of Negal's neck and put her hands on the hard muscles of his chest. He understood right away, released her mouth, and rested his forehead against hers.

"Fates, Margo. What are you doing to me?"

She chuckled. "The question is, what are you doing to me? I've never kissed anyone in a dressing room before."

As he lifted his head and smiled down at her, his fangs were peeking out, and the sight sent a shiver down her spine, but not because she was scared.

Perhaps she should be, though. She had a feeling that they were only partially elongated and that they got much larger than that.

"Do you want to do more than kissing?" Negal teased. "I can barricade that door."

For a split second, she was tempted, but then old fears returned in a rush, and she shook her head. "I'm not the adventurous type."

"Could have fooled me."

She took a step back. "What, the kiss? That wasn't adventurous. Well, maybe a little."

He shook his head. "I was referring to you trying to save a woman you've just met from being trafficked and getting yourself in a shitload of trouble."

"That was different." She ducked behind the screen. "I didn't know I was risking myself. I was just trying to help Jasmine get away." She carefully unzipped the dress and took it off. "My mistake was going to her suite and looking for the cameras." She draped it on the hanger and closed the zipper so it would stay in place. "I should have insisted on just leaving right away. Then Alberto surprised us, and he was so charming and attentive that he fooled me." She removed one of the other dresses from the hanger and pulled it on.

Stepping out from behind the screen, she found Negal frowning. "How did he manage that? You are so suspicious and careful by nature, and you are not easily fooled. Maybe he slipped you something even before putting the sleeping drug in the wine."

"Maybe. Or perhaps I'm a sucker for charm and a handsome face." She turned to the mirror and examined the evening dress. "What do you think?"

"I'm good on the handsome face front but not so much on the charm."

Margo laughed. "I mean about the dress. Do you like it?"

"It's beautiful. Take it."

"It's not nicer than the emerald one."

"It's not. I meant, take them both. You look stunning in each one. In fact, you should be wearing dresses like that all of the time. They bring out the inner Margo that tries to shine less brightly in borrowed leggings and a T-shirt. You were meant to wear luxury."

She turned to him and smiled. "And you say that you're not charming. I think that you are very much so." *And also an amazing kisser.*

Should she compliment him on that?

Yeah, why not?

Despite being a god and looking like one, Negal wasn't full of himself.

"You are also a great kisser." She licked her lips.

Emitting a groan, he reached for her, but as the door opened, he hissed and took a step back.

His fangs were even longer than they had been before.

Luckily, the saleswoman was holding a stack of five boxes in front of her and couldn't see Negal's face.

Margo sprang into action. "Let me help you with those." She took the woman's elbow and turned her toward the couch before taking the top two boxes.

"Thank you." The saleslady put the other three on the floor. "Do you need my assistance trying them on?"

"Not at all." Margo smiled at her brightly. "Your time will be better spent assisting other customers. I still have all those other things you brought to try on."

"Thank you." The woman cast her a grateful look. "Take your time. I only allow the most discriminating customers into this dressing room, and it's all yours for as long as you need it." She turned to look at Negal, who, in the meantime, had managed to get his fangs under control. "If you buy five items or more, I will give you a twenty percent discount."

"Thank you."

Once she was gone, Negal released a breath. "I don't know why I lose control like that around you."

Margo liked having such an effect on him. It made her feel more powerful and, in turn, less fearful.

Walking over to him, she cupped his cheek. "That's because you like me, and you think that one day I will become the love of your life."

He leaned into her hand. "What do you think? Is that going to happen?"

"You are very easy to love, Negal," she whispered. "But I need more time. I believe in starting small and allowing for measured growth. It's healthier that way."

He nodded. "Wise words."

66

ROBERT

Robert stood at the foot of the podium, his six groomsmen flanking him and a glowing goddess behind him, her palpable power like a brand on his back.

It occurred to him that it was rude to have his back to the Clan Mother, and he shifted his stance so he had his side to her but could still watch the entrance to the dining hall and behold his bride as she walked in surrounded by her bridesmaids.

He hadn't seen Sharon since morning because she'd insisted that it was bad luck for the groom and bride to be together on the day of their wedding. It was a silly human superstition, but then Sharon had been a human until not too long ago.

Having been the one who had induced her immortality was special to him, and he had no doubt that the bond between them was formed because of that. Bridget and Amanda believed that it was the other way around and that Dormants who bonded with their immortal partners had a better chance of transitioning, but even though he knew next to nothing about science, Robert was sure that the bond was the result of the induction. Otherwise, it didn't make sense that so many couples were fated mates.

But what did he know?

He was just a simple soldier with decent organizational skills, who Kian had taken pity on and had given a job in the clan's building and development projects.

Robert's swirling thoughts came to an abrupt stop as the bridal march started playing. The doors to the dining room opened, and Sharon's six bridesmaids walked in and joined the groomsmen.

He held his breath as he waited for his bride to emerge, and as she walked in, with her head held high and a bright smile that was all for him, his heart stopped racing, and a calm washed over him.

Everything was good in his world as long as she was in it.

Returning her smile, he waited until she reached the podium and took her hand.

"Hi," he mouthed.

Her smile broadened, but she didn't reply. Instead, she turned toward the goddess, and he turned with her.

They both bowed to the Clan Mother, who smiled fondly at them.

"My children," she addressed both of them, and Robert's heart flooded with warmth. "You are here today, standing in front of me and waiting for me to officially join you, but your hearts have been joined for a long time."

The goddess shifted her gaze to the audience and smiled. "We are gathered here not to unite these two souls but to acknowledge their union and celebrate it. Sharon and Robert's union defies the ordinary and is a testament to the extraordinary power of forgiveness, transformation, and love. Today, we honor the bond of a couple whose journey to this altar is a remarkable tale of redemption, courage, and the healing power of love.

"Once, Robert walked a path shrouded in darkness, yet within him burned a light, a beacon of honor and compassion that not even the deepest shadows could extinguish. When faced with the unimaginable cruelty inflicted upon one of our own, it was this light that guided him to do the right thing, to defy his sworn allegiance, and to choose the path of righteousness. To aid in her escape, he forsook his former life, everything he worked for, and everyone he knew, proving that his inner light and spirit had not been crushed. That day, good triumphed over evil.

"Robert's journey led him to our doors, seeking sanctuary, understanding, and a new beginning among those he once thought were his enemies.

"When he met Sharon, she rekindled a flame from the flickering embers of his past—a flame of love, trust, and mutual respect. Sharon saw more than Robert's past. She saw the noble heart that lay within, and together they have woven a new narrative, one that speaks to the transformative power of love and a new dawn.

"Their love story is a beacon for all who seek redemption and a reminder that the past does not define us, but rather, it is our actions, our choices, and the love we share that truly shapes our destiny. In each other, they have found not only a partner but also a mirror reflecting their best selves, a sanctuary of peace and a wellspring of joy.

"Today, as Robert and Sharon stand before us, let us all bear witness to the incredible journey that has led them to this moment. Their joining is a testament to the belief that out of discord can come harmony, and from distrust can bloom the most profound trust."

The goddess lowered her eyes to the two of them. "In the spirit of unity and under the benevolent gaze of the Fates, I bless this union with the deepest joy and highest hopes. May your lives together be filled with endless days of happiness, nights of passion, and a love that grows stronger with each passing moment. As you embark on this journey together, nurture your love with understanding and kindness, and it will shine brightly. May you be blessed with eternal happiness."

The goddess smiled. "Before I pronounce you bonded for life, would you like to recite your vows to each other?"

"Yes, we would, Clan Mother." Robert dipped his head to the goddess and then turned to his bride.

67

SHARON

Sharon's heart started beating faster.

The Clan Mother's speech had been beautiful and moving, and Sharon had teared up a little, but with all due respect to the goddess and the head of the clan, Sharon valued more what Robert was about to say.

He wasn't a man of many words, but he felt deeply and loved wholeheartedly, and she prayed that he had managed to put it all into his vows, not because she needed to hear it, but because he needed to say it and he needed the clan to hear it.

They were both outsiders who had found a home in this amazing community, but even after all this time, they were still struggling to feel like they truly belonged, and this ceremony was a huge step in that direction.

Robert looked into her eyes with so much love and adoration that her breath caught in her throat.

"Sharon," he said with a slight tremble in his voice. "In this moment, before this community that accepted us with open arms and, more importantly, with open hearts, I stand before you, a male transformed not by my own doing but by the grace of your love and the acceptance of a clan that I once viewed through the eyes of an adversary.

"Once, I walked a path shadowed by remorse and led by misguidance, a life marked by battles and a heart burdened with regret. I was a stranger to my own soul, lost in a darkness I thought impenetrable. But then you entered my life, a beacon of light in my unfathomable darkness, guiding me to a safe shore with your brave spirit and enormous heart.

"You saw beyond the ugliness of my past, beyond the façade of strength I projected to the world. You saw the male I longed to be but feared I could never become. With you, my love, I have discovered a strength I never knew I possessed, the courage to banish the shadows of the past, and embrace a hope for a future I once believed was beyond my reach.

"I vow to you, my heart, my soul, and my eternal devotion. I promise to honor the faith you've placed in me, to support you in your dreams, to stand by your side in times of joy and hardship.

"I pledge to listen with understanding, to speak with honesty, and to act with integrity. I will laugh with you in times of joy and comfort you in times of sorrow. I will share in your dreams and support you as you strive to achieve your goals.

"I commit to you a life of partnership, of growth, and of love. May our days be filled with adventure, our nights with passion, and our home with laughter. Sharon, you are my love, my light, and my life. I am yours, completely and forever."

He pulled out a ring from his pocket. "With this symbol of everlasting love, I pledge myself to you." He slipped the ring on her finger.

As the crowd erupted in cheers and applause, Sharon mouthed, "I love you. It was perfect."

He smiled. "I love you more than life."

The crowd went wild, with the groomsmen cheering and the bridesmaids wiping happy tears from their eyes.

Sharon waited for everyone to quiet down.

"Robert, my love. Before the eyes of our friends, new and old, I stand with you, my heart open, my soul alive with a joy I once thought was the stuff of fairy tales. In you, I have found not only a partner but also a reflection of true strength, resilience, and the purest form of courage.

"From the moment we met, I saw in you a spirit that resonated with something deep within me. I saw the shadows of your past, but more luminously, I saw the light of your potential, the warmth of your heart, and the true valor of your being.

"In this journey we have embarked upon together, you have taught me the true meaning of resilience. You have shown me that the past does not define us but is instead the soil from which our future grows. Your courage in facing what once was, your determination to become the male you are today, has inspired me to be a better person.

"Today, as I take your hand in mine, I vow to be your sanctuary and your strength, as you have been mine. I promise to stand beside you through all the trials and triumphs that our future holds. I vow to be your confidant, your ally, and your closest friend.

"I commit to you a heart that listens, a mind that supports, and a love that knows no bounds. I will laugh with you in times of joy and hold you close in times of sorrow. I will challenge you to be the best version of yourself, just as you have challenged me.

"I promise to cherish the love we have nurtured together, to always fight for us, and to never take for granted the miracle that is our togetherness. I will honor your growth, as well as my own, as we navigate this beautiful life side by side.

"Robert, you are my rock, my refuge, and my greatest adventure. I pledge to you my loyalty, my respect, and my unconditional love. Together, may we build a life filled with laughter, learning, and endless love. I am yours, in all ways and forever."

Sharon turned to Eva, who handed her the ring, and then back to Robert. "With this ring, I bind myself to you for eternity." She slipped the ring on his finger.

Just as before, their guests started cheering, hooting, and clapping, and as the ruckus went on, she stared into the eyes of the man she loved more than anything and anyone in the world.

The Clan Mother lifted her glowing arms, and the crowd hushed down.

"By the sacred power the Fates vested in me, I now pronounce you, Robert and Sharon, bonded for life, partners in love, and allies in spirit. May your union be as enduring as the earth, as vast as the sky, and as infinite as the stars. Congratulations, you may proceed with the kiss."

Someone whistled, and then a chant began, "kiss, kiss, kiss…"

Smiling, Robert shrugged. "Should we oblige them?"

"Well, if we must, we must." She launched herself into his waiting arms.

68

NEGAL

As Sharon and Robert pledged their love and commitment to each other, Negal found himself unexpectedly touched by the sincerity and depth of their promises. The earnestness in their voices, the tears of joy in their eyes, and the undeniable bond that connected them stirred something within him he hadn't anticipated.

He glanced at Margo, taking in her soft features that were bathed in the glow from the candelabra that served as the centerpiece of their table. She was watching the ceremony with a tender smile, her eyes glinting with a sheen of tears, just as moved as he was by the vows the couple had exchanged.

Would that be them one day?

The thought of exchanging vows with Margo, of standing before her and promising a lifetime of love, support, and understanding, filled him with a sense of longing but also dread.

What if she was just a human with no godly genes and a limited lifespan?

He'd never expected to fall for an immortal, let alone a human.

He was supposed to be smarter than that. He should guard his heart at least until he was sure that she could become immortal, and he needed to prepare himself for the possibility that it was not going to happen and that he would need to leave her.

It shouldn't be too difficult.

After all, they had known each other for two days and had shared a single kiss. When he left, the experience would be less than a blink of an eye in his lifetime. It would eventually fade into the vast cloud of all that he had experienced before.

Still, he could allow himself a few moments of wistfulness and envision the words they might one day say to each other.

He wasn't very eloquent, but with enough effort, he imagined he could come up with a few things. He would tell Margo how she had changed his life, how she had brought light into his world in a way he never thought possible. He would vow to stand by her, cherish her, and also challenge her because Margo needed to be challenged to be happy. To be engaged.

She wasn't the type who longed for serenity. She was a fighter, just like him.

How did he know that after spending so little time with her?

He wasn't sure.

The warrior's eyes were a clue, and her willingness to help a stranger in jeopardy was another.

As the bride leaped into the groom's arms, Negal felt a gentle pressure on his hand, and then Margo's fingers intertwined with his. He wasn't sure what the gesture meant, but he appreciated it and squeezed her hand in response.

Once the newlyweds took to the dance floor, all the guests rose to their feet and clapped as the Clan Mother, the sole heir to Anumati's throne, walked out of the ballroom accompanied by a couple of Guardians and her two Odus.

"The Clan Mother is not like you," Margo said quietly so that only he could hear her. "She is what I imagined a real goddess would look like."

He nodded. "She is special."

Margo lifted her eyes to him. "In what way?"

How was he supposed to answer that? Most of the clan was not aware of Annani's special status as the Eternal King's only legitimate heir, and he wasn't sure that they knew the distinction between the different classes of gods either, but that wasn't something that needed to be kept a secret, so he could share it with her.

"The Clan Mother comes from a royal line, and that's why she glows. Toven can glow as well, but he chooses not to for some reason."

Margo smiled. "So, Mia got herself a prince? Why didn't she tell me?"

"Toven is not a prince. There are many royals on Anumati."

"Oh." She looked disappointed.

He lifted her hand to his lips and smiled. "You, on the other hand, look like a princess." He kissed the back of it. "Should we join the newlyweds on the dance floor?"

Margo grinned. "Yes, we should."

She looked truly stunning tonight. The dress flowed around her like a second skin, its fabric catching the light with every movement and making her seem as if she were gliding rather than stepping.

Margo was a vision, and judging by the radiant spark in her eyes, she was well aware of that.

Pride swelled in his chest at the thought that he had contributed in some small way to the joy she exuded. The surge of satisfaction was slightly overshadowed by the little lie he'd told about his allowance, but it had been worth it just to see her this happy. There was no other way to convince her to allow him to pay for her new wardrobe, and he was sure that Aru would understand.

Their allowance had indeed been generous, but now that their stay on Earth had been extended indefinitely, their funds would have to last them much longer, and they would have to find a way to supplement them.

One day, he would have to confess the lie to Margo, but it didn't need to be anytime soon, at least not until the end of the cruise. He wanted her to enjoy all five weddings like she was enjoying this one, and she wouldn't if he fessed up.

Navigating through the clusters of guests, he led her to the dance floor, and as he put his arms around her the world seemed to shrink until it was just the two of them, enclosed in their own sphere of shared rhythm and warmth.

The song ended too soon, the last note lingering in the air like a whispered promise. As the applause broke their bubble, Negal reluctantly released Margo, though he kept one hand entwined with hers. Her cheeks were flushed with excitement, and her eyes shone with an inner light.

"One more dance?" she asked.

"As many dances as you want." He took her hand, needing to preserve the contact even though the next song had an upbeat tempo that was more appropriate for a freestyle dance.

"Are you always this agreeable?" She twirled in place, her cheeks rosy, and her lips lifted in a smile that tonight seemed permanently etched on her face.

"With you, I am. I'd battle dragons to see you this happy every day." Perhaps it wasn't the most romantic thing to say, but it was true.

She affected a pout. "Did you forget that I like dragons?"

He snorted. "I promise you that you wouldn't like the ones I'm talking about. But if you want me to play nice with an honorable fairytale dragon in a Perfect Match adventure, I will gladly do that." He leaned and kissed her cheek. "I'll go to great lengths to make you glow with happiness like that every day."

Stretching on her toes, she surprised him by planting a kiss on his lips. "That's so incredibly sweet that I could fall in love with you just for that." She leaned away with a naughty smirk. "But I will be even happier if you will agree to become a dragon shifter in our shared adventure."

"Anything you want and I can provide is yours."

He frowned as it occurred to him that a virtual adventure might be just the thing to get Margo over her inhibitions. It was a shame that they didn't have the service on the cruise ship.

"Are you sure?" She tilted her head. "You don't look like you are excited by the idea."

"I am. I was just thinking that I wished they had a virtual room on the ship."

Margo looked disappointed. "They don't?"

"Not as far as I know."

"Oh, well." She wound her arms around his neck. "Then we will need to create our adventure in the real world."

"That's even better." He dipped his head and took her lips in a gentle kiss.

As the song ended and they stepped off the dance floor, Negal wrapped his arm around Margo's waist and held her close to him as they made their way to their table.

He had a feeling that tonight would be imprinted in his memory forever, a perfect moment in time to cherish even if, at the end of the cruise, they would have to part.

The thought felt like a spear to his heart.

He didn't want to part with Margo for even a few minutes. He wanted to be with her every moment of the day and night in any form she would allow.

The irony of that wasn't lost on him. Where were his prior convictions about not wanting a mate?

Could Margo truly be his fated one?

Why not?

If Aru and Dagor had found their one and only on Earth, perhaps that was what the Fates had always intended for them.

Maybe that was why they had ended up together on the ship patrolling this sector.

Or maybe there was a larger game in play, and it had to do with the simmering rebellion and the heir to the Anumati throne?

Finding the princess on Earth must be even more significant than him and his teammates finding their true love matches here.

But what if it was all connected?

After all, their lives were threads in the tapestry the Fates were weaving, and only they knew the endgame.

THE WITCHING HOUR

1

NEGAL

Outside the panoramic windows of the ship's converted dining hall, the moon spilled its silver light across the waves, its reflection creating a shimmering path of luminescence that moved with the gentle swell of the water.

As Negal led Margo through the crowded dance floor, the ship's swaying felt like its own dance, a slow, rhythmic motion that didn't match the cadence of the lively Latin piece blasting through the loudspeakers.

"Are you up for it?" Negal extended his hand to Margo.

She cast him a challenging smile. "I am if you are. Do you know how to salsa?"

He snorted. "I carry a Portuguese passport. Mastery of mambo and salsa was a requirement for obtaining citizenship."

Margo laughed. "Salsa didn't originate in Portugal. It was invented in New York."

"I didn't know that, but I do know how to dance it."

"Then lead on because I'm rusty."

Negal might have exaggerated his mastery of the dance, but watching the other couples was enough to refresh his memory, and he guided Margo effortlessly through the steps. Following his lead she quickly found her rhythm, with her body responding naturally to the beat. As she gained confidence, so did he, and he spun her out and then back into his arms.

Her dress flaring with every turn, her smile broad and her eyes shimmering with excitement, she looked so lovely, so joyful, that his heart swelled with emotion.

Was this love?

It had to be.

He'd never been in love before, but he couldn't imagine a stronger emotion than what he was feeling for Margo. It was as if the world had narrowed down to the space they occupied, creating a bubble in which only they existed.

As the song reached its climax, Negal executed a final, daring spin, bending Margo over his arm in a graceful arch.

The room erupted into applause, and as Margo curtsied gracefully, he bowed to their audience.

When the next piece started playing, Negal was grateful that it was a slower, less demanding dance.

The immortals were still going just as strong as they had before dinner, but Margo was human, and it had been a long day for her. The salsa had drained her, and he noticed that she was growing fatigued even though she tried to hide it.

Her steps were no longer as sure as they had been during the previous dance, and her movements were becoming slightly sluggish, but her eyes were so full of joy and her smile so bright that it would pain him to suggest she should rest.

Besides, he didn't want to let go of her just yet.

The clarity that had begun to crystallize in his mind was like the afterglow of a supernova—blinding in its intensity and too grand to settle comfortably.

He'd always considered himself a creature of duty, and the concept of finding a mate and intertwining his life with another's had seemed almost alien to him.

Yet, here he was, on the cusp of a revelation that threatened to redefine his very existence.

The realization that he desired Margo not just for a few fleeting moments of passion, but at all times and in every conceivable way, was exhilarating and terrifying at the same time.

The possibility that Margo could be his fated one was a concept he might have scoffed at in another life, but now it held a weight of truth he could not ignore. The fact that Aru and Dagor had found their fated mates on Earth hinted at a design rather than a coincidence—a thread in the Fates' intricate tapestry of destinies.

Against the backdrop of the brewing rebellion on Anumati and their discovery of the heir to the Anumati throne on Earth, the personal destinies of Negal and his teammates seemed to be somehow intertwined with the Fates' grand design.

The question was how he would navigate the complexities of being bound by the duties of his post while also fulfilling his duty to his mate.

Right now, it seemed as if the two would be difficult to reconcile, maybe even impossible. At some point in the future his time on Earth would come to an end, and he wouldn't be able to take Margo with him.

There was also the question of whether Margo was indeed his mate.

If it turned out that she wasn't a Dormant and had no godly genes in her, there was no way she was his one and only. He could still love her, but it wouldn't be the unbreakable bond of fated mates.

The old Negal would have prayed that she had no godly genes so he wouldn't be bound to her, but the new Negal was allowing himself to hope for a miracle and possibly opening himself up to a world of hurt should that miracle not come to pass.

When the song ended, he leaned closer to whisper in her ear. "You seem tired. Ready to call it a night?"

"What makes you think that I'm tired?"

He chuckled. "You are swaying on your feet, and it's not because of the ship."

Margo sighed, a reluctant smile playing on her lips. "I don't want the magic to end." She took a step away from him and twirled in place. "This dress makes me feel like a fairy-tale princess, dancing with the prince on an enchanted voyage."

Her eyes sparkled with joy, but there were dark shadows under them, and even though Negal wished he could prolong the enchantment for Margo, he couldn't ignore the physical toll the long day and night had taken on her.

Taking her hand, he led her away from the dance floor. "The magic doesn't end with the night. To me, you are always a princess, and it has nothing to do with the dress."

"Men are so literal." She rolled her eyes for effect. "It has everything to do with the dress. I don't feel like this every day."

Had he said something wrong?

He was experienced enough to know to avoid most of the usual landmines that females liked to plant in front of males to test them, and he was sure that telling a female that she was always a princess to him regardless of her attire had been the right response.

Margo laughed. "You look so confused."

"I am," he admitted as he pulled out a chair for her. "You look offended, and I can't understand why."

"Oh, my sweet Negal." She leaned her head against his bicep. "I'm not offended. I just feel that once I leave this ballroom, the magic will disappear, and I'll turn back into Cinderella minus the glass slipper." She lifted her head and looked at him. "I keep forgetting that you are not from around here and that you might not know what I'm talking about." She snorted. "That was a major understatement. How many light years away from Earth is your home planet?"

"Hundreds, but I'm familiar with the Cinderella fairy tale, and I know that you have nothing in common with her."

Margo frowned. "You are right. In my case, the prince got me the beautiful evening gown, not the fairy godmother, and he doesn't need a glass slipper to find me."

"You are also not a timid girl who needs a prince to rescue her."

"But you did."

"First of all, I'm not a prince. I'm more of a cinders guy, just without the mean family. Secondly, I can't take credit for your rescue because it was a team effort, and most of the credit belongs to Kalugal. Thirdly, you get to keep the dress, and fourthly, tomorrow we will dance at yet another wedding, and you will be wearing yet another beautiful dress."

She let out a tired laugh, leaning more heavily against him. "You're right. My fairy tale started the moment you caught me when I fainted, and it will probably end when the ship docks in Long Beach. I have four more nights of magic to enjoy, and then my memories of it will be erased, and I will not remember that it ever happened."

Negal's chest tightened despite him feeling confident that their story would have a much happier ending.

Even if he didn't manage to induce Margo's transition before the end of the cruise, he would find a way to do it after. Aru hadn't answered him yet about the possibility of delaying their departure for Tibet, but even if their commander didn't approve a delay, Aru and Dagor could go ahead while Negal stayed behind for a few more weeks to induce Margo. Once that was achieved and she transitioned, they could join the expedition.

Aru might object, but he would cave.

As someone who had just found his mate, Aru knew how impossible it was to deny the call of one's fated partner and leave her for any reason.

"That's not how our story is going to end, and you know it. You're just tired, so everything seems gloomy to you."

She lifted a pair of sad eyes to him. "I'm not a guaranteed Dormant, Negal. I don't have any special paranormal talents, and I'm not related to any immortals. If the induction doesn't work, I can't stay with you or even work for Perfect Match with Frankie. Toven might arrange a job for me in the company's offices in the city, and I might even become a beta tester, just not in the immortals' village. They will thrall me to forget everything I know about them."

He wrapped his arm around her shoulders. "That's a worst-case scenario, Margo. And I refuse to be a pessimist. I believe that you are a Dormant and that you will transition, and so should you."

2

MARGO

Platitudes usually did nothing for Margo. She was too cynical and practical to feel encouraged by empty words of comfort. And yet, Negal's confidence in her ability to turn immortal was welcomed, and it made her feel all warm and fuzzy inside.

She hadn't intended to voice her fears and insecurities, especially not during the party, but Negal had been so sweet and said such nice things that it had all felt too good to be true, which meant that it couldn't be.

She was no princess, and Negal was not her prince.

He was amazing, not just because he was a god, but that only diminished the probability of him being hers. She was just an average woman, a nobody, and she didn't believe in fairy tales.

Then again, she wasn't any less worthy than Mia or Frankie, so why not?

Margo sighed. "As much as I want to continue the fairy tale, I don't want to fall on my face when the clock strikes midnight either, so I should get going while I can still walk."

"The last thing I want is for my princess to wear out her slippers." Negal rose to his feet and offered her a hand up.

Margo laughed. "That was a good one." She took his offered hand. "But you don't have to leave just because your feeble human date is exhausted. You should stay and have fun. I can find my way back to my cabin by myself."

His lips thinned out, and his brows dipped in an affronted expression. "First of all, escorting you to your cabin is my privilege and my duty. And secondly, I won't have any fun without you, so there is no reason for me to stay."

Her heart happily somersaulting in her chest, Margo lifted on her toes and kissed Negal's cheek. "You are adorable."

What she really wanted to say was that she loved him, but she still wasn't ready to make such a declaration. They had just met two days ago, for goodness' sake, and she didn't really know him well enough to have strong feelings for him. It was an infatuation, and surprisingly, for her, lust.

The kiss they had shared earlier had been like no kiss she'd ever experienced, but it had probably been nothing special for Negal. He was an exceptionally good kisser, which was one hell of an achievement given that his fangs elongated when he was aroused, and he had definitely been aroused by their kiss.

Was she ready to take it to the next level, though?

She should be if she was like any other twenty-seven-year-old who wasn't a virgin, but she needed a little more time. Negal was hot, had the face of an angel, and on top of that, he was also smart and kind, but getting naked with a male and allowing him into her body required a deeper emotional connection, and that couldn't happen overnight.

Negal looked at her with amusement in his eyes. "Adorable is not the adjective a male wants to hear from a female he desires." He took her hand and brought it to his lips for a soft kiss.

"How about sweet?" she teased.

"No, not sweet either."

"Handsome?"

"Getting close. But no. I was thinking along the lines of irresistibly sexy, devastatingly attractive, etc."

"You are all that and more." She averted her gaze. "We should congratulate the newlyweds and say goodbye before we leave."

"Sharon and Robert are on the dance floor." Negal wrapped an arm around her waist. "But if you want, we can say hello to Kian and Syssi. You said that you wanted to meet them, and I see them walking toward their table."

Margo swallowed. "Perhaps not tonight."

He leaned down and whispered in her ear, "Don't feel intimidated. Kian is a little gruff but he's a good guy, and if you want to catch him in a good mood, this is the best time. He's with his wife and the rest of his family, and he's having fun."

That was true. Besides, she would be less intimidated by the guy while looking her best and with Negal by her side than if she was summoned to his office or cabin during the day and on her own.

Still, Margo wanted Mia and Toven to be there when the introductions were made. After all, she and Frankie had gotten invited to the cruise only because Mia had insisted, and Toven had backed her up.

"Let's find Mia and Toven first. I want them to introduce me to Kian and his wife."

Negal regarded her for a moment before nodding. "I don't see why you need them, but if their presence will make you more comfortable, then why not?"

"I'm here thanks to Mia and Toven. I mean, I'm here because you saved me from the Modanas, but if I hadn't gotten in trouble and needed rescuing, I would have waited in the resort to be picked up as Mia had arranged."

Negal's arm around her waist tightened. "But then we might never have met. I'm sorry that you had such a scare, so I can't say that I'm happy you got kidnapped by the cartel, but I believe that everything had to happen the way it did so we would find each other."

3

KIAN

Kian noticed Toven and Mia heading his way with Negal and Margo. He hadn't been introduced to her yet, but he'd seen her dancing with Negal last night, and then the two had gone outside and hadn't returned. Today though, they had put on a show, and he had gotten a good look at her.

She was very pretty, but that wasn't what had impressed him about her. What warmed Kian's heart was the way she looked at Negal. It was obvious that she was smitten by the god, which wasn't surprising, and the feeling seemed mutual.

Hopefully, the Fates would be merciful and grant the two a happy ending. It would be a shame if Margo turned out to be just a plain mortal.

Had they begun the process?

Getting induced by a god was Margo's best bet, and if it didn't work, there would be no point trying with anyone else. They would get their answer about her sooner rather than later, which was good. The fewer memories she accumulated of their world, which would have to be later thralled away, the better.

"Margo is beautiful," Syssi said. "Mia and Frankie didn't mention how gorgeous their friend is."

"Her friends are both attractive females." Amanda plucked a chocolate-covered strawberry off the platter. "So, they probably didn't even see that." She took a bite of the strawberry and moaned. "This is so good. I need Onidu to get the recipe from the dessert chef." She looked at Kian. "Is there a chance we can lure the kitchen crew to move to the village?"

He shrugged. "We can try, although I had a different proposition for them in mind."

"Do tell." Amanda took another strawberry.

"I'll tell you about it later." He rose to his feet and waited for the group to reach the table before offering his hand to Margo. "Welcome aboard, Margo."

She took his hand and dipped her head. "Thank you for having me, and an even bigger thank you for saving me and my friend from the cartel."

"You're welcome." He let go of her hand. "How are you doing? I bet your head is spinning from all you've learned."

"It is, but at least it's all good." She offered him a bright smile. "I'm so glad to finally be proven right. For years, I've been telling everyone who cared to listen that the governments of the world are hiding contact with aliens from the public. And now I know it's true."

Kian chuckled. "I hate to disappoint you, but the governments don't know about us, and if they have contact with some other aliens, we don't know about them."

Margo's face fell. "Well, at least I have proof that aliens exist." She turned to look at Negal. "I'm dating one."

"Yay!" Amanda clapped her hands. "That's wonderful. A god is your best chance of successful transition."

"My thoughts exactly," Toven said.

Margo's cheeks turned crimson. "If you don't mind, I would rather change the subject."

"Sorry," Amanda said with a smirk. "I didn't know that you were bashful."

Margo frowned. "I prefer to describe myself as reserved."

"Same here." Syssi lifted her hand. "Amanda makes me blush about twenty times a day every day, and I've known her for years."

Amanda pretended to pout. "You make me sound so bad."

"That's because you are bad." Syssi mock-glared at her.

Kian realized that he hadn't introduced his table companions yet. "This is my sister Amanda, next to her is her husband Dalhu, and this lovely lady is my wife, Syssi."

"Nice to meet you all." Margo put a hand over her chest. "I just hope that I won't have to forget you soon. I would very much like to become part of your world, and not just to become immortal. I would love to become part of the biggest conspiracy on the planet."

As everyone laughed, Kian regarded the young woman with curiosity. He found her likable and wondered whether it was just that he enjoyed her unconventional personality or if there was an affinity at play.

He could never tell the difference between normal feelings of friendliness toward people and affinity for Dormants.

"I wish we were the biggest conspiracy on the planet," Syssi murmured. "We also thought that we were the biggest deal around until not too long ago, but now we've discovered conspiracies so big that they dwarf our secretive existence."

Margo's eyes sparkled with interest. "What could be bigger than the existence of the gods and their descendants among humans?"

Evidently, Negal hadn't told her about the threat of the Eternal King, and Kian appreciated that. The council had been informed, but he had asked them not to spread the news. There was no reason to alarm the entire clan. But that wasn't even the biggest secret. The Anumati queen communicating with Annani with the help of the telepathic twins was the biggest one of all, but Negal didn't know about it, and he was not going to find out.

Kian still hadn't told Syssi about the first session being tomorrow after the wedding ceremony. The queen could only hold the telepathic meeting at one o'clock in the morning local time, which meant that he and Aru would have to sneak away while everyone else was still celebrating. Perhaps Syssi could advise him on how to excuse his and Aru's absence so it wouldn't look suspicious.

"There is always a bigger fish," Syssi said with a smile.

"Indeed." He nodded and added, "Enjoy the rest of your night."

Thankfully, Margo understood from his tone of voice that no further questions should be asked about the subject.

"Thank you." She returned his smile. "I'm afraid that this feeble human is tired and needs to go to bed. It was very nice to meet all of you." She dipped her head. "Good night and thank you again for saving me and hosting me aboard this lovely ship."

4

NEGAL

"That wasn't so bad," Margo said as she walked into the elevator. "Kian was a little intimidating, but I've met worse in the advertising agency I work for." She pressed the button for her deck. "Do you think he was trying to be nice for the poor human's sake?"

"I told you that he was a good guy. I don't know why he has such a reputation."

They were alone in the elevator, and Negal considered pulling Margo into his arms for a quick kiss, but the ride was too short, and by the time he completed the thought, the automated voice announced the third deck.

"Perhaps he was nice to me because of you." She took his hand. "After all, you are a visiting god, right? A dignitary of sorts."

He shook his head. "Not a dignitary. We are not here in any official capacity. The people back home don't even know that immortals exist."

They had spent a lot of time together today, and yet there hadn't been enough of it for him to tell her anything significant about himself or to learn more about her. It was impossible to cram everything there was to know about a person into a few hours, and on top of that, he knew that she might be made to forget everything he told her, so what was the point?

Margo stopped in front of her cabin and pulled out her phone from her purse. "Tomorrow, we are going to sit down somewhere, and you are going to tell me about yourself."

He chuckled. "Is that an order?"

"Yes."

As she lifted her phone to open the door, he put his hand over hers. "Not yet."

She lifted a pair of questioning eyes to him. "We don't have to say good night out here. You can come in and we can have a quiet cup of tea together."

If the invitation had come from any other female, he would have assumed that tea meant something else, but in Margo's case, tea meant tea.

Still, he would take whatever she was willing to give him, including sharing a cup of tea, but he needed to kiss her, and he wouldn't be able to do that with Dagor and Frankie inside. They hadn't attended the wedding, and they would probably be in their bedroom with the door closed, making up for lost time during Frankie's transition, but they might be taking a break from their marathon lovemaking, and he didn't want to take the chance.

He cupped her cheek and lowered his head, so their lips were almost touching. "Frankie and Dagor might be in there, and I want to kiss you good night."

He waited for her to close the fraction-of-an-inch distance between their lips.

Mischief dancing in her eyes, she wound her arms around his neck and teased his lips with hers. "Like this?" she whispered.

"Yes, but I need a little more."

Gripping her hips, he pulled her closer to him and took over the kiss. She tasted of the sweets she'd eaten for dessert and the vermouth she'd drunk and her own unique taste, which was sweeter than both.

Delicious. Addictive.

She moaned, and as her fingers threaded through his short hair, he regretted it not being longer so she could tug on the strands, claiming him as he was claiming her with this kiss.

Hoisting her up, Negal hooked one of Margo's legs around his waist and ground his erection against her center. Despite the layers of clothing between them, he could feel her heat and imagine how wet she was for him.

A groan escaped his throat, and in answer, she rubbed back against him. Wanton, uninhibited. He had a feeling that if there was no one in the cabin behind the door he was pressing her against, she wouldn't have objected to him taking her to bed.

"Margo," he breathed as he propped her up with one hand so he could free the other one to smooth over her exposed thigh.

Her heated core was like a magnet to his roaming fingers, but as he got so close that he could actually feel the heat radiating from her, she stiffened, and he immediately retracted his hand.

"I apologize," he murmured. "I got carried away." Gently, he eased her back down to the ground, taking a moment to carefully adjust her dress, ensuring everything was properly in place.

"Don't be." She smoothed two shaky fingers over her puffy lips. "I'm the one who should be sorry."

She was panting, a beautiful blush painting her cheeks crimson.

"Never." He cupped the back of her head and pressed a soft kiss to her forehead. "I shouldn't have rushed you when you weren't ready. I want it to be perfect between us, and that can only happen when you are fully ready for me."

"Thank you." Her shoulders relaxed, and a teasing smile lifted her lips. "Tea?" she asked.

"I would love some."

As Margo opened the door, Frankie and Dagor looked up at them from the couch with twin fake-innocent expressions.

Negal stifled a chuckle as he took in their languid state. They looked like a couple of satisfied cats, lounging lazily on the sofa after making love for hours.

They hadn't attended the wedding because Frankie was supposedly still recovering from her transition, but anyone could have guessed the real reason.

"How was the wedding?" Frankie asked.

"Beautiful." Margo put her purse on the bar and filled the kettle with water. "Such heartfelt vows." She shook her head. "You could see the love shining through their eyes."

"We saw it on the ship's channel," Dagor said. "Not live, but the rerun is already available. You can watch all the previous weddings as well."

"That's so cool." Margo pulled two mugs out of the cabinet. "Do you want tea? I'm making some for Negal and me."

"No, thank you." Frankie lifted her half-empty cup of coffee. "We are good."

"Do you need help?" Negal asked.

Margo eyed him from under lowered lashes. "I'm tired, but I'm not dead. I can still make tea."

Touchy female. The funny part was that she was touchy about things no other female he knew cared about.

He lifted his hands in surrender. "Just asking."

"Come, take a seat." Frankie beckoned with a wave of her hand.

Negal unbuttoned his tux and sat down on one of the armchairs. "Can I ask you a favor?"

"Of course," Frankie said.

"I need you to keep an eye on Margo. Can you leave your bedroom door ajar so you can hear her and check on her from time to time?"

"Sure thing," Frankie said with not much enthusiasm, and he could understand why. She and Dagor probably planned to continue their lovefest, and they wouldn't be able to do that with the door open.

"I'm fine." Margo put down two teacups on the coffee table. "I don't need babysitting." She sat on the other armchair. "Frankie is fresh out of her transition and needs rest."

"Bridget said that you need to be watched for reaction to the drugs for seventy-two hours, and it hasn't been that long yet. You are still mortal, and I'm worried about you."

Negal was also worried about Karen and how her transition was progressing. Once he was done here, he planned on going down to the clinic and checking up on her.

"I have no problem keeping an eye on you." Frankie leaned on Dagor's shoulder. "I'll check on you during the night."

"I will do that," Dagor said. "You need to rest." He looked at Negal. "If that's okay with you."

"Hey." Margo snapped her fingers. "I thought that gods were an advanced species, not cavemen. You should ask me if I'm okay with that, not Negal."

Dagor dipped his head. "Apologies. Are you okay with me checking up on you?"

"Although it is not necessary, yes, and thank you."

Negal was glad that the nightgown she'd gotten at the boutique earlier that day was not as revealing as the one she had borrowed from Frankie the night before. He would have definitely had an issue with Dagor checking up on her if she was sleeping with that flimsy thing on.

Margo cast him a sidelong glance. "Does that meet with your approval?"

"Of course." He reached over the armrests of both chairs and took her hand. "I just want to make sure that you are okay."

Her eyes softened. "Thank you for worrying about me."

"Always." He leaned over and kissed her knuckles. "Sleep well and dream sweet dreams." *Naughty ones of me,* he wanted to add.

5

MARGO

When the door closed behind Negal, Margo's heart was still racing, and her core still throbbing with need. If she weren't so damn repressed, the kiss they had shared outside the door would have ended with them naked in bed, and Margo had a feeling that she would have been just fine with that.

Why the hell had she frozen when Negal's fingers got close to where she had so desperately needed them?

She was still so wet that she worried about the evidence of her arousal showing on her dress, which would be mortifying on several counts. First of all, she didn't want to soil the magnificent gown, and secondly, she didn't want Frankie and Dagor to see it.

Dagor cleared his throat. "I'm going to watch some television in bed." He smiled at Frankie. "You can stay with Margo until she's ready to retire for the night."

Some sort of silent communication passed between the two of them, and then Frankie nodded. "I'm going to make more coffee. Do you want me to bring you some to bed?"

"Thank you, but I'm all coffeed out." He winked at her before ducking into the bedroom and closing the door behind him.

Frankie rose to her feet and walked over to the kitchenette. "Do you want coffee or another cup of tea?"

"I'll have tea," Margo said.

"Why didn't you invite Negal to spend the night with you?"

That was so direct and so like Frankie. The girl had no filter and just blurted out anything that went through her head.

"It's a bit early for that." Margo crossed her legs, hoping to ease the itch in her center that was growing uncomfortable. "I'm not ready to take it to the next level yet."

Frankie lifted a brow. "You seem very ready to me."

Margo was sure that she'd done a good job of keeping her expression schooled, not panting like a cat in heat or devouring Negal with her eyes.

"What do you mean?"

Frankie chuckled. "Did you forget already what I told you about immortals' enhanced sense of smell? Poor Dagor had to escape to the bedroom not to react to that."

As a wave of mortification washed over Margo, she closed her eyes.

"Oh, my God. I did forget about that. I'm so embarrassed."

"Don't be. It's natural, and both of us are happy that the two of you are drawn to each other. That's precisely what I wanted and hoped for. I just don't understand what you are waiting for."

Damn.

Neither Frankie nor Mia knew about Margo's problems with intimacy, and she needed it to stay that way. If she told them, they would immediately start offering her unsolicited advice on how she could overcome her problem, and worse, they would pity her.

"You heard Negal. I'm still not out of the woods with the drug I was injected with. I feel fine, but I want to be absolutely sure that I'm sober before I let myself be intimate with anyone. I don't want to do anything under the influence of drugs and regret it later."

Frankie surprised her with a hearty laugh. "Believe me, you will not regret this even if you decide that Negal is not for you. Words cannot describe what sex with a god or an immortal is like. Think multiple earth-shattering orgasms, euphoria, and an unrivaled psychedelic trip all combined into an unparalleled pleasure package. And that's not all. The next morning, you will feel like you've just been through a rejuvenating spa instead of feeling like you were hit by a freight train. The venom contains healing properties, so even the most intense session won't leave you with bruises and sore lady bits."

"That sounds incredible, but I still prefer to take it slow and savor the buildup. You know what I think about hookups."

Frankie returned with their drinks and set them down on the coffee table.

"Negal doesn't think of you as a hookup. I've seen him around other females, and he never looked at any of them the way he looks at you."

Margo's heart fluttered. "And how is that?"

"Like you are precious to him." Frankie sat down next to her on the couch. "Besides, you don't have time to play it safe, Margo. Negal is your best chance for a successful transition, and he's leaving shortly."

"He said that he would talk with Aru about postponing the mission to Tibet by a few weeks."

Frankie shook her head. "Aru is not going to agree to that. He's already postponed it so he and his team could be on this cruise. He won't ask for another delay. The only exception might be if you are already transitioning. He might let Negal stay behind until you are out of danger, and then he would have to join us with you or without you. Negal is a trooper, and he has to obey orders. He doesn't have a choice."

6

NEGAL

It was late, or rather early, since it was about two o'clock in the morning, and the smart thing to do would be to head back to his cabin and go to sleep, but Negal was still buzzed from being around Margo most of the day and the two kisses they had shared.

Negal shook his head.

He'd bedded hundreds of females, goddesses, and those of created species, but here he was, excited about sharing two kisses with a female and counting himself lucky and blessed for the privilege.

If he went to his cabin right now, he knew what he would be doing. He would get in the shower and repeat what he had done the day before. It wasn't a bad idea, and it would definitely ease some of the pressure building up inside of him, but it would also leave a bad taste in his mouth, and not because of his venom or the towel he would have to bite.

On some level, it was disrespectful to Margo.

Not that he would mind in the slightest if she pleasured herself while thinking about him. He would be the smuggest guy on this ship if she did. But he had a feeling she wouldn't, and therefore, he shouldn't either.

Besides, he needed to check on Karen.

He hadn't heard anything about how her transition was progressing, and since she wasn't young in human terms, the process was supposedly dangerous for her, and she might need a blood transfusion from him.

The question was how to do it without anyone knowing. Kian was adamant about keeping the power of a god's blood a secret, so it would have to be done in a way that wouldn't arouse suspicion.

Gilbert was no doubt sitting by his mate's side, and Negal was sure that the guy wouldn't agree to leave her alone with him no matter what.

He could get into Gilbert's mind and thrall him to forget that he was there, but then he would also need to do something about the security camera, and he wasn't an expert on that like Dagor.

Well, the obvious solution was to ask Dagor for help.

When he arrived at the clinic level, Negal was relieved to see Gilbert outside by the coffee machine.

He hadn't texted the guy to ask for permission to visit his mate, and knocking on her patient's room in the middle of the night was not really appropriate for someone who wasn't an immediate family member.

Hearing his approaching footsteps, Gilbert turned to look at him. "Negal. What brings you here?"

"I'm worried about Karen. How is she doing?"

"Bridget says that she's doing fine. She's sleeping, but she's conscious. I wake her up from time to time to make sure."

"That's good news." Negal took Gilbert's place in front of the machine, put a cup under the nozzle, and pressed the button for an Americano. "Do me a favor." He removed the paper cup and lifted it to his lips for a quick sip. "Let me know if anything changes."

Gilbert nodded. "I will. Thanks for checking up on Karen."

Negal smiled. "For better or worse, I'm in part responsible for what she's going through."

"I know what you mean." Gilbert chuckled. "When Karen gave birth to Idina and then to the twins, I felt guilty for getting her pregnant. It was absurd since we both wanted to have those children, and Karen didn't blame me, but I couldn't help it." He took a sip from his coffee. "Nothing worth having comes without a struggle, though. So, there is that."

Negal understood what Gilbert was trying to say. "With a few exceptions, that's mostly true. You didn't have to struggle to bring the children into the world like your mate did, but I'm sure you faced other struggles while raising them."

Gilbert huffed out a laugh. "They are a daily challenge but also the joy of my life."

"I believe you." Negal clapped him on the back. "Text me if Karen's situation changes."

Gilbert frowned. "I get it that you feel responsible, but what can you do for her if she gets worse? You'll just join me in worrying."

"Not knowing will make me worry all of the time, but as long as I don't get a text from you, I will know that Karen is okay."

7

MARGO

Margo showered, got dressed in the nightgown she'd bought earlier that day, and climbed into bed, all while Frankie was watching over her from the living room through her bedroom's open door.

"Are you going to stay out there all night?" Margo asked.

"No, I'm going to bed, but I will leave our bedroom door open so I can hear you."

"There is really no need. I'm feeling fine."

Except for the throbbing in her center and the disquiet in her chest, but neither had anything to do with the drug and everything to do with Negal and the fire he'd ignited in her with that kiss that had been more than a kiss.

"I know," Frankie said. "But I promised Negal." She peeked into the bedroom. "Good night, Margo."

"Good night. Can you close the door just a little bit? I feel exposed with it wide open."

"Sure thing." Frankie closed it almost all the way, and a moment later, the lights in the living room went off.

Margo let out a breath.

Solitude at last.

If she had one of her books with her, she could've scratched that itch, just to make sure that everything still worked. It had been a while since she'd pleasured herself, and as the saying went, you had to use it or lose it, and Margo wanted to make sure that she hadn't lost it.

The good news was that it had taken very little for Negal to ignite the fire within her, which was unusual for her, but getting from there to a climax was a different story. She had trouble achieving that even when self-pleasuring, and never with a man.

With a sigh, Margo closed her eyes and tried to remember one of the hotter stories she'd read recently, but it wasn't the same as reading. She liked the slow buildup of a good story, but she lacked the imagination to create it in her head.

What if she fantasized about Negal, though? She could start with the kiss they had shared outside the door, but in her fantasy, she wouldn't freeze up, Frankie and Dagor wouldn't be in the cabin, and things would progress as they should have. Maybe she could even give it a Perfect Match twist and make Negal a dragon shifter.

Nibbling on her lower lip, Margo pulled up her nightgown under the blanket and feathered her fingers over the gusset of her panties. The movement was so minimal that there was no way Frankie and Dagor could hear her all the way in their room, even with their supernatural hearing, and if her arousal intensified, the scent would hopefully stay trapped under the blanket.

Perhaps she could also add a little magic to her fantasy.

Instead of stiffening when Negal's fingers grazed her panties, she would moan and grind herself against him. He would magically get the door open and, with a partial shift, get his wings up and fly them both to the bed.

Naturally, he would also remove their clothing with his magic while flying them so they would both be naked when they reached the bed.

Margo chuckled.

It was such an absurd fantasy that it was amusing instead of arousing. Hopefully, Frankie and Dagor hadn't heard her chuckle, but if they did, they wouldn't know what had caused it.

Taking a deep breath, she tried to concentrate.

Negal opens the door and strides into my bedroom. He's cradling me to him as if I'm precious to him, and I'm a little scared, but I don't stop him because I want him so much.

I burn for him.

He gently lays me on the bed and then takes a step back to look at me.

"Do you want me?" he asks.

"More than anything," I admit as I scoot back and lie against a stack of pillows. "I want to see you. All of you."

Margo chuckled again. She'd never said those words to a man, but she'd read them so many times in romance novels that they almost didn't sound ridiculous to her.

With a cocky smile, he takes off his tux jacket and then starts unbuttoning his shirt slowly, teasingly, one button at a time. Forget about being undressed by magic, this was going to be a lot more fun. *I watch him with hooded eyes, but I don't make a move.*

He shrugs the shirt off and toes off his shoes, but he leaves the pants on as he prowls toward me. "Your turn, love."

Would he call her his love? Or would he have some other term of endearment for her?

Beautiful? Gorgeous? Sweet?

Maybe they had some other terms of endearment where he came from, and he would say a sexy-sounding foreign word that she wouldn't understand the meaning of.

As he carefully removes my dress, I help him so it won't tear, and as I'm left with only the sexy bra and panties set that's also brand new, he sucks in a breath.

"I wanted to see these things on you from the moment the saleslady brought them to the changing room."

"And I wanted you to see me in them from that same moment. That's why I got them."

Margo had gotten them because she'd needed underthings, and in reality, Negal probably wouldn't even remember that she'd bought several sexy sets. All he would care about would be how fast he could take them off her. In her fantasy, though, he would appreciate the lingerie.

He trails his fingers up my calf, my thighs, and as they brush against the lacy trim of my panties, I suck in a breath, but I don't freeze.

Negal looks into my eyes for a long moment and then dips his head, and I suck in another breath as I guess what he's going to do next.

Margo was never a fan of oral pleasuring, not on the receiving end and not on the giving end. It was just too intimate, too personal, and she'd never felt comfortable enough to do that, even with boyfriends she'd been having sex with for a while. But this was a fantasy, and she could be as wild as she pleased, and surprisingly, the prospect of such intimacy with Negal didn't turn her off.

As he presses a soft kiss to my moist folds through the lacy fabric of my panties, I moan and thread my fingers through his hair to encourage him to keep going.

A hungry look taking over his eyes, he hooks his fingers in the elastic of my panties and slides them down my legs.

At that point, Negal's eyes would no doubt be glowing, and his fangs would elongate, but Margo was okay with leaving those parts out of her fantasy for now.

My bra is next, and then his mouth is on my breast. I hiss at the wet heat of his mouth, the rolling of his tongue. He repeats the same with the other breast, and I'm on fire.

Margo pressed her fingers to the needy bundle of nerves at the apex of her thighs, but she still did it over her panties, not ready for full contact. With her other hand, she cupped her breast over her nightgown and pressed her lips tightly shut to prevent a moan from escaping.

Negal lets go of my nipples and looks at me with hunger in his glowing eyes. "I need to taste you. Will you allow it?"

"Yes," I whisper.

And then his mouth is on me, with his lips and tongue setting me on fire. I'm not climbing. I'm shooting up like a rocket.

Margo's hand snaked into her panties, and as she dipped her fingers to coat them in her wetness, she had to turn her head into the pillow to muffle the groan that was forcing its way out of her throat.

Negal devours me with his mouth, sucking and licking, and I spread my thighs even wider like some wanton woman from a romance story to allow him better access. My fingers claw into his hair, and I shamelessly grind myself against his mouth.

"Negal," I whisper as he flicks his tongue over the most sensitive part of me, and then I shatter into a million pieces, with his name still on my lips.

But he's not done with me. Slipping a finger into my wet heat and then another, he stretches me wider to prepare me for his erection, and the anticipation tightens the coil that sprang loose only a moment ago.

He's in no rush, though. He hooks his long fingers and touches a spot I've only read about but never found before, and the coil releases again with an intense wave of pleasure washing over me.

I'm so ready for him to take me.

With a satisfied smile on his glistening lips, he rears on his knees and pushes his pants down.

I gasp.

I imagined him being generously endowed, and he is mouthwateringly so, and for the first time in my life, I want to pleasure a male with my mouth.

"I want to taste you." I reach for him...

"Margo? Are you alright?"

With a start, Margo turned her head and opened her eyes to see Frankie standing in her doorway with a worried expression on her face.

The worry in her friend's eyes was a relief. It meant that she hadn't smelled the arousal that was trapped under the blanket. She must have heard Margo moaning or groaning and had come to check up on her.

"I'm fine. It was just a dream."

Frankie made a sad face. "A nightmare?"

Margo hoped it was dark enough to hide her blush, even from Frankie's new and enhanced vision.

"No. Just a very vivid dream."

"Okay then." Frankie released a breath. "I'm going back to bed. Try to get some sleep."

"Good night, Frankie. And thanks for checking up on me."

8

KIAN

Syssi took off her shoes as soon as they reached the door to their cabin. "I know that I say this about every wedding, but tonight was magical."

Kian smiled. "I agree. I love weddings." He opened the door.

Parker rose to his feet as they walked in.

"Allegra slept the entire time." He sounded disappointed.

"Good." Syssi put a hand on the boy's shoulder. "It means that you have a peaceful aura, and she felt safe with you."

He pursed his lips. "Is that a real thing? I mean, auras?"

"Of course. Babies and animals are more attuned to them than adults. If you were emitting nervous energy, Allegra would have been restless or fussy."

"I was a little nervous," Parker admitted. "I watched over Cheryl's brothers, but they are older, and she was there to help."

"You would have been fine." Kian pulled out his wallet, took out a hundred-dollar bill, folded it, and put it in Parker's hand. "Okidu was here in case you needed help, so there was no reason to be anxious."

Hearing his name, Okidu poked his head out of his bedroom. "Is there anything I can do for you, master?"

"No, thank you. You can close the door now."

"As you wish, master." Okidu dipped his head before doing as Kian instructed.

"Thank you." Parker put the folded bill in his pocket. "I'm available whenever you need a babysitter."

"Good. We will probably be using your services again tomorrow." Kian opened the door for him. "Good night, Parker."

"Awesome." The kid flashed them one last smile before walking out. "Good night."

Syssi shook her head as Kian closed the door. "You practically threw Parker out."

"It's almost morning, and I want to get in bed." He pulled her into his arms.

She laughed. "I guessed as much." She unbuttoned his tuxedo jacket and put her hands on his chest. "You look devastatingly handsome in the tux but even better with nothing at all."

"Ditto, my ravishing beauty."

Perhaps telling Syssi about his problem with Aru could wait for the morning?

Narrowing her eyes, she patted his chest before removing her hands. "Okay, big guy. Out with it."

"Out with what?"

"You were frowning throughout the evening, so I know something is troubling you." She walked over to the kitchenette and popped a pod into the coffeemaker. "Talk to me."

With a sigh, he pulled out a stool and sat down. "It's about my mother speaking with the queen through Aru and his sister. The queen scheduled the first telepathic meeting for tomorrow night after Kri and Michael's wedding, and the following sessions will be at the same time each night, or rather at one o'clock in the morning of the following day."

Syssi tilted her head. "Your mother leaves right after the ceremonies conclude, so that's not a problem."

"Right, but Aru and I will need to be there, and people will notice that we are leaving. My mother offered to invoke her diva status and demand that Aru show up at her cabin each night to tell her about Anumati's history before she goes to bed, and naturally, I would need to be there as well, but that's not a good enough excuse. My mother never issues such unreasonable demands, and people will get suspicious, and by people, I mean my sisters."

Syssi removed the two cups from under the twin spouts of the coffeemaker and put them on the counter. "Maybe we can use Allegra as your excuse. We can transfer her to your mother's cabin and have Parker babysit while she's presiding over the ceremony, and then when the time comes, your mother can call you and say that Allegra is fussy. I will come with you because everyone knows that I wouldn't send you alone to deal with our daughter."

He frowned. "I'm perfectly capable of calming Allegra without your help."

"I know, love." Syssi sat next to him and cradled the coffee mug in her hands. "But someone needs to transcribe what the queen is telling your mother. It's too important to just commit to memory."

He hadn't thought about that, but Syssi was absolutely right. They needed to record the sessions and keep the recordings safe, using the same security protocol as they had for Okidu's journals.

"You are right. I can use my phone to record everything Aru says, and we can transcribe it later. But the excuse of a fussy baby might work once, not every night, and it doesn't solve the problem of Aru leaving at the same time as we do."

Syssi sighed. "I still think that I should be there, taking notes in real time. There is no substitute for that. Transcribing recorded audio is time-consuming, often requiring several hours to transcribe one hour of speech. Live transcribing will eliminate the delay, allowing us to discuss what was learned immediately following the conversation and enabling better absorption of the material and deeper understanding." She pushed a strand of hair behind her ear. "It's like taking notes during class and reviewing them right after as compared to copying the notes someone else made. It's not the same, and the first method is much better."

Kian nodded. "In a way, it will be like attending a lecture, and the information dump will not be easy to absorb. That still leaves the problem of secrecy. How are we going to excuse our early departure?"

"The easiest solution is to tell the family what's going on. It's not like any of us can tell anyone from Anumati about the communication, but if Aru is so concerned, you can ask your mother or Toven to compel everyone to keep Aria and Aru's telepathic connection a secret."

Kian shook his head. "Negal and Dagor don't know about it, and it's crucial to Aru that they don't find out. He doesn't even know that I told you, and he will be furious when he finds out. He didn't even tell Gabi."

"I'm sure he told her."

"He did not. His sister's life is on the line. He wouldn't risk it for anything other than a direct command from his queen."

9

GILBERT

Gilbert leaned over the bed and kissed his wife's cheek. "Karen, honey, wake up."

It was early morning, and they had been doing it all through the night to make sure that she was sleeping and not unconscious.

There was no response.

Panic rising, he shook her shoulder. "Karen?"

Still no response.

"Crap." He ran out of the room, frantic to find Bridget or one of the nurses, but there was no one in there. It was still too early.

Pulling out his phone, he dialed Bridget's number, which he'd programmed in his short favorites list.

"Hello," she answered after several rings, sounding like he'd woken her up from sleep, which he probably had.

"Karen lost consciousness," Gilbert said without bothering with any preamble.

"That's no reason to panic, Gilbert," she said in a much more alert tone. "I'll be there in half an hour."

Half an hour was an eternity, but there wasn't much he could do about that.

"Can you send one of the nurses over? There is no one here."

"Karen is fine, Gilbert. I can see her stats on my phone. I'm coming over more for your sake than hers."

Some of his panic abated, but not all. "I appreciate that, I truly do, but I would feel better if there was a medical professional here to watch over her."

"Gertrude and Hildegard are asleep, and it will take them as long as it will take me to get ready. Do you prefer one of them to come over instead of me?"

He closed his eyes. "I want you."

"I thought so." She ended the call.

"Damn it." Walking back into Karen's room, he scrolled down to another number on his favorites list.

"Gilbert?" Kaia answered almost immediately. "What's happening?"

"Your mother lost consciousness. I called Bridget, and she said that her stats looked okay. She's coming over in half an hour."

"I'll get Darlene to watch over the kids and come down. I'll bring Cheryl with me."

"Good. I want you to take a look at the stats. I don't know if Bridget's telling me the truth, and I don't know what those readouts mean."

"I'll take a look. Hang in there, Gilbert. She's going to be fine. We have to believe it."

"I know." He sighed. "See you in a bit." He ended the call.

Twenty-five minutes later, Bridget arrived and got busy checking Karen's vitals. "She's doing okay." She smiled at Gilbert, but the smile looked forced.

She also hadn't said that Karen was doing great.

"What are you not telling me?" he asked.

Bridget released a breath. "Her blood pressure is a little elevated."

She'd told him before that it would happen as the transition got in full swing.

"Isn't that normal during transition?"

"It's a little higher than what is normal at this stage."

His heart started pounding. "Can't you give her something to lower it?"

Bridget shook her head. "Not unless it reaches critical levels. The best thing for her is to let her body do what it needs to do without interfering." She pulled out her phone. "I'm calling Gertrude. Karen will need round-the-clock supervision until her vitals level out."

So, he hadn't been panicking for nothing, and she'd lied about looking at the readouts on her phone. If she'd seen that Karen's blood pressure was higher than was normal for a transitioning Dormant, she should have told him that.

"Why did you tell me that her vitals were okay when they weren't?"

She gave him a frosty look. "They were fine when I checked half an hour ago. The elevated readout is the most recent one. The blood pressure monitoring is not continuous. The machine was programmed to measure it once every two hours, but I've changed it now to every half an hour."

"I see." That sounded reasonable, and he believed her. "I'm sorry for questioning you."

She lifted a hand. "That's okay. Doctors are not infallible, and it's the duty of family members to remain vigilant and watch over their loved ones. It's especially true when it comes to children. Parents and grandparents know them much better than the doctor who might be seeing them for the first time. If their response to whatever is done to them is atypical, it's important to bring it to the physician's attention."

He nodded. "Thanks for the advice, doc, but since my family is going to be in your care for the foreseeable future, I don't need to remember it. I'm sure you will remind us."

That seemed to placate her, and she gave him a genuine smile. "You have a very nice family, Gilbert, and it's my pleasure to take care of them."

"Thank you."

As Bridget walked out and sat behind the desk in the front room, Gilbert sat on the chair he'd been sitting on throughout the night, took Karen's hand, and kissed the back of it.

"You are going to be okay, my love. You are a fighter." He repeated the same sentence several more times in his head until he started to actually believe it.

When Kaia and Cheryl arrived, he pulled them both into his arms. "Your mother is going to be okay. She's a fighter." He said it with newfound conviction.

10

PETER

Marina stirred in Peter's arms. "What time is it?"

"Seven-fifteen." He kissed the tip of her nose.

She groaned. "I need to get up. I'm on breakfast cleanup, and I'm also working the lunch and dinner shifts today."

"You were supposed to get the night off yesterday and didn't. Are you telling me that you and Larissa are stranding me and Jay tonight as well?"

One of the human servers had sprained her wrist, and the other was suffering from an upset stomach, but Peter had hoped they would both feel better today so he could have Marina to himself the entire evening and night.

"I'm sorry, but with two staff members still out of commission, no one can take time off." She kissed the underside of his jaw. "I'll come to your cabin after I'm done in the kitchen tonight." She smiled. "Anyway, that's the best part, right?"

Peter couldn't argue with that, but as much as he loved Marina in his bed, he also loved seeing her having fun with him outside of it.

"Not good enough," he said, cupping her lush bottom. "Be prepared to be whisked away for a dance or two. I'm sure you are allowed breaks."

"I can't." Marina pulled out of his arms and rose to her feet. She was gloriously naked save for the long blue hair cascading down her front and covering one of her breasts. "We are short-staffed, and I will be running around like crazy. I also need to collect Jasmine's dress from the laundry and return it to her. I should have done it yesterday, but there was no time." She walked into the bathroom but didn't close the door behind her and continued talking to him.

Peter listened with only half an ear to her prattle. Not surprisingly, he was hard again, and all he could think about was getting her back under him.

They hadn't done anything overly naughty last night because Marina had been exhausted after the long day she'd had at work, and she probably wouldn't be up to anything overly strenuous before her shift, but he could think of a few things he could do to her in the shower that would keep her humming with arousal for the rest of the day until she came back to his bed again.

Ah, good times.

Peter's hand wrapped around his arousal, and he gave it a few lazy strokes. He would need to refrain from biting her, but since he had bitten her last night, that shouldn't be too difficult.

When he heard the shower faucet turn on, Peter released his shaft and got out of bed. In the bathroom, steam rose in the shower, and Marina hummed a tune he wasn't familiar with. After emptying his bladder and brushing his teeth, he walked into the small enclosure, positioned himself behind her, and cupped her breasts.

She leaned into him. "That's nice."

"Nice? I don't do nice." He turned her around, clasped her wrists, and lifted her hands over her head.

Marina's eyes became hooded, and as he bent down and twirled his tongue over her right nipple, her breath hitched.

"I don't have much time," she whispered.

"I'm going to be quick." He moved his mouth to her other nipple and licked it before giving it a hard suck.

Marina hissed, but it wasn't in pain, it was in anticipation, and when he nipped it with his front blunt teeth, she jerked even though she must have known what he'd been planning.

It was amazing how quickly they had learned each other's bodies and how to deliver them the most pleasure.

He licked it, coating it with his healing saliva, as she'd known he would.

Immortal males were uniquely well suited for the intricate dance of providing just the right sprinkling of pain to enhance a female's pleasure.

Letting go of Marina's wrists and her nipple at the same time, Peter straightened up and took a step back. "Turn around and put your hands against the wall."

She hesitated. "What are you going to do to me?"

"Something you were craving. Now, do as you're told." He laced his tone with command.

She spun around, braced her hands against the wall as he'd told her, and pushed her ass out.

The vixen had guessed what he had in mind.

"Excellent." He rubbed a hand over her round bottom. "You've earned a spanking for pleasuring yourself without my permission yesterday."

"But I didn't know that I wasn't supposed to," she protested, as the scent of her arousal flared.

"Ignorance of the law is no excuse." He delivered a sharp smack to her left cheek and another one to her right. "But I'll take into account the extenuating circumstances." He massaged her beautiful bottom before delivering two more smacks.

She emitted a sound that was part groan, part moan, and as he slid his fingers over her wet folds, she stuck her bottom out even more and threw her head back.

He pressed his body to hers and nipped her ear. "Do you want me to continue?"

Her answer was immediate. "Yes, please."

"That was the right answer." He took a step back and delivered several smacks to each cheek.

He would have loved to prolong the play, but given the ferocity of Marina's scent, she was about to come, and he wanted all that delicious nectar on his tongue.

Going down to his knees, he lifted one of her legs and licked into her from behind.

"Fuck!" Marina exclaimed.

He chuckled. "Not yet, but soon." He speared his tongue into her wet entrance and wrapped an arm around her to keep her from collapsing in a heap when she climaxed.

Pushing two fingers into her, he sucked and licked on her petals, and when he pressed his palm to her clit, she exploded, and he got to lick up all the bounty.

When he'd had his fill, he rose to his feet and aligned his erection with her entrance. With his arm still wrapped around her waist to brace her, he surged all the way inside of her in one hard thrust.

Marina climaxed again almost immediately, her sheath gripping and squeezing his shaft. Peter tried to prolong the pleasure, but he didn't last more than a few more thrusts before tumbling over the edge after her.

"Marina," he roared as he came, his seed shooting into her and filling her with his essence.

The urge to bite her again was strong, but he somehow managed to keep his wits about him and refrained from sinking his fangs into her neck. Instead, he licked and sucked the spot, which was sure to leave a hickey, but at least it wouldn't make her black out when she needed to report to work.

He was still hard when he brushed her wet hair aside and turned her head to him so he could take her lips in a soft kiss. "Was that quick enough for you?"

She laughed. "It was perfect."

"Yes, it was, and so are you." He withdrew, immediately missing the connection. "Finish washing up. I'll make us breakfast."

11

NEGAL

Negal dropped another pod into the coffeemaker and glanced at the door to Aru and Gabi's room.

It was after eight in the morning, and his commander should have been awake already. On second thought, Aru and Gabi might have been up for a while and were engaging in some morning fun.

The soundproofing on the damn ship was so good that he couldn't hear them, even with his superior hearing. Not unless they got really loud, which they hadn't so far.

When the door finally opened, he cast a smile at the emerging couple. "Good morning. Can I interest you in coffee?"

"Yes, please." Gabi tightened the tie around her short robe and sat down at the dining table. "Did you sleep here last night?"

He pulled out two mugs and put them under the twin spouts of the coffeemaker. "Frankie is back in her room with Dagor, so Margo was not left alone, and I had no excuse to stay."

Gabi's brows furrowed. "I thought things were going well with the two of you. Why is she still playing hard to get?"

Negal's shoulders stiffened. "Margo is not playing any games." He took the two full mugs and placed them in front of Gabi and Aru. "She just needs more time to feel comfortable with me."

"You don't have time," Aru said.

"Then I will make time." Negal popped another pod into the machine. "I like it that we are taking it slow. It allows us time to get to know each other, and there is also something to be said for delayed gratification."

Given the doubtful expressions on Gabi and Aru's faces, they didn't share his opinion, but that was their prerogative. Each couple had its own dynamic, and what was good for one wasn't necessarily good for another.

"I can't delay our departure." Aru took a sip from his coffee. "We've already pushed it with the commander."

"You said that you would try if Margo started transitioning. That means that you've thought of a way to convince the commander why we need to stay in the area for longer."

"I've thought of many things, but none of them are very convincing."

Gabi took her mug and rose to her feet. "I'll leave you two to talk while I get dressed." She leaned down to kiss Aru on his cheek before turning around and padding to their room.

When the door closed behind her, Aru turned to Negal. "Did you talk with Margo about coming with us?"

"I did." Negal took his mug and joined Aru at the table. "Her main objection is that she would need medical supervision while transitioning, and her second objection is about the job Toven promised her if she joined the clan."

Aru leaned back in his chair, holding his mug. "The truth is that Margo can go without medical supervision. Your blood can ensure that she makes it."

It had occurred to Negal that he could give Margo a boost with a transfusion of his blood, but that still didn't make it acceptable for her to transition without Bridget or one of the clan's other doctors watching over her.

"Your blood helped Gabi, and Dagor's helped Frankie, but they still needed a doctor's supervision."

Aru sighed. "What do you suggest we do then?"

"You, Dagor, and your mates can go ahead while I stay behind to be with Margo and join you later. It will be easier to come up with a good excuse for why only I stayed behind."

"Like what?"

Negal rubbed a hand over his jaw. "Now that we need our resources to last much longer than was originally planned, we need to find a way to supplement our allowance. I think it can be an excellent excuse to give the commander. You can tell him that I stayed behind to work on a deal. He knows that we are using the flea market trading as a cover and as a way to refill our coffers."

"That's a possibility." Aru put his mug on the table. "But again, I would rather do it only if we know for sure that Margo is transitioning. We can use that excuse once, but not over and over again."

"Agreed. Although I can think up more plausible excuses. We could have gotten a lead about something suspicious in the Los Angeles area that we need to investigate."

Aru chuckled. "We used that one to explain our prolonged stay in California and our trip down to Mexico. I'm surprised the commander didn't realize that it was highly unlikely for us to find any clues so far from the crash site. There is no way any of the pods landed in this area."

"True." Negal took a sip of his coffee, giving himself time to collect his thoughts. "But information about the pods could have traveled elsewhere. Perhaps we found someone who knew something that could point us in the right direction. Or maybe a pod was taken to a facility for investigation. The commander is well aware that humans are not as primitive now as they were the last time gods visited this planet."

Aru sighed. "And that's another reason for worry. How long do you think he would be able to hide this knowledge from the king?"

"He won't be able to hide it at all, but he can downplay it. As long as humans don't have interstellar travel capability or even communication, he won't consider them a threat."

His words didn't seem to reassure Aru. "Once the Eternal King finds out how close they are to achieving these benchmarks, he will be watching them much more closely. I hope the heir and her clan can do something about it and thwart human advancement in that area."

Negal shrugged. "Humans would also need to come up with a way to keep their travelers in stasis so they could traverse hundreds of light years, and that's an even more advanced technology than traveling at the necessary speed."

12

MARGO

"Good morning," Frankie said as Margo emerged from her bedroom. "Did you sleep well?"

"Yes. Thanks for checking up on me."

"It was our pleasure," Dagor said. "Are you feeling okay?"

"Of course." She forced a smile. "I was fine yesterday, too. Negal was worried for no reason."

"Perhaps," Frankie said. "But it's better to be vigilant, right?"

Nodding, Margo sat down at the breakfast table and accepted the cup of coffee from Frankie.

The truth was that it had been a miserable night. After getting interrupted during her attempt at self-pleasuring, Margo couldn't summon the energy to try again and had fallen asleep, but each time Dagor had peeked into her room to check up on her, she'd woken up and then had trouble falling asleep because her mind had been racing.

"You seem to be doing great." She smiled at Frankie. "From what you've told me, I expected the recovery from transition to be much longer, but you seem to be ready to trek through Tibet."

She wondered if Frankie really wanted to do that. Her friend wasn't fond of camping or hiking. She was a city girl through and through.

The thing was, Aru and his teammates didn't have a choice. They were soldiers, and they had to follow their orders. So, if Frankie wanted to be with Dagor, she had to follow him, and if things went well with Negal, Margo would have to do the same.

She loved the idea of the six of them going on an adventure together, but she wasn't looking forward to roughing it out in nature. She also wasn't happy about passing on the opportunity to be part of Perfect Match, but she wasn't naive enough to believe that she could have everything she wanted.

"I'm not a hundred percent okay to go yet, but I will be by the end of the cruise." Frankie sat next to her with a cup of coffee cradled in her hands. "What are your plans for today?"

"I don't have any."

Frankie regarded her new sundress with a little smirk. "All dressed up with nowhere to go?"

"I thought I'd call Negal and have him meet me at the Lido deck."

Frankie's smirk turned into a grin. "That's a very good plan. Call him right now."

Margo chuckled. "Give me a moment to wake up. I can't call him before I've had my first cup of coffee of the day. I sound like a zombie." She exaggerated slurring her words.

"You can finish your coffee and then call him." Frankie rose to her feet with her coffee cup in hand. "I should get dressed and plan the rest of my day." She sauntered toward her bedroom with Dagor happily trotting behind her.

Margo had a feeling that they wouldn't be emerging anytime soon.

They were probably hopping back in bed to make up for all the sex they had missed last night because they were watching over her.

It would be so nice to be in that stage of her relationship with Negal.

No more awkwardness, no more uncertainty.

To think that Frankie had reached that stage in only a few days was mind-blowing. She'd bedded Dagor the same day they met, or the next, Margo wasn't sure, and then she started transitioning, and now it was all behind them, and they were bonded for eternity.

Even the couples in the romance books she read did not progress so fast from initial meeting to everlasting commitment. If she hadn't seen Frankie with Dagor, Margo would have thought it was just an infatuation, or that her bestie had fallen in lust, not in love, but their feelings for each other were so evident that the air around them sizzled with their love.

Lucky.

They were so incredibly lucky.

With a sigh, she pulled out her fancy new phone and called Negal.

He answered on the second ring. "Good morning. How was your night?"

"Good. And yours?"

"Lonely," he said, melting her heart a little. "I would have loved to sleep on your couch again, but with Frankie and Dagor there, I knew that you wouldn't feel comfortable."

"Are you sure that you would have wanted to spend another night on the couch?"

"I would have loved much more spending it with you in bed, but since that wasn't on the menu, the next best thing was the couch. At least I would have been close to you."

He sounded so sincere. There hadn't been even a tiny note of artifice in his tone, and if that was how Dagor had talked to Frankie, Margo could understand why her bestie had fallen in love with him so quickly.

"That's so sweet of you to say, Negal. To tell you the truth, I would have loved that too."

"Which part? Me on the couch or me in your bed?"

He'd been so truthful, so open, and he deserved no less from her. "The couch, for starters, and then my bed."

It had been on the tip of her tongue to tell him what she'd done last night, but she didn't have the guts. Besides, it had been a failure because she hadn't climaxed, and even if Frankie hadn't interrupted her, she didn't know whether she would have succeeded in reaching that peak.

Usually, Margo needed a steamy book to get in the mood, and she'd never been able to bring herself to completion without one. And it wasn't just the steamy parts. She needed the whole story, and it had to be good and believable for her to be able to enjoy it.

The irony wasn't lost on her.

Here she was, falling for her supernatural hero in a matter of days while she'd sneered at insta-love stories as unrealistic and cheesy.

As the saying went, reality was stranger than fiction, and unbelievably, it could also be better.

Negal cleared his throat. "I've never thought I would enjoy a slow buildup, but here I am, more aroused than I ever was by the prospect of sleeping on your couch."

Margo laughed. "That's desperation talking, and I'm really sorry for that."

"Don't be sorry. I mean it. I enjoy the torture. It's only going to be so much more epic when it finally happens."

What was she supposed to say to that?

What if all this anticipation culminated in a grand disappointment?

Margo wasn't some great seductress, and her former lovers hadn't praised her bedroom prowess.

Instead of responding to his statement, she chose to change the subject. "Would you like to meet me on the Lido deck for a cup of coffee?"

He chuckled. "I made you uncomfortable. I apologize. I would love to meet you on the Lido deck. Do you want me to come get you, or do you want to meet up there?"

"I'll meet you there. How about an hour from now?"

Would an hour suffice to calm the churning butterflies in her stomach? Perhaps she could watch some television. The weddings she'd missed could be a nice distraction.

"Perfect. I'll see you there." Negal ended the call.

Taking a deep breath, Margo rose to her feet, walked back into her bedroom, reached for the remote, and clicked the television on.

13

MARINA

"Is it ready?" Marina asked the woman in charge of the laundry.

Thankfully, the ship was equipped with dry cleaning equipment because Marina wouldn't have entrusted Jasmine's beautiful dress to regular washing even though the label said that it could be handwashed. The dress probably cost a fortune, and if it got ruined in the laundry, Marina would have to pay Jasmine back. Not that she was destitute now that she was earning a decent salary for her work at Safe Haven, but it would be a shame to deplete her savings for something as stupid as not being careful with a loaned dress.

"It is." Aina turned around and took one of the hangers off the rod. "Good as new." She handed the plastic-covered garment to Marina.

"Thank you."

Aina smiled. "You're most welcome. Are you going to be dancing with your immortal at the wedding tonight?"

"No, not tonight. I'm working."

"That's a shame. Your immortal is so handsome, but then they all are. So much nicer than the Kra-ell." Aina leaned closer. "Are they good in bed?"

Marina snorted. "I don't know about all of them, but mine is."

"I thought so." Aina sighed with a dreamy expression on her lined face. "If only I was ten years younger." She laughed. "Make that twenty."

"You are a married woman." Marina playfully punched her bicep. "You don't want Boris to hear you talking like that."

"Boris is not here." Aina waggled her brows. "But I'm just kidding. Even if I was young and pretty like you, I wouldn't have chosen one of them over my Boris. I can look, though, right?"

"You can look as much as you want, just not at my guy."

The smile slid off Aina's face. "Be careful, Marina. You can have fun with the immortal, but don't let him into your heart. Once this job is over, it's back to Safe Haven and bye-bye hunky immortals."

Marina shrugged. "Some of them are stationed at Safe Haven. Peter might ask his chief to send him to me." Or even better, Peter would invite her to live with him in the village.

Aina shook her head. "Don't get your hopes up."

"I'll try." Marina lifted the hanger so the dress wouldn't drag on the floor. "I'd better get this back to its owner. Thanks again." She turned around before Aina could give her more useless advice.

What did all of them think? That she didn't know how unlikely a happy ending with Peter was?

She wasn't dumb, but she was an optimist, and she had a few more days to get Peter to fall in love with her.

In a way, it was good that she couldn't accompany him to last night's wedding or tonight's. The less his mother and his other relatives saw him with her, the less pressure they would put on him to end things between them.

It wasn't hard to guess that Peter's mother was not happy about him spending time with the blue-haired vixen, and hopefully, she didn't know that they were spending their nights together as well.

When Marina reached Jasmine's cabin, she knocked on the door but wasn't surprised that there was no answer. The woman spent most of her time in the staff's lounge, playing cards, talking with everyone who knew a few words in English, or watching television.

Marina knocked again, just in case, and when there was still no answer, she turned around and headed to the lounge.

This time, however, she found Jasmine playing cards not with one of her friends but with Amanda, the gorgeous immortal lady who had been the second bride to get married on the ship and who supervised the decorating of the dining room for all the weddings.

She stopped by their table. "Hello. I'm just returning the dress." She draped it over the back of a chair. "Thank you so much for loaning it to me."

Jasmine frowned. "I didn't expect you to return it until the end of the cruise, and you didn't need to dry clean it either."

"I wanted to bring it back in the same pristine condition I got it."

Amanda regarded her with a small smile playing on her full, red lips. "I expected you to dance at Sharon and Robert's wedding last night. Is everything alright between you and Peter?"

Marina didn't detect any derision in Amanda's tone, and the immortal seemed like she didn't object to Peter's interest in the human serving girl.

"Peter and I are fine. I just needed to work because two servers were out of commission, and we were short-staffed."

Amanda frowned. "What happened to them?"

Did she really care?

"Nothing serious. One slipped, fell, and sprained her wrist, and the other had stomach cramps. The doctor gave her painkillers, but they made her dizzy and sleepy, so she couldn't work."

"That's a shame. You created quite a stir, and it was fun to watch."

Marina's gut twisted, and she swallowed. "A stir?"

"Quite. Everyone was whispering about the beautiful blue-haired girl dancing with Peter."

Right. Maybe a few of the males had said that, but she very much doubted it had been everyone.

"I'm sure many didn't approve of Peter inviting a servant to the wedding as a guest."

Mischief danced in Amanda's deep blue eyes. "Perhaps some did not, but is it important what they think? Many did not approve of my husband either, and some still do not, but it's their problem, not mine."

14

AMANDA

Marina's face brightened. "Is your husband like me?"

The humans working on the ship were compelled to keep the identity of immortals a secret, and since Jasmine was there, Marina couldn't say anything that would indicate they were different in any way.

Amanda laughed. "No, he's not a cute blue-haired young woman. He used to be the antagonist in our story, but he switched sides, and now he's devoted not only to me but to everyone I care for as well, and he will fight his former brothers with everything he has to protect me and mine."

"I see." Marina's eyes dimmed. "So, he's like you."

Amanda nodded. "Fierce and protective," she added for Jasmine's benefit.

The woman had been watching their exchange with curiosity in her strangely colored eyes, and Amanda had a feeling she knew more than she was letting on.

Jasmine's talent with card games was uncanny.

So far, she had beaten Amanda in every game, and Amanda was starting to get suspicious. She had an excellent poker face, with even other immortals having a hard time guessing the strength of her hand, let alone humans.

"You both look formidable," Marina said. "It was nice chatting with you, ladies, but I need to go." She turned to Jasmine. "Thanks again for the dress."

"No problem. If you need another outfit, come see me. I don't have any more evening gowns, but I have a couple of short, fancy dresses that will look great on you."

"Thank you." Marina smiled. "I might take you up on that offer."

After the girl left, Amanda turned back to Jasmine. "It's so sweet of you to offer Marina your clothing."

Jasmine shrugged. "I'm not invited to the weddings, so all my party dresses are going to waste. I'm glad someone gets to enjoy them."

"I'm sorry about that." Amanda lifted her cards. "I wish I could invite you, but the amount of paperwork you would have to sign wouldn't be worth it. Confidentiality is paramount in our business."

Jasmine believed that the cruise was a Perfect Match company retreat and that the couples getting married were success stories of the company's matchmaking algorithm. It was a good cover story, and Amanda had no problem using it. As someone who worked in the human world, she had to lie more than she cared to, but at least it came easy to her.

"Did you meet your husband in a Perfect Match adventure?" Jasmine asked.

Amanda smiled behind her cards. "I'm not at liberty to say, but I can tell you that the circumstances of our first meeting were extraordinary. Dalhu kidnapped me."

Horror filled Jasmine's eyes. "He did what?"

Damn. Amanda had forgotten what had almost happened to the woman. Her so-called boyfriend had sold her to a cartel boss, and if not for Margo and the clan's intervention, she would now be in the scumbag's bed, probably drugged within an inch of her life.

"It wasn't like that. Dalhu was very respectful, and he didn't do anything I didn't agree to. He just wanted me to give him a chance, and since I considered him my enemy, I wouldn't have given it to him under normal circumstances."

"What kind of enemy? Was he working for a competitor?"

"Yes, but I really can't say more about it without revealing things I'm not allowed to."

In a way, it was true. Navuh and the Brotherhood were competing with Annani and the clan for control of all humans, so technically, they were a competitor.

Jasmine pursed her lips. "All this confidentiality business is so frustrating." She looked at the back of Amanda's cards. "Are you going to make a move?"

"I thought it was your turn?"

"No, it's yours."

Amanda looked at the cards on the table, back at the ones she was holding, and then sighed. "I can only add this one here." She put the card down.

Jasmine smiled. "I win again." She put down a series of three and added two after the one Amanda had just added to the series.

Jasmine won just as easily playing rummy as she won playing poker. With her skills, she should have been loaded, but she didn't strike Amanda as rich. She was down to earth, laughed easily, and was friendly with everyone.

"What a surprise." Amanda put the rest of her cards down and leaned back in her chair. "Have you ever been tested for paranormal abilities?"

As Jasmine's smile turned into a grimace, the golden flakes in her eyes started swirling. "The fact that I'm good at card games doesn't mean that I'm using any unnatural means to win."

Amanda let out a breath. "There is nothing unnatural about extrasensory abilities. They are rare, and those who are not gifted are sometimes jealous or afraid of those who are, but that's like vilifying people for being extraordinarily good at math and science or sports."

The flakes in Jasmine's eyes stopped swirling, and her smile returned. "The problem is that there are many people who are good at sports or science, but as you've said, freaks are rare."

Amanda huffed. "I object to that term. I happen to be a neuroscientist, and I research paranormal abilities. I would like to test you for telepathy and precognition."

Usually, people were excited when she told them what she did and that she suspected they had hidden talents, but Jasmine looked like she'd bitten on a lemon.

"How do you perform your tests?"

"At my lab, I have equipment that projects random images, but I can do it here with these cards. If you correctly guess which card I'm holding more times than is statistically expected, that will indicate that you have precognition ability. The more correct guesses, the stronger the ability. As for telepathy, I will hold an image in my head and have you guess what it is. Both are simple tests that can be performed anywhere."

Jasmine leaned back and crossed her arms over her chest. "What happens if you confirm your suspicion that I have some paranormal ability?"

It could mean that she was a Dormant, and Amanda would send immortal males her way to assess affinity. She would also get Lisa to sniff her out and maybe even Syssi to see if her foresight would kick in. If Jasmine's abilities were marginal, she could also bring Mia over and ask her to sit near the woman to enhance her performance and make sure that the test results hadn't been a fluke. But all of that needed to happen without Jasmine being aware of the others' role in her testing.

"I will invite you to come to my laboratory in the university and test you further. I've been researching the subject for many years."

Jasmine was still regarding her with suspicion in her eyes. "And what then? You'll report me to the government so they can use my so-called talents to spy on their enemies?"

Aha, so that was why Jasmine was so skittish about admitting paranormal abilities, and it also reinforced Amanda's conviction that she had paranormal talents and was afraid of the implications.

"I assure you that I will never report you to the government or any other organization that might want to exploit your talents. You will appear in my research as subject number X, and your name will not be mentioned."

Jasmine still didn't look reassured. "I will want that in writing before I agree to participate in any test."

"No problem. You can draft an agreement, and I'll sign it."

"Not good enough. I'm not a lawyer, and I won't know how to close all the loopholes. But since you are working for Perfect Match, you must have access to their nondisclosure paperwork, true?"

Amanda nodded.

"Can you get me a copy?"

Toven could probably print it out for her, but it was no doubt specific to the Perfect Match experience and would not assuage Jasmine's fears.

"I can, but I doubt it's generic enough to cover what you need."

"I'll just use it as a base." Jasmine shrugged. "Or we can scrap the whole idea and just keep playing cards." She collected the discarded cards and started reshuffling them. "For every time you win, I will perform one test. Deal?"

It could be so easy to get into Jasmine's head and win every time, but that would be unethical. Amanda wanted to win the woman's trust the normal way.

"I'll play another game with you, but since we both know you will win, I will not make that deal with you. I'll get you the paperwork you asked for, you will craft an agreement you are comfortable with, and I'll sign it, provided that you don't ask for anything crazy."

Jasmine arched a brow. "Like what?"

"No clue, but I've learned from my brother to read the small print of every contract I sign."

"That's good advice." Jasmine shuffled the cards with a professional magician's flair. "Let's play."

15

NEGAL

Negal arrived at the Lido deck half an hour early, ordered a drink, and secured a table. Margo had said coffee, but if he ordered it now, it would be cold by the time she arrived.

Did Bob even serve coffee?

As Negal looked around to check if anyone was drinking hot beverages, he saw Karen's twins and her little girl arrive at the pool deck with Darlene and Eric, who were carrying a bunch of pool toys.

Why were the kids with their aunt and uncle? Gilbert had said that Kaia was watching them.

He rose to his feet and walked over to where the family had settled down by the pool.

"Good morning." He smiled at the little ones, who were peering at him with curiosity in their eyes. "Are you going swimming?"

"I am." The little girl lifted her arms to show him the pink floating devices she was wearing. "Uncle Eric is going swimming with me." She waved a dismissive hand at her brothers. "They don't know how to swim. They can only float on their ducks."

Negal shifted his gaze to Eric. "You're a brave male taking on these three." Instead of asking if everything was okay, he asked, "Where are their older sisters?"

"With Karen," Darlene said quietly. "Gilbert is freaking out, and they are keeping him company."

Negal's gut twisted. "Is something wrong with their mother?" he asked in a whisper that was audible only to immortals.

"Karen lost consciousness early this morning," Eric whispered just as quietly. "Her blood pressure is elevated more than it normally would be for this stage of transition, and Bridget is a little worried."

Gilbert was probably too distraught to remember that he'd promised to contact Negal if Karen's situation changed.

"She's going to be fine," Darlene said. "Bridget is watching over her. Besides, she was given the best kind of venom." She winked at Negal. "Premium stuff. Not the diluted kind that I got. Still, I made it just fine despite that."

Negal was sure that Darlene's grandfather had something to do with her successful and easy transition. Toven had given her a transfusion of his blood, which compensated for Max's weaker venom.

Then again, Darlene was close to the godly source, and she would have probably made it just fine even without the god's intervention.

"I should go visit her," he said.

Eric clapped him on the back. "Maybe later. Right now, it's pretty crowded down there."

"Right." Gilbert and Karen's older daughters were there, and the ship's clinic was small.

Negal's main reason for visiting was to give Karen a boost with an injection of his blood, and he couldn't do that while she was surrounded by her family. Not unless he thralled all of them, and he would rather not do that if he didn't have to.

"Uncle Eric." The little girl tugged on Eric's hand. "Come to the pool with me."

"Yes, munchkin." Eric bent down, lifted the child, and put her on his shoulders. "See you later, Negal." He walked over to the shallow end of the pool, where he could wade in without having to jump or use the stairs.

When Darlene led the little boys and their floating ducks to the water, Negal turned around and walked back to his table.

A few minutes later Margo arrived, looking fresh and beautiful in the colorful sundress she'd gotten the day before.

He got up and greeted her. "You look lovely this morning." He kissed her cheek.

"Thank you." Her gaze roamed over him. "So do you."

He'd put on his best pair of jeans and a white, button-down short-sleeved shirt. After all, this could count as a date, and he'd dressed with care to honor his partner.

He pulled out a chair for her. "I'm not sure Bob is serving coffee, but I'll ask."

"It's okay if he isn't." She smiled up at him. "I just want to be with you. It doesn't matter what beverage we consume."

"What would you like if coffee is not an option?"

"A ginger ale would be refreshing. In fact, I prefer it to coffee."

"Coming up."

When Negal returned a moment later with a frosty can of ginger ale and two packs of pretzels, he saw Margo watching the children playing in the pool with a smile on her beautiful face.

"Do you like children?" He put the can in front of her.

"Who doesn't?"

He chuckled. "You'd be surprised how many people don't want children around. They are messy and noisy."

Shrugging, she popped the lid and took a small sip. "I love the sounds of children playing, but I have to admit that I hate it when they cry or whine. Whose are they?"

"These are Karen's kids."

Her eyes widened. "The Dormant who's transitioning right now?"

"She lost consciousness this morning, and her older daughters are with her and Gilbert, so their aunt and uncle are taking care of the little ones." Negal raked his fingers through his short hair. "I plan to visit her later. Would you like to join me?"

Perhaps he could somehow use Margo to distract the family while he gave Karen the blood transfusion.

Probably not a good idea since he couldn't tell her why he needed her to distract them. Dagor would be a better choice, and he also knew where to get syringes.

He needed to call him.

Margo frowned. "Are you close friends with Karen?"

Was there a note of jealousy in her tone?

He was Karen's inducer, which was more than a friend, and yet he didn't know the woman well. At some point, he would have to tell Margo about what he had done, but not yet.

"I'm a friend of her mate, Gilbert, and his brother Eric, who is the one playing with the little girl in the pool."

"He seems good with kids." Margo opened the bag of pretzels. "If you want me to accompany you, and if that's okay with Karen's family, I'll go with you to visit her. They might not want strangers to hang around her during a time like this."

"I'm sure it's okay with them." Negal needed to tell Dagor to get a syringe for him and to come over as well, and he didn't want to do that in front of Margo.

She was sharp and observant, and she might put two and two together.

He rose to his feet. "If you'll excuse me, I need to visit the bathroom."

"Of course." Margo smiled up at him. "When do you want to go visit Karen?"

Eric had said that he should wait, but Negal didn't want to take the risk of delaying the blood transfusion. If he waited for the right moment, he might be too late.

"When I get back if that's alright with you."

"Of course, it is."

16

MARGO

A soft smile played on Margo's lips as she watched Karen's brother-in-law playing with his little niece. The child was squealing with glee, and Eric was grinning so broadly that it threatened to split his face.

As her mind substituted Negal for Eric, and a little blond-haired girl who looked like Negal for the dark-haired child in the pool, Margo stifled a chuckle.

That was one hell of a leap. If she didn't find a way to quickly overcome her intimacy problem, and Negal's commander refused to let him stay around for a little longer, Negal would have to leave, and there would be no future for them.

She couldn't go with him because she couldn't keep up with five immortals, and she couldn't expect them to slow down for her. She also couldn't risk transitioning on a trail with no medical facilities for miles around.

Ugh. If she wasn't such a coward, she would have just taken the dive and hoped for the best. She could imagine that it was an arranged marriage and that she was no different from millions of women who had barely any contact with their husbands before their wedding night.

They had survived, and so would she.

Or even better, she could convince her brain that she was in a Perfect Match adventure with Negal and that none of it was real.

With a sigh, Margo pulled out her phone and texted Frankie. *Are you busy?*

Her phone rang a moment later. "For you, never."

Margo laughed. "I wasn't sure you and Dagor were out of bed."

"I'm still in bed, and Dagor is ordering room service."

"I didn't know that was an option. I was under the impression that the staff couldn't handle orders."

"They usually don't, but they don't mind if you call to request a meal and then come get it yourself. He's going to pick it up when it's ready."

"That's good to know." She looked around to make sure that no one was paying her attention and lowered her voice. "Did you bring any romance novels with you on the cruise? Mine are on my phone, which is probably at the bottom of the ocean, and I need something to read to relax."

Frankie chuckled. "You have a real romance going on. What do you need a book for?"

"Reading helps me fall asleep, and I need something sweet and silly that will not make me anxious." It was the truth, just not the whole truth.

"Yeah, I like reading before bed, too, but only if I don't have something better to do to relax me." She laughed. "I have some e-books on my phone, but I can't give that to you for obvious reasons."

Damn. "What about Mia? Do you think she might have brought some paperbacks with her?"

"I don't think she reads romance novels now that she has Toven. But maybe he has some. He writes under several pen names, and the dude is an old-fashioned romantic, so maybe he has a completed manuscript that he needs someone to beta read for him."

"Right, I forgot that he's a writer. But it would be super awkward to read sex scenes written by Mia's fiancé. Do you know what I mean?"

She wouldn't be able to keep from imagining that he was describing making love to Mia.

"Yeah, I totally do. I can ask around for you, but the truth is that the only one I've seen with a paperback book on board was Kaia, and knowing her, it was a science book. Most everyone reads on their phone these days. Come to think of it, they should have a library on this ship."

"That would be wonderful if they do. Is there a suggestion box somewhere? Not that it's going to help me right now, but it could benefit future passengers."

"We should tell Mia. She knows everyone by now, and as Toven's mate, she can talk to the bosses whenever she wants."

"You mean Kian and his wife?"

"Yeah. Anyway, Dagor is back, and I need to go."

Lucky girl.

"Have fun. We'll talk later." Margo ended the call.

Perhaps Jasmine had brought with her some of those historical romance novels she'd talked about. But if she was like Margo, she'd left the paperbacks at home and only read e-books while on vacation.

Some of the covers of romance novels were so racy that reading them in public was embarrassing. Then again, Jasmine didn't seem like the type who got embarrassed about stuff like that. The woman was an extrovert and a flirt, and there was a small chance that she had what Margo needed.

If not for her promise to accompany Negal to the clinic, Margo would have gone to see Jasmine right away, but it would have to wait. Perhaps she could leave Negal with Karen and her family and excuse herself to go see Jasmine.

17

SYSSI

"So, what exactly do you want me to do?" Syssi followed Amanda into the elevator.

"As I said, Jasmine might need a demonstration of precognition and how it works. Did you bring a coin to toss?"

Syssi patted her pocket. "It's right here."

"Good. I also want you to get an impression of her." Amanda tucked a stack of papers under her arm and pressed the button for the staff level. "Maybe she will trigger a vision."

Syssi frowned. "Why would she do that? I've never had a person trigger a vision before. They either come on their own, or I ask for them and actively try to induce them. Do you want me to do that?"

"No way." Amanda leaned against the elevator wall. "It's not important enough to find out what she's about. If it were, I would have an excuse to probe her mind, but it's not. I'm just curious. She's an odd bird."

"In what way?"

"She appears friendly and open, the kind of woman you want in your social circle because she's fun to be around—not stuck up, not timid, quick to smile, and easy on the eyes." Amanda smiled. "I know that's incredibly shallow of me, but I can't help it. It gives me pleasure to gaze upon beauty even if she gives me a run for my money."

Syssi gaped. "No way. No mere human can do that."

Amanda smirked just as the elevator door opened. "Bingo. Things just don't add up. Even if she's had tons of plastic surgery, which I don't think she has, I have to wonder why a beauty like her is not on the covers of magazines or playing in movies. She says she's an actress, so she's putting herself out there. Why hasn't she landed any roles?"

"Now I'm really curious."

"I had Lisa sniff her." Amanda headed down the corridor to the staff lounge.

"What did she say?"

"She wasn't sure."

"So, you think Jasmine is a Dormant."

Amanda nodded. "Everyone who's met her so far has liked her, including me. I just have this itchy feeling that there is more to her than meets the eye, and I'm not talking about the possibility of dormant godly genes."

They were about to enter the lounge when Syssi stopped and put a hand on Amanda's arm. "If you have a bad feeling about her, that's a good enough excuse to enter her mind. After all, she's on our turf, and if she's up to no good, we need to know."

"But that's the thing. I don't have a bad feeling. I like the woman." Amanda shrugged. "I'm just curious, and you know me. I won't rest until I get to the bottom of things."

"Yeah. That's what makes you such a good researcher."

As they entered the lounge, Syssi had no trouble identifying Jasmine from Amanda's description. She was indeed beautiful, but Amanda had exaggerated. Jasmine wasn't in the same league as her sister-in-law.

Jasmine sat on the couch between two men who were practically drooling over her, but she seemed oblivious to their lustful glances and looked completely absorbed in the sitcom she was watching.

It was an old *Big Bang Theory* episode that was playing in English with subtitles in Russian.

"Hello, Jasmine," Amanda said. "I'm back."

The woman turned to look at them, and a bright smile spread over her face. "Awesome." She rose to her feet and offered Syssi her hand. "You must be the sister-in-law Amanda mentioned. The one who works with her in the university."

"That's me." Syssi took the woman's hand. "Nice to meet you, Jasmine. I'm Syssi."

"The pleasure is all mine." Jasmine gifted her with another dazzling smile.

Unless the woman was a superb actress, the warm smile was genuine. Syssi felt as if she was truly glad to meet her and wanted to get to know her, and since Jasmine wasn't a movie star, she probably wasn't such a great performer.

"Let's sit over there." Amanda pointed to the table. "I printed out the Perfect Match nondisclosure agreement for you, and I also drafted a one-page agreement between us that I think will satisfy your needs."

Jasmine eyed the big stack of papers under Amanda's arm. "Do you expect me to read all of that right now?"

"I highlighted the relevant passages." Amanda put the stack of papers on the table. "Does anyone want something to drink?"

Syssi shook her head. "I just had coffee, so I'm good for now."

"Diet Coke for me, please." Jasmine sat down.

Syssi suppressed a chuckle. Evidently, Jasmine had no idea how important Amanda was, or she would have never asked her to serve her.

Perhaps that was precisely what endeared her to Amanda. Jasmine treated her just like she would any other person she befriended. No special treatment.

Watching her read through the document gave Syssi the opportunity to observe the woman without having to hide her interest. She was nearly as tall as Amanda, but she had curves. Where Amanda appeared slim and athletic, Jasmine had large breasts, rounded hips, and a lush bottom. Maybe that was why she hadn't made it big in movies. Supposedly, the camera added at least fifteen pounds to a person's appearance, and actresses had to be super-slim to look good on the screen.

Still, her face was so gorgeous that it was hard to look away from her. Jasmine's eyes had the most unusual ring of floating gold flakes around the pupils, and the irises were chocolate brown with some amber hues. Her hair was wavy, thick, long, and almost black, with a few golden strands that were probably not natural. Her skin looked perfect even though she didn't have much makeup on.

"Here is your Coke." Amanda put a cold can in front of Jasmine and sat across from her. "If you need me to explain anything, let me know."

"No, I'm good." Jasmine sighed. "I read the one you wrote, and I think it's good enough." She lifted her eyes to Amanda. "If you wanted to sell me to the government, no paper would protect me anyway."

"True." Amanda popped the lid on her can of soda. "But you can take my word to the bank, and I vow to protect your identity and never sell you out to the government or any other agency who might be interested in your talent."

"I can vouch for Amanda," Syssi said. "When she tested me and saw that my scores were off the charts, she hired me, and we're still working together. If she was a recruiter for the government, I wouldn't be here."

That got Jasmine's attention. "What's your talent?"

"Precognition." Syssi smiled and pulled out the coin from her pocket. "I brought this to demonstrate and also to test you. Do you know the statistical probability of guessing heads or tails correctly?"

"Fifty-fifty?"

"Correct." Syssi flipped the quarter in the air.

18

AMANDA

When Syssi guessed the first four tosses correctly, Jasmine's eyes widened, and when she continued guessing the next ten, she gaped.

"Unbelievable." Jasmine shook her head. "You could make a killing at poker."

Syssi chuckled. "I never tried applying my precognition in a card game. With my luck, it wouldn't work. Besides, it would be cheating."

A blush tinted Jasmine's cheeks. "I'm just good at reading people's responses, and that's a legitimate part of the game, so it's not cheating."

"It might also be precognition, and that's what I want to test." Amanda reached for the card deck. "To eliminate the possibility that you are reading my responses, I will turn my back on you so that you won't see my face when I lift a card and ask you what it is. Or better yet, close your eyes and try to guess."

"I'm curious to see what my results will be." Jasmine glanced at the printed page Amanda had prepared. "Would you mind signing this before we start? I know that it's probably worthless, but I will still feel better having a signed document from you."

"No problem." Amanda whipped out the tiny pen she'd stashed in the pocket of her leggings just for that purpose and signed the page. "I don't even know your last name, so I really can't sell the information to anyone."

Jasmine cast her an amused look. "Kevin had my passport in his hands. I'm sure he took a peek."

"Probably," Amanda admitted. "But I promise you that you have nothing to fear from me or any of us. We are not in cahoots with the government or anyone else."

Jasmine let out a breath. "I'm too curious to keep objecting. Let's start with me closing my eyes while guessing which card you are looking at."

"Good idea." Amanda cast a sidelong glance at Syssi. "Your job is to write down the results." She handed her the pen and a clean page.

When Jasmine closed her eyes, Amanda pulled out a random card from the pack. It was the four of spades.

"What card am I looking at?" she asked in her best neutral tone.

Jasmine's forehead furrowed. "It's a numbers card, and it's black, which means that it's either spades or clubs, but I can't guess the number."

"That's very good. It's four of spades." Amanda put the card on the table. "For some reason, colors are easier to guess, and not just in the case of cards where there are only two. Perhaps they make a bigger impression on our brains."

Jasmine opened her eyes. "Do you want to repeat the test the same way, or do you want to try it while my eyes are open, and you are with your back to me?"

"Let's try it a few more times this way."

Jasmine guessed the color of the next two cards correctly, but she said that one of them was a face card when it was another number card, and she was completely off for the next five.

"I guess I don't have precognition talent." She shrugged. "Oh, well. I told you that's not the reason I'm good at card games."

"It's not unusual for the results to diminish after several tries," Syssi said. "Normally, I start guessing wrong after ten correct guesses. It's like the brain becomes tired."

Amanda nodded. "We have observed that happening with all our test subjects that had some talent. You can improve with practice and keep guessing accurately for longer, but eventually, you will start guessing wrong."

Jasmine pursed her lips. "You are the expert, so I have to take your word for it. Do you want to try the other methods?"

"Not yet. I want you to rest. But we can test other abilities that require different mental muscles. This time, I will think about an object, and you will try to guess what it is."

"Do I need to close my eyes?"

"No. I want you to look into mine and try to catch what I'm thinking. It's going to be an object, but it can be anything from a lemon to a spaceship. Ready?"

Jasmine nodded.

Amanda thought of a red rose, which was easy to visualize, and those with even weak telepathic ability could sense the bold color.

"What am I thinking of?"

Jasmine scrunched her nose. "A flower."

"Good. What kind of flower?"

"I don't know."

"What color is the flower?"

Jasmine closed one eye and pursed her lips. "White?"

"No." Amanda was disappointed. "It was a red rose."

"Damn." Jasmine grimaced. "I was close."

"What made you think that it was a flower?" Syssi asked.

Jasmine smirked. "Amanda's nostrils flared a little like she was imagining smelling something, and I knew it was something good because her eyes widened a tiny bit, and her forehead remained smooth."

"Those are exceptional observational skills." Syssi looked at Amanda. "True?"

"Indeed. It's not a paranormal talent, but it's a useful one. Can you tell when people are lying?"

Jasmine huffed out a laugh. "If I could, would I have believed Alberto when he told me that he loved me? But you are right. If I knew for a fact when people lied, I could learn the tells. My observational skills are good because of my acting background. Mimicking behavior is a very important aspect of acting, so I trained myself to pay attention to body language and facial expressions."

Syssi tilted her head. "Were you good at poker before you studied acting?"

"I joined the drama program in middle school, and I didn't play poker back then, so I don't know how good I would have been at poker without the training that started in that program."

Amanda had a strong urge to delve into Jasmine's head and find out if she was telling the truth.

She didn't emit any scents that would indicate it, but it was possible that she was a method actress, capable of convincing herself that she was telling the truth.

"Let's try another object." Amanda thought of a chair. A simple wooden chair that didn't evoke any emotions in her. "Well?" she asked.

Jasmine lifted her hands in surrender. "No clue. You must have thought about something very mundane and boring."

"That's correct. I thought of a chair."

"Does that count as a good guess?" Syssi asked.

"It's not a paranormally good guess, but it's not bad. With proper training, Jasmine could become an excellent interrogator."

The woman recoiled. "No way. I would never do something like that."

"Why not?" Amanda asked.

"I don't want to deal with the ugly underbelly of society. I want to be surrounded by pretty things and good people."

Amanda snorted. "Then you've chosen the wrong profession. The movie industry is a nest of vipers."

"I know." Jasmine sighed. "When I started acting in middle school, it was great because everyone in the acting club was like me. It was the first time I felt comfortable in my own skin. No one thought that I was overdramatic or that I was an attention seeker." She chuckled. "Well, I was, but so was everyone else in the club. Actors like attention. Anyway, it got even better in high school, but then the real world was a different story. Instead of well-meaning drama teachers, I was suddenly dealing with people who thought they could exploit my ambition to get me to do things I would never do otherwise, and I realized how naive I was when I dreamt of a career on the big or small screen. Still, I love acting too much to do anything else. I might be only getting small parts and playing in commercials, but it's better than nothing."

19

KIAN

Kian stood on the top deck, watching the harbor crew at work preparing the ship for departure.

The pilot's boat approached, carrying the harbor pilot tasked with guiding the cruise liner out of the seaport. Kian didn't like an outsider boarding his ship, but harbor pilots were experts in local water conditions and port intricacies, and they were essential for the safe exit of the ship from the congested seaport area.

Once onboard, the pilot would collaborate with the captain and the bridge team, helping them navigate the ship out safely, and after it was done, he would depart on the small boat that was trailing the ship out to sea.

Kian had learned a lot about the operations of cruise ships on this voyage, and it was much more complicated than running hotels, but Shai had run the numbers, and it was a profitable business, provided of course that the passengers were the paying kind, and not his family.

He contemplated purchasing two more ships for the clan, and if that operation proved successful, to keep adding more. He needed to put someone in charge of the operations, though, and he was not happy with the shortlist of candidates he'd compiled. None had experience in the cruise line industry, and Ragnar, who was the most knowledgeable and experienced in the hospitality business, had enough on his plate with running the clan's hotels.

The human staff that used to serve the Kra-ell were doing a remarkable job, given that they had no prior experience save for the voyage that had taken them out of captivity. Kian planned on visiting Safe Haven and offering them the option of permanent employment in the clan's cruise liner business.

Amanda wouldn't be happy because she'd hoped he would invite some of them to work in the village, especially the talented cooks, but he believed that they would be better off traveling the world and seeing places they wouldn't otherwise get the chance to visit.

It had never sat well with him that they had to be confined to Safe Haven after spending their lives in captivity, but for now, it was the best option for them and for the immortals. The humans were not ready to live independently, and their knowledge of aliens had to be protected. Working on a cruise line could solve both issues.

"I thought I would find you here." Onegus leaned against the railing next to Kian. "Edgar called. He inspected the helicopter and confirmed that we got all we were promised." He chuckled. "He's as excited as a kid with a new puppy. When should I tell him to fly the craft over?"

"I want us to be far enough from the shore so that no one sees the helicopter landing on the ship." Kian cast Onegus a sidelong glance. "He should take off in about two hours unless that will be too far for its range?"

"This bird has great range, so it's fine even with Ed making a detour and flying south before heading out to sea from an unpopulated spot."

"Good plan."

"I'm glad we finally got the helicopter," Onegus said. "With the Clan Mother on board, it's crucial that we have an escape vehicle."

Kian crossed his arms over his chest. "If we are under attack, evacuating her with the helicopter is not a good move. I prefer to have her where I can protect her. But it's good to have an aircraft for other emergencies."

"It depends on the situation." Onegus rubbed a hand over the back of his neck. "The helicopter can seat twelve, which is plenty of Guardian power to protect the Clan Mother, but if the enemy has missiles, then the helicopter will become a death trap."

"True," Kian agreed.

The best option was to remain hidden, but the unexpected encounter with the cartel and then the Doomers in Acapulco had undermined the secrecy of their location. They'd managed to salvage the situation by altering the ship's travel plan, but it was still possible for the Brotherhood to deduce where the adversaries who'd annihilated the Acapulco cell had come from.

"Are you coming to Michael's bachelor party?" Onegus asked.

"I wasn't invited." Kian cast him a smile. "Which I'm thankful for. I don't want to spend every afternoon at a different bachelor party. I want to spend as much of my vacation time as possible with my wife and daughter."

As if talking about them had summoned them, Syssi walked over with Allegra in her arms. "Allegra wants her daddy." She handed him their daughter.

As Kian took her and hugged her to his chest, his heart swelled with love. "Did you miss me, sweetie?"

"Daddy." She lifted her arms, cupped his cheeks, and planted a slobbery kiss on his lips before turning to watch the activity taking place below.

"I'll see you at the wedding," Onegus said before turning on his heel and walking away.

"Look, Daddy." Allegra pointed at one of the other cruise ships. "Big."

"Yes, it's big." Smiling, he shifted his gaze to Syssi. "Her vocabulary is growing by the day. Is that normal for a child her age?"

She chuckled. "Not at all. But we know that Allegra is special." She leaned and kissed their daughter's cheek. "Right, sweetheart?"

"Mama," Allegra said in a tone that conveyed her amusement.

"She says even more with tonality than with words, and right now, she's communicating that she thinks you are being silly, but she likes it."

Syssi laughed. "I know." She took Onegus's spot, leaning against the railing and crossing her arms over her chest. "Amanda and I visited Jasmine earlier, and Amanda tested her paranormal abilities."

For some reason, apprehension flickered through him. "And?"

"Her results were interesting. She guessed the first few cards correctly, which was impressive, but then her accuracy diminished, which is common even for those who have a smidgen of real paranormal ability. But that wasn't the interesting part. Her observational skills are phenomenal. She noticed subtle changes in Amanda's expressions, tiny cues that even I missed. It's not a paranormal ability, but it's an important talent."

Kian mulled over her words, the wheels in his mind turning. Jasmine's unique skill set could be an asset, but only if she proved to be a Dormant. Otherwise, she would need to find a use for her unique skill set in the human world.

"What about affinity? Did you feel any toward her?"

Syssi hesitated. "Jasmine is friendly, upbeat, and very likable. She's also not easily impressed or intimidated by others, which I admire. On the flip side, she's very hesitant about referring to her abilities as extrasensory. I have a feeling that she's had bad experiences with people who caught her doing things she shouldn't have been able to do, and that's why she's hiding what she's actually capable of." Syssi canted her head. "I keep wondering whether her small oddities justify a thrall to find out what she's hiding."

Kian shrugged. "We will thrall her before we let her off the ship, so if she's hiding something that we should be aware of, we will find out then. In the meantime, I'm not worried about her, even if she has some nefarious plans. She's just a human, and she's being watched."

"Jasmine doesn't have nefarious intentions," Syssi said. "At least, I don't think she does. But maybe we should ask Edna to probe her. Her probe is not a thrall, so it's not considered breaking the rules." She shifted closer to him. "After all, Edna probed me when she first met me, making sure that I wasn't taking advantage of you."

Kian wrapped his arm around her shoulders. "You are welcome to take advantage of me any time you want, my love."

20

NEGAL

As Negal walked toward the clinic with Margo at his side, he was running through different scenarios in his head for a way to administer a blood transfusion to Karen without anyone being any the wiser.

Through the open door of the clinic's front room, Negal saw Karen's older daughters standing next to the nurse's desk. Kaia looked distraught, her eyes wide and darting around the room as if seeking some anchor in the storm of her thoughts. Her younger sister looked worried but calm and collected.

Raking her fingers through her long blond hair, Kaia mumbled under her breath, "I need to crack the code. I'm so close, but I don't have it yet, and I need it. What am I missing?"

Negal exchanged a quick glance with Margo before returning his attention to Kaia. He had no idea what she was talking about.

What was the code she believed she had deciphered?

"You will find the answer." Cheryl, her younger sister, moved closer and wrapped her arms around Kaia in a tight hug. "You always do."

The words of comfort seemed to pierce through the haze of the young woman's distress. "Yes, I know. It's just that I'm almost there, and once I get it..." She finally noticed Negal and Margo standing outside the door and stopped. "Hi." She forced a smile. "If you are here to ask about my mother, there is no change. She is still unconscious."

The door to the inner room opened, and Doctor Bridget stepped out, her gaze sweeping over the small crowd before settling on Karen's oldest daughter. "Kaia, you need to calm down. Your mother is not dying. She's stable and doing just as well as most of the other Dormants in this stage of transition. There is no need for alarm. An easy and straightforward transition like Frankie's is the exception, not the norm."

The tension slowly dissipated from Kaia's expression, and she took a deep breath. "What about her blood pressure? You said that it was elevated more than it was for other Dormants during this stage."

"It's stable," Bridget said. "There is no need for you to be hovering around here. Go inside, talk to your mother for a little bit, and then go take care of your brothers and sister. They need you more than your mother does right now."

Kaia's thunderous expression indicated that she didn't like getting lectured by Bridget, but her only response was a nod.

Negal was glad that the doctor was sending Kaia away. It would be great if she did the same to the younger sister. With only Gilbert remaining, it would be easier to execute his plan.

Where was Dagor, though?

He needed the guy to get him a syringe and to create a distraction.

"Can we see Karen?" he asked the doctor.

"Perhaps a little later." She cast him an apologetic smile. "I don't allow more than two visitors at a time. After Kaia and Cheryl are done, you can go in and keep Gilbert company for a little bit." She looked at Margo. "I'm sorry, but you'll have to wait outside."

Margo looked disappointed, but she nodded. "I understand. I don't really know Karen, but I'm curious about the process."

"When Negal goes into Karen's room, I'll answer any questions you might have."

Negal needed to get Gilbert out of the room as well, but first, he needed the damn syringe.

"Hello," Dagor said from behind him. "I was looking for you." He signaled with his eyes that he wanted Negal to follow him.

Negal let go of Margo's hand. "I need to have a word with Dagor. I will be right back."

She smiled. "I'll stay here and talk with the doctor."

Negal followed Dagor to the coffee station. "Do you have it?" he asked quietly.

"I do." Dagor took a paper cup, put it under the coffeemaker spout, and dropped a pod into the slot. "Do you want coffee?"

"I don't, but Margo might want some."

He felt Dagor's hand slide into his pocket and deposit his loot.

"I have more. I'll leave them in your bathroom in one of the drawers."

"Thank you."

When the machine stopped brewing, Dagor removed his cup and placed a new empty one under the spout. "How are you going to do it?"

"I'm not sure yet. Do you have any ideas?"

Dagor looked around to make sure that no one was within hearing distance. "I was thinking about delivering a cup to Gilbert and *accidentally* spilling it on him, but I'll wait for it to cool down."

"That's a good plan. Make another one, and I'll pretend to drink it when I go into Karen's room. I'll spill it over Gilbert."

Dagor nodded. "That's a better plan. You have a good reason to visit them. I don't."

Negal hadn't told Dagor about his role in Karen's transition, but his friend had probably guessed it, and Negal wasn't going to bother with denials.

When the elevator dinged at the end of the corridor, Negal looked in the direction of the sound. "More visitors will make this more complicated."

His eyes widened when he saw Toven striding down the corridor with a determined expression on his face and his glow on full display.

"What's going on with him?" Dagor asked in a whisper. "He never glows."

"I'm wondering the same thing."

"The Clan Mother asked me to perform the blessing ritual in her name," Toven announced, sweeping into the clinic's front room with a flourish Negal had never seen him show before.

Dagor leaned closer to Negal. "Are you thinking the same thing I'm thinking?"

"Yeah, I think he's about to do what I had in mind." Negal walked over to watch the performance from the opened door with Dagor right behind him.

Bridget eyed Toven with skeptical eyes. "Karen is not in critical condition."

"I thank the merciful Fates for that, but why wait? Karen is like family to me, and it's my privilege and duty to bless her."

"How are they related?" Dagor whispered in Negal's ear.

"No clue, but we need to support him."

"I wish I could bless Karen," Negal said out loud. "But only those with royal blood can do that. It's a sacred ritual that no one else is allowed to witness."

Margo turned to him with questioning eyes. "You didn't tell me about a blessing and neither did Frankie."

"Frankie didn't need it, and I didn't know whether either of the gods would volunteer to bless Karen. It's not as if I can speak in their name."

Bridget rose to her feet. "Very well. I'll let Gilbert know."

"Can Cheryl and I stay here?" Kaia asked Toven.

"I prefer for everyone to stay outside. My full concentration is needed for the ritual, and I don't want to get distracted."

Kaia nodded. "Thank you for doing this for our mother."

Toven's eyes softened. "I'm glad to help in any way I can."

As Bridget entered Karen's room and everyone other than Toven left the clinic, Toven snuck a quick look at Negal and dipped his head in acknowledgment. "I entrust you two with guarding the door." He shifted his gaze to Karen's bewildered daughters. "It's part of the ritual. It needs to be done in total secrecy."

Negal bowed to the royal. "Dagor and I are honored to be the guardians of the blessing."

Once Bridget and Gilbert joined them out in the corridor, Negal closed the door, and he and Dagor stationed themselves in front of it.

"The Clan Mother and Toven have performed the ritual for several of the transitioning Dormants," Bridget said. "I don't know what she did, but it seemed to help. They all did better after that."

Gilbert wrapped an arm around each of Karen's daughters. "We are grateful for any help we can get."

21

KIAN

Kian hopped into the cabin of the newly acquired helicopter. "It's much more luxurious than I expected."

"It's not just about the fancy leather seats," Edgar said. "It's also about the performance and safety. Compared to the one we have in the village, this one provides a remarkably smooth and quiet ride thanks to the advanced technological innovations."

As Edgar continued to list all the marvelous avionic features, Kian understood only a fraction of what he was talking about, but the pilot was so excited that he felt bad about stopping him and pretended to listen with interest.

When he was finally done, Kian thanked him and stepped out of the craft. All that had interested him was that the copter could transport up to twelve passengers, had an average cruising speed of approximately 138 knots, could travel a maximum range of 475 nautical miles with standard fuel tanks, and had a maximum endurance of about four hours and thirty minutes, ensuring that it could stay airborne for extended periods when needed. It could also reach a maximum flight altitude of 20,000 feet. Those were impressive specs that made it a valuable asset, and it had certainly cost accordingly.

The truth was that the clan needed to upgrade its fleet, and Kian had no intention of leaving the helicopter with the ship. It was coming home with them.

He should call Aru to invite him to see the helicopter and use the opportunity to tell him about Syssi joining them for tonight's session with the queen. Except, it didn't look like Edgar would be leaving his new baby anytime soon, and the conversation Kian needed to have with Aru had to be private.

Instead, Kian headed back to his cabin and sent the god a text message, asking Aru to join him.

When the doorbell rang a short while later, Kian opened the door and motioned for Aru to enter. "Thank you for coming on such short notice."

Aru looked worried. "I knew you wouldn't ask me to come if it wasn't important. I assume that this is not a social meeting." He glanced around the cabin. "Otherwise, you would have invited me together with my mate, and yours would be here."

"Syssi took Allegra to see her grandparents, so we have the place to ourselves." Kian motioned to the couch. "Please, take a seat. Can I offer you a drink?"

"Sure. I'll have whatever you are having."

Kian walked over to the bar and pulled out his best bottle of whiskey. "I have a confession to make, and I hope you won't be too upset about it." He poured two shots, joined Aru in the living room, and handed him one. "Syssi knows about your telepathic communication with Aria."

The temperature in the cabin dropped by at least ten degrees. "You vowed not to tell anyone." Aru's tone was frosty. "My own mate doesn't know."

Kian raised a hand, signaling for him to calm down. "Syssi didn't hear it from me or anyone else. She saw Aria in a vision, and she recognized her as your twin sister. She says that you look a lot alike. When she confronted me about it, lying to her would have been futile and would have only upset her, so I confirmed her guess."

"Who else knows?" Aru asked.

"Just Syssi and my mother," Kian assured him. "You know that Syssi is a seer. You must have assumed that sooner or later, she would see your sister."

Kian watched as Aru processed the information, his initial anger giving way to reluctant acceptance.

"I was afraid of that, but I hoped that she wouldn't get a vision about me and my sister." Aru rubbed a hand over his face. "Aria and I have guarded this secret throughout our lives, and the only reason we were discovered was that the Supreme Oracle saw us in one of her visions. Since then, we have lived in fear that other seers will discover us. The Supreme promised to somehow hide us from other seers, but apparently, she wasn't successful. If Syssi saw us, others could as well."

"Syssi knew you, and she knew that you were communicating with someone on Anumati. When she saw Aria with the queen and the Oracle, it was clear to her that she was the one you were communicating with. Others don't have the same knowledge."

Aru let out a breath. "I hope you are right. I fear for my sister."

"I bet you do." Kian cast him a sympathetic look. "I would be worried too, but not because Syssi is privy to the information. You have nothing to fear on her account."

"I hope so." Aru finished the whiskey in his glass and put it down on the table. "So, this is it? You wanted to tell me that she knows?"

Kian shook his head. "When I told Syssi about the meeting tonight, asking her advice about the best way to excuse our absence from the celebration, she had a few good suggestions. She offered to come along and transcribe what was being said. She pointed out that the information the queen would share with my mother was too important to entrust to memory. It should be written down."

"I hadn't thought of that, but I agree with your mate. I hoped to conduct the meeting in Anumatian, which would have made it easier for Aria and me, but it might not have been possible anyway because your mother is not fluent in it."

"She's not." Kian regarded Aru, noting the furrows on his forehead. "Perhaps you should tell Gabi about Aria. Keeping a secret from your mate is not healthy for the relationship. It would also make your departure less suspicious if you leave with Gabi. People would just assume that you wanted to continue celebrating in private."

He was such a hypocrite, giving advice to Aru about keeping secrets from his mate when he was doing it himself. Only in his case, he was doing it to protect Syssi more than his mother.

Aru shook his head. "I can't. I will tell Gabi that I need to do something in secret and ask her to cover for me. She will back me up."

"Of course. Syssi and I will claim that Allegra is fussy. I will also ask for the wedding ceremony to be scheduled earlier. If we start at eight o'clock in the evening instead of ten at night, by the time we need to leave the party will start dwindling, and it will look less suspicious."

Aru smiled for the first time since arriving at Kian's cabin. "That's the best idea you've had so far."

22

MARGO

Margo walked down the softly lit corridor with Frankie on one side and Mia riding her wheelchair on the other. "Toven looked like one of those evangelical preachers on television when he showed up declaring that he was sent by the Clan Mother to give Karen a blessing, and he was glowing like a neon sign. I've never seen him act like that."

"Are you serious?" Mia laughed. "I had no idea that he was going to do it."

Margo had known Mia since she was five years old, and she'd never been a good liar. "Toven didn't tell you that he was going to bless Karen?"

"He said he was going to visit her and Gilbert and offer his support. He didn't say anything about a blessing."

For some reason Mia was lying, and Frankie wasn't calling her out on that, which was suspicious as hell.

Margo stopped walking and put her hands on her hips. "Okay, you two. What are you hiding from me?"

"Nothing." Mia looked at her with fake innocence in her eyes. "Toven really didn't tell me. Perhaps the Clan Mother called him while he was on his way to see Karen and Gilbert and asked him to bless Karen."

Frankie nodded. "Yeah. That's probably what happened."

Margo shook her head. "Fine. Be like that." She resumed walking. "It's a shame I can't tell Jasmine about it. She would have gotten a kick out of Toven's performance."

Frankie snorted. "I can teach you a few workarounds, but perhaps I shouldn't right before we are going to see Jasmine. You really shouldn't tell her anything that will make her suspicious."

Margo stopped in front of Jasmine's cabin door and rang the bell. "I'd rather not know. Don't tell me."

Knowing Frankie, she wouldn't be able to help herself and would tell her anyway.

She rang the doorbell again and waited a couple more seconds before turning away. "Jasmine is never in her cabin. She spends her days in the staff lounge."

When they reached the lounge, Margo was surprised to find Jasmine sprawled on one of the comfy-looking couches and not sitting at one of the tables, playing poker with the staff.

"Hi." She waved them over. "Are you here to see me?"

"Who else?" Margo sat down next to her on the couch. "Are you resting after a long day of poker wins?"

"I wish." Jasmine pushed her thick hair behind her shoulder. "Do you know a lady named Amanda?"

Margo nodded. "Where did you meet her?"

"She came to see me. My poker playing has made me famous, and she wanted to see if I had any paranormal talents. She is a professor of neuroscience who researches paranormal abilities, and she wanted to test me."

Kian's gorgeous sister was a professor?

To Margo, it was almost as impressive as being a demigoddess, which actually meant a demi-alien. "I met Amanda at the wedding last night, but she didn't say anything about being a professor." She turned to Frankie. "Did you know that she was a researcher?"

Frankie shook her head. "I didn't."

"I did," Mia said. "She tested me too."

Margo already knew what Mia's talent was, but she hadn't known that she'd been tested by a neuroscientist. According to what Mia had told her, it had been Kian's wife who had figured out her talent.

"What kind of tests did she run on you?" Margo asked Jasmine to preempt her asking Mia the same question.

"Oh, the usual stuff you see in movies," Jasmine said with a playful roll of her eyes. "Card guessing, identifying objects without seeing them, guessing what she was thinking about, etc. It was pretty out there, but I cooperated because I was curious to see if I had any paranormal talents."

"And?" Frankie prodded. "Do you have any?"

Jasmine shrugged. "My so-called 'talents' are more about observation and intuition than anything mystical. I guessed a few cards more or less correctly, but I got most of them wrong, so I guess it was just luck."

Margo was fascinated by the fine line between science and the supernatural, and now she knew an expert in the field. Would Amanda mind if she asked her a few questions?

"Your exceptional ability to read people might be a paranormal talent," Mia pointed out. "If it was normal, everyone could do it, right?"

Jasmine smiled with a hint of pride flickering in her eyes. "I trained myself to notice all those little details. Observing human behavior is essential for an actor. After all, I need to be able to portray emotions in a thousand different ways according to the characters I'm supposed to play."

As a conversation about different acting methods ensued, Margo's mind wandered to Negal and her quest for a romance novel that would put her in the right mood.

"Daydreaming about your new boyfriend?" Jasmine pulled her out of her reveries.

"How did you know?"

"Easy. You had this dreamy expression on your face, with your lips lifting in a ghost of a smile. Things are going well with Negal, I assume?"

Margo nodded. "You could say that." She felt a blush creep up her cheeks as she remembered the kiss they had shared.

Jaz laughed. "So, are you taming the rogue?"

"Negal is not a rogue. He's gentle and patient and kind of sweet. But speaking of rogues, do you have any romance novels that I can borrow? I need something relaxing to read before going to sleep."

"I have a couple." Jasmine rose to her feet. "But I have to warn you. They are quite racy."

"Perfect." Margo smiled up at her. "That's precisely the kind I need."

Jasmine's lips twisted into a knowing grin. "So, it's that kind of relaxing."

Margo rolled her eyes. "You have a dirty mind."

"That I do." She laughed.

As Jasmine left to retrieve the books from her cabin, Mia leaned closer to Margo. "Having paranormal talent is a possible indicator of immortal genes," she whispered conspiratorially. "The other is affinity, which we all seem to feel toward Jaz. Your friend might be a Dormant. Wouldn't that be great?"

"Yeah, it would." Margo felt a pang of jealousy.

If Negal knew that Jasmine was also a potential Dormant, would he have courted her?

She was much better looking than Margo, had a better disposition, and seemed to have no hang-ups about sex. She was a superior catch.

Jasmine returned a few minutes later with two tattered paperbacks. "Excuse the condition they are in." She smiled. "It's not that I read them so frequently. I buy them secondhand."

"Thank you." Margo took the books and put them in her tote without checking out the covers.

"Did you have your job interview already?" Jasmine asked.

"Not yet. Everyone is busy with the weddings."

"Right." Jasmine nodded. "I became friends with two of the servers. They were invited to tonight's wedding as guests, but they have nothing to wear because they didn't expect to be dancing at the weddings they were supposed to wait." She told them about Marina and Larissa.

"I saw the one with the blue hair dancing with Peter," Mia said. "She's very pretty, and she had a beautiful dress on."

"It was mine," Jaz said. "But she returned it, and now she needs another one."

"Maybe I can help her," Frankie said. "I have plenty of dresses."

23

KRI

"Mom, stop." Kri put her hand on her mother's shoulder. "The tray looks perfect as it is."

Her mother lifted a pair of frantic eyes at her. "I'm sorry. It's the stress. It's making it worse." She took a deep breath. "I thought we would have more time to put up the decorations."

Kian had called less than an hour ago, informing Kri that the wedding party needed to start two hours earlier than planned, which also affected the timing of her and Michael's bachelorette and bachelor parties.

She didn't really mind, but the sudden schedule change wreaked havoc on her mother's ability to control her OCD. With Vanessa's help, she'd made great progress in the last year or so, but when stressed, the obsessive need to arrange everything in neat groups of three resurged with a vengeance.

"So did I, but we made it on time." Kri leaned to kiss her mother's cheek. "The cabin looks awesome, and appetizers are ready, and all that's left to do is welcome our guests."

"Your guests, sweetheart." Her mother smiled. "Not mine. This is your day. You are the bride."

The tone of wistfulness in her mother's voice made Kri wish that there was a mate for her out there, but given that her mother rarely left her house, she wouldn't find him even if he was in the village.

Kri had tried to introduce her to some of Kalugal's men, but her mother was terrified of them as if they were still members of the Brotherhood, and it didn't matter how many times Kri had explained that they had escaped Navuh's camp because they were not like the others.

Her mother needed to find a gentle soul who wouldn't mind her oddities and her constant state of fearfulness.

As the doorbell rang, her mother's hand flew to her chest. "Oh, my. That's such a shrill sound."

"It's okay, Mom." Kri patted her slim shoulder. "My guests are starting to arrive, so prepare yourself for more shrill sounds or step out onto the balcony until the last one gets here."

Kri walked over to the door and opened it.

"Amanda? I can't believe it. You're the first one."

Amanda was usually the last to arrive, whether at a social gathering or a council meeting. Kri suspected that she did that on purpose to make a grand entrance and get everyone's attention.

"Hello, darling." Amanda leaned and kissed the air near Kri's cheek. "Dalhu took Evie to the pool, and I had nothing to do, so here I am." She walked toward Kri's mother. "Mona." She leaned in to kiss the air next to Kri's mother's cheek. "I haven't seen you the entire voyage. Where have you been hiding?"

Her mother darted her eyes to the dessert table, probably searching for something that wasn't grouped in threes yet. "I attended the weddings, but I stayed in my cabin the rest of the time. I don't like crowds. Dolores, my cabin mate, brought me food from the dining hall."

Amanda shook her head. "You should mingle more."

"I know." Mona walked over to the bar and started arranging the glasses in groups of three.

Kri decided not to comment. It was not only futile but usually made the problem worse.

"I'm dying to see your dress," Amanda said. "I bumped into Stella earlier, and she said it's one of her best creations."

Everyone was so excited about the damn wedding gown that Kri didn't have the heart to admit that she hated everything about it.

"You'll have to wait until the others get here."

It wasn't that there was anything wrong with the dress, or that Stella's creation wasn't beautiful. It was just that any dress, no matter how gorgeous, looked ridiculous on Kri. With her height and broad shoulders, it wasn't a pretty picture. It was like stuffing John Cena into a white wedding dress and expecting him to look wonderful in it.

She could have insisted on getting married in a white tuxedo or even pink, but the way she saw it, letting Stella design the dress, and Mey and Jin produce it in their shop, was more for their benefit than hers. It was a prototype for their new line of wedding dresses for tall women.

Amanda pouted. "Don't I deserve at least a peek?"

Thankfully, the doorbell rang again, so Kri didn't have to respond.

As she opened the door, she found the rest of her bridesmaids in the corridor, already dressed in their gowns, which had also been designed by Stella and produced by Mey and Jin.

The big square case Eva was holding most likely contained the makeup she was going to use on Kri's face, and the bag in Callie's contained the hair styling tools she was going to use on her.

Oh, the joy.

Amanda put her hands on her hips. "How come no one told me to dress in my bridesmaid outfit?"

"Didn't you get my text?" Carol asked.

Amanda pulled out her phone. "Oh, damn. I didn't notice it." She cast an apologetic glance at Kri. "Do you want me to go get it?"

Kri shook her head. "You can do it right before the ceremony."

"Can we see the dress?" Carol asked. "Stella has been gushing over it for days."

"I was," Stella admitted. "I love that dress. When Richard and I get married, I will design one for myself in the same style."

Well, duh. Stella was of average height, and her shoulders were slim and feminine. She would look awesome in something like that.

"It's in the bedroom." Kri walked over to the door and opened it. "Go ahead. Take a look."

"We want to see it on you," Stella said. "You refused to come for fittings, and I'm terrified that it doesn't fit. I brought my sewing machine on the cruise in case I need to make last-minute alterations."

Kri grimaced. "I'm sorry, but I just didn't have time. You know how hectic things were before the cruise."

The look Stella gave her made it clear she hadn't bought the explanation even for a second. "I'm armed with pins and ready to use them. Get in that dress."

Kri chuckled. "Yes, ma'am."

24

MARGO

"Are you sure?" Margo eyed the pile of dresses Frankie had dropped on the bed. "What if Marina and Larissa don't take good care of them? Your cousins will be upset if you return them damaged."

"Don't be silly." Frankie waved a dismissive hand. "What could they do to them?"

"Stains, tears," Mia supplied. "But if they do, I'll happily cover the cost of replacements."

It was nice to be in Mia's situation and not have any more worries about money. Margo had never dreamt about being rich, but being able to pay her bills and do nice things for others from time to time could have been nice.

Hopefully, her new job at Perfect Match would pay enough to cover the basics. The problem was that her future was uncertain at the moment, and she might not be able to take the job because she had to leave, either because she had no godly genes and didn't become immortal or she had them and had to follow Negal to Tibet.

She pulled out her new phone to check if Negal had left her a message and was disappointed that there was none.

After the visit to the clinic, she'd gone to see Jasmine with Frankie and Mia, and Negal had returned to the Lido deck with Dagor. Since Dagor wasn't back yet either, they were probably still up there.

"We don't have to deliver the dresses right now," Margo said. "They are still short-staffed, so Larissa and Marina have to work tonight and won't need them until tomorrow. Let's join the guys on the Lido deck."

Frankie perked up. "I like the way you think. I haven't had a drink in forever." She turned to Mia. "You can call Toven and ask him to meet you up there."

"I'll do that." Mia pulled out her phone.

As they headed out, Margo leaned toward Frankie. "Are you allowed to have alcohol so soon after your transition?"

"Bridget didn't say anything to that effect, so I assume it's fine."

"You should ask," Mia said.

"Why? So, she can tell me no?" Frankie called the elevator. "If I don't ask, I can claim ignorance."

It wasn't smart, but Margo knew better than to argue with Frankie. She was a sweetheart but had a stubborn streak a mile long.

When they reached the Lido deck, they found Negal and Dagor sitting at a table, sipping on beers and munching on pretzels.

Both rose to their feet when they saw them approaching, and then Negal walked over to Margo. "I've missed you." He feathered a kiss on her cheek.

She arched a brow. "You did?"

"Why does that surprise you?" He pulled out a chair for her.

"You didn't text me." She sat down.

"Was I supposed to?"

Dagor chuckled. "Yeah, you were."

Negal turned to him. "How do you know?"

"Frankie made a list of rules for me. One of them is to always let her know where I am and what I am doing."

Margo looked at Frankie, who nodded. "Don't forget that they are not from this planet. How are they supposed to know what human women expect from their significant others?"

"I suspect that females on Anumati are not all that different from us. After all, we are biologically compatible, which means that we are more similar than different."

"Culture plays a big role," Dagor said. "Expectations are different." He glanced at Negal. "Right?"

Negal nodded. "Couples don't get as close emotionally on Anumati unless they are fated mates, and that's extremely rare."

"That's strange," Mia said. "There are so many fated matches in the clan. Most of them are, in fact."

It was indeed strange, but if Mia didn't know the reason for that, Margo doubted anyone else did. "What about children?" she asked. "Are parents close to their children on Anumati?"

Negal nodded. "Very much so. The birth rate is so low that every child is treated like a miracle."

That was surprising for a society with such advanced knowledge in genetics.

"Given what Anumatians can do with gene manipulation, I would assume that anyone who wanted a child on Anumati could get one." Margo looked at Negal. "Even humans know how to make babies in a lab, and then implant them in a female's womb. I'm sure Anumatian scientists know how to make test tube babies."

Negal nodded. "You are correct, but to make a test tube baby, as you call it, a couple needs to apply, get approved, and have the funds for it. The wait line is centuries long, and the procedure is above most citizens' means. On the other hand, having a child naturally does not cost anything and doesn't require approval."

"It's sad," Mia said. "I imagined that a society as advanced as the gods' would do away with money, and that everyone would get what they need while contributing what they can."

Dagor chuckled. "It doesn't work like that. Not here and not on my home planet. People need incentives to put in an effort. Regrettably, praise and recognition, or even social pressure, are not enough to encourage people to put in the work. Fear of destitution on the one hand and monetary rewards on the other are much stronger motivators, and at the end of the day, we are better for it. Laziness and lack of motivation lead to low self-esteem, which in turn might lead to depression, drug abuse, and distractive behaviors to alleviate the boredom."

Margo agreed, but Mia didn't look convinced. "The clan has a good system, but I doubt it could work for a large society. Every member gets a share in the clan's profit, and it's enough to live on comfortably without having to work, but if they do choose to work, they get paid for their efforts and have more than just the basics."

"That's amazing," Margo said. "I would love to have the security of knowing that my bills are covered, and that I could do whatever I'm passionate about without having to worry about money."

Negal grimaced. "We don't have that on Anumati. But to tell you the truth, I have no idea what I would do with myself if I didn't have to work. I don't love what I do, and I don't hate it either, but I'm not passionate about it."

"Speaking of work," Margo said. "Did Aru speak to your commander about postponing the trip or letting you stay behind?"

Negal shook his head. "Aru didn't speak to the commander, and he won't unless you start transitioning."

Margo's heart sank. She was out of time, and she needed to get over her inhibitions or lose her chance with Negal. If he left before inducing her, she would have to choose someone else, and there was no way she would be able to do that.

It was either Negal or no one.

25

MICHAEL

Surrounded by his fellow Guardians, including the chief, Michael felt a profound sense of camaraderie. These males had become his family, taking him under their proverbial wings, teaching him, and supporting him through his transition and beyond. Still, as laughter filled the air and stories of past exploits were shared, Michael's mind drifted to his old friends from college.

He wished they could be there with him, along with his parents, to celebrate his bachelor party and attend his wedding.

It had been a spontaneous decision to secure one of the nights on the cruise for their wedding, and although Michael had agreed to it, he hadn't been happy about celebrating without at least his parents attending.

Perhaps once they returned home, he and Kri could have another wedding in Vegas with his parents, his best friends Eddie and Zach, and maybe also Kri's mother if she was up to it. After all, the cruise wedding did not provide any official documentation, so in the human world, they wouldn't be considered married.

The more occasions to celebrate, the better, right?

Since stepping through the veil separating their worlds, Michael had met with his college friends from time to time, but they had drifted apart.

Zach and Eddie did not belong in his new world, where gods and immortals were real, and he had become an immortal himself, but he did not want to let go of them just because he had been changed.

He still remembered vividly introducing Kri to them over four years ago. He'd been anxious about how his friends would react to his new girlfriend and the fact that he was not returning to college.

Even though his buddies had been with him when he'd been thrust into this new world, they had no recollection of how it had happened. Yamanu had thralled them to forget the Doomers' attack, replacing their memories with a story about a drunken brawl and a sudden family emergency that Michael had to attend to, necessitating his leaving right away.

He'd met Kri the next day, and his life had been irrevocably changed in more ways than he could count.

It had taken him months to arrange a get-together with Zach and Eddie and introduce Kri to them.

Michael chuckled.

He'd fabricated a story about joining a secret government training program and meeting Kri there, but the truth wasn't that far removed from the lie. He'd joined the Guardian force as a trainee, hoping to one day become a Guardian like her.

He'd been told that it would take him decades to reach her level, and at the time, he'd naively believed that he'd do it faster, but four years later, he was still a trainee, and Kri was still light years ahead of him in her level of skill and ability.

Michael had learned to live with it. He'd realized that he didn't need to be better than she was or even as good. He just wished to be a full-fledged member of the force and get all the perks the position entailed.

Looking around at the immortal warriors who had become his best friends, he felt a twinge of nostalgia for his old, simpler life, but he wouldn't have traded his new one for anything.

"You seem miles away, kid." Bhathian clapped him on the shoulder, jolting him back to the present.

Michael shrugged. "I was thinking about the old times and about being a full-fledged Guardian. I always thought that Kri and I would get married after I got accepted, but the wedding cruise came up, and suddenly, she was talking about getting married on the ship, and I just went along with it. I couldn't say no."

Bhathian let out a low chuckle. "I'm married too, kid. The secret to a happy marriage is saying yes at least ten times for every no."

Smiling, Arwel leaned over Bhathian's shoulder. "You should have a relationship advice column on the clan's virtual bulletin board."

"That's not a bad idea." Bhathian raised his glass in a salute. "I might just do that."

Anandur snorted. "It'll have to be a very short column. It will answer every question with, 'yes, dear'."

Brundar's lips lifted in a ghost of a smile, but as usual, he didn't say anything. Instead, he walked over and clapped Michael on his back, offering his silent support.

"A toast." Onegus raised his glass and waited until everyone hushed. "To Michael, who works harder than any other trainee in the history of the force."

The statement surprised Michael. Onegus had never praised his progress, and Michael had been under the impression that he was pretty average.

"Thank you." He lifted his glass and clinked it with Onegus's.

"You are welcome, but I'm not done." Onegus kept his glass aloft. "I've been watching you, Michael. You've done very well on the missions I've sent you on, and your team leaders have had nothing but praise for you."

Hope rose in Michael's chest. Was Onegus praising him just because it was his bachelor party, or was he getting promoted?

Onegus reached into his pocket, pulled out a scroll tied with a red ribbon, and handed it to Michael. "Welcome to the force, Michael."

The sudden eruption of cheers and applause from everyone was overwhelming. Bhathian slapped him on the back, Arwel smiled and clapped his hands, and then Yamanu enveloped him in his arms. "Congratulations, little brother."

For a long moment, Michael was speechless. This was so unexpected that he suspected he was dreaming. He must have fallen asleep and dreamt about the bachelor party and the scroll clasped in his hand.

"Can someone please pinch me?"

Bhathian's booming laugh was soon joined by four more, with Brundar the only one not laughing.

"This is not a dream," Onegus said. "You've done so well on the test missions I've sent you on that there was no point in delaying your acceptance. You've earned it in record time like you've said you would from the very beginning."

"Thank you," Michael managed to choke out. "I'll make sure that you never regret the decision to grant me fully-fledged status after only four years of training." He swept his gaze over the smiling faces of his friends. "I won't let any of you down."

Onegus nodded. "We all know that you won't. That's why you are holding this scroll. Otherwise, I would never have given it to you."

26

PETER

Peter scrolled through the selection of movies on the ship's server, clicked on a comedy he'd already seen, watched a few minutes, and clicked it off. He was bored and restless. He missed Marina.

Dropping the remote on the couch beside him, he leaned back and closed his eyes.

He was doing it again. Falling for a female that was no good for him and with whom he could have no future.

'You are in love with the notion of being in love.' Kagra's words reverberated through his mind. *You need to learn to live in the moment.*

"If only I could."

He wouldn't admit it to anyone, not even to himself, but in the back of his mind, he entertained the hope that Marina was a Dormant. It wasn't likely, because what were the chances of that?

Practically none.

If she had the genes, she would have started transitioning already, given how many times he had bitten her.

Then again, several of the Dormants had taken weeks to transition. Mey and Yamanu had almost lost hope before the first signs began manifesting.

But even if Marina was just a human, which was most likely the case, she wasn't like all the other human females Peter had been with. She knew who he was, and nothing was preventing him from bringing her to the village. Several of the humans from the Kra-ell compound were already living there, so Kian couldn't use the secrecy excuse to forbid it, and there was no reason to deny Marina.

Well, except that it wasn't good for Peter.

He was well aware that it was a prescription for heartache and that watching her get old and die would slay him, but he just couldn't think of not being with her.

If he had any brains, he would end things between them before his attachment to her grew even stronger, but it wasn't his brain that was in charge. It was his heart.

With a groan, he picked up his phone and dialed her number.

She answered on the second ring. "Peter. What's up?"

"I just wanted to hear your voice. How's your day going?"

"Hectic. How is yours?"

"I'm bored, and I want to see you."

She chuckled. "It would have sounded better if you'd said that you missed me, and that's why you wanted to see me."

"But that's what I said."

"No, you said that you were bored."

He rolled his eyes. "Can I come down to the kitchen? I can help out. Wash dishes or cut vegetables. I don't care what task I'm assigned as long as I can be near you."

She sighed. "That's so sweet of you, and I would love it, but you'd just be underfoot because you don't know your way around a commercial kitchen. Besides, you'll make everyone nervous. Humans and immortals usually don't mix well."

"I can be useful, though. I can carry heavy stuff."

Marina laughed. "I know you can, but it's not going to work. The kitchen is a well-oiled machine, and you'd be like a wrench thrown into the gears."

Peter slumped against the back of the couch. "Can I at least come visit and steal you away for a few minutes?"

There was a moment of silence, and then she let out a sigh. "I've already taken a break to return the dress to Jasmine, and Mila will not be happy about me taking another one, especially since we were informed that the wedding would start two hours earlier than scheduled, but perhaps I can come up with an excuse that's more convincing than a long visit to the bathroom."

Peter perked up. "Just tell me when, and I'll be there."

"Hold on, I'm thinking. Do you still have the dresses you borrowed for me from your relatives?"

"Of course. You returned the one you borrowed from Jasmine, and there are still four weddings to go."

"Three. I'm not accompanying you to tonight's wedding. But I hope that Larissa and I can attend tomorrow's wedding, and Larissa has nothing nice to wear. Could you possibly bring her one of the dresses? That would be a great excuse for me to take a break."

Peter sighed. "They were meant for you, and none of them will fit Larissa, but we can pretend that I'm bringing a dress for her, right?"

"Yeah, I guess. Poor Larissa will be disappointed. I need to find her something. I just hope that the two servers are back to work tomorrow. If they are not, I will drag them out of their beds even if one needs to work one-handed and the other is loopy from pain medication."

"They'd better. If not, I'm coming to help prepare breakfast and lunch so you and Larissa can take the evening off. I might be inexperienced in the kitchen, but with my speed and strength, I can do the work of two people with ease, and it's not like I have anything better to do when you're not around."

"I'll tell that to Mila." Marina chuckled. "You helping in the kitchen should be threat enough to make sure we get the time off no matter what."

27

MARINA

Marina's hands moved with practiced efficiency as she chopped vegetables. Usually the monotony of the task, along with the clatter of pots and pans and the sizzle of frying food, calmed her down and centered her, but today it wasn't enough to distract her from thinking about Peter.

Reaching for another tomato, she placed it on the chopping board, but as she lifted the knife, she heard the kitchen doors swinging open. It could have been anyone, but she knew it was Peter even before she turned around.

He strode in with his typical swagger, a broad smile on his handsome face, and looking good enough to eat.

Everyone seemed to pause for a heartbeat, every pair of eyes flicking toward him and then quickly back to what they were doing before the interruption.

Peter didn't seem to notice, his focus on her and his smile getting broader the closer he got to her.

A flutter of anticipation stirred in her stomach.

Without a word, he took the knife from her hand, put it on the chopping board, and pulled her to him for a quick kiss. "I missed you too much to wait," he murmured against her lips.

Behind his back, several of her friends snickered, and the indignant huff had no doubt come from Mila.

"Take it outside," the cook barked in Russian. "You have five minutes."

Chuckling, Marina rested her forehead against Peter's chest. "Mila told me to take it outside."

Peter turned around to look at the cook and dipped his head. "*Spasibo*."

Mila waved him off with her mixing spoon, a stern expression on her round face, but Marina caught the slight twitching of the cook's lips. She wasn't really mad.

As Peter took her hand, she smiled at Mila and mouthed '*Spasibo*' as well.

This time, Mila allowed her lips to lift in a lopsided smile.

Outside, he led her to the small alcove they had discovered during one of his previous visits to the kitchen.

Leaning against the wall, he spread his legs and pulled her between them. "I need to kiss you."

"You just did."

"That was just a taste." His hand wrapped around the back of her neck, and then his lips were on hers.

Marina closed her eyes and wrapped her arms around his neck, the tips of her fingers playing with the strands of hair on the back of his head.

He needed a trim.

For a moment, his hands settled on her waist, but they didn't stay there. His fingers stroked up her sides, skimming the swell of her breasts and eliciting a moan, which he caught with his mouth.

She tightened her hold on his neck to bring him closer so she could rub her hardened nipples against his chest, but the thick fabric of her apron was in the way.

They had made love that morning, and yet the kiss ignited a hunger in her that had her forgo caution and lift one leg to wrap it against Peter's waist, so her achy center was aligned with the delicious bulge in his pants.

"Marina." He broke the kiss and leaned his forehead against hers. "I can't get enough of you."

"Me too," she said breathlessly and then sighed. "Unfortunately, I think the five minutes are up."

"What a shame." The look he gave her was lustful, but it was also so tender and full of feeling that it made her heart flutter.

Could it be that he was falling for her?

Did his emotions run as deep as hers?

Probably not. Immortals didn't fall in love with humans, and she would never be his mate, but she wouldn't mind being with him as his lover, or a friend with benefits, or even his housekeeper whom he occasionally shagged.

Scrap the 'occasional' part. She would accept daily shagging as payment for her cleaning and cooking services.

"You didn't bring the dress," she said, to hide the manic laughter bubbling up in her throat.

"I forgot." Peter grinned. "Which means that I have an excuse to whisk you out of the kitchen again."

"Mila will chase you off with a rolling pin in hand."

"No way." He planted a chaste kiss on her cheek. "She likes me."

Of course, she did. Everyone liked Peter. What was there not to like?

Back in the kitchen, she ignored the knowing looks and the smirks as she walked over to her station and resumed chopping vegetables for the salad.

She was lost in the rhythm of her task when Amanda breezed into the kitchen to give last-minute instructions for tonight's wedding and check that everything would be ready on time.

When she was done, she walked over to Marina's station and leaned against the counter. "Are you accompanying Peter to the wedding tonight?"

Marina shook her head. "We are understaffed, so I can't get tonight off, but I will be there tomorrow." She regarded Amanda with a challenge in her eyes, waiting for the lecture about how inappropriate it was for her to date an immortal.

"It's a shame that you can't be his date tonight. I haven't seen Peter so happy in a long time."

Marina's eyes widened in surprise. Amanda was an important immortal, the sister of their leader. If she wasn't against Peter dating a human, then maybe others wouldn't be either.

She schooled her expression to hide her surprise. "My friend Larissa was supposed to accompany Jay, but she's in the same situation as I am." She watched Amanda's expression to see if her reaction would be different to yet another human and immortal pairing.

"I'm sure that Jay is thrilled," Amanda said, sounding genuine.

"Larissa surely is, but if she doesn't find something nice to wear, she might not attend." Marina sighed. "Thanks to Peter's cousins' generous contributions, I'm covered, but none of their dresses will fit Larissa." She turned to smile at her friend across the kitchen.

Following her gaze, Amanda also smiled at Larissa and gave her a small wave hello. "I will ask around for her," Amanda said. "Perhaps I can scavenge something for her to wear."

That was so kind and unexpected that Marina was lost for words for the second time in mere minutes.

"Thank you so much. Can I do something to repay your kindness? Does your cabin need sprucing up? Do you need breakfast delivered tomorrow morning?"

Amanda laughed. "Thank you for the offer, darling, but my butler would be mortified if anyone tried to take the job of sprucing up and making breakfast from him."

Amanda had her own servant on board?

"Oh. I didn't know that you had a butler."

"Onidu rarely leaves the cabin," Amanda said. "He's also my nanny."

"You are lucky to have such a capable person in your employ."

"I know." Amanda pushed away from the counter. "I'll see what I can find for Larissa and come back. If not today, then tomorrow."

"Thank you."

As the doors flung closed behind the gorgeous brunette, Marina sighed. "It must be nice to be a princess."

28

ANNANI

Annani put the brush away, rose to her feet, and walked into the living room. The afternoon sun filtered through the curtains, casting a serene light over the table that her Odus had set in preparation for Syssi's parents' visit.

The cruise offered a rare occasion for Annani to interact with her in-laws, and she was looking forward to a stimulating conversation with Anita and Adam.

They always had so many fascinating stories to tell about their exploits in the Congo. Listening to Anita talk about her work with children, Adam about his wildlife photography, and the dangerous situations both often found themselves in might take her mind off tonight's first telepathic meeting with her grandmother.

It was a shame she could not share that piece of information with them or the rest of her clan. If it was up to her, she would have told everyone about it, but Aru insisted on secrecy, and she had to honor his wishes even though she did not believe it was necessary.

Well, it was true that letting Dagor and Negal in on the secret carried some risk. If they ever got picked up by the Anumati patrol ship, the knowledge of Aru and Aria's telepathic connection could be extracted from them.

When the doorbell rang and Oridu let Anita and Adam in, Annani greeted each one with a warm smile and a gentle embrace.

She might be petite and look delicate, but she could easily crush a human's ribcage if she was not careful.

"I hope you have not eaten yet. My Odus prepared afternoon tea."

"Not since lunch." Adam patted his belly. "I'm going to gain so much weight on this cruise that I will need to go on a diet when we return to Liuma."

Anita sighed. "That won't be difficult." She cast Annani a sad smile. "It's hard to eat well when people are hungry around you."

"Is hunger still such a severe problem in the Congo?" Annani asked.

Syssi's mother nodded. "Yes, hunger remains a significant issue in DRC. Many are experiencing food insecurity, and many children are acutely malnourished. Poor harvests, violence-driven displacement, disease, unemployment, and collapsing infrastructure are to blame, and there are no fast and easy solutions to any of that."

Annani shook her head. "It is hard to believe that hunger is still an issue in today's world."

Adam snorted. "And what about barbarism? When I was a boy, I believed the world was getting better and that there were no more barbarians left."

Annani leaned back, Oridu filled her cup with tea, and then she waited for him to fill Anita and Adam's cups.

"I assume that you are referring to what happened in Acapulco."

Adam let out a sigh. "Among other instances. There are too many to count even though the media tends to focus on only one or two while completely ignoring the worst travesties."

"It's all ugly politics." Anita lifted her hand. "But let's talk about more pleasant subjects." She forced a smile. "I've loved all of your wedding speeches, Annani. How do you come up with all those beautiful words for all the ceremonies?"

Annani smiled. "Every couple has a unique story that inspires my words."

Anita leaned forward. "Do you write them in advance?"

Annani laughed. "I used to wing it, but with a different wedding every night, I need to make sure I don't repeat myself, so I write down a few bullet points and read through them before the ceremony. Some repetition is unavoidable, of course, but I try not to bore my audience."

Nodding, Anita smiled. "I must admit that I tear up each night, and you know me. I'm not usually the emotional type. And it's not just during your speech but also during the vows the couples exchange. They are so heartfelt." She cast a smile at her husband. "When we got married, exchanging personal vows wasn't a thing. I wish it was."

"Our golden anniversary is approaching." Adam reached for her hand and brought it to his lips for a kiss. "We can renew our vows, and this time not use the standard wording."

"That is a marvelous idea." Annani clapped her hands. "I would love to preside over your vow renewal ceremony." She leaned closer to Anita. "Perhaps it could coincide with your retirement? Allegra and Phoenix would love to have their grandmother near."

Anita let out a sigh. "My granddaughters are surrounded by a loving and supportive community. I'm sure they would love to have me close, and I would love that as well, but the children I help in Liuma need me, and I can't abandon them."

"I am sure you can find a replacement," Annani said.

"I wish that was true. People are willing to volunteer for a few months, sometimes a year, but it's a rare soul that is willing to make Liuma their home."

29

KRI

Kri stood just outside the dining hall doors, her fingers twisting the simple wedding band she was about to put on Michael's finger. Her bridesmaids were smiling, but she was too nervous to even pretend, and it had nothing to do with being unsure about the male she was marrying.

It was the damn wedding gown.

It was grand, a true masterpiece, but she was not used to wearing dresses, especially not one as constricting as what Stella had designed for her. The corset was tight, making it difficult to take a full breath, and with her ample cleavage, Kri was afraid that if she fully expanded her chest, the zipper would give up.

Served her right for not making time for fittings. Stella had taken her measurements, and Kri had thought it would be enough, but apparently it hadn't been.

Her large breasts were pushed up uncomfortably, making her self-conscious despite her bridesmaids' gushing over how lovely she looked in the damn dress.

Instead of succumbing to peer pressure and her mother's pleading, she should have gotten married in an elegant white pantsuit like she'd wanted to. The dress, while stunning and crafted to fit her six-foot-tall broad-shouldered frame, did not complement her Guardian's body.

Her bridesmaids, on the other hand, looked effortlessly beautiful in their dresses.

Taking a shallow breath, Kri turned inward to calm her nerves.

After all, it was just a ceremony. She and Michael had pledged their lives to each other a long time ago.

Their relationship hadn't been all smooth sailing, and they had weathered some rough waters, but once Michael had given up on his preconceived notions of masculinity and femininity, it had been as close to bliss as she could have hoped for.

Kri smiled, thinking of their first meeting.

Curious about the newcomer housed in the keep's dungeon, she'd volunteered to deliver him lunch, and the connection had been immediate.

Michael had been taken aback by her. She was so different from the girls he'd encountered in college. She'd teased him, and he'd almost choked on his food, but then he'd expressed his admiration for her in such an earnest and uncommon manner that he had won her over.

In no time, they had found themselves deeply in love, and despite a few rough spots along the way, she had zero hesitation about pledging her life to Michael.

Taking as deep of a breath as she could in the damn corset, Kri steeled herself for the walk down the aisle and the reaction of her clan members to seeing her stuffed like a big sausage into a too-tight white dress.

It was nothing compared to facing traffickers and other scum, and if she could handle that, she could handle a few snide remarks. She would walk into the hall with her head held high.

So yeah, today she was a bride, but above all she was a Guardian, and Guardians feared nothing.

When the music started, and the doors opened, Kri trained her eyes on Michael's smiling face and strode forward.

When she and her bridesmaids reached the podium, she took Michael's extended hand while her bridesmaids took positions next to their mates, who were Michael's groomsmen.

Standing on top of the dais, the Clan Mother was so petite that her eyes were on the same level as Kri's and Michael's, and as she turned to them, her gaze was full of warmth.

When the room fell silent, Annani turned back to face the guests. "My beloveds, today, we gather under the auspices of love and community to witness the union of two extraordinary souls—Kri and Michael."

She turned her gaze affectionately towards Kri. "Kri, our fierce and brave Guardian. You embody strength, courage, and loyalty. From the moment you took your first baby steps, it was clear to everyone that you would grow up to be a warrior. You have always stood tall, not just in stature but in spirit. You have never backed out of a challenge, and when you found your one and only, you conquered him the same way you conquered every goal you have set for yourself."

As a few snickers sounded from the assembled guests, Kri gave Michael's hand a gentle squeeze, and he returned it along with a wink.

Annani turned to Michael with a brilliant smile. "My dear Michael. You entered our world unexpectedly but have since become a cherished member of our community. Your openness, humor, and bravery have not only won Kri's heart but have earned you the respect and affection of all who have come to know you. You remind us that strength is shown not just through acts of valor but through determination, hard work, and the courage to embrace a vastly different world from the one you were born to."

The goddess then addressed them both. "May the love that has brought you together continue to grow and deepen with each passing day. May you face every challenge hand in hand and side by side. And may your lives be blessed with endless joy, unwavering support, and love that deepens and grows along with your joined journey."

Annani lifted her hands. "In the presence of your family and friends, I bless this union. Kri and Michael, would you like to exchange vows?"

Kri dipped her head, "Yes, Clan Mother."

30

MICHAEL

Michael felt a lump form in his throat as he saw Kri walking down the aisle, looking every inch the warrior princess that she was.

Her strength and beauty left him breathless.

The dress, which he hadn't been allowed to see, was exquisite. It complemented her tall, powerful frame, capturing the essence of Kri, which was fierce yet beautiful and feminine, formidable yet graceful and kind.

Beside him stood his groomsmen, a solid wall of muscle and fierce loyalty. They were more like family to him than friends and mentors, but he once again regretted not having his family by birth and his old friends with him at this monumental moment.

His father.

His mother.

Zach and Eddie.

Reminding himself of his plan to have another ceremony with them in Vegas, Michael took a deep breath and focused on the present. He hoped he would remember all the beautiful words that Yamanu and Bhathian had helped him craft and that they would please Kri, conveying the depth of his feelings for her.

As she reached him, Michael took Kri's hands in his, feeling the familiar rush of energy that always flowed between them. He looked into her blue, smiling eyes, which had captivated him from the first moment he'd seen her and hadn't loosened their hold on him ever since.

"I love you," he mouthed, but she was already turning to the Clan Mother.

Listening to the goddess deliver her speech, he waited for her to finish her blessing over their union and give them the go-ahead to recite their vows.

He'd won the privilege of going first in a fierce game of *War of the Godzillas* they had played the day before, which made him anxious.

What if Kri's vows were more beautifully worded than his?

It wasn't a competition, he reminded himself. And even if it was, he should happily accept Kri winning.

Turning to the love of his life, Michael smiled. "My beautiful Kri. From the moment I met you, I knew that my life would never be the same. The man I became, thanks to you, is very different from the boy I was before. You challenged me, you laughed with me, and you showed me what it means to be truly strong. You've taught me that true strength is in the heart and mind and that bravery manifests in many ways. But most of all, you taught me all I know now and will ever know about love."

As her eyes glistened with unshed tears, he rubbed his thumb over her racing pulse. "I vow to honor the incredible woman you are, to support you in your battles, and to be your partner in every adventure life throws our way. I vow to respect our differences as much as our similarities and to cherish the love that binds us. For better and for worse, you are stuck with me."

As their audience laughed, Michael took a deep breath and continued, "I pledge to stand by you, to be your confidant, your ally, and your partner in all things. I will be your shelter in the storm, your light in the darkness, and the one who holds you close through all the seasons of our lives."

He paused, looking into her glistening eyes and hoping that she could see the sincerity and love he felt for her. "Kri, my mate, my one and only, the owner of my heart. Today, in front of our friends and family, I pledge myself to you for eternity." He pulled a ring out of his pocket. "Kri, my love. With this ring, I thee wed."

As Michael finished with the traditional words, the weight of the moment settled upon him. He felt blessed beyond measure to have Kri by his side and to call her his mate.

As Kri's eyes held his, shimmering with unshed happy tears, he was awed by the power of her presence, the strength of her spirit, and the tenderness of her heart.

She took a steadying breath. "Michael. Before you entered my life, I thought that I had all that I needed to be happy, but I was wrong. You brought me joy, friendship, and companionship, and you even managed to convince me to enroll in online college. Thanks to you, I now hold a bachelor's degree in criminal justice."

As the crowd clapped and cheered, she lifted their joined hands in the air. "Michael earned a degree in business, so give him a cheer as well."

She waited for the applause and cheers to subside before continuing. "And that was in addition to training for long hours every day." She smiled at him before turning to look at their guests. "Respect, people."

The applause and cheers were deafening.

He dipped his head. "Thank you."

This was the Kri he knew and loved. The female who took charge and led the crowd even at her own wedding and with the Clan Mother standing inches away from her.

His mate wasn't afraid of anything.

Kri smiled and squeezed his hand. "Michael, my love. I vow to support you, to stand by your side, and to be your partner in all things. I vow to be your shield in times of war and your solace in times of peace. I vow to laugh with you, to dream with you, and to shoulder any burden or challenge that comes our way. Together, we are stronger, braver, and more complete than the sum of our parts. I promise to cherish and love you forever and beyond." She reached into her corset and pulled out a ring from between her breasts to the cheers and laughter of their guests.

"Michael, my love, with this ring I thee wed."

Their audience erupted with hoots, cheers, and applause, and then someone started a chant, "Kiss, kiss, kiss…"

Michael lifted a hand to shush them. "The Clan Mother hasn't said the last words yet."

The room fell silent in an instant.

Stepping forward, the goddess raised her arms, signaling the culmination of the ceremony. "Kri and Michael, I pronounce you mated and bonded for life. May your union be blessed by the Fates and as enduring as the fabric of the universe." She paused, allowing her words to settle over the congregation. "You may now seal your promises with a kiss," she announced with a twinkle in her eye.

As Michael wrapped his arms around his bride's narrow waist, she wound hers around his neck, and the kiss they shared was an affirmation of their vows, tender yet full of strength—a perfect balance of passion and promise.

31

NEGAL

Just like the one the night before, the wedding ceremony had been touching, and the vows Kri and Michael had exchanged echoed in Negal's mind long after the words had faded into the ether and the festivities had commenced.

The hall was alive with laughter and the soft clink of glasses, and as the music started, couples took to the dance floor.

"Would you like to dance?" he asked Margo.

"I would love to." She swiped a finger under one eye and then the other.

He smiled. "Got emotional?"

She nodded. "For a cynical skeptic, I love weddings too much." She cast a glance in Kian's direction. "Apparently, I share this weakness with the big boss, so maybe it's something that grouches like us have in common."

"You're not a grouch." Negal rose to his feet and offered her a hand up. "Maybe you just need more reminders that not everything is as bad as you think it is."

Chuckling, Margo took his hand. "Oh, it's much worse. The older I get, the more I discover how naive I was, believing in a better future and the integrity of the system."

"I'm not well versed in human affairs, but I experienced the same on Anumati. Sometimes, I miss the days of my youth, when I worshipped the Eternal King and believed wholeheartedly that he had my best interests at heart along with all the citizens of Anumati, whether residing on the home world or the colonies."

"I'm glad that you understand my way of thinking." Margo smiled up at him. "Not many do."

As he led her to the dance floor, Negal scanned the room, noting all the males whose eyes followed her, and he had the absurd urge to wrap her in his arms and hide her from view.

Margo looked exquisite in a dress made from a shimmery gold fabric. The bodice hugged her curves gently while the skirt flowed like liquid gold, cascading to the floor in a series of gentle waves. Her long blond hair was gathered atop her head, and a few strands cascaded like a golden waterfall, framing her face and highlighting the clear blue of her eyes.

His thoughts drifting to Kri and Michael's vows, to the joy and love he glimpsed in their exchange, Negal couldn't help but yearn for an everlasting bond like theirs.

As the slow dance began, Margo looked into his eyes and frowned. "Did something upset you?"

"Why do you ask?"

"Your eyes are glowing."

He wasn't sure whether they were doing that in response to the male gazes that had trailed Margo or what her nearness was doing to him, but it was unacceptable in either case.

"My apologies." He blinked a couple of times until he was sure they were no longer glowing.

"You have nothing to apologize for. I was just curious about the reason." A smile lifted her lips. "Were you having naughty thoughts about me?"

He chuckled. "I'm always having naughty thoughts about you, but I'm usually in better control of my responses."

As her cheeks pinked, she got closer and rested her forehead against his chest. "I'm having naughty thoughts about you as well," she admitted in a whisper. "But they are probably much tamer than yours."

His shaft swelled in an instant. "Now I'm dying to hear all about those naughty thoughts."

She shook her head. "I'm not going to tell you."

Negal hoped she would show him, and that she wouldn't keep him waiting for too long. Delayed gratification had its merits, but he preferred to end the delay sooner rather than later.

As they swayed in place to the rhythm of the music, not really dancing but rather enjoying each other's closeness, the world around them seemed to fade.

The music and the couples dancing next to them all receded until it was just the two of them, moving to the beat.

As the song ended and they stepped apart, Negal was reluctant to let go. "Another dance?"

Margo stepped closer to him. "Of course."

As Dagor and Frankie glided onto the dance floor to join them, the dynamic shifted, their bubble expanding to include their friends.

Watching how happy and in love they looked, Negal was glad for Dagor and Frankie, but he was also a little envious.

The obstacles that they had faced together were behind them. Frankie had successfully transitioned, and her future with Dagor was set on the right path. They would still face challenges, but their relationship was cemented, their bond just as everlasting as Kri and Michael's.

Still, Dagor would never be able to bring Frankie home to his parents on Anumati because she was a hybrid, part human, part goddess, and mating with created species was not allowed on the home planet. The same was true for Negal, but he no longer cared about that.

His gaze flickered from Dagor and Frankie back to Margo, who was watching the other couple with a smile.

Was she thinking about all the obstacles that still stood in his and her way before they could bask in each other's company with the same ease?

The crux of it all was her transition, but for that to have a chance of happening, they needed to overcome Margo's intimacy problem.

Not that he was overly concerned about that. The way she was looking at him, her eyes full of desire and perhaps even love, it wouldn't be long now, but the biggest question was whether she possessed the godly genes at all. He believed that she did, that the Fates wouldn't be cruel to him by sending him a mere human to taunt him, but until it happened, the uncertainty was gnawing at him.

The thought of a future without her was unbearable. He loved her, more than he had ever thought possible, and the realization that her transition might never occur and that their time together could be limited was weighing heavily on his heart.

32

MARGO

Margo smiled and moved to the beat, but her mind was a whirlwind of thoughts and anxiety.

She had made up her mind that tonight would be her first time with Negal, but she had no idea how to make it happen. She was sharing a cabin with Frankie and Dagor and Negal was sharing a cabin with Aru and Gabi. She was nervous enough as it was without the added complexity of the lack of privacy.

Margo tried to keep her expression serene, to lose herself in the music, the dancing, and in Negal's eyes, which looked at her with such depth and warmth. But given the crease between his brows, Negal was sensing her disquiet.

"What's the matter?" he asked. "Are you tired? Do you want to sit down?"

"No, I'm fine." She smiled up at him. "Are you enjoying yourself?"

The crease between his eyebrows deepened. "I have you in my arms, so of course, I'm having a good time, but I know that something is troubling you." He leaned closer and brushed his lips over her ear, eliciting a shiver. "You can tell me anything, sweetheart."

The sudden flash of desire loosened her tongue. "I was just thinking about our lodging situation," she whispered. "It's not very conducive to romance. When we are ready to take the next step, and I'm not saying that it is now, but when we are, I would have liked for us to have a cabin to ourselves," she finally confessed.

His expression shifted from concern to understanding, and then his eyes started glowing again, but this time, she had no doubt about the nature of the catalyst.

Leaning so his mouth was at her ear, he whispered, "I believe that there are plenty of staff cabins available if you are willing to lower your standards a little."

The idea of having a space just for them ignited a spark of hope, but the logistics of arranging that seemed daunting.

Her cheeks heating up, Margo pressed closer to him and whispered back, "I would be more than happy in a bare necessities cabin if that's what's available, but who can we ask about it?"

It felt so awkward to talk about it. Those things should be spontaneous, not planned like a military operation.

"I'll find out." His hand ran small soothing circles on her back. "Leave it all up to me."

She'd known he would say that and was relieved that he would spare her the embarrassment of inquiring about a spare cabin herself, but on the other hand, she hated relying on others for things she could easily do but preferred not to because of nonsensical considerations like outdated attitudes toward sex.

When the song ended, Margo stepped out of Negal's arms. "Would you excuse me for a few moments? I need to visit the ladies' room."

"I'll come with you," Frankie said. "I need to freshen up as well."

Had Frankie heard their conversation and was about to suggest a solution?

Perhaps Margo should have started there and asked her bestie for advice.

When they reached the bathroom, though, Frankie immediately ducked into one of the stalls, which implied that her visit to the bathroom had nothing to do with the lodging dilemma.

With a sigh, Margo entered the stall next to her friend and relieved her bladder.

As they both stepped up to the sinks to wash their hands, Frankie cast her a sidelong glance in the mirror. "What's going on with you? You look stressed."

"It's a stressful situation." Margo tucked a few loose strands into her chignon. "It's such a weird feeling to know that everyone is expecting me to get in bed with Negal."

Frankie chuckled. "Everyone probably assumes that you are already sharing his bed. Immortals are, by and large, a lustful and uninhibited bunch. None of them would think that you are holding off on the fun." She smiled at her in the mirror. "The truth is that I don't know why you are doing that either."

"Lack of privacy, for one," Margo shot back.

"The moment you close the door to your bedroom, you have all the privacy you want. You can moan and groan to your heart's content, and we will not hear you. If you scream, though, we might, so don't. I mean, do, just no screaming. Not that I care if you do, but you seem to, so yeah." Frankie put a finger over her lips. "Turn down the volume."

Margo shook her head. "I envy the ease with which you approach sex. I wish I could be as open and outspoken about it."

Frankie narrowed her eyes at her. "You've never seemed to have a problem talking about it before. Is it just because it's Negal? Does he intimidate you because he's a god?"

She could have lied and said yes, but maybe it was time that her friends knew the truth. "Negal doesn't intimidate me. I have a problem with getting intimate with a man I've just met. Your rule about having sex for the first time with a guy used to be at least three dates, mine was more like thirty."

Frankie's eyes widened. "No wonder you had a problem keeping boyfriends. Who was willing to wait that long?"

"I exaggerated a little for emphasis." She hadn't.

Shaking her head, Frankie glared at Margo and then pulled a tube of lipstick out of her clutch. "You had me there for a moment." She refreshed the color on her lips.

"I might have exaggerated, but you get the gist of it. I'm also a very private person in that regard." She reached for Frankie's lipstick. "Do you happen to know who is in charge of assigning cabins?"

"Ingrid. Why? Do you want to move out? I don't think there are any cabins left."

"Negal said that there are plenty of available cabins in the staff quarters." Margo dabbed a few touches of color on her lips and then smacked them together.

"You must be really desperate to settle for a staff cabin. They have single beds, but I guess you can push two together to make a king-sized one. Still, it's like making love for the first time in a closet or the backseat of a car. Not the kind of accommodations that are conducive to pleasant memories."

"Yeah, I guess you are right." Margo handed Frankie the tube. "Do you have a better solution?"

33

NEGAL

As Margo and Frankie headed out to the ladies' room, Negal tried to come up with a plan.

He hadn't expected Margo to announce that she was ready so soon, especially not in the middle of the dance floor at Kri and Michael's wedding, but now he had to solve their lodging problem so he could make this night special for her.

The thought of having Dagor and Frankie in the next room in her cabin suite or Aru and Gabi in his was far from ideal for their first night together. He didn't particularly mind, but Margo obviously did.

He needed a plan. But who to ask?

Negal's gaze drifted across the room, landing on Gabi, who was laughing at something Aru had said. She knew many of the immortals and had family in the village. Perhaps she could tell him who the person in charge of lodging was.

It was also possible that the task had been assigned to one of the humans, but he had to start somewhere.

"I'm heading to the bar," Dagor said. "Want to join?"

"Perhaps later. I need to talk to Gabi."

Negal walked over to where Gabi was sitting with Aru and a female he knew but whose name he had forgotten.

"Good evening." He dipped his head to the female and turned to Gabi. "Can I steal you away for a few moments?"

She lifted a brow. "Lady troubles?"

"No troubles. I just need to ask you something, in private if possible."

His quest for new lodging would make his intentions obvious, and although he didn't mind who knew, Margo would be embarrassed, so he needed to be discreet.

"Of course." She cast Aru a smile. "Can I get you something from the bar after I'm done talking to Negal?"

"No, thanks, I'm good." He trained his dark eyes on Negal. "Is everything okay?"

"Everything is great. I just need Gabi's help with something."

Aru nodded.

As they walked out of the dining room, Gabi turned to him. "What's up?"

He glanced around, lowering his voice. "Margo and I need a cabin of our own, preferably as soon as tonight. Do you know who takes care of assigning cabins?"

Gabi's eyes widened, and then a smile spread over her face. "Congratulations. I'm glad that my advice worked." She tapped her lips with a long-nailed finger. "I don't know who is in charge of assigning lodging, but I might know someone who knows. Wait here." She flounced away without waiting for his response.

Moments later, she returned with the female who had been sitting next to her and Aru.

"Negal, this is Darlene. My brother's mate."

Now he remembered who she was. Gabi's family had visited often during her recovery, and although he and Dagor had tried to make themselves scarce during the family's visits, he'd been introduced to Darlene.

"Hi, Negal," Eric's mate smiled. "Gabi tells me that you need help with something."

"I need a private cabin. Sharing one with Aru and Gabi doesn't work for me right now."

Hopefully, she wouldn't need further explanations.

Frowning, Darlene glanced at Gabi. "Did the boys have a fight?"

Gabi laughed. "Not at all. Negal's changing needs are romantic in nature."

Darlene's eyes widened with understanding. "I see. Well, in that case, Ingrid is the person to talk to. I can give her your phone number, and she will contact you tomorrow."

"I need the cabin tonight. Time is of the essence."

"I see." Darlene was trying really hard not to smile, but her lips twitched, betraying her amusement. "I'll go find Ingrid."

"Thank you. Should I wait here?"

Darlene hesitated but then nodded. "Ingrid is a sweetheart. She'll be happy to help."

When Darlene left, Gabi remained standing by his side. "Where is Margo?"

"In the ladies' room with Frankie."

Gabi shifted to lean against the wall. "What prompted the sudden urgency?"

Negal wondered the same thing. Their kissing had been full of passion, so maybe that was what had cut through Margo's resistance.

But what was more likely was that she'd decided that she couldn't wait after hearing that Aru had refused to contact their commander about postponing their departure or letting Negal stay behind.

"Pragmatism, I guess," he finally said. "The cruise is almost over."

Darlene returned, accompanied by an elegant blond who regarded him with a twinkle in her eyes.

"Negal, this is Ingrid, the clan's interior designer and the person in charge of allocating lodging," Darlene introduced her. "Ingrid, this is Negal, who doesn't need introductions."

Ingrid shook his offered hand. "Darlene told me that you need a private cabin and that it's somewhat urgent, but I really can't help you tonight. The upper decks are at full capacity, and all I can offer are staff cabins that are pretty utilitarian and not really conducive to romance if you know what I mean." She chuckled. "It will be like taking a virgin to a motel. A shared cabin is preferable to that. But what I can try to do tomorrow is to move some people around to free a guest cabin for you and Margo."

He didn't want to move people from their cabins. "If you can get us a staff cabin, I can try to spruce it up."

She gave him an apologetic look. "I'm sorry, but that too will have to wait for tomorrow. With the extra passengers we've collected, I'm not sure what's available, and if it's in habitable condition."

To say that Negal was disappointed was an understatement. "I understand. Thank you for your help, and I apologize for dragging you away from the party."

Ingrid waved a dismissive hand. "Don't mention it. I'm always glad to help a couple in love."

Were they a couple in love?

Yeah, they were. Margo hadn't told him that she loved him, and he hadn't told her how he felt about her either, but he knew it to be true.

Relief flooded through Negal, though he felt a twinge of disappointment at the delay. "Yes, that will be perfect. Thank you, Ingrid, and thank you, Darlene and Gabi. Margo will be thrilled."

As Ingrid and Darlene left, Negal turned to Gabi. "Thank you."

She waved him off. "I wish I could do more." As she turned to leave, the dining room doors pushed open, and Dagor walked out.

"Did you see Margo and Frankie?"

Negal frowned. "They are not back from the ladies' room yet?"

Dagor shook his head. "I thought that they were out here with you."

"I'll go check on them," Gabi offered. "They are probably having a girl talk." She winked before walking toward the bathrooms.

"What's going on?" Dagor asked. "Were you also looking for our missing mates?"

First Ingrid with her comment about them being a couple in love and now Dagor, it seemed like everyone assumed that Margo and he were a done deal.

If only he could share their confidence.

"I needed to find a private cabin for me and Margo, and I enlisted Gabi's help."

Dagor regarded him with a knowing look. "Given your expression, you were unsuccessful."

"The person in charge of lodging can't do anything tonight, and the prospects of her finding anything decent for us tomorrow are not good either."

Dagor's lips lifted in a grin. "As always, your thinking is too linear. The solution is quite simple." He clapped Negal on the back. "You just need to think a little creatively. Tonight, you will pretend that you're going to sleep on the living room couch because Frankie and I can't watch over Margo for another night, and you are still worried about her having a delayed reaction to the drugs she was injected with. And that's not even a lie. We will make ourselves scarce as soon as we enter the suite, so you will have the living room to yourself and can pretend that we are not even there. Then, if things go right," he paused, giving Negal a knowing look, "you can join Margo in the bedroom later. That way, she will not be embarrassed about inviting you to stay the night. On our part, Frankie and I will not emerge from our bedroom until you text me that it's okay."

Negal considered the idea. It wasn't perfect, but it was simple and didn't require any preparation or moving to another cabin.

"That might just work." He clapped Dagor on the back. "Thanks."

"Anytime."

34

MARINA

Marina maneuvered through the crowded wedding hall, balancing a laden tray, her arms shaking with the effort.

The damn immortals could have invested in carts so moving dishes from the kitchen to the dining room wouldn't have been such an onerous task.

Were they even aware of how heavy these things were?

For them, the trays probably weighed nothing, but they hadn't stopped to think how heavy they were for human females.

Marina let out a breath.

She was just irritated because she'd been working almost nonstop for two days and didn't get to spend enough time with Peter. The cruise was almost over, and she was running out of time to make him fall in love with her.

Heck, who was she kidding. She was in love with him already, and he was merely infatuated. When the cruise ended and they had to part, he might be sad for a day or two, but she would be devastated.

"Serves you right for scheming," she murmured under her breath.

The scent of roasted meats and exotic spices filled the air, clashing with the sound of love songs floating through the room. Marina didn't know why, but in her mind, romantic music went with wine and dessert, not meat and potatoes.

Not that she had anything against either. She loved both in any form or shape.

"You look beautiful tonight," a deep male voice said behind her.

She nearly dropped the tray as she spun around to find Peter watching her with an amused grin.

"You startled me. Not a smart move when I'm carrying a heavy load."

"Dance with me." With a swift motion, he plucked the tray from her hands and set it down on a nearby table. Then he grasped her hand and pulled her toward the dance floor.

Marina tried to resist. "Peter, stop it. I can't dance with you. I'm working, and look at me!" She gestured at her apron, but that wasn't the worst part of her appearance.

Her hair was pulled back in a messy bun, a few loose tendrils sticking to her flushed face from the heat of the kitchen. She had hastily applied some eyeliner that morning, but it had no doubt smeared over the course of her long workday.

Couples swirled around them as Peter pulled her close, his large hand settling at the small of her back. "You deserve a break."

"I look messy, and you are set on embarrassing me in front of your family, and especially your mother."

Peter laughed. "First of all, you look as beautiful as always, and secondly, I love my mother, but she has no say in my love life."

The word 'love' hung between them, charged and bold and painfully irrelevant.

Marina couldn't resist teasing him about it, even though it would no doubt backfire. "Love, huh? That's a strong word."

Peter didn't shy away. Instead, he pulled her closer. "Yes, love. I'm not taking it back because it's the truth. I've fallen for you, and I don't want to let you go."

The breath stalled in Marina's lungs. She swallowed hard, peering up at him through the fan of her lashes. "Then don't," she blurted.

"I don't intend to."

As Peter's words lingered in the air, the music around them seemed to fade, and the chatter and laughter of the other guests became a distant murmur.

Regrettably, his expression looked teasing rather than serious, and Marina knew he didn't mean it the way she wished he would.

Afraid that her disappointment showed on her face, she shifted the conversation away from that dangerous territory. "Amanda was really sweet today," she said. "When I told her about Larissa not having anything to wear tomorrow, she promised to find something for her. I was so touched that the clan's princess volunteered to assist a lowly human."

Peter's brows furrowed. "Every member of our clan helps humans. We made it our mission to save victims of trafficking and rehabilitate them, and we fund most of the effort from our own coffers. Not to mention that we liberated you and your people from the Kra-ell."

Evidently, she'd hit a nerve. "I'm sorry. I didn't mean it that way. It's just that Amanda is such a princess, and she comes into the kitchen issuing orders without asking anyone if we can actually do what she wants, so I assumed she was stuck up. I was surprised at how nice she was and how accepting of our relationship."

The furrow between his brows smoothed out a little but didn't disappear. "What did she say?"

"She said that it was a shame I couldn't be your date for tonight because she hadn't seen you so happy in a long time."

Marina waited with bated breath for him to confirm what Amanda had said, and after what seemed like forever, he nodded. "That's true. Being with you makes me happy."

"Same here." She stretched up on her toes and kissed him lightly on the lips. "But I need to go."

As the song ended, Peter released her, his demeanor pleasant but distant.

With unease churning in her gut, Marina returned to work, her mind a whirlwind of what-ifs and maybes.

Peter had confessed that he was falling for her, and he'd even said that he didn't want to part with her, but when she'd blurted that she wanted him to take her with him, his reaction was far from enthusiastic.

Had he guessed her intentions? Did he think that he was just a means to an end for her?

It might have started that way, but it no longer was.

It was as real as it got.

35

KIAN

Kian glanced at his watch and then surveyed the party, the dim lights casting long shadows across the faces of the dwindling number of guests. It was only a few minutes past midnight, and the dance floor was not as packed as it had been an hour ago, but it was still quite lively, and laughter bubbled from a few clusters of seated guests. If he could wait another half an hour, his and Syssi's departure wouldn't arouse suspicion, but the clock was marching relentlessly toward half-past twelve, which was the latest they could afford to stay.

He caught Syssi's eye across the table and gestured with his head toward the exit.

Nodding, she pulled her phone from her clutch and affected a concerned frown. "Allegra is fussy," she said out loud and looked at Kian. "We need to go."

Amanda quirked a perfectly arched brow. "Isn't Parker babysitting her with Okidu?"

"She's asking for Mommy and Daddy." Syssi smiled. "She won't go back to sleep unless we show up." She stood, smoothing the folds of her purple gown.

Kian rose to his feet and took Syssi's hand. "Good night, everyone. Continue to enjoy the party."

A small chorus of good nights followed them as they made their way out of the dining hall and into the blessedly quiet corridor.

Kian let out a breath once they were alone. "Well played, my love." He pressed a quick kiss to Syssi's temple.

As they entered their cabin, Parker looked up at them with surprise in his eyes. "Why did you come back so early?" he asked, a hint of disappointment in his voice, perhaps at the evening ending sooner than expected and his babysitting fee shrinking.

"Syssi had a feeling Allegra was going to wake up and ask for us," Kian said, hoping the explanation sounded plausible given Syssi's psychic abilities.

He also pulled a crisp hundred-dollar bill from his wallet and handed it over with a conspiratorial wink.

Parker's eyes lit up at the sight of the bill, his disappointment quickly forgotten. "No problem, Mr. Kian. Allegra was great," he said with a broad smile. "Good night!" He waved cheerfully as he exited.

Once the boy was gone, they hurried to trade their elegant evening wear for comfortable clothing, and Syssi gently transferred their sleeping daughter from the portable crib into her stroller, covering her in a soft blue blanket.

Allegra didn't so much as stir throughout the transfer.

Kian swept his gaze over his two favorite girls, his heart swelling with love. He would walk through fire a thousand times over for them.

A glance at his watch had him tensing again. They had ten minutes to get to his mother's cabin and get ready for the session.

"We should get moving," he said in a hushed tone. "Aru will meet us there."

"I'm ready." Syssi put a yellow paper pad into a compartment of the stroller and pushed it toward the door.

"Where did you get that from?" Kian opened the door for her.

"Turner, of course. I asked him if he had a spare one, and he did. He didn't even ask what I needed it for."

"Naturally." Kian took command of the stroller.

As they made their way down the corridor to Annani's cabin, the short walk was done in silence, each lost in their own thoughts about what was to come.

Kian was nervous.

His mother had been waiting for this first meeting with her grandmother with such great excitement that he was worried she would be disappointed.

What if the queen of Anumati turned out to be a condescending monarch who would belittle her granddaughter?

Annani was the Clan Mother, the most superior being on Earth, and she wouldn't take well to being regarded with anything other than the utmost respect.

Syssi stopped in front of Annani's door. "Why are you so stressed?" she asked. "I know it's a monumental event, but you look like you are about to enter the lions' den, or the lionesses' as the case may be."

"I don't want my mother to be disappointed. She's been looking forward to this meeting with her grandmother, expecting to learn about the planet of the gods, their culture, their politics, but that is not what's going to happen during this initial meeting, and if the queen doesn't get what she wants, there might not be another one."

Syssi frowned. "What do you mean?"

"The queen needs to assess my mother, and she will be asking more questions than answering them. If she's impressed with my mother, she will schedule another meeting. If she's not, she might decide that it's not worth the risk she's taking."

Smiling, Syssi lifted her hand and cupped his cheek. "You have nothing to worry about. Your mother is the most impressive person I've ever met, heard of, or read about. There is no way the shrewd queen of Anumati wouldn't recognize her greatness."

He let out a breath. "I hope you are right. To me, my mother is second only to my wife, but the queen of the gods might not share my opinion."

Syssi laughed. "I'm sure she won't share your opinion about me, but I'm just as sure that she will agree that your mother is the most important person on Earth."

36

ARU

Aru clenched his jaw as he watched Kian and Syssi make their excuses and exit the wedding reception. As a wave of anger washed over him, a muscle ticked in his cheek. He couldn't forgive Kian for betraying his trust and telling Syssi about the telepathic connection Aru shared with his twin sister.

Being a seer, Syssi had seen Aria in a vision and guessed the truth, but Kian shouldn't have confirmed it for her. Visions were often unreliable, and without confirmation, Syssi might have dismissed it.

The knowledge of Aria's telepathic connection with Aru was supposed to be safeguarded at all costs, hidden away from the Eternal King and his numerous spies. Aru had stressed the importance of secrecy to Kian, and yet, his trust had been shattered. Part of him understood that the bond between mates made it difficult to keep things from each other, but this was a matter of life and death.

His sister's life depended on her ability to stay hidden from the ruthless dictator occupying the Anumati throne and, even more so, her part in assisting the queen, who was supporting the resistance.

The queen herself was in danger.

Queen Ani was too beloved by the citizens and too connected to the ruling families to dispose of outright. But the Eternal King was a master at orchestrating unfortunate "accidents" when it suited his purposes.

The king also had to remain oblivious to the fact that his son had sired a daughter on Earth before his untimely demise. If he ever learned of Annani's existence, the sole remaining legitimate heir to his throne, Aru shuddered to think what he would do.

Destroying Earth to eliminate Annani was a very real possibility.

The heir represented their best chance for a peaceful revolution. Her ascendancy to power could herald a new era for Anumati. Unlike her grandfather, Annani was no tyrant and had no greed for power. But like her grandfather, she was powerful and impressive. If the people of Anumati accepted her as their queen, she would rule them with a firm but kind hand and always look after their best interests.

Or so Aru hoped.

Power was corruptive, and once upon a time, the Eternal King hadn't been the monster he was today. He'd united Anumati's ruling families and brought prosperity to all, but he'd become too attached to his throne, so much so that he eliminated his own flesh and blood, his only son by his official mate, just so there would be no suitable contender to replace him.

A warm hand settling over his clenched fist drew Aru's attention back to the present. He blinked to find Gabi watching him with concern.

"What's wrong, my love?" She leaned closer to him. "You look troubled."

Aru forced his lips to curve in a reassuring smile as he turned his hand to lace their fingers together. "I have something I need to do that will take about an hour, and I will have to do it every night at the same time from now on. I wish I could tell you what it is, but I can't."

Gabi worried her lower lip briefly between her teeth as she studied him. "Does it have to do with Anumati?"

He nodded. "You don't have to leave with me. You can stay and enjoy the party."

Aru's chest twinged with a pang of remorse. Keeping things from his mate didn't sit well with him, instilling a dull ache of guilt. But it was a necessity. His sister's life was more important than even his bond with his mate.

Gabi smiled. "I know it must be important or you wouldn't keep it from me. I don't need to know the particulars."

The truth of her words was like a soothing balm gliding over the frayed edges of his nerves. He surged forward to capture her lips in a fierce kiss.

"Thank you," he rasped when they finally broke apart, his forehead resting against hers. "I don't know what I did to deserve such a perfect, understanding mate, but I'm grateful to the Fates for you every day."

Gabi's face glowed with pleasure at his words, smoky lashes sweeping low to veil her shining eyes. "I'm the lucky one, my love. I'll leave with you," she said with a teasing lilt. "I'll just head back to our cabin and relax until you return. I'll be waiting for you in something skimpy and lacy." She waggled her brows.

Aru groaned low in his throat, capturing her mouth once more in a hungry kiss. When the need for air became too pressing to ignore, he finally tore his lips away with a shuddering inhale.

"You're deliciously wicked, my love," he growled hoarsely, drinking in the sight of her tousled curls and passion-glazed eyes. "Now, I will have to conduct my business with a raging hard-on."

She laughed, smoothing her hands over the plackets of his tux jacket. "Try to finish your business as soon as possible. I'm not a patient woman."

37

ANNANI

Annani smoothed her hand over the soft silk of her flowing gown as she settled onto the plush couch. Though her heart was racing with excitement, she projected an aura of calm, clutching a steaming teacup in her hands.

This moment had been weeks in the making, and she could scarcely allow her turbulent emotions to overwhelm her now that it had finally arrived.

As the doorbell rang, she watched Oridu usher Kian and Syssi in with Allegra nestled in her stroller.

"Hello, Mother." Kian leaned to kiss her cheek. "Are you excited?"

"Of course." She peered down at Allegra's peacefully slumbering face, resisting the urge to brush her fingers over the downy curve of her cheek.

To wake her now would only lead to fussing that could disrupt the critical meeting ahead. Annani contented herself with drinking in the sight of her granddaughter. To compensate, tomorrow she would hold her to her chest and kiss her cheeks until the little girl pushed her away.

"She is so perfect," Annani whispered.

Kian's chest puffed up with fatherly pride. "That she is."

"You could have left her with Okidu," Annani said. "There was no need to interrupt her sleep."

Syssi sat next to her on the couch. "Allegra didn't even stir when I transferred her to the stroller. Besides, our excuse for leaving the party early was a fussy baby, so if anyone asks, Allegra demanded to see her Nana."

Annani laughed, some of the tension leaving her shoulders. "No one would doubt that story. Allegra's demands have to be obeyed, or else."

"You make her sound like a spoiled brat." Kian sat down on Annani's other side.

"Fates forbid." Annani put a hand on her chest. "She is simply assertive, which is important for a future leader."

That seemed to mollify her son, and as he gazed at the sleeping baby, his lips curved in a soft smile. "For as long as I can, I will spare her the need to take on the mantle of leadership."

Annani patted Kian's knee. "I have a feeling that when little Allegra is all grown up, she will be thrilled to ease your burden and take the mantle of leadership upon her shoulders. Leaders are born, Kian. They are not made."

"Perhaps." He sighed.

"Can I pour tea for you, Mistress Syssi?" Oridu bowed nearly in half.

"That would be lovely, thank you."

When he was done pouring tea into Syssi's cup, Oridu turned to Kian, still in the bowed position. "Master Kian?"

"Yes, please."

When Oridu was done pouring, the doorbell rang again, and Ogidu rushed to open the door.

Aru strode into the room, his brow furrowed in concentration as he bowed to Annani. "Good morning, Your Highness. Aria says they will be ready to begin in a few minutes."

"Thank you, Aru." She motioned for him to take a seat on the armchair. "Would you like some tea?"

As he nodded, Oridu hastened to fill his cup and hand it to him.

As she waited for Aru to begin, Annani's heart pounded in her chest. Soon, she would converse with her grandmother for the first time. The matriarch of her lineage, the queen of Anumati, held answers to so many questions that Annani could not think of them all.

She should have written them down, but the truth was that she did not expect to learn much tonight. The queen would want to get the measure of her, which meant that the one answering questions would be Annani.

She did not need to prepare for that.

She had many regrets, but if given a chance for a do-over, she would have most likely done things the same way, even knowing the consequences.

Well, that was not true. She would have never allowed Khiann to leave with the caravan. She would have even involved her father to forbid his departure.

Khiann's murder had started the chain of events that led to the gods' demise, and all she had needed to do to stop it was be more assertive and less accommodating.

But then, hindsight was always 20-20.

At the time, she had felt that she was doing the right thing by her husband, letting him do the things he loved and not stifling him by confining him to the palace.

38

QUEEN ANI

As the temple doors closed behind Ani's attendants, she embraced Sofringhati. "Finally, the day has arrived."

Sofri patted her back. "You are cold, my friend." Sofri turned to her scribe. "Could you please raise the heat in the braziers, Aria? It is a little chilly in here."

Aria bowed. "Of course."

"And also move the cushions closer to the heat," Sofri added.

"Yes, Supreme Oracle." Aria bowed again and rushed to comply with Sofringhati's commands.

Everywhere else on Anumati, the temperature in the room would have been adjusted automatically, the sensors adjusting the heating or cooling based on its occupants' biomarkers, but walking into the Supreme Oracle's temple was like stepping hundreds of thousands of years back in time.

The chamber was completely devoid of technology, with the illumination coming from burning sconces attached to the towering columns and the heating from ancient braziers that burned oil and had to be adjusted manually.

Nevertheless, to Ani the temple felt more like home than her own suite of rooms in the palace. Here, amidst the thick, isolating walls and towering columns and carvings of ancient prophecies, Ani could drop the mask of the untouchable monarch for a couple of hours and enjoy the company of her only friend.

"Please, sit down, Ani." Sofri pointed to the cushions that Aria had dragged closer to the braziers.

Ani made herself comfortable on the large square pillow and tucked her legs under her. "Whenever I am here, I am reminded of our days in the dormitories. We used to sit like this and chat for hours until the headmistress sent us to bed."

Taking a seat on the other cushion, Sofri sighed. "I miss those days. Life was simpler when our biggest worry was passing exams. We were so naive."

"I miss being that girl." Ani sighed. "That being said, I knew even then that I would not be free to choose who I would mate, and that my marriage would be a political alliance. I just did not imagine that I would be chosen by the king." She chuckled. "Let alone one day lead a rebellion against him."

"You loved him once."

Ani shook her head. "I was blinded by his charm, but it did not take me long to realize that what he projected was very different from who he really was. I still admired him for many years, though. He was good for Anumati until he stopped being so."

Sofri canted her head. "He was never good to the Kra-ell. Ahn opened your eyes to the injustice done to them."

Tears misted Ani's eyes.

Usually, she was very good at masking her emotions, but no one other than Sofri spoke Ahn's name anymore, and hearing it said out loud was like a javelin to her heart.

Ani's thoughts drifted to Annani, her granddaughter, the living legacy of her lost son, his direct descendant who was hidden away on Earth. The knowledge that Ahn's legacy lived on, that his bloodline had not been extinguished, was like an injection of vitality for Ani, an unexpected beacon of light in the darkness.

Would Annani prove to be all that Ani hoped for?

Would she be like Ahn?

Little Ani, Ahn had named his daughter, and according to Aru, Annani bore an uncanny resemblance to Ani. Hopefully, it would not be just skin deep.

So many questions bubbled within her, so many words of guidance she longed to impart.

Ani turned her attention to Aria, the young scribe who was about to become the conduit for a conversation that spanned light years and yet was as instantaneous as a quantum communicator.

"I am ready, Aria."

The scribe nodded. "I will check with Aru if they are ready as well."

As she waited, Ani allowed her mind to wander through the past, through all the decisions and sacrifices she had made. Her relationship with the Supreme Oracle, Sofringhati, had always been her anchor, providing a safe harbor in the treacherous waters of Anumati's society. But even Sofri, with all her foresight, had been unable to predict the loss of Ani's son, not until after the fact.

There was a limit to what an oracle could see, and Ani suspected that the Fates allowed Sofringhati to see only what suited their plans and promoted their agenda.

For now, Annani was alive and well on Earth, but Sofri could not see what the future had in store for her, and that filled Ani's heart with fear.

Now that she had found Ahn's daughter, the thought of losing her as she had lost Ahn was unbearable, and if she dragged Annani into the rebellion she would be putting her at great risk.

What chance did a goddess with no knowledge of Anumati's intricate politics and power plays have against the Eternal King?

Perhaps it was best to leave her be and not involve her in the resistance. Ani could train her over many years, making sure that Annani knew all there was to know about Anumati's history, social structure, economy, and politics, and bring her home to present to their people only once the Eternal King was eliminated, but not before.

Ani could not bear the thought of losing Annani, and that was even before they had exchanged a single word.

39

ANNANI

Annani watched Aru's face, noting the subtle shift in his expression as he connected with his sister and bridged the vast distance between Anumati and Earth through their extraordinary link.

Finally, Aru announced, "The queen is ready."

Annani set her tea aside. "I am ready as well."

"Greetings from Queen Ani of Anumati," Aru said in the gods' language, which resembled the tongue of her youth but not precisely.

Still, she understood enough to get the message the greeting conveyed, setting a tone for their conversation.

The greeting was not from Ani, the grandmother who was overjoyed to discover that her beloved son had fathered a daughter before he died. The greeting was from the queen of Anumati.

It made Annani acutely aware of the fine line she needed to walk. She needed to show the proper deference expected when addressing a monarch, yet this was also her grandmother, her father's mother, and some warmth needed to be injected into the conversation to establish rapport.

"Please convey my deepest respects and heartfelt greetings to Her Majesty," Annani replied in English.

Her knowledge of the gods' language was not sufficient to conduct a high-level conversation.

Next to her, Syssi was writing with a pen on a yellow notepad, and Annani wondered whether she had understood Aru's words or guessed the meaning.

For the sake of record keeping, it would be better to conduct the conversation in English.

"I am overjoyed to finally meet you, my dear granddaughter," Aru translated, probably arriving at the same conclusion as Annani.

Nevertheless, the words sounded strange coming out in his masculine voice and yet sweet in Annani's ears. Her grandmother acknowledged their blood ties and addressed her as she wished to be addressed. "I wish I could gaze upon your face and see for myself the resemblance Aru reported, but regrettably, I do not possess telepathic abilities and I cannot peer into Aria's mind to see what Aru is sending to her through their connection. I can only hear what she repeats."

Annani glanced at Syssi, who had seen the queen and Aria in her prophetic vision. With Syssi's permission, Annani could peek into her mind and see her grandmother, but perhaps it was not a good idea to mention her hybrid children and their hybrid mates just yet.

The queen had been informed of the immortals' existence, but she might choose to ignore everyone other than Annani and perhaps Toven.

Even Ahn, who had been a progressive god, had ignored Areana, his own daughter, because she was a weak goddess born to a concubine. He hadn't fathered any hybrid children, but if he had, Annani had no doubt that he would have ignored their existence even more pointedly than Areana's.

She had no illusions that her father had been without fault, but he had been a rebel who fought for the rights of those who were considered second class on Anumati. Life was full of contradictions. She could imagine the queen as an elitist, even though she had believed in her son's cause enough to shoulder it after his exile.

On the other hand, Annani had nothing to be ashamed of, and if her grandmother sneered at her hybrid children, then Annani did not want to have anything to do with her.

"I am grateful to Aru and Aria for providing us this opportunity to communicate on a private channel that the Eternal King cannot spy on. For the sake of transparency, though, I would like to mention that my son and his wife are here with me, and my daughter-in-law is transcribing our conversation. My son's name is Kian, and his mate's name is Syssi. Syssi is a seer, and she had a vision of you, the Oracle, and Aria. If she permits it, I can peek into her mind and see what each of you looks like."

There was a long moment of silence as Aru transmitted what she had said to Aria, who in turn repeated it to the queen. Annani waited with bated breath for her grandmother's response.

"Greetings to my great-grandson and his mate."

Annani let out a breath. The queen had acknowledged Kian as her great-grandson, knowing that he was a hybrid.

"Please convey our greetings and deepest respects to Her Majesty," Kian told Aru.

A short moment passed before Aru spoke again. "I know that you have many questions, my dearest granddaughter, and I will answer them in time, but today, I want to learn about you. Aru told Aria what he knew, but I want you to tell me more about your life."

Annani had expected that. Her grandmother needed to assess her and verify that she was worthy of the role the queen hoped she would one day assume. If she was not impressed, she would not invest the time and effort to groom her for the role of Anumati's future monarch.

Annani was not yet sure that she wanted the job, but she wanted to be deemed worthy.

"I have lived for over five thousand Earth years, and I have had many adventures and trials, accomplishments and setbacks, but I have never given up no matter how hopeless things seemed at the time. Where would you like me to start, Your Majesty?"

"Tell me about your father and your relationship with him. He named you after me. Did he groom you to one day become queen?"

"Yes, he did." Annani smiled. "My father, your son, taught me all I know about duty, responsibility, fairness, and respect for all, including the lowliest of humans. I have spent countless hours in the throne room, listening to proceedings that bored me to the point of despair. But he taught me what it meant to be a leader and that sometimes there are no good choices, and a leader cannot hide from her responsibility or let another shoulder it. She has to choose the least harmful one and continue forward."

Annani paused, allowing Aru time to repeat her words to Aria.

A few moments later, he said, "Tell me about your mother."

Annani smiled. The queen wanted to ensure that her parents had been officially married when they had her. Otherwise, she could not be Ahn's official heir.

"My mother was not even seventeen when she set her sights on my father and decided that he would be hers. She was not of legal age, but since it was known that he was about to choose a wife, she knew that she could not wait until she reached the age of consent and set out to seduce him before it was too late. Long story short, he succumbed to her temptation, finding out too late her real age. To avoid the legal complications of his transgression, my father proposed, and they were married. It was not long before he realized that she was his fated one and only, and that the Fates had gifted him with the greatest joy a god could hope for."

There was a long moment of silence before Aru relayed the queen's answer. "I am glad that my son found happiness with your mother, but I am not glad that their relationship had started with deceit."

Annani chuckled. "Then Your Majesty should brace herself because my tale is full of conspiracies and manipulations, although given what I have heard of Anumati, that should not come as a surprise."

Aru's lips quirked up in a smile. "That is true, my astute granddaughter. Please continue with your tale."

40

QUEEN ANI

As Aria continued relaying Annani's tale about her ill-fated engagement to Mortdh and her cunning way of subverting it, Ani's ire rose.

What had possessed Ahn to arrange such a match for his beloved daughter?

Ani had known Mortdh quite well. He had been like his grandfather, marked by the same unquenchable ambition and hunger for power but lacking the charm and sophistication of the king. Even as a child, his eyes had been full of shadows far too dark for his young age.

He had been nothing like Ekin, Ahn's half-brother by one of the king's numerous concubines. Mortdh's father had been loyal and fully dedicated to Ahn and his cause. His passion was science and engineering, and he had no ambitions other than inventing things and supporting Ahn's rebellion. It was regrettable that Mortdh had inherited none of Ekin's nobler qualities while sharing his father's sharp intelligence.

It was a bitter pill to swallow to realize that Ahn had made such a monumental error in judgment, but Ani understood his reasoning. Her son had been an idealist, and he had been willing to sacrifice even his own daughter's happiness on the altar of his people's greater good. But Ani was disappointed that he had naively believed mollifying Mortdh would ensure peace.

Sacrificing Annani would not have prevented war. At best, it would have postponed it, and at worst, it would have cost Annani's life.

"Ahn was smart, but he was also a dreamer, an optimist, and an idealist," Ani said. "He believed that given the chance and the benefit of the doubt, people would rise to the occasion. In rare instances, he could have been right, but all too often his naive belief that people were inherently good was dangerous. It was both his greatest strength and his most significant weakness."

Admitting this truth of Ahn's flaws had not been easy. His soft spot for family had blinded him to the potential dangers of binding his daughter to someone like Mortdh.

Annani's reply came a moment later. "I am just glad that my father listened to my plea when I asked him to allow Khiann to court me."

Ani listened intently as Annani recounted her daring pursuit of Khiann, the son of a merchant god whom her father would have never considered as a mate for her. She had disguised herself as a commoner to bypass the rigid structures of their society and sought out the god who had captured her heart.

Ani's heart swelled with pride.

Even at a young age, her granddaughter had displayed uncommon boldness and determination, unwilling to let her future be dictated by others.

Like her, Annani refused to be a pawn in the political games that dominated their world. She had taken matters into her own hands, changing the course of history.

Annani was precisely what Anumati needed. A bold and courageous leader with a clear vision of the right path.

The queen chuckled as Aria continued recounting Annani's exploits, detailing how she had instructed Khiann to approach Ahn, and her heart soared when she heard how Ahn had handled the situation. He had cunningly employed Khiann as a tutor to test the waters of their potential as fated mates, allowing the relationship to develop under the guise of mentorship while protecting the secrecy of the potential bond.

And then came the resolution—the revelation of Annani and Khiann's status as fated mates and Ahn's subsequent affirmation of the paramount importance of the Fates' will and dissolution of Annani's engagement to Mortdh.

The decision to offer Mortdh Annani's half-sister, Areana, as an alternative was a masterstroke, maintaining diplomatic relations while safeguarding his only legitimate heir.

Some might have viewed the move as heartless, but it was just one more example of a leader choosing the lesser of two evils.

The queen cast a sidelong glance at her best friend, who was listening to Aria with rapt attention and a smile on her face.

"Your granddaughter is a take-charge goddess, Ani. She is exactly what Anumati needs."

Ani reached for her friend's hand and gave it a light squeeze.

Her heart was full as she considered the future with Annani as queen. It would be the dawn of a new era for Anumati, one led by a goddess who understood what it meant to be a leader, and valued love, the importance of being in the driver's seat of one's own destiny, and the power of being proactive instead of reactive.

Annani continued to recount her brief marriage and the subsequent tragedy that befell her and the other gods, or at least the version that she had been told and had accepted as true. "Mortdh murdered my Khiann in cold blood. He had planned the ambush days in advance and killed my love with his own hands. The assembly of gods heard the witnesses' account of the brutal murder and sentenced Mortdh to entombment, but to do that, they had to catch him and bring him to justice first. But since he commanded a large force of immortal warriors, the assembly deliberated for days about the best way to do that. Mortdh, on the other hand, did not wait. To escape his punishment, he used a weapon of mass destruction on the assembly hall, killing all the gods inside. I managed to escape because I was afraid of him coming after me, so I ran away to the far north. My sister Areana was on her way to Mortdh's stronghold, so that was how she survived. Toven, Mortdh's brother, was away on one of his expeditions at the time, and that was how he was spared as well. We were the only three gods remaining on Earth until the arrival of Aru and his team."

Listening to the story unfold, Ani's heart went out to her granddaughter, a kindred spirit who had suffered a terrible loss and had known grief as great as hers.

When Aria fell silent, Ani let out a sigh. "Mortdh might have murdered your mate, but he probably was not responsible for the cataclysm that befell the rest of your people and destroyed a large portion of the region. Mortdh loved himself too much to go on a suicide mission, and he was too smart not to realize that he would not survive the blast in a small craft that had limited speed and maneuverability. He was most likely a pawn, used as a scapegoat for the real perpetrators."

Annani's shocked response carried over through Aria's voice. "If it was not Mortdh, then who was the real perpetrator?"

41

ANNANI

Annani had often entertained the same doubts about Mortdh's intentions that fateful day, but if not him, then who could have destroyed the assembly hall along with all the gods inside of it?

The truth was that no one knew for a fact that it had been a bomb. The particulars of the devastation suggested a nuclear weapon, but it could have been some other alien technology that had similar cataclysmic results.

The narrative she had clung to, the one that had painted Mortdh as the ultimate villain in their tragic tale, had been unraveling ever since Jade's account of Anumati's history and then Igor's, but there had been too many pieces of the puzzle missing to solve the mystery.

"If it was not Mortdh, then who was the real perpetrator?" Annani asked.

"I have no definite proof," Aru translated the queen's words. "But there is plenty of circumstantial evidence. Shortly before the catastrophe, an Anumatian patrol ship passed near Earth, and a team of scouts was deployed. By then, communications with Earth had been severed. The king blamed the destruction of the communication satellites on Ahn, the rebel who didn't want to face the accusations of war crimes that his father had trumped up against him. The truth was that the king had ordered the satellites destroyed.

"Sometime later, the Eternal King announced in a public address that the heir, along with his half-brother and sister and all the other gods who had been exiled to Earth, had perished.

"Since there was supposedly no communication with Earth, the king claimed that a seer told him of the demise of all of the gods on Earth, but it was not my friend, and when she checked with the other oracles, none of them admitted to delivering the news to the king. Still, that does not mean that the king had not had a seer in his employ who had just not reported the truth to my friend. Ahn's father pretended to be devastated by the loss and announced a day of mourning to show that he was a good father who loved his children even though they had betrayed him.

"I asked the Supreme Oracle to try to see what had really happened to them, but for some reason, Earth was hidden from her view. All she could do was confirm what the king said. The Supreme Oracle and I suspect that the Fates were shielding you and the two other surviving gods from the Eternal King's seers. If the Supreme Oracle couldn't see Earth, none of the lesser ones could either. Therefore, the only way the king could have known about the fate of the Earthbound gods' was because he had a hand in their demise."

It was not news to Annani that her grandfather was a terrible god. She had heard the tale from Jade's perspective, but it was not the same as hearing from her grandmother how the Eternal King had spun his deceitful narrative to consolidate his power and eliminate any threats to his rule, even those from his own flesh and blood. It made her heart heavy. The public mourning and the feigned benevolence were all a calculated act to cloak his tyrannical reign in a veneer of paternal sorrow and righteousness.

The greatest revelation so far was that Earth was obscured from the Supreme Oracle's vision, and therefore shielded from the prying eyes of the king's seers.

"It's a relief knowing that we are obscured," Kian said.

Aru opened his eyes and looked at him. "Do you want me to translate that for the queen?"

Kian shook his head. "I'm just an observer. Only translate my mother's words."

Nodding, Aru turned to Annani. "Anything Your Highness would like to say to Her Majesty?"

"I am grateful to the merciful Fates for shielding me, my sister, and my cousin from the machinations of the Eternal King."

"So am I," Aru translated the queen's words after a moment.

The realization that her grandfather had ordered the bombing to ensure his dominion filled her with revulsion. Mortdh had become a scapegoat in the Eternal King's scheme, but she felt no pity for him. He might not have been responsible for the bombing, but his cold-blooded murder of Khiann was indisputable.

She had heard the witnesses' account with her own two ears, and their words still reverberated in her mind five thousand years later, bringing bile to her throat and an unbearable ache to her chest.

"Mortdh was a tyrant and a murderer, but it seems that he was not the architect of our people's destruction," Annani said. "He was caught in a web much larger than his own making, perhaps even unknowingly used by my grandfather."

A few moments passed before Aru conveyed the queen's response. "Our time today draws to an end. We will have to continue our talk on the morrow, my dear Annani."

"Thank you, Grandmother. I shall await our next conversation."

The understanding that she had escaped not just Mortdh's ambitions but the far reach of the Eternal King, made Annani feel blessed and a little humbler than she had been before the start of the conversation with her grandmother. She was alive, not by chance, not by her own decisiveness and clear vision, but by the Fates' design.

42

KIAN

Kian grappled with the information the queen had relayed, and so did his mother and Syssi. The only one who didn't look surprised was Aru, and Kian had a feeling that the god had known about the patrol ship and the potential assassins that had been sent to end Ahn and the other gods.

Shaking her head, his mother got up and started pacing. "If Mortdh didn't kill the gods, maybe he didn't kill Khiann either?" She looked at Kian with hope and desperation shining in her eyes. "His body was never found because his murder coincided with the earthquake. What if he is buried in the desert, alive in stasis?"

Kian's heart clenched. He understood his mother's desire to cling to any shred of hope, to believe that her beloved mate might still be alive somewhere, waiting to be found, but clinging to false hope would just reopen old wounds that had scabbed over.

Rising to his feet, he walked over to her and put a hand on her shoulder.

"I know you want to believe that, but you heard the witnesses describe the murder yourself. They saw Mortdh kill Khiann with their own eyes."

His mother's shoulders slumped, the brief spark of hope dimming in her eyes. She sighed. "I know, Kian. I just allowed myself to hope for a moment."

The familiar mask of composure settling over her features again, she offered him a smile. "We should call it a night." She cast a quick glance at her sleeping granddaughter, and the fake smile turned genuine. "Allegra will be more comfortable in her crib."

Leaning down, Kian kissed his mother's cheek. "Are you going to be okay?"

She nodded. "This is a lot to process, but we had our doubts for a long time, so it should not have come as such a big shock. We have always wondered what actually happened that day and what prompted Mortdh to act out of character. Now, we know that he did not intend to commit suicide. Perhaps he was coerced by a compeller even more powerful than he was, or maybe he just happened to be at the right place at the right moment for the assassins to frame him for what they did."

Syssi nodded. "I still wonder how the real perpetrators managed to coordinate it so perfectly that it appeared as if it was Mortdh's fault."

"We can talk more about this over brunch tomorrow," Kian suggested. "After we've all had a chance to process everything we've learned."

"That is a good idea." Annani took a deep breath. "Thank you for being here with me tonight." She smiled at Syssi. "It would have been much more difficult without you." She turned to Aru. "I am grateful to you and your sister for your help tonight. Thank you for enabling this conversation and all the future ones that will follow."

"We are glad to help." The god didn't sound convincing, which was understandable.

He and his sister were taking a great risk, and it wasn't as if either of them had a choice in the matter. They had been recruited, and saying no to the queen of Anumati had not been an option.

After they had said their goodbyes and walked out of the cabin, Kian waited for Ogidu to close the door behind them before turning to Aru. "You knew about the assassins."

"I did," he admitted. "But since it's all conjecture and speculation, I didn't want to bring it up. Maybe Mortdh was responsible after all, or maybe the assassins shot him down and caused the weapon to explode. We will never know the truth because the only one who knows it is the king."

"And the assassins," Syssi said.

Aru shook his head. "I doubt that they are still around. The Eternal King does not leave any breadcrumbs that could lead back to him."

Kian felt a flicker of irritation at Aru's admission. He understood the god's reluctance to share unconfirmed theories, but part of him wished they had been better prepared for the emotional fallout of this revelation.

"I get why you didn't want to bring it up," Kian said, running a hand through his hair. "But maybe a little warning would have been warranted. I hated seeing the hope flare in my mother's eyes only to have to quash it."

A hint of regret flickered through Aru's eyes, but then they hardened. "I apologize, but it really wasn't my place to share this information."

Was he still angry about Syssi finding out about Aria?

Probably.

Kian regarded the god with a frown. "I assume that your teammates don't know about this either."

"Of course not." Aru glanced at the cameras mounted on the walls. "I'd rather not talk about it out here."

"Don't worry about it." Kian waved a hand at the camera. "I asked for the cameras to be turned off on this deck between midnight and three o'clock in the morning every night from now until the end of the cruise." He chuckled. "I can only imagine what the Guardians in security think of my request."

Syssi groaned. "Now I understand the smirks I noticed during the wedding. They are probably imagining us chasing each other in the nude down the corridor."

Aru's eyes widened, but he was smart enough not to respond.

"No one was smirking at you." Kian kissed the top of Syssi's head before turning to the god. "Nevertheless, we shouldn't conduct such conversations out in the hallway. Would you like to come to our cabin for a glass of whiskey?"

The god smiled. "Thank you for the invitation, but I will have to take a raincheck. It's after two o'clock in the morning, and my mate is waiting for me in our cabin."

"I understand." Kian offered Aru his hand. "Thank you for your help tonight."

Aru shook it. "It was definitely an interesting hour. I'm looking forward to the next session tomorrow."

43

NEGAL

As the party dwindled, with more than half the guests having left, Negal started his slow seduction of Margo by massaging her toes.

After admitting to being ready, she'd been so nervous that he'd started to doubt her assertion, and his doubts had only increased when he'd told her that he couldn't secure a private cabin for tonight and had seen her visibly relax.

That was why he hadn't told her about the plan Dagor had suggested, deciding it would be better to just let it unfold naturally. He would offer to once again sleep on the couch in the living room and leave the initiative of inviting him to her bedroom up to Margo.

Despite the urgency of the situation, their first time together shouldn't happen under pressure.

Sitting in a chair with her feet on his knees, he kneaded and rubbed, eliciting soft moans of pleasure that stirred a predictable reaction from him. Thankfully, the lighting was dim, and his tux jacket covered the evidence.

"Are foot massages your secret talent?" Margo teased.

Working his fingers gently on her arches, he smirked. "It's just one among many."

Her eyes sparkled with interest. "What are your other talents?"

Negal hoped to demonstrate his other talents tonight, but he didn't say that. Keeping Margo relaxed was his number one priority right now, and since she was well aware of how much he wanted her, there was no chance of her misunderstanding his lack of initiative for disinterest.

When she felt truly ready, she would take the next step.

"That looks so good." Frankie plopped on a chair next to Margo and toed off her ridiculously high heels. "I could use some of that." She cast a smile at Dagor. "Any volunteers?"

Pretending innocence, he arched a brow and looked around. "Maybe I can find someone for you."

She grabbed a napkin off the table and threw it at him. "Sit."

"Yes, ma'am." He pulled out a chair on Frankie's other side and lifted her feet onto his lap.

Margo smiled. "I thought that turning immortal would mean no more toe pain from high heels."

"I still feel pain just as I did before." Frankie's expression turned blissful as Dagor went to work on her feet. "But thankfully, not for long because I recover so quickly. This, though, feels divine." She sighed. "Still, I'm a little peeved about not gaining more inches during my transition. It would have been nice not to need high heels."

"Amanda wears heels," Margo said. "And she's very tall."

"So is the bride." Frankie shifted her gaze to Kri, who was still on the dance floor with her groom after long hours of dancing. "Kri is smart. She's wearing flats."

Listening to their conversation, Negal absentmindedly kept rubbing Margo's toes while thinking of the best way to steer the four of them toward the cabin so he could put Dagor's plan in motion.

His teammate cast him a knowing look and then gently lifted Frankie's feet off his lap. "Are you ready to call it a night?" He lowered her feet to the floor and leaned down to collect her shoes. "I can carry you if you don't want to put your shoes back on."

Frankie gave the platforms a baleful look. "I don't want to put them on, but I don't want you to carry me out of here either."

Dagor affected a disappointed pout. "But I love carrying you around. You fit so well in my arms."

Frankie sighed with a small smile playing on her lips. "I'll walk to the elevator, and then you can carry me."

He grinned as if she had given him the best of gifts.

"I should call it a night, too." Margo lifted her feet off Negal's lap and slid them into her discarded shoes. "I don't think I'm up for any more dancing."

Hallelujah.

Negal got up and offered her his hand. "Neither am I."

After congratulating the newlyweds and saying their goodbyes, the four of them left the dining hall and headed toward the elevators. Negal kept some distance from the other couple and leaned to whisper in Margo's ear. "Those two are not going to leave the door to their bedroom open tonight. I need to sleep on the living room couch again to keep an eye on you."

Margo smiled at him. "I'm fine, really, and I don't need to be watched over, but I would love to wind down on the couch with you with a cup of tea and a good movie."

Had Margo been entertaining the same ideas as he was?

Negal's grin threatened to split his face in half. "It would be my pleasure to snuggle with you on the couch."

When she glanced up at him, her cheeks looked a little rosy, and he had a feeling it wasn't from the two drinks she'd had throughout the evening. "You should probably change out of the tux first. You look very handsome in it, but it's not the right outfit for snuggling."

"You are right," he agreed.

As soon as they entered the elevator, Dagor scooped Frankie into his arms and the two started kissing as if they were alone in there.

Margo and Negal exchanged smiles.

When the elevator stopped on their deck, Dagor walked out with Frankie in his arms, and Margo followed.

Negal stayed inside, holding the door from closing. "I'll change clothes and be there shortly."

Margo smiled. "I'll brew us some tea."

44

MARGO

As Margo walked into the cabin, her heart felt as if it was beating too fast in her chest, and her hands felt clammy. If she hadn't known better, she would have feared a health problem, but she'd had her annual checkup recently, and everything was great.

Her symptoms were the fault of a six-foot-three alien with blond, wavy hair and piercing blue eyes, and the soul of an angel.

Negal wouldn't agree with her on the last one, but she had seen enough of his beautiful soul to make that assertion. He was a very good person, and she wasn't saying that just because she was falling in love with him.

"Good night, Margo." Frankie waved from Dagor's arms.

"See you in the morning," Dagor said as he carried Frankie into their bedroom.

"Good night," Margo said with a smile.

As the door closed behind them, Margo sighed.

It was nice to see Frankie so happy. She and Dagor were so obviously in love, so effortlessly.

If only she could be a little bit like Frankie and not a nervous wreck whose hands shook as she thought about inviting the male she was falling in love with to her bed.

She wasn't a blushing virgin, for goodness' sake. She was a grown woman.

Inside her bedroom, Margo slipped out of her evening gown and hung it carefully in the closet. The hours of dancing had left her feeling sticky and overheated, and she needed a shower, but what if Negal arrived before she was done?

Frankie and Dagor were probably already tearing each other's clothes off so they wouldn't let him in.

She needed to let him know.

Pulling out her phone, she texted him. *I'm taking a quick shower, so if I don't answer the door, please wait for a few minutes and try again.*

His return text arrived a moment later. *I was just about to step into the shower as well, so take your time. I will be there in twenty minutes.*

Margo sent Negal an emoji of a thumbs up and put the phone on the charger.

A smile ghosted across her lips as she imagined him taking a cold shower to cool down. It hadn't escaped her notice that he'd been rock hard when he'd massaged her feet, and she'd tormented him with the sounds she'd made.

Perhaps it hadn't been nice of her, but she needed him in the mood for what she was planning. Not that Negal needed much encouragement to get aroused. He'd even admitted on several occasions that he had trouble controlling his responses to her.

As she stepped into the shower and the warm water cascaded over her skin, Margo imagined it washing away her insecurities.

She was a confident and assertive woman in all ways but one, and it was time she conquered that last frontier and allowed herself to flourish sexually. But a lifetime of reserve and self-doubt was hard to shake off, even in the face of her overwhelming attraction to Negal.

Once she was done washing and scrubbing every inch of her skin, she stepped out of the shower, dried herself off, and slipped into the new nightgown and robe he'd bought for her.

The silky fabric felt so luxurious against her skin that it was almost decadent. If not for Negal's insistence, she never would have splurged on something like that for herself, and even though he'd insisted on paying for everything, she made a mental note to calculate just how much she owed him.

Margo was determined to pay him back once she got her first paycheck from her job at Perfect Match.

With a few minutes left to spare, she settled onto the couch and reached for the historical novel she'd borrowed from Jasmine. She flipped through the pages, searching for the naughty bits, hoping to find some inspiration or courage from the fictional characters. But as she skimmed the flowery language and period-specific dialogue, Margo found herself more bemused than aroused. Without the context of the full story, the intimate scenes felt disconnected and overly dramatic.

The book painted Lord Alistair as a man of fierce passions and brooding intensity, a warrior whose mere presence could ignite a woman's heart with untold desires.

"Annabella's breath hitched as she beheld the sight of the rugged Scottish lord. With his broad shoulders straining against his tartan and his eyes as stormy as the Highland skies, Lord Alistair was a vision of masculinity."

Imagining the scene, Margo snorted softly at how ridiculous it sounded.

"In the dimly lit stables, their eyes met across the straw-covered floor. Annabella felt a wild stirring within her, an untamed yearning that drew her closer to the brawny lord."

Margo couldn't stifle a laugh. "Untamed yearning, really? What does that even mean?"

"Lord Alistair was overcome by the beauty of the wash girl disguising herself as a lady, and he took a step forward, closing the distance between them. 'Annabella,' he growled in a voice that was laden with desire, 'I ken not what magic ye possess to draw me so.'"

Margo rolled her eyes and read aloud in a deep voice and a Scottish twang. "'I ken not what magic ye possess?'"

"As their lips met in a passionate embrace, Annabella melted against the strength of Lord Alistair's embrace, her doubts and fears dissipating like mist in the morning sun."

Shaking her head, Margo closed the book.

The flowery, over-the-top prose was ridiculous, and the two-dimensional characters were not relatable, but there was something endearing about the simplicity and predictability of the story.

Margo could understand Jasmine's preference for period romances, but it wasn't her cup of tea. To truly lose herself in the narrative, Margo needed a story with more substance, and more relatable characters and situations, which was kind of funny since she loved reading about shifters and fae, and all sorts of otherworldly beings.

Glancing at the door, Margo thought about the real story unfolding between her and a god, which was much more fantastical than the story of a Scottish lord falling for the beautiful but lowly wash girl and also all the shifter romances she favored.

45

NEGAL

Negal walked out of the shower much calmer and more collected than when he'd entered it. Pleasuring himself to the image of Margo might have been a violation of sorts, but he'd excused it by the need to take the edge off, which was necessary to keeping his cool and not ravaging the woman the moment he entered her cabin.

It was good that she'd texted him and provided him with an excellent excuse not to rush.

After toweling off, he slipped into a pair of comfortable training pants and a soft t-shirt but then reconsidered his choice of attire and changed into a pair of jeans that would hopefully provide some level of concealment.

Given that she referred to an erection as a one-eyed trouser snake, he didn't want her to get a fright once she saw the large outline of the snake in his pants.

Besides, the jeans had more pockets, and he needed them for all the stuff he was carrying around.

Thinking of stuff, should he bring a bottle of wine?

Nah. First of all, it would take him too long to search for one, and secondly, Margo had already had too much alcohol for one day. When she turned immortal, she could have as much as she wanted, but as a human, it wasn't healthy for her to overindulge.

Well, that was what he had read online, so it might not be true. Anyone could write anything they wanted on the web, and Negal wasn't well versed enough in medical research to evaluate the merit of the studies those assertions were citing.

As he rang the doorbell, the door swung open a moment later, and Negal's breath caught in his throat.

Margo looked like a wet dream in the silky nightgown and robe set he had bought for her. The fabric skimmed over her curves, and the outline of her breasts was so well-defined that it took a lot of willpower to tear his eyes away from the enticing swells and up to Margo's smiling eyes.

"Hi." She lifted on her bare toes and kissed his cheek. "You smell amazing."

"Thank you." The words came out of his mouth, sounding like a hiss because his fangs had punched out.

He swallowed and commanded them to retract. "You look ravishing." As she blushed, he regretted his choice of words. "I mean beautiful. And you smell wonderful as well."

He sounded like a boy on his first date.

"Thank you." Margo took a step back and motioned for him to come in.

"Would you like some tea?" she asked. "I just finished brewing it."

"I would love some." He didn't even like tea, but right now, he would eat gravel and chew on nails if she served them to him.

Desperate much?

Sitting on one of the barstools, he watched her flutter around the small kitchen area, her robe flying behind her like a pair of colorful butterfly wings.

When she poured each of them a cup and handed one to Negal, their fingers brushed, sending a jolt of electricity through his body. He had to fight the urge to pull her into his arms right then and there.

"Let's see what they've got." He reached for the remote as they sat together on the couch. "Do you have any preferences?" He dropped his flip-flops and stretched out his legs.

"Something romantic." Margo's gaze went to his bare feet and stayed there.

Was she looking at his feet because she found them appealing for some reason, or was she embarrassed about asking for a romantic movie?

It was probably the latter. It seemed that Margo had the same plans for tonight as he had, and he wondered if Frankie had told her about his and Dagor's conversation.

Keeping his expression schooled, he leaned back against the sofa's plush cushions and started scrolling through the ship's entertainment options.

The pictures and titles flashing across were all a blur. He didn't care which movie they watched and just waited for Margo to tell him on which one to stop, or go back if he was scrolling too quickly, but she sat quietly beside him, sipping on her tea, her eyes just as unfocused as his.

All he could think about was the woman beside him, the way her thigh pressed against his, the smell of her skin, and the soft sound of her breathing.

After he had gone through the entire selection, he turned to Margo. "Nothing?"

"I'm sorry." She smiled apologetically. "I wasn't paying attention. Can you scroll through the movies again?"

"Sure."

This time he went slower and tried to actually focus on the titles, but nothing appealed to him as the right movie to set the mood, and given Margo's expression, she hadn't found any of the offerings titillating either.

Worse. The lackluster options seemed to have dampened Margo's mood, while Negal had no such problem. Just being near her, inhaling her scent, and feeling the heat of her skin was enough to undo all the good work he had done in the shower.

When he went over the selection for the third time, and it became obvious that they were out of options, he put the remote down. "I have a feeling that we will need to come up with a romantic story ourselves. Why don't you tell me about that idea you had for a Perfect Match virtual adventure? The one where I'm a dragon shifter?"

Margo laughed. "You must be really desperate to bring that up."

She had no idea.

"I am," he admitted. "But it can be fun."

She worried her lower lip between her teeth. "I'm not a great storyteller, but I was just reading a romance novel that I could use as the starting point for our story."

"Go on..."

Margo's cheeks became slightly rosy. "I needed something to read to help me fall asleep, and this is the only paperback book I found. I borrowed it from Jasmine."

Given that preamble, the book must have been either really racy or really stupid. Otherwise, Margo wouldn't have gone to all that trouble telling him that it wasn't hers.

"What is it about?" he asked.

Her blush deepened. "It's a historical romance set in the Scottish Highlands." She cleared her throat and put a haughty expression on her face. "In the wild Highlands of Scotland, there was a rugged lord with a roguish reputation and a wash girl, pure and untouched. When their eyes met across the crowded courtyard, it was as if the world ceased to exist. 'Oh, Alistair,' she whispered, her bosom heaving like the stormy sea, 'ye are the very air I breathe.'"

Negal laughed. "Let's put a spin on it. Imagine that the lord is a werewolf who is the protector of ancient lands, and you are a traveler from afar, unaware of the legends and of the magic that lurks in the misty moors."

"That's a very good start." Margo leaned in, caught up in the story. "You have a knack for storytelling. Continue, please."

He shook his head. "It's your turn."

"Okay." She straightened. "In a land of myths and legends, where the mountains touch the sky, and the lochs reflect the stars, lives a werewolf, known to the locals only as the Guardian of the Glen. By day he is Negal, a nobleman, respected and admired. But under the full moon, he roams the Highlands in his true form." She waved a hand at him to indicate it was his turn.

"One day, an American lady named Margo arrives in the Highlands. She's an adventurous soul, seeking the stories hidden in the wild lands. Little does she know that her arrival has been foretold by an ancient prophecy."

Margo smiled. "The prophecy speaks of a stranger who will enter the Guardian's domain and change his fate forever. Negal is intrigued by the mysterious woman and decides to watch over her, ensuring her safety in the treacherous terrain."

Negal continued, "But as he watches her, Negal finds himself drawn to Margo's fearless spirit. Unaware of his secret identity, Margo only sees the kindness and strength in the man."

She leaned in, her eyes sparkling with excitement. "One evening Margo wanders too close to the forest's edge and finds herself surrounded by a pack of vicious wolves. Negal reveals his true form, transforming into the werewolf to protect her from the pack."

"Despite the shock and fear," Negal continued the story, "Margo sees in the werewolf's eyes the same kindness and strength she admires in Negal, and she realizes that the Guardian of the Glen is none other than the man she has been falling in love with."

Engrossed in the story, she continued, "Margo decides to stay and learn the secrets of the Highlands. Together, they uncover the truth behind the prophecy, finding love and redemption in the wild Scottish lands."

Negal shook his head. "This story is missing something. Where are the passionate kisses? The longing looks?"

"You are right." Margo looked at him from under her lashes. "Can you add them?" Her voice sounded husky.

Negal growled softly, the sound rumbling deep in his chest. "Negal's lips found Margo's, claiming her with a passionate kiss that conveyed the depth of his feelings for her. His hands roamed over her curves, mapping every inch of her skin and stoking the flames of their desire."

Margo's hand landed on his thigh, her fingers tracing small circles over his jeans. "The American surrendered to the overwhelming passion consuming her," she breathed, her lips mere inches from Negal's. "She knew that the Scottish lord was her soulmate, and she was ready to give herself to him, body and soul."

As Negal closed the distance between them, capturing Margo's lips in a searing kiss, she responded with equal fervor, her arms winding around his neck and her body arching into his.

46

MARGO

As Negal's hands clasped Margo's waist, and he lifted her onto his lap without breaking the kiss, she wound her arms around his neck and surrendered to the passion.

He devoured her, the fierceness of the kiss and his tight hold on her so overwhelming that it became too much. Leaning away, she gasped for breath.

Negal's hold on her slackened. "Too much?"

She shook her head. "No, it wasn't too much."

Before she could let herself second-guess her decision, she pulled out of his arms, rose to her feet, and offered him a hand up.

Negal looked up at her, hesitating only for a moment before taking her hand and letting her pull him to his feet.

As she led him to her bedroom, he seemed to be in a daze, and as she closed the door behind them, he remained frozen in place.

The lights were off, but the curtains were parted, and the moon illuminated the hard angles of Negal's perfect face.

"Are you sure about this?" he whispered, his hand still clasped in hers and his blue eyes glowing with inner light.

"I'm sure." Margo pulled her hand out of his and shrugged off her robe, letting it slide to the floor.

His breathing hitched, and as she pushed the straps of her nightgown down her arms and let it slide to the floor as well, he hissed but still didn't move.

Frozen in place, he just stared at her with those luminous eyes of his, and for a moment, Margo felt self-conscious about her nearly nude body.

With only a small triangle of fabric covering any part of her, she was completely exposed, physically and emotionally, and if he rejected her offering, she knew she would never recover from it. She would never again trust herself with a male, human or immortal, because she had somehow terribly misunderstood and miscalculated his plans for her.

"You are so beautiful, Margo." Negal's whisper obliterated her insecurity, and she would have sagged to the floor from relief if not for his hands landing on her waist and then coasting up her ribcage.

Her breathing stilled as she waited for him to move them higher. Her breasts felt as if they had swollen to double their size, and if he didn't touch them soon, they were going to explode.

When his hands coasted down instead of up, she nearly cried with frustration, but then he leaned down and swirled his tongue over her nipple, and she cried out for the opposite reason.

Supporting her with a hand on the small of her back, he took the hardened peak into his mouth, and as he sucked it in, Margo threw her head back and arched into him to give him better access, but when his fangs grazed over her sensitive flesh, she whimpered, partly from fear that he would draw blood and partly from the spike of her arousal that the sense of danger caused.

What was wrong with her that this sort of thing turned her on?

As Negal lavished the same attention on her other nipple, Margo turned into a quivering mass of need. The pulsing in her core quickened with every swipe of his tongue, every pull of his mouth, and every gentle graze of his fangs until she thought that she could climax just from the foreplay, which had never happened to her before.

Heck, she'd never climaxed with a man before, period. Not during the foreplay stage and not during intercourse. Would today be the first time it happened?

Her musing ended abruptly when Negal's mouth left her nipple, and then he dropped to his knees in front of her.

"What are you doing?"

He grinned up at her. "Worshiping my goddess." He pressed a kiss to the apex of her thighs over her lacy panties, and then he gripped the strings connecting the two triangles and tugged them apart. "Sorry about that." He tossed the destroyed panties aside, not looking sorry at all.

Leaning lower, he kissed her naked mound with such gentleness and reverence that her knees buckled from the emotional impact, but then his hands were spanning her bottom and holding her up for his ministrations.

It dawned on her that he was still fully dressed, but she was too dazed to comment on it. Instead, she pushed her fingers into his thick hair and held on for dear life as he licked over the bundle of nerves at the top of her slit.

Margo was already so close that if Negal kept going for a few more seconds, she was going to detonate.

He dug his fingers into the soft flesh of her bottom and then swiped his tongue over that sensitive bundle of nerves, once, twice, three times, and then he growled and whipped his tongue over the same spot one more time.

"Negal!" Margo gasped his name as the coil sprang, and the explosion was like nothing she had ever experienced before.

With his hands on her bottom, keeping her from collapsing, he kept licking and growling until the last tremors rocking her body subsided.

47

NEGAL

As Margo shuddered from her orgasm, immense satisfaction filled Negal.

Lapping at the fountain of her pleasure, he felt intoxicated, and he also had no more doubts about her being a Dormant. No human had ever tasted so delicious.

"Negal," she breathed, her fingers slackening their hold on his hair. "Thank you."

With one last kiss to her puffed petals, he lifted his head and smiled at her. "I'm the one who's grateful." He licked his lips.

Margo chuckled, but he detected a note of nervousness in her expression. "You look like a satisfied cat who has just finished licking a bowl of cream."

"That's precisely how I feel." He rose to his feet, wrapped his arms around her, and kissed her.

Margo sagged into him, but she wasn't as boneless as he'd hoped her climax would leave her. The muscles in her back felt tight, and even with the overwhelming scent of her desire filling the room, he could scent a slight undertone of apprehension.

When he let her come up for air, Margo pushed her hands under his t-shirt. "You are a little overdressed for the occasion."

She didn't sound as confident as he would have liked, but she sounded determined, and that was good enough for him.

Margo wanted this. Still, he needed to do everything he could to allow her to feel safe and comfortable. To let her be in charge.

Whipping his t-shirt over his head and tossing it on the floor, he let her explore his chest for a few moments and then wrapped his arms around her and lifted her. Turning them both around so he was with his back to the bed, Negal bent his knees and leaped backward, landing on the bed with Margo on top of him.

"Oof," she exhaled. "You could have warned me."

He smiled up at her. "What would have been the fun in that?"

Removing his arms from her was hard, but to implement his plan, he had to let her be in complete control of what came next.

Hopefully, it wouldn't backfire.

Some females did not enjoy sex unless their partner took the lead, and he had a feeling that Margo belonged to that group, but she'd also had some bad experiences in her past that had made her wary of males, which necessitated relinquishing control to her, at least initially.

He lifted his arms and tucked his hands under his head. "I'm yours to do with as you please."

Margo's eyes widened. Bracing her hands on his chest, she leaned up and back and regarded him with a shy smile.

He had a hard time keeping his eyes on hers and not dipping them to look at her perky breasts. She might not have minded, but it would have made staying on his back with his hands tucked under his head much more difficult.

He was a god, but he was no saint.

"I didn't expect this," Margo said.

"I want you to feel in complete control of our joining."

If Margo didn't like his idea, she could tell him that she didn't want to be in control, but she responded as he had expected, scooting back and going for his zipper.

Negal held his breath as she lowered it, and so did she. He had boxer shorts on, so the reveal would come in stages, which was also part of his plan.

Slow seduction.

With her eyes trained on his bulge, Margo pushed his jeans down, and as he lifted to help her take them off him, she pulled them all the way down and tossed them aside. When she came back, she hesitated before feathering her fingers over his erection, which was mostly covered by the soft cotton of his boxer shorts but not completely. It had elongated so much that the head was peeking over the waistband.

"Don't be afraid to touch it." He smiled with partially elongated fangs. "I promise that my one-eyed trouser snake doesn't bite."

She chuckled. "No, it doesn't. That's the danger from the other end."

The smile slid off his face. "Does it scare you?"

"No," she whispered, her eyes still glued to his shaft.

"I mean the bite, the fangs, the venom."

Finally, she tore her eyes from his erection. "No, your fangs don't scare me."

"Then what does?"

Margo swallowed. "Nothing. I want this."

She reached into his boxers, and as she wrapped her hand around his shaft, Negal hissed.

Her grip immediately loosened. "Did I hurt you?"

He laughed. "Yeah, but not in the way you think. I love the feel of your hand on my…male organ."

Most young humans had no problem with the words dick or cock, but Margo was more reserved, and she might find those two objectionable, or worse, they could turn her off.

48

MARGO

M*ale organ?*

Not wanting to offend Negal, Margo stifled a laugh. His pose and awkward choice of words both helped to boost her confidence and perhaps that had been his intention.

On the other hand, Negal was an alien, so perhaps he didn't know what words to use in reference to his erection—a very long, thick erection that pulsed against her palm and tempted her to do things that she usually didn't like doing.

Fisting it, Margo gently tugged on the velvety skin, gliding her palm from base to tip and back.

Negal groaned, but she was sure that this time it was with pleasure.

As she licked her lips, tasting herself from his kiss, it wasn't bad. In fact, it was quite arousing.

Dipping her head, she swept her tongue over the tip, and Negal's bottom lifted, pushing his shaft past her lips before she was ready to take it.

"Sorry about that." He dropped his bottom back on the mattress. "You are in charge, Nesha. Not me."

Nesha? What did that mean?

Was it an endearment term in Anumatian?

She would have asked if her mouth wasn't wrapped around Negal's pleasure stick.

Yeah, that was what she was going to call it from now on. Then again, he might take offense to the word stick, so maybe rod would be more appropriate.

Except, a rod had a painful connotation in her mind, and Margo didn't want anything negative to be associated with Negal.

Gripping his shaft, she pumped it with her hand in tandem with her mouth while letting her thoughts meander in strange directions.

Pleasure baton? Pleasure tool?

"Margo," he hissed. "If you keep going like this, I'm going to come in your mouth, and that's not going to benefit your transition."

He was right, of course. It was time to woman up and welcome this magnificent male into her body.

All they had done so far had been incredibly intimate, but this was the ultimate act and the one she'd always had the most trouble with.

His shaft still gripped in her hand, Margo lifted to her knees and positioned her entrance over the tip.

Looking into Negal's glowing eyes, she lowered herself until the tip breached her entrance and then stopped to let her body get accustomed to the sensation of being invaded.

Except, she wasn't being invaded. Not this time. She was welcoming him into her, controlling how deep and how fast she would take him, and it made all the difference.

"Margo," he whispered her name. "You are killing me, but I couldn't have asked for a better way to die."

This time, she didn't stop the chuckle bubbling up her chest. "You are immortal. I can't kill you even if I tried." She lowered herself two more inches over his shaft and stopped.

Negal's hands were still trapped under his head, but the bunching of his biceps indicated how hard he was struggling to keep them there.

Should she tell him it was okay to release them?

Margo wanted him to grip her thighs or her ass, but not just yet. First, she wanted to finish what she had started. She lifted up and then glided back down, up and back down, and each time, she managed to get more of him inside of her.

Negal's forehead was covered in a sheen of sweat, no doubt from the effort to keep from taking over.

She was grateful for his restraint, for his willingness to relinquish control to her so she wouldn't get overwhelmed—so she would be comfortable with their joining.

And she was.

Somehow, he had made it so that she didn't feel any of the awful awkwardness of getting naked with a man for the first time, of letting him inside of her as if they belonged together.

Too many people didn't realize that sex shouldn't be a casual thing, that such intimacy required a level of connection that could only come after a long period of courtship—that it should be the final step to cement a relationship and not the first.

Except, she was a hypocrite because she was doing exactly what she was preaching against.

She was taking a male she barely knew into her body. But the truth was that even though she didn't know much about Negal's past, she knew his soul and the kind of person he was, and that was enough.

When he was as deep inside her as he could go, she leaned over him and kissed him.

Understanding her silent communication, Negal released his hands from their makeshift prison and gripped her thighs.

As he took charge, flipping them around so she was under him, his hold on her was firm but not bruising, and as he found his rhythm, the coil inside of her began winding tighter and tighter.

Everything had been wonderful so far, but having him in control of the joining and letting go was so much more pleasurable that it took mere moments for another orgasm to gather momentum in her belly, and as she felt the coil springing, she instinctively tilted her head to the side, exposing her neck for his bite.

He hissed, and as she climaxed, she felt his seed jet into her, and he struck with his fangs.

The pain was blinding in its intensity, but it only lasted a split second, and then a wave of euphoria washed over her, and she was climaxing again, and again, and again until her body could not take any more, and then she felt as if her soul had left her body, and she was soaring above the clouds.

49

NEGAL

After the storm had subsided and Margo drifted off on the wings of euphoria, Negal retracted his fangs and licked the puncture wounds closed.

Bracing on his forearms, he buried his nose in her silky hair and breathed her in. The connection that had been forming between them even before they had met had solidified with their joining, and the feeling of no longer being alone was incredible.

There was no more just Negal. From now on, it was Negal and Margo.

The two were one, a unit.

"I love you," he murmured against her upturned lips.

The soft, blissed-out expression on her face made her look angelic.

"My angel," he whispered before kissing her lightly and withdrawing gently.

As he padded to the bathroom to clean up, Negal wondered what Margo was seeing in her euphoric dream. Was she continuing the story they had started earlier? Was she lost in the Scottish Highlands, her mind continuing to weave the tale of him as a werewolf lord and her as the adventurous American? Or had their own story taken center stage, their real-life romance more captivating than the fictional narrative?

Stepping into the shower, Negal considered their future together. The cruise was drawing to a close, but their journey as a couple was only beginning, and even though he had to concede that nothing was guaranteed, he felt optimistic about the future.

Margo would transition, he was sure of that, and the only question was when.

Frankie and Gabi had both started transitioning after the first or second bite and so did Karen, so he hoped Margo would be the same despite what he had heard about other Dormants' transitions that had taken weeks and many bites.

He and Margo did not have weeks.

They had days.

Returning to the bedroom, Negal slipped beneath the covers, careful not to disturb her even though there was no chance she would wake up, even if he purposely tried to rouse her.

She was knocked out, and given his experience with human females, she would keep soaring on the clouds of euphoria for many more hours. If he could quiet his mind, he might be able to catch a few hours of sleep before she woke up.

As Negal gathered Margo into his arms, he relished the feel of her soft skin against his and the way her body molded perfectly to his own.

Holding her close, he allowed himself to dream of a shared life, where they embarked on missions together with Aru and Gabi, Frankie and Dagor.

He was excited by the prospect, but he would have preferred to have more time alone with Margo so they could enjoy more moments like this—quiet, intimate, and in a comfortable bed. But life was full of compromises, and he would take being with Margo just about anywhere over being without her surrounded by luxury.

Pressing a gentle kiss to her forehead, Negal whispered once more, "I love you, my sweet angel."

50

MARGO

The morning light filtered through the curtains, casting a soft glow over Negal's handsome face. He looked so peaceful in repose, almost boyish if not for the dark blond shadow over his jaw.

Margo wanted to cup that stubble-covered cheek and kiss those firm lips, but she also wanted a few more moments of just basking in his perfection and thinking about the night they had shared before she woke him up.

Negal's chest was still rising and falling with the same rhythm as it had when Margo had first opened her eyes, but she had a feeling that he had sensed the moment she had awakened and was pretending to sleep for some reason.

Maybe he was afraid that in the light of day she would freak out about last night?

That wasn't going to happen. The toughest part, which was garnering the courage to get intimate with a male she'd met only two days ago, was over, and it hadn't even been all that tough.

In fact, it had been almost easy.

The storytelling, the shared laughter, and then their fictional tale intertwining with reality—it had all led to their joining and culminated in Negal's bite.

Frankie was right, no drug could ever compare to the intensity, the sheer exhilaration of the venom bite, let alone what had followed. The memory sent a shiver of longing through Margo. She wondered if Negal would bite her every time they made love.

The bliss was indescribable, but she couldn't black out again and be out of commission for hours.

Frankie and Mia had warned her about that, but she'd thought they had been exaggerating.

If she awakened him right now, made love to him again, and he bit her, she would be out for half of the day, and as much as she craved Negal's body, she also didn't want to lose time just talking with him.

A smile curved her lips as she imagined them continuing the story they had started creating last night. She hadn't expected Negal to be such an imaginative storyteller.

It dawned on her then that he tended to undervalue himself. Negal identified as a god of humble origins, a trooper in the interstellar fleet, and a nothing-special guy.

There was so much more to him than he realized, and if the Fates smiled upon them and she transitioned, Margo would make it her mission to explore all of Negal's hidden talents and abilities.

It wasn't about trying to change him or make him strive for more than he was comfortable with. That was totally up to him. It was about self-discovery and not putting limits on himself, and if the newfound confidence led to different choices, they would be Negal's, not hers. Being aware of a talent for storytelling didn't mean that he should become a writer if he had no patience or passion for it.

Margo had watched Mia work for months on one short children's book, and she knew she would never have had the patience to work on one project for so long and then do all the revisions that the publisher had demanded, especially given that success wasn't guaranteed.

At least in advertising, things happened quickly. Usually, it took a few days to develop the concept, get approval, and then a few weeks until the campaign was ready to launch.

Despite working on the fringes of the process and not having much say in the creative part, Margo loved the fast pace and the immediate results, provided that they were good. No one liked failure, but thankfully the agency she worked for had rarely produced a campaign that flopped.

Hopefully, though, that part of her life was over, and she would get to do what she loved in Perfect Match.

But why was she thinking about the advertising campaigns when she was lying next to a naked god?

Well, she knew why. Work was simple, and thinking about it was a distraction, a way to avoid thinking about the big L-word that was pushing up from her heart and demanding to be heard.

The rational part of her screamed that it was too soon, and even though the circumstances were unlike any she had faced before, she shouldn't let herself fall in love with Negal, at least until she transitioned.

To fall in love and to be made to forget about it was too terrible to even think about. Her mind might be forced to forget Negal, but the ache in her heart would remind her that she was missing a vital part of her life, and not knowing what it was would drive her insane.

The problem was that Margo had a feeling that she had already lost the battle and just hadn't admitted it to herself yet.

Her feelings for Negal couldn't be boxed into a timeline, and they couldn't be compared to any of her past experiences or even to Frankie's or Mia's, which were similar and yet as vastly different as the three of them were different from each other.

It was like stepping into a Perfect Match adventure, where everything was condensed into a few hours but felt as if it had lasted weeks or even months.

Negal stirred, and as his eyes fluttered open to meet hers, a smile bloomed on his face. "Hello, beautiful." He lifted his hand and cupped her cheek.

She leaned into it and covered his hand with hers. "Good morning."

"How are you feeling?" he asked.

She laughed softly. "Like I've returned from the best and most restful vacation in heaven. I can't even describe the things I saw after shooting up to the sky."

His grin broadened. "It's something else, isn't it?"

"Have you ever experienced a venom bite?"

He nodded. "Getting bitten during a fight is not the same as being bitten during sex, but the effects of the venom are similar enough. I was loopy the rest of the day."

Margo pursed her lips. "I'm not loopy at all. In fact, I'm incredibly clear and feel on top of the world."

"I'm glad." He let go of her cheek and wrapped his arms around her. "No regrets about last night?"

"None." She leaned in and kissed him on the lips. "I would love to stay and cuddle, but I need to visit the bathroom quite urgently."

Margo had more than cuddling in mind, but only if Negal could refrain from biting her. She didn't want to spend the next several hours passed out in bed.

Reluctantly, he released her from the cage of his arms. "Go, but come back quickly."

"I will."

She got out from under the covers, unconcerned about her nudity as she sauntered to the bathroom, giving Negal a great view of her ass.

The hiss he emitted was followed by a groan, and both were deeply satisfying.

In the bathroom, Margo took care of the most urgent need first, and as she washed her hands, the reflection staring back at her was that of a happy woman. She had experienced many happy moments during her life, but she'd never looked so vibrant.

51

NEGAL

As Margo ducked into the bathroom, Negal closed his eyes and let out a relieved breath.

During the night, or rather the early morning hours, he had remained mostly awake, checking up on Margo to make sure she was doing okay and only dozing off and on for a few minutes here and there.

Even though he hadn't encountered a human female who had a negative reaction to the venom, and none of the immortals had warned him that it could be potentially harmful, it only made sense that not everyone would tolerate the venom well.

Humans were so fragile.

He'd read about a young woman who was allergic to peanuts and died after kissing her boyfriend, who had eaten peanuts beforehand. So, if an allergic reaction could be so deadly, he wasn't taking chances.

To be frank, he hadn't been as concerned about the women he had been with before meeting Margo, not because he hadn't cared but because it hadn't occurred to him before that they might have an adverse reaction to his venom.

Come to think of it, allergy was just one potential health risk. What if a human had a weak heart that couldn't survive so much stimulation?

Had he thought about all those potential risks before making love to Margo, he would have insisted she get a thorough physical from the clan's doctor before taking her to bed.

Margo projected such a tough-girl persona that at first, he'd been fooled by it, but when he'd gotten to know her better, he'd realized that underneath the façade she was hiding a vulnerability.

Last night, he had done everything he could to make the experience as wonderful for her as it was for him, which meant a lot of restraint on his part, but it hadn't diminished the experience. It still had been the best he'd ever had, probably because it had been more than just sex.

It was the coming together of not just their bodies but also their souls.

Negal chuckled. Had he just graduated from making up romance stories to composing poetry?

Who would have thought that he had it in him?

When the door opened, and Margo stepped out of the bathroom, he lifted the blanket and motioned for her to duck in.

For some reason, her cheeks were rosy, and she had a sheepish expression on her face, but he couldn't smell her arousal, so it couldn't be that she was planning another round of lovemaking.

"You're cold." He wrapped his arms around her and drew her against his body.

She wiggled, rubbing against his erection. "And you are hard."

He chuckled. "I'm always hard around you, and in case your friends failed to mention it, gods' and immortals' stamina far exceeds that of human males. We don't need much time to recuperate. We can go many times in a row."

"Oh, wow." The rosy hue of her cheeks deepened, and as a delicate whiff of feminine arousal reached his nose, he smoothed his hands down her back and squeezed her bottom.

She put her hands on his chest. "I have a question."

"Ask, and I shall answer."

"Do you have to bite your partner every time you climax?"

"That's a good question, and the answer is no. My venom doesn't get replenished nearly as fast as my seed. I can probably provide two bites a day."

"Oh." Her face fell, and she lowered her eyes to his chest.

"Hey." He hooked a finger under her chin and lifted her head so that she had to look at him. "If you are craving another bite, I'm more than capable of providing it."

"I do crave it, but not now." She worried her lower lip. "As incredible as it is, I don't want to be out for hours. I want to enjoy your company."

So that was what Margo was worried about. They were docked in the port of Mazatlan, and she wanted to go sightseeing. She didn't want to spend the rest of the day in bed.

Besides, perhaps it would be for the best if they didn't make love now anyway. The goal was to induce her transition, which required his venom and his seed to be concentrated and not diluted by overindulgence.

"You are absolutely right." He dipped his head and kissed the top of her nose. "We should get off the ship and go exploring. But first, I'll make you breakfast." He smiled. "You need to replenish your energy after the vigorous activities of last night."

Margo scrunched her nose. "So, no morning hanky-panky?"

Negal laughed. "Who are you, and what have you done with my cautious and reserved Margo?"

She rolled her eyes. "Gone, hopefully, never to be seen again. I like the new me much better."

"I loved the old you, I love the new you, and I will love every new facet of you."

Her eyes widened. "You love me?"

He tightened his arms around her. "I do, and I don't expect you to feel the same about me so soon after we've met, but I will woo you until you have no choice but to love me back."

"Silly Negal." She cupped his cheek. "Isn't it obvious that I love you too?"

He made a doubtful face even though she was right. He knew. "I don't want to assume anything. I still need to hear the words."

"How could I not love you?" she whispered. "You are as beautiful on the inside as you are on the outside, and you treat me with more care and respect than anyone ever has. You didn't belittle my insecurities about intimacy or try to bulldoze over them as most men would have tried to do. You've been attentive, considerate, and patient, but you still managed to convey at every turn how much you desired me. I don't know anyone who would have been capable of navigating the convoluted maze of my psyche as well as you have."

Negal's heart swelled in response to her praise, and he felt more manly than he ever had because he had done right by the female he loved.

"Thank you." He pressed his forehead to hers. "I just wanted you to feel safe and comfortable with me." He chuckled. "Usually, though, females are aroused by danger, not by those who offer them safety."

"You are danger and safety and everything in between wrapped into one hell of a sexy package. I don't know any woman who wouldn't have been wildly attracted to you, and I'm so grateful that you are mine." She looked into his eyes with an expectant expression on her beautiful face.

Did she need confirmation? Or did she want him to say the same things to her?

Negal tightened his arms around his female. "You are strength, vulnerability, and everything in between wrapped into the most alluring, beautiful, and sexy gift from the Fates. I am yours, Margo, for as long as you will have me, which I hope is forever."

"Oh, Negal." Her eyes misted with tears. "I pray that you will be mine forever, too, and I feel greedy for wanting so much for myself. What have I done to deserve you?"

He laughed. "I'm not the saint you think I am, and I'm definitely no prize. Perhaps you have done something bad, and I'm your punishment?"

"No way." She slapped his chest playfully. "You need to stop deprecating yourself."

"Aha, so I do have faults."

She rolled her eyes. "No one is perfect. But as long as the plusses outweigh the minuses, it's a win, and in your case, the scale dips heavily on the plus side, making you a big win."

"I can live with that."

52

MARGO

Margo sat on the barstool next to the counter, feeling stupidly happy but also terrified that her happiness would be temporary.

She was in love with Negal, and he was in love with her, but if she didn't transition, it would all be lost because Kian would demand the removal of all her memories regarding the secret world of gods and immortals, including her and Negal's love for each other.

Negal didn't need to obey Kian's orders, though. He wasn't a member of Kian's community, and he could do as he pleased. Well, he answered to Aru, but she had a feeling that Aru was more flexible than Kian.

Would Aru allow her to retain her memories and tag along with them to Tibet even if she was just a plain human?

Would Negal?

If he really loved her, he would.

"What are you frowning about?" Negal pulled a skillet out of the cabinet.

She leaned her elbows on the counter and braced her chin on her fist. "Would you keep me with you if I didn't transition?"

He froze with the skillet midair above the stovetop. "You are transitioning. I have no doubt about it."

Margo rolled her eyes. "I love your optimism. But what if I don't? Will you let Kian erase my memories of you and try to forget about me?"

Negal's eyes blazed with inner light. "I won't," he hissed. "I can't. I love you too much to let you go." He shuddered. "But if you don't transition, nature will eventually take you from me." He shook his head. "Let's stop with the depressing hypotheticals because, one way or another, you are going to transition."

Margo chuckled. "Is there another way? Other than the fun way?"

"My people can probably turn anyone immortal, but I don't have access to their biotech. One day, in the not-too-distant future, human science will catch up, though."

"It's possible." She sighed. "But I doubt it will happen during my lifetime, and even if it does, it wouldn't be widely available to anyone who wants it. As much as immortality appeals to me, I'm terrified of what it would do to my world. The consequences can be catastrophic."

Negal put the pan on the heating element. "Two things would have to happen simultaneously with turning all humans immortal. Birth rates would have to plummet, and interstellar travel with colonizing capabilities would have to be developed and deployed. Otherwise, you are right. The consequences would be disastrous."

Margo sighed. "And to think that I was so happy only moments ago." She looked at the skillet and searched her mind for a different topic to talk about. "We could get breakfast in the dining hall, or we could go up to the Lido deck and get a drink."

Negal huffed. "This early in the morning? No way. You need to eat something healthy to replenish your energy."

It was sweet how much he wanted to take care of her, but given his cooking skills, she would have preferred to eat elsewhere. Then again, he would be offended if she said so, so maybe she should pretend like she loved whatever he made.

Was that the right thing to do, though?

Partners, lovers, shouldn't lie to each other, not even little white lies said out of love and not malice, but the truth should always be wrapped in a lot of love to mitigate the sting.

"Why?" Negal lifted a brow. "You don't like my cooking?"

She smiled. "I love everything about you, and I know that you will be amazing at anything you put your mind to. Therefore, I'm more than willing to be the taster of your culinary experiments."

Shaking his head, Negal rubbed a hand over the back of his neck. "I stopped listening after you said that you loved everything about me and that I would be amazing at anything I do."

Margo laughed. "You heard the rest. Don't pretend that you did not." She leaned over the counter. "Did I offend you with the remark about your culinary skills?"

"Not really. I appreciate your honesty."

"Good." She gave him a bright smile. "If I don't criticize anything, you won't believe my praise when it's actually deserved."

His eyes glinted with amusement. "True that." He opened the refrigerator, and pulled out a stick of butter, a carton of eggs, and a pack of sliced bread. "So, let's hear that praise."

Margo knew what kind of praise he meant, but she pretended innocence. "You are a great storyteller." She tried hard not to laugh at his disappointed expression.

But then he shrugged and dropped some butter into the hot skillet.

"The story we came up with last night could make a great addition to the Perfect Match virtual adventures. It has romance, mystery, and supernatural elements. Naturally, we would have to change the names, but other than that, it's good to go."

Margo huffed out a breath. "I didn't even get the job offer yet. Everything is in a state of flux. I want to transition and have a long and happy life with you, but I would be lying if I said that I was excited about trekking through Tibet or any other remote place in search of the missing pods. I would much rather sit in an air-conditioned space and brainstorm ideas for new Perfect Match adventures with Frankie and Mia, participate in test runs, and then come home to you in the evenings. But we can't have all that we want, right?"

For a long moment, the only sound in the living room was the sizzling of butter in the skillet.

"I'm sorry," Negal eventually said. "I wish I could join you in the immortals' village, but that's not possible even if I didn't have to leave on the mission."

"Why not?"

"It's complicated." He turned around and broke two eggs over the skillet and then two more.

"Is it a secret?" Margo asked.

"Not from you." He scrambled the eggs with a fork. "My people don't know about the immortals. They are not supposed to exist. Aru, Dagor and I can be tracked by the patrol ship, and we don't want to lead anyone to the immortals' village."

Margo frowned. "How are you being tracked?"

"Implants." Negal pulled out two plates and put them on the table. "The clan's doctors might be able to remove them, but then our commander would assume that we are dead, and that's not something we want or can do at the moment. In the future, though, that might be an option."

She nodded. "As long as there is a way out, the situation is not hopeless, right?"

"True." He put half of the scrambled eggs on her plate and half on his. "After we find the pods, we might be able to stage our deaths and get free, but it's also possible that the trackers can't be removed. We won't know until we get scanned, and even then, I wouldn't trust the crude equipment they have here. Our technology is so advanced compared to what humans have that even the best scanners might not locate our trackers."

"Is it possible that trying to remove the implants would cause them to explode or harm you in any way?" When Negal looked surprised by her suggestion, Margo rolled her eyes. "Don't tell me that's never occurred to you."

"It hasn't, but the truth is that I haven't given removing the trackers much thought before I met you."

He didn't sound like it was something he wanted to do, and she couldn't blame him. Negal and his friends had family on Anumati and its colonies, and they didn't want to be forever cut off from them, which would happen if they faked their deaths. The only transportation method that could get them back home was the Anumati patrol ship, which was due to pick them up in five hundred years or so.

It was so far in the future that she shouldn't worry about it, but she still felt a tightening in her chest at the thought of being separated from Negal.

"I'm going crazy." She pushed her fingers through her hair. "This is only our third day together, and I'm already so in love with you that I'm worried about us separating half a millennium from now." Provided that she transitioned and got to live that long; she decided against adding the qualifier.

There was no reason to upset Negal. He was so convinced that she would transition that he got angry every time she mentioned the possibility that she wouldn't.

He leaned over the counter and took her hands. "You are not crazy, Margo. I feel the same about you, and you know why?"

"Why?"

"Because we are fated for each other. That's how it works when you meet the person the Fates have chosen for you, and last night solidified our bond. That's why I'm convinced that you will start transitioning soon and that you will do so successfully."

Margo swallowed. "I hope you are right."

Negal's confidence in her impending transition was infectious, and Margo wanted to believe that he was right, but she couldn't ignore the odds that were stacked against her. She had no paranormal abilities, and the supposed affinity immortals felt for Dormants wasn't something she could quantify or rely on as proof of her genetics. She hadn't mingled extensively outside her immediate circle. Aside from the time spent with Negal, Frankie, Mia, and Jasmine, she hadn't even attempted to make new connections.

There was the undeniable bond with Negal, but was that enough to prove that she was a Dormant?

"I know I am," Negal said. "And speaking of transitioning, would you mind if we stopped by the clinic to check on Karen before going ashore?"

Margo wasn't sure that she wanted to get off the ship and endure the humidity and heat of the streets of Mazatlan, but she was curious about Karen's progress.

"I would love to visit Karen. I want to know how she's doing."

53

ANNANI

"Hello, Mother." Kian kissed Annani's cheek. "I thought we were going to talk about yesterday's revelations," he whispered next to her ear.

She smiled. "I cannot invite you and your family for brunch without inviting your sisters and their families," she whispered back. "They would think that I am playing favorites. If you wish, you can stay after everyone leaves."

Annani wished she could share her conversations with the queen of Anumati with all of her children. It did not feel right to keep it from her daughters, but unless she lied and claimed to have established the communication herself, she could not. It would be repaying Aru's kindness and sacrifice with betrayal.

She was the reason he would not get picked up by the patrol ship on its way back to Anumati. The queen had arranged for him to stay so he could be her liaison to Earth. His telepathic connection with his sister would be his only contact with home, and since their parents did not know about their connection, Aria could not even keep them updated on his well-being.

In a way, though, it was for the best.

Their parents would not be happy to learn that their son had a hybrid mate, whom he could never bring home and introduce to them.

Perhaps in the distant future, when Annani took over the Anumatian throne, she would change those archaic prohibitions and re-establish communications and travel to Earth. Aru's parents could come for a visit, and perhaps by then, he would be able to present them with a grandchild.

"What's that smile about?" Alena asked, pulling Annani out of her reveries.

"I am imagining a better future."

Amanda snorted. "Please, share your vision. We all need a dose of optimism these days."

The world was indeed entering another dark period, just as Syssi had foreseen. Wars were raging in several hotspots around the globe, and drug cartels were so powerful and pervasive that they controlled entire countries, with their governments either helpless to do anything or worse—willingly cooperating with the cartels. Those criminal organizations were not only responsible for the loss of countless lives to overdosing and other drug-related deaths, but several of them were also run by terrorist organizations that were using drug money to finance their deadly operations.

There was so much chaos going on around the world, but Annani still hoped that this time, it would not last as long as it had previously. It was a vicious cycle of good times followed by bad times and then the good times returned only to be followed by bad times again.

The cycles were becoming shorter, though.

While epochs in the distant past had lasted thousands of years and then hundreds, they had shrunk to decades and even less in modern times. The duration followed advancements in technology, and since there had never been a leap as vast as the advent of artificial intelligence, perhaps this time around things would get back to normal faster than ever.

"Technology will usher in a better future," Annani said at last. "Despite the fears of technology displacing workers, it has always improved lives, and it will continue doing so in the future. Most diseases will be eradicated, most of the work will be done by robots, and people will have to work fewer hours a week to make a living. They will have plenty of time to enjoy their children and pursue hobbies."

"Utopia," Kian snorted, "does not exist. They have technology aplenty on Anumati and no diseases. Yet, according to Aru and his teammates, it is far from the paradise you are describing."

Annani smiled indulgently. "I did not describe a paradise. People are people, and there will always be strife, competition, and jealousy. But if the great evils are eliminated or reduced, everyone's lives will be better. I will be satisfied when there are no more deadly diseases, wars, terror attacks, hunger, exploitation, illicit drugs, human trafficking, and other evils that currently plague humanity."

Sari sighed. "I would be happy with that list accomplished as well, but I don't hold my breath for it happening anytime soon. I don't know what, if anything, can end all those evils. It's just not possible."

"The Eternal King managed to do all that," Kian said. "It's not that I'm justifying his methods, especially since he had no qualms about killing his own children, but I have to admit that what he achieved was extraordinary."

Annani tensed. Would her daughters catch Kian's slip-up?

"What do you mean he killed his own children?" Amanda asked.

"I meant that the Eternal King wanted to kill the rebels, including Ahn, his legitimate heir, and Ahn's half-siblings Ekin and Athor. He would have succeeded if Mortdh had not beaten him to it."

Satisfied with his answer, Amanda leaned back in her chair. "In this case, the intent is incriminating enough. No sane person sends assassins after his own son."

"It's happened many times throughout human history," Annani said. "To gain or keep a throne, sons have murdered their fathers, and fathers have murdered their sons. Power is a corruptive force."

"Maybe it's the other way around," Alena said. People who ascend to positions of power are corrupt or sociopaths to start with, and many times, this trait is inherited by their offspring."

Annani let out an indignant huff. "My father was not a sociopath. He was ruthless at times, but he had feelings, and he cared deeply for my mother and me."

"Navuh cares for Areana," Sari said. "But he's still a sociopath. He would have killed Kalugal if he had discovered that his son was a strong enough compeller to usurp him."

"Perhaps," Annani said. "We will never know."

In the same way, they would never know whether Mortdh had dropped the bomb on the assembly or if someone shot his plane down, causing the weapon to explode.

Regrettably, she could not entertain the same doubts about Khiann's death. The three witnesses who had testified against Mortdh had given almost the same exact description with slight variations, even though they had given their testimonies separately. They might have told a coordinated lie, but why would they have done so? And if they had, her father would have known they had lied, wouldn't he?

Then again, her father had wanted Mortdh to be found guilty of the murder, so perhaps he had compelled those males to testify against Mortdh?

The thought had never occurred to her before, and Annani wondered why it had not. She had idolized her father, but she had been aware of how ruthless he was. Her father had promised her hand in marriage to Mortdh, knowing that the god would never love her. He had done so to secure peace. But when it had become clear to him that securing peace through marriage would not work, perhaps he had thought of another way to get rid of Mortdh and the threat he represented.

Could her father have ordered Khiann's murder to pin it on Mortdh?

No, she would never believe Ahn capable of that. But she could definitely believe he was capable of using the murder to his advantage.

The implications were so profound that Annani felt her chest constrict, and she had to excuse herself to go out on the terrace for some fresh air.

"I will go with you." Alena started to rise.

"No, stay." Annani put a hand on her shoulder. "I need a few moments alone."

Everyone's worried eyes followed her as she grabbed her sunglasses and stepped out onto the balcony, but she could not explain why she needed a few minutes of solitude.

She could not tell her children and their mates that she had only just now realized that her father might have compelled the witnesses who had testified against Mortdh. It had taken her over five thousand years to start doubting what she had seen and heard with her own eyes and ears, when she should have done so during the testimony.

She was so young back then and addled with grief, but she had never been naive. She had grown up in the palace, had witnessed the machinations of court, and had known that things were not always the way they seemed.

Annani took a deep breath.

Most times, though, things were exactly like they seemed. She was probably working herself up for nothing. The witnesses might have told the truth, and Mortdh had beheaded Khiann.

At least now, she had a sliver of hope that things had not happened the way the witnesses had testified, and if Khiann still had his head attached to his neck, he might have survived and was buried somewhere in the desert, in stasis and waiting for her to revive him.

54

PETER

Peter turned on his side, propped his elbow on the mattress, his head on his fist, and looked at Marina.

The midmorning sun filtered through the curtains, casting its rays on her blue hair, her pale, freckled skin, and her lips that were slightly parted.

She seemed so peaceful, her chest rising and falling in a steady rhythm. The nervous energy that emanated from her when she was awake was gone, and he wondered if it was because he had pleasured her so thoroughly last night or because of the venom-induced dreams that she was experiencing.

The poor girl had been exhausted when he'd picked her up from the kitchen after she and the rest of the staff finished cleaning up. When he'd offered to carry her out of the elevator, she hadn't even tried to object.

Resting her head on his chest, she'd closed her eyes and had fallen asleep on the way. He'd drawn her a bath, stripped her, and washed the smell of the kitchen out of her hair and skin before carrying her to his bed.

Marina had woken up then, and they had made gentle, sweet love because she was in no state to do anything strenuous.

He liked taking care of her.

There was something about Marina that drew him in. They had similar sexual proclivities, which was a big plus, but that wasn't all. He simply liked being with her and making her life a little easier and a little brighter. It provided him with satisfaction.

He could almost hear Kagra's disparaging voice in his head; *you enjoy playing the savior, Peter.*

"Screw that," he murmured quietly.

Kagra was a typical Kra-ell female warrior, who didn't believe in love or in exclusive relationships, and who valued her independence above all.

He should forget all the things she had told him and not let them get to him time and again, like some parasite crawling under his skin. The fact that she couldn't understand emotional attachment didn't mean that it was not worthy of pursuit.

Irritated, he slid out of bed and ducked into the bathroom.

After a shower and a shave, he felt like a new male and decided to cook breakfast for Marina and serve it to her in bed.

She'd worked so hard for the past two days that she deserved a little pampering. Today, she was only working on the cleanup after lunch, so she could laze in bed for a long time.

As he moved around the kitchenette, gathering ingredients, he deliberated whether he should make something for Jay and decided against it.

His roommate hadn't awoken yet, and when he did, Peter hoped he would go to the dining room and give them privacy.

He would make a simple meal because that was all he knew how to do, with eggs, bread, some sliced cheese, fruit, and coffee, of course.

No breakfast was complete without a cup of java.

As he whisked the eggs, added a dash of salt, and buttered the bread, he found himself humming a tune.

When he was done, Peter plated the food with care, arranging the slices of toast and the scrambled eggs with a side of fresh fruit.

Satisfied with the presentation, he was about to carry the tray to the bedroom when he heard the rustling of bedding, and a moment later Marina appeared at the doorway, rubbing sleep from her eyes.

"What are you doing?" A look of confusion gave way to delight as she took in the scene before her. "Are you bringing me breakfast in bed?"

"That was the plan." He met her gaze, his heart swelling at the sight of her, tousled hair and all. "But since you are already up, we can eat here." He put the tray on the table.

"No way. I'm not passing this up. No one has ever served me breakfast in bed." She lifted a finger. "Give me five minutes to clean up in the bathroom, and then you can bring the tray in."

Marina looked so happy, so excited, that Peter promised himself that he would serve her breakfast in bed every morning from now until the end of the cruise.

It was a damn shame that the voyage was almost over.

55

MARINA

After waking up to the aroma of breakfast cooking, Marina had rushed to the living room to see what was going on, and now she regretted it.

It would have been so much nicer to have Peter surprise her with breakfast in bed. No one had ever done something like that for her. Then again, she would have needed to excuse herself to visit the bathroom and brush her teeth, so maybe it was better this way.

At least now, when Peter brought the tray in, her hair wouldn't look like a bird's nest, and her breath would not stink.

Getting back in bed, she arranged a stack of pillows at her back, pulled the blanket up to her chin, and waited for Peter to arrive.

When he entered, the laden tray carefully balanced in his hand, the sight stirred a well of emotions that threatened to overwhelm her, and as he placed the tray across her lap, Marina felt her eyes misting with tears.

She was so touched by the gesture, the care it implied, her importance to him, the feelings he had for her. Perhaps he had meant it when he'd said he didn't want to let her go?

Or was she reading too much into it?

Peter frowned. "Why are you crying?"

"I'm not crying." She lifted a hooked finger and rubbed it under her eye to make sure. "I'm just still sleepy so my eyes get misty."

Looking doubtful, he lifted one of the mugs off the tray and handed it to her. "The coffee will wake you up."

"Thank you." She took it and cradled the warm mug between her palms before taking a sip. "Oh, wow. You made it just as I like it." Her voice quivered, and she sniffled.

He canted his head. "What's going on, Marina? I thought you would like a little pampering."

"I love it." She sniffled again. "It's just that this is such a sweet gesture, and I'm a little overwhelmed."

Peter smiled. "You've done sweet things for me, and now I'm repaying the favor."

Did he mean the sex?

No, that wasn't it.

"What sweet things?"

He chuckled. "Have you forgotten the lunch you made for me when I was on guard duty?"

"It was nothing. Just a couple of sandwiches."

"And this is just scrambled eggs with toast, cheese, and fruit. Not a big deal either." He leaned over the tray and planted a gentle kiss on her lips. "I like doing nice things for you."

Emboldened by his actions and his words, or perhaps just tired of keeping her desires bottled up inside of her, Marina found the words spilling out of her, "Take me with you to your village." When his eyes widened, she rushed to add, "I won't be a burden. There are plenty of things I can do to earn my keep. I can clean houses, cook, or babysit. And I could be your girlfriend just for as long as you want me. I don't expect a commitment. I know that it's not possible between us."

Marina waited, her heart beating a frantic rhythm and her breath frozen in her throat, readying herself for the rejection that she was sure would come, and yet hoping that it wouldn't, that by some miracle Peter would say that he couldn't live without her and would take whatever years she could give him.

Watching him absorb her confession, she saw his expression change from surprise to concern, and then to regret.

Her heart sank to the pit of her gut like it was made from lead. She could practically hear the splash as it landed and disturbed the acid in her stomach, sending it up to her throat.

She was going to be sick, and she couldn't move because the damn tray was on her lap.

"Marina," Peter said as he reached for her hand. "I would have loved it, but the longer we stay together, the harder it will be to part. I care for you deeply, and I enjoy being with you more than I have with any woman, but the reality is that you will age, and I will not, and it's not something we can ignore." He smiled sadly. "I know that humans do not like to think about their mortality, and even less so about the mortality of their loved ones, and I totally understand that, but in this case, you need to remove your blinders and look far into the future. You won't like what you see."

Marina appreciated Peter's honesty, but his words cut her, nonetheless.

What did he think, that she was stupid? Ignorant? That she wasn't aware of her mortality and his immortality?

As if there was anything else she could think about.

"Nothing you've said is news to me," she said in a much steadier voice than she felt. "I'm not asking for forever, Peter. I'm asking for now. I need to get away from Safe Haven for a while to heal."

He arched a brow. "Heal from what?"

Marina swallowed. "My former boyfriend dumped me for someone he met in college. It hurt, but it wasn't so bad while he was gone most of the time. Then he finished his studies and came back with her to Safe Haven, and seeing them together every day, kissing, touching, exchanging loving looks, is just painful." She closed her eyes. "I thought we would get married, have kids, all the silly dreams girls have. Seeing him with her is a constant reminder of that lost dream." She opened her eyes and looked into Peter's. "It's not that I still love him. I don't think I ever truly loved him, but I loved the dream, and Nicolai carelessly shattered it. So, I lick my wounds and mourn the dream, and I need to be away from him and his new girlfriend to heal. That's why I want to move with you to your village."

Everything she'd said was the truth, but not the entire truth. She had also fallen for Peter and wanted him to love her back, but evidently his feelings for her didn't run as deep.

Was there something wrong with her that no one wanted to commit to her?

Whatever.

If Peter cared for her even a little, he would not deny her. It wasn't as if she was asking him to mend her broken pieces or to commit to a future that both of them knew was impossible. She was asking for a reprieve and a chance to find joy in the present without the shadows of her past looming over her.

Was it really so much to ask?

Gazing into Peter's eyes, she searched for understanding and acceptance, but all she saw was a conflict that was peppered with sadness and sweetened with affection.

56

PETER

In a way, Marina's story echoed Peter's. They had both been dumped by their partners and then had to see them too often for comfort.

No wonder they had been so drawn to each other. Still were. It wasn't just about the incredible physical attraction and shared kink. It was about the invisible wounds they were both still licking.

"I understand your predicament because I'm in the same boat." He chuckled. "And I don't mean this ship. Thankfully, the Kra-ell stayed behind to guard the village, so I didn't have to see Kagra during the cruise." He lifted his eyes to the ceiling. "Thank the merciful Fates."

Marina tilted her head. "I remember you mentioning dating her, but I didn't realize it was that serious."

Peter chuckled, the sound more bitter than he'd intended. "It was serious for me but not for Kagra. She's a true Kra-ell, and she doesn't do relationships. I was a passing curiosity to her."

"Yeah, she's a badass. I would have never imagined you with someone like her. How did it even work between you? Did you take turns topping each other?"

Peter laughed. "You guessed it. She wanted to try something different, a gentler approach to lovemaking, and I was curious about being with a female who could easily dominate me. It was fun to experiment, but in the end, she must have realized that gentle didn't do it for her and that she preferred the Kra-ell's brutal sex games to my much milder ones."

Marina shivered. "Don't remind me."

Damn, he was such an ass. He'd forgotten that Marina had been a victim, forced to service the Kra-ell males. Mostly, it had been hybrids who weren't as bad as the purebloods, but still, she'd had to say yes more than no or suffer unpleasant consequences.

"I'm sorry." He squeezed her hand. "It was insensitive of me to bring that up. You probably want to forget about that part of your life."

"No, that's okay. I have no problem talking about it. I'd only been with hybrids, and most were careful with humans. They didn't want to break us. I shivered, thinking of the way it was between the purebloods. With the males and females being almost equally strong, their fight for dominance was ferocious."

He quirked a brow. "Did you witness it?"

"I wasn't in the room with them, but I heard the snarls, the growls, and the thrashing. I also saw them emerge from the chamber, bloodied, shredded, and either satisfied or humiliated. It was rough."

If a pureblooded Kra-ell male failed to subdue a pureblooded female, she would kick him out, and subsequently no other female would invite him to her bed. It was survival of the fittest, and only the strongest and most ruthless got to father children.

Still, Jade had chosen Phinas as her mate, and they seemed to be happy together despite those differences. Peter had hoped that the same would hold true for him and Kagra, but she hadn't felt for him what Jade felt for Phinas.

"I've always been adventurous," he admitted. "Maybe that was what attracted me to Kagra. She was different."

"Do you still care for her?" Marina asked in a near whisper.

He nodded. "I will always care for her as a friend. It wasn't her fault that I had unrealistic expectations." Kagra had said some things that had been unkind, but in retrospect, Peter realized that she wasn't being malicious. She'd been trying to help him get over the rejection. "The only one I should be angry at is myself. Kagra told me from the very start that she wasn't interested in anything serious, but my stupidly prideful mind was convinced that I would make her change her mind." He smiled. "My heart recovered from the breakup quickly, but my pride suffered a serious blow and took longer to get over itself."

Marina nodded. "I first noticed you in the dining room because you looked so defeated whenever you thought no one was looking your way."

Ouch. He'd hoped that she'd noticed him because he was so irresistibly handsome, charming, debonair. Not because he'd seemed beaten down.

Was that why she'd approached him in the first place?

"So that was my appeal?" Peter asked. "I was an easy target?"

Marina blushed. "It made you seem more approachable. After Nicolai, I couldn't handle another guy who was full of himself and believed I should worship at his feet because he graced me with his marvelous dick."

Peter couldn't stifle the laugh that bubbled up from his chest. "I think all males are guilty of thinking that their dicks are worthy of worship, myself included." He plucked a grape off the vine and lifted it to Marina's mouth. "And I have to say, you do that so reverently."

Remembering Marina on her knees, pleasuring him with her mouth and taking him deep, had his shaft turn into a club.

Wrapping her lips around the grape, she sucked it into her mouth while somehow managing to smile while doing it.

"You have such a talented mouth, Marina."

"Talented enough to get me an entrance into your village?"

Peter's smile wilted. He didn't like thinking that she was with him to gain entrance to the village. She could do that on her own without having to do any favors for him or anyone else.

"You don't need to do anything of the sort to come live in the village. You just have to get Kian's approval, and I don't see why he would deny it. A few of the former human occupants of Igor's compound decided to move to the village, and Kian okayed it."

She lifted her fingers. "Only two requests were granted, but I don't know how many applied."

"I don't know either. But since Kian offered anyone who wanted to come live in the village the option, there is no reason for him to refuse you. He wouldn't want you traveling back and forth for security reasons, but if you want to move permanently, he won't object. There are plenty of jobs you can get in the village. In fact, people will be fighting over you."

Her eyes shone with excitement. "Really? Like what?"

"All the ones you mentioned before, and more. The village café is always understaffed, Callie could use another server in her restaurant, and Atzil is looking for barmen and barmaids."

"That's awesome. I even know who to talk to about it."

Peter arched a brow. "Me?"

"Well, yes, but also Amanda. She's Kian's sister, and she seems to like me."

Warring emotions washed over Peter. On the one hand, he was glad that Marina now knew how to get what she wanted without his help, so if she stayed with him, it would be just because she wanted him and not what he could get for her. On the other hand, though, he was afraid that she would leave.

It was pathetic that he wanted her regardless of her motives, but he needed to at least know where her heart was.

Choosing a ripe strawberry, he lifted it to her mouth. "Open wide."

Marina chuckled. "Are you going to feed me the entire breakfast?"

"That's the plan." As he pushed the strawberry past her lips, he couldn't help imagining something else breaching the seal of her mouth. "When do you need to show up for your lunch shift?"

She finished chewing and swallowed. "I have time. You can finish feeding me breakfast and then feed me dessert."

Her gaze shifted downward to where his erection was pressing against the zipper of his pants, and as she licked her lips, he almost sagged with relief.

Marina wanted him just for him, regardless of any ulterior motives.

57

ONEGUS

"Hey, you're early," Onegus greeted Connor, a smile breaking across his face as he reached out for a friendly clap on his former roommate's shoulder. "Thanks for coming to help."

Connor had always been there for him during his bachelor days, making sure that he'd eaten, that his suits had been collected from the dry cleaners, and that his socks matched. As much as Onegus loved Cassandra, she was too busy with her own career to do those things for him, and he missed having Connor around.

"I knew you would be lost without me." Connor walked into the cabin and scanned it with a knowing look. "And I was right."

Onegus tried to see the place through Connor's eyes, but he couldn't find fault with anything.

There was plenty of whiskey, enough glasses for all the groomsmen, a box of great cigars courtesy of Kian, bowls filled with nuts and pretzels, and two large trays of cold cuts and crackers.

"What am I missing?"

"Decorations, of course." Connor smiled.

Onegus rubbed a hand over the back of his head. "I didn't bring any, and I don't think the guys will notice their absence. As long as the alcohol is flowing, no one is going to complain about the lack of decorations."

Connor shrugged. "Straights are so boringly predictable."

Onegus laughed, shaking his head. "True. But to be honest, even my

Cassandra lacks your touch. You have no idea how often I come home to a cold house and think of how you always welcomed me with a home-cooked meal."

Connor's hand went to his chest. "You miss me."

"I do, but don't tell Cassandra. She will feel guilty, and she shouldn't. We both have demanding careers, and I'm just as much at fault as she is for the lack of homey feeling at our place."

Connor sighed. "Unlike you and Cassandra, I spend most of my days at home, and cooking relaxes me when I need a break from practicing or composing." He started rearranging the bottles to make the counter more presentable.

"No new love interests, then?"

There was a moment's hesitation, a flicker of something passing through Connor's eyes before he shrugged. "Actually, I'm seeing someone, but it's all very hush-hush. His friends don't know about his proclivities, and he's not ready to come out."

"One of the former Doomers?" Onegus guessed.

Connor confirmed with a nod. "We met at the café, and we started talking about my music, and one thing led to another, and yeah…that's all I can say at the moment."

"Are you happy?" Onegus asked.

Connor chuckled. "Ask me in three months. Right now, it's too new and stressful. We come from different worlds."

The former Doomers had left the Brotherhood a long time ago, and nearly a century was long enough to forget Mortdh's teaching and adopt more enlightened attitudes. By now, Connor's guy should have been okay to admit his preferences, but Onegus chose not to say anything.

"If he mistreats you, let me know." Onegus bared his fangs. "I'll take care of him."

Smiling, Connor clapped him on the back. "Thanks. I'll let him know you said that. And if…"

The buzzing sound of Onegus's phone interrupted their conversation, and as he pulled it out and looked at the screen, he saw that it was a message from Kri.

"Hold that thought." Onegus lifted his hand. "It's Kri, and she's asking if she can skip my bachelor party. I need to call her."

"Go ahead." Connor waved a dismissive hand. "In the meantime, I'll make everything look prettier."

Onegus started to type a response to Kri but then decided to call her and stepped into the bedroom. After closing the door, he called the head Guardian. "Enjoying your married bliss, Kri?"

"I am. Michael wants me all to himself today, but I feel bad about bailing on you after you made him full Guardian yesterday. Did I thank you for that already?"

"You don't need to thank me. Michael earned the promotion all on his own."

"He did, but the timing is a little suspicious. You must have cut corners to welcome him into the force on his wedding day."

"I did not. Bhathian approached me before the cruise to tell me that he thought Michael was ready. I just needed a little time to go over his test scores and evaluations from all his teachers. I didn't talk to you because I wanted it to be a surprise."

"Fine," she relented. "I'm not complaining. Michael always dreamt about being a full-fledged Guardian when he and I stood in front of the Clan Mother. You made his dream a reality, and I owe you for that, so if you want me to come to your bachelor party, I will."

"It's okay. You don't have to come if you want to spend the day with your new husband. All the other head Guardians are going to be here, though."

He could have invited Michael and solved the problem that way, but there were so many males who would feel offended for not getting invited that he had to keep it to a very specific group. All the head Guardians, Kian, Toven, Shai, and Connor.

Kri sighed. "I know that you all want to make me feel included, but the truth is that I don't feel comfortable attending the bachelor parties. I'm not one of the dudes, even though I can fight with the best of them." She chuckled. "After all, I showed up at the altar in a white dress, not a white tux, although I really wanted to."

"You looked beautiful."

"Yeah, yeah. I looked like a pro wrestler stuffed into a dress, but it is what it is, right? We play the hand we are dealt ."

Onegus chuckled. "You didn't look like a wrestler. You are a beautiful female, Kri. Beauty is not the exclusive domain of the petite and dainty. My Cassandra is neither, and to me, she's beauty personified."

Kri sighed. "Cassandra has style and attitude. I have shoulders and attitude. Not the same, but I accept your compliment. Thank you."

"You are welcome. You are coming to the wedding, right?"

"I wouldn't miss it for anything. Even I am curious about Cassandra's dress, and I normally couldn't care less."

"You and me both. She didn't let me see it. I'll see you tonight, Kri."

Ending the call, Onegus opened the door and walked into the transformed living room of his cabin.

"How did you do all this?" He turned in a circle.

"Magic." Connor waved a hand around the decorations. "And Amanda. I called her and told her about the sorry state of your cabin, and she sent Onidu with a bunch of stuff."

Onegus frowned. "How long have I been on the call with Kri that you managed to do all that?"

"Not long. Onidu helped." Connor shook his head. "The guy is fast. He was like a blur. I only had to point, and it was done before I lowered my finger. I would really love to have an Odu. Wouldn't it be great if every house in the village had one?"

"Yeah, it would."

Connor's wish was getting closer by the day to becoming a reality, but it was classified information that Onegus couldn't share with his former roommate.

58

MARINA

Marina wiped her hands on a dish towel and glanced at the new bin of dirty plates someone had rolled up to her scraping and sorting station by the sink.

"I thought I was done," she muttered under her breath. "That's the last one," Dimitri said. "After you are done with it, you can go."

"Thanks." Marina let out a breath.

Her friends were being super nice about her and Larissa leaving early so they could get ready for the wedding tonight. Dimitri and Chester had volunteered to finish loading the dishwashers and put everything away on the racks once they were clean. The two had at least another hour of work before the kitchen switched gears and started preparations for the wedding tonight, but they were willing to do that for her and Larissa.

The only thing missing was the dress that Amanda had promised to bring, and Marina feared that she had forgotten about it and wasn't coming.

Poor Larissa would need to somehow squeeze herself into one of the dresses that Peter had borrowed for Marina from his relatives, and asking Amanda about getting into the village would have to wait for another opportunity.

She was almost done with the bin when she heard the doors to the kitchen swish open and then the clicking of high-heeled shoes, announcing the arrival of the female she'd been waiting for.

"Hello, Amanda." Marina turned around and glanced at the dress draped over the brunette's arm. "I see that you found something for Larissa."

"It was more difficult than I expected." Amanda lifted the hanger with the dress. "What do you think? Will it fit her?" She looked around the busy kitchen. "Where is she?"

"Larissa went to get a shower." Marina admired the shimmery purple fabric but didn't reach for it. "It's loose, so it should work." She reached for the dish towel to dry her hands. "Thank you so much." She took the dress. "I need to hang it somewhere safe until I'm done."

"Go," Mila said. "You are done."

"Thank you." She blew the head cook an air kiss and turned back to Amanda. "Would you like to come to my cabin and see how the dress fits Larissa?"

Amanda lifted her hand and glanced at her watch. "I guess I have time for a short visit."

"That's awesome." Marina cast her an appreciative smile before heading out of the kitchen.

When they were out in the corridor, she headed for the stairs instead of taking the elevator. She needed a few minutes of Amanda's time before they got to the cabin and the conversation shifted to Larissa and her dress.

"I want to ask you for another favor if that's okay." She cast Amanda a sidelong glance.

"Shoes?" Amanda asked. "I'm afraid that you are on your own in that department."

Marina chuckled. "No, not shoes. I would like to move to the village, and I was wondering who I should talk to about approving it."

Amanda canted her head. "Does this have to do with Peter? Because if it does, he could make a request on your behalf."

"Well, it does, and it doesn't. I like Peter a lot, and I hope we can be together for a little while, but I know that it won't work in the long term. I'm not happy at Safe Haven at the moment, and I need a change of scenery. I was told that there are plenty of positions in the village I could fill."

As they exited the stairwell and headed down the long corridor of staff cabins, Amanda's heels clacked and clicked on the hardwood flooring.

"The best way to approach this is to ask either Eleanor or Emmett to arrange a transfer. They will ask for approval, and if it's granted, you can pack your bags and accompany the Guardians who are heading home at the end of their tour of duty at Safe Haven. I think that they have two-week rotations there."

Marina's heart sank.

She'd hoped Amanda would intervene on her behalf, which would have guaranteed her request's approval, but she'd miscalculated. The princess either didn't have the sway Marina thought she had, or she didn't want to get involved in the lives of the humans.

"You should talk to Atzil," Amanda said as they stopped in front of Marina's door. "He's the guy who looks like an army drill sergeant and follows Ingrid around. The interior designer."

"I know who Ingrid is, and I know the guy you are talking about. Peter said that he's looking for barmaids for his bar."

Amanda flashed her a brilliant smile. "That's the one. Talk to him, tell him that you are interested in the position, and ask if he could send a request to Eleanor to arrange a transfer for you."

Marina frowned. "Doesn't your brother need to approve the request?"

"He does, but after Atzil and Eleanor ask on your behalf, it's going to be rubber-stamped."

Marina wasn't sure what a rubber stamp meant, but she guessed it meant that Kian would approve her transfer without putting up any roadblocks.

What Amanda suggested made a lot of sense, but it would take time to go through the official channels, and Marina knew that she would miss Peter terribly in the meantime. It was better that way, though. He hadn't been overjoyed at her suggestion of moving in with him, and it seemed like he intended to end things between them or keep them casual.

In either case, she should be glad to have an option that didn't involve him.

Except, she wasn't. Her heart ached, and the rejection stung.

Plastering a smile on her face, she looked up at Amanda. "Thank you for the great advice. I'll try to talk to Atzil about working at his bar during the wedding tonight."

59

CASSANDRA

"Oh, Mom. This is amazing." Cassandra turned in a circle in her mother's cabin. "You and Darlene have outdone yourselves."

The space was transformed, adorned with beautiful decorations that sparkled and shimmered, making the cabin look festive. Fancy little appetizers that had been prepared by the staff were spread out on tables that her mother and sister must have gotten from other cabins in addition to the one that had come with it.

"I'm glad you like it." Her mother pulled her into a warm hug while her sister waited her turn, standing to the side and smiling.

"Come here." Cassandra reached for Darlene's hand, pulling her into a group hug. "Thank you for doing this for me."

"It was my pleasure." Darlene untangled herself from the hug. "I got to see your dress and all the bridesmaids' dresses that you've been hiding from us."

Cassandra cast her a mock glare. "I wanted the reveal to be the highlight of my bachelorette party. You know, in the absence of strippers."

As her bridesmaids began to arrive, the cabin filled with laughter and excited chatter, each guest bringing their own unique energy to the gathering. Alena, Sylvia, Callie, Wonder, Mey, Jin, Eva, and Mia—each held a special place in Cassandra's heart, and having them there to celebrate with her meant the world to her.

She had never had so many friends. For most of her life, it had been her mother and her, living almost in hiding, and now they had a whole clan as their family.

Despite the hardships they had suffered, they had been extremely lucky to end up in this amazing community, and Cassandra thanked the Fates, the stars, and every supernatural force out there for the blessing she had been given.

Once the party was in full swing, Cassandra could feel the anticipation in the room rising. Her bridesmaids were casting glances at the closed door to her mother's bedroom and whispering conspiratorially about pretending to need to visit the bathroom so they could take a peek at her wedding dress and their bridesmaids' dresses.

She had kept the details under wraps, wanting to surprise everyone at her bachelorette party and adding an element of excitement to the celebration.

"Okay, okay." Cassandra lifted her hands in the air, scanning the eager faces of her friends. "I know you've all been dying to see what I picked out for tonight, and I promised that I would reveal the dresses at my party. Please follow me." She led them to the bedroom, where the dresses hung on a mobile rack, hidden beneath silk covers to add to the mystery and grandeur of the reveal.

Turning to her bridesmaids, she announced, "First, your dresses." With a dramatic flourish, she pulled back the covers, unveiling the array of bridesmaid dresses she had chosen.

They weren't custom made, but then that wasn't her mode of operation. Cassandra was an expert at finding spectacular designer stuff that was ready to wear with just a few alterations.

The bridesmaid dresses were the creation of Ursula Bemonir, an up-and-coming designer who was still trying to find her way to the top. They were elegant and modern, each tailored to flatter the individual wearer while maintaining a cohesive look for the group. The fabric was a soft, shimmering gold, designed in a sophisticated, floor-length sheath style. Each dress had a unique touch, with a subtle variation in necklines, sleeves, or straps, allowing each bridesmaid to shine in her own way.

"They are all stunning." Alena smoothed a hand over her protruding belly. "Which one is mine?"

Cassandra removed it from the rack and handed it to her. "It's not a maternity dress, but it's loose enough to fit your cute little belly."

Alena chuckled. "I think my belly passed the cute and little stage a month ago, but I'll take the compliment."

"I wanted you all to feel stunning and yet comfortable." Cassandra removed the dresses one at a time from the rack and handed them to their owners. "Would you like to change into them now?"

Darlene shook her head. "You have to show us your gown first."

Her sister had already seen it, but she was saying that for the benefit of the others.

"Very well."

The room fell into an expectant silence as Cassandra moved towards the last covered garment, and as she pulled down the zipper, she couldn't hear anyone breathing.

The gown was breathtaking in its simplicity. Delicate spaghetti straps set the stage for a graceful, cowled neckline, while the bias-cut design and soft satin fabric elegantly draped the silhouette. The voluminous train and alluring low back added a daring touch to the otherwise reserved dress.

"Wow, Cassandra, it's gorgeous," Mia breathed. "You are going to look stunning in it."

"Put it on," her mother said. "I want to see you in it."

It was still several hours until the wedding, but the dress was such a simple garment that it was no problem to put it on and then take it off.

"As you wish."

A round of applause followed her acquiescence, and when she put it on along with the matching shoes, her friends ahhed and oohed.

Amanda shook her head. "I don't know how you do it, Cassandra, but you find hidden gems in places I wouldn't even think to look."

"Thank you." Cassandra beamed. "Now it's your turn, ladies. Put on your dresses, and if any last-minute alterations are needed, my mother will whip out her sewing kit."

60

MARINA

A sea of dresses was spread over Marina and Larissa's beds. Some were from Frankie and Mia, others were from Peter's relatives, and one was from Amanda, or rather the person she borrowed it from.

Amanda refused to disclose the information for some reason. Perhaps the lady who had donated the dress was embarrassed about letting someone else wear it, or maybe she was just the shy type who didn't want Larissa to thank her.

"So, what's the verdict?" Marina asked.

Lace and chiffon, silk and brocade, they came in all shapes, fabrics, and colors, and the one she had on now was red, had a tight bodice, and was short in the front and long in the back.

Larissa regarded her with a hand on her hips and pursed lips. "It's hard to decide. They all look so good on you, but this one is a little too much."

"I agree." Marina lowered the zipper in the back and peeled off the dress.

Thankfully, the dress Amanda had brought for Larissa fit her with the help of a travel sewing kit and some creative adjustments. Amanda hadn't stayed to see the transformation, leaving moments after arriving, saying that she needed to make an appearance at the bachelorette party for tonight's bride.

It was so weird that they were celebrating the bachelor and bachelorette parties on the same day as the weddings, but maybe it was the immortals' tradition.

"Since you are wearing purple, I'll go with black." Marina draped the red dress over the bed and lifted the one that was the most flattering on her. "I can't do red with my blue hair, and the gold one is a bit too much, so black it is."

Larissa nodded. "Black is always a safe bet." She patted the curlers on top of her head. "Will you help me with my hair and makeup?"

"Of course." Marina pulled on a t-shirt and motioned for Larissa to sit on the only desk chair in the cabin.

"Just not too much foundation," Larissa warned. "I don't want to look like I have plaster on my face."

The prospect of being Jay's date for tonight excited her roommate, but it also made her a little jittery, which wasn't surprising. It was the first wedding that Larissa was attending as a guest. It wasn't Marina's first, but she was even more nervous tonight than she was the first time.

She'd lowered her guard this morning and blurted to Peter that she'd noticed him because he'd looked defeated. The guarded look in his eyes had said it all.

He was a smart guy, and he'd put two and two together, realizing that she thought him easy prey. She'd managed to salvage the situation with some clever wording that hadn't been a lie, but in retrospect, it would have been better to come clean.

The weight of the deceit pressed down on her.

She was in love with Peter, and with that came the fear of losing him if he learned the truth. But the flip side was that keeping it from him was not healthy in the long run.

Yeah, as if there was a long run.

There was no future for them, and even though Peter might have feelings for her, he wouldn't allow himself to fall in love with her because that would be plain stupid.

Marina finished removing the hair rollers and brushed out Larissa's locks with her fingers. "I think it looks perfect the way it is." Her voice wobbled a little, and her friend noticed.

Looking at her through the mirror, Larissa frowned. "What's wrong? You've been moody the entire day."

Marina had thought that she'd done a good job of hiding her inner turmoil, but apparently, Larissa knew her too well to be fooled by her fake smiles.

Her friend's earnestly concerned expression broke the dam, and Marina found herself wanting to confess everything. "I've fallen into my own snare," she said after telling Larissa her plan. "I love Peter, and he cares about me, but not the same way I care about him."

Larissa's eyes were soft as she regarded Marina in the mirror. "You need to tell Peter the truth and get it off your chest. Honesty is scary, but it's liberating. If what you have with Peter is real, he'll understand that you were desperate, and he will forgive you. If not, then he's not worthy of your love, and it's better to find that out sooner rather than later."

Larissa was a simple girl, but what she'd said made perfect sense, her words echoing the thoughts that had been circling in Marina's mind.

The fear of Peter's reaction had held her back, but she couldn't allow their relationship, as fleeting and short as it might be, to be built on a foundation of lies and omissions.

No matter how terrifying the prospect, she owed Peter the truth.

61

MARGO

"I'm so relieved," Negal said as he held the clinic door open for Margo. "Karen is doing amazingly well."

"She is," Margo agreed. "Even the doctor seems surprised that Karen woke up so quickly from her coma."

Bridget had murmured something about Karen's transition being unusual because she'd been unconscious for nearly twenty-four hours and then woke up as if nothing had happened. No relapses. Not even sleepiness.

Karen was chatting with her family and her visitors as if she was recuperating from a light cold, not a complete overhaul of her body. She still looked a little tired, but the fine lines around her eyes were nearly gone.

"Thank the merciful Fates, she's okay," Negal said, sounding a little smug as if he had something to do with Karen's rapid recovery.

It must be her imagination.

He was simply happy that Karen was doing well. So what if it was strange that he showed so much interest in a woman who was a mother of five and in a loving relationship with the father of three of those children? He'd told her that he was friends with Karen's partner but observing them interacting hadn't convinced Margo of that.

There was more to this story than he was letting on. Perhaps the number of children Karen had was what fascinated him about the woman.

Where Negal came from, people counted themselves lucky if they had one child, and given the scarcity of children on the cruise, the immortals were facing the same problem.

Margo's gut twisted. Would she and Negal ever be blessed with a child? Would he want children with her?

It was one of the many things they needed to talk about, but maybe not today. It was too soon to have that kind of talk.

Had Frankie and Dagor discussed children already?

Mia and Toven had, but they had been together for a while, and Toven already had at least two children he knew of, and there could potentially be more. Mia had told her that Toven had been convinced that he was infertile, and since he had been around for seven thousand years, that meant a hell of a lot of women he had been with, and as it turned out, when gods took humans as partners, their chances of creating offspring increased dramatically. The guy could have hundreds of children he didn't know about.

As they entered the elevator, Negal wrapped his arm around her waist. "Do you want to go shopping or sightseeing in Mazatlán? We still have a few hours before the wedding."

Margo scrunched her nose. "I would rather go up to the Lido deck and have a drink. But if you want to see the town, I'll come with you."

"I'm okay with skipping it." He pressed the button for the top deck. "But I'm surprised that you don't want a shore excursion."

She didn't want Negal to buy more things for her, and given their prior experience in Puerto Vallarta, he would insist, and she would cave, and then she would owe him even more money that he would refuse to accept.

"It's too hot and humid." She smiled sweetly at him. "And besides, there is so much we still need to talk about, and I'd rather do that over drinks."

"Like what?"

She rolled her eyes. "Did you forget already? You promised to tell me more about your life."

He made a face. "Unless you want to hear about countless missions, most of them boring, there isn't really much to tell."

"Are you kidding me? There is so much I want to know that has nothing to do with your missions. Tell me about your parents, what they do for a living, the kind of people they are, and whether they were strict or lenient with you when you were growing up. Who was your first crush? What happened to her?"

Shaking his head, Negal chuckled and led her out of the elevator and onto the Lido deck. "Slow down, my love. I can only answer one question at a time."

He called her his love, and her heart fluttered like it had wings. The happiness bubbling inside her made her feel as if she were walking on air rather than the solid deck of the ship.

Leaning against the railing, Negal turned to look at her with amusement in his eyes. "What's that smile about? Did I say something funny?"

"You called me your love," she said, her eyes locking with his. "I like the sound of it."

Negal's expression softened. "I love you."

She batted her eyelashes. "Say it again. I love the way it sounds."

"I love you." He smiled. "Now say it back to me."

She lifted her hand and cupped his cheek. "I love you, and I don't care how absurd it is for me to feel that way after knowing you for three days." She stretched on her tiptoes and kissed his lips.

When he wrapped his arms around her and pressed her to his chest, her unanswered questions and the uncertainties of their future faded away.

62

KIAN

Yamanu draped his arm over Onegus's shoulders. "I hope Cassandra doesn't blow up anything during the wedding."

The Guardian had been drinking nonstop since the start of Onegus's bachelor party and was now a little unsteady on his feet. The others were only in slightly better shape, with the exceptions being Onegus and Kian.

Onegus because the chief was always on alert, and Kian for the same reason.

Trouble seemed to follow them no matter how hard they tried to stay away from it.

Anandur laughed. "We should be fine as long as we keep her away from the punchbowl."

When Cassandra had first joined the clan, she'd started training to learn how to control her strange power, but Kian knew that she hadn't been doing that nearly as intensively as she should have. Lately, she'd been busy revamping the entire style of advertising for the cosmetics company she worked for and had halted her training altogether.

Regrettably, she loved her job and had no intention of quitting. Her only concession to the secretive nature of the clan had been to do some of her work from home.

Onegus grimaced. "Cassy hasn't accidentally blown anything up in a long while, so don't even think of teasing her about it."

Anandur lifted his hands in the air. "I wouldn't dare."

Everyone laughed, including Kian, probably because each of them had been privy to one of her chilly looks at one time or another.

Nothing and no one intimidated Cassandra, which was what made her such a perfect mate for Onegus. The chief only appeared to be easygoing because of his innate charm, but he wouldn't have risen to his position if he was lenient or overly accommodating.

When Onegus's phone buzzed with a message, Kian assumed it was his bride checking up on him, but as the chief pulled out the device and read the text, his deep frown indicated otherwise.

Kian was not the only one who noticed, and the change in Onegus's demeanor had a chilling effect on everyone present.

As they all fell silent, the jazz music playing in the background suddenly sounded too loud, and Connor did everyone a service by turning it off.

Noticing the sudden quiet, Onegus shifted his gaze away from the screen and looked at Kian. "The guys watching the surveillance feed from Modana's estate report that Carlos Modana has arrived with two individuals, who they strongly suspect are Doomers."

Kian's blood chilled in his veins. "This is bad news. If they manage to break through Kalugal's compulsion and thralling, they could uncover the truth about Julio's religious awakening." He pulled out his phone and called his cousin.

When Kalugal finally answered, the shrill sound of a baby crying in the background made Kian grimace. "Hello, Kian. Can I call you later?"

"I'm sorry, but this cannot wait. Carlos Modana showed up at the estate with two individuals who could be Doomers. Is there a chance they can break through what you've done to Julio?"

"Hold on," Kalugal said.

The baby's crying stopped abruptly, probably because Kalugal walked into another room and closed the door.

"They can't break through my compulsion and thralling unless they have a compeller stronger than me among them, and we know that they don't. The Brotherhood's only powerful compeller is my father, and he never leaves the island, so the only way they can have another one is if Lokan is not as well informed as he thinks he is, and the Brotherhood has gained one in recent years."

The possibility of a young Doomer developing an extraordinary compulsion ability was almost nonexistent, and even if that had somehow happened,

Navuh would have done away with the guy. He didn't want anyone around him to have the power to usurp him.

Kian let out a breath. "I know it's not a good time, but I need you to meet me in the control room. I want you to take a look at those suspected Doomers."

"I'll head out there in a few minutes."

"Thank you. I'll see you there." Kian ended the call.

When Onegus followed Kian to the door, he stopped him with a hand on his arm. "Stay. This is your bachelor party, and I can handle this without you."

Onegus shook his head. "Duty always comes before pleasure for me, Kian. I'm coming with you."

63

NEGAL

After sitting down and ordering drinks, Negal took Margo's hand and asked the question that had been bothering him ever since Margo had admitted her difficulties with intimacy.

After last night, he knew that there was nothing wrong with her. She was sexy, passionate, and responsive, so the only thing he could think of was some creep in her past had left a bad impression.

"I want to ask you something that might be upsetting to you, so if you don't want to answer, that's fine."

She frowned. "After such a preamble, I'm scared of what you want to ask me."

Had she guessed what he had on his mind, or was she imagining something worse?

"Did something happen to you to make you afraid of intimacy? Did you have a bad experience?"

Margo seemed relieved, so she must have imagined a worse question, although he could not think of what it could be.

"Only two really bad things have happened to me. One was Mia almost dying and then having her legs amputated. I forced myself to remain strong for her sake and for Frankie's, but I was terrified and devastated. The second bad thing was getting drugged and kidnapped by Alberto and delivered to his boss."

Her intimacy problems had started long before her latest ordeal, so that wasn't the cause. Could there be a connection to what had happened to Mia?

"Were you afraid to get close to anyone because you feared losing them like you almost lost Mia?"

Margo shook her head. "It has nothing to do with that. It was the pedophiles who ogled me when I was too young for such attention. It repulsed and scared me, but I wasn't molested, if that's what you are thinking." She grimaced. "There were a few instances of that almost happening, one of them with my uncle, but I was always cautious, so it never came to that."

He bared his fangs. "Is that uncle still around?"

"Yeah, but he lives in Europe now. I had an active imagination when I was a teenager, and it's possible that he really had no nefarious intentions when he wanted me to go with him into a dark corner of the park, so, sheathe those fangs and forget that I ever told you that."

Could it be that there had been more to it than Margo remembered? Sometimes, people repressed memories to protect themselves from pain. Only a trained therapist could help her process that, but perhaps Negal could help in some other way.

Reaching for her other hand, he held both and looked into her eyes. "No one will dare to ogle you while I'm around," he vowed.

It didn't have the impact he'd hoped for.

Margo laughed, a burst of genuine amusement that lightened the moment. "They'll just do it behind your back."

He bared his fangs. "Let them try."

"That's sweet." She lifted one of their conjoined hands and kissed his knuckles. "But I'm a grown woman now, and ogling me does not merit being torn apart, so please, retract your fangs and don't bite anyone's head off."

"Yes, ma'am." Negal commanded his fangs to recede.

"Wow, that's impressive control. How did you make them shrink so fast?"

He chuckled. "First of all, the word shrink has a very negative connotation when applied to any part of my male anatomy, which includes my fangs. And secondly, control comes with age and lots of practice."

"There's so much about you I don't know," she said, looking up at him with eyes filled with wonder. "I don't even know how old you are."

He'd walked into a trap of his own making. Why had he mentioned age? What if she had a problem with how old he was compared to her?

Negal took a deep breath. "Brace yourself for a shock," he warned.

Margo's brow furrowed. "That old?" she asked, her tone laced with a hint of humor.

Perhaps he was overthinking it, and she didn't care how old he was.

He nodded, the truth finally spilling out. "I'm afraid so. Not counting the time I spent in stasis, I'm five hundred and twenty-two years old. But, since I've served in the fleet for a very long time, I've logged in thousands of years of stasis."

Negal braced himself for a look of shock, but to his astonishment, Margo shrugged. "Toven is over seven thousand years old," she said casually as if discussing the weather. "Numbers are irrelevant, but all the experiences you've had during your service must be fascinating. I bet there are thousands of stories you can tell me from missions all over the galaxy."

He looked into her sparkling eyes and saw only excited curiosity. She really didn't care that he was ancient compared to her.

"Let me see." He rubbed a hand over his jaw. "Where should I start?"

"Anywhere you want. You can just pick one." She leaned closer. "The dragon world should be exciting. Tell me about that."

He laughed. "If fear of being torched alive is exciting, then yes. But honestly, I'm not a thrill-seeker, and I didn't enjoy that. Despite what you might think, I'm not indestructible."

"But you're a god. You should be impervious to dragon fire."

Negal shook his head. "Even if I was, which I'm not, it would have been painful in the extreme. My body can heal fast, but not fast enough to remake itself from ash."

Margo swallowed. "Suddenly, I'm no longer interested in hearing about dragons. I don't want to think about you being in mortal danger." She sucked in a breath. "What else can kill a god?"

"Many things. No one can survive without a head or a heart, so if either is removed or explodes, it is death for a god."

Margo grimaced. "Let's not talk about that. Tell me about your world."

That was much easier because he'd spent a lot of time thinking about Anumati's injustices.

"Our society has a class system that distinguishes the royals from the commoners. Royals glow, and commoners do not. Royals can suppress their glow and pretend to be commoners if they want to, but commoners can't pretend to be royal. Within the royals, there are degrees of luminosity, and those who shine the brightest are the elite. Each class attends different schools, which dictate the universities they move on to, creating a system that favors the elite and is nearly impossible to break into for someone like me, Dagor, and Aru. The ironic part is that we are all supposed to be equal because, supposedly, we have equal rights under the law, but that's the biggest lie of all. The vast majority of Anumatian citizens are considered superfluous, and only the elites who support the Eternal King have a voice. The rest of us have very limited options. Every move we make is monitored, evaluated, and judged, and we have to obey orders without question."

"You are a soldier. So, of course, you have to obey."

Negal shook his head. "It's true for all commoners, and that's why the resistance was born. People are fed up with the system, the lies, the lack of say in how they live their lives."

Eyes full of understanding, Margo squeezed his hand. "It's not as bad here in the West, at least not yet, but things are rapidly heading in that direction. I hoped that the gods would be more enlightened. I hoped that they'd created a better world."

Negal smiled. "One day we will, but for that to happen, the current system needs to be abolished, and the Eternal King's reign needs to come to an end."

64

KIAN

In the control room, Kian, Onegus, and Kalugal huddled around the screen showing Modana's office as captured by the surveillance cameras Julio had installed there.

The idea to hack into the existing surveillance network was brilliant, especially since the cameras they had been able to procure in Puerto Vallarta hadn't been the kind that were easy to hide. Still, Kian didn't like to rely only on that, and they had installed backup listening devices in case Modana disconnected his own cameras, or someone sabotaged his network.

The Modana brothers had just left, probably to continue shouting at each other out of their guests' earshot, and as the two males switched to talking in their own language, the guttural sounds proved beyond a shadow of a doubt who they were.

Kian strained to catch familiar words or phrases, but his knowledge of the Doomer language was limited. They talked fast, and with too many words meaningless to him, their conversation was a frustrating puzzle he couldn't solve, but that was in part why he had asked Kalugal to join him.

His cousin should still be fluent in it.

"They've figured it out," Kalugal said after a moment. "They suspect that Julio Modana was thralled or compelled."

A cold shiver ran down Kian's spine. "How?"

Kalugal listened for a few more moments. "It seems that Carlos told them about his brother's sudden religious awakening, and it didn't take a genius to connect the dots to the immortals they suspected of eliminating their team in Acapulco."

Kian motioned for Reuben to pause the replay before turning back to Kalugal. "Did they say that, or are you extrapolating?"

"They said it. They came along with Carlos to investigate who was behind Julio's transformation, and if they could, to undo it." Kalugal smirked. "Obviously, they can't, and that's why Julio and Carlos are at each other's throats."

Onegus leaned away and crossed his arms over his chest. "Are you absolutely sure that they can't break through your thralling? I know that they can't override your compulsion, but thralling is simpler to detect and undo."

Kalugal shook his head. "No, they can't break through my thralling because I reinforced it with compulsion, but they might try to introduce a different thrall to lead Julio away from the path we've set him on. I don't think they will be successful, but they might try."

Onegus shook his head. "I wish I had your confidence. Why do you think they will not succeed in thralling him into going back to the way he was?"

Kalugal regarded the chief with his trademark smirk that conveyed how much smarter he believed himself to be. Not that his belief was unfounded, but it wouldn't have hurt Kalugal to have some humility.

"My compulsion and thralling were strong because they were not applied in a vacuum. Julio was raised religiously, but as a young man, he believed himself to be invincible and above the law. As he got older, though, he started to be concerned with the fate of his eternal soul, and he was convinced that he was going to hell for all the evil he had done."

Kian chuckled. "If there is a hell, he would sure go there."

Kalugal gave him one of those condescending smiles. "You don't know for a fact whether there is no hell or there is. No one does."

"True," Kian conceded. "No one has come back from beyond the veil to enlighten us either way."

Kalugal nodded. "Many humans believe in them, though, and Julio is one of them. I reinforced his belief in his God's endless capacity for forgiveness. I also made him believe that the Mother of God spoke to him, telling him that his redemption must start on the earthly plane. His good deeds have to equal his evil deeds for his soul to stand a chance at the end-of-life trial that he will face. Julio grabbed on to that chance with both hands. He won't let go unless someone much more powerful than I am forces him to do it, and even then, there is a higher chance he will go insane than go back to the way he was."

Kalugal's lengthy explanation eased some of Kian's concern, but Julio resuming his evil ways was not the only thing to be worried about in regard to the Doomers' presence.

Kian was glad that the ship was currently at sea and that the Doomers didn't know where the immortals who had annihilated their Acapulco team and their cohorts were, where they had come from, and how they had found out about the Modana brothers' connection to the atrocities committed in Acapulco.

"Let's hear the rest of it," Kalugal said. "Maybe there was more said that could clue us in to what they are planning."

Kian motioned for the Guardian to un-pause the replay.

As it started from the exact point at which it had been stopped, one sentence that Kian understood without Kalugal's translation raised his hackles.

"Is it all about the woman?" one of the Doomers asked. "The one the tour guide said his clients were picking up in Cabo San Lucas? Or maybe the other one, the actress that Julio was obsessed with?"

The other Doomer shrugged. "The actress is a nobody that he wanted to fuck, but I don't know what part the other one plays in the story. The goddess's corrupt and immoral female descendants might be fighting along with their males, so maybe that Margo woman is one of them, and she was sent to the hotel to spy on us."

"The actress could be a plant, too," the first Doomer said.

Kian signaled for the Guardian to pause the replay. "I think I understood what they were saying, but I want to be sure."

When Kalugal translated, Kian nodded. "Yeah, I was afraid of that. If they find out about Margo, they can find out about Frankie and Mia too. They've been friends since they were little girls, and their families know each other. It will be very easy for the Doomers to find the connection. We can keep Mia's grandparents in the village, but Frankie has a huge family. How the hell are we going to protect them all?"

Kalugal lifted his hand. "Let's hear the rest of it first. Maybe they didn't follow the thread."

Kian waved a hand, and the replay continued.

The first Doomer shook his head. "Margo's background was checked, and her human connections were real, not the fabricated kind to make her look human."

"She could be working with the clan," the second Doomer said. "Her parents think that she's in a witness protection program. We use humans to do our dirty work for us all the time. The enemy could be doing the same thing."

The first Doomer huffed out a breath. "They pretend to be such do-gooders, when, in fact, they are rotten to the core. They not only allow their women to be morally loose but encourage it."

When Kalugal was done translating, the eyes of everyone in the room were glowing with rage.

Onegus shook his head. "Their disconnect from reality is infuriating. Do they really think that denying their own females immortality, forcing them into prostitution, and turning them into breeders for the cause is morally superior?"

"They do," Kalugal said. "They believe that a female's only value is her womb and that it belongs to the males of her family to do with as they please, all in the name of Mortdh's cause."

As the two Doomers continued spouting Navuh's malicious propaganda against the clan, Kian signaled to Reuben to stop the replay.

"That's sick," Reuben murmured. "I wish we could wipe the Brotherhood off the face of the Earth." He smiled apologetically at Kalugal. "No offense to you, sir. You are no longer a member."

"None was taken, but you need to remember that they are what they are being preached to believe and act upon day in and day out for millennia, and that preaching is constantly reinforced by my father's compulsion. And to start with, people are rather easily brainwashed, humans and immortals alike, and males in particular are easily incited to violence, although females are not much better." Kalugal smiled sadly. "That still doesn't excuse the evils the Doomers commit, but the Brotherhood is not the only evil organization in the world."

Kian grimaced. "We can't even take the Doomers out. There are too few of us. The only way for us to change the world is the way my mother envisioned, by spreading the right ideas. The problem is that one step forward is usually followed by two steps back, and right now, we are on a backward trajectory."

65

ONEGUS

Onegus let out a breath. "We need to ignore their hateful propaganda. These paragons of morality believe that rape is justified as punishment of female disobedience, and so is beheading those who dare to voice opposition, even in the most trivial way, to the way things are run."

He let out another breath, breathed in, then out, repeating the process a few times until his fangs stopped itching and his venom glands stopped pulsating.

The enemy was not here for him to attack, and fueling his own anger served no one.

"I apologize." He turned to Kian. "We need to focus on Margo's family, and perhaps Frankie's and Mia's as well. Mia's grandparents are at their Arcadia home during the cruise, which leaves them exposed."

Kalugal looked at his phone's screen and winced. "Jacki and I are invited to Lokan and Carol's cabin, so if you can continue without me, I should be going."

"Go." Kian clapped him on his back. "Thanks for the help. I might call you later, though, to ask your and Lokan's advice."

"No problem." Kalugal said his goodbyes to the others and hurried out of the control room.

As Kian and Onegus stepped outside, Onegus turned to Kian. "I wonder what made Margo's family think that she was in the witness protection program. She couldn't call them with the phone she was given, and her friends were warned not to let her use theirs. But maybe she asked one of them to call her family for her and tell them the story."

Kian nodded. "I was wondering the same thing and reached the same conclusion, and I'm not happy about it. They should have known better. If Margo's parents didn't know anything, they would have been in less danger."

"Not really." Onegus started toward the elevator. "Margo's future sister-in-law raised the alarm, calling the police and notifying them that Margo was missing. They would have been worried sick about her and would have probably booked a flight to Cabo to search for her. The witness protection story was actually not a bad idea."

"I'm not sure about that. Our problem now is how to protect Margo's family while our entire force is here. I could lift the lockdown and ask Jade to organize a team to watch over them, but the last thing I want is for the Doomers to discover the Kra-ell's existence."

They stopped in front of the elevators, and Onegus pressed the button. "I guess it's Turner to the rescue once more."

"I guess so." Kian pulled out his phone and texted the strategist.

His phone rang a moment later, just as the elevator doors opened.

"What's up, Kian?" Turner asked.

"Can you come to my cabin?"

"When do you need me?"

"Right now." Kian leaned against the wall. "We have a situation."

Turner chuckled. "A new one?"

"It's still the same shit, just with a different flavor."

Turner laughed. "Give me five minutes." He ended the call.

Kian turned to Onegus. "Go back to your party. There isn't much you can help with now, and your guests are waiting for you."

Everything inside Onegus rebelled against the dismissal. He was the chief Guardian, and it was his duty to be on top of things, even if someone else was managing a part of the mission.

It was a matter of principle.

Ever since Turner had joined the clan, Kian had been entrusting him with handling all their hired human teams, and with all of the Guardians stuck on the ship, there really wasn't much Onegus could do for Margo's family.

Still, that wasn't the reason he was willing to acquiesce. Today was a special day in his life, and for once, he should dedicate himself to celebrating with his friends and letting someone else be in charge.

Being a Guardian meant always being on duty, always vigilant, and moments of happiness were all the more precious for their rarity and shouldn't be squandered.

"Call me if you need anything." Onegus pressed the button for his deck.

"You know I will. Try to enjoy what's left of your day."

As he made his way back to the party, Onegus deliberated whether to tell his friends about the Doomers and the threat to Margo's family.

Most of his guests were head Guardians, and he would need to tell them at some point even though there was nothing any of them could do.

Perhaps he could wait with the upsetting news and not ruin the party.

Toven was there as well, and he should know about the threat to Mia's grandparents, even though Onegus considered that a very remote risk. If the Doomers found the connection, they would disregard Margo's obviously human childhood friends. In fact, their friendship might protect Margo as well. Nothing in her history connected her to immortals.

66

KIAN

As Kian opened the door to his cabin, he found Syssi standing in the tiny foyer with Allegra in her arms. Their daughter was dressed in an adorable little swimming suit adorned with a pink tutu, indicating they were on their way to the pool.

"Hello, my lovelies." He kissed Syssi's cheek and then Allegra's. "Are you going swimming with Mommy?"

Allegra patted her tutu.

"It's very pretty." Kian smiled.

"What happened?" Syssi adjusted Allegra in her arms. "Why aren't you at Onegus's bachelor party?"

"I'll tell you in a moment. First, I need a hug from my daughter." He took Allegra from her and peppered her face with tiny kisses, eliciting adorable giggles.

His heart was so full of love that it could burst from happiness, and for a moment, he allowed himself to enjoy it and forget about the latest gathering storm.

"Don't keep me in suspense," Syssi said. "What happened?"

"Carlos Modana arrived at his brother's mansion with two Doomers," he said softly, not to upset Allegra. "They found out about Margo and suspect that she's somehow connected to us."

Syssi's eyes widened. "What are you going to do?"

Kian sighed, shifting Allegra to one arm while wrapping the other one around Syssi's shoulders. "Turner is on his way. I want to ask him to station some of his people to watch over Margo's family and possibly Frankie's and Mia's as well. The Doomers might dig deeper for information about Margo, and if they do, they will find out about her two best friends."

Syssi nodded. "It's a good idea to cover all the bases. Mia's grandparents are in their Arcadia home, and we can't tell them to go to the village because it's on lockdown, and even if we could lift the lockdown, we shouldn't because they might already be watched."

"My thoughts exactly."

"Nana." Allegra pointed at the door.

"We are going, sweetie." Syssi shifted her gaze back to Kian. "I'm meeting my parents and Andrew and Nathalie at the pool, so you will have the place to yourself to strategize with Turner for as long as you need to." She lifted on her toes and kissed his cheek. "Poor baby. You never get a break."

He chuckled. "I object to being called a baby, and it's all fine as long as I can come home to you and Allegra at the end of the day." He planted a soft kiss on top of their daughter's head before giving her back to her mother. "Enjoy the pool, my loves."

As Kian opened the door for them, he found Turner standing outside. The guy's severe expression softened when he saw Allegra. "Hello, little lady. You look absolutely adorable in this bathing suit. Are you going swimming?"

"Nana," Allegra said with a satisfied smile.

"We are going to meet Grandma at the pool," Syssi said. "By the way, how is your grandson?"

Turner's face split in a grin. "Big. That boy is going to be even taller than Douglas."

"I would love to see his pictures if you got them," Syssi said. "But perhaps some other time. Allegra is impatient, and you have a new emergency to deal with."

"Right." Turner's smile morphed into a frown. "I still don't know what this latest one is about."

"Come in, and I'll tell you." Kian ushered him inside and waved goodbye to his family.

Turner walked over to the bar and pulled out a bar stool. "Do I need a shot of whiskey to hear your news?"

"No, but you can get one anyway." Kian poured them both a drink from one of his finest bottles and told Turner about Carlos and the Doomers, as well as his concern about Margo's family.

"You need to call Margo and tell her what's going on," was the first thing Turner said.

"I know, but I need to know what to tell her. Can you arrange for someone to watch over her family?"

"Of course." Turner pulled out his phone. "I'm texting my assistant to find out who is available in Los Angeles for immediate deployment."

"Does your assistant work on a Saturday?"

"She's not in the office, but she knows she must always be on call."

Turner's mode of operation was to keep a skeleton office staff, and subcontract operations to a select group of former Special Ops who had exchanged their uniforms for civilian clothing and continued doing what they had done before but for better pay.

When Turner was done texting, he shifted his gaze to Kian. "Are you calling Margo?"

"I'm waiting for your assistant to tell us if anyone is available to send to her parents' house."

"Just ask Margo to come here and don't tell her why. By the time she arrives, I'll have an answer regarding availability, and I will need to know where to send the team. The fastest way to get all the information I need is to talk to Margo."

67

MARGO

Margo's head was spinning with all that Negal had told her about his home world, the colonies, and the many missions he had completed. If she had Mia's talent for storytelling, she could have written a science fiction series based on Negal's adventures alone.

"Your life has been so exciting." She gave his hand a light squeeze before reaching for the chilled cucumber water Bob had served her. "You must be bored out of your mind here on Earth."

Negal laughed. "I've condensed centuries of existence and told you only the highlights. What do you think happened the rest of the time?"

She lifted one eyebrow. "Boring stuff?"

"A lot of it." He frowned. "Your phone is ringing."

"It is?" She bent over, lifted her purse off the floor, and pulled out her phone. "Apparently it is." She looked at the screen, expecting to see Mia or Frankie's name. Instead, Kian's name flashed brightly, causing her eyes to widen in surprise.

"Why is he calling me?" she murmured as she accepted the call. "Hello, Kian?"

"Hi. I'm sorry to disturb whatever you're doing, but I need you to come to my cabin. I'll text you the number. My cabin is at the top residential deck."

"I know where it is."

"Good. Please, don't delay."

"I won't. I'll be there in a few moments," she said, her mind racing with possible explanations for why Kian wanted to see her so urgently.

When he ended the call without giving her the opportunity to ask why he needed to see her, she turned to Negal. "That was unexpected. Why do you think he wants to see me? Could it be about the job offer?"

Negal's expression was doubtful. "It wouldn't be Kian calling you about that," he said. "It would be someone else. It must be about a different issue."

"Like what?" Margo asked, her worry deepening. She hadn't considered other reasons for the call, her mind fixated on the potential job.

"I don't know," Negal said. "But I can come with you if you want me to."

She wanted him with her, needing the support and reassurance his presence provided. But what if Kian wouldn't be okay with it?

"I don't know if that's okay," she admitted, biting her lip. "I didn't ask Kian if I could bring you along, and I'm not about to call him back and ask."

Negal leaned toward her, his eyes glowing brightly even in the middle of the day. "If he doesn't want me there, he can just tell me to leave, right?"

Margo swallowed. "I guess."

"Don't worry about it." Negal rose to his feet. "Kian doesn't scare me."

She took his offered hand. "That makes one of us."

He chuckled. "You said that he wasn't as scary as everyone said he was."

"I expected worse and was surprised that he was courteous with me, but he's an intense guy. I hope he will still want to play nice for the benefit of the poor human."

As they made their way to Kian's cabin, Margo tried to come up with possible reasons for the summons, but each one she thought of was more absurd than the last.

What if he wanted to ask her if she and Negal had started working on her induction? That was too private, and she hoped he wouldn't be that uncouth, but according to the rumors, Kian often disregarded social conventions, so he might ask that. Or what if he wanted to tell her she had to choose one of the immortals to be her initiator because she couldn't join the village otherwise?

When they were finally standing in front of Kian's door and Negal rang the bell, Margo's heart lodged in her throat, and her mouth got so dry that she feared being unable to talk.

The door was opened by a guy she assumed was Kian's butler.

"Good afternoon, Mistress Margo, Master Negal. Please, come in. Master Kian and Master Turner are waiting for you."

Who was Turner?

Margo didn't remember being introduced to him.

"Thanks for coming so quickly," Kian didn't waste time on pleasantries. "Please, sit down." He motioned to the chairs the butler had pulled out for Margo and then for Negal.

"Hello." Margo offered her hand to Turner. "Have we been introduced?"

He took her hand and shook it lightly. "Not officially, but I've seen you at the weddings. Victor Turner at your service, but everyone calls me Turner."

That still didn't explain why he was there and why Kian wanted her to meet the guy. Hopefully, he wasn't one of the immortal males Kian wanted her to hook up with.

Perhaps she should save them time and tell him that she was in love with Negal and wouldn't accept anyone else as her inducer.

"So, here is the situation," Kian said. "You know we hacked into Modana's security feed, right?"

Negal nodded, and so did Margo, even though she didn't remember anyone telling her about it. So much had happened in such a short time that much of it was a blur in her mind.

"Carlos Modana showed up at his brother's mansion with two men," Kian continued. "The Guardians monitoring the feed called me to watch a conversation that occurred in Modana's office. Long story short, they mentioned you by name and also that your family is under the impression you are in the witness protection program."

A chill ran down Margo's spine as she realized the potential danger to her family.

Kian was still glaring at her with his intense eyes. "Why would your family think that? Did you disobey my orders and call them from someone else's phone?"

Swallowing, she shook her head. "I didn't."

Kian lifted a brow. "So, how did they arrive at that conclusion?"

She tried to think of something that wouldn't implicate Frankie, but then Frankie hadn't broken the rules. She hadn't given Margo her phone or called Margo's parents for her. She'd sent a messenger, which was very clever.

"I asked Frankie to help me," Margo said. "She called her cousin Angelica, who knows my parents, and she went in person to relay the message to them, ensuring there was no digital footprint to trace."

"That was clever." Turner nodded in approval. "No one can trace that."

Kian, who had initially looked angry, seemed to accept Turner's opinion because his expression changed from menacing to approving.

"What do you think Carlos and his goons will do?" Margo asked. "What do they know about me?"

68

KIAN

"Do you think the Doomers will go after Margo's family?" Negal asked before Kian could formulate his answer to Margo.

He didn't know how much she'd been told about what had happened in Acapulco and whether she knew about the involvement of the clan's enemies.

On the one hand, it would be difficult to explain the danger to her family without giving her context, but on the other hand, it wasn't advisable to give her substantial additional information that would need to be erased if she failed to transition.

"It's possible," Kian answered Negal's question first and then turned to Margo, deciding that telling her the truth about the situation was the decent thing to do.

When he was done recounting the events, sparing Margo only the most gruesome details, her cheeks were stained with tears, and her eyes blazed with fury.

"I hope they are all dead," she hissed. "And I hope that they died in agony."

Kian's smile was cold. "Those who actively participated are, but the leaders who either ordered the massacre or allowed it remain at large, and I intend to rectify the situation."

Going after the Brotherhood leaders, those responsible for what had happened in Acapulco and countless drug-related deaths, hadn't occurred to him until that moment.

Kian didn't command the manpower to attack the Brotherhood's base and take out Navuh and his entire mercenary army. He also couldn't just nuke the island because he would kill thousands of the Brotherhood's victims along with their abductors and jailers. But he could target the leaders when they were away from the island.

Before, the Brotherhood's upper-level commanders had rarely left their stronghold, but now that they had shifted to financing their operation with drug and trafficking money, they needed to oversee the human scum in their employ, and the mid-level commanders were out in the world for extended periods of time.

Regrettably, the upper echelon of the Brotherhood's leadership hardly ever left the island, but he could start taking out the mid-level operators one by one.

Come to think of it, Losham had been operating in California for years now, but going after Navuh's adopted sons would be an open declaration of war, and Kian wasn't ready for that.

The mid-level scum would have to do for now.

It wouldn't be easy, and he would need much better intelligence than he had now, but it was doable.

As the decision solidified in his mind, it settled the burning ache that had taken residence in his chest the day he'd learned of the massacre. Vengeance would not bring those lives back, but it might deter the evildoers from striking with such brutality again, and that was priceless.

In addition, it just might disrupt and slow down the drug supply and human trafficking superhighway, which would also save countless lives.

First, though, he needed to take care of Margo and her family, who had been inadvertently dragged into his world and the war he'd been waging his entire life against the Brotherhood and other devil-spawned evildoers.

Feeling his fangs grow in his mouth, Kian commanded them to retract, and when that didn't work, he closed his eyes and thought of Allegra's slobbery kisses, which never failed to do the trick.

"Did anyone check on my family to see if they are okay?" Margo asked.

"Not yet," Turner admitted. "If you can give me their phone numbers, I'll have my assistant call them pretending to be a telemarketer."

Margo grimaced. "They will end the call before your assistant can ask them anything."

Turner smiled. "But we will know that they haven't been kidnapped. Are they usually home on the weekend? Or do they go shopping or out to eat?"

"My parents are most likely home, but my brother and his fiancée are probably out and about."

Kian and Turner exchanged glances.

"Your brother's fiancée was the one who called the police and filed a missing person's report, so you are right about them being in danger as well."

Margo reached into her purse and pulled out a notepad and a pen. "I'm writing down all four cell numbers. My parents still have a landline but rarely answer calls since most are from telemarketers." She tore out the page from her notepad and handed it to Turner.

"I'll text my assistant the information right away," he said.

Margo shifted in her chair and turned her gaze to Kian. "If all of your Guardians are on this ship, who will you send to protect my family?"

"Turner has human subcontractors he works with. They are all highly trained former Special Ops people. They know what they are about."

Margo's expression turned skeptical. "What good are humans against immortals who can thrall and compel?"

"Most immortals can't compel, but thralling is usually more than enough to get humans to cooperate with them. Given the circumstances, I wish we had a better solution, but that's the best we can do. I hope that the Doomers didn't get to them yet and that we can whisk them away somewhere safe." He looked at Turner. "We can use the cabin again."

"Good idea," the guy answered without pausing his rapid typing on the phone's screen.

Kian shifted his gaze back to Margo. "We have a very nice cabin in the mountains where we can house your family until we are convinced that the coast is clear and they can return home."

69

MARGO

"They are going to hate the disruption to their lives." Margo focused her gaze on Turner. "And what will your men tell them? I assume they don't even know about immortal goons who can thrall my parents and anyone assigned to protect them."

She just hoped that they weren't too late.

"The cartel threat is enough of an excuse," Kian said. "We can tell your parents that they are going into the witness protection program like you did. They already believe that you witnessed a crime committed by a drug lord, so we will ride that wave."

Casting another glance at Turner, Margo surmised that he hadn't gotten an answer from his assistant yet.

"That could work. They will not make too much of a fuss about being moved when their lives are in danger, although knowing Lynda, she will complain anyway."

She would bitch and complain, but whoever Turner sent to guard her would deal with that. Former Special Forces operators would not be intimidated by a thirty-two-year-old valley girl with a superiority complex.

"How long will they need to stay in hiding?" Margo asked.

"It depends on whether anyone actually comes looking for them." Kian turned to Turner. "What do you think? Would one week be enough?"

"Two is better," the guy said. "If no one comes for them over the next two weeks, then they probably won't come at all." He shifted his gaze to Margo.

"My people will install surveillance cameras in both homes to monitor suspicious activity."

"What about their workplaces?" Negal asked.

"There is very little chance the Doomers will try to abduct or harm your family members in front of other people. I'm not worried about them being taken from their prospective workplaces."

That made one of them.

Margo was definitely worried about that, but Turner was supposedly an expert, so she should trust his risk assessment. The problem was that Margo didn't trust anyone implicitly. Everyone made errors in judgment and needed to be monitored, even if they were supposed to know more than she did.

Still, if her family was hidden in some remote mountain cabin, it didn't matter if someone came looking for them where they worked. They wouldn't be there anyway.

"Can I talk with my parents and brother?" she asked. "They are probably worried sick about me, and hearing from me might alleviate their fears.

"Not now. When Turner's people are in position, they can give your family members a secure phone, and then you can call them and explain."

That made sense.

Margo looked at Turner. "Any news yet?"

He checked his phone. "My assistant is typing a message. Hold on."

It took forever, or at least that was how it felt to Margo before Turner lifted his eyes from the screen and smiled.

"Good news. They all answered, and your brother and his fiancée were home. My assistant located a contractor who was available to take the case on, and he's deploying two teams to collect your family. Their estimated time of arrival is two hours."

Margo's heart fluttered, and not in a good way. "Two hours is a long time. They might be taken while your guys are on the way. Call the police. Report a burglary or some suspicious activity. That might keep the goons away until your people arrive."

Turner smiled. "This is not the movies, Margo, and things don't happen in an instant. The Doomers don't even know how you are connected to us and if you are connected at all. They will likely decide that you were taken along with Jasmine for the Modanas' nefarious reasons, which is true. Then again, the fact that neither you nor Jasmine are with the cartel bosses is suspicious to them, and they might want to investigate it, but it would be a very low priority for them."

"Speaking of Jasmine," Negal said. "Shouldn't we protect her family as well?"

Kian winced. "The bigger problem is that we can't just drop her at home as planned. She can't go home." He shifted his gaze to Margo. "Neither can you, but that's less of a problem." He cast a quick glance at Negal. "What's your progress with the induction?"

Margo felt her cheeks catch fire. How could Kian be so uncouth?

Negal squeezed her hand. "We are working on it, and I'm confident that Margo will start transitioning before the cruise is over. That means that she will need to stay in your clinic, either the one downtown or in your village. Once she's okay to travel, she will accompany me on the search expedition."

Pulling her hand out of Negal's, she glared at him. "She is right here, so don't talk about me like I am not. Besides, it's not guaranteed that I will transition, and even if I do, I'm not sure what I want to do after that." She turned to look at Kian. "I really want that Perfect Match beta tester job."

Margo knew that if she transitioned, she would follow Negal, but she was angry at him for discussing their sex life and their future with Kian as if she wasn't there, and in front of Turner.

Negal's eyes widened. "We talked about all of that. I thought that was what we agreed on."

"We talked about it, but we didn't finalize anything. Besides, we can't make decisive plans when the most important step is still pending. It all depends on whether I transition."

70

KIAN

Kian stifled a chuckle.

Negal was still a rookie when it came to relationships, and he had a lot to learn about what triggered women.

"I'm sorry if I offended you and made premature assumptions," Negal said. "Can we at least agree that if you transition by the end of the cruise, the plan we discussed is the one we will follow?"

As apologies went, Negal's was so-so, but Margo seemed like a down-to-earth kind of girl who didn't usually blow things out of proportion. Perhaps if she weren't so worried about her family, she would have let Negal's offense slide.

Margo let out a breath. "You are lucky that I love you too much to let you go, or I would have sent you to Tibet alone. I hope my transition starts and ends soon so I can accompany you without causing additional delays."

Kian's heart swelled with emotion, but he kept his expression schooled. Perhaps Syssi was right, and he was a romantic at heart, because Margo's grumpy but heartfelt response touched him.

Negal lifted Margo's hand to his lips and kissed her knuckles. "I am incredibly fortunate, and I thank the Fates daily for you."

She cast a sidelong glance at Kian. "How long will the job offer hold? Is there a chance I will still get it after Negal's mission is done?"

Kian didn't have the heart to tell her that it might take centuries for Negal and his team to locate all the missing Kra-ell pods. "I'm not in charge of the

Perfect Match studios, but Syssi and Toven are, and I'm sure they will find a spot for you upon your return. I expect the company to grow exponentially over the next decade, so there will be plenty of job openings at any given time."

"Thank you." Margo put a hand over her chest. "It's good to know that I will have a job waiting for me no matter when I return."

Turner cleared his throat. "Congratulations on your newly formed bond with Negal, and best of luck on your transition. Now, let's get back to the issue of Jasmine and her family." He trained his gaze on Margo. "Do you know where they live?"

Margo canted her head. "I think she told me that her father and stepmom live in New York, or maybe it was New Jersey. I don't remember. She's not close to them or her stepbrothers, though, and she rarely sees them."

"Any siblings other than the stepbrothers?" Kian asked.

"Jasmine didn't mention any, so I assume there aren't. Her mother died when she was five, and her father married a woman who had two sons."

"I don't think that we have anything to worry about with regard to Jasmine's family, but I will send Kri to talk to her." Kian pulled out his phone.

Turner lifted his hand. "Perhaps send someone else. Kri deserves a day off after her wedding."

Shamefully, Kian had already forgotten that Kri had gotten married the day before. "You are right. I'll send someone else."

Typically, he would have called Onegus and asked him to send a Guardian to question Jasmine, but he didn't want to interrupt the chief's bachelor's party again.

"We can talk to her," Negal offered. "We can explain what's going on and why we need information about her family, without mentioning immortals and Doomers. We can then send the details to Turner so he can inform his people."

"If I allow you to do that, you need to come up with a good cover story. I don't want her to know more than she already does just from being exposed to the rescued women."

"At the end of the cruise, you are going to thrall her memories away anyway, so I don't know why it's important to keep things from Jasmine," Negal said. "But if you tell us what we can say to her and what not to, we will make sure to follow your instructions."

Kian sighed. "This particular story will leave an impression that will haunt her in her dreams, but you are right. In the end, it doesn't really matter."

"Was Jasmine tested for immunity?" Turner asked. "We need to make sure that she's susceptible to thralling before we let her know too much."

Kian nodded. "Kri tested Jasmine, and according to her, the woman was easy to thrall."

"Jasmine might be a Dormant," Margo blurted. "Frankie and Mia think so. She has two indicators. One is her uncanny ability with card games, and the other is how quickly I took a liking to her, and that doesn't happen to me often. In fact, it's very rare. I don't connect with most people. And it's not only me. Mia and Frankie also felt an affinity with her." She chuckled. "It's kind of ironic that I am considered a potential Dormant just because I'm friends with Mia and Frankie. I don't have any paranormal talents, and Jasmine has that and the friendliness factor."

"My sister and wife reported similar experiences with her." Kian cast a glance at Turner. "Maybe we should send some of the unmated guardians to talk to Jasmine."

"Have you seen her?" Negal asked.

"Just a peek or two through the surveillance feed. She seems confident and outgoing. Quite charming, I must say."

The feed had shown him a woman who moved with ease and confidence, smiled a lot, and laughed with ease.

"She is a beautiful woman who knows how to use her looks to her advantage," Negal noted.

The comment intrigued Kian, not because Negal thought Jasmine was beautiful but because he'd noticed that she used her looks to her advantage. "Perhaps I should visit Jasmine myself."

Personal observation could provide him with valuable insights that surveillance and secondhand reports could not. If there was more to Jasmine than met the eye, he needed to know what it was.

71

NEGAL

As soon as Negal closed Kian's cabin door behind them, Margo's shoulders slumped and she leaned against the wall, closing her eyes.

She'd been so resilient through all the life-altering events that had happened to her in the last several days, whether good or bad. But everyone had their breaking point, and evidently, Margo had reached hers when her family was threatened. The strength she had mustered in front of Kian evaporated, leaving her shaken and distraught.

"I'm so scared for my family. I hope Turner's people move fast," she whispered. "Two hours are an eternity."

He wanted to comfort her, to provide some solace in the storm, but he knew platitudes would offer little reassurance. "Do you want to get a drink before we talk to Jasmine? If she sees you like this, she will panic."

Margo opened her eyes and gave him a feeble smile. "We could make up a story for her that will be partly true and partly fiction like we did last night. That was so much fun."

He cupped her cheek. "Yes, it was. But we will not use our own names this time."

The idea had been to make her smile again, but she shook her head.

"For this story to be relevant to her situation, it can't be fun. It has to relay that her family might be in danger."

"We don't have to go," Negal said softly. "Kian will send someone to collect the information from Jasmine anyway, or maybe he will go himself. Besides, I don't think they will go after her parents."

Margo nodded. "It's a stretch. We are not sure they will come after my parents either."

"Absolutely. Kian is just being overly cautious, which is commendable, but you don't need to worry too much about this." Negal was glad that Margo was willing to listen to reason. "I suggest we go back to the Lido deck and try to relax with a drink. We could also go to your cabin. Which option do you prefer?"

"I'm too upset for the Lido. Let's go back to the cabin." She sighed. "I hope Frankie is there. Talking to my besties always helps."

It occurred to Negal that her friends' families might also be in danger, but he'd managed to get Margo's panic down a notch, and he didn't want to get it up again. The first chance he got, though, he was going to text Kian and remind him to check on the other two families.

Negal hated feeling helpless. He could go ashore, get a taxi to the airport, catch the first flight back to Los Angeles, and safeguard Margo's family himself, but it would take too long. He wouldn't get there before Turner's people, who would arrive in less than two hours, and hopefully they would make it in time.

When they entered the cabin, Margo sighed with relief when she saw Frankie sitting on the couch, and her next move was to abandon Negal by the door and rush to embrace her friend while releasing a great shuddering sob.

"What's wrong?" Frankie caressed Margo's back. "What happened?"

As the words tumbled from Margo in a rush, Negal offered a clarification here and there, but mostly, he remained silent. He would never admit it, but he was a little jealous that Margo was seeking solace in her friend's arms and not his.

He was her mate, and it was his job to comfort her. But then she'd known Frankie for most of her life, and she'd met him only a few days ago. In time, he would become the one she ran to, but he couldn't expect it to happen overnight.

Frankie patted Margo's back. "Kian and Turner know what they are doing. I know it's scary, and not knowing is the worst, but you need to have faith in them."

Margo's chuckle sounded more like a hiccup. "You know me. I'm a cynic. Even the most capable people make mistakes, and when it's the lives of my loved ones on the line, I need to stay vigilant and on top of things. But I might start transitioning, and then what?" Margo's gaze flicked to Negal. "Who will ensure that my family is being taken care of?"

His heart swelled with pride that she was looking to him for help. "No matter what happens, I will make sure that your family is safe. You have my word. But even if you start transitioning, I don't expect you to be completely out of commission." He pushed to his feet, sat on Margo's other side, and took her hand. "I fully expect you to issue commands and run the show from your hospital bed in the clinic."

72

MARGO

Margo smiled and cupped Negal's cheek. "I appreciate your confidence in me, but I doubt I will be as lucky as Frankie. I will probably pass out like Karen."

"You will not, but even if you do, Karen was out for less than a day."

It was so sweet of him to believe in her, but he was being overly optimistic. "Let's just hope that I start transitioning and that it happens after my parents and my brother are safe in that mountain cabin that Kian talked about." She turned to Frankie. "You don't happen to know where it is, do you?"

Frankie shook her head. "No clue."

Suddenly, a wave of dizziness washed over Margo, and when she closed her eyes, it got even worse. "I don't feel so good." She put a hand on her upper chest.

The ship was swaying slightly, so some of the dizziness could be attributed to that, but she was also feeling faint, which was probably because of the anxiety and worry coursing through her veins.

Negal regarded her with concern in his eyes. "What's wrong?"

"It must be the stress." She looked at Frankie. "Can I bother you for a cup of coffee?"

"Sure thing." Frankie rose, pushed her feet into her platform slides, and walked into the kitchen. "Did you eat anything today?"

Margo frowned. "I had eggs and toast for breakfast and munched on some pretzels on the Lido deck, but that was it."

Frankie cast her a knowing look. "The pretzels were no doubt served with a side of alcohol."

Margo chuckled. "Of course."

"I made the same mistake the day I met Dagor." She cast her mate a loving look. "I didn't eat, and I had a couple of drinks, and then I saw the goddess that night, and when she introduced Dagor as a god, the shock was so great that I fainted." Frankie popped a pod into the coffee maker.

It sounded like what was happening to Margo, but the difference was that she'd had a proper breakfast and skipping lunch had never affected her like that before.

"It's the worry," Margo said. "I wish I had Turner's phone number so I could call him to see if he's deployed people to safeguard my parents. I can't call them, and I can't ask you or Mia to call them either because it will only expose them to greater risk."

"I can send Angelica again," Frankie offered. "She doesn't live far from your parents, so it's really no bother." She removed the cup from the coffee maker, added cream and sugar, and brought the cup to Margo. "Do you want me to call her?"

Margo looked at Negal. "What do you think?"

"It's not a bad idea. Frankie's cousin visiting would probably be less scary than some big military-looking guys showing up on their doorstep, and she can prepare them for the arrival of the military types. I can ask Aru to get me Turner's number and suggest to him that he use Angelica as his undercover agent."

Frankie laughed. "She will love that."

"She will," Margo confirmed. "Angelica is so feisty that I'm worried she'll get herself in trouble, but desperate times call for desperate measures." She looked at Negal. "Call Aru, please."

"Yes, ma'am." He pulled out his phone and placed the call. "Hi, Aru, I hope I'm not interrupting anything. I need a small favor."

He proceeded to explain what the new concern was in fewer words than Margo could have ever managed to cram all the information into, but that was probably thanks to his military training. Succinctly conveying information was crucial in combat situations.

"I'll get you the number," Aru said. "Is it okay if Gabi and I join you and Margo?"

Negal glanced at Margo to get her approval.

"Of course, it is," she said. "The more heads we put together, the better."

"You heard the lady," Negal said. "We are waiting for you." He ended the call.

Margo sipped on the coffee, but it wasn't helping as much as she'd hoped. She was still feeling dizzy from all the stress, and her stomach was starting to feel uneasy, too. Perhaps Frankie was right, and the two drinks she'd had on the Lido deck and no real food since breakfast were to blame.

"I need to lie down." She kicked her shoes off and turned to lie down with her feet propped on Negal's lap.

"I'll get you a pillow from the bed," Negal said, starting to move her feet off his lap.

"No, don't move. Just give me one of the throw pillows."

He did that and tucked it under her head. "Better?"

"Yes." She forced a smile. "I guess I'm getting too old to handle what I could with ease only a couple of years ago."

Frankie chuckled. "You can stop worrying about that. Now that you and Negal have finally started working on your transition, you will be immortal in no time."

Margo's cheeks heated up with embarrassment. She'd thought they were being discreet, but she should have known that Frankie would guess they hadn't slept on the couch in the living room the entire night.

"Fates willing." Negal took her hand and kissed the back of it.

"I'm texting Mia." Frankie lifted her phone. "We need to assemble the bestie war council." Her small fingers raced over the phone's screen. "And then I'm ordering food from the kitchen. You need to eat more than pretzels and popcorn."

"I didn't eat popcorn."

"I know, but that's all we have left here. We need to restock."

73

NEGAL

The thought that began forming in Negal's mind excited and scared him at the same time. Could Margo's sudden dizziness and nausea be the first signs of transition?

Bridget had said that every Dormant's transformation was unique, but there were some commonalities. Most developed fever and body aches, and Margo hadn't complained about either.

That didn't mean those were absent, though, only that she wasn't aware of them yet because they were just beginning to manifest.

Negal wanted to lean over and press his lips to her forehead to check her body's temperature, but with her feet propped on his lap his movements were somewhat restricted, and he couldn't do that without telegraphing his intentions.

In case he was wrong, he didn't want to raise her hopes for nothing. It was too early for her to start transitioning. They'd only had sex once, and it had been last night.

The vain part of him wanted to believe that his venom and seed were so incredibly potent that they had triggered her transition, or that his and Margo's connection was so powerful because it was fated, and therefore his venom worked its magic in record time.

But the rational and pragmatic part of his brain doubted both.

Aru and Dagor were also gods, neither of them inferior or superior to him, and as far as he knew, neither of their mates had transitioned after a single venom bite.

Then again, Karen was transitioning after he had bitten her only once, but her symptoms hadn't manifested immediately, and it had taken four days for the first signs of transition to appear.

Still, it proved that sometimes one bite was enough.

Closing his eyes, Negal sent a silent prayer to the Fates. *Please, make my mate immortal because I can't live without her. She's my one and only.*

Only fated mates could fall in love so quickly and deeply in such an incredibly short time, and it was clear to him that Margo was his. He wasn't a young man with his first crush, believing that no other male had ever loved a female as much as he loved his. He'd been around long enough to recognize how different his feelings for Margo were from any feelings he'd ever had for any female.

It was like in the stories about fated mates that he used to think were fables. The love was all-consuming, all-encompassing, and, like the universe, ever-expanding.

Surely, the Fates saw that too, and would bless Margo and him with an eternal union.

"What are you thinking about so intently?" Margo asked.

Negal smoothed a hand over the silky strands of her hair, tucking a stray strand behind her ear. "I was praying to the Fates."

She chuckled. "I'm not dying, Negal. You don't need to pray for me."

Hadn't she guessed what he was praying for?

Margo was brilliant, so there was no way she hadn't. She was just too afraid to hope.

As the doorbell rang, Frankie pushed to her feet. "That must be Aru and Gabi."

When she opened the door though, a different couple entered.

Toven's mate zipped toward Margo, stopping her wheelchair a hair away from colliding with the furniture. "Frankie said you nearly fainted. Did anyone call Bridget?" She put her hand on Margo's forehead. "You feel a little warm."

Negal's breath caught in his throat.

"I'm fine," Margo waved a dismissive hand. "The stress finally got to me, and I just fell apart." She smiled at Negal. "Thanks for catching me."

"Any day." He reached out his hand and put it on her forehead, but she didn't feel warm to him. On the contrary, she was a bit too cool. "You don't have a fever."

Toven sat down on the armrest and trained his eyes on Negal. "So, what's going on that is stressing Margo so much?"

"Her family might be in danger." Negal continued to tell Toven and Mia what Kian had told them.

The royal frowned at Negal. "Why didn't Kian tell me? You and I ought to hop on a plane to Los Angeles and take care of those Doomers if they show up."

Margo looked like she was fighting back tears. "Thank you, Toven."

"The same idea occurred to me," Negal said. "But Turner's team will beat us to it. There is no way we can get there before them."

"True." Toven rubbed the back of his neck. "But perhaps we should go just in case things go south and the Doomers overpower Turner's operatives."

Negal nodded. "There is merit to what you are saying."

"Of course, there is." Toven pulled out his phone. "I'm calling Kian."

74

MARGO

Margo tried to listen to Toven's conversation with Kian, but her mind was racing, her stomach was roiling, and she had trouble following what was being said.

Lying on the couch with her head nestled on the throw pillow, she fought to keep the dizziness at bay as her thoughts spun faster than the ship's propeller.

Everything felt surreal, like a nightmare she couldn't wake up from.

Her family was in danger, but instead of rushing to them, she was stuck here, feeling weak, helpless, and useless. Not that she could have done anything to protect them from immortals with mind-manipulation abilities, but she might have made it in time to get them out before the Doomers got to them.

"Time is of the essence," Toven said, ending the call. "Kian is on his way," he announced.

Everyone else in the room had probably heard both sides of the conversation thanks to their freakish immortal hearing, but Margo was still human, and she'd only heard Toven's side, and not all of it, mostly because her mind was frazzled, but also because Gabi and Aru had arrived while he'd been on the line, and she'd gotten even more distracted.

"What did Kian say?" Margo asked.

Toven put the phone in his trouser pocket. "Let's wait for him to get here. He was already on his way while we talked."

The doorbell rang a moment later, and when Dagor opened the door, Kian walked in.

Looking around the room, he smiled. "It looks like a god convention in here."

Margo couldn't help the half-hysterical laughter that bubbled up from her queasy-feeling belly. It wasn't even all that funny, but she was at her wits' end, and those ends were completely frayed.

"I was on my way to visit Jasmine." Kian glared at Toven. "But then you called with all kinds of suggestions, so I had to make a stop here to convince you not to get involved. You are too valuable to risk for such a minor operation."

Toven's expression turned thunderous. "Mia's grandparents are in their Arcadia home, exposed, and I don't need your permission to go ashore and fly home to check on them."

Kian didn't back down. "Turner's people are going to take care of them and Frankie's parents." He looked at Negal. "You, Dagor, and Aru can volunteer, though. In fact, you should check flight availability and book seats just in case. I hope there will be no need for you to go, but if something goes wrong and we need to rescue family members, your thralling ability over immortals will be helpful."

Toven pulled out his phone. "I'm checking available flights for the four of us."

"I need you here, Toven. To secure the ship," Kian added.

"No, you don't. You have Kalugal and your mother. Between the two of them, they can thwart any Doomer attack. Stop coddling Annani. You are doing her a disservice."

For a long moment, Kian gaped at the god as if he couldn't believe anyone dared to talk to him like that, but then he shook his head and turned to Frankie. "We don't think your parents are in danger, but we sent a team to sit outside their house just in case." He shifted his gaze to Mia. "The same is true for your grandparents."

Frankie's eyes widened. "I should call them."

Kian raised a hand. "Don't. You will just scare them, and if the Doomers are monitoring them, their phones are being tapped, and your call will alert them that we are onto them."

"I can call my cousin and have her go over to my parents' house, pick them up, take them for a ride, and tell them what's going on in the car."

"You could do that," Kian agreed. "But I suggest waiting for the teams to arrive at their designated locations and reporting to us before doing anything that could potentially sabotage them." He glanced at his watch. "Their ETA is less than an hour." He lifted his head and looked at Margo. "I'm positive they will arrive in time to get your family out and relocate them to the cabin. You have nothing to worry about."

When someone told Margo that she had nothing to worry about, her response was usually the opposite, which was what was happening now.

"A lot can happen in an hour." Margo swallowed the bile rising in her throat. "And in the meantime, they're sitting ducks. I don't want to wait that long. Frankie's cousin Angelica lives less than a fifteen-minute drive from my parents. She can get to them before Turner's people. I should have asked Frankie to call her as soon as you told me about the Doomers."

Kian shook his head. "I didn't want to worry you with hypothetical scenarios, but the Doomers might already be in your parents' or your brother's house, waiting for your return so they can interrogate you about us. If Frankie sends her cousin, they will apprehend her as well and have one more hostage to negotiate with."

Margo hadn't thought about that scenario, but now that Kian had painted that picture for her, it was the only one she could see. She wanted to scream, but instead, she bit her tongue until she tasted blood.

This was her fault. She had poked her nose in where it hadn't belonged, got herself kidnapped by a drug lord, and brought this danger to her family's doorstep.

The guilt was suffocating in its intensity, and suddenly, she couldn't breathe or see through the dark spots multiplying in her field of vision. The world tilted and spun as the voices around her faded into a distant buzz.

Dimly, Margo heard someone call her name but couldn't answer because she was spiraling into a black abyss.

Awareness returned in sluggish increments. First, there was touch, Negal's fingers brushing against her cheek. Then sound, the low murmur of concerned voices. Finally, after a gargantuan effort, Margo managed to crack her eyes open just a sliver and squinted against the too-bright lights.

"There you are," Negal breathed. As his handsome face swam into focus, the relief and love shining in his eyes made her heart twinge. "You scared me, Nesha," he whispered.

"Sorry," she croaked, wincing at the dry rasp of her throat. "How long was I out?

Negal helped her sit up just enough to sip from a glass of water. "A couple of minutes, but it felt like an eternity."

Margo glanced around at the worried faces of her friends and their mates, but Kian was gone.

"Where is Kian?" she asked.

"He called Bridget to come check on you and then went to see Jasmine." Negal smoothed her hair with such tender fingers that tears pricked her eyes. "He said that as soon as Turner's people check in, he will let us know."

Margo wished she could close her eyes, and when she opened them again, everyone she loved would be safe.

75

NEGAL

Negal cradled Margo against his chest and thought of ways to get his hands on a syringe. He needed to administer a transfusion of his blood as soon as possible, regardless of whether Margo was transitioning or there was something else wrong with her.

His blood could fix whatever needed fixing.

Seeing her like that, looking sickly and defeated, was slaying him. He needed his vibrant and assertive mate back.

How did humans deal with the mortality of their loved ones? It was intolerable.

Where was the doctor? Why was it taking her so long to get to Margo?

It felt like an eternity until the doorbell finally rang.

When Dagor opened the door, Bridget strode in with her medical bag in hand.

"Here is my patient." She sat on the coffee table, put her doctor's bag beside her, and gripped Margo's wrist.

"I think Margo is transitioning," Negal said in a near whisper.

"I'm not," Margo murmured. "It's just the stress and anxiety. It got to be too much, and I fell apart. I'm sorry they dragged you here for nothing, Doctor Bridget."

"Nothing to be sorry about." The doctor let go of her wrist. "Your pulse is all over the place, which can be the result of intense emotions."

Negal shook his head. "You've been kidnapped and drugged. You were terrified of becoming a monster's plaything, rescued, and then faced with the existence of gods and immortals, yet you handled it all with your head held high and in good spirits. Your reaction was never this extreme."

"Not true." Margo smiled at him. "I fainted when I first saw you." She lifted her hand and cupped his cheek. "My angel." She gave him a look so full of love and adoration that his heart turned to goo.

Bending down, he pressed a kiss to her forehead, which, regrettably, still felt cool to him. "That was different. You fainted because of the drugs and the alcohol and being in the sun for too long. Something else is going on with you now."

A ghost of a smile played on Margo's lips. "When it was just me in danger, I could handle it. But when it's my family, it's so much worse." Her voice broke, and she swallowed thickly. "I feel responsible for dragging them into this mess."

"None of this is your fault, my warrior mate." Negal brought her hand to his lips and brushed his lips over her knuckles. "I love how fiercely protective you are of those you love, but falsely blaming yourself is not helping anyone."

Bridget cleared her throat, reminding them that they were not alone. "Since you suspect Margo is transitioning, I assume you have started the induction process."

As Negal nodded, Margo tensed in his arms.

"When did you start?" she asked.

"Last night," Negal said.

As a deep blush tinted Margo's cheeks, she pinched his thigh in a warning.

He took her other hand to prevent her from pinching him again. "You have nothing to feel embarrassed or ashamed about, my love, and certainly not when the information is medically relevant."

The doctor nodded and looked at Margo. "It's not likely that you are transitioning so soon after your first venom infusion, but I can't rule anything out. I need to check what's going on with you, but I suggest we move to the bedroom for the examination so you will have some privacy."

Margo's fingers tightened around Negal's. "Can Negal come with me?"

Bridget's expression softened. "Of course. I know better than to keep the mate of a transitioning Dormant away, not unless they are uncomfortable about being examined in front of their lovers."

Negal looked into Margo's eyes, and when she smiled and nodded, he gathered her into his arms once more, cradling her like the precious treasure she was, and carried her to the bedroom.

She relaxed against him, tucking her face into the crook of his neck. "I'm not transitioning."

He chuckled. "I see that you haven't lost your stubbornness."

"I'm not stubborn," she insisted as he laid her on the bed. "I'm just being realistic. Even Bridget says that no one transitions after one venom bite."

"I didn't say that," Bridget said as she closed the door. "I said that it's not likely, not that it's impossible."

76

MARGO

Bridget's touch was gentle but professional and firm as she checked Margo's vitals. "Can you describe your symptoms for me?" she asked, wrapping a blood pressure cuff around Margo's arm.

Margo took a slow, steadying breath. "I feel dizzy, like the world is spinning, even when I'm lying down. And I'm weak like my limbs are made of lead." She swallowed against the dryness in her throat.

"Sore throat? Runny nose?" Bridget asked after recording the blood pressure test results.

Margo shook her head. "Just dry."

"What about aches and pains?"

"Only my head," Margo said. "It has just started pounding."

She glanced at Negal, who was standing by the door, a concerned expression on his handsome face. She missed the warmth and strength of his hand but felt silly about reaching for him and kept her hands loose at her sides.

Bridget's forehead furrowed as she jotted notes on her tablet. "Your temperature is slightly elevated but within the normal range, and your blood pressure is a little low, which could explain the dizziness and fainting. Usually, the transition is accompanied by elevated blood pressure, not low, but I still think that you are transitioning."

Margo wished it was true, but nothing the doctor had said should have led to that conclusion. "Why do you think that I'm transitioning if my symptoms don't align with how it usually happens?"

The doctor put her tablet on the nightstand. "None of the humans on the ship are sick, so you couldn't have caught a virus from them, and the fact that you just started working on the transition last night, and developed symptoms today cannot be dismissed as coincidental. Besides, we've seen transitions play out in so many different ways that it's difficult to say anything is unusual. Kri's mate, Michael, started growing venom glands before we realized that he was transitioning."

"Are you sure?" Margo's throat felt even dryer. "Has it ever happened to anyone so quickly?"

Bridget pursed her lips. "Well, we do have an instance where a Dormant was induced by one bite from a powerful immortal during a random hookup, and the symptoms of her transition were so mild that she just thought she had the flu. That immortal is what we call 'close to the source.' As is Kian, who performed the induction of my mate. Just the one bite and Victor didn't even wake up until his transition was complete."

She glanced between them. "Still, I would have expected at least twenty-four hours to pass before any symptoms manifested, but Negal is a god, so he has extra mojo that mere immortals do not have."

Margo's mind spun with the implications. If this wasn't the start of her transition, then what was wrong with her? A cold tendril of fear slithered down her spine. "What else can it be?"

Bridget shrugged. "It might be the overload of stress, as you have suspected. The mind-body connection is very powerful, and intense anxiety and prolonged stress can have an adverse effect."

"So, what do we do now?" Negal asked. "Should Margo move to the clinic for observation?"

Bridget shook her head. "I don't think that's necessary at this stage. Karen is still there. She's stable, and if needed, I can release her earlier than I intended, but there is no reason to rush." She fixed Negal with a stern look. "Just keep an eye on Margo, and if her symptoms worsen, call me."

They were talking about her as if she wasn't there, but this time Margo had no energy to remind them that she was listening. Besides, the doctor was giving Negal instructions on how to care for her, so it was all good.

Negal nodded. "Of course. I won't leave her side."

Satisfied with his response, Bridget started packing up her equipment. When she was done, she smiled at Margo. "Rest, stay hydrated, and don't hesitate to call me if anything feels off. Your body is going through a lot right now, whether it's the start of transition or a reaction to stress."

"Thank you," Margo said.

"You are most welcome." The doctor smiled before walking toward the door, and as she opened it, the aroma of food reached Margo's nostrils, but then Bridget closed the door behind her, and the smell faded.

"I smell food." Margo put a hand on her belly. "Am I imagining it because I'm hungry?"

"You're not imagining it." Negal sat down on the bed. "The delivery from the kitchen must have arrived. But I thought that you were feeling nauseous."

"I am. And I'm hungry at the same time. Isn't that strange?"

"I guess so. I've never felt both at the same time."

Margo wondered if Negal had ever felt nauseous at all. "Can you help me up?" She lifted her arm.

"Wouldn't it be better if I carry you?"

"I can walk." She swung her legs over the side of the bed and sat up at the same time, which caused her head to spin.

"Slow down." Negal took her hand. "You are so damn stubborn." He helped her to her feet, keeping a secure arm around her waist as they made their way back to the living room.

The scene that greeted them was almost bizarrely normal given the circumstances, with their friends gathered around the table, digging into the food Frankie had ordered from the kitchen.

The scent of ginger and spices turned Margo's stomach, and she swallowed hard against a surge of nausea. Negal guided her to the couch, settling her against the cushions like she was made of spun glass.

"I'll bring you a plate," he offered.

"I've lost my appetite. I'm no longer hungry."

Toven paused in the middle of typing on his phone. "I'm making plane reservations to LA." He looked at Negal. "Are you coming with us?"

Negal looked at Margo, Toven, and then back to Margo. "Bridget said that I need to keep an eye on you."

"Negal needs to stay here." Dagor looked at Toven. "Aru and I will accompany you."

Margo opened her mouth to protest, to insist that Negal should go, that her family needed him more than she did, but the words felt false even in her own mind and then died on her tongue as a wave of dizziness crashed over her.

Negal was there in an instant, gathering her into his arms. "Breathe, Nesha," he soothed, his lips pressing a cool kiss to her temple. "I'm not going anywhere. I'm staying right here with you."

"What does Nesha mean?" she asked.
"Soul," he whispered. "You are my soul."

77

NEGAL

As Negal held Margo close, he watched warring emotions flicker across her eyes. She was relieved and grateful that he was staying with her, but she also felt guilty about keeping him from aiding her family.

That was life, though. Nothing ever was easy, and everything had a price. To him, though, there was nothing more important than Margo, and he wasn't going to leave her side until she transitioned.

She and Bridget might still be doubtful about the cause of her symptoms, but he wasn't. The Fates had answered his prayers, making his mate immortal so she could be with him forever.

Catching Dagor's eye over Margo's head, he conveyed his thanks for his friend's intervention with a nod and a smile, and Dagor responded in the same way before going back to shoveling noodles into his mouth.

"I want you to eat something." Negal stroked Margo's hair.

"I can't, but you should eat."

"Not without you."

She smiled up at him. "That's blackmail, but fine. If you get me a piece of toast, I'll munch on it while you eat lunch."

"Your body needs more than toast to combat whatever is going on."

Her blue eyes were full of challenge as she looked at him. "That's the deal I'm willing to make. Take it or leave it."

He laughed. "Given that you are back to being stubborn, I think you are starting to feel better." He rose to his feet and walked over to the table.

Gabi handed him a plate. "I'll make toast for Margo while you pile food on your plate," Gabi said.

As he got busy collecting samples from all the different dishes, Negal thought of a way to sneak out for a few minutes to get a syringe so he could give Margo a blood transfusion.

Glancing at Dagor, he suddenly remembered that his friend had stolen a whole stack of them.

Come to think of it, he should have given Margo a transfusion in preparation for the transition, but things had moved faster than he'd expected, and he hadn't been prepared. He'd been caught off guard by how swiftly Margo had welcomed him into her bed.

Negal was almost done loading his plate when the doorbell rang. Since he was the only one standing, he walked over to open the door.

"Kian," he said in surprise. "Did you hear from Turner's people?"

"Not yet." The guy walked in and stopped in front of Toven. "You can't go. It's too big of a risk. We can't let the Doomers learn of your existence."

Toven opened his mouth to argue, but Kian cut him off with a raised hand. "Orion can go in your stead. He's also a powerful compeller, and more than capable of handling a few low-ranking Doomers."

Toven shook his head. "Orion just got married. To your sister. And they are enjoying their honeymoon. The only other compeller that you will be okay with going is Kalugal, and it's even more risky for him to get recognized by his former so-called brothers."

Kian was about to answer when he suddenly noticed Margo on the couch. "How are you feeling?"

"I'm okay, more or less." Margo shifted, so she sat propped against the pillow. "Did you talk to Jasmine about her family?"

Kian shook his head. "Not yet. I was on my way to see her when I decided that talking some sense into Toven was more important."

"There is nothing to talk about," Toven grumbled. "As you said, some low-ranking Doomers are no match for me. It'll be child's play."

Just then, Kian's phone rang, and everyone in the room tensed.

"Talk to me," he barked into the phone as he walked out the door and closed it behind him.

Afraid that the stress of waiting for Kian to deliver the news might cause Margo to faint again, Negal put the plate on the table and rushed to her side.

Thankfully, the door opened a moment later, and Kian entered the room with a very different expression on his face than the one he had sported when he'd left. "Turner's teams reached Margo's parents, brother, and sister-in-law, and they are safe and packing their things as we speak."

"They are okay," Margo breathed. "But they need to hurry. If the Doomers get to them while they are still home, Turner's men will be defenseless against them."

"They are okay, love." Negal cupped her cheek. "If the Doomers hadn't got to them yet, they won't now."

"Can I talk to them?" she asked Kian.

"Not yet," he said apologetically. "We don't want them to delay their departure. Let's wait until they're en route to the safe house."

Margo nodded. "You are right. I wasn't thinking."

Negal pressed a kiss to her hair, breathing in her scent and letting it soothe his own ragged edges.

For now, they could all breathe a little easier.

78

MARGO

Margo clutched the phone to her ear, tears of relief streaming down her face as she listened to her parents' voices. They were scared, confused, angry, but safe.

"I don't understand," her mother said, her tone wavering between fear and indignation. "Why do we have to hide? We didn't see any crime committed, and we can't testify about anything, so why do we need to be in the witness protection program?"

"It's just a precaution, Mom. The people handling the case were afraid that the cartel would kidnap you to blackmail me so I wouldn't testify against them."

It wasn't a complete fabrication because the fear was that the Doomers planned to use her family as a negotiation chip, just not for the reasons she had told her parents.

"I see." There was a long moment of silence. "How long do we need to stay away? Rob's wedding is in three weeks, and so much still needs to be done. Lynda is going to be hysterical."

Margo closed her eyes. She'd forgotten about that.

Everything was already paid for, and all the invitations had been sent months ago. They couldn't postpone the wedding now.

"Two weeks max, Mom. I know it's terrible timing, but what can we do?"

Her father's calm voice came on the line. "We know it's not your fault, Margo. I'm just grateful that you're okay and that we have people looking out for us." He paused, and she could almost see him running a hand through his sparse hair. "Are you safe, though? Are they taking good care of you at the place they are hiding you in?"

A watery chuckle bubbled up in her throat. "I couldn't be safer locked up in Fort Knox. I have a lot of people taking care of me." Her gaze drifted to Negal, Kian, her best friends, and their mates. "I'm surrounded by wonderful people."

After a few more assurances and tearful I love you's, Margo ended the call.

As the adrenaline that had been fueling her during the call drained away, leaving behind bone-deep exhaustion, a wave of dizziness swept over her, and she leaned against Negal's chest. "I'm so glad this is over," she whispered. "Well, almost." She looked at Kian. "Two weeks, right?"

He nodded. "Turner's people planted hidden cameras around both homes. Let's hope no one suspicious shows up over the next two weeks."

"I sincerely hope not. If they have to stay in hiding longer than that, my future sister-in-law is going to assassinate me." Margo let out a shuddering breath and burrowed deeper into Negal's embrace.

Sweeping her gaze over her friends' faces, old and new, she felt a rush of gratitude for all they had done for her.

Toven, a god, a royal god, had been ready to drop everything and fly to her family's rescue.

"Thank you," she said, her voice thick with unshed tears as she met Toven's gaze. "For being willing to put yourself at risk for me and mine. I can't even begin to express what that means to me."

Toven smiled. "There's no need to thank me, Margo. We're family now. Besides, I would have been in no danger, and I'm not saying that to boast."

"I don't know about that." She chuckled. "I don't mean about your formidable godly powers. I'm well aware of those. I don't know if we are a family yet. That depends on whether I will turn immortal."

"You will." Kian surprised her by the conviction in his voice. "I can welcome you to the clan with full confidence that you will meet the necessary criteria, which are immortality and loyalty to the clan."

Mia heaved a sigh. "I wish Dagor, Aru, and Negal could join the clan as well so we could all be together."

Margo swallowed past the sudden tightness in her throat. She wished for that, too, but it was impossible to get everything she wanted.

"We'll make it work, Mia," she said. "If everything goes well, and I transition, Frankie and I will call you every day from the trail." She looked at Frankie. "Right?"

"For sure. We have satellite phones, and they work everywhere."

It was a bittersweet promise, and Margo's heart ached for Mia, who would be left behind. But Mia had Toven, her family, and an entire warm and tightly knit community of the clan, so it was all good.

Margo had Negal, Frankie, Dagor, Gabi, and Aru, and that was enough. She would miss her family when she trekked through Tibet or wherever else their search for the missing pods led them, but as much as she loved her parents and her brother, knowing they were well and safe would have to be enough for now. Perhaps she would be able to go for a short visit before leaving the country.

Besides, immortality meant that one day, she and her besties would get to do everything they had dreamt of doing together as little girls, including having families that would be close to each other and husbands who would be best friends.

If she transitioned, all of their shared dreams would be fulfilled, just not all at the same time.

Kian rose to his feet. "Thanks to the merciful Fates, one more crisis has been averted." He chuckled. "I hope my chat with Jasmine won't lead to the next one."

COMING UP NEXT

DARK WITCH TRILOGY

Children of the Gods Series Books 83-85

Read the enclosed excerpt.

INCLUDES

83: Dark Witch: Entangled Fates

84: Dark Witch: Twin Destinies

85: Dark Witch: Resurrection

Join the VIP Club

To find out what's included in your free membership, flip to the last page.

DARK WITCH: EXERPT

1

JASMINE

Jasmine pushed the pile of Fritos away from the edge of the table. "It's a shame that you ladies cannot stay longer and win back some of your losses." She collected her playing cards, reshuffled them a few times, and then returned them to their cardboard box.

As Lina translated what Jasmine had said into Russian, her two other poker buddies regarded her with mock animosity. Grabbing a handful of the winnings, Jasmine stuffed the chips into her mouth while mock-glaring back at the two and crunching loudly.

Lina was the only one of the three who was semi-fluent in English, but Jasmine had a feeling that the other two understood more than they were letting on.

Panya snorted and released a string of words in Russian that made the other two laugh.

"What did she say?" Jasmine asked Lina.

The girl's cheeks reddened, which happened often because her skin was so pale that it appeared almost translucent. "Panya said that if you keep eating your winnings, you are going to get thunder thighs, and it will serve you right for cheating."

Jasmine frowned. "I'm not cheating. I'm just good."

The two older women snorted derisively, and then Panya released another rapid-fire string of Russian words.

Lina translated, "She says that mind reading is cheating even if you are not doing it on purpose."

Panya must have gotten the idea that Jasmine could read minds from Amanda's visit to the lounge the other day.

Rumors about Jaz's uncanny streak of poker winnings had reached the neuroscientist who specialized in paranormal abilities. She had gotten curious and had come down to the staff lounge to test Jaz for telepathy and precognition.

The results had been unimpressive, and when Amanda had insisted on bringing others to test her further, the results remained underwhelming.

So, Jasmine might have fudged them just a little to avoid suspicion, but not by much. She really wasn't a telepath or a seer.

She was something else. She was a conduit for the divine spirit of the goddess.

Right.

It sounded good, but was it true?

Probably not.

Jasmine was just exceptionally good at reading people without having to peek into their minds.

"I'm not a mind reader. I'm a body language reader, and as much as the three of you try not to project what you are thinking, you still do."

After Lina translated into Russian, Panya retorted again, but this time her tone sounded more good-natured than derisive.

Lina translated. "She doesn't mind losing because it doesn't cost her anything. Even the potato chips are free. She says that playing with you teaches her how to guard her expressions and body language so that when she gets back home, she will win real money playing with her friends."

"I only play for fun." Jasmine cast Panya a mock glare. "Tell her to have mercy on her friends and not play for money. It will only bring her bad luck."

Under the table, Jasmine curled her thumb between her index and middle fingers, forming the *malocchio* sign to shield against negative energies and ill intentions.

Playing poker professionally could have made her rich, but after all the lectures she'd heard from her father about how it could get her in trouble with bad people or even killed, she only played for fun, or in this case, for Fritos and information.

Not that the Russians were particularly forthcoming. The bits and pieces she had collected so far were pitiful compared to what she could usually gather with nothing more than a few charming smiles and several carefully spaced questions.

As much as she was grateful to these people for rescuing her from the cartel and giving her a ride back home, she was dying of curiosity about them, and all the secrecy they insisted on was just ridiculous.

She was stuck in the crew quarters, not allowed to go to the upper decks, and no one was willing to tell her anything.

Panya waved a dismissive hand as she rose to her feet with Lina and Anya following her. "*Nevezeniye—eto yerunda,*" she said before heading toward the door.

Lina translated, "She said that bad luck is nonsense."

"It's not," Jasmine murmured under her breath.

It was no use trying to convince the stubborn Russian that bad luck was very real. She would find out soon enough.

Jasmine munched on the last of her winnings, walked over to one of the plush couches in the corner, sat down, and stretched out her long legs.

With the kitchen staff leaving to start working on tonight's wedding dinner, the lounge was emptying, and the place that was usually bustling with activity and lively chatter was turning depressingly quiet.

Ever since Jasmine was brought on board, she'd been observing the same exodus happening every afternoon, but usually some of the staff remained because not everyone worked all three shifts.

Today, though, she'd heard rumors that someone very important was getting married, but no one would tell her who they were or even why they were important.

Well, since Lina and Marina were the only ones who spoke English, they were the only two she'd asked, and both had refused to answer, saying that it was classified information.

Whatever.

It didn't matter who was getting married. What bothered Jasmine was that with the staff gone, she was about to be the only one left in the lounge. The rescued women who occupied some of the cabins on this level only left their rooms to eat in the crew's dining room and never visited the lounge, but even if some of them decided to brave it, they only spoke Spanish, and she didn't.

The truth was that Jasmine hated being alone, and she hated being stuck in places with no windows, but the staff quarters and facilities were all below the water line, and she was not allowed to venture to the upper decks where the Perfect Match Virtual Studios management mingled with the distinguished guests, who were all former users of the service who had found true love in a

Perfect Match adventure and were getting married on this super-secretive, exclusive cruise. Not that she knew any of that for a fact, but she had gathered enough tidbits of information to deduce that.

The other thing that Jasmine hated was sleeping alone in her tiny, windowless cabin, but it didn't seem like she would be able to find anyone to share it with for the last three nights of the cruise. The number of male staff members was pitifully small, and they were either too old, too young or in committed relationships.

Jasmine sighed, her fingers drumming an idle rhythm on her thigh. If only she could venture to the upper deck and mingle with the guests, she could perhaps find the handsome helicopter pilot whom she'd flirted with during the boat ride from Modana's yacht to the ship.

Edgar had been enchanted with her, and he seemed like a nice guy. The two guards who had collected her and the others were not bad looking either. In fact, she wouldn't have minded a tumble with any of them, but none had come down to see her, not even to say 'Hi, how are ya?'

Had she lost her touch?

Maybe they had been told to stay away from her?

It was ridiculous how tight-lipped everyone was about the whole Perfect Match thing. So what if the couples had met through the company's exclusive dating service?

If anything, it would make a fantastic PR opportunity.

Jasmine would love to become part of that PR effort, perhaps as the spokesperson in their commercials, or a character in one of their adventures. After all, they based their avatars on real people, or at least that was what she'd been led to believe.

Some sneered at the service and its users, but not her. It would be nice to have the computer find her the perfect guy. After the disastrous results of consulting her tarot cards on matters of the heart, Jasmine was much more inclined to trust artificial intelligence to find the perfect man for her.

The damn tarot had promised her a prince, and she'd foolishly believed they had meant Alberto, only for her so-called prince to turn into an ugly, wart-covered toad.

Jasmine's stomach churned at the memory of how easily she'd been fooled by the handsome, charismatic guy pretending to be an honest, well-to-do businessman. Alberto had swept her off her feet with lavish dinners, extravagant bouquets of flowers, and charming smiles. She'd been so sure that he was the prince the tarot cards had foretold, but instead of a happily-ever-after, she'd found herself snared in a nightmare.

Shaking off the painful recollections, Jasmine sat up and pulled out the worn velvet pouch nestled in her purse. Despite their disappointing guidance as of late, she cherished those tarot cards above all of her other possessions.

They had been her constant companions since she was a young girl, an unintended gift left behind by her mother.

Or intended, as she chose to believe.

Her mother had left the cards hidden inside a secret compartment in her jewelry box, which she must have known would go to Jasmine after her death.

With no one to instruct Jasmine on how to use them, they had initially been just a collection of pretty pictures, a reminder of the mother she'd lost, and a secret treasure hidden from her father. But when Jaz got old enough to be allowed access to the internet, she'd found all the instructions she needed.

Over the years, Jasmine had come to rely on the cards' guidance, finding comfort in their cryptic messages and, more often than not, finding out that they had been right. But sometimes, she had done so to her detriment.

Well, only once.

They had never steered her wrong before leading her to that scumbag Alberto. May his dark soul rot in hell.

Glancing around to ensure that she was truly alone, Jasmine pulled the deck out of the velvet pouch and began to shuffle. A smile spread over her face as the familiar motions relaxed her better than meditation, yoga, or just about anything else.

Well, save for sex. But that wasn't in the cards until she got off the ship.

Jasmine snorted. Not in the cards—now that was funny.

She closed her eyes, focusing her energy on the question that had been plaguing her since she was brought on board.

Was her prince on this ship?

Was that why the cards had led her to Alberto, so she could end up here where her prince awaited?

With a deep breath, she laid out the first card, The Six of Cups. The image of two children exchanging gifts stared back at her, a symbol of innocence, nostalgia, and the promise of a new beginning. Jasmine's heart skipped a beat. That card hadn't popped up before. Could this mean that her prince was someone from her past? Perhaps it was a guy that she'd met in school and hadn't noticed back then but who had admired her from afar? And who was also secretly a prince?

Jasmine chuckled. Talk about romantic fantasies. She sounded like a character from one of her period romance novels. She'd never really thought that the cards were promising her an actual prince. They must have meant a prince of a man, and she would be more than happy with that.

The next card was The Lovers. The naked figures of Adam and Eve were intertwined beneath the watchful eye of an angel, the image relaying a profound connection and a union blessed by the divine. After pulling that one, she knew what the final card would be even before laying it down, the same way she knew when she was about to get a winning hand.

And there it was—The Knight of Cups, a dashing figure astride a white horse, holding out a golden chalice as if in offering. The embodiment of romance, chivalry, and the arrival of a suitor. And behind him, rising from the horizon like a beacon, was a castle.

Her prince.

The first few times the same sequence had unfolded, Jasmine had been so excited that her hands had trembled, but now, it seemed more like a curse than a blessing.

It was nothing, a fluke, a cruel joke that some malicious spirit was playing on her.

Her father had warned her against relying on the cards, and at the time she thought he was being superstitious, but maybe he'd been right. After all, cartomancy had only been her introduction to the occult. Since then, she had delved into more serious stuff, but she still had a lot to learn about being a proper witch.

The devil's playground, her father called anything he considered witchcraft, but he was wrong. Hellish or divine, it all depended on the practitioner.

2

KIAN

Kian left Margo's cabin and headed toward the elevators, intending to finally have a long overdue chat with Jasmine.

When she'd been brought to the ship, he hadn't paid her much attention because he hadn't deemed it necessary. After all, the woman had just been someone whom Margo had befriended, a magnet for trouble who had gotten Margo entangled with the cartel. But since day one, people around him had been talking about Jasmine as if she was someone special, and that included Syssi and Amanda, whose opinions he valued.

According to his wife and sister, Jasmine had an uncanny ability to read the most minute changes in expression and body language, which allowed her to excel at poker. She'd won against Amanda, who was an excellent player herself. That and her likability led them to believe that Jasmine might be a Dormant.

Given the way the Fates worked, Kian had no problem believing that she had found her way to the ship with their guidance, but the skeptic in him was still very much to the fore, and before he accepted the supernatural explanation, he needed to make sure that Margo's befriending Jasmine in Cabo had indeed been a coincidence, and that the woman wasn't a plant.

Stopping by the elevator, he considered for a moment calling Anandur and Brundar to accompany him. Protocol demanded that they be with him in all meetings outside the village, but since the ship was under his control, it was like an extension of the village, and therefore he didn't need bodyguards to be with him when he visited the woman.

Not that he would have needed protection from the human under any circumstances, but he had vowed to follow his mother's rule in that regard, and even though he used every available loophole to avoid dragging the brothers everywhere with him, he never disregarded it completely unless he had no choice.

Besides, the two were enjoying themselves at Onegus's bachelor party, and Anandur was most likely drunk by now. Not that it would make the Guardian any less effective. Anandur was lethal even when inebriated, but Kian was loath to pull either of the brothers away from the festivities.

As he pressed the button to summon the elevator, it occurred to him that he didn't know where to look for her. He knew where the clinic was located, but other than that, he wasn't familiar with the crew quarters, which was where she was staying.

Kian could call the security office to ask, but it was a little embarrassing to admit that he didn't know his way around his own ship. Syssi would know where Jasmine could be found, but she was in the pool with Allegra and he didn't want to disturb her, which left Amanda.

His sister was at Cassandra's bachelorette party, but that shouldn't prevent her from answering him unless the party was so loud and boisterous that she didn't notice it.

His phone rang a moment after he'd sent her the text.

"Why do you want to know where to find Jasmine?" Amanda asked without much preamble.

"I'm intrigued. Isn't that reason enough?"

She chuckled. "It is. I'll come with you."

Kian frowned, glancing at his watch once more. "Are you sure? I don't want to pull you away from Cassandra's celebration. It would be rude for you to leave in the middle of the party."

Amanda laughed, the sound light and breezy. "Don't worry about that. Cassandra is indulging in a bubble bath, and her mother and sister have everything under control. Geraldine and Darlene are getting ready to attack Cassandra's hair, and Eva has her bag of tricks with her, although I doubt Cassandra will let her touch her face. The female is gorgeous, and she knows how to use makeup to her advantage. She doesn't need Eva's help."

Kian stifled the urge to roll his eyes. "I'll take your word for it."

Amanda laughed again. "Too much information?"

"You could say so. Makeup is not my field of expertise."

"I get it. Where are you now?"

"Outside the elevators on Margo and Frankie's deck."

"What are you doing there?"

He'd just finished updating Margo about the successful evacuation of her parents and her brother and his fiancée from their homes, but Amanda wasn't aware of the latest crisis, and he didn't want to tell her about it while waiting for the elevator.

"I'll tell you on the way to the crew quarters. Meet me next to the staircase on the promenade deck."

"See you in a few," Amanda said before ending the call.

As Kian made his way to their designated meeting spot, his thoughts drifted back to Margo. He hoped that her transition symptoms were not a false alarm and that she was indeed turning immortal. He also hoped that no Doomers would show up at her parents' and brother's houses so her family could return to their homes.

Right now, they were on their way to the clan's mountain cabin with Turner's team to keep watch over them.

Kian didn't like that the cabin's location had to be compromised for Margo's family and that there was no one there to thrall away the memory of where it was from all the humans involved, but he'd had to come up with a location on the spot, and the cabin was his go-to safe house.

Lost in his musings, Kian didn't notice Amanda approaching him until he heard the clicking of her high heels on the marble floor. She looked fantastic in an elegant cocktail dress reminiscent of the fifties. If he wasn't mistaken, Audrey Hepburn had worn something similar in one of her iconic films.

"You look distracted." She leaned toward him and kissed his cheek. "Everything okay?"

Kian started down the stairs, which were thankfully deserted. "Margo may be transitioning, and we had a close call with her family." He proceeded to tell Amanda about Carlos Modana showing up with two Doomers at his brother's mansion and then the two talking about Margo. "We got her family out and installed cameras to monitor both houses. I hope no one shows up so they can return home, and we don't need to relocate them permanently."

"What a mess." Amanda sighed. "It's like the Fates are constantly throwing challenges at us. Couldn't they have given us a break during this ten-day cruise?"

"My thoughts exactly, but then we have been gifted two new Dormants during this vacation, so perhaps it could be called a good trade. Maybe three if Jasmine proves to be one as well."

"True." Amanda slowed down her pace and stopped on the landing. "But Frankie and Margo are mated to gods, and they are not part of our clan. I don't see why we all had to suffer so the gods would get a boon."

Kian turned to his sister. "I don't know, but I'm sure the Fates had a good reason."

Amanda smiled. "What a transformation you have gone through. My jaded, skeptical brother has faith now."

"I do, and I don't. It depends on my mood on any given day." He continued down the stairs.

Amanda followed. "And what is it today?"

"That still remains to be seen."

3

JASMINE

As Amanda entered the lounge with a man who could only be described as a god, Jasmine got a little lightheaded.

Was that what swooning meant? She'd always wondered about that word when it appeared in the historical romances she favored.

His features were chiseled, his eyes a piercing blue, and his presence seemed to fill the room with tangible energy.

"Jasmine, this is my brother Kian," Amanda said. "Kian, this is Jasmine."

Jasmine pushed to her feet, but her knees refused to lock, and her heart fluttered in her chest. Could this be him? The prince the tarot cards had promised, the one who would sweep her off her feet?

Except, unlike most men, Kian seemed indifferent to her charms. His gaze was cool and reserved, and as he inclined his head in greeting, there was no spark of interest and no flicker of attraction in his eyes.

Confused and a little hurt, Jasmine tried to mask her disappointment.

She really should stop relying on the damn tarot. They had either lost their potency, or all their prior successes had been flukes.

As if reading her mind, Amanda smiled knowingly. "Kian is Syssi's husband. They have the most adorable little girl named Allegra." She opened her purse and pulled out her phone. "I have to show you her picture."

Jasmine felt like knocking on her own head to check if anything was loose in there. She'd been so stupefied by Kian's looks that she'd forgotten that Amanda had introduced Syssi as her sister-in-law.

Then again, Amanda could have more than one brother, right?

"Here is the little princess." Amanda thrust the screen in front of Jasmine's face.

"Absolutely adorable." Jaz smiled at Amanda, silently thanking her for the reprieve she'd given her by showing her the picture. She then turned her smile on Kian. "She is a mixture of you and your wife." She pushed aside the foolish notions of princes and destiny. "But I'm sure that you didn't come down here to show me pictures of your daughter."

"I did not. Let's sit down." Kian waved a hand toward the couch and then lowered himself to a sitting position with more grace than a man his size should have been capable of. "As you know, Julio Modana was convinced by my associate to abandon his evil ways and embrace God."

She chuckled. "Kevin's hypnotic ability is mind-boggling."

"It is." Kian offered her a tight smile. "Julio's brother Carlos was obviously not happy about the one-eighty pivot his brother had made, and he paid him a visit. Fortunately, we'd planted listening devices around the estate, and we heard two of Carlos's goons talking about Margo and you. They even knew that Margo's family was under the impression that she was in the witness protection program."

Jasmine's eyes widened. "Why would they think that? Margo was supposed to board this ship, and her family knew her plans. They wouldn't have wondered where she was."

Kian looked at her as if she was dimwitted. "Margo was reported missing from her hotel room by her sister-in-law, and all of her things remained there. Her family was not informed of her finally being able to board the ship, and they also didn't know which ship she was supposed to board because we kept those details confidential on purpose." Kian turned to his sister with a smile tugging on his lips. "This time, you have to agree that my paranoia had merit."

Amanda winced. "I'm not sure that Mia kept the name of the ship from her friends. I just hope that Frankie and Margo didn't repeat it to their families."

Letting out a long-suffering sigh, Kian briefly closed his eyes. "I should never have agreed to allow Frankie and Margo on the ship. Evidently, I'm not paranoid enough."

Jasmine listened to the exchange, waiting for a break so she could ask what was going on. The level of secrecy Kian insisted on implied something more serious than protecting the identities of famous guests.

"Why was it important to keep the name of the ship a secret? Is something illegal going on here?"

Suddenly, Jaz remembered the poor women in the other cabins and wondered whether they really had been rescued from traffickers. What if they were being trafficked?

"Don't worry." Amanda leaned over and patted her thigh. "Our unfortunate entanglement with the cartel is all Margo's fault and has nothing to do with why we needed to keep the ship and its guests secret. We need to keep the paparazzi off our trail. You have no idea how resourceful they can be, how tenacious, and how low they are willing to stoop to get a story." She smiled. "But then, if Margo hadn't tried to help you, we would have never known that you were trafficked, and no one would have come to your rescue, so it's all good, right?"

"Now I feel guilty." Jasmine sighed. "If I hadn't gotten involved with Alberto, none of this would have happened. It's all my fault, not Margo's."

Kian lifted his hand. "Let's not play the blame game. Since the thugs mentioned you, we are concerned that they might go after your family as well as Margo's. They know how to locate Margo's family because her brother's fiancée filed a missing person's report, and they can find all the information they need by following her trail. We got her parents, brother, and future sister-in-law to a safe location. How easy will it be for them to locate your folks?"

"Why would they go after our families?" Jasmine asked. "What do they hope to gain by that?"

"Leverage," Kian said. "That's the cartel's mode of operation. They take hostages to pressure family members to give them what they want, whether it's money or information."

"I see." Jaz tucked a lock of hair behind her ear. "I'm not too worried about them finding my family. I use a stage name and I legally changed my last name years ago. My father and stepmother live in New Jersey, and we rarely see each other or even talk on the phone. If the cartel people check my records, they will see that most of my calls are to my agent, my acting coach, and my friends."

Jaz didn't have many friends, and she rarely talked with them on the phone, but it would have sounded pitiful if she'd only mentioned her agent and her coach.

"What about your brothers?" Kian asked. "Margo told me that you have two stepbrothers."

Jasmine snorted. "I see them once a year on Christmas at our parents' house, and we never call each other. There isn't much love lost between us."

"Good." Kian nodded. "I mean, not good that your relationship with your family is strained. It's good that we don't have to worry about it."

"Yeah." She winced. "Sometimes having an unhappy family is an advantage rather than a disadvantage."

"To quote Tolstoy's Anna Karenina," Amanda said, "all happy families are alike, but each unhappy family is unhappy in its own way."

4

KIAN

When Jasmine had explained her family situation, Kian couldn't shake the nagging suspicion that something was off about her story. She was hiding something, but then it could be just family drama that had nothing to do with him and the safety of his people.

He studied her carefully, noting the way she forced her eyes to stay focused on his, and smiled pleasantly when he knew that he was making her nervous.

Not that her reaction to him was surprising.

Kian made most people uncomfortable, even gods and immortals, and Jasmine was just a human female. She was beautiful, which no doubt contributed to her self-confidence, but she was also an actress, and she knew how to hide her tells remarkably well.

"It's a shame that you are not close to your parents." He offered her a smile. "Family is very important to me." He cut a sidelong glance at Amanda. "Sometimes they drive me crazy, but most of the time, I'm grateful for having them in my life."

"Ooh, Kian." Amanda batted her eyelashes and put a hand over her heart. "That's as close as you've ever gotten to telling me that you love me."

He frowned. "Really? I must have told you that I love you hundreds of times."

"Maybe when I was little, but you stopped when I became a teenager."

"That's because you were a hellion."

Jasmine's eyes darted from him to Amanda and back. "What's the age difference between you? You don't look more than five years apart."

Amanda laughed. "Kian only looks young. His soul is at least two thousand years old."

He wanted to kick her leg to make sure she was more careful about what she was saying in front of Jasmine, but there was no way he could do that without Jasmine seeing.

"So, about these paranormal talents of yours," Kian said before Amanda had a chance to make another comment that she shouldn't. "My sister and my wife are very impressed by your ability to read people."

Jasmine shrugged, a coy smile playing on her lips. "What can I say? I've always been good at picking up on the little things. Body language and micro expressions are all there if you know what to look for. People call it a sixth sense or female intuition, but it's just good observational skills." She leaned forward. "I call it the 'staying quiet and letting others talk' skill."

"That's very astute. Did you learn it from your acting teachers?"

Jasmine nodded. "My coach's number one advice was to observe people. The more I learn and store in my mind, the more I have to draw on when I need to build a character."

"Interesting." Kian crossed his arms over his chest. "When did you discover that you could use your observational skills in poker?"

"It was a gradual process. I joined the drama club by the end of middle school, and I discovered poker when I was an adult, but I didn't have such well-developed observational skills back then. Not until I got professional coaching. So, I think that it was a self-feeding loop. Better acting meant more poker wins, and more poker wins made me a better actress." She leaned back to reach into her pocket and pulled out a deck of cards. "Would you like a demonstration?"

He arched a brow. "You want me to play poker with you?"

"Yeah, why not. Amanda can join us, right?"

Amanda glanced at her watch. "I don't have a lot of time, but I would like Kian to see you in your element."

Kian was not a great poker player. In fact, he tended to telegraph his emotions and had a hard time keeping them in check.

"I'm a very mediocre poker player," he admitted. "You two will have no problem beating me."

Jasmine grinned. "Good, then I should take advantage of your supposed lack of skill. If I win, you will let me onto the upper decks and allow me to attend the weddings."

Kian arched an eyebrow, amused by her audacity. Eva would have called it hutzpah, and she would have been right on the money.

Not many people would have dared to challenge him so directly.

"Did you really expect me to agree to that?" he asked.

Jasmine sighed dramatically, leaning back against the plush cushions. "It was worth a try." She fixed him with an assessing look, her head tilted to the side. "I hate being cooped up here with no windows to the outside, and I really don't understand why Margo gets to be up there while I have to stay down here." She pouted. "I will sign whatever NDA you want me to sign, and I will not breathe a word about the celebrities getting married on this cruise." She put a hand on her chest. "I swear it. I'm just dying of curiosity. I want to hobnob with the rich and famous and experience the glitz."

The woman didn't seem intimidated by him even in the slightest, which made Kian doubt her self-preservation instincts, but at the same time there was something refreshing about her irreverence and lack of fear, even if it was all an act.

Was she flirting with him? Or was she just using her charm to soften him up?

She was undeniably beautiful, and there was also a spark, a vibrancy to her that he found appealing in a completely nonsexual way.

Was that the affinity that Amanda had talked about?

Probably. It couldn't be anything else.

Kian was a happily mated male, bound heart and soul to Syssi, and the only thing he could feel for Jasmine was friendliness, which most likely stemmed from affinity.

Perhaps Jasmine was feeling that, too, but was misinterpreting it as attraction. If she were an immortal female, she would have sensed his bonded status immediately and never dared to approach him with even a hint of flirtation.

He waved at the deck in her hand. "Shuffle the cards, and let's play."

Jasmine shook her head. "We need something to wager, and I don't play for money."

That was strange. If she was as good as everyone was claiming, then she could make a killing playing poker professionally.

"Ever?" Kian asked.

"Ever. It's dangerous. I play for fun."

He supposed that it could turn dangerous if she played with the wrong kind of people. Criminal types were usually sore losers.

"That's smart. What do you usually wager with?"

"Chips, popcorn, crackers, grapes, etc."

"I'll get some chips." Amanda pushed to her feet and walked over to the vending machine.

While Jasmine shuffled the cards and Amanda collected bags of chips from the dispenser, Kian was tempted to delve into Jasmine's mind and search for a hidden agenda.

It would be so easy to reach out with his power, to slip past her mental defenses and pluck the truth from her consciousness. Except, it was against the rules to thrall a human without just cause, and curiosity didn't count.

5

AMANDA

"I win." Jasmine pumped her fist in the air and gathered her winnings, several flavors of Pringles Grab & Go packed in small individual containers.

Kian shook his head. "I'm positive that I wasn't telegraphing anything. How did you know that I had a crappy hand?"

Poor guy. He didn't even know how bad he was.

"You are a terrible poker player." Amanda patted Kian's knee. "You took one look at your cards, and your eyes narrowed like you wanted to shoot lasers at them and incinerate the useless hand, and the cloud over your head didn't clear as the game progressed, so Jasmine and I knew that you kept getting bad cards."

"I was narrowing my eyes not because I was angry at my cards but because I was looking at Jasmine and wondering if she had an amazing memory and incredible math skills. Usually, those are needed to be a good poker player."

Jasmine laughed. "I'm terrible at math. My memory is okay, but nothing special. It was just intuition and observation." She pushed to her feet. "If you'll excuse me, I need to visit the ladies' room." She glanced at Amanda. "Do you want to come with me?"

"No, thank you, darling." Amanda smiled. "I'll wait for you here. The truth is that I should be heading back to the party, but I want us to play one more game so Kian can win back the chips he lost."

Her brother waved a dismissive hand. "Contrary to what you think about me, I don't have to always win."

"I'll be right back." Jasmine rushed out of the lounge.

Kian cast Amanda a sidelong glance. "Did you have anything to do with her sudden need to visit the ladies' room?"

She shrugged and assumed an innocent expression. "I might have projected the suggestion to see if she picked it up."

"That was clever." Kian regarded his sister with appreciation. "Did you suspect that she was faking her underwhelming results with your tests?"

Amanda nodded. "She's unnaturally good with cards, so I suspected that she'd fudged the answers. Anyway, while she's gone, I wanted to suggest that you ask Edna to take a peek at Jasmine's psyche. Edna's talent is more akin to empathic reading than thralling, so it's totally within the rules."

"It is, but it's also not subtle. Jasmine will know that she's being probed."

"It's either that or thralling, which I don't mind doing if you are too squeamish about breaking the rules. You know that I don't believe in strict adherence to them, and since no one ever checks, I see no harm in taking a quick look. Jasmine wouldn't even feel it."

He tilted his head. "Why is this so important to you? Do you suspect that something about her is not as it seems?"

"Not really." Amanda sighed. "She's hiding things, but that's not an indication of anything malicious. We all have things we hide, old pains that we don't want others to see, shame, and guilt. But I want Jasmine to mingle with our eligible bachelors, and I know that you won't let her onto the upper decks without making sure she's harmless. So, we need Edna to take a peek, or I can do that and break the rules for a good cause." A sly grin lifted Amanda's red-painted lips. "Since Jasmine obviously has some paranormal talent, and the Fates brought her to us, we have an obligation to check whether she's a Dormant. I have a strong hunch that she is."

Kian surprised her by nodding. "I agree. Even I like her, and you know me. I rarely take a liking to new people."

Amanda snorted. "Generally, that's true, but in the case of gorgeous ladies, you are a bit more flexible."

"What are you talking about?" He glared at her. "Her looks have no effect on me. How can you even suggest that?"

"Relax." She put a hand on his arm. "I'm not suggesting that you are attracted to her, only that you find her pleasing to look at. It's natural, and you don't need to get defensive about it. Even little kids prefer pretty teachers to the ones less fortunate in the looks department. That's how humans are wired, and given who our ancestors are, you shouldn't be surprised. Gods are obsessed with beauty and physical perfection."

Kian dismissed Amanda's theory with a wave of his hand, not because it was untrue but because it was irrelevant to their discussion. "The cruise is almost over, so I don't see the point in sending Edna to test Jasmine. Before she disembarks, we will thrall her to forget about us, and while we are at it, we can take a look at whatever she is hiding."

"You forget the Doomers," Amanda said. "We can't just send Jasmine home, and we can't let her return to her job. We need to get her somewhere safe for a couple of weeks until we are sure that the coast is clear."

"True." He sighed. "I did forget about that. I'll talk to Edna, but it still won't change the fact that we have only three days left."

"We can do a lot in three days, even if you don't allow Jasmine to go up. I'm going to tell Max that he needs to keep an eye on her up close and personal."

"Why Max?"

Amanda shrugged. "He's been a groomsman but never the groom for too long, and it's his turn. Jasmine might not be the one for him, but he deserves first dibs."

DARK WITCH TRILOGY

83: Dark Witch: Entangled Fates

84: Dark Witch: Twin Destinies

85: Dark Witch: Resurrection

NOTE

Dear reader,

I hope my stories have added a little joy to your day. If you have a moment to add some to mine, you can help spread the word about the Children Of The Gods series by telling your friends and penning a review. Your recommendations are the most powerful way to inspire new readers to explore the series.

Thank you,

Isabell

Also by I. T. Lucas

THE CHILDREN OF THE GODS ORIGINS

1: Goddess's Choice

2: Goddess's Hope

THE CHILDREN OF THE GODS

Dark Stranger

1: Dark Stranger The Dream

2: Dark Stranger Revealed

3: Dark Stranger Immortal

Dark Enemy

4: Dark Enemy Taken

5: Dark Enemy Captive

6: Dark Enemy Redeemed

Kri & Michael's Story

6.5: My Dark Amazon

Dark Warrior

7: Dark Warrior Mine

8: Dark Warrior's Promise

9: Dark Warrior's Destiny

10: Dark Warrior's Legacy

Dark Guardian

11: Dark Guardian Found

12: Dark Guardian Craved

13: Dark Guardian's Mate

Dark Angel

14: Dark Angel's Obsession

15: Dark Angel's Seduction

16: Dark Angel's Surrender

Dark Operative

17: Dark Operative: A Shadow of Death
18: Dark Operative: A Glimmer of Hope
19: Dark Operative: The Dawn of Love

Dark Survivor

20: Dark Survivor Awakened
21: Dark Survivor Echoes of Love
22: Dark Survivor Reunited

Dark Widow

23: Dark Widow's Secret
24: Dark Widow's Curse
25: Dark Widow's Blessing

Dark Dream

26: Dark Dream's Temptation
27: Dark Dream's Unraveling
28: Dark Dream's Trap

Dark Prince

29: Dark Prince's Enigma
30: Dark Prince's Dilemma
31: Dark Prince's Agenda

Dark Queen

32: Dark Queen's Quest
33: Dark Queen's Knight
34: Dark Queen's Army

Dark Spy

35: Dark Spy Conscripted
36: Dark Spy's Mission
37: Dark Spy's Resolution

Dark Overlord

38: Dark Overlord New Horizon
39: Dark Overlord's Wife
40: Dark Overlord's Clan

ALSO BY I. T. LUCAS

ALSO BY I. T. LUCAS

ALSO BY I. T. LUCAS

PERFECT MATCH

Vampire's Consort
King's Chosen
Captain's Conquest
The Thief Who Loved Me
My Merman Prince
The Dragon King
My Werewolf Romeo
The Channeler's Companion
The Valkyrie & The Witch
Adina and the Magic Lamp

TRANSLATIONS

DIE ERBEN DER GÖTTER

Dark Stranger

1- Dark Stranger Der Traum
2- Dark Stranger Die Offenbarung
3- Dark Stranger Unsterblich

Dark Enemy

4- Dark Enemy Entführt
5- Dark Enemy Gefangen
6- Dark Enemy Erlöst

Dark Warrior

7- Dark Warrior Meine Sehnsucht
8- Dark Warrior – Dein Versprechen
9- Dark Warrior - Unser Schicksal
10-Dark Warrior-Unser Vermächtnis

LOS HIJOS DE LOS DIOSES

ALSO BY I. T. LUCAS

EL OSCURO DESCONOCIDO

1: EL OSCURO DESCONOCIDO EL SUEÑO

2: EL OSCURO DESCONOCIDO REVELADO

3: EL OSCURO DESCONOCIDO INMORTAL

EL OSCURO ENEMIGO

4- EL OSCURO ENEMIGO CAPTURADO

5 - EL OSCURO ENEMIGO CAUTIVO

6- EL OSCURO ENEMIGO REDIMIDO

LES ENFANTS DES DIEUX

DARK STRANGER

1- Dark Stranger Le rêve

2- Dark Stranger La révélation

3- Dark Stranger L'immortelle

The Children of the Gods Series Sets

Books 1-3: Dark Stranger trilogy—Includes a bonus short story: **The Fates Take a Vacation**

Books 4-6: Dark Enemy Trilogy —Includes a bonus short story—**The Fates' Post-Wedding Celebration**

Books 7-10: Dark Warrior Tetralogy

Books 11-13: Dark Guardian Trilogy

Books 14-16: Dark Angel Trilogy

Books 17-19: Dark Operative Trilogy

Books 20-22: Dark Survivor Trilogy

Books 23-25: Dark Widow Trilogy

Books 26-28: Dark Dream Trilogy

Books 29-31: Dark Prince Trilogy

Books 32-34: Dark Queen Trilogy

Books 35-37: Dark Spy Trilogy

Books 38-40: Dark Overlord Trilogy

Books 41-43: Dark Choices Trilogy

Books 44-46: Dark Secrets Trilogy

Books 47-49: Dark Haven Trilogy

MEGA SETS

CHECK OUT THE SPECIALS ON
ITLUCAS.COM
(https://itlucas.com/specials)

FOR EXCLUSIVE PEEKS AT UPCOMING RELEASES & A FREE I. T. LUCAS COMPANION BOOK

Join my *VIP Club* and gain access to the VIP portal at itlucas.com

To Join, go to:
http://eepurl.com/blMTpD

Find out more details about what's included with your free membership on the book's last page.

ALSO BY I. T. LUCAS

TRY THE CHILDREN OF THE GODS SERIES ON AUDIBLE

2 FREE audiobooks with your new Audible subscription!

FOR EXCLUSIVE PEEKS AT UPCOMING RELEASES & A FREE I. T. LUCAS COMPANION BOOK

JOIN MY *VIP CLUB* AND GAIN ACCESS TO THE VIP PORTAL AT ITLUCAS.COM

TO JOIN, GO TO:

http://eepurl.com/blMTpD

INCLUDED IN YOUR FREE MEMBERSHIP:

YOUR VIP PORTAL

- READ PREVIEW CHAPTERS OF UPCOMING RELEASES.
- LISTEN TO GODDESS'S CHOICE NARRATION BY CHARLES LAWRENCE
- EXCLUSIVE CONTENT OFFERED ONLY TO MY VIPS.

FREE I.T. LUCAS COMPANION INCLUDES:

- GODDESS'S CHOICE PART 1
- PERFECT MATCH: VAMPIRE'S CONSORT (A STANDALONE NOVELLA)
- INTERVIEW Q & A
- CHARACTER CHARTS

IF YOU'RE ALREADY A SUBSCRIBER AND YOU ARE NOT GETTING MY EMAILS, YOUR PROVIDER IS SENDING THEM TO YOUR JUNK FOLDER, AND YOU ARE MISSING OUT ON IMPORTANT UPDATES. TO FIX THAT, ADD isabell@itlucas.com TO YOUR EMAIL CONTACTS OR YOUR EMAIL VIP LIST.

Check out the specials at
https://www.itlucas.com/specials

Printed in Great Britain
by Amazon